MW00770316

LONGUS
XENOPHON OF EPHESUS

LCL 69

LONGUS

DAPHNIS AND CHLOE

XENOPHON OF EPHESUS

ANTHIA AND HABROCOMES

EDITED AND TRANSLATED BY

JEFFREY HENDERSON

HARVARD UNIVERSITY PRESS
CAMBRIDGE, MASSACHUSETTS
LONDON, ENGLAND
2009

First published 2009

LOEB CLASSICAL LIBRARY® is a registered trademark
of the President and Fellows of Harvard College

Library of Congress Control Number 2008938509

ISBN 978-0-674-99633-5

*Composed in ZephGreek and ZephText by
Technologies 'N Typography, Merrimac, Massachusetts.
Printed on acid-free paper and bound by
The Maple-Vail Book Manufacturing Group*

CONTENTS

PREFACE

This edition replaces the Loeb Classical Library edition containing Longus and Parthenius, first published in 1916, which for Longus had a Greek text by J. M. Edmonds paired with a seventeenth-century translation by one George Thornley. Xenophon of Ephesus, making his debut in the Library, replaces Parthenius, who is to reappear freshly edited in a new Loeb volume of Hellenistic works. The pairing of Xenophon's *Anthia and Habrocomes*, perhaps the earliest and certainly the least polished of the extant novels, with Longus' highly sophisticated *Daphnis and Chloe* well illustrates both the basic conventions of the genre and its creative range.

For my texts I have adapted the Teubner editions of Longus by M. D. Reeve (1982, corr. 1994) and of Xenophon of Ephesus by J. N. O'Sullivan (2005). In my textual notes I include only readings that significantly affect interpretation or translation; for more detailed information the reader should consult the critical editions.

It is now more than forty years since I was introduced to *Daphnis and Chloe* by my first Greek teacher, William McCulloh, who was then at work on his *Longus* (New York, 1970), the first comprehensive literary treatment of the novel. Instantly captivated, I resolved to follow Goethe's advice to revisit *Daphnis and Chloe* once every year "so as to learn from it again and again, and to sense freshly its great beauty" (*Conversations with Eckermann*, 20 March 1831). Although my visits have turned out to be less frequent, Goethe's promise has always come true. It is a special pleasure to contribute to the Library an edition of this last great work of classical Greek literature and to dedicate it, *parvum pro magno*, to William E. McCulloh.

For comments on the final draft of Longus I thank William McCulloh; for comments on Xenophon, Stephen Trzaskoma.

BIBLIOGRAPHY

Good bibliographical sources for past and current work on the ancient novel, all Web-based, are the journal *Ancient Narrative* and the *Newsletters* and archives of the Petronian Society.

General

Anderson, G. *Eros Sophistes: Ancient Novelists at Play.* Chicago, 1982.

———. *Ancient Fiction: The Novel in the Greco-Roman World.* London, 1984.

Billault, A. *La création romanesque dans la littérature grecque à l'époque impériale.* Paris, 1991.

Bowie, E. "The Greek Novel," in *The Cambridge History of Classical Literature*, I 683–98.

———, "The Chronology of the Earlier Greek Novels since B. E. Perry: Revisions and Precisions," *Ancient Narrative* 2 (2002) 47–63.

Conca, F., De Carli, E., Zanetto, G., eds. *Lessico dei romanzieri greci.* Milan and Hildesheim, 1983–.

Cueva, E. C. *The Myths of Fiction: Studies in the Canonical Greek Novels.* Ann Arbor, 2004.

Fusillo, M. *Il Romanzo Greco: Polifonia ed Eros.* Venice, 1989 = *Naissance du roman*, tr. (with some additions) by M. Abrioux. Paris, 1991.

BIBLIOGRAPHY

Gärtner, H., ed. *Beiträge zum griechischen Liebesroman*. Olms Studien 20. Hildesheim, 1984.

Gill, C. and Wiseman, T. P., eds. *Lies and Fiction in the Ancient World*. Exeter, 1993.

Goldhill, S. *Foucault's Virginity. Ancient Erotic Fiction and the History of Sexuality*. Cambridge, 1995.

Hägg, T. *Narrative Technique in Ancient Greek Romances*. Stockholm, 1971.

———, *The Novel in Antiquity*. Oxford, 1983.

Hofmann, H., ed. *Groningen Colloquia on the Novel*. Groningen, 1988–.

Holzberg, N. *The Ancient Novel: An Introduction*. London and New York, 1995.

Konstan, D. *Sexual Symmetry. Love in the Ancient Novel and Related Genres*. Princeton, 1994.

Kuch, H., ed. *Der antike Roman*. Berlin, 1989.

Lalanne, S. *Une éducation grecque: rites de passage et construction des genres dans le roman grec ancien*. Paris, 2006.

Létoublon, F. *Les lieux communs du roman: stereotypes grecs d'aventure et d'amour*. Leiden, 1993.

Morgan, J. R. and Stoneman, R., edd. *Greek Fiction: The Greek Novel in Context*. London/New York, 1994.

Panayotakis, S., Zimmerman, M., and Keulen, W. eds. *The Ancient Novel and Beyond*. Leiden, 2003.

Perry, B. E. *The Ancient Romances. A Literary-Historical Account of their Origins*. California, 1967.

Pouderon, B., ed. *Les Personnages du Roman Grec*. Lyon, 2001.

Reardon, B. P., ed. *The Collected Ancient Greek Novels*. California, 1989, 2008[2].

———. *The Form of Greek Romance*. Princeton, 1991.

BIBLIOGRAPHY

Rohde, E. *Der griechischen Roman und seine Vorläufer.* Leipzig 1876, Darmstadt, 1974⁵.

Saïd, S. "Rural Society in the Greek Novel," in Swain, ed., pp. 83–107. Original French version in E. Frézouls, ed. *Sociétés urbaines, sociétés rurales dans l' Asie Mineure et la Syrie hellénistiques et romaines.* Strasbourg, 1987, pp. 33–66.

Schmeling, G. ed., *The Novel in the Ancient World.* Boston/Leiden, 1986, rev. 2003.

Swain, S., ed. *Oxford Readings in the Greek Novel.* Oxford, 1999.

Tatum, J., ed. *The Search for the Ancient Novel.* Baltimore/London, 1994.

Whitmarsh, T. "The Greek Novel: Titles and Genre," *AJP* 126 (2005) 587–611.

———, ed. *The Cambridge Companion to the Greek and Roman Novel.* Cambridge, 2008.

Fragments

Stephens, S. and Winkler, J. J., edd. *Ancient Greek Novels: The Fragments* (Princeton, 1994).

Reception

Barber, G. *Daphnis and Chloe: The Markets and Metamorphoses of an Unknown Best-Seller* (The Panizzi Lectures, 1988). London, 1989.

Beaton, R., ed. *The Greek Novel, A.D. 1–1985.* London, 1988.

Bianchi, N. *Il codice del romanzo. Tradizione manoscritta e ricezione dei romanzi greci.* Bari, 2006.

BIBLIOGRAPHY

Ferrini, M. F. *Bibliografia di Longo, Dafni e Cloe. Edizioni e traduzioni*. Macerata, 1991.

García Gual, C. *Los Orígenes de la Novela*. Madrid, 1972.

Hubbard, T. K. *The Pipes of Pan: Intertextuality and Literary Filiation in the Pastoral Tradition from Theocritus to Milton*. Ann Arbor, 1998.

MacAlister, S. *Dreams and Suicides. The Greek Novel from Antiquity to the Byzantine Empire*. London/New York, 1996.

Reeve, M. "The re-emergence of ancient novels in western Europe, 1300–1810," in Whitmarsh, ed., pp. 282–98.

Schmeling 2003 (above), pp. 685–711 (Christian), 713–33 (Byzantine), 735–73 (French and British), 775–99 (16th-century Iberian).

Zimmermann, B. and Picone, M., edd., *Der antike Roman und seine mittelalterliche Rezeption*. Basel/Boston/Berlin, 1997.

LONGUS

There is a full bibliographical survey of work on Longus covering the period 1950–1995 by J. R. Morgan in *Aufstieg und Niedergang der römischen Welt* II 34.3 (1997) 2208–76, and extensive bibliographies in Morgan (2004), Pattoni, and Schmeling.

Editions

G. Dalmeyda, 2nd ed. (Budé: Paris, 1960), with French translation.

L. Rojas Álvarez (Mexico, 1981), with Spanish translation.

BIBLIOGRAPHY

M. D. Reeve (Teubner: Leipzig, 1982, corr. edd. 1986, 1994).

J.-R. Vieillefond (Budé: Paris, 1987), with French translation.

O. Schönberger, 4th ed. (Berlin, 1989), with German translation.

J. R. Morgan (Aris & Phillips: Oxford, 2004), with English translation.

M. P. Pattoni (Milan, 2005), with Italian translation.

General

Alvares, J. "Reading Longus' *Daphnis and Chloe* and Achilles Tatius' *Leucippe and Clitophon* in counterpoint," *Ancient Narrative* Suppl. 1 (2006) 1–33.

Bowie, E. L. "Theocritus' Seventh *Idyll*, Philetas and Longus," *Classical Quarterly* 35 (1985) 67–91.

———. "Metaphor in *Daphnis and Chloe*," *Ancient Narrative* Suppl. 4 (2005) 68–86.

Chalk, H. H. O. "Eros and the Lesbian Pastorals of Longus," *JHS* 80 (1960) 32–51, reprinted in Gärtner, pp. 388–407.

Cresci, L. R. "The Novel of Longus the Sophist and the Pastoral Tradition," in Swain, pp. 210–242. Original Italian version in *A&R* 26 (1981) 1–25.

Effe, B. "Longus: Towards a History of Bucolic and its Function in the Roman Empire," in Swain, pp. 189–209. Original German version in *Hermes* 110 (1982) 65–84.

Hunter, R. L. *A Study of Daphnis and Chloe.* Cambridge, 1983.

McCulloh, W. E. *Longus.* New York, 1970.

BIBLIOGRAPHY

MacQueen, B. D. *Myth, Rhetoric, and Fiction. A Reading of Longus's "Daphnis and Chloe."* Lincoln/London, 1990.

Merkelbach, R. *Die Hirten des Dionysos*. Stuttgart, 1988.

Pandiri, T. A. "Daphnis and Chloe: The Art of Pastoral Play," *Ramus* 14 (1985) 116–41.

Teske, D. *Der Roman des Longos als Werk der Kunst.* Orbis Antiquus 32. Münster, 1991.

Winkler, J. J. *The Constraints of Desire* (London, 1990), Ch. 4 "The education of Chloe: Hidden Injuries of Sex," pp. 101–26.

Wouters, A. "Longus, *Daphnis et Chloé. Le proemion* et les Histoires Enchâssées, à la Lumiére de la Critique Récente," *Les Études Classiques* 62 (1994) 131–167.

Zeitlin, F. I. "The Poetics of Eros: Nature, Art, and Imitation in Longus' *Daphnis and Chloe*," in Halperin, D. M. et al., edd. *Before Sexuality* (Princeton, 1990) 417–64.

XENOPHON OF EPHESUS

Editions

G. Dalmeyda (Budé: Paris 1926, 2003³), with French translation.

A. Papanikolaou (Teubner: Leipzig 1973).

J. N. O'Sullivan (Teubner: Munich and Leipzig 2005).

General

Bierl, A. "Räume im Anderen und der griechische Liebesroman des Xenophon von Ephesos. Träume?" in A. Loprieno, ed. *Mensch und Raum von der Antike bis zur*

Gegenwart. Colloquium Rauricum 9 (Munich and Leipzig, 2006) 71–103.

Gärtner, H. "Xenophon von Ephesos," *RE* 9A.2 (1967) 2055–2089.

Griffiths, J. G. "Xenophon of Ephesus on Isis and Alexandria," in *Hommages Vermaseren* (Leiden, 1978) 409–37.

Hägg, T. "Die Ephesiaka des Xenophon Ephesius—Original oder Epitome?", *Classica et Mediaevalia* 27 (1966) 118–61.

———. "The Naming of the Characters in the Romance of Xenophon Ephesius," *Eranos* 49 (1971) 25–59.

Henne, H. "La Géographie de l'Égypte dans Xénophon d'Ephèse," *Revue d'Histoire de la Philosophie et d'Histoire Générale de la Civilisation* 4 (1936) 97–106.

Kytzler, B. 2003. "Xenophon of Ephesus," in Schmeling, ed., pp. 336–60.

O'Sullivan, J. N. *Xenophon of Ephesus: His Compositional Technique and the Birth of the Novel*. Berlin and New York, 1995.

Ruiz Montero, C. "Xenophon von Ephesos: Ein Überblick," *ANRW* II 34.2 (1994) 1088–1138.

Sartori, F. "Italie et Sicilie dans le roman de Xénophon d'Éphèse," *Journal des Savants* (1985) 161–86.

Schmeling, G. *Xenophon of Ephesus*. Boston, 1980.

LONGUS

INTRODUCTION

Author and Date

We have no external evidence for the Longus to whom *The Story of Daphnis and Chloe*[1] is attributed in the MSS.[2] The name was not uncommon in the imperial period and, like many another Roman name, was also borne by Greeks, e.g. the Pompeii Longi of Lesbos, the descendants of the Greeks given citizenship by Pompey the Great. The novel's Lesbian setting is not traditionally associated with pastoral[3] and drawn vividly and particularly enough that

---

[1] For the title, which the MSS transmit with three toponymic descriptors—*Poimenika* "Pastoral Tale" in the title (V and F), *Aipolika* "Goatherding Tale" (V) and *Lesbiaka* "Lesbian Tale" (F) in the subscriptions—see the Introduction to Xenophon of Ephesus, n. 1.

[2] In the title V gives the author's name as Longos, F (in both title and subscription) as Logos. It has been suggested that Logos (an attested name but also "book" or "account") originated in a misreading of the title (for example, Florentinus Laurentianus 627 gives as the title Λόγου ποιμενικῶν περὶ Δάφνιν καὶ Χλόην) and that Longos was merely a subsequent attempt to produce a more plausible name. But Longos is likelier to have been altered to Logos than vice versa, and elsewhere F tends to alter proper names.

[3] Though the programmatic figure Lycidas in Theocritus 7

3

Longus could have been a native or resident. On the other hand, the island's erotic, and particularly Sapphic, associations[4] well suited a literary love story; the narrator's persona is that of a non-resident who requires instruction from a local expert (Prologue); and his tale is so addressed to an audience of non-residents as to suggest discovery rather than native familiarity (e.g. 2.1). In any case, the novel's refined style and dense allusiveness suggest that Longus was a native speaker of Greek, and its allusions to material found in Latin poets but not in their extant Greek models were probably to lost Greek models, in particular the poems of Philitas of Cos, as signalled by his emblematic namesake in the novel.[5]

No internal details fix the novel's date, but its literary and stylistic affinities, taken together, are consistent with a date in the middle to late second century CE or early in the third: the heyday of the Greek novel (as witnessed by the papyri) and a period of cultural efflorescence in Greece generally (the "second sophistic"). It has features in common with the fictitious letters (especially those of farmers and fishermen) by Aelian and Alciphron, with the

comes from Cydonia, the island off the coast of Lesbos (?), which thus may have figured in the tradition, perhaps in Philitas' poetry.

4 Sappho's poetry is an important intertextual constituent of the novel.

5 Although Philitas (born c. 340 BCE) was a major influence on Hellenistic and Latin poetry, especially erotic elegy and pastoral, little of his work survives (see L. Sbardella, *Filita. Testimonianze e frammenti poetici* [Rome, 2000]). The passing of the syrinx in 2.37.3 apparently symbolizes the literary succession Philetas–Theocritus–Longus.

Euboicus of Dio of Prusa, and with Lucian, and among the extant novels with Achilles Tatius' *Leucippe and Clitophon* (two papyri are datable to c. 150, and its portrayal of the Boukoloi may reflect their revolt of 172) and Apuleius' *Metamorphoses* (based on a Greek original and datable to the same era), which are comparable in their narrative sophistication and complexity, their literary texture, and their creative engagement with features of romantic fiction that had become stereotypical.

Summary

Daphnis and Chloe, born to prominent families of Mytilene but abandoned as infants in the countryside, are suckled respectively by a goat and a ewe, discovered each by a different shepherd, and raised by that shepherd's family. Grazing their goats and sheep together in their early teens, they develop a strong mutual attraction but know nothing about the workings of love, which they gradually discover by trial and error. They are pointed in the right direction by a wise old shepherd, Philetas, and Daphnis is tutored in the basics of lovemaking by a married woman from the city. Along the way they encounter external obstacles as well—the demands of seasonal labor, separation in winter, Daphnis' abduction by pirates and Chloe's by a party of wealthy young men from Methymna, unwelcome attention from amorous rivals—but these they overcome with help from the benevolent and ever-present deities of the countryside: Pan and the Nymphs, and Dionysus. Daphnis' true identity is discovered when his parents visit their country estate, and Chloe's recognition soon follows. The couple are married and finally consummate their love.

Longus' unique amalgam of romantic prose fiction and pastoral poetry well suited his theme: the nature and discovery of love. His countryside is based in reality as seen through the eyes of his urban narrator and exemplified by visiting town-dwellers, including the owners of the land, and is not immune to poverty, ignorance, hard labor, and base behavior. At the same time it is envisioned as an edenic place, under the control of but uncontaminated by civilization, where innocence can still be found and where nature is not embellished or supplanted by artifice except to cater to the expectations of vacationing urban landlords. To his pastoral purposes Longus adapted conventional features of the romantic novel: the plot is simple and linear instead of complex and episodic; a unitary location in Greece replaces far-flung and exotic travel; gradual, dynamic, and mutual discovery of love replaces static love at first sight followed by long separation and belated reunion;[6] and the couple's adventures on the way to happiness are more internal and psychological than external, unfolding in time rather than confronted in space. Longus adapts his pastoral inheritance as well, although its norms and sensibility predominate and always transform the conventional novelistic elements: the earlier bucolic conception of love as a disease requiring a cure (cf. especially the programmatic figure of Daphnis in Theocritus 1) is redefined by a conception of true love as a natural and organic process, and the simplicity of country life is viewed not from the superior and ironic perspective of urbanity (exemplified, for example, by Simichidas in Theocritus 7) but in a sentimental

---

[6] Though Achilles Tatius does something similar in the first quarter of his novel.

and playful light, as an ideal world of the imagination and the spirit, reachable only through art and imagination.

The world of *Daphnis and Chloe* is in fact a self-consciously literary construction, and the narrative, though simple and straightforward on the surface, is extraordinarily complex and subtle. In a programmatic Prologue, the narrator describes a painting[7] that he happened upon while hunting, i.e. he is a townsman who visits the countryside for recreation. The painting's beauty, lovelier even than the Nymphs' grove which it adorned, impelled him to respond in writing and to seek out an interpreter of its meaning, signalling that the story is not an imitation of life but an artifact, that its narrator is himself part of the fiction and his authority only partial, and that there is meaning, both literary and personal, that lies beyond what he tells us and that readers are invited to discover by their own contemplation.

The surface behind which contemplative readers can glimpse, or project, elusive depths is intricately crafted and highly polished: a smooth and tuneful narrative style (hiatus is generally avoided), basically Attic, with rhetorical heightening in the speeches, deft use of metaphor, and the sort of rhythmical, symmetrical, and variegated patterning familiar in the Gorgianic and Asianic traditions of the second sophistic era, though they are more poetic, and worn much more lightly, than in Achilles Tatius and Heliodorus. The overall structure is carefully shaped, its rhythm and symmetry more musical than geometric, following the human and natural pattern of the seasons, the protagonists' parallel process of discovery, the repetition,

---

[7] Achilles Tatius also begins his novel with an ecphrasis.

variation, and counterpointing of themes, speeches, and events, and the central role played by nature, whose vitality, immanent divinity, and musicality complement the human action at every turn.

Longus also incorporates a wider range of literary texts than the other novelists, as befits his fundamentally Hellenistic orientation: prominent besides pastoral and romance are Homer (especially the *Odyssey*), Sappho, Euripides, Plato (especially *Phaedrus*), and (especially in Book IV) New Comedy. His literary reminiscences are not merely quotation or allusion but always creatively appropriated, so that they become part of the fabric of his own artistic sensibility and the meaning that his narrator attaches to the story. Although his literary interests and moral outlook are always foremost, the settings, action, and characters are never implausible, as they often are in the other novels (especially Xenophon's). From Theocritus, for example, he takes pastoral incidentals, but his portrayal of pastoral innocence and erotic awakening in a sympathetic natural setting is original, as is his adaptation of motifs and descriptive details to suit, or playfully subvert, the narrative requirements of a romantic novel.

Longus uses none of his literary or mythological sources to construct a consistent framework for his story, but near the end of each of the first three books, and corresponding to the stages of the couple's progress in love, is an aetiological erotic myth involving Pan, told secondhand, about a musical girl, aggression against her, the girl's metamorphosis, and the survival of her music: the wooddove, alluding to the myth of Pitys (1.27), Pan and Syrinx (2.34, then mimed by the protagonists in 37–39), and Echo (3.23). As often, the myths serve to universalize the couple's experience and complicate our responses to it. Their tragic and violent tenor is at variance with the novel's overall comic-pastoral mode, in which real harm rarely comes to anyone and the tutelary divinities are benign, but mythical glimpses of this dimension add perspective and contrast.

Because of their mythic and initiatory features, the Greek and Roman novels have been read as cultic texts derived from, or even as esoteric allegories of, the rituals and lore of mystery religions, in the case of *Daphnis and Chloe* the Dionysiac mysteries or Dionysiac/Orphic theology, in which Eros is an avatar of Dionysus. It is true that an atmosphere of divine immanence pervades the novel, that education is a central theme, that some themes or images are found also in Dionysiac cult and myth, and that the narrative invites discovery of more than meets the eye. But this theory lacks explanatory power: there is nothing in the novel that cannot be more naturally accounted for as an element of the literary narrative, which is always rationally and plausibly motivated; none of its narrative or didactic voices has superior authority; and the assumption that the novel contains a systematic esoteric meaning is at variance with its pervasive humor, irony, playfulness, and ambiguity, and is incompatible with the universal appeal claimed in the Prologue.

Reception

Although *Daphnis and Chloe* has yet to turn up on papyri and the earliest likely reminiscence is in a ninth-century poem by Constantine of Sicily,[8] the novel has enjoyed a richer literary, artistic, and musical reception than any

---

[8] R. C. McCail, *Byzantion* 58 (1988) 112–122.

of the other Greek novels.[9] Direct references and adaptations begin to appear in the twelfth century (the verse romance *Drosilla and Charicles* by Nicetas Eugenianus) and translations even before the first printed edition of the Greek text (Florence, 1598), into Italian by Annibal Caro (Parma, 1784, but completed before 1538), into English by Angel Day (London, 1587), and, most influentially, into French by Jacques Amyot (Paris, 1559); subsequently translations have appeared in all the major languages, in editions cheap or lavish (some with illustrations by prominent artists), expurgated or (much less often) faithful.[10] The novel was a source for Belleau's *Bergerie* (1565, 1572), Lorenzo Gambara's *Foundlings* (Naples, 1574, in Latin hexameters), Spenser's *The Faerie Queene* (1590, 1596), and perhaps Shakespeare's *Tempest* (c. 1610), in modern times for Ravel's ballet *Daphnis et Chloé*, Yukio Mishima's novel *The Sound of Waves* (1954), and for the films *Young Aphrodites* (1963), *The Blue Lagoon* (1980), and *Dafnis i Khloya* (1993). Despite its perennial popularity and the admiration of no less an authority than Goethe,[11] *Daphnis and Chloe* was largely ignored by classical scholars, being considered trivial and/or pornographic, until the 1960s, when the ancient novel began to be viewed as a worthwhile object of study.

[9] Surveys in García Gual, 263–75; Rojas Álvarez, xxviii–xxxvi; Schönberger, 45–52; Vieillefond, lxxx–xcviii; Morgan (1997) 2273–76; and Pattoni, 180–89.

[10] Surveys in Barber; Ferrini; and Morgan (1997) 2212–16.

[11] *Conversations with Eckermann*, 9, 18, and 20 March 1831.

INTRODUCTION

The Text

Two independent manuscripts preserve the whole (F) or most (V) of the text, and one contains four gnomic excerpts (O). F and V derive from the same archetype, V through an intermediary manuscript; O is related to V, possibly through the lost intermediary (since O predates V). The other manuscripts predating the first printed edition of the Greek text (Juntine, ed. Raffaello Colombani, Florence, 1598) all derive from V with occasional contamination from F, but they occasionally provide useful corrections and conjectures; both the Juntine edition and the vernacular versions made before its publication (see above) were based on one or another of these derivative manuscripts. The standard chapter divisions derive from Villoison's edition (Paris, 1778) as numbered in Passow's edition (Leipzig, 1811).

F (formerly A)	Florentinus Laurentianus Conv. Soppr. 627 (XIII)
V (formerly B)	Vaticanus Graecus 1348 (XVI)
O	Olomucensis M 79 (XV)

ΤΑ ΚΑΤΑ
ΔΑΦΝΙΝ ΚΑΙ ΧΛΟΗΝ[1]

‹ΠΡΟΟΙΜΙΟΝ›

Ἐν Λέσβῳ θηρῶν ἐν ἄλσει Νυμφῶν θέαμα εἶδον κάλλιστον ὧν εἶδον· εἰκόνα γραπτήν, ἱστορίαν ἔρωτος. καλὸν μὲν καὶ τὸ ἄλσος, πολύδενδρον, ἀνθηρόν, κατάρρυτον· μία πηγὴ πάντα ἔτρεφε, καὶ τὰ ἄνθη καὶ τὰ δένδρα· ἀλλ' ἡ γραφὴ τερπνοτέρα καὶ τέχνην ἔχουσα περιττὴν καὶ τύχην ἐρωτικήν· ὥστε πολλοὶ καὶ τῶν ξένων κατὰ φήμην ᾖσαν, τῶν μὲν Νυμφῶν ἱκέται, τῆς δὲ εἰκόνος θεαταί. 2. γυναῖκες ἐπ' αὐτῆς τίκτουσαι καὶ ἄλλαι σπαργάνοις κοσμοῦσαι, παιδία ἐκκείμενα, ποίμνια τρέφοντα, ποιμένες ἀναιρούμενοι, νέοι συντιθέμενοι, λῃστῶν καταδρομή, πολεμίων ἐμβολή, πολλὰ ἄλλα καὶ πάντα ἐρωτικά. 3. ἰδόντα με καὶ θαυμάσαντα πόθος ἔσχεν ἀντιγράψαι τῇ γραφῇ· καὶ ἀναζητησάμενος ἐξηγητὴν τῆς εἰκόνος τέτταρας βίβλους ἐξεπονησάμην, ἀνάθημα μὲν Ἔρωτι καὶ Νύμφαις καὶ Πανί, κτῆμα δὲ τερπνὸν πᾶσιν ἀνθρώποις, ὃ καὶ νοσοῦντα ἰάσεται, καὶ λυπούμενον παραμυθήσεται,

[1] Λόγγου ποιμενικῶν τῶν κατὰ Δάφνιν καὶ Χλόην V: Λόγγου ποιμενικῶν περὶ Δάφνιν καὶ Χλόην F: ἐκ τοῦ τρίτου λόγου τοῦ Λόγγου O ad III 5.4, et cf. subscriptionem

THE STORY OF
DAPHNIS AND CHLOE

PROLOGUE

On Lesbos while hunting I saw in a Nymphs' grove a display, the fairest I ever saw: an image depicted, a story of love. Fair also was the grove, thick with trees, flowery, well watered: a single spring nourished it all, flowers and trees alike. But that depiction was lovelier still, owning outstanding technique and an amorous subject, so that its prestige drew many visitors, even strangers, to worship the Nymphs and to view the image. 2. In it were women giving birth and other women adorning babies in swaddling clothes, babies abandoned and beasts feeding them, shepherds taking them up, youngsters plighting their troth, a pirate raid, an enemy invasion, and much more, all of it amorous. 3. I looked and marveled, and a longing seized me to rival the depiction in words; I sought out an interpreter of the image and have carefully fashioned four books, an offering to Love and the Nymphs and Pan, a delightful possession for all mankind that will heal the sick and encourage the depressed, that will stir memories in

13

τὸν ἐρασθέντα ἀναμνήσει, τὸν οὐκ ἐρασθέντα προ-
παιδεύσει. 4. πάντως γὰρ οὐδεὶς ἔρωτα ἔφυγεν ἢ
φεύξεται, μέχρις ἂν κάλλος ᾖ καὶ ὀφθαλμοὶ βλέπω-
σιν. ἡμῖν δ᾽ ὁ θεὸς παράσχοι σωφρονοῦσι τὰ τῶν
ἄλλων γράφειν.

those experienced in love and for the inexperienced will be a lesson for the future.[1] 4. For absolutely no one has ever escaped Love nor ever shall, as long as beauty exists and eyes can see. For our part, may the god grant us proper detachment in depicting the story of others.

[1] Recalling the programmatic claims of Thucydides (1.22) and Polybius (9.2.6) but combining enjoyment with utility.

ΛΟΓΟΣ ΠΡΩΤΟΣ

1   Πόλις ἐστὶ τῆς Λέσβου Μιτυλήνη, μεγάλη καὶ
καλή· διείληπται γὰρ εὐρίποις ὑπεισρεούσης τῆς θαλάσσης, καὶ κεκόσμηται γεφύραις ξεστοῦ καὶ λευκοῦ
λίθου. νομίσεις οὐ πόλιν ὁρᾶν ἀλλὰ νῆσον. 2. ταύτης
τῆς πόλεως τῆς Μιτυλήνης ὅσον ἀπὸ σταδίων δια-
κοσίων² ἀγρὸς ἦν ἀνδρὸς εὐδαίμονος, κτῆμα κάλ-
λιστον· ὄρη θηροτρόφα, πεδία πυροφόρα, γήλοφοι
κλημάτων, νομαὶ ποιμνίων· καὶ ἡ θάλασσα προσ-
έκλυζεν ἠιόνος ἐκτεταμένης ψάμμῳ μαλθακῇ.

2   Ἐν τῷδε τῷ ἀγρῷ νέμων αἰπόλος, Λάμων τοὔνομα,
παιδίον εὗρεν ὑπὸ αἰγὸς τρεφόμενον. δρυμὸς ἦν καὶ
λόχμη βάτων καὶ κιττὸς ἐπιπλανώμενος καὶ πόα μαλθακή, καθ' ἧς ἔκειτο τὸ παιδίον. ἐνταῦθα ἡ αἲξ θέουσα
συνεχὲς ἀφανὴς ἐγίνετο πολλάκις καὶ τὸν ἔριφον
ἀπολιποῦσα τῷ βρέφει παρέμενε. 2. φυλάττει τὰς
διαδρομὰς ὁ Λάμων οἰκτείρας ἀμελούμενον τὸν ἔριφον, καὶ μεσημβρίας ἀκμαζούσης κατ' ἴχνος ἐλθὼν
ὁρᾷ τὴν μὲν αἶγα πεφυλαγμένως περιβεβηκυῖαν μὴ
ταῖς χηλαῖς βλάπτοι πατοῦσα, τὸ δὲ ὥσπερ ἐκ μη-
τρῴας θηλῆς τὴν ἐπιρροὴν ἕλκον τοῦ γάλακτος. 3. καὶ
θαυμάσας, ὥσπερ εἰκὸς ἦν, πρόσεισιν ἐγγὺς καὶ εὑρίσκει παιδίον ἄρρεν, μέγα καὶ καλὸν καὶ τῆς κατὰ

---

² εἴκοσιν V: an ἑκατὸν? E. L. Bowie *CQ* 79 (1985) 86–90

BOOK I

Mitylene is a city on Lesbos, large and beautiful, for it is   1
divided by channels where the sea flows in and adorned by
bridges of bright polished stone. You will have the impression not of a city but an island. 2. About two hundred
stades[2] from this city of Mitylene was a rich man's country
manor, a very fine property: hills supporting game, plains
bearing wheat, slopes spread with vineyards, pastures with
flocks; and the sea washed upon the soft sand of an extensive beach.

While pasturing his flock on this estate a goatherd   2
named Lamo[3] found a baby being suckled by a she-goat. It
was a copse with a bramble thicket, wandering ivy, and soft
grass where the baby lay. The goat kept running out of
sight in this direction and abandoning her kid to stay with
the newborn. 2. Lamo, feeling sorry for the neglected kid,
kept an eye on these comings and goings, and at high noon
he tracked her and saw the goat standing over the child
carefully, so as not to hurt it by treading with her hooves,
while it sucked her flowing milk as if from a mother's
breast. 3. Naturally he was amazed, and coming closer he
discovered a male child, large and handsome, in swaddling

[2] 37 km; the variant reading "twenty stades" is incompatible
with the statement in IV 33.2–3 that the trip from the farm to the
city took an entire day.
[3] The name appears elsewhere only in an epigram of
Philippus (*AP* 6.102) of a horticulturist, cf. 4.1–3.

τὴν ἔκθεσιν τύχης ἐν σπαργάνοις κρείττοσι· χλαμύ-
διόν τε γὰρ ἦν ἁλουργὲς καὶ πόρπη χρυσῆ καὶ ξιφίδιον ἐλεφαντόκωπον.

3   τὸ μὲν οὖν πρῶτον ἐβουλεύσατο μόνα τὰ γνωρίσματα βαστάσας ἀμελῆσαι τοῦ βρέφους· ἔπειτα
αἰδεσθεὶς εἰ μηδὲ αἰγὸς φιλανθρωπίαν μιμήσεται,
νύκτα φυλάξας κομίζει πάντα πρὸς τὴν γυναῖκα Μυρτάλην, καὶ τὰ γνωρίσματα καὶ τὸ παιδίον καὶ τὴν αἶγα
αὐτήν. 2. τῆς δὲ ἐκπλαγείσης εἰ παιδία τίκτουσιν
αἶγες, πάντα αὐτὴ διηγεῖται· πῶς εὗρεν ἐκκείμενον,
πῶς εἶδε τρεφόμενον, πῶς ᾐδέσθη καταλιπεῖν ἀποθα-
νούμενον. δόξαν δὴ κἀκείνῃ, τὰ μὲν συνεκτεθέντα
κρύπτουσι, τὸ δὲ παιδίον αὑτῶν νομίζουσι, τῇ δὲ αἰγὶ
τὴν τροφὴν ἐπιτρέπουσιν. ὡς δ᾽ ἂν καὶ τό ὄνομα τοῦ
παιδίου ποιμενικὸν δοκοίη, Δάφνιν αὐτὸν ἔγνωσαν
καλεῖν.

4   Ἤδη δὲ διετοῦς χρόνου διηνυσμένου,[3] ποιμὴν ἐξ
ἀγρῶν ὁμόρων νέμων, Δρύας τὸ ὄνομα, καὶ αὐτὸς
ὁμοίοις ἐπιτυγχάνει καὶ εὑρήμασι καὶ θεάμασι. Νυμφῶν ἄντρον ἦν, πέτρα μεγάλη, τὰ ἔνδοθεν κοίλη, τὰ
ἔξωθεν περιφερής. 2. τὰ ἀγάλματα τῶν Νυμφῶν αὐτῶν
λίθοις ἐπεποίητο· πόδες ἀνυπόδητοι, χεῖρες εἰς ὤμους
γυμναί, κόμαι μέχρι τῶν αὐχένων λελυμέναι, ζῶμα
περὶ τὴν ἰξύν, μείδιαμα περὶ τὴν ὀφρύν· τὸ πᾶν σχῆμα
χορεία<ς>[4] ἦν ὀρχουμένων. 3. ἡ ὤα[5] τοῦ ἄντρου τῆς
μεγάλης πέτρας ἦν τὸ μεσαίτατον, ἐκ δὲ [τῆς] πηγῆς[6]

3 in ras. V²: δικνουμένου cett: διαγενομένου Reeve cl.
1.15.1, 21.1, 2.2.4, 3.2.5

4 Suppl. Hunter cl. Ach. Tat. 1.1.7

5 ἡ ὤα codd: ἵνα Castiglioni cl. 4.3.1

clothes too fine for a foundling's condition: a little purple mantle with a golden clasp, and a little sword with an ivory hilt.

His first plan was to ignore the newborn and just make 3 off with its tokens of identity. Then feeling ashamed were he not to match even a goat's humanity, he waited until nightfall and brought everything to his wife, Myrtale:[4] the tokens, the child, and the goat as well. 2. She was astounded at the thought of goats having babies, so he told her the whole story: how he saw it being suckled, how he felt ashamed to leave it to die. With her agreement they hid the accompanying objects, called the child their own, and assigned its feeding to the goat. To assure that even the child's name would sound pastoral, they decided to call him Daphnis.[5]

When two years had been accomplished, a shepherd 4 named Dryas[6] was pasturing his flock on an adjoining farm when he happened upon similar discoveries and sights. It was a cave of the Nymphs, a great boulder hollow inside and domed outside. 2. The statues of the Nymphs themselves were made of stones, with feet unshod, arms bare to the shoulders, tresses loose on their necks, a belt around the waist, a smile upon the face. The whole arrangement was of dancers in circular motion. 3. The mouth of the cave was at the very center of the great boulder, and water bub-

---

[4] "Myrtle," a conventional name found in both erotic and pastoral poetry.

[5] An archetypal figure in pastoral poetry, cf. especially Theocritus 1.

[6] The name (based on δρῦς "oak tree") perhaps suggests Nymphs, a variety of whom were the Dryads, cf. 2.39.3.

ἀναβλύζον ὕδωρ ῥεῖθρον ἐποίει χεόμενον, ὥστε καὶ
λειμὼν πάνυ γλαφυρὸς ἐκτέτατο πρὸ τοῦ ἄντρου,
πολλῆς καὶ μαλακῆς πόας ὑπὸ τῆς νοτίδος τρεφο-
μένης. ἀνέκειντο δὲ καὶ γαυλοὶ καὶ αὐλοὶ πλάγιοι καὶ
σύριγγες καὶ καλαύροπες,[6] πρεσβυτέρων ποιμένων
ἀναθήματα.

5   Εἰς τοῦτο τὸ νυμφαῖον ὄϊς ἀρτιτόκος συχνὰ φοι-
τῶσα δόξαν πολλάκις ἀπωλείας παρεῖχε. κολάσαι δὴ
βουλόμενος αὐτὴν καὶ εἰς τὴν προτέραν εὐνομίαν
καταστῆσαι, δεσμὸν ῥάβδου χλωρᾶς λυγίσας ὅμοιον
βρόχῳ τῇ πέτρᾳ προσῆλθεν, ὡς ἐκεῖ συλληψόμενος
αὐτήν. 2. ἐπιστὰς δὲ οὐδὲν εἶδεν ὧν ἤλπισεν, ἀλλὰ τὴν
μὲν διδοῦσαν πάνυ ἀνθρωπίνως τὴν θηλὴν εἰς ἄφθονον τοῦ γάλακτος ὁλκήν, τὸ δὲ παιδίον ἀκλαυτὶ
λάβρως εἰς ἀμφοτέρας τὰς θηλὰς μεταφέρον τὸ στόμα
καθαρὸν καὶ φαιδρόν, οἷα τῆς ὄϊος τῇ γλώττῃ τὸ
πρόσωπον ἀπολιχμωμένης μετὰ τὸν κόρον τῆς τροφῆς. 3. θῆλυ ἦν τοῦτο τὸ παιδίον, καὶ παρέκειτο καὶ
τούτῳ [σπάργανα] γνωρίσματα· μίτρα διάχρυσος,
ὑποδήματα ἐπίχρυσα, περισκελίδες χρυσαῖ.

6   Θεῖόν δή τι νομίσας τὸ εὕρημα καὶ διδασκόμενος
παρὰ τῆς ὄϊος ἐλεεῖν τε τὸ παιδίον καὶ φιλεῖν, ἀναι-
ρεῖται μὲν τὸ βρέφος ἐπ᾽ ἀγκῶνος, ἀποτίθεται δὲ τὰ
γνωρίσματα κατὰ τῆς πήρας, εὔχεται δὲ ταῖς Νύμφαις
ἐπὶ τύχῃ χρηστῇ θρέψαι τὴν ἱκέτιν αὐτῶν. 2. καὶ ἐπεὶ
καιρὸς ἦν ἀπελαύνειν τὴν ποίμνην, ἐλθὼν εἰς τὴν
ἔπαυλιν τῇ γυναικὶ διηγεῖται τὰ ὀφθέντα, δείκνυσι τὰ
εὑρεθέντα, παρακελεύεται θυγάτριον νομίζειν καὶ λαν-
θάνουσαν ὡς ἴδιον τρέφειν. 3. ἡ μὲν δὴ Νάπη (τοῦτο

---

6 Trzaskoma cl. 4.26.2: καὶ (om. F) κάλαμοι
7 The name (meaning "glen") appears elsewhere though not

bling up from a spring created a running stream, so that before the cave stretched a silky meadow, thick with soft grass nourished by the moisture. Hung on the walls were milk pails, transverse flutes, panpipes, and staffs, offerings of bygone shepherds.

A newly lambed ewe kept visiting this shrine of the Nymphs, often making it seem that she had vanished. Meaning to punish her and recall her to her former good behavior, he twisted a green switch into a halter like a snare and went off to the boulder hoping to catch her there. 2. But on arrival he did not see at all what he expected: no, he saw the ewe in quite human fashion offering her teat for unstinted sucking of milk, and the child, without a whimper, eagerly applying to one teat and then the other a mouth clean and shiny, as the ewe licked off its face with her tongue when it had fed enough. 3. This child was female, and lying beside it too were tokens of identity: a headband threaded with gold, gilded sandals, and anklets of solid gold.

Thinking his discovery something divine, and learning from the ewe to feel compassion and love for the child, he picked up the baby in the crook of his arm, packed the tokens in his knapsack, and asked the Nymphs in prayer to favor with good luck his rearing of their suppliant. 2. And when it was time to drive his flock home, he returned to his farmhouse and told his wife what he had seen, showed her what he had found, and urged her to regard it as a little daughter and raise it, as far as anyone knew, as her own. 3. From that moment on, Nape (that was her name)[7] moth-

in pastoral poetry; there was a town of this name on Lesbos and a variety of Nymphs were called Napaea.

γὰρ ἐκαλεῖτο) μήτηρ εὐθὺς ἦν καὶ ἐφίλει τὸ παιδίον,
ὥσπερ ὑπὸ τῆς ὄϊος παρευδοκιμηθῆναι δεδοικυῖα, καὶ
τίθεται καὶ αὐτὴ ποιμενικὸν ὄνομα πρὸς πίστιν αὐτῷ
Χλόην.

7   Ταῦτα τὰ παιδία ταχὺ μάλα ηὔξησε, καὶ κάλλος
αὐτοῖς ἐξεφαίνετο κρεῖττον ἀγροικίας. ἤδη τε ἦν ὁ μὲν
πέντε καὶ δέκα ἐτῶν ἀπὸ γενεᾶς, ἡ δὲ τοσούτων δυοῖν
ἀποδεόντων, καὶ ὁ Δρύας καὶ ὁ Λάμων ἐπὶ μιᾶς νυκτὸς
ὁρῶσιν ὄναρ τοιόνδε τι. 2. τὰς Νύμφας ἐδόκουν ἐκεί-
νας, τὰς ἐν τῷ ἄντρῳ ἐν ᾧ ἡ πηγή, ἐν ᾧ τὸ παιδίον
εὗρεν ὁ Δρύας, τὸν Δάφνιν καὶ τὴν Χλόην παρα-
διδόναι παιδίῳ μάλα σοβαρῷ καὶ καλῷ, πτερὰ ἐκ τῶν
ὤμων ἔχοντι, βέλη σμικρὰ ἅμα τοξαρίῳ φέροντι, τὸ δὲ
ἐφαψάμενον ἀμφοτέρων ἑνὶ βέλει κελεῦσαι λοιπὸν
νέμειν τὸν μὲν τὸ αἰπόλιον, τὴν δὲ τὸ ποίμνιον.

8   Τοῦτο τὸ ὄναρ ἰδόντες ἤχθοντο μὲν εἰ ποιμένες
ἔσοιντο καὶ αἰπόλοι ⟨οἳ⟩ τύχην ἐκ σπαργάνων ἐπαγ-
γελλόμενοι κρείττονα, δι᾽ ἣν αὐτοὺς καὶ τροφαῖς ἔτρε-
φον ἁβροτέραις καὶ γράμματα ἐπαίδευον καὶ πάντα
ὅσα καλὰ ἦν ἐπ᾽ ἀγροικίας· ἐδόκει δὲ πείθεσθαι θεοῖς
περὶ τῶν σωθέντων προνοίᾳ θεῶν. 2. καὶ κοινώσαντες
ἀλλήλοις τὸ ὄναρ καὶ θύσαντες τῷ τὰ πτερὰ ἔχοντι
παιδίῳ παρὰ ταῖς Νύμφαις (τὸ γὰρ ὄνομα λέγειν οὐκ
εἶχον) ὡς ποιμένας ἐκπέμπουσιν αὐτοὺς ἅμα ταῖς
ἀγέλαις ἐκδιδάξαντες ἕκαστα, πῶς δεῖ νέμειν πρὸ
μεσημβρίας, πῶς ἐπινέμειν κοπάσαντος τοῦ καύμα-
τος, πότε ἄγειν ἐπὶ ποτόν, πότε ἀπάγειν ἐπὶ κοῖτον, ἐπὶ
τίσι καλαύροπι χρηστέον, ἐπὶ τίσι μόνῃ φωνῇ. 3. οἱ δὲ
μάλα χαίροντες ὡς ἀρχὴν μεγάλην παρελάμβανον

---

8 "First Growth in Spring," a conventional personal name and
a cult-title of Demeter but not found in extant pastoral poetry.

ered and loved the child, as though frightened of being outshone by the ewe, and for credibility she too gave the child a pastoral name: Chloe.[8]

These children grew very rapidly and their beauty conspicuously surpassed the rural norm. The boy was now fifteen years of age and the girl just two years younger, when in the very same night Dryas and Lamo had the following dream. 2. They dreamed that those Nymphs in the cave where the spring was, where Dryas had found the baby, were handing Daphnis and Chloe over to a very headstrong and handsome boy sporting wings on his shoulders and carrying a small bow and arrows, who lightly touched them both with a single arrow and ordered them henceforth to tend the flocks, he the goats and she the sheep.[9]

Both were depressed by the vision of this dream, if it meant that they were to be mere shepherds and goatherds who from swaddling had shown promise of a better future—the reason why they had raised them on daintier fare and taught them reading and writing and whatever refinements a country life held; but they decided to obey the gods in the case of those saved by the gods' providence. 2. So they shared the dream with each other and in the Nymphs' shrine made an offering to the winged boy (they did not know what to call him), and then sent them forth with the flocks as shepherds, after instructing them in every particular: how they should let them graze before midday, how to graze them again after the midday heat has abated, when to take them for a drink, when to bring them home to sleep, on which ones to use the staff, on which ones the voice alone. 3. They accepted this role with great

7

8

[9] The boy is Eros.

καὶ ἐφίλουν τὰς αἶγας καὶ τὰ πρόβατα μᾶλλον ἢ
ποιμέσιν ἔθος, ἡ μὲν ἐς ποίμνιον ἄγουσα τῆς σωτηρίας τὴν αἰτίαν, ὁ δὲ μεμνημένος ὡς ἐκκείμενον αὐτὸν
αἲξ ἀνέθρεψεν.

9   Ἦρος ἦν ἀρχὴ καὶ πάντα ἤκμαζεν ἄνθη, τὰ ἐν
δρυμοῖς, τὰ ἐν λειμῶσι καὶ ὅσα ὄρεια· βόμβος ἦν
ἤδη μελιττῶν, ἦχος ὀρνίθων μουσικῶν, σκιρτήματα
ποιμνίων ἀρτιγεννήτων· ἄρνες ἐσκίρτων ἐν τοῖς ὄρε-
σιν, ἐβόμβουν ἐν τοῖς λειμῶσιν αἱ μέλιτται, τὰς
λόχμας κατῇδον ὄρνιθες. 2. τοσαύτης δὴ πάντα κατ-
εχούσης εὐωρίας οἷα ἁπαλοὶ καὶ νέοι μιμηταὶ τῶν
ἀκουομένων ἐγίνοντο καὶ βλεπομένων· ἀκούοντες μὲν
τῶν ὀρνίθων ᾀδόντων ᾖδον, βλέποντες δὲ σκιρτῶντας
τοὺς ἄρνας ἥλλοντο κοῦφα, καὶ τὰς μελίττας δὲ μιμού-
μενοι τὰ ἄνθη συνέλεγον· καὶ τὰ μὲν εἰς τοὺς κόλπους
ἔβαλλον, τὰ δὲ στεφανίσκους πλέκοντες ταῖς Νύμφαις ἐπέφερον.

10   Ἔπραττον δὲ κοινῇ πάντα, πλησίον ἀλλήλων νέ-
μοντες, καὶ πολλάκις μὲν ὁ Δάφνις τῶν προβάτων τὰ
ἀποπλανώμενα συνέστελλε, πολλάκις δὲ ἡ Χλόη τὰς
θρασυτέρας τῶν αἰγῶν ἀπὸ τῶν κρημνῶν κατήλαυνεν·
ἤδη δέ τις καὶ τὰς ἀγέλας ἀμφοτέρας ἐφρούρησε
θατέρου προσλιπαρήσαντος ἀθύρματι. 2. ἀθύρματα
δὲ ἦν αὐτοῖς ποιμενικὰ καὶ παιδικά. ἡ μὲν ἀνθερίκους
ἀνελομένη ποθὲν ἀκριδοθήραν[7] ἔπλεκε καὶ περὶ τοῦτο
πονουμένη τῶν ποιμνίων ἠμέλησεν, ὁ δὲ καλάμους
ἐκτεμὼν λεπτοὺς καὶ τρήσας τὰς τῶν γονάτων δια-
φυὰς ἀλλήλοις τε κηρῷ μαλθακῷ συναρτήσας μέχρι
νυκτὸς συρίζειν ἐμελέτησε. 3. καὶ ποτοῦ δὲ ἐκοινώνουν
γάλακτος ἢ οἴνου καὶ τροφὰς ἃς οἴκοθεν ἔφερον

---

7 -θήκην F, cf. Theocr. 1.52

delight as if it were a high office, and grew fonder of the goats and the sheep than shepherds usually are, for she credited a sheep with her survival, and he remembered that when he lay abandoned a goat had nursed him.

Spring had begun and all the flowers were abloom, in the woods, in the meadows, and on the hills. Now there was buzzing of bees, music of songbirds, gamboling of newborn sheep; lambs gamboled on the hills, bees buzzed in the meadows, birds enchanted the thickets. 2. Such was the season's beauty that filled the world, and being tender and young they began to mimic its sights and sounds: hearing the birds sing, they sang; seeing the lambs gambol, they skipped nimbly; and mimicking the bees, they gathered flowers, putting some inside their clothes and weaving others into garlands to bring to the Nymphs. 9

They did everything together, pasturing their flocks side by side. Often would Daphnis round up sheep that strayed, and often would Chloe drive the bolder goats down from the cliffs; it also happened that one would mind both flocks while the other was busy with a pastime. 2. Their pastimes were pastoral and childlike: she would collect stalks of asphodel here and there and weave a locust-trap,[10] ignoring the sheep as she worked at it; he would cut tender reeds, punch holes in the clefts at the joints, join them with soft wax, and practice playing the syrinx until nightfall.[11] 3. For drink they would share milk or wine, and the food they brought from home they brought to 10

[10] Alluding to a scene on the ivy-cup, symbolic of Theocritean pastoral, in *Idyll* 1; there is a further reminiscence of this cup below, 15. 3.

[11] Panpipes, the emblematic instrument of Greek pastoral.

εἰς κοινὸν ἔφερον. θᾶττον ἄν τις εἶδε τὰ ποίμνια καὶ
τὰς αἶγας ἀπ' ἀλλήλων μεμερισμένας ἢ Χλόην καὶ
Δάφνιν.

11   Τοιαῦτα δὲ αὐτῶν παιζόντων τοιάνδε σπουδὴν
Ἔρως ἀνέπλασε. λύκαινα τρέφουσα σκύμνους νέους
ἐκ τῶν πλησίον ἀγρῶν ἐξ ἄλλων ποιμνίων πολλὰ
ἥρπαζε, πολλῆς τροφῆς ἐς ἀνατροφὴν τῶν σκύμνων
δεομένη. 2. συνελθόντες οὖν οἱ κωμῆται νύκτωρ σι-
ροὺς ὀρύττουσι τὸ εὖρος ὀργυιᾶς, τὸ βάθος τεττάρων.
τὸ μὲν δὴ χῶμα τὸ πολὺ σπείρουσι κομίσαντες
μακράν, ξύλα δὲ ξηρὰ μακρὰ τείναντες ὑπὲρ τοῦ
χάσματος τὸ περιττὸν τοῦ χώματος κατέπασαν τῆς
πρότερον γῆς εἰκόνα, ὥστε κἂν λαγὼς ἐπιδράμῃ,
κατακλᾶν τὰ ξύλα καρφῶν ἀσθενέστερα ὄντα καὶ τότε
παρέχειν μαθεῖν ὅτι γῆ οὐκ ἦν ἀλλὰ μεμίμητο γῆν.
τοιαῦτα πολλὰ ὀρύγματα κἂν τοῖς ὄρεσι κἂν τοῖς
πεδίοις ὀρύξαντες, τὴν μὲν λύκαιναν οὐκ εὐτύχησαν
λαβεῖν (αἰσθάνεται γὰρ καὶ γῆς σεσοφισμένης), πολλὰς δὲ αἶγας καὶ ποίμνια διέφθειραν, καὶ Δάφνιν παρ'
ὀλίγον ὧδε.

12   Τράγοι παροξυνθέντες εἰς μάχην συνέπεσον. τῷ
οὖν ἑτέρῳ τὸ ἕτερον κέρας βιαιοτέρας γενομένης συμ-
βολῆς θραύεται, καὶ ἀλγήσας φριμαξάμενος ἐς φυγὴν
ἐτρέπετο· ὁ δὲ νικῶν κατ' ἴχνος ἑπόμενος ἄπαυστον
ἐποίει τὴν φυγήν. ἀλγεῖ Δάφνις περὶ τῷ κέρατι καὶ τῇ
θρασύτητι ἀχθεσθεὶς ξύλον καὶ τὴν καλαύροπα λαβὼν ἐδίωκε τὸν διώκοντα. 2. οἷα δὲ τοῦ μὲν ὑπ-
εκφεύγοντος, τοῦ δὲ ὀργῇ διώκοντος οὐκ ἀκριβὴς τῶν
ἐν ποσὶν ἡ πρόσοψις ἦν, ἀλλὰ κατὰ χάσματος ἄμφω
πίπτουσιν, ὁ τράγος πρότερος, ὁ Δάφνις δεύτερος.
τοῦτο μὲν ἔσωσε Δάφνιν, χρήσασθαι τῆς καταφορᾶς
ὀχήματι τῷ τράγῳ. 3. ὁ μὲν δὴ τὸν ἀνιμησόμενον εἴ τις

share. You would sooner have seen the sheep and the goats parted from one another than Chloe and Daphnis.

While they played at these pastimes, Love fashioned a 11 serious development. A she-wolf with young cubs to feed was carrying off lots of sheep from other flocks on the neighboring farms, since she needed lots of food for raising her cubs. 2. So the villagers gathered one night and dug pits six feet wide and twenty-four feet deep. Most of the dug soil they carried off and scattered at a distance, and then they put long dry sticks over the hole and spread the rest of the soil on top to make it look like the ground looked before, so that if even a hare ran over them it would snap the sticks, which were flimsier than straw, and then would have found out that it was not ground but a semblance of ground. They dug many such pits both in the hills and on the plains, and while they had no luck in catching the she-wolf (a wolf recognizes specious ground), they did destroy lots of goats and sheep, and almost Daphnis too, in the following way.

Two he-goats got worked up and fell to fighting. In an 12 especially violent clash, one of them had a horn broken and took to flight, bucking in pain, but the victor followed close on his heels and kept him on the run. Daphnis was upset about the horn and annoyed at such impetuosity, so grabbing a stick and his staff he took off in pursuit of the pursuer. 2. What with one trying to get away and the other in furious pursuit, there was no close attention to what lay underfoot and both fell into a pit, first the goat and then Daphnis. What saved Daphnis' life was using the goat as a vehicle on the way down. 3. He waited tearfully for anyone

ἄρα γένοιτο δακρύων ἀνέμενεν, ἡ δὲ Χλόη θεασαμένη
τὸ συμβὰν δρόμῳ παραγίνεται πρὸς τὸν σιρόν καὶ
μαθοῦσα ὅτι ζῇ καλεῖ τινα βουκόλον ἐκ τῶν ἀγρῶν
τῶν πλησίον εἰς ἐπικουρίαν. 4. ὁ δὲ ἐλθὼν σχοῖνον
ἐζήτει μακρὰν ἧς ἐχόμενος ἀνιμώμενος ἐκβήσεται, καὶ
σχοῖνος μὲν οὐκ ἦν, ἡ δὲ Χλόη λυσαμένη ταινίαν
δίδωσι καθεῖναι τῷ βουκόλῳ, καὶ οὕτως οἱ μὲν ἐπὶ τοῦ
χείλους ἑστῶτες εἷλκον, ὁ δὲ ἀνέβη ταῖς[8] τῆς ταινίας
ὁλκαῖς ταῖς χερσὶν ἀκολουθῶν. 5. ἀνιμήσαντο δὲ καὶ
τὸν ἄθλιον τράγον συντεθραυσμένον ἄμφω τὰ κέρατα·
τοσοῦτον ἄρα ἡ δίκη μετῆλθε τοῦ νικηθέντος τράγου.
τοῦτον μὲν δὴ τυθησόμενον χαρίζονται σῶστρα τῷ
βουκόλῳ, καὶ ἔμελλον ψεύδεσθαι πρὸς τοὺς οἴκοι
λύκων ἐπιδρομήν, εἴ τις αὐτὸν ἐπόθησεν· αὐτοὶ δὲ
ἐπανελθόντες ἐπεσκοποῦντο τὴν ποίμνην καὶ τὸ αἰπόλιον, καὶ ἐπεὶ κατέμαθον ἐν κόσμῳ νομῆς καὶ τὰς
αἶγας καὶ τὰ πρόβατα, καθίσαντες ἐπὶ στελέχει δρυὸς
ἐσκόπουν μή τι μέρος τοῦ σώματος ὁ Δάφνις ἥμαξε
καταπεσών. 6. τέτρωτο μὲν οὖν οὐδὲν οὐδὲ ἥμακτο
οὐδέν, χώματος δὲ καὶ πηλοῦ πέπαστο καὶ τὰς κόμας
καὶ τὸ ἄλλο σῶμα. ἐδόκει δὲ λούσασθαι πρὶν αἴσθη-
σιν γενέσθαι τοῦ συμβάντος Λάμωνι καὶ Μυρτάλῃ.

13   Καὶ ἐλθὼν ἅμα τῇ Χλόῃ πρὸς τὸ νυμφαῖον τῇ μὲν
ἔδωκε καὶ τὸν χιτωνίσκον καὶ τὴν πήραν φυλάττειν,
αὐτὸς δὲ τῇ πηγῇ προστὰς τήν τε κόμην καὶ τὸ σῶμα
πᾶν ἀπελούετο. 2. ἦν δὲ ἡ μὲν κόμη μέλαινα καὶ
πολλή, τὸ δὲ σῶμα ἐπίκαυτον ἡλίῳ· εἴκασεν ἄν τις
αὐτὸ χρῴζεσθαι τῇ σκιᾷ τῆς κόμης. ἐδόκει δὲ τῇ Χλόῃ
θεωμένῃ καλὸς ὁ Δάφνις, ὅτι πρῶτον[9] αὐτῇ καλὸς
ἐδόκει τὸ λουτρὸν ἐνόμιζε τοῦ κάλλους αἴτιον. καὶ τὰ

---

[8] Post ἀνέβη ταῖς usque ad 1.17.4 ἐγένετο deficit V

28

who might show up to pull him up, and Chloe, who had seen the accident, came running to the pit, and finding that he was alive hailed a cowherd from the neighboring farm for help. 4. He came and cast about for a long rope that Daphnis could hold onto and be pulled up. There was no rope, but Chloe undid her breast-band and gave it to the cowherd to let down. So they stood at the edge and pulled, and he ascended, following with both hands their pulls on the breast-band. 5. They also pulled up the poor goat, with both its horns broken: such then was its penalty in the matter of the vanquished goat. As a life-saver's reward they presented it to the goatherd to sacrifice, and in case anyone missed it they made up a story to tell their families about an attack by wolves. They themselves went back and looked over their herd and flock, and when they found the goats and the sheep grazing properly, they sat by the trunk of an oak tree and checked to be sure that in his fall Daphnis had not bloodied any part of his body. 6. In fact he had not been wounded at all and there was no trace of blood, but he was caked with dirt and mud in his hair and all over his body. It seemed best to wash before Lamo and Myrtale found out what had happened.

He went with Chloe to the Nymphs' shrine and gave   13 her his shirt and his knapsack to look after, while he stood by the spring and began washing his hair and his whole body. 2. His hair was dark and thick, his body tanned by the sun—one might have supposed it colored by the shadow of his hair. As Chloe watched, Daphnis seemed beautiful, and since he seemed beautiful to her for the first time, she thought the washing was the cause of the beauty. And

---

⁹ Maltese: πρότερον F

νῶτα δὲ ἀπολουούσης ἡ σὰρξ ὑπέπιπτε μαλθακή,
ὥστε λαθοῦσα ἑαυτῆς ἥψατο πολλάκις, εἰ τρυφερώτε-
ρος εἴη πειρωμένη. 3. καὶ τότε μὲν (ἤδη γὰρ ἐπὶ
δυσμαῖς[10] ἦν ὁ ἥλιος) ἀπήλασαν τὰς ἀγέλας οἴκαδε,
καὶ ἐπεπόνθει Χλόη περιττὸν οὐδὲν ὅτι μὴ Δάφνιν
ἐπεθύμει λουόμενον ἰδεῖν πάλιν. 4. τῆς δὲ ἐπιούσης ὡς
ἧκον εἰς τὴν νομήν, ὁ μὲν Δάφνις ὑπὸ τῇ δρυῒ τῇ
συνήθει καθεζόμενος ἐσύριττε καὶ ἅμα τὰς αἶγας
ἐπεσκόπει κατακειμένας καὶ ὥσπερ τῶν μελῶν ἀκρο-
ωμένας, ἡ δὲ Χλόη πλησίον καθημένη τὴν ἀγέλην μὲν
τῶν προβάτων ἐπέβλεπε, τὸ δὲ πλέον εἰς Δάφνιν ἑώρα,
καὶ ἐδόκει καλὸς αὐτῇ συρίττων πάλιν, καὶ αὖθις
αἰτίαν ἐνόμιζε τὴν μουσικὴν τοῦ κάλλους, ὥστε μετ᾽
ἐκεῖνον καὶ αὐτὴ τὴν σύριγγα ἔλαβεν, εἴ πως γένοιτο
καὶ αὐτὴ καλή. 5. ἔπεισε δὲ αὐτὸν καὶ λούσασθαι
πάλιν καὶ λουόμενον εἶδε καὶ ἰδοῦσα ἥψατο καὶ ἀπῆλθε πάλιν ἐπαινέσασα, καὶ ὁ ἔπαινος ἦν ἔρωτος
ἀρχή. ὅ τι μὲν οὖν ἔπασχεν οὐκ ᾔδει, νέα κόρη καὶ ἐν
ἀγροικίᾳ τεθραμμένη καὶ οὐδὲ ἄλλου λέγοντος ἀκούσασα τὸ τοῦ ἔρωτος ὄνομα· ἄση δὲ αὐτῆς εἶχε τὴν
ψυχὴν καὶ τῶν ὀφθαλμῶν οὐκ ἐκράτει καὶ πολλὰ
ἐλάλει Δάφνιν. 6. τροφῆς ἠμέλει, νύκτωρ ἠγρύπνει,
τῆς ἀγέλης κατεφρόνει· νῦν ἐγέλα, νῦν ἔκλαεν· εἶτα
ἐκάθητο,[11] εἶτα ἀνεπήδα· ὠχρία τὸ πρόσωπον, ἐρυθήματι αὖθις ἐφλέγετο. οὐδὲ βοὸς οἴστρῳ πληγείσης
τοσαῦτα ἔργα. ἐπῆλθόν ποτε αὐτῇ καὶ τοιοίδε λόγοι
μόνη γενομένη.

14   "Νῦν ἐγὼ νοσῶ μέν, τί δὲ ἡ νόσος ἀγνοῶ· ἀλγῶ, καὶ
ἕλκος οὐκ ἔστι μοι· λυποῦμαι, καὶ οὐδὲν τῶν προ-

---

10 ἤδη γὰρ ἐπὶ δυσμαῖς Reeve: [γὰρ ἐπὶ δυ]σμαῖς F
11 Henderson cf. 1.18.2: ἐκάθευδεν F: ἐκάθιζεν Rohde

when she washed his back, his skin yielded softly to her touch, so that she kept touching herself stealthily to find out whether he was more velvety than she. 3. At that point they drove their flocks home (by now the sun was setting), and Chloe had experienced nothing extraordinary except that she longed to see Daphnis washing again. 4. When they got to the pasture next day, Daphnis sat beneath the usual oak and played the syrinx while he watched his goats that lay about as if listening to the tunes; Chloe sat nearby and kept an eye on her flock of sheep, but mostly she was looking at Daphnis. As he played he once again seemed to her beautiful, and this time she thought the music was the cause of the beauty. And so when he had finished she picked up the syrinx herself, hoping that she too might become beautiful. 5. She also persuaded him to have another wash, and she watched him while he washed, and after watching she touched him, and again she came away in admiration, and that admiration was the beginning of love. She did not know what was happening to her, being but a young girl raised in the country, who had never even heard anyone speak of love. Her heart began to ache, she could not control her eyes, she was always talking about Daphnis. 6. She neglected food, she was sleepless at night, she neglected her flock. Now she would be laughing, now she would be crying. One moment she would sit quietly, the next she would leap into action. Her face would turn pale and then blush red. Not even a cow stung by a gadfly acts this way. One day when she was alone, she found herself speaking this way:

"I'm ailing these days, but I don't know what my ailment is. I hurt, and I have no wound. I feel sad, and none of   14

βάτων ἀπόλωλέ μοι· κάομαι, καὶ ἐν σκιᾷ τοσαύτῃ
κάθημαι. 2. πόσοι βάτοι με πολλάκις ἤμυξαν, καὶ οὐκ
ἔκλαυσα· πόσαι μέλιτται ⟨τὰ⟩ κέντρα ἐνῆκαν, καὶ οὐκ
ἔκραγον¹²· τουτὶ δὲ τὸ νύττον μου τὴν καρδίαν πάντων
ἐκείνων πικρότερον. καλὸς ὁ Δάφνις, καὶ γὰρ τὰ ἄνθη·
καλὸν ἡ σύριγξ αὐτοῦ φθέγγεται, καὶ γὰρ αἱ ἀηδόνες.
ἀλλ᾽ ἐκείνων οὐδείς μοι λόγος. 3. εἴθε αὐτοῦ σύριγξ
ἐγενόμην, ἵν᾽ ἐμπνέῃ μοι· εἴθε αἴξ ἵν᾽ ὑπ᾽ ἐκείνου
νέμωμαι. ὦ πονηρὸν ὕδωρ, μόνον Δάφνιν καλὸν ἐποίη-
σας, ἐγὼ δὲ μάτην ἀπελουσάμην. οἴχομαι, Νύμφαι
φίλαι· καὶ οὐδὲ ὑμεῖς σώζετε τὴν παρθένον τὴν ἐν ὑμῖν
τραφεῖσαν. 4. τίς ὑμᾶς στεφανώσει μετ᾽ ἐμέ; τίς τοὺς
ἀθλίους ἄρνας ἀναθρέψει; τίς τὴν λάλον ἀκρίδα θερα-
πεύσει, ἣν πολλὰ καμοῦσα ἐθήρασα ἵνα με κατα-
κοιμίζῃ φθεγγομένη πρὸ τοῦ ἄντρου; νῦν δὲ ἐγὼ μὲν
ἀγρυπνῶ διὰ Δάφνιν, ἡ δὲ μάτην λαλεῖ."

15   Τοιαῦτα ἔπασχε, τοιαῦτα ἔλεγεν, ἐπιζητοῦσα τὸ
ἔρωτος ὄνομα. Δόρκων δὲ ὁ βουκόλος ὁ τὸν Δάφνιν ἐκ
τοῦ σιροῦ καὶ τὸν τράγον ἀνιμησάμενος, ἀρτιγένειος
μειρακίσκος καὶ εἰδὼς ἔρωτος καὶ τὰ ἔργα καὶ τὰ
ὀνόματα, εὐθὺς μὲν ἐπ᾽ ἐκείνης τῆς ἡμέρας ἐρωτικῶς
τῆς Χλόης διετέθη, πλειόνων δὲ διαγενομένων μᾶλλον
τὴν ψυχὴν ἐξεπυρσεύθη καὶ τοῦ Δάφνιδος ὡς παιδὸς
καταφρονήσας ἔγνω κατεργάσασθαι δώροις ἢ βίᾳ.
2. τὸ μὲν δὴ πρῶτον δῶρα αὐτοῖς ἐκόμισε τῷ μὲν σύριγγα βουκολικήν, καλάμους ἐννέα χαλκῷ δεδεμένους
ἀντὶ κηροῦ, τῇ δὲ νεβρίδα βακχικήν, καὶ αὐτῇ τὸ
χρῶμα ἦν ὥσπερ γεγραμμένον¹³ χρώμασιν. 3. ἐντεῦθεν δὲ φίλος νομιζόμενος τοῦ μὲν Δάφνιδος ἠμέλει

---

¹² ἀλλ᾽ (melius καὶ) οὐκ ἔκραγον Edmonds: ἀλλὰ ἔφαγον
F   ¹³ ὥσπερ γεγραμμένον] ὡς ἐπεστιγμένον Follet

32

my sheep have gone missing. I feel hot, and I'm sitting in deep shade. 2. How often have brambles scratched me, and I never cried! How often have bees plunged their stingers, and I never screamed! But this thing that now stings my heart is sharper than all of those. Daphnis is beautiful, but so are the flowers; his syrinx sounds beautiful, but so do the nightingales. And yet they are nothing special to me. 3. I wish I could be his syrinx, so he could breathe into me! I wish I could be a goat, so I could be in his flock! Wicked water, you made only Daphnis beautiful, but washing did nothing for me! I'm passing away, dear Nymphs, and not even you try to save the girl who was raised among you. 4. After I'm gone, who will garland you? Who will bring up the poor lambs? Who will take care of the chatty locust that I took such trouble to catch, so that it would sing me to sleep in front of the cave? And now on account of Daphnis I can't sleep, and its chatter is wasted."

Such were her feelings and such her speech as she sought the word for love. But Dorco,[12] the cowherd who had pulled Daphnis and the goat out of the pit, a young man with his first beard who knew about love, both what it does and the words for it, on that very day had conceived an immediate passion for Chloe, and as the days passed his heart grew more inflamed, and scorning Daphnis as a mere child, he resolved to make her his, by gifts or by force. 2. First of all he brought them gifts: for him a cowherd's syrinx, nine reeds joined by bronze instead of wax, and for her a bacchic fawnskin whose color was as if applied with paints. 3. Being now regarded as a friend, he took less and

[12] "Roe Deer", a name not found in extant pastoral poetry.

κατ᾽ ὀλίγον, τῇ Χλόῃ δὲ ἀνὰ πᾶσαν ἡμέραν ἐπέφερεν
ἢ τυρὸν ἁπαλὸν ἢ στέφανον ἀνθηρὸν ἢ μῆλον ὡραῖον·
ἐκόμισε δέ ποτε αὐτῇ καὶ μόσχον ἀρτιγέννητον καὶ
κισσύβιον διάχρυσον καὶ ὀρνίθων ὀρείων νεοττούς. ἡ
δὲ ἄπειρος οὖσα τέχνης ἐραστοῦ λαμβάνουσα μὲν τὰ
δῶρα ἔχαιρε, μᾶλλον δὲ ἔχαιρεν ὅτι Δάφνιδι εἶχεν
αὐτὴ χαρίζεσθαι. 4. καὶ (ἔδει γὰρ ἤδη καὶ Δάφνιν
γνῶναι τὰ ἔρωτος ἔργα) γίνεταί ποτε τῷ Δόρκωνι πρὸς
αὐτὸν ὑπὲρ κάλλους ἔρις, καὶ ἐδίκαζε μὲν Χλόη, ἔκειτο
δὲ ἆθλον τῷ νικήσαντι φιλῆσαι Χλόην. Δόρκων δὲ
πρότερος ὧδε ἔλεγεν·

16   "Ἐγώ, παρθένε, μείζων εἰμὶ Δάφνιδος, καὶ ἐγὼ μὲν
βουκόλος, ὁ δὲ αἰπόλος· τοσοῦτον ⟨οὖν ἐγὼ⟩[14] κρείττων ὅσον αἰγῶν βόες· καὶ λευκός εἰμι ὡς γάλα καὶ
πυ⟨ρ⟩ρὸς ὡς θέρος μέλλον ἀμᾶσθαι, καί ⟨με⟩[15] ἔθρεψε
μήτηρ, οὐ θηρίον. 2. οὗτος δέ ἐστι μικρὸς ⟨ὡς παῖς⟩[16]
καὶ ἀγένειος ὡς γυνὴ καὶ μέλας ὡς λύκος· νέμει δὲ
τράγους, ὀδω⟨δὼς αὐτὸς⟩[17] δεινόν, καὶ ἔστι πένης ὡς
μηδὲ κύνα τρέφειν. εἰ δ᾽ ὡς λέγουσι καὶ αἶξ αὐτῷ γάλα
δέδωκεν, οὐδὲν ἐρίφων διαφέρει." 3. ταῦτα καὶ τοιαῦτα
ὁ Δόρκων, καὶ μετὰ ταῦτα ὁ Δάφνις· "ἐμὲ αἶξ ἀνέθρεψεν ὥσπερ τὸν Δία, νέμω δὲ τράγους τῶν τούτου βοῶν
μείζονας, ὄζω δὲ οὐδὲν ἀπ᾽ αὐτῶν, ὅτι μηδὲ ὁ Πάν,
καίτοιγε ὢν τὸ πλέον τράγος. 4. ἀρκεῖ δέ μοι τυρὸς καὶ
ἄρτος ὀβελίας καὶ οἶνος λευκός,[18] ὅσα ἀγροίκων πλουσίων κτήματα. ἀγένειός εἰμι, καὶ γὰρ ὁ Διόνυσος·
μέλας,[19] καὶ γὰρ ὁ ὑάκινθος· ἀλλὰ κρείττων καὶ ὁ

    14 Suppl. Cobet   15 Suppl. Courier cl. 3.29.3
    16 Suppl. Reeve   17 Suppl. Henderson: ὀδω⟨δὼς ἀπ᾽
αὐτῶν Cobet: ὄδω⟨δεν ἄρα Follet: ὀδω[c. 6–8 litt.] F
    18 an γλυκύς? Morgan cl. 4.17.6 (V F)

less notice of Daphnis, but every day he would bring Chloe soft cheese or a garland of flowers or a ripe apple. One day he brought her a newborn calf, a wooden ivy-bowl inlaid with gold,[13] and some nestling mountain birds. Being unfamiliar with a lover's technique, she was happy to receive the gifts, and even happier that she herself had something to give Daphnis. 4. One day, for now it was Daphnis' turn to discover what love does, Dorco got into a beauty contest with him. Chloe would be the judge, and the victor's prize would be to kiss Chloe. Dorco spoke first:

"I, my girl, am bigger than Daphnis, and I'm a cowherd   16 while he's a goatherd, so I'm as superior to him as cows are to goats. I'm as white as milk and my hair is ruddy like a cornfield ready for reaping. And a mother raised me, not a beast. 2. But this fellow is short ⟨like a boy⟩, beardless like a woman, and dark like a wolf. He tends he-goats and smells terrible himself, and he's too poor to keep even a dog. And if what they say is true, that a goat suckled him, he's really no better than a kid." 3. This and the like from Dorco, and then it was Daphnis' turn: "A goat did nurse me, just like Zeus,[14] and the goats I tend are bigger than his cows. I don't smell of them at all, because Pan doesn't either, and he's mostly goat. 4. And I have plenty of cheese, bread baked on a spit, and white[15] wine—the sort of goods that make countrymen rich. I'm beardless, but so is Dionysus; dark, and so is the hyacinth. And yet Dionysus is better

---

13 See 1.10.2 n.
14 By the goat-nymph Amaltheia.
15 Perhaps "sweet" should be read.

---

19 Courier: μέγας F

Διόνυσος Σατύρων ⟨καὶ⟩ ὁ ὑάκινθος κρίνων. 5. οὗτος δὲ καὶ πυρρὸς ὡς ἀλώπηξ καὶ προγένειος ὡς τράγος καὶ λευκὸς ὡς ἐξ ἄστεος γυνή· κἂν δέῃ σε φιλεῖν, ἐμοῦ μὲν φιλεῖς τὸ στόμα, τούτου δὲ τὰς ἐπὶ τοῦ γενείου τρίχας. μέμνησο δέ, ὦ παρθένε, ὅτι σὲ ποίμνιον ἔθρεψεν, ἀλλ᾽ εἶ καλή.”

17　　Οὐκέθ᾽ ἡ Χλόη περιέμεινεν, ἀλλὰ τὰ μὲν ἡσθεῖσα τῷ ἐγκωμίῳ, τὰ δὲ πάλαι ποθοῦσα φιλῆσαι Δάφνιν, ἀναπηδήσασα αὐτὸν ἐφίλησεν, ἀδίδακτον μὲν καὶ ἄτεχνον, πάνυ δὲ ψυχὴν θερμᾶναι δυνάμενον. 2. Δόρκων μὲν οὖν ἀλγήσας ἀπέδραμε ζητῶν ἄλλην ὁδὸν ἔρωτος· Δάφνις δὲ ὥσπερ οὐ φιληθεὶς ἀλλὰ δηχθεὶς σκυθρωπός τις εὐθὺς ἦν καὶ πολλάκις ἐψύχετο καὶ τὴν καρδίαν παλλομένην κατεῖχε, καὶ βλέπειν μὲν ἤθελε τὴν Χλόην, βλέπων δ᾽ ἐρυθήματι ἐπίμπλατο. 3. τότε πρῶτον καὶ τὴν κόμην αὐτῆς ἐθαύμασεν ὅτι ξανθὴ καὶ τοὺς ὀφθαλμοὺς ὅτι μεγάλοι καθάπερ βοὸς καὶ τὸ πρόσωπον ὅτι λευκότερον ἀληθῶς καὶ τοῦ τῶν αἰγῶν γάλακτος, ὥσπερ τότε πρῶτον ὀφθαλμοὺς κτησάμενος, τὸν δὲ πρότερον χρόνον πεπηρωμένος. 4. οὔτε οὖν τροφὴν προσεφέρετο πλὴν ὅσον ἀπογεύσασθαι καὶ ποτὸν εἴ ποτε ἐβιάσθη μέχρι τοῦ διαβρέξαι τὸ στόμα προσεφέρετο. σιωπηλὸς ἦν ὁ πρότερον τῶν ἀκρίδων λαλίστερος, ἀργὸς ὁ περιττότερα τῶν αἰγῶν κινούμενος. ἠμέλητο καὶ ἡ ἀγέλη· ἔρριπτο καὶ ἡ σῦριγξ, χλωρότερον τὸ πρόσωπον ἦν πόας θερινῆς.[20] εἰς μόνην Χλόην ἐγίγνετο λάλος, καὶ εἴ ποτε μόνος ἀπ᾽ αὐτῆς ἐγένετο[21] τοιαῦτα πρὸς αὑτὸν ἀπελήρει·

18　　“Τί ποτέ με ⟨τὸ⟩[22] Χλόης ἐργάζεται φίλημα; χείλη μὲν ῥόδων ἁπαλώτερα καὶ στόμα κηρίων γλυκύτερον, τὸ δὲ φίλημα κέντρου μελίττης πικρότερον. πολλάκις ἐφίλησα ἐρίφους, πολλάκις ἐφίλησα σκύλακας ἀρτι-

than Satyrs and the hyacinth better than lilies. 5. But this
fellow is ruddy like a fox, goateed like a goat, and white like
a townswoman. And if you must kiss someone, you can kiss
my mouth but only the hairs on his chin. Remember, my
girl, that a sheep nursed you, but you are beautiful."

Chloe delayed no longer, but delighted by his homage   17
and anyway having long yearned to kiss him, she jumped
up and gave him a kiss, untrained and artless but with
power to inflame a soul. 2. So Dorco ran off in pain, looking
for another route to love, while Daphnis, as if not kissed
but rather stung, was from that moment a sullen sort; he
kept getting chills and kept trying to control his pounding
heart; he wanted to look at Chloe but when he looked he
blushed all over. 3. That was the first time he saw with won-
der that her hair was blonde, her eyes as big as a cow's, her
face truly whiter even than goats' milk, as if that was the
first time he had eyes to see and hadn't eyes before. 4. So
he took no food except a mere taste, and if he had to drink
he took only enough to moisten his lips. Before, he had
been more chatty than a locust, but now he was taciturn;
before, he had been busier than the goats, but now he was
listless. His flock was neglected, his syrinx tossed aside, his
face paler than summer grass. He was chatty only with
Chloe, and if ever he was alone without her, he would prat-
tle to himself this way:

"What in the world is Chloe's kiss doing to me? Her lips   18
are softer than rose petals and her mouth is sweeter than
honeycombs, but her kiss is sharper than a bee sting. I have
many times kissed kids, many times newborn puppies and

---

20 Courier: χλόας (-ης superscr.) καιρινῆς (θε- superscr.) F
21 Hic redit V   22 Suppl. Reeve

γεννήτους καὶ τὸν μόσχον ὃν ὁ Δόρκων ἐχαρίσατο·[23]
ἀλλὰ τοῦτο φίλημα καινόν· ἐκπηδᾷ μου τὸ πνεῦμα,
ἐξάλλεται ἡ καρδία, τήκεται ἡ ψυχή, καὶ ὅμως πάλιν
φιλῆσαι θέλω. 2. ὦ νίκης κακῆς, ὦ νόσου καινῆς, ἧς
οὐδὲ εἰπεῖν οἶδα τὸ ὄνομα. ἆρα φαρμάκων ἐγεύσατο
Χλόη μέλλουσά με φιλεῖν; πῶς οὖν οὐκ ἀπέθανεν;[24]
οἷον ᾄδουσιν αἱ ἀηδόνες, ἡ δὲ ἐμὴ σῦριγξ σιωπᾷ· οἷον
σκιρτῶσιν οἱ ἔριφοι, κἀγὼ κάθημαι· οἷον ἀκμάζει τὰ
ἄνθη, κἀγὼ στεφάνους οὐ πλέκω, ἀλλὰ τὰ μὲν ἴα καὶ ὁ
ὑάκινθος ἀνθεῖ, Δάφνις δὲ μαραίνεται. ἆρά μου καὶ
Δόρκων εὐμορφότερος ὀφθήσεται;"

19   Τοιαῦτα ὁ βέλτιστος Δάφνις ἔπασχε καὶ ἔλεγεν,
οἷα πρῶτον γευόμενος τῶν ἔρωτος ἔργων καὶ λόγων. ὁ
δὲ Δόρκων ὁ βουκόλος ὁ τῆς Χλόης ἐραστὴς φυλάξας
τὸν Δρύαντα φυτὸν κατορύττοντα πλησίον κλήματος
πρόσεισιν αὐτῷ μετὰ τυρίσκων[25] τινῶν γεννικῶν καὶ
τοὺς μὲν δῶρον εἶναι δίδωσι, πάλαι φίλος ὢν ἡνίκα
αὐτὸς ἔνεμεν, ἐντεῦθεν δὲ ἀρξάμενος ἐνέβαλε λόγον
περὶ τοῦ τῆς Χλόης γάμου· 2. καὶ εἰ λαμβάνοι γυναῖκα
δῶρα πολλὰ καὶ μεγάλα ὡς βουκόλος ἐπηγγέλλετο,
ζεῦγος βοῶν ἀροτήρων, σμήνη τέτταρα μελιττῶν,
φυτὰ μηλεῶν πεντήκοντα, δέρμα ταύρου τεμεῖν ὑποδήματα, μόσχον ἀνὰ πᾶν ἔτος μηκέτι γάλακτος δεό-
μενον· 3. ὥστε σμικροῦ δεῖν ὁ Δρύας θελχθεὶς τοῖς
δώροις ἐπένευσε τὸν γάμον. ἐννοήσας δὲ ὡς κρείτ-
τονος ἡ παρθένος ἀξία νυμφίου καὶ δείσας μὴ φωρα-
θεὶς ποτε κακοῖς ἀνηκέστοις περιπέσοι, τόν τε γάμον
ἀνένευσε καὶ συγγνώμην ἔχειν ᾐτήσατο καὶ τὰ ὀνο-
μασθέντα δῶρα παρῃτήσατο.

20   Δευτέρας δὴ διαμαρτὼν ὁ Δόρκων ἐλπίδος καὶ
μάτην τυροὺς ἀγαθοὺς ἀπολέσας ἔγνω διὰ χειρῶν

the calf that was Dorco's gift. But this kiss is something strange: my breath is surging, my heart is leaping, my soul is melting away, and yet I want to kiss her again. What a malign victory, what a strange sickness; I don't even know what to call it. Did Chloe sip poison just before she kissed me? Then how come she didn't die? How the nightingales are singing, and my syrinx is silent! How the kids are frisking about, and I sit still! How the flowers bloom, and I weave no garlands. The violets and the hyacinth flower, and Daphnis withers. Will even Dorco be looking handsomer than me?"

In this manner did that fine fellow Daphnis suffer and 19 speak upon first tasting love's effects and expressions. But Dorco, Chloe's cowherd suitor, waited until Dryas was planting a tree beside a vine slip and went over to him with some fine little cheeses. These he gave as a present, being his old friend from the days when Dryas herded cattle himself. He followed this opener by broaching the subject of Chloe's marriage. 2. He promised a cowherd's plethora of great gifts if he got her as his wife: a yoke of plough oxen, four swarms of bees, fifty apple trees, a bull's hide to cut up for shoes, and a weaned calf annually. 3. Dryas, charmed by these gifts, very nearly consented to the marriage. But he reckoned that the girl deserved a better bridegroom and feared that one day he would be found out and get into desperate trouble, so he rejected the marriage, begged pardon, and declined the proffered gifts.

Now Dorco had suffered his second disappointment 20 and had wasted some good cheeses, so he resolved to get

<hr>

23 ἐδωρήσατο F   24 ἀπέθανον V
25 συρίγγων F

ἐπιθέσθαι τῇ Χλόῃ μόνῃ γενομένῃ, καὶ παραφυλάξας
ὅτι παρ' ἡμέραν ἐπὶ ποτὸν ἄγουσι τὰς ἀγέλας ποτὲ
μὲν ὁ Δάφνις ποτὲ δὲ ἡ παῖς, ἐπιτεχνᾶται τέχνην
ποιμένι πρέπουσαν. 2. λύκου δέρμα μεγάλου λαβὼν
ὃν ταῦρός ποτε πρὸ τῶν βοῶν μαχόμενος τοῖς κέρασι
διέφθειρε, περιέτεινε τῷ σώματι ποδῆρες κατανωτι-
σάμενος ὡς τούς τ' ἐμπροσθίους πόδας ἐφηπλῶσθαι
ταῖς χερσὶ καὶ τοὺς κατόπιν τοῖς σκέλεσιν ἄχρι πτέρ-
νης καὶ τοῦ στόματος τὸ χάσμα σκέπειν τὴν κεφαλὴν
ὥσπερ ἀνδρὸς ὁπλίτου κράνος. 3. ἐκθηριώσας δὲ αὐτὸν ὡς ἔνι μάλιστα, παραγίνεται πρὸς τὴν πηγὴν ἧς
ἔπινον αἱ αἶγες καὶ τὰ πρόβατα μετὰ τὴν νομήν. ἐν
κοίλῃ δὲ πάνυ γῇ ἦν ἡ πηγή, καὶ περὶ αὐτὴν πᾶς ὁ
τόπος ἀκάνθαις καὶ βάτοις καὶ ἀρκεύθῳ ταπεινῇ καὶ
σκολύμοις ἠγρίωτο· 4. ῥᾳδίως ἂν ἐκεῖ καὶ λύκος ἀληθινὸς ἔλαθε λοχῶν. ἐνταῦθα κρύψας ἑαυτὸν ἐπετήρει
τοῦ ποτοῦ τὴν ὥραν ὁ Δόρκων καὶ πολλὴν εἶχεν
ἐλπίδα τῷ σχήματι φοβήσας λαβεῖν ταῖς χερσὶ τὴν
Χλόην.

21   Χρόνος ὀλίγος διαγίνεται καὶ Χλόη κατήλαυνε τὰς
ἀγέλας εἰς τὴν πηγήν, καταλιποῦσα τὸν Δάφνιν φυλλάδα χλωρὰν κόπτοντα τοῖς ἐρίφοις τροφὴν μετὰ τὴν
νομήν. 2. καὶ οἱ κύνες οἱ τῶν προβάτων ἐπιφύλακες[26]
καὶ τῶν αἰγῶν ἑπόμενοι, οἷα δὴ κυνῶν ἐν ῥινηλασίαις
περιεργίᾳ, κινούμενον τὸν Δόρκωνα πρὸς τὴν ἐπίθεσιν
τῆς κόρης φωράσαντες πικρὸν μάλα ὑλακτήσαντες
ὥρμησαν ὡς ἐπὶ λύκον καὶ περισχόντες πρὶν ὅλως
ἀναστῆναι δι' ἔκπληξιν ἔδακνον κατὰ τοῦ δέρματος.[27]
3. τέως μὲν οὖν τὸν ἔλεγχον αἰδούμενος καὶ ὑπὸ τοῦ
δέρματος ἐπισκέποντος φρουρούμενος ἔκειτο σιωπῶν
ἐν τῇ λόχμῃ· ἐπεὶ δὲ ἥ τε Χλόη πρὸς τὴν πρώτην θέαν
διαταραχθεῖσα τὸν Δάφνιν ἐκάλει βοηθὸν οἵ τε κύνες

Chloe into his clutches when she was alone. Noticing that they drove their flocks to drink on alternate days, one day Daphnis and the next day the girl, he worked out a stratagem befitting a herdsman. 2. He got the skin of a big wolf that a bull once gored to death in defense of his cows and stretched it over his back, wrapping it around his body down to his toes so that the forepaws spread over his hands and the hind paws over his legs down to the heels, and the gaping maw covered his head like an infantryman's helmet. 3. Having turned himself into a beast as best he could, he went to the spring where the goats and sheep drank after grazing. The spring was in a deep hollow, and the whole area around it grew wild with thorns, brambles, dwarf juniper, and thistles. 4. Even a real wolf could easily have lurked there unseen. Dorco hid himself in that spot and waited for watering time, very confident that he would scare Chloe with his disguise and get her into his clutches.

In a little while, Chloe left Daphnis cutting green 21 leaves as fodder for the kids and began driving her flocks to the spring. 2. The dogs that went with her to guard the sheep and goats, with typical canine nosiness in tracking a scent, got wind of Dorco as he moved on the girl and, barking deafeningly, rushed at him as at a wolf. Before his panic allowed him to stand fully upright, they were all over him and biting away at the skin. 3. For a while he lay mute in his copse, embarrassed at the prospect of exposure and still protected by the skin that covered him; but when Chloe, quite spooked by her first sight of him, started calling Daphnis to help and the dogs pulled off the skin and began

---

26 ἐπιφύλαξ memoratur ap. Apollon. 104.10: ἐπὶ φυλακὴν F
27 τοῦ δέρματος F: κράτος V

περισπῶντες τὸ δέρμα τοῦ σώματος ἥπτοντο αὐτοῦ,
μέγα οἰμώξας ἱκέτευε βοηθεῖν τὴν κόρην καὶ τὸν
Δάφνιν ἤδη παρόντα. 4. τοὺς μὲν δὴ κύνας ἀνακαλέ-
σαντες συνήθως²⁸ ταχέως ἡμέρωσαν, τὸν δὲ Δόρκωνα
κατά τε μηρῶν καὶ ὤμων δεδηγμένον ἀγαγόντες ἐπὶ
τὴν πηγὴν ἀπένιψαν τὰ δήγματα [ἵνα ἦσαν τῶν ὀδόντων αἱ ἐμβολαὶ]²⁹ καὶ διαμασησάμενοι φλοιὸν χλωρὸν
πτελέας ἐπέπασαν, 5. ὑπό τε ἀπειρίας ἐρωτικῶν τολ-
μημάτων ποιμενικὴν παιδιὰν νομίζοντες τὴν ἐπιβολὴν
τοῦ δέρματος οὐδὲν ὀργισθέντες ἀλλὰ καὶ παραμυθη-
σάμενοι καὶ μέχρι τινὸς χειραγωγήσαντες ἀπέπεμ-
ψαν.

22   Καὶ ὁ μὲν κινδύνου παρὰ τοσοῦτον ἐλθὼν καὶ
σωθεὶς ἐκ κυνός φασιν οὐ λύκου στόματος ἐθεράπευε
τὸ σῶμα· ὁ δὲ Δάφνις καὶ ἡ Χλόη κάματον πολὺν
ἔσχον μέχρι νυκτὸς τὰς αἶγας καὶ τὰς ὄϊς συλλέγον-
τες· 2. ὑπὸ γὰρ τοῦ δέρματος πτοηθεῖσαι καὶ ὑπὸ τῶν
κυνῶν ὑλακτησάντων ταραχθεῖσαι αἱ μὲν εἰς πέτρας
ἀνέδραμον, αἱ δὲ μέχρι καὶ τῆς θαλάσσης αὐτῆς
κατέδραμον. καίτοιγε πεπαίδευντο καὶ φωνῇ πείθεσθαι καὶ σύριγγι θέλγεσθαι καὶ χειρὸς παταγῇ συλ-
λέγεσθαι· ἀλλὰ τότε πάντων αὐταῖς ὁ φόβος λήθην
ἐνέβαλε. 3. καὶ μόλις ὥσπερ λαγὼς ἐκ τῶν ἰχνῶν
εὑρίσκοντες εἰς τὰς ἐπαύλεις ἤγαγον. ἐκείνης μόνης
τῆς νυκτὸς ἐκοιμήθησαν βαθὺν ὕπνον καὶ τῆς ἐρωτικῆς λύπης φάρμακον τὸν κάματον ἔσχον. 4. αὖθις δὲ
ἡμέρας ἐπελθούσης πάλιν ἔπασχον παραπλήσια.
ἔχαιρον ἰδόντες, ἐλυποῦντο ἀπαλλαγέντες [ἤλγουν]·³⁰
ἤθελόν τι, ἠγνόουν ὅ τι θέλουσι. τοῦτο μόνον ᾔδεσαν,
ὅτι τὸν μὲν φίλημα, τὴν δὲ λουτρὸν ἀπώλεσεν.

23   Ἐξέκαε δὲ αὐτοὺς καὶ ἡ ὥρα τοῦ ἔτους. ἦρος ἦν ἤδη

to fasten onto him, he gave a loud cry and pleaded for help
from Chloe and Daphnis, who was now on the scene. 4.
Calling off the dogs in their usual way they quickly quieted
them, and Dorco, bitten on the thighs and shoulders, they
led to the spring and washed his bites clean, and chewed
some green elm bark to daub on them. 5. In their innocence of amorous adventures they regarded the skin costume as a pastoral game, so they were not at all angry and
even tried to cheer him up, and they led him by the hand
for a while before sending him on his way.

After so narrow a brush with danger, and safely   22
snatched from the jaws of a dog (not the proverbial wolf),
Dorco nursed his wounds, while Daphnis and Chloe were
kept hard at work till nightfall rounding up the she-goats
and the ewes; 2. for panicked by the skin and startled by
the baying of the dogs, some had run up cliffs and others
had run down all the way to the sea. They were trained to
obey the human voice, to be calmed by the syrinx, and to
gather at a hand-clap, yet on that occasion their fright had
consigned everything to oblivion. 3. It took some doing to
track them down like hares and drive them into their folds.
That night, for once, they slept soundly, and in weariness
had relief from the pain of love. 4. But when daylight returned their feelings were much the same as before: they
were happy to see one another and sad to be apart; they
wanted something but did not know what they wanted.
They knew only that a kiss had been his undoing, and a
bath hers.

The time of year inflamed them too. It was now the end   23

---

28 ἀνακλάσει (-κλή- V2) συνήθει V   29 Del. Hercher
30 ἤλγουν del. Reeve, ἐλυποῦντο del. Cobet

43

τέλη καὶ θέρους ἀρχή, καὶ πάντα ἐν ἀκμῇ· δένδρα ἐν
καρποῖς, πεδία ἐν ληΐοις· ἡδεῖα μὲν τεττίγων ἠχή,
γλυκεῖα δὲ ὀπώρας ὀδμή, τερπνὴ δὲ ποιμνίων βληχή.
2. εἴκασεν ἄν τις καὶ τοὺς ποταμοὺς ᾄδειν ἠρέμα
ῥέοντας καὶ τοὺς ἀνέμους συρίττειν ταῖς πίτυσιν ἐμ-
πνέοντας καὶ τὰ μῆλα ἐρῶντα πίπτειν χαμαὶ καὶ τὸν
ἥλιον φιλόκαλον ὄντα πάντας ἀποδύειν. ὁ μὲν οὖν
Δάφνις θαλπόμενος τούτοις ἅπασιν εἰς τοὺς ποταμοὺς
ἐνέβαινε καὶ ποτὲ μὲν ἐλούετο, ποτὲ δὲ καὶ τῶν ἰχθύων
τοὺς ἐνδινεύοντας ἐθήρα, πολλάκις δὲ καὶ ἔπινεν ὡς τὸ
ἔνδοθεν καῦμα σβέσων· 3. ἡ δὲ Χλόη μετὰ τὸ ἀμέλξαι
τὰς ὄϊς καὶ τῶν αἰγῶν τὰς πολλὰς ἐπὶ πολὺν μὲν
χρόνον εἶχε πηγνῦσα τὸ γάλα· δειναὶ γὰρ αἱ μυῖαι
λυπῆσαι καὶ δακεῖν εἰ <μὴ>[31] διώκοιντο· τὸ δὲ ἐντεῦθεν
ἀπολουσαμένη τὸ πρόσωπον πίτυος ἐστεφανοῦτο κλά-
δοις καὶ τῇ νεβρίδι ἐζώννυτο καὶ τὸν γαυλὸν ἀναπλή-
σασα οἴνου καὶ γάλακτος κοινὸν μετὰ τοῦ Δάφνιδος
ποτὸν εἶχε.

24   Τῆς δὲ μεσημβρίας ἐπελθούσης ἐγίνετο ἤδη τῶν
ὀφθαλμῶν ἅλωσις αὐτοῖς· ἡ μὲν γὰρ γυμνὸν ὁρῶσα
τὸν Δάφνιν εἰς ἄθρουν[32] ἐνέπιπτε τὸ κάλλος καὶ ἐτή-
κετο μηδὲν αὐτοῦ μέρος μέμψασθαι δυναμένη· ὁ δὲ
ἰδὼν ἐν νεβρίδι καὶ στεφάνῳ πίτυος ὀρέγουσαν τὸν
γαυλὸν μίαν ᾤετο τῶν ἐκ τοῦ ἄντρου Νυμφῶν ὁρᾶν. 2.
ὁ μὲν οὖν τὴν πίτυν ἀπὸ τῆς κεφαλῆς ἁρπάζων αὐτὸς
ἐστεφανοῦτο, πρότερον φιλήσας τὸν στέφανον· ἡ δὲ
τὴν ἐσθῆτα αὐτοῦ λουομένου καὶ γυμνωθέντος ἐνεδύ-
ετο, πρότερον καὶ αὐτὴ φιλήσασα. 3. ἤδη ποτὲ καὶ
μήλοις ἀλλήλους ἔβαλον καὶ τὰς κεφαλὰς ἀλλήλων
ἐκόσμησαν διακρίνοντες τὰς κόμας, καὶ ἡ μὲν εἴκασεν

---

[31] Suppl. Bowie

of spring and the start of summer, and everything was in its prime: fruit in the trees, crops in the fields. Pleasant was the sound of cicadas, sweet the fragrance of fruit, delightful the bleating of sheep. 2. One would have thought that the very rivers sang as they flowed gently along, the winds made syrinx-music as they blew through the pines, the apples swooned to the ground from love, and the sun in liking for beauty made everyone undress. So Daphnis, made hot by all this, took to wading into rivers; sometimes he bathed, sometimes he tried to catch the fish that swirled around him, and often he drank the water, hoping to quench the burning within him. 3. And Chloe, after milking the ewes and most of the she-goats, took a long time pressing the milk into cheese, for the flies were awful, plaguing her and biting if ⟨not⟩ shooed away; then she would wash her face, adorn her head with pine twigs, put her fawnskin around her waist, fill her pail with wine and milk, and share a drink with Daphnis.

When midday came they fell prey to each other's eyes. 24 Beholding Daphnis naked, she would succumb to his overwhelming beauty and melt away, unable to fault any part of him; and seeing her in fawn skin and pine garland offering the pail, he would imagine that he beheld one of the Nymphs from the cave. 2. So he would snatch the pine garland from her head and put it on his own, after giving the garland a kiss; and when he was bathing and undressed, she would put on his clothes, after likewise giving them a kiss. 3. Occasionally they also pelted each other with apples and spruced up their heads by combing each other's hair. She compared Daphnis' hair to myrtle berries be-

---

³² ἐ(ὶ)ς ἄθρουν Hercher: ἐπαθροῦν F: ἐπανθοῦν V

αὐτοῦ τὴν κόμην ὅτι μέλαινα μύρτοις, ὁ δὲ μήλῳ τὸ
πρόσωπον αὐτῆς ὅτι λευκὸν καὶ ἐνερευθὲς ἦν. 4. ἐδί-
δασκεν αὐτὴν καὶ συρίττειν, καὶ ἀρξαμένης ἐμπνεῖν
ἁρπάζων τὴν σύριγγα τοῖς χείλεσιν αὐτὸς τοὺς καλάμους ἐπέτρεχε καὶ ἐδόκει μὲν διδάσκειν ἁμαρτάνου-
σαν, εὐπρεπῶς δὲ διὰ τῆς σύριγγος Χλόην κατεφίλει.

25   Συρίττοντος δὲ αὐτοῦ τὸ μεσημβρινὸν καὶ τῶν
ποιμνίων σκιαζομένων ἔλαθεν ἡ Χλόη καταννυστά-
ξασα. φωράσας τοῦτο ὁ Δάφνις καὶ καταθέμενος τὴν
σύριγγα πᾶσαν αὐτὴν ἔβλεπεν ἀπλήστως οἷα μηδὲν
αἰδούμενος καὶ ἅμα [κρύφα]³³ ἠρέμα ὑπεφθέγγετο· 2.
"οἷοι καθεύδουσιν ὀφθαλμοί, οἷον δὲ ἀποπνεῖ τὸ στό-
μα· οὐδὲ τὰ μῆλα τοιοῦτον, οὐδὲ αἱ ὄχναι.³⁴ ἀλλὰ
φιλῆσαι δέδοικα· δάκνει τὸ φίλημα τὴν καρδίαν καὶ
ὥσπερ τὸ νέον μέλι μαίνεσθαι ποιεῖ· ὀκνῶ δὲ μὴ καὶ
φιλήσας αὐτὴν ἀφυπνίσω. 3. ὦ λάλων τεττίγων· οὐκ
ἐάσουσιν αὐτὴν καθεύδειν μέγα ἠχοῦντες. ἀλλὰ καὶ οἱ
τράγοι τοῖς κέρασι παίουσι μαχόμενοι· ὦ λύκων ἀλω-
πέκων δειλοτέρων, οἳ τούτους οὐχ ἥρπασαν."

26   Ἐν τοιούτοις ὄντος αὐτοῦ λόγοις τέττιξ φεύγων
χελιδόνα θηρᾶσαι θέλουσαν κατέπεσεν εἰς τὸν κόλπον
τῆς Χλόης, καὶ ἡ χελιδὼν ἑπομένη τὸν μὲν οὐκ ἠδυνήθη λαβεῖν, ταῖς δὲ πτέρυξιν ἐγγὺς διὰ τὴν δίωξιν
γενομένη τῶν παρειῶν αὐτῆς ἥψατο. 2. ἡ δὲ οὐκ εἰδυῖα
τὸ πραχθὲν μέγα βοήσασα τῶν ὕπνων ἐξέθορεν, ἰδοῦσα δὲ καὶ τὴν χελιδόνα ἔτι πλησίον πετομένην καὶ τὸν
Δάφνιν ἐπὶ τῷ δέει γελῶντα τοῦ φόβου μὲν ἐπαύσατο,
τοὺς δὲ ὀφθαλμοὺς ἀπέματτεν ἔτι καθεύδειν θέλοντας,
3. καὶ ὁ τέττιξ ἐκ τῶν κόλπων ἐπήχησεν ὅμοιον ἱκέτῃ
χάριν ὁμολογοῦντι τῆς σωτηρίας. πάλιν οὖν ἡ Χλόη
μέγα ἀνεβόησεν, ὁ δὲ Δάφνις ἐγέλασε καὶ προφάσεως

cause it was black, and he compared her face to an apple because it was fair and pink. 4. He also began to teach her to play the syrinx, and when she started to blow into it he would snatch the syrinx away and run his own lips over it; he gave the impression of correcting her mistakes, but by proxy of the syrinx he was giving Chloe kisses.

While he played the syrinx at midday and the flocks   25
took to the shade, Chloe fell asleep unobserved. Noticing this, Daphnis put down his syrinx and, fearing no embarrassment, looked her all over insatiably and quietly whispered, 2. "Such eyes sleep here! Such a breath from this mouth—not even apples, not even pears can match it! But I'm afraid to kiss: her kiss stings my heart and, like new honey, drives me mad, and I worry that a kiss will wake her. 3. Oh those chattering cicadas! They won't let her sleep on with all their loud noise. And the goats too, slamming their horns as they fight! Oh wolves more cowardly than foxes, for not having carried them off!"

As he went on with these pronouncements a cicada, on   26
the run from a swallow looking to capture it, dropped into Chloe's shirt. The swallow followed and could not catch it, but in its pursuit came close enough to touch her cheeks with its wings. 2. Unaware of what had happened, she started from her slumbers with a loud scream, but when she saw the swallow flying near and Daphnis laughing at her fear, she stopped being afraid and rubbed her eyes, which still wanted to sleep. 3. The cicada chirped from her shirt like a suppliant giving thanks for its life. So Chloe screamed loudly again, but Daphnis laughed and, seizing

---

33 Del. Boissonade: κύψας Giangrande
34 Wyttenbach: λόχμαι V F

λαβόμενος καθῆκεν αὐτῆς εἰς τὰ στέρνα τὰς χεῖρας
καὶ ἐξάγει τὸν βέλτιστον τέττιγα, μηδὲ ἐν τῇ δεξιᾷ
σιωπῶντα. ἡ δὲ ἥδετο ἰδοῦσα καὶ ἐφίλησε λαβοῦσα
καὶ αὖθις ἐνέβαλε τῷ κόλπῳ λαλοῦντα.

27   Ἔτερψε δὲ αὐτούς ποτε φάττα βουκολικὸν ἐκ τῆς
ὕλης φθεγξαμένη, καὶ τῆς Χλόης ζητούσης μαθεῖν ὅ
τι λέγει διδάσκει αὐτὴν ὁ Δάφνις μυθολογῶν τὰ
θρυλούμενα. 2. "ἦν παρθένος, παρθένε, οὕτω καλὴ καὶ
ἔνεμε βοῦς πολλὰς οὕτως ἐν ὕλῃ. ἦν δὲ ἄρα καὶ ᾠδική,
καὶ ἐτέρποντο αἱ βόες αὐτῆς τῇ μουσικῇ, καὶ ἔνεμεν
οὔτε καλαύροπος πληγῇ οὔτε κέντρου προσβολῇ,
ἀλλὰ καθίσασα ὑπὸ πίτυν καὶ στεφανωσαμένη πίτυϊ
ᾖδε Πᾶνα καὶ τὴν Πίτυν, καὶ αἱ βόες τῇ φωνῇ παρέμε-
νον. 3. παῖς οὐ μακρὰν νέμων βοῦς, καὶ αὐτὸς καλὸς
καὶ ᾠδικὸς ὡς ἡ παρθένος, φιλονεικήσας πρὸς τὴν
μελῳδίαν μείζονα ὡς ἀνήρ, ἡδεῖαν ὡς παῖς φωνὴν
ἀντεπεδείξατο καὶ τῶν βοῶν ὀκτὼ τὰς ἀρίστας ἐς τὴν
ἰδίαν ἀγέλην θέλξας ἀπεβουκόλησεν. 4. ἄχθεται ἡ
παρθένος τῇ βλάβῃ τῆς ἀγέλης, τῇ ἥττῃ τῆς ᾠδῆς,
καὶ εὔχεται τοῖς θεοῖς ὄρνις γενέσθαι πρὶν οἴκαδε
ἀφικέσθαι. πείθονται οἱ θεοὶ καὶ ποιοῦσι τήνδε τὴν
ὄρνιν, ὄρειον ὡς ἡ παρθένος, μουσικὴν ὡς ἐκείνη, καὶ
ἔτι νῦν ᾄδουσα μηνύει τὴν συμφοράν, ὅτι βοῦς ζητεῖ
πεπλανημένας."

28   Τοιάσδε τέρψεις αὐτοῖς τὸ θέρος παρεῖχε. μετοπώρου δὲ ἀκμάζοντος καὶ τοῦ βότρυος ⟨ἤδη περκάζον-
τος⟩[35] Τύριοι[36] λῃσταὶ Καρικὴν ἔχοντες ἡμιολίαν ὡς

---

[35] Suppl. Bernhard
[36] Πύρριοι F: Πυρραῖοι Young

this pretext, put his hands down around her breasts and retrieved that trusty cicada, which did not fall silent even in
his hand. She was delighted to see it, took and kissed it, and
tossed it back into her shirt still chirping.

One day a wood pigeon entertained them from the   27
wood by singing a pastoral tune, and when Chloe sought to
learn what it meant, Daphnis instructed her by recounting
a story commonly told.[16] 2. "Once, my girl, there was a girl
as beautiful as you who herded many cows in a wood, just
as you do. She was a singer too, and her cows were entertained by her music; she herded them not by the stroke of
a crook or the prod of a goad, but sitting beneath a pine
and garlanded with pine twigs she would sing of Pan and
Pitys,[17] and the cows stayed in range of her voice. 3. Not far
off a boy herded cows, and he too was fair and a singer like
the girl. He vied with her in singing and countered with a
voice as strong as a man's but as sweet as a boy's, and
charming her eight best cows into his own herd he herded
them away. 4. The girl was distressed at the loss to her
herd, the defeat of her song, and prayed to the gods to become a bird before she got home. The gods granted her
prayer and turned her into this bird, a dweller in the moun-
tains like the girl and musical like her. And to this day her
song recounts her misfortune, that she is looking for her
stray cows."

Such were the pleasures that summer brought them.   28
But in high autumn, when the grapes were already turning
dark, some Tyrian pirates, manning a Carian cutter so as to

[16] There is no obvious source, though Ovid, *Met*. 13.640–7
(Anius' daughters) is somewhat similar.

[17] "Pine" (a nymph), cf. Propertius 1.18.20.

ἂν δοκοῖεν βάρβαροι[37] προσέσχον τοῖς ἀγροῖς καὶ
ἐκβάντες σὺν μαχαίραις καὶ ἡμιθωρακίοις κατέσυρον
πάντα τὰ εἰς χεῖρας ἐλθόντα· οἶνον ἀνθοσμίαν, πυρὸν
ἄφθονον, μέλι ἐν κηρίοις. ἤλασάν τινας καὶ βοῦς ἐκ
τῆς Δόρκωνος ἀγέλης. 2. λαμβάνουσι καὶ τὸν Δάφνιν
ἀλύοντα περὶ τὴν θάλασσαν· ἡ γὰρ Χλόη βραδύτερον
ὡς κόρη τὰ πρόβατα ἐξῆγε τοῦ Δρύαντος φόβῳ τῶν
ἀγερώχων ποιμένων. ἰδόντες δὲ μειράκιον μέγα καὶ
καλὸν καὶ κρεῖττον τῆς ἐξ ἀγρῶν ἁρπαγῆς, μηκέτι
μηδὲν μήτε εἰς τὰς αἶγας μήτε εἰς τοὺς ἄλλους ἀγροὺς
περιεργασάμενοι κατῆγον αὐτὸν ἐπὶ τὴν ναῦν κλαί-
οντα καὶ ἠπορημένον καὶ μέγα Χλόην καλοῦντα. 3. καὶ
οἱ μὲν ἄρτι τὸ πεῖσμα ἀπολύσαντες καὶ τὰς κώπας
ἐμβαλόντες ἀπέπλεον εἰς τὸ πέλαγος, Χλόη δὲ κατήλαυνε τὸ ποίμνιον σύριγγα καινὴν τῷ Δάφνιδι δῶρον
κομίζουσα· ἰδοῦσα δὲ τὰς αἶγας τεταραγμένας καὶ
ἀκούσασα τοῦ Δάφνιδος ἀεὶ μεῖζον αὐτὴν βοῶντος,
προβάτων μὲν ἀμελεῖ καὶ τὴν σύριγγα ῥίπτει, δρόμῳ
δὲ πρὸς τὸν Δόρκωνα παραγίνεται δεησομένη βοηθεῖν.

29   Ὁ δὲ ἔκειτο πληγαῖς νεανικαῖς συγκεκομμένος ὑπὸ
τῶν λῃστῶν καὶ ὀλίγον ἐμπνέων αἵματος πολλοῦ
χεομένου. ἰδὼν δὲ τὴν Χλόην καὶ ὀλίγον ἐκ τοῦ πρότερον ἔρωτος ἐμπύρευμα λαβὼν "ἐγὼ μὲν" εἶπε,
"Χλόη, τεθνήξομαι μετ' ὀλίγον, οἱ γάρ με ἀσεβεῖς
λῃσταὶ πρὸ τῶν βοῶν μαχόμενον κατέκοψαν ὡς βοῦν,

37 ὡς ἂν δοκοῖεν βάρβαροι fort. delendum ut ex glossemate
ortum

18 Tyrian pirates appear in other Greek novels, and the Carian
cutter ("one-and-one-half boat") was a typical pirate craft (one

look like barbarians,[18] put in at the farm. They came ashore
with cutlasses and breastplates and started pillaging everything that came to hand: fragrant wine, plentiful wheat,
honey in the combs. They also rustled some cows from
Dorco's herd. 2. And they caught Daphnis as he wandered
by the seashore, for Chloe was driving Dryas' sheep out
more slowly, being a girl and wary of the headstrong shepherds. Spotting a tall, handsome lad worth more than their
plunder from the farm, they lost all interest in the goats
and the other farms and marched him onto their ship, wailing desperately and calling loudly for Chloe. 3. No sooner
had they untied the mooring rope, dipped their oars, and
started to sail out to sea than Chloe came driving her flock
down, carrying a new syrinx as a present for Daphnis.
When she saw the goats scattered and heard Daphnis ever
more loudly yelling for her, she forgot about her sheep,
dropped the syrinx, and ran off to Dorco to ask for help.

But he was lying on the ground, thoroughly battered   29
by the pirates' lusty blows, scarcely breathing and losing a
lot of blood. When he saw Chloe he briefly held onto a
spark of warmth from his earlier passion and said, "Chloe,
I will soon be dead—as I defended my cows those impious pirates butchered me like a cow—but you must res-

bank of oars was modified to facilitate grappling). Tyre, a city on
the Phoenician coast, was an important Hellenistic and Roman
capital, and Caria, the southwest region of modern Turkey, had
long since been hellenized, but Longus evidently thought of Caria
as barbarian, unless the phrase about barbarians is spurious (it
may have originated as a gloss). In any case there is no need to
emend "Tyrian" to "Pyrrhaean," i.e. from Pyrrha, a town on
Lesbos and an unlikely venue for pirates.

σὺ δέ μοι καὶ Δάφνιν σῶσον κἀμοὶ τιμώρησον κἀκείνους ἀπόλεσον. 2. ἐπαίδευσα τὰς βοῦς ἤχῳ σύριγγος
ἀκολουθεῖν καὶ διώκειν τὸ μέλος αὐτῆς κἂν νέμωνταί
ποι μακράν. ἴθι δή, λαβοῦσα τὴν σύριγγα ταύτην
ἔμπνευσον αὐτῇ μέλος ἐκεῖνο ὃ Δάφνιν μὲν ἐγώ ποτε
ἐδιδαξάμην, σὲ δὲ Δάφνις· τὸ δὲ ἐντεῦθεν τῇ σύριγγι
μελήσει καὶ τῶν βοῶν ταῖς ἐκεῖ. 3. χαρίζομαι δέ σοι
καὶ τὴν σύριγγα αὐτήν, ᾗ πολλοὺς ἐρίζων καὶ βου-
κόλους ἐνίκησα καὶ αἰπόλους. σὺ δὲ ἀντὶ τῶνδε καὶ
ζῶντα ἔτι φίλησον καὶ ἀποθανόντα κλαῦσον, κἂν ἴδῃς
ἄλλον νέμοντα τὰς βοῦς ἐμοῦ μνημόνευσον."

30   Δόρκων μὲν τοσαῦτα εἰπὼν καὶ φίλημα φιλήσας
ὕστατον ἀφῆκεν ἅμα τῷ φιλήματι καὶ τῇ φωνῇ τὴν
ψυχήν· ἡ δὲ Χλόη λαβοῦσα τὴν σύριγγα καὶ ἐνθεῖσα
τοῖς χείλεσιν ἐσύριζε μέγιστον ὡς ἠδύνατο, καὶ αἱ
βόες ἀκούουσι καὶ τὸ μέλος γνωρίζουσι καὶ ὁρμῇ μιᾷ
μυκησάμεναι πηδῶσιν εἰς τὴν θάλασσαν. 2. βιαίου δὲ
πηδήματος εἰς ἕνα τοῖχον τῆς νεὼς γενομένου καὶ
ἐκ τῆς ἐμπτώσεως τῶν βοῶν κοίλης τῆς θαλάσσης
διαστάσης στρέφεται μὲν ἡ ναῦς καὶ τοῦ κλύδωνος
συνιόντος ἀπόλλυται, οἱ δὲ ἐκπίπτουσιν οὐχ ὁμοίαν
ἔχοντες ἐλπίδα σωτηρίας. 3. οἱ μὲν γὰρ λῃσταὶ τὰς
μαχαίρας παρήρτηντο καὶ τὰ ἡμιθωράκια λεπιδωτὰ
ἐνεδέδυντο καὶ κνημῖδας εἰς μέσην κνήμην ὑπεδέ-
δεντο, ὁ δὲ Δάφνις ἀνυπόδετος <ἦν> ὡς ἐν πεδίῳ νέμων
καὶ ἡμίγυμνος ὡς ἔτι τῆς ὥρας οὔσης καυματ<ώ-
δ>ο<υ>ς.³⁸ 4. ἐκείνους μὲν οὖν ἐπ᾽ ὀλίγον νηξαμένους
τὰ ὅπλα κατήνεγκεν εἰς βυθόν, ὁ δὲ Δάφνις τὴν μὲν
ἐσθῆτα ῥᾳδίως ἀπεδύσατο, περὶ δὲ τὴν νῆξιν ἔκαμεν,
οἷα πρότερον νηχόμενος ἐν ποταμοῖς μόνοις· 5. ὕστερον δὲ παρὰ τῆς ἀνάγκης τὸ πρακτέον διδαχθεὶς εἰς
μέσας ὥρμησε τὰς βοῦς καὶ δύο βοῶν δύο κεράτων

cue Daphnis, avenge me, and destroy them. 2. I taught my
cattle to attend to the sound of the syrinx and follow its
tune however far away they might be grazing. Here, take
this syrinx and breathe into it the tune that I once taught
Daphnis and Daphnis taught you. What happens next will
be up to the syrinx and the cattle out there. 3. The syrinx itself is my gift to you; with it I won competitions against
many cowherds and shepherds. In return for all this, give
me a kiss while I'm still alive and weep for me when I'm
dead, and if you see someone else grazing my cattle, remember me."

With these words Dorco kissed his last kiss and, along   30
with the kiss and his voice, took leave of his life. Chloe took
the syrinx, put it to her lips, and began playing as loudly as
she could. The cattle heard and recognized the tune, and
in a concerted charge lunged mooing into the sea. 2. What
with a violent lunge to one side of the ship and a trough
opened in the sea from the plunge of the cattle, the ship
capsized and sank as the waves met. Those aboard fell in,
with unequal chances to survive: 3. the pirates had the cutlasses hanging at their sides and were wearing the mail
breastplates and greaves fastened halfway up their shins,
while Daphnis was barefoot, as befits a herdsman on the
plain, and half-dressed, as it was still seasonally hot. 4. So
the pirates swam only a short way before their gear pulled
them to the bottom, while Daphnis easily shucked his
clothes, though the swim tired him, since he had swum
only in rivers before. 5. But before long he learned by ne-
cessity what had to be done: he plunged into the midst of
the cattle, grabbed two horns of two cattle in his [two]

---

38 Suppl. Bernhard

ταῖς [δύο]³⁹ χερσὶ λαβόμενος ἐκομίζετο μέσος ἀλύπως
καὶ ἀπόνως ὥσπερ ἐλαύνων ἄμαξαν. 6. νήχεται δὲ ἄρα
βοῦς ὅσον οὐδὲ ἄνθρωπος· μόνον λείπεται τῶν ἐν-
ύδρων ὀρνίθων καὶ αὐτῶν ἰχθύων· οὐδ' ἂν ἀπόλοιτο
βοῦς νηχόμενος εἰ μὴ τῶν χηλῶν οἱ ὄνυχες περι-
πέσοιεν διάβροχοι γενόμενοι. μαρτυροῦσι τῷ λόγῳ
μέχρι νῦν πολλοὶ τόποι τῆς θαλάσσης βοὸς πόροι
λεγόμενοι.

31   Ἐκσῴζεται μὲν δὴ τοῦτον τὸν τρόπον ὁ Δάφνις, δύο
κινδύνους παρ' ἐλπίδα πᾶσαν διαφυγών, λῃστηρίου
καὶ ναυαγίου· ἐξελθὼν δὲ καὶ τὴν Χλόην ἐπὶ τῆς γῆς
γελῶσαν ἅμα καὶ δακρύουσαν εὑρὼν ἐμπίπτει τε
αὐτῆς τοῖς κόλποις καὶ ἐπυνθάνετο τί βουλομένη
συρίσειεν. 2. ἡ δὲ αὐτῷ διηγεῖται πάντα· τὸν δρόμον
τὸν ἐπὶ τὸν Δόρκωνα, τὸ παίδευμα τὸ τῶν βοῶν, πῶς
κελευσθείη συρίσαι, καὶ ὅτι τέθνηκε Δόρκων. μόνον
αἰδεσθεῖσα τὸ φίλημα οὐκ εἶπεν. ἔδοξε δὴ τιμῆσαι τὸν
εὐεργέτην, καὶ ἐλθόντες μετὰ τῶν προσηκόντων Δόρκωνα θάπτουσι τὸν ἄθλιον. 3. γῆν μὲν οὖν πολλὴν
ἐπέθεσαν, φυτὰ δὲ ἥμερα πολλὰ ἐφύτευσαν καὶ ἐξήρτησαν αὐτῷ τῶν ἔργων ἀπαρχάς· ἀλλὰ καὶ γάλα
κατέσπεισαν καὶ βότρυς κατέθλιψαν καὶ σύριγγας
πολλὰς κατέκλασαν. 4. ἠκούσθη καὶ τῶν βοῶν ἐλεεινὰ
μυκήματα καὶ δρόμοι τινὲς ὤφθησαν ἅμα τοῖς μυκή-
μασιν ἄτακτοι· καὶ ὡς ἐν ποιμέσιν εἰκάζετο καὶ αἰπόλοις ταῦτα θρῆνος ἦν τῶν βοῶν ἐπὶ βουκόλῳ τετε-
λευτηκότι.

32   Μετὰ δὲ τὸν Δόρκωνος τάφον λούει τὸν Δάφνιν ἡ
Χλόη πρὸς τὰς Νύμφας ἀγαγοῦσα, εἰς τὸ ἄντρον
εἰσαγαγοῦσα, καὶ αὐτὴ τότε πρῶτον Δάφνιδος ὁρῶν-
τος ἐλούσατο τὸ σῶμα, λευκὸν καὶ καθαρὸν ὑπὸ κάλλους καὶ οὐδὲν λουτρῶν ἐς κάλλος δεόμενον· 2. καὶ

hands, and rode between them as comfortably and effort-
lessly as driving a wagon. 6. A cow in fact swims better than
any person, bettered only by waterfowl and fish themselves. A cow would never drown while swimming unless
its hooves got waterlogged and dropped off. To this day,
many places by the sea named Bosporus[19] prove this point.

In this way Daphnis was saved, rescued against all hope   31
from two hazards, piracy and shipwreck. He emerged to
find Chloe on shore, laughing and crying at the same time.
He fell into her arms and wanted to know her reason for
playing the syrinx. 2. She told him the whole story: her
dash to Dorco, the cattle's training, how she was told to
play the syrinx, and that Dorco was dead; she only omit-
ted the kiss, feeling embarrassed. They thought it right
to honor their benefactor, so they went with his relatives
and buried poor Dorco. 3. They put ample earth on his
grave, planted many cultivated trees, and dedicated the
first fruits of their labors to him. They also poured libations
of milk, crushed some grapes, and broke many syrinxes.
4. There was the sound of cattle mooing in pity and the
sight of them running in disorder as they mooed; all this
the shepherds and herdsmen imagined was the cattle's
dirge for a deceased herdsman.

After Dorco's burial Chloe took Daphnis to the   32
Nymphs, took him into the cave and bathed him, and for
the first time she bathed her own body while Daphnis was
looking. It was white and pure in its beauty, needing no
baths to enhance beauty. 2. Gathering all the flowers that

19 "Cattle Crossing," cf. "Oxford."

---

39 Del. Reeve

ἄνθη τε συλλέξαντες, ὅσα ἄνθη τῆς ὥρας ἐκείνης
ἐστεφάνωσαν τὰ ἀγάλματα καὶ τὴν τοῦ Δόρκωνος
σύριγγα τῆς πέτρας ἐξήρτησαν ἀνάθημα, καὶ μετὰ
τοῦτο ἐλθόντες ἐπεσκόπουν τὰς αἶγας καὶ τὰ πρόβατα.
3. τὰ δὲ πάντα κατέκειτο μήτε νεμόμενα μήτε βληχώμενα, ἀλλ᾽ οἶμαι τὸν Δάφνιν καὶ τὴν Χλόην ἀφανεῖς ὄντας ποθοῦντα. ἐπεὶ γοῦν ὀφθέντες καὶ ἐβόησαν
τὸ σύνηθες καὶ ἐσύρισαν, τὰ μὲν ⟨πρόβατα⟩[40] ἀνα-
στάντα ἐνέμετο, αἱ δὲ αἶγες ἐσκίρτων φριμασσόμεναι
καθάπερ ἡδόμεναι σωτηρίᾳ συνήθους αἰπόλου. 4. οὐ
μὴν ὁ Δάφνις χαίρειν ἔπειθε τὴν ψυχήν, ἰδὼν τὴν
Χλόην γυμνὴν καὶ τὸ πρότερον λανθάνον κάλλος
ἐκκεκαλυμμένον. ἤλγει τὴν καρδίαν ὡς ἐσθιομένην
ὑπὸ φαρμάκων, καὶ αὐτῷ τὸ πνεῦμα ποτὲ μὲν λάβρον
ἐξέπνει καθάπερ τινὸς διώκοντος αὐτόν, ποτὲ δὲ ἐπ-
έλειπε καθάπερ ἐκδαπανηθὲν ἐν ταῖς προτέραις ἐπι-
δρομαῖς· ἐδόκει τὸ λουτρὸν εἶναι τῆς θαλάσσης φοβε-
ρώτερον· ἐνόμιζε τὴν ψυχὴν ἔτι παρὰ τοῖς λῃσταῖς
μένειν, οἷα νέος καὶ ἄγροικος καὶ ἔτι ἀγνοῶν τὸ
ἔρωτος λῃστήριον.

[40] Suppl. Villoison

flower in that season, they garlanded the statues and hung Dorco's syrinx on the rock as a dedication, and then they went to inspect the goats and sheep. 3. They were all lying on the ground, not grazing or bleating but I think missing the absent Daphnis and Chloe; after all, when they came into view and gave their usual cry and played their tunes, the sheep got up and started to graze, and the goats started to frisk about, bucking as if joyful at the safe return of their accustomed goatherd. 4. But Daphnis could not bring his spirit to feel happy, now that he had seen Chloe naked and her hitherto hidden beauty unveiled. He was sore at heart as though it were gnawed by poisons. Sometimes the breath within him would rush out violently, as if someone were chasing him, and sometimes it would fail him as if spent in the recent attacks. The bath seemed more frightful than the sea. He thought that his life must still be in the pirates' hands, rustic lad that he was and still unaware of love's piracy.

ΛΟΓΟΣ ΔΕΥΤΕΡΟΣ

1 Ἤδη δὲ τῆς ὀπώρας ἀκμαζούσης καὶ ἐπείγοντος
τοῦ τρυγητοῦ πᾶς ἦν κατὰ τοὺς ἀγροὺς ἐν ἔργῳ· ὁ μὲν
ληνοὺς ἐπεσκεύαζεν, ὁ δὲ πίθους ἐξεκάθαιρεν, ὁ δὲ
ἀρρίχους ἔπλεκεν· 2. ἔμελέ τινι δρεπάνης μικρᾶς ἐς
βότρυος τομὴν καὶ ἑτέρῳ λίθου θλῖψαι τὰ ἔνοινα τῶν
βοτρυ⟨δί⟩ων[41] δυναμένου καὶ ἄλλῳ λύγου ξηρᾶς πληγαῖς κατεξασμένης ὡς ἂν ὑπὸ φωτὶ νύκτωρ τὸ γλεῦκος
φέροιτο. 3. ἀμελήσαντες οὖν ὁ Δάφνις καὶ ἡ Χλόη τῶν
αἰγῶν καὶ τῶν προβάτων, χειρὸς ὠφέλειαν ἄλλοις
μετεδίδοσαν· ὁ μὲν ἐβάσταζεν ἐν ἀρρίχοις βότρυς καὶ
ἐπάτει ταῖς ληνοῖς ἐμβαλὼν καὶ εἰς τοὺς πίθους ἔφερε
τὸν οἶνον, ἡ δὲ τροφὴν παρεσκεύαζε τοῖς τρυγῶσι καὶ
ἐνέχει ποτὸν αὐτοῖς πρεσβύτερον οἶνον, καὶ τῶν ἀμπέ-
λων δὲ τὰς ταπεινοτέρας ἀπετρύγα. 4. πᾶσα γὰρ κατὰ
τὴν Λέσβον ἡ ἄμπελος ταπεινή, οὐ μετέωρος οὐδὲ
ἀναδενδρὰς ἀλλὰ κάτω τὰ κλήματα ἀποτείνουσα καὶ
ὥσπερ κιττὸς νεμομένη· καὶ παῖς ἂν ἐφίκοιτο βότρυος
ἄρτι τὰς χεῖρας ἐκ σπαργάνων λελυμένος.[42]

2 Οἷον οὖν εἰκὸς ἐν ἑορτῇ Διονύσου καὶ οἴνου γενέ-
σει, αἱ μὲν γυναῖκες ἐκ τῶν πλησίον ἀγρῶν εἰς ἐπικουρίαν [οἴνου][43] κεκλημέναι τῷ Δάφνιδι τοὺς ὀφθαλμοὺς ἐπέβαλλον καὶ ἐπήνουν ὡς ὅμοιον τῷ Διονύσῳ τὸ

---

41 Suppl. Schäfer
42 πᾶσα . . . λελυμένος del. Schmidt
43 Om. Parisinus Gr. 2903 (s. XVI), del. Villoison

BOOK II

With the fruit season now at its peak and vintage-time   1
drawing near, everyone was busy on the farms. Some repaired wine presses, some scrubbed jars, some plaited baskets; 2. someone saw to a small sickle for cutting clusters of
grapes, someone else to a stone fit for crushing the juice
from the clusters, another to a dry willow twig, pounded
into shreds, by whose light the must could be drawn after dark. 3. So Daphnis and Chloe stopped tending their
goats and sheep and lent the others a helping hand: he
hoisted bunches of grapes in baskets, dumped them into
the presses and trod them, and collected the wine into the
jars, while she made meals for the vintners, poured them a
drink of more mature wine, and harvested the fruit from
the vines nearer the ground.[20] 4. Indeed every vine on
Lesbos is near the ground, not high up or trained on trees
but trailing its shoots downwards and creeping like ivy.
Even a baby with its hands barely free of swaddling clothes
could reach a cluster.

As befits a festival for Dionysus and the birth of wine,   2
the women who had been called in from the nearby farms
to lend a hand cast glances at Daphnis and praised him as

[20] Puzzling in view of the following statement that all the
vines were near the ground, which also contradicts what is re-
ported in 1.19.1 (vines trained on trees) and 4.2.2 (vines high up),
so that the following digression in §4 may be an interpolation.

κάλλος, καί τις τῶν θρασυτέρων καὶ ἐφίλησε καὶ τὸν
Δάφνιν παρώξυνε, τὴν δὲ Χλόην ἐλύπησεν· 2. οἱ δὲ ἐν
ταῖς ληνοῖς ποικίλας φωνὰς ἔρριπτον ἐπὶ τὴν Χλόην
καὶ ὥσπερ ἐπί τινα Βάκχην Σάτυροι μανικώτερον
ἐπήδων καὶ ηὔχοντο γενέσθαι ποίμνια καὶ ὑπ᾽ ἐκείνης
νέμεσθαι, ὥστε αὖ πάλιν ἡ μὲν ἤδετο, Δάφνις δὲ
ἐλυπεῖτο. 3. ηὔχοντο δὲ δὴ ταχέως παύσασθαι τὸν
τρυγητὸν καὶ λαβέσθαι τῶν συνήθων χωρίων καὶ ἀντὶ
τῆς ἀμούσου βοῆς ἀκούειν σύριγγος ἢ τῶν ποιμνίων
αὐτῶν βληχωμένων. 4. καὶ ἐπεὶ διαγενομένων ὀλίγων
ἡμερῶν αἱ μὲν ἄμπελοι τετρύγηντο, πίθοι δὲ τὸ γλεῦκος εἶχον, ἔδει δὲ οὐκέτ᾽ οὐδὲν πολυχειρίας, κατήλαυνον τὰς ἀγέλας εἰς τὸ πεδίον καὶ μάλα χαίροντες τὰς
Νύμφας προσεκύνουν, βότρυς αὐταῖς κομίζοντες ἐπὶ
κλημάτων ἀπαρχὰς τοῦ τρυγητοῦ. 5. οὐδὲ τὸν πρότερον χρόνον ἀμελῶς ποτε παρῆλθον ἀλλ᾽ ἀεί τε
ἀρχόμενοι νομῆς προσήδρευον καὶ ἐκ νομῆς ἀνιόντες
προσεκύνουν καὶ πάντως τι ἐπέφερον, ἢ ἄνθος ἢ
ὀπώραν ἢ φυλλάδα χλωρὰν ἢ γάλακτος σπονδήν. 6.
καὶ τούτου μὲν ὕστερον ἀμοιβὰς ἐκομίσαντο παρὰ τῶν
θεῶν, τότε δὲ κύνες φασὶν ἐκ δεσμῶν λυθέντες ἐσκίρτων, ἐσύριττον, ᾖδον, τοῖς τράγοις καὶ τοῖς προβάτοις
συνεπάλαιον.

3   Τερπομένοις δὲ αὐτοῖς ἐφίσταται πρεσβύτης σισύ-
ραν ἐνδεδυμένος, καρβατίνας ὑποδεδεμένος, πήραν
ἐξηρτημένος καὶ τὴν πήραν παλαιάν. οὗτος πλησίον
καθίσας αὐτῶν ὧδε εἶπε· 2. "Φιλητᾶς, ὦ παῖδες, ὁ
πρεσβύτης ἐγώ, ὃς πολλὰ μὲν ταῖσδε ταῖς Νύμφαις

the equal of Dionysus in beauty; one of the more forward ones even kissed him, which excited Daphnis but pained Chloe. 2. Meanwhile the men in the wine presses flung manifold compliments at Chloe and pranced madly about her like satyrs about a maenad, praying to be turned into sheep and pastured by her, so that now she was pleased and he was pained. 3. They prayed for the vintage to be finished quickly, so that they could return to their usual haunts and instead of discordant shouting hear the syrinx or the bleating of their own flocks. 4. A few days later the vines were harvested, the juice was in the jars, and there was no further need of many hands, so they drove their flocks down to the plain and joyfully paid obeisance to the Nymphs, bringing them bunches of grapes on the stem as first fruits of the vintage. 5. Nor had they in time past ever passed by neglectfully but at the start of each day's pasturing they would pay their respects, and when they returned from the pasture they would make obeisance and never fail to offer them something: a flower, fruit, green leaves, or a libation of milk. 6. For this they received a reward from the goddesses later on, but for now they were like dogs off the leash, as they say, frisking, playing the syrinx, singing, and romping with their goats and sheep.

While they were enjoying themselves an old man approached, clad in a goat-skin jacket, with rawhide sandals on his feet and a bag slung from his shoulder, and a very old bag it was. He sat down beside them and said, 2. "My children, I am old Philetas.[21] Many a song have I sung to these

---

[21] The name appropriately suggests love (*philia*) but also recollects and emblematizes the Hellenistic poet and scholar Philitas (*var.* Philetas) of Cos; see Introduction.

ἦσα, πολλὰ δὲ τῷ Πανὶ ἐκείνῳ ἐσύρισα, βοῶν δὲ
πολλῆς ἀγέλης ἡγησάμην μόνῃ μουσικῇ. ἥκω δὲ ὑμῖν
ὅσα εἶδον μηνύσων, ὅσα ἤκουσα ἀπαγγελῶν. 3. κῆπός
ἐστί μοι τῶν ἐμῶν χειρῶν, ὃν ἐξ οὗ νέμειν διὰ γῆρας
ἐπαυσάμην ἐξεπονησάμην, ὅσα ὧραι φύουσι⁴⁴ πάντα
ἔχων ἐν αὐτῷ καθ᾽ ὥραν ἑκάστην· 4. ἦρος ῥόδα <καὶ>⁴⁵
κρίνα καὶ ὑάκινθος καὶ ἴα ἀμφότερα, θέρους μήκωνες
καὶ ἀχράδες καὶ μῆλα πάντα, νῦν ἄμπελοι καὶ συκαῖ
καὶ ῥοιαὶ καὶ μύρτα χλωρά. 5. εἰς τοῦτον τὸν κῆπον
ὀρνίθων ἀγέλαι συνέρχονται τὸ ἑωθινόν, τῶν μὲν ἐς
τροφήν, τῶν δὲ ἐς ᾠδήν· συνηρεφὴς γὰρ καὶ κατά-
σκιος καὶ πηγαῖς τρισὶ κατάρρυτος· ἂν περιέλῃ τις
τὴν αἱμασιὰν ἄλσος ὁρᾶν οἰήσεται.

4   "Εἰσελθόντι δέ μοι τήμερον ἀμφὶ μέσην ἡμέραν
ὑπὸ ταῖς ῥοιαῖς καὶ ταῖς μυρρίναις βλέπεται παῖς
μύρτα καὶ ῥοιὰς ἔχων, λευκὸς ὥσπερ γάλα καὶ ξανθὸς
ὡς πῦρ, στιλπνὸς ὡς ἄρτι λελουμένος. γυμνὸς ἦν,
μόνος ἦν· ἔπαιζεν ὡς ἴδιον κῆπον τρυγῶν. 2. ἐγὼ μὲν
οὖν ὥρμησα ἐπ᾽ αὐτὸν ὡς συλληψόμενος, δείσας μὴ
ὑπ᾽ ἀγερωχίας τὰς μυρρίνας καὶ τὰς ῥοιὰς κατα-
κλάσῃ· ὁ δέ με κούφως καὶ ῥᾳδίως ὑπέφευγε, ποτὲ μὲν
ταῖς ῥοδωνιαῖς ὑποτρέχων, ποτὲ δὲ ταῖς μήκωσιν
ὑποκρυπτόμενος ὥσπερ πέρδικος νεοττός. 3. καίτοι
πολλάκις μὲν πράγματα ἔσχον ἐρίφους γαλαθηνοὺς
διώκων, πολλάκις δὲ ἔκαμον μεταθέων μόσχους ἀρτι-
γεννήτους· ἀλλὰ τοῦτο ποικίλον τι χρῆμα ἦν καὶ
ἀθήρατον. καμὼν οὖν ὡς γέρων καὶ ἐπερεισάμενος τῇ
βακτηρίᾳ καὶ ἅμα φυλάττων μὴ φύγῃ, ἐπυνθανόμην
τίνος ἐστὶ τῶν γειτόνων καὶ τί βουλόμενος ἀλλότριον

⁴⁴ φύουσι Naber, cf. 3.34.2, X. An. 1.4.10: φέρουσι V F
⁴⁵ Suppl. Hercher

Nymphs, and many a tune have I played for Pan over there, and many the herd of cattle that I have herded by music alone. I have come to disclose to you what I have seen and to pass on to you what I have heard. 3. I have a garden, made by my own hands, that I have worked on ever since I retired from being a herdsman on account of old age. It has everything that the seasons produce in its due season: 4. in spring roses, lilies, hyacinth, both kinds of violet; in summer poppies, wild pears, and every kind of apple; and currently vines, figs, pomegranates, and green myrtle berries. In the morning flocks of birds gather in this garden, some for food and some for song, for it is sheltered, shady, and watered by three springs. If the stone fence were removed it would look to be a sacred grove.

"When I went into my garden around midday today, beneath the pomegranate trees and the myrtle bushes, I caught sight of a boy with pomegranates and myrtle berries in his hands, as pale as milk, as tawny-haired as fire, gleaming as if just bathed. He was unclothed, he was alone, he was having fun picking fruit as if the garden were his own. 2. So I lunged and tried to grab him, afraid that in his naughtiness he would damage my myrtle bushes and my pomegranate trees, but he kept dodging me nimbly and easily, now darting under the rose bushes, now hiding beneath the poppies like a partridge chick. 3. Well, I have often had trouble chasing unweaned kids and I have often worn myself out running after newborn calves, but this one was a complicated little thing and uncatchable. So being an old man, I got tired and, leaning on my stick while watching to see that he didn't escape, I asked which of the neighbors he belonged to and what he meant by picking fruit in

4

κῆπον τρυγᾷ. 4. ὁ δὲ ἀπεκρίνατο μὲν οὐδέν, στὰς δὲ
πλησίον ἐγέλα πάνυ ἁπαλὸν καὶ ἔβαλλέ με τοῖς
μύρτοις καὶ οὐκ οἶδ᾽ ὅπως ἔθελγε μηκέτι θυμοῦσθαι.
ἐδεόμην οὖν εἰς χεῖρας ἐλθεῖν μηδὲν φοβούμενον ἔτι
καὶ ὤμνυον κατὰ τῶν μύρτων ἀφήσειν ἐπιδοὺς μήλων
καὶ ῥοιῶν παρέξειν τε ἀεὶ τρυγᾶν τὰ φυτὰ καὶ δρέπειν
τὰ ἄνθη τυχὼν παρ᾽ αὐτοῦ φιλήματος ἑνός.

5 "Ἐνταῦθα πάνυ καπυρὸν γελάσας ἀφίησι φωνὴν
οἵαν οὔτε χελιδὼν οὔτε ἀηδὼν οὔτε κύκνος ὅμοιος ἐμοὶ
γέρων γενόμενος. 'ἐμοὶ μέν, ὦ Φιλητᾶ, φιλῆσαί σε
πόνος οὐδείς· βούλομαι γὰρ φιλεῖσθαι μᾶλλον ἢ σὺ
γενέσθαι νέος. ὅρα δὲ εἴ σοι καθ᾽ ἡλικίαν τὸ δῶρον. 2.
οὐδὲν γάρ σε ὠφελήσει τὸ γῆρας πρὸς τὸ μὴ διώκειν
ἐμὲ μετὰ τὸ ἓν φίλημα. δυσθήρατός εἰμι καὶ ἱέρακι καὶ
ἀετῷ καὶ εἴ τις ἄλλος τούτων ὠκύτερος ὄρνις. οὔτοι
παῖς ἐγὼ καὶ εἰ δοκῶ παῖς, ἀλλὰ καὶ τοῦ Κρόνου
πρεσβύτερος καὶ αὐτοῦ τοῦ παντὸς χρόνου· 3. καί σε
οἶδα νέμοντα πρωθήβην ἐν ἐκείνῳ τῷ ὄρει τὸ πλατὺ
βουκόλιον καὶ παρήμην σοι συρίττοντι πρὸς ταῖς
φηγοῖς ἐκείναις ἡνίκα ἤρας Ἀμαρυλλίδος, ἀλλά με
οὐχ ἑώρας καίτοι πλησίον μάλα τῇ κόρῃ παρεστῶτα.
σοὶ μὲν οὖν ἐκείνην ἔδωκα, καὶ ἤδη σοι παῖδες ἀγαθοὶ
βουκόλοι καὶ γεωργοί· 4. νῦν δὲ Δάφνιν ποιμαίνω καὶ
Χλόην, καὶ ἡνίκα ἂν αὐτοὺς εἰς ἓν συναγάγω τὸ
ἑωθινόν, εἰς τὸν σὸν ἔρχομαι κῆπον καὶ τέρπομαι τοῖς
ἄνθεσι καὶ τοῖς φυτοῖς κἂν ταῖς πηγαῖς ταύταις λού-

---

22 Cronus, father of Zeus, was the king of the pre-Olympians.
Longus' Eros combines the primal entity of philosophical and
cosmogonic thought (cf. Hesiod, *Theogony* 120–122) with the
eternally young son of Aphrodite frequently encountered in
Hellenistic poetry and art.

someone else's garden. 4. He made no reply, but stood beside me and began to laugh very softly and to pelt me with
myrtle berries, and somehow he charmed my anger away.
So I encouraged him to embrace me and be frightened no
more, and I swore by the myrtle berries that I would send
him off with a gift of apples and pomegranates and give
him permission to pick the fruit and pluck the flowers any
time he wanted, if I could get one kiss from him.

"At that, with clear silvery laughter he produced a voice   5
that no swallow owns, no nightingale, no swan grown old
like me. 'For my part, Philetas, it is no trouble to kiss you,
for I want to be kissed more than you want to grow young
again, but do consider whether the gift is appropriate at
your age. 2. Your old age will not help you resist stalking
me after that one kiss. I am hard to catch even for a hawk or
an eagle, or any other bird that may be swifter than they
are. I am not really a boy, even though I look like a boy, but
senior even to Cronus and time itself.[22] 3. I know that in
your earliest youth you used to graze your broad herd of
cattle on that mountain there, and I was with you when you
played your syrinx beside those oak trees when you were
in love with Amaryllis,[23] but you could not see me even
though I stood right next to the girl. It was I who gave her
to you, and now you have sons, fine shepherds and farmers.
4. At present I am shepherd to Daphnis and Chloe, and
when I herd them together in the morning, I come to your
garden and enjoy the flowers and trees, and I bathe in
these springs. It is because your flowers and trees are wa-

[23] The name appears in Theocritus and Virgil and perhaps derives from Philitas.

DAPHNIS AND CHLOE

ομαι. διὰ τοῦτο καλὰ καὶ τὰ ἄνθη καὶ τὰ φυτὰ τοῖς
ἐμοῖς λουτροῖς ἀρδόμενα. 5. ὅρα δὲ μή τί σοι τῶν
φυτῶν κατακέκλασται, μή τις ὀπώρα τετρύγηται, μή
τις ἄνθους ῥίζα πεπάτηται, μή τις πηγὴ τετάρακται·
καὶ χαῖρε, μόνος ἀνθρώπων ἐν γήρᾳ θεασάμενος τοῦτο
τὸ παιδίον.'

6 "Ταῦτα εἰπὼν ἀνήλατο καθάπερ ἀηδόνος νεοττὸς
ἐπὶ τὰς μυρρίνας καὶ κλάδον ἀμείβων ἐκ κλάδου διὰ
τῶν φύλλων ἀνεῖρπεν εἰς ἄκρον. εἶδον αὐτοῦ καὶ
πτέρυγας ἐκ τῶν ὤμων καὶ τοξάρια μεταξὺ τῶν πτε-
ρύγων⁴⁶ καὶ οὐκέτι οὔτε ταῦτα οὔτε αὐτόν. 2. εἰ δὲ μὴ
μάτην ταύτας τὰς πολιὰς ἔφυσα μηδὲ γηράσας μαται-
οτέρας τὰς φρένας ἐκτησάμην, Ἔρωτι, ὦ παῖδες,
κατέσπεισθε καὶ Ἔρωτι ὑμῶν μέλει."

7 Πάνυ ἐτέρφθησαν ὥσπερ μῦθον οὐ λόγον ἀκούοντες καὶ ἐπυνθάνοντο τί ἐστί ποτε ὁ Ἔρως, πότερα
παῖς ἢ ὄρνις, καὶ τί δύναται. πάλιν οὖν ὁ Φιλητᾶς ἔφη·
"θεός⁴⁷ ἐστιν, ὦ παῖδες, ὁ Ἔρως, νέος καὶ καλὸς καὶ
πετόμενος· διὰ τοῦτο καὶ νεότητι χαίρει καὶ κάλλος
διώκει καὶ τὰς ψυχὰς ἀναπτεροῖ. 2. δύναται δὲ τοσοῦτον ὅσον οὐδὲ ὁ Ζεύς· κρατεῖ μὲν στοιχείων, κρατεῖ δὲ
ἄστρων, κρατεῖ δὲ τῶν ὁμοίων θεῶν· οὐδὲ ὑμεῖς τοσοῦτον τῶν αἰγῶν καὶ τῶν προβάτων. 3. τὰ ἄνθη⁴⁸ πάντα
Ἔρωτος ἔργα, τὰ φυτὰ πάντα⁴⁹ τούτου ποιήματα, διὰ
τοῦτον καὶ ποταμοὶ ῥέουσι καὶ ἄνεμοι πνέουσιν· 4.
ἔγνων δὲ ἐγὼ καὶ ταῦρον ἐρασθέντα καὶ ὡς οἴστρῳ
πληγεὶς ἐμυκᾶτο, καὶ τράγον φιλήσαντα αἶγα καὶ
ἠκολούθει πανταχοῦ. αὐτὸς μὲν γὰρ ἤμην νέος καὶ
ἠράσθην Ἀμαρυλλίδος, καὶ οὔτε τροφῆς ἐμεμνήμην

⁴⁶ πτερύγων Hercher: πτερύγων καὶ τῶν ὤμων V F
⁴⁷ θεός . . . ὁμοίων θεῶν habet O

66

tered by my baths that they are beautiful. 5. Look and see whether any of your trees is damaged, any fruit picked, any flower's stem trampled, any spring muddied. Goodbye, then, and be glad that you are the only elderly person ever to have seen this child.'

"With these words he hopped up into the myrtles like a 6 nightingale's chick, and moving from branch to branch worked his way up through the leaves to the top. I saw wings on his shoulders and a little bow and arrows between his wings, and then I couldn't see them or him anymore. 2. Unless I have grown these gray hairs for nothing and turned feebleminded in my old age, you are consecrated to Love, my children, and Love is looking after you."

They enjoyed this very much, as if they were listening 7 to a story and not fact, and asked just what Love is, a boy or a bird, and what power he has. So Philetas continued, "Love is a god, my children, young, beautiful, and winged. That is why he enjoys youth, pursues beauty, and makes souls take wing. 2. He has more power even than Zeus: he rules the elements, rules the stars, rules his fellow gods, moreso even than you rule your goats and sheep. 3. All the flowers are the work of Love, all the trees are his creations, and on his account rivers flow and winds blow. 4. I have even known a bull in love, and he bellowed as if stung by a gadfly, and a he-goat who fancied a she-goat and followed her everywhere. And of course I was once young myself and in love with Amaryllis; I forgot about food, took

---

48 τὰ ἄνθη . . . πανταχοῦ habet O
49 Hercher: ταῦτα V F

οὔτε ποτὸν προσεφερόμην οὔτε ὕπνον ᾑρούμην. 5.
ἤλγουν τὴν ψυχήν, τὴν καρδίαν ἐπαλλόμην, τὸ σῶμα
ἐψυχόμην· ἐβόων ὡς παιόμενος, ἐσιώπων ὡς νεκρού-
μενος, εἰς ποταμοὺς ἐνέβαινον ὡς καόμενος. 6. ἐκάλουν τὸν Πᾶνα βοηθὸν ὡς καὶ αὐτὸν τῆς Πίτυος
ἐρασθέντα· ἐπήνουν τὴν Ἠχὼ τὸ Ἀμαρυλλίδος ὄνομα
μετ' ἐμὲ καλοῦσαν· κατέκλων τὰς σύριγγας ὅτι μοι τὰς
μὲν βοῦς ἔθελγον, Ἀμαρυλλίδα δὲ οὐκ ἦγον. 7. Ἔρωτος γὰρ οὐδὲν φάρμακον, οὐ πινόμενον, οὐκ ἐσθιό-
μενον, οὐκ ἐν ᾠδαῖς λαλούμενον, ὅτι μὴ φίλημα καὶ
περιβολὴ καὶ συγκατακλιθῆναι γυμνοῖς σώμασι."

8   Φιλητᾶς μὲν τοσαῦτα παιδεύσας αὐτοὺς ἀπαλ-
λάττεται, τυρούς τινας παρ' αὐτῶν καὶ ἔριφον ἤδη
κεράστην λαβών· οἱ δὲ μόνοι καταλειφθέντες καὶ τότε
πρῶτον ἀκούσαντες τὸ Ἔρωτος ὄνομα τάς τε ψυχὰς
συνεστάλησαν ὑπὸ λύπης καὶ ἐπανελθόντες νύκτωρ
εἰς τὰς ἐπαύλεις παρέβαλλον οἷς ἤκουσαν τὰ αὐτῶν.
2. "ἀλγοῦσιν οἱ ἐρῶντες, καὶ ἡμεῖς· ⟨τροφῆς⟩ ἀμελοῦ-
σιν·[50] ἠμελήκαμεν ὁμοίως. καθεύδειν οὐ δύνανται· τοῦτο νῦν πάσχομεν καὶ ἡμεῖς. κάεσθαι δοκοῦσι· καὶ παρ'
ἡμῖν τὸ πῦρ. ἐπιθυμοῦσιν ἀλλήλους ὁρᾶν· διὰ τοῦτο
θᾶττον εὐχόμεθα γενέσθαι τὴν ἡμέραν. 3. σχεδὸν
τοῦτό ἐστιν ὁ ἔρως καὶ ἐρῶμεν ἀλλήλων οὐκ εἰδότες. ἢ
τοῦτο μέν ἐστιν ὁ ἔρως, ἐγὼ δὲ ἐρῶ μόνος;[51] τί οὖν τὰ
αὐτὰ ἀλγοῦμεν; τί δὲ ἀλλήλους ζητοῦμεν; ἀληθῆ πάντα εἶπεν ὁ Φιλητᾶς. 4. τὸ ἐκ τοῦ κήπου παιδίον ὤφθη

50 Suppl. Courier: ἀμελοῦσιν ἵν' V F

51 ἢ τοῦτο . . . ἐρῶ μόνος Jackson: εἰ τοῦτο . . . ἐρώμενος (ὁ
ἐρ. V) V F

nothing to drink, and got no sleep. 5. I was soul-sick, my heart throbbed, my body was frozen. I would scream as if beaten, I fell as quiet as a dying man, I plunged into rivers as if on fire. 6. I would call on Pan for help, since he himself had been in love with Pitys. I would praise Echo for repeating Amaryllis' name after me. I would smash my syrinxes for charming my cattle but not bringing me Amaryllis. 7. No, there is no remedy for Love, none to drink, to eat, or chant in songs, except kissing, embracing, and lying down together with naked bodies."[24]

When Philetas had given them this lesson he went on his way, accepting from them some cheeses and a kid that already had its horns, while they were left on their own, having heard Love's name for the very first time. Their souls were painfully downcast, and when they returned to their farms that night they compared their own experiences with what they had heard. 2. "Lovers are in pain, and so are we. They neglect food: we have neglected it likewise. They cannot sleep, and now that is happening to us too. They think they're burning up: that fire is in us too. They long to see each other, and that is why we pray for the day to come sooner. 3. This must be love and we must be in love with each other without realizing it. Or maybe this is love and I am the only one in love? Then why do we feel the same pain? Why do we seek after each other? Everything that Philetas said is true. 4. The little boy in the garden ap-

8

---

[24] Alluding to and "correcting" the negative formulation in Theocritus 11.1–3, "There is no other medicine for love, it seems to me, Nicias, neither smeared in nor sprinkled on, than the Daughters of Pieria" (the Muses), i.e. than by singing an appropriate song.

καὶ τοῖς πατράσιν ἡμῶν ὄναρ ἐκεῖνο καὶ νέμειν ἡμᾶς
τὰς ἀγέλας ἐκέλευσε. πῶς ἄν τις αὐτὸ λάβοι; μικρόν
ἐστι καὶ φεύξεται. καὶ πῶς ἄν τις αὐτὸ φύγοι; πτερὰ
ἔχει καὶ καταλήψεται. 5. ἐπὶ τὰς Νύμφας δεῖ βοηθοὺς
καταφεύγειν. ἀλλ᾽ οὐδὲ Φιλητᾶν ὁ Πὰν ὠφέλησεν
Ἀμαρυλλίδος ἐρῶντα. ὅσα εἶπεν ἄρα φάρμακα, ταῦτα
ζητητέον, φίλημα καὶ περιβολὴν καὶ κεῖσθαι γυμνοὺς
χαμαί. κρύος μέν, ἀλλὰ καρτερήσομεν[52] δεύτεροι μετὰ
Φιλητᾶν."

9   Τοῦτο αὐτοῖς γίνεται νυκτερινὸν παιδευτήριον, καὶ
ἀγαγόντες τῆς ἐπιούσης ἡμέρας τὰς ἀγέλας εἰς νομὴν
ἐφίλησαν μὲν ἀλλήλους ἰδόντες, ὃ μήπω πρότερον
ἐποίησαν, περιέβαλον τὰς χεῖρας ἐπαλλάξαντες, τὸ δὲ
τρίτον ὤκνουν φάρμακον, ἀποδυθέντες κατακλιθῆναι·
θρασύτερον γὰρ οὐ μόνον παρθένων ἀλλὰ καὶ νέων
αἰπόλων. 2. πάλιν οὖν νὺξ ἀγρυπνίαν ἔχουσα καὶ
ἔννοιαν τῶν γεγενημένων καὶ κατάμεμψιν τῶν παρα-
λελειμμένων· "ἐφιλήσαμεν, καὶ οὐδὲν ὄφελος. περι-
εβάλομεν, καὶ οὐδὲν πλέον. σχεδὸν τὸ συγκατακλιθῆναι μόνον φάρμακον ἔρωτος. πειρατέον καὶ τούτου·
πάντως ἐν αὐτῷ τι κρεῖττον ἔσται φιλήματος."

10   Ἐπὶ τούτοις τοῖς λογισμοῖς οἷον εἰκὸς καὶ ὀνείρατα
ἑώρων ἐρωτικά· τὰ φιλήματα, τὰς περιβολάς· καὶ ὅσα
δὲ μεθ᾽ ἡμέραν οὐκ ἔπραξαν, ταῦτα ὄναρ ἔπραξαν·
γυμνοὶ μετ᾽ ἀλλήλων ἔκειντο. 2. ἐνθεώτεροι δὴ κατὰ
τὴν ἐπιοῦσαν ἡμέραν ἀνέστησαν καὶ ῥοίζῳ τὰς ἀγέλας κατήλαυνον ἐπειγόμενοι πρὸς τὰ φιλήματα καὶ
ἰδόντες ἀλλήλους ἅμα μειδιάματι προσέδραμον. 3. τὰ
μὲν οὖν φιλήματα ἐγένετο καὶ ἡ περιβολὴ τῶν χειρῶν
ἠκολούθησε, τὸ δὲ τρίτον φάρμακον ἐβράδυνε, μήτε

[52] D. Heinsius: μαρτυρήσομεν V F

peared to our fathers in that dream, and he told us to graze the flocks. How could anyone catch him? He is small and will get away. And how could anyone get away from him? He has wings and will overtake you. 5. We must run to the Nymphs for help. But Pan didn't even help Philetas when he was in love with Amaryllis. Those remedies he mentioned, we must look for them: kissing, embracing, and lying naked on the ground. It's icy, but we will endure it, following Philetas' example."

That was their nocturnal lesson, and the next day, as   9 they led their flocks to pasture, they kissed each other on sight, which they had never done before, and threw their arms around each other tightly, but they balked at the third remedy, undressing and lying down: that was too bold not only for girls but also for young goatherds. 2. So another night of insomnia, thinking over what had happened, and remorse for what had been left undone. "We kissed, and that was no help. We embraced, and that was no better. Lying down together must be the only remedy for love. We must try that too: there will certainly be something in it more potent than kissing."

After these calculations they naturally had erotic   10 dreams about their kisses and embraces, and what they had not done by day they did in their dreams: they lay naked with each other. 2. They got up next morning even more possessed, and whistled their flocks down in eagerness for kisses, and on sight they ran to each other with a smile. 3. There were kisses, of course, followed by embraces, but the third remedy took its time, since Daphnis

τοῦ Δάφνιδος τολμῶντος εἰπεῖν μήτε τῆς Χλόης βου-
λομένης κατάρχεσθαι, ἔστε τύχη καὶ τοῦτο ἔπραξαν.

11   Καθεζόμενοι ὑπὸ στελέχει δρυὸς πλησίον ἀλλήλων
καὶ γευσάμενοι τῆς ἐν φιλήματι τέρψεως[53] ἀπλήστως
ἐνεφοροῦντο τῆς ἡδονῆς· ἦσαν δὲ καὶ χειρῶν περιβολαὶ θλῖψιν τοῖς στόμασι παρέχουσαι. 2. κατὰ τὴν
τῶν χειρῶν προσβολὴν βιαιότερον δή τοῦ Δάφνιδος
ἐπισπασαμένου κλίνεταί πως ἐπὶ πλευρὰν ἡ Χλόη,
κἀκεῖνος δὲ συγκατακλίνεται τῷ φιλήματι ἀκολουθῶν,
καὶ γνωρίσαντες τῶν ὀνείρων τὴν εἰκόνα κατέκειντο
πολὺν χρόνον ὥσπερ συνδεδεμένοι· 3. εἰδότες δὲ τῶν
ἐντεῦθεν οὐδὲν καὶ νομίσαντες τοῦτο εἶναι πέρας ἐρωτικῆς ἀπολαύσεως, μάτην τὸ πλεῖστον τῆς ἡμέρας
δαπανήσαντες διελύθησαν καὶ τὰς ἀγέλας ἀπήλαυνον
τὴν νύκτα μισοῦντες. ἴσως ἄν τι καὶ τῶν ἀληθῶν
ἔπραξαν εἰ μὴ θόρυβος τοιόσδε πᾶσαν τὴν ἀγροικίαν
ἐκείνην κατέλαβε.

12   Νέοι Μηθυμναῖοι πλούσιοι, διαθέσθαι τὸν τρυγητὸν ἐν ξενικῇ τέρψει θελήσαντες, ναῦν μικρὰν καθελ-
κύσαντες καὶ οἰκέτας προσκώπους καθίσαντες τοὺς
Μιτυληναίων ἀγροὺς παρέπλεον ὅσοι θαλάσσης πλησίον. 2. εὐλίμενός τε γὰρ ἡ παραλία καὶ οἰκήσεσιν
ἠσκημένη πολυτελῶς, καὶ λουτρὰ συνεχῆ παράδεισοί
τε καὶ ἄλση, τὰ μὲν φύσεως ἔργα, τὰ δ' ἀνθρώπων
τέχνη· πάντα ἐνηβῆσαι καλά. 3. παραπλέοντες δὲ καὶ
ἐνορμιζόμενοι κακὸν μὲν ἐποίουν οὐδέν, τέρψεις δὲ
ποικίλας ἐτέρποντο, ποτὲ μὲν ἀγκίστροις καλάμων
ἀπηρτημένοις ἐκ λίνου λεπτοῦ πετραίους ἰχθῦς ἁλιεύ-
οντες ἐκ πέτρας ἁλιτενοῦς, ποτὲ δὲ κυσὶ καὶ δικτύοις
λαγὼς φεύγοντας τὸν ἐν ταῖς ἀμπέλοις θόρυβον λαμ-

53 γεύσεως F

did not dare to suggest it nor did Chloe want to take the lead, until by accident they did this too.

Sitting close beside each other by the trunk of an oak, 11 they tasted the delight of kissing and kept indulging in that pleasure insatiably, and there were embraces too, abetting the pressure of their lips. 2. When during these embraces Daphnis hugged Chloe rather forcefully, she somehow tipped over on her side and, following his kiss, he tipped over with her. Recognizing the image in their dreams, they lay there for a long while as if lashed together. 3. Knowing nothing of what comes next, and imagining that this was the limit of erotic satisfaction, they parted after wasting most of the day and drove their flocks away with hateful thoughts of the night. Perhaps they would have done the real thing if the following disturbance had not gripped the whole countryside.

Some rich young men from Methymna,[25] wanting to 12 celebrate the vintage by having fun away from home, launched a small yacht, enlisting their houseboys as oarsmen, and went sailing along the seaside farms of Mytilene. 2. This coast is well supplied with harbors and sumptuously equipped with residences, with swimming pools one after another, parks and groves, some the product of nature and others of human handiwork, all of them fine places to be young. 3. They were having all kinds of fun and doing no mischief as they sailed along and put into shore, sometimes casting for rockfish from a prominent rock, using hooks on a fine line hung from reeds, sometimes trying with dogs and hounds to catch hares fleeing the hubbub in

[25] The second-largest city on Lesbos.

βάνοντες· 4. ἤδη δὲ καὶ ὀρνίθων ἄγρας ἐμέλησεν
αὐτοῖς καὶ ἔλαβον βρόχοις χῆνας ἀγρίους καὶ νήττας
καὶ ὠτίδας, ὥστε ἡ τέρψις αὐτοῖς καὶ τραπέζης ὠφέλειαν παρεῖχεν. εἰ δέ τινος προσέδει, παρὰ τῶν ἐν τοῖς
ἀγροῖς ἐλάμβανον, περιττοτέρους τῆς ἀξίας ὀβολοὺς
καταβάλλοντες. 5. ἔδει δὲ μόνον ἄρτου καὶ οἴνου καὶ
στέγης· οὐ γὰρ ἀσφαλὲς ἐδόκει μετοπωρινῆς ὥρας
ἐνεστώσης ἐνθαλαττεύειν, ὥστε καὶ τὴν ναῦν ἀνεῖλκον
ἐπὶ τὴν γῆν νύκτα χειμέριον δεδοικότες.

13   Τῶν δή τις ἀγροίκων ἐς ἀνολκὴν λίθου θλίβοντος
τὰ πατηθέντα βοτρύδια χρῄζων σχοίνου, τῆς πρότερον ῥαγείσης, κρύφα ἐπὶ τὴν θάλασσαν ἐλθών,
ἀφρουρήτῳ τῇ νηῒ προσελθών, τὸ πεῖσμα ἐκλύσας,
οἴκαδε κομίσας, ἐς ὅ τι ἔχρῃζεν ἐχρήσατο. 2. ἔωθεν
οὖν οἱ Μηθυμναῖοι νεανίσκοι ζήτησιν ἐποιοῦντο τοῦ
πείσματος καὶ (ὡμολόγει γὰρ οὐδεὶς τὴν κλοπὴν)
ὀλίγα μεμψάμενοι τοὺς ξενοδόχους παρέπλεον καὶ
σταδίους τριάκοντα παρελάσαντες προσορμίζονται
τοῖς ἀγροῖς ἐν οἷς ᾤκουν ὁ Δάφνις καὶ ἡ Χλόη· ἐδόκει
γὰρ αὐτοῖς καλὸν εἶναι τὸ πεδίον ἐς θήραν λαγῶν. 3.
σχοῖνον μὲν οὖν οὐκ εἶχον ὥστε ἐκδήσασθαι πεῖσμα,
λύγον δὲ χλωρὰν μακρὰν στρέψαντες ὡς σχοῖνον
ταύτῃ τὴν ναῦν ἐκ τῆς πρύμνης ἄκρας εἰς τὴν γῆν
ἔδησαν, ἔπειτα τοὺς κύνας ἀφέντες ῥινηλατεῖν ἐν ταῖς
εὐκαίροις φαινομέναις τῶν ὁδῶν ἐλινοστάτουν. 4. οἱ
μὲν δὴ κύνες ἅμα ὑλακῇ διαθέοντες ἐφόβησαν τὰς
αἶγας, αἱ δὲ τὰ ὀρεινὰ καταλιποῦσαι μᾶλλόν τι πρὸς
τὴν θάλασσαν ὥρμησαν, ἔχουσαι δὲ οὐδὲν ἐν ψάμμῳ
τρώξιμον ἐλθοῦσαι πρὸς τὴν ναῦν αἱ θρασύτεραι
αὐτῶν τὴν λύγον τὴν χλωρὰν ᾗ δέδετο ἡ ναῦς ἀπ-
έφαγον.

14   Ἦν δέ τι καὶ κλυδώνιον ἐν τῇ θαλάσσῃ κινηθέντος

the vineyards. 4. Then they turned to wildfowl and snared wild geese, ducks, and bustards, so that their fun also provided for their table. Whatever else they needed they got from the country people, paying more money than it was worth. 5. They needed only bread, wine, and shelter, for they thought it unsafe to stay at sea with autumn set in and would even beach their yacht if they feared a stormy night.

Now one of the farmers needed a rope, his own having 13 broken, for hoisting a stone being used to crush the grapes after treading. So he stole down to the shore, approached the yacht, which had been left unguarded, untied her cable, took it home, and used it for what he needed. 2. Next morning the young men from Methymna launched an inquiry after the rope, and when no one would own up to the theft they made a few complaints about their hosts and sailed on. After cruising thirty stades[26] they put in at the farm where Daphnis and Chloe lived, for this plain seemed to them a fine spot for hunting hares. 3. But since they had no rope to use as a mooring cable, they plaited a long, green willow shoot for a rope, used it to moor the yacht's stern to land, then released their hounds to pick up a scent and started setting out nets on the paths that looked promising. 4. The hounds ran around baying and frightened the goats, which left the high ground and rushed down to the shore. Having nothing to eat on shore, the bolder ones went over to the yacht and ate up the green willow shoot that moored it.

There was also a bit of swell on the sea, as a breeze from 14

26 About 5.5 km.

ἀπὸ τῶν ὀρῶν πνεύματος. ταχὺ δὴ μάλα λυθεῖσαν
αὐτὴν ὑπήνεγκεν ἡ παλίρροια τοῦ κύματος καὶ ἐς τὸ
πέλαγος μετέωρον ἔφερεν. 2. αἰσθήσεως δὴ τοῖς Μηθυμναίοις γενομένης, οἱ μὲν ἐπὶ τὴν θάλασσαν ἔθεον,
οἱ δὲ τοὺς κύνας συνέλεγον· ἐβόων δὲ πάντες, ὡς
πάντας τοὺς ἐκ τῶν πλησίον ἀγρῶν ἀκούσαντας
συνελθεῖν. ἀλλ' ἦν οὐδὲν ὄφελος· τοῦ γὰρ πνεύματος
ἀκμάζοντος ἀσχέτῳ τάχει κατὰ ῥοῦν ἡ ναῦς ἐφέρετο.
3. οἱ δ' οὖν οὐκ ὀλίγων κτημάτων οἱ Μηθυμναῖοι
στερόμενοι ἐζήτουν τὸν νέμοντα τὰς αἶγας καὶ εὑ-
ρόντες τὸν Δάφνιν ἔπαιον, ἀπέδυον· εἷς δέ τις καὶ
κυνόδεσμον ἀράμενος περιῆγε τὰς χεῖρας ὡς δήσων.
4. ὁ δὲ ἐβόα τε παιόμενος καὶ ἱκέτευε τοὺς ἀγροίκους
καὶ πρώτους γε τὸν Λάμωνα καὶ τὸν Δρύαντα βοηθοὺς
ἐπεκαλεῖτο. οἱ δὲ ἀντείχοντο σκληροὶ γέροντες καὶ
χεῖρας ἐκ γεωργικῶν ἔργων ἰσχυρὰς ἔχοντες καὶ
ἠξίουν δικαιολογήσασθαι περὶ τῶν γεγενημένων.

15   Ταὐτὰ δὲ καὶ τῶν ἄλλων ἀξιούντων δικαστὴν
καθίζουσι Φιλητᾶν τὸν βουκόλον· πρεσβύτατός τε
γὰρ ἦν τῶν παρόντων καὶ κλέος εἶχεν ἐν τοῖς κω-
μήταις δικαιοσύνης περιττῆς. πρῶτοι δὲ κατηγόρουν
οἱ Μηθυμναῖοι σαφῆ καὶ σύντομα βουκόλον ἔχοντες
δικαστήν· 2. "ἤλθομεν εἰς τούτους τοὺς ἀγροὺς θηρᾶσαι θέλοντες. τὴν μὲν οὖν ναῦν λύγῳ χλωρᾷ δήσαντες ἐπὶ τῆς ἀκτῆς κατελίπομεν, αὐτοὶ δὲ διὰ τῶν
κυνῶν ζήτησιν ἐποιούμεθα θηρίων. ἐν τούτῳ πρὸς τὴν
θάλασσαν αἱ αἶγες τούτου κατελθοῦσαι τήν τε λύγον
κατεσθίουσι καὶ τὴν ναῦν ἀπολύουσιν. 3. εἶδες αὐτὴν
ἐπὶ τῇ θαλάσσῃ φερομένην, πόσων οἴει μεστὴν ἀγαθῶν; οἷα μὲν ἐσθὴς ἀπόλωλεν, οἷος δὲ κόσμος κυνῶν,
ὅσον δὲ ἀργύριον. τοὺς ἀγροὺς ἄν τις τούτους ἐκεῖνα
ἔχων ὠνήσατο. ἀνθ' ὧν ἀξιοῦμεν ἄγειν τοῦτον πονη-

the hills had kicked up. As soon as the yacht was un-
moored, the backwash of the surf lifted her and took her
out to the open sea. 2. When this news reached the Methymnaeans, some went running to the shore, the rest collected the hounds, and all were shouting, so that everyone
from the neighboring farms heard them and arrived on the
scene en masse. But it was no use: the breeze was at its
peak and the backwash carried the yacht away with irre-
sistible speed. 3. The Methymnaeans had lost no trivial
amount of property, so they went looking for the person in
charge of those goats. When they found Daphnis they
started beating him and stripping off his clothes, and one
of them even picked up a dog-leash and started pulling his
hands behind his back to tie him up. 4. He screamed as he
was beaten and appealed to the farmers, calling first of all
on Lamo and Dryas for help. And they held their own, being hard old men with hands strengthened by farm work,
and demanded a judicial inquiry into the events.

The other side made the same demand, so they appointed Philetas the cowherd as judge: he was the most
venerable person there and among the villagers owned a
reputation for exceptional fairness. First the Methymnaeans argued the case for the prosecution, making it plain
and simple for their herdsman judge: 2. "We came to these
fields to do some hunting. We moored our yacht with green
willow and left her on the beach while we set our hounds
on the quest for game. Meanwhile, this fellow's goats came
down to the shore, ate up the willow, and cast the yacht
adrift. 3. You saw her drifting on the sea. Have any idea
how valuable her cargo is? Such fine clothing, such gear for
the hounds, so much money, all lost. Anyone with that
cargo could buy up these farms. In recompense, we claim

15

ρὸν ὄντα αἰπόλον, ὃς ἐπὶ τῆς θαλάσσης νέμει τὰς
αἶγας ὡς ναύτης."

16 Τοσαῦτα οἱ Μηθυμναῖοι κατηγόρησαν· ὁ δὲ
Δάφνις διέκειτο μὲν κακῶς ὑπὸ τῶν πληγῶν, Χλόην δὲ
ὁρῶν παροῦσαν πάντων κατεφρόνει καὶ ὧδε εἶπεν·
"ἐγὼ νέμω τὰς αἶγας καλῶς. οὐδέποτε ᾐτιάσατο κωμή-
της οὐδὲ εἷς ὡς ἢ κῆπόν τινος αἲξ ἐμὴ κατεβοσκήσατο
ἢ ἄμπελον βλαστάνουσαν κατέκλασεν. 2. οὗτοι δέ
εἰσι κυνηγέται πονηροὶ καὶ κύνας ἔχουσι κακῶς πε-
παιδευμένους, οἵτινες τρέχοντες πολλὰ καὶ ὑλακτοῦν-
τες σκληρὰ κατεδίωξαν αὐτὰς ἐκ τῶν ὀρῶν καὶ τῶν
πεδίων ἐπὶ τὴν θάλασσαν ὥσπερ λύκοι. 3. ἀλλ' ἀπ-
έφαγον τὴν λύγον· οὐ γὰρ εἶχον ἐν ψάμμῳ πόαν ἢ
κόμαρον ἢ θύμον· ἀλλὰ ἀπώλετο ἡ ναῦς ὑπὸ τοῦ
πνεύματος καὶ τῆς θαλάσσης· ταῦτα χειμῶνος οὐκ
αἰγῶν ἐστιν ἔργα. ἀλλ' ἐσθὴς ἐνέκειτο καὶ ἄργυρος·
καὶ τίς πιστεύσει νοῦν ἔχων ὅτι τοσαῦτα φέρουσα
ναῦς πεῖσμα εἶχε λύγον;"

17 Τούτοις ἐπεδάκρυσεν ὁ Δάφνις καὶ εἰς οἶκτον ὑπ-
ηγάγετο τοὺς ἀγροίκους πολύν, ὥστε ὁ Φιλητᾶς, ὁ
δικαστής, ὤμνυε Πᾶνα καὶ Νύμφας μηδὲν ἀδικεῖν
Δάφνιν ἀλλὰ μηδὲ τὰς αἶγας, τὴν δὲ θάλασσαν καὶ
τὸν ἄνεμον, ὧν ἄλλους εἶναι δικαστάς. 2. οὐκ ἔπειθε
ταῦτα Φιλητᾶς <τοῖς> Μηθυμναίοις λέγων, ἀλλ' ὑπ'
ὀργῆς ὁρμήσαντες ἦγον τὸν Δάφνιν πάλιν καὶ συν-
δεῖν ἤθελον. 3. ἐνταῦθα οἱ κωμῆται ταραχθέντες ἐπι-
πηδῶσιν αὐτοῖς ὡσεὶ ψᾶρες ἢ κολοιοὶ καὶ ταχὺ μὲν
ἀφαιροῦνται τὸν Δάφνιν ἤδη καὶ αὐτὸν μαχόμενον,
ταχὺ δὲ ξύλοις παίοντες ἐκείνους εἰς φυγὴν ἔτρεψαν·

---

27 That is, no more competently than a goatherd would sail a

78

the right to carry off this bungling goatherd, who tends his goats like a sailor."[27]

Such was the Methymnaeans' case for the prosecution. 16 Daphnis was in a bad way from his beating but when he saw Chloe there, he disregarded all that and said, "I graze my goats just fine. Never has a single villager ever complained that a goat of mine has eaten up anyone's garden or trampled a budding vine. 2. These hunters are the bunglers, with their poorly trained hounds that chased the goats off the hills and plains down to the shore by running all about and baying harshly, like wolves. 3. Item: they ate the willow. Yes, because on the beach they had no grass, arbutus, or thyme. Item: the yacht was lost because of the wind and the sea. Yes, that was the work of a storm, not goats. Item: clothing and money were on board. But who in their right mind will believe that a yacht with such a cargo had a willow shoot for a mooring cable?"

To this Daphnis added a burst of tears and made the 17 country folk feel very sorry for him. And so Philetas the judge swore by Pan and the Nymphs that Daphnis had done no wrong and neither had the goats, but rather the sea and the wind, who were answerable to different judges. 2. This verdict of Philetas did not satisfy the Methymnaeans,: they angrily charged at Daphnis and again started to take him away and were ready to tie him up. 3. Here the villagers got stirred up and lit into them like starlings or jackdaws. They soon reclaimed Daphnis, who was now fighting too, and soon routed them with cudgel-blows,

ship. There may, however, be a pun on *aigas* ("goats" or "waves"), in which case we might translate "who is like a sailor at sea tending billow-goats."

ἀπέστησαν δὲ οὐ πρότερον ἔστε τῶν ὅρων αὐτοὺς
ἐξήλασαν ἐς ἄλλους ἀγρούς.

18   Διωκόντων δὴ τοὺς Μηθυμναίους ἐκείνων, ἡ Χλόη
κατὰ πολλὴν ἡσυχίαν ἄγει πρὸς τὰς Νύμφας τὸν
Δάφνιν καὶ ἀπονίπτει τε τὸ πρόσωπον ἡμαγμένον ἐκ
τῶν ῥινῶν ῥαγεισῶν ὑπὸ πληγῆς τινος καὶ τῆς πήρας
προκομίσασα ζυμίτου μέρος καὶ τυροῦ τμῆμά τι δίδωσι φαγεῖν, τὸ δὲ μάλιστα ἀνακτησάμενον[54] αὐτόν,
φίλημα ἐφίλησε μελιτῶδες ἁπαλοῖς τοῖς χείλεσι.

19   Τότε μὲν δὴ παρὰ τοσοῦτον Δάφνις ἦλθε κακοῦ· τὸ
δὲ πρᾶγμα οὐ ταύτῃ πέπαυτο ἀλλ' ἐλθόντες οἱ Μηθυμναῖοι μόλις εἰς τὴν ἑαυτῶν, ὁδοιπόροι μὲν ἀντὶ
ναυτῶν, τραυματίαι δὲ ἀντὶ τρυφώντων,[55] ἐκκλησίαν
τε συνήγαγον τῶν πολιτῶν καὶ ἱκετηρίας θέντες
ἱκέτευον τιμωρίας ἀξιωθῆναι, 2. τῶν μὲν ἀληθῶν λέγοντες οὐδὲ ἕν, μὴ καὶ προσκαταγέλαστοι γένοιντο
τοιαῦτα καὶ τοσαῦτα παθόντες ὑπὸ ποιμένων, κατ-
ηγοροῦντες δὲ Μιτυληναίων, ὡς τὴν ναῦν ἀφελομένων
καὶ τὰ χρήματα διαρπασάντων πολέμου νόμῳ. 3. οἱ δὲ
πιστεύοντες διὰ τὰ τραύματα καὶ νεανίσκοις τῶν πρώ-
των παρ' αὐτοῖς οἰκιῶν τιμωρῆσαι δίκαιον νομίζοντες
Μιτυληναίοις μὲν πόλεμον ἀκήρυκτον ἐψηφίσαντο,
τὸν δὲ στρατηγὸν ἐκέλευσαν δέκα ναῦς καθελκύσαντα
κακουργεῖν αὐτῶν τὴν παραλίαν· πλησίον γὰρ χειμῶνος ὄντος οὐκ ἦν ἀσφαλὲς μείζονα στόλον πιστεύ-
ειν τῇ θαλάσσῃ.

20   Ὁ δὲ εὐθὺς τῆς ἐπιούσης ἀναγόμενος αὐτερέταις
στρατιώταις ἐπέπλει τοῖς παραθαλασσίοις τῶν Μιτυληναίων ἀγροῖς καὶ πολλὰ μὲν ἥρπαζε ποίμνια, πολὺν

---

54 τὸ δὲ . . . -σάμενον Seiler: τότε . . . -σαμένη V F
55 ὁδοιπόροι . . . τρυφώντων V: πόλιν τραυματίαι τῶν

and they did not let up until they had driven them over the boundaries into other farms.

While they were chasing the Methymnaeans, Chloe took Daphnis in very calm circumstances to the Nymphs, where she washed from his face the blood from his nose, broken by a punch, and gave him from her knapsack a piece of leavened bread and a slice of cheese to eat. But what most revived him was the kiss she gave him, sweet as honey, with her soft lips. 18

So narrow was Daphnis' escape from harm that day. But the matter did not end there: when the Methymnaeans returned home the hard way, trekkers instead of sailors, casualties instead of voluptuaries, they convened an assembly of the citizens and, placing olive branches, petitioned to be accorded vengeance. 2. In their account they spoke not a word of truth, for fear that on top of everything else they would become laughing-stocks for having been foiled in so many ways by shepherds. Instead, they accused the Mitylenaeans of seizing their yacht and plundering their possessions in an act of war. 3. The assemblymen were convinced by their wounds and thought it right to avenge young men from the leading families in town, so they voted for an undeclared war against the Mitylenaeans and authorized the commander to launch ten ships to ravage their coast: with winter approaching, it was unsafe to commit a larger fleet to the sea. 19

The very next day the commander put to sea with infantrymen at the oars and invaded the coastal farms of the Mitylenaeans. He seized many animals, large quantities of 20

ἐγχωρίων τρυφώντων καὶ ἐν ἡσυχίᾳ ὄντων τούτους εἰς βοήθειαν ἥξειν ἱκέτευον F

δὲ σῖτον καὶ οἶνον, ἄρτι πεπαυμένου τοῦ τρυγητοῦ, καὶ ἀνθρώπους δὲ οὐκ ὀλίγους ὅσοι τούτων ἐργάται. 2. ἐπέπλευσε καὶ τοῖς τῆς Χλόης ἀγροῖς καὶ τοῦ Δάφνιδος καὶ ἀπόβασιν ὀξεῖαν θέμενος λείαν ἤλαυνε τὰ ἐν ποσίν. ὁ μὲν Δάφνις οὐκ ἔνεμε τὰς αἶγας ἀλλ' ἐς τὴν ὕλην ἀνελθὼν φυλλάδα χλωρὰν ἔκοπτεν ὡς ἔχοι τοῦ χειμῶνος παρέχειν τοῖς ἐρίφοις τροφήν, ὥστε ἄνωθεν θεασάμενος τὴν καταδρομὴν ἐνέκρυψεν αὑτὸν στελέχει κοίλῳ[56] ξηρᾶς ὀξύης· 3. ἡ δὲ Χλόη παρῆν ταῖς ἀγέλαις καὶ διωκομένη καταφεύγει πρὸς τὰς Νύμφας ἱκέτις καὶ ἐδεῖτο φείσασθαι καὶ ὧν ἔνεμε καὶ αὐτῆς διὰ τὰς θεάς. ἀλλ' ἦν οὐδὲν ὄφελος· οἱ γὰρ Μηθυμναῖοι πολλὰ τῶν ἀγαλμάτων κατακερτομήσαντες καὶ τὰς ἀγέλας ἤλασαν κἀκείνην ἤγαγον ὥσπερ αἶγα ἢ πρόβατον παίοντες λύγοις.

21 Ἔχοντες δὲ ἤδη τὰς ναῦς παντοδαπῆς ἁρπαγῆς μεστὰς οὐκέτ' ἐγίνωσκον περαιτέρω πλεῖν ἀλλὰ τὸν οἴκαδε πλοῦν ἐποιοῦντο, καὶ τὸν χειμῶνα καὶ τοὺς πολεμίους δεδιότες. οἱ μὲν οὖν ἀπέπλεον εἰρεσίᾳ προσταλαιπωροῦντες (ἄνεμος γὰρ οὐκ ἦν), 2. ὁ δὲ Δάφνις ἡσυχίας γενομένης ἐλθὼν εἰς τὸ πεδίον ἔνθα ἔνεμον καὶ μήτε τὰς αἶγας ἰδὼν μήτε τὰ πρόβατα καταλαβὼν μήτε Χλόην εὑρὼν ἀλλὰ ἐρημίαν πολλὴν καὶ τὴν σύριγγα ἐρριμμένην ᾗ συνήθως ἐτέρπετο ἡ Χλόη, 3. μέγα βοῶν καὶ ἐλεεινὸν κωκύων, ποτὲ μὲν πρὸς τὴν φηγὸν ἔτρεχεν ἔνθα ἐκαθέζοντο, ποτὲ δὲ ἐπὶ τὴν θάλασσαν ὡς ὀψόμενος αὐτήν, ποτὲ δὲ ἐπὶ τὰς Νύμφας, ἐφ' ἃς διωκομένη[57] κατέφυγεν. ἐνταῦθα καὶ ἔρριψεν ἑαυτὸν χαμαὶ καὶ ταῖς Νύμφαις ὡς προδούσαις κατεμέμφετο·

22 "Ἀφ' ὑμῶν ἡρπάσθη Χλόη καὶ τοῦτο ὑμεῖς ἰδεῖν ὑπεμείνατε, ἡ τοὺς στεφάνους ὑμῖν πλέκουσα, ἡ σπέν-

grain and wine (the vintage having just ended), and not a
few of the people who were workers there. 2. He also invaded the farms of Daphnis and Chloe, where he made a
blitz landing and plundered whatever he found. Daphnis
was not grazing his goats but had gone up to the woods and
was chopping green leaves so that he would have food for
his kids that winter. So he saw the raid from up there and
hid in the hollow trunk of a dry beech tree. 3. But Chloe
was with her flocks, and when they started to chase her
fled for sanctuary to the Nymphs, where she pleaded with
them in the name of the goddesses to spare her flocks and
herself. But it was no use: pouring scorn on the statues, the
Methymnaeans drove off her flocks and led her away too,
whipping her with willow shoots like a goat or a sheep.

Now that they had filled their ships with all kinds of   21
booty they decided to sail no farther and set their course
for home, worried about the weather and their enemies.
So they sailed away toiling at their oars, for there was no
wind, 2. while Daphnis, once the coast was clear, went to
the plain where they had been grazing. He saw no goats, he
found no sheep, he discovered no Chloe, only great desola-
tion and the syrinx, Chloe's habitual delight, lying dis-
carded. 3. He gave a loud shout and wailed piteously, now
running to the oak tree where they used to sit, now to the
sea hoping to see her there, now to the Nymphs, where she
had fled when chased. And there he threw himself onto the
ground and berated the Nymphs for their betrayal:

"Chloe was snatched from you, and you were content to   22
look on? Chloe, who weaves you garlands, who makes liba-

---

56 Scaliger: ξύλῳ V F
57 Wakefield: ἑλκομένη V F

δουσα τοῦ πρώτου γάλακτος, ἧς καὶ ἡ σῦριγξ ἥδε ἀνάθημα; 2. αἶγα μὲν οὐδὲ μίαν μοι λύκος ἥρπασε, πολέμιοι δὲ ⟨καὶ⟩ τὴν ἀγέλην καὶ τὴν συννέμουσαν, καὶ τὰς μὲν αἶγας ἀποδεροῦσι καὶ τὰ πρόβατα κατα- θύ⟨σ⟩ουσι, Χλόη δὲ λοιπὸν πόλιν οἰκήσει. 3. ποίοις ποσὶν ἄπειμι παρὰ τὸν πατέρα καὶ τὴν μητέρα ἄνευ τῶν αἰγῶν, ἄνευ Χλόης, λιπεργάτης ἐσόμενος; ἔχω γὰρ νέμειν ἔτι οὐδέν. 4. ἐνταῦθα περιμενῶ κείμενος ἢ θάνατον ἢ πόλεμον δεύτερον. ἆρα καὶ σύ, Χλόη, τοιαῦτα πάσχεις; ἆρα μέμνησαι τοῦ πεδίου τοῦδε καὶ τῶν Νυμφῶν τῶνδε κἀμοῦ; ἢ παραμυθοῦνταί σε τὰ πρόβατα καὶ αἱ αἶγες αἰχμάλωτοι μετὰ σοῦ γενό- μεναι;"

23   Τοιαῦτα λέγοντα αὐτὸν ἐκ τῶν δακρύων καὶ τῆς λύπης ὕπνος βαθὺς καταλαμβάνει, καὶ αὐτῷ αἱ τρεῖς ἐφίστανται Νύμφαι, μεγάλαι γυναῖκες καὶ καλαί, ἡμί- γυμνοι καὶ ἀνυπόδετοι, τὰς κόμας λελυμέναι καὶ τοῖς ἀγάλμασιν ὅμοιαι. 2. καὶ τὸ μὲν πρῶτον ἐῴκεσαν ἐλεούσαι⟨ς⟩ τὸν Δάφνιν· ἔπειτα ἡ πρεσβυτάτη λέγει ἐπιρρωννύουσα· "μηδὲν ἡμᾶς μέμφου, Δάφνι. Χλόης γὰρ ἡμῖν μᾶλλον ἢ σοὶ μέλει. ἡμεῖς τοι καὶ παιδίον οὖσαν αὐτὴν ἠλεήσαμεν καὶ ἐν τῷδε τῷ ἄντρῳ κειμέ- νην αὐτὴν ἀνεθρέψαμεν. 3. [ἐκείνη πεδίοις κοινὸν οὐδὲν καὶ τοῖς προβατίοις τοῦ Λάμωνος.][58] καὶ νῦν δὲ ἡμῖν πεφρόντισται τὸ κατ' ἐκείνην ὡς μήτε εἰς τὴν Μήθυμναν κομισθεῖσα δουλεύοι μήτε μέρος γένοιτο λείας πολεμικῆς. 4. καὶ τὸν Πᾶνα ἐκεῖνον τὸν ὑπὸ τῇ πίτυϊ ἱδρυμένον, ὃν ὑμεῖς οὐδέποτε οὐδὲ ἄνθεσιν ἐτι- μήσατε, τούτου ἐδεήθημεν ἐπίκουρον γενέσθαι Χλόης· συνήθης γὰρ στρατοπέδοις μᾶλλον ἡμῶν καὶ πολλοὺς ἤδη πολέμους ἐπολέμησε τὴν ἀγροικίαν καταλιπών,

tions of the first milk, whose dedication this syrinx was? 2. No wolf ever snatched a single goat of mine, but now enemies have snatched the flock too as well as the girl who tended them with me. They will skin the goats and sacrifice the sheep, and from now on Chloe will live in a town. 3. How can I bring myself home to my father and mother without my goats, without Chloe, to be unemployed? Because I have nothing left to graze. 4. I will lie here and wait either for death or a second war. Chloe, are you feeling the same torment? Do you think of this plain and these Nymphs, and of me? Or do the sheep and the goats, your fellow captives, comfort you?"

While he was speaking this way, a deep sleep spirited 23 him away from his tears and pain, and the three Nymphs appeared to him, tall and beautiful ladies, semi-clothed and barefoot, with their hair unbound and looking like their statues. 2. First of all they looked as if they felt sorry for Daphnis, and then the eldest encouraged him by saying, "Find no fault with us, Daphnis: we care about Chloe more than you do. We were the ones who took pity on her when she was a baby and who nursed her as she lay in this cave. 3. [She has nothing in common with plains and with Lamo's little sheep.] And today too she is on our minds, that she not be taken to Methymna to be a slave and not become a piece of war booty. 4. Pan there, his image set up under the pine, whom you two have never honored with so much as a bunch of flowers, we have asked him to be Chloe's protector. He is more at home in army camps than we are and many a time has he left the countryside to fight a war. When he comes at the Methymnaeans he will not be

---

58 Del. Reeve

καὶ ἔπεισι τοῖς Μηθυμναίοις οὐκ ἀγαθὸς πολέμιος. 5. κάμνε δὲ μηδὲν ἀλλ᾽ ἀναστὰς ὄφθητι Λάμωνι καὶ Μυρτάλῃ, οἳ καὶ αὐτοὶ κεῖνται χαμαί, νομίζοντες καὶ σὲ μέρος γεγονέναι τῆς ἁρπαγῆς. Χλόη γάρ σοι τῆς ἐπιούσης ἀφίξεται μετὰ τῶν αἰγῶν, μετὰ τῶν προβάτων, καὶ νεμήσετε κοινῇ καὶ συρίσετε κοινῇ· τὰ δὲ ἄλλα μελήσει περὶ ὑμῶν Ἔρωτι."

24   Τοιαῦτα ἰδὼν καὶ ἀκούσας Δάφνις ἀναπηδήσας τῶν ὕπνων καὶ κοινῇ ὑφ᾽ ἡδονῆς καὶ λύπης δακρύων τὰ ἀγάλματα τῶν Νυμφῶν προσεκύνει καὶ ἐπηγγέλλετο σωθείσης Χλόης θύσειν τῶν αἰγῶν τὴν ἀρίστην. 2. δραμὼν δὲ καὶ ἐπὶ τὴν πίτυν ἔνθα τὸ τοῦ Πανὸς ἄγαλμα ἵδρυτο, τραγοσκελές, κερασφόρον, τῇ μὲν σύριγγα, τῇ δὲ τράγον πηδῶντα κατέχον, κἀκεῖνον προσεκύνει καὶ ηὔχετο ὑπὲρ τῆς Χλόης καὶ τράγον θύσειν ἐπηγγέλλετο, 3. καὶ μόλις ποτὲ περὶ ἡλίου καταφορὰς παυσάμενος δακρύων καὶ εὐχῶν ἀράμενος τὰς φυλλάδας ἃς ἔκοψεν ἐπανῆλθεν εἰς τὴν ἔπαυλιν καὶ τοὺς ἀμφὶ τὸν Λάμωνα πένθους ἀπαλλάξας, εὐφροσύνης ἐμπλήσας, 4. τροφῆς τε ἐγεύσατο καὶ ἐς ὕπνον ὥρμησεν οὐδὲ τοῦτον ἄδακρυν, ἀλλ᾽ εὐχόμενος μὲν αὖθις τὰς Νύμφας ὄναρ ἰδεῖν, εὐχόμενος δὲ τὴν ἡμέραν γενέσθαι ταχέως, ἐν ᾗ τὴν Χλόην ἐπηγγείλαντο αὐτῷ. νυκτῶν ἐκείνη πασῶν ἔδοξε μακροτάτη γεγονέναι· ἐπράχθη δὲ ἐπ᾽ αὐτῆς τάδε.

25   Ὁ στρατηγὸς ὁ τῶν Μηθυμναίων ὅσον δέκα σταδίους ἀπελάσας ἠθέλησε τῇ καταδρομῇ τοὺς στρατιώτας κεκμηκότας ἀναλαβεῖν. 2. ἄκρας οὖν ἐπεμβαινούσης τῷ πελάγει λαβόμενος ἐπεκτεινομένης μηνοειδῶς, ἧς ἐντὸς ἡ θάλασσα γαληνότερον τῶν λιμένων ὅρμον εἰργάζετο, ἐνταῦθα τὰς ναῦς ἐπ᾽ ἀγκυρῶν μετεώρους διορμίσας ὡς μηδεμίαν ἐκ τῆς γῆς τῶν

a good enemy to have. 5. Do not be downcast, but get up and show yourself to Lamo and Myrtale, who are also lying on the ground, thinking that you are also part of the plunder. Tomorrow Chloe will return to you with the goats, with the sheep, and you will graze them together and play the syrinx together. As for the rest, Love will take care of you."

When Daphnis saw and heard this, he bolted up from 24 his slumbers and, weeping all at once with pleasure and pain, knelt before the Nymphs and promised to sacrifice the finest of his she-goats if Chloe were rescued. 2. And he ran to the pine tree where Pan's statue was set up, goat-legged and horned, with a syrinx in one hand and a frisking he-goat in the other, and knelt before him too, prayed for Chloe, and promised to sacrifice a he-goat. 3. Only around sunset did he finally stop weeping and praying, and then he picked up the leaves that he had cut and went back to the farmhouse, relieving Lamo and his family of grief and filling them with joy. 4. He had something to eat and went straight to sleep, though not even that sleep was without tears, while he prayed to see the Nymphs again in a dream and prayed for the quick arrival of the day when they had promised him Chloe. Of all nights ever, that one seemed the longest, and during that night here is what happened.

After sailing for about ten stades,[28] the Methymnaean 25 commander decided to rest his troops, who were tired out after their raid. 2. So he made for a long crescent-shaped cape jutting into the deep, in which the sea formed a haven stiller than any harbor, and there brought his ships to anchor off shore, so that none would be damaged from land

28 About 1.8 km.

ἀγροίκων τινὰ λυπῆσαι, ἀνῆκε τοὺς Μηθυμναίους εἰς
τέρψιν εἰρηνικήν. 3. οἱ δὲ ἔχοντες πάντων ἀφθονίαν ἐκ
τῆς ἁρπαγῆς ἔπινον, ἔπαιζον, ἐπινίκιον ἑορτὴν ἐμι-
μοῦντο. ἄρτι δὲ παυομένης ἡμέρας καὶ τῆς τέρψεως ἐς
νύκτα ληγούσης, αἰφνίδιον μὲν ἡ γῆ πᾶσα ἐδόκει
λάμπεσθαι πυρί, κτύπος δὲ ἠκούετο ῥόθιος κωπῶν ὡς
ἐπιπλέοντος μεγάλου στόλου. 4. ἐβόα τις ὁπλίζεσθαι,
τὸν στρατηγὸν ἄλλος ἐκάλει, καὶ τετρῶσθαί τις ἐδόκει
καὶ σχῆμά τις ἔκειτο νεκροῦ μιμούμενος. εἴκασεν ἄν
τις ὁρᾶν νυκτομαχίαν οὐ παρόντων πολεμίων.

26   Τῆς δὲ νυκτὸς αὐτοῖς τοιαύτης γενομένης ἐπῆλθεν
ἡ ἡμέρα πολὺ τῆς νυκτὸς φοβερωτέρα. οἱ τράγοι μὲν
οἱ τοῦ Δάφνιδος καὶ αἱ αἶγες κιττὸν ἐν τοῖς κέρασι
κορυμβοφόρον εἶχον, οἱ δὲ κριοὶ καὶ αἱ ὄιες τῆς Χλόης
λύκων ὠρυγμὸν ὠρύοντο. 2. ὤφθη δὲ καὶ αὐτὴ πίτυος
ἐστεφανωμένη. ἐγίνετο καὶ περὶ τὴν θάλασσαν αὐτὴν
πολλὰ παράδοξα· αἵ τε γὰρ ἄγκυραι κατὰ βυθοῦ
πειρωμένων ἀναφέρειν ἔμενον, αἵ τε κῶπαι καθιέντων
εἰς εἰρεσίαν ἐθραύοντο, καὶ δελφῖνες πηδῶντες ἐξ ἁλὸς
ταῖς οὐραῖς παίοντες τὰς ναῦς ἔλυον τὰ γομφώματα.
3. ἠκούετό τις καὶ ὑπὲρ τῆς ὀρθίου πέτρας τῆς ὑπὸ τὴν
ἄκραν σύριγγος ἦχος, ἀλλὰ οὐκ ἔτερπεν ὡς σῦριγξ,
ἐφόβει δὲ τοὺς ἀκούοντας ὡς σάλπιγξ. 4. ἐταράττοντο
οὖν καὶ ἐπὶ τὰ ὅπλα ἔθεον καὶ πολεμίους ἐκάλουν τοὺς
οὐ βλεπομένους, ὥστε πάλιν ηὔχοντο νύκτα ἐπελθεῖν
ὡς τευξόμενοι σπονδῶν ἐν αὐτῇ. 5. συνετὰ μὲν οὖν
πᾶσιν ἦν τὰ γινόμενα τοῖς φρονοῦσιν ὀρθῶς, ὅτι ἐκ
Πανὸς ἦν τὰ φαντάσματα καὶ ἀκούσματα μηνίοντός τι
τοῖς ναύταις, οὐκ εἶχον δὲ τὴν αἰτίαν συμβαλεῖν
(οὐδὲν γὰρ ἱερὸν σεσύλητο Πανός), ἔστε ἀμφὶ μέσην

by the farmers, and then gave the Methymnaeans leave for peaceful recreation. 3. Having plenty of everything from their plunder, they started drinking, carousing, and aping a victory celebration. Just as day was ending and the recreation was tapering off for the night, the whole landscape seemed to burst into flame, and the sound of oars splashing could be heard, as of a huge fleet on the attack. 4. Someone gave the call to arms, someone else summoned the commander; here someone looked to be wounded, there someone lay in an attitude suggesting a corpse. An observer would have imagined a night battle, although no enemy was at hand.

Such was their night, but the day that followed was 26 much more terrifying than the night. Daphnis' he-goats and she-goats sported ivy with clusters on their horns, and Chloe's rams and ewes were howling like wolves. 2. She herself was seen wearing a crown of pine. About the sea itself many extraordinary things were happening too: their anchors stuck to the seabed when they tried to raise them, their oars broke off when they lowered them to row, and dolphins leaping from the water struck the ships with their tails and loosened the timber joints. 3. And over the sheer cliff beneath the cape came the sound of a syrinx, but it did not give pleasure like a syrinx but brought fear like a bugle. 4. Of course they were rattled, ran for their weapons, and called the enemy those they could not see, so that they prayed for the return of night in hope of making a truce then. 5. But the meaning of what had happened was clear to those who had their wits about them: the strange sights and sounds came from Pan because for some reason he was angry with the sailors. But they could not guess the reason, for no shrine of Pan had been plundered, un-

ἡμέραν εἰς ὕπνον οὐκ ἀθεεὶ τοῦ στρατηγοῦ κατα-
πεσόντος αὐτὸς ὁ Πὰν ὤφθη τοιάδε λέγων·

27   "ὮὮ πάντων ἀνοσιώτατοι καὶ ἀσεβέστατοι, τί ταῦτα
μαινομέναις φρεσὶν ἐτολμήσατε; πολέμου μὲν τὴν
ἀγροικίαν ἐνεπλήσατε τὴν ἐμοὶ φίλην, ἀγέλας δὲ
βοῶν καὶ αἰγῶν καὶ ποιμνίων ἀπηλάσατε τὰς ἐμοὶ
μελομένας, 2. ἀπεσπάσατε δὲ βωμῶν παρθένον ἐξ ἧς
Ἔρως μῦθον ποιῆσαι θέλει, καὶ οὔτε τὰς Νύμφας
ᾐδέσθητε βλεπούσας οὔτε τὸν Πᾶνα ἐμέ. οὔτ᾽ οὖν
Μήθυμναν ὄψεσθε μετὰ τοιούτων λαφύρων πλέοντες
οὔτε τήνδε φεύξεσθε τὴν σύριγγα τὴν ὑμᾶς ταράξα-
σαν, 3. ἀλλὰ ὑμᾶς βορὰν ἰχθύων θήσω καταδύσας εἰ
μὴ τὴν ταχίστην καὶ Χλόην ταῖς Νύμφαις ἀποδώσεις
καὶ τὰς ἀγέλας Χλόῃ,[59] καὶ τὰς αἶγας καὶ τὰ πρόβατα.
ἀνίστω δὴ καὶ ἐκβίβαζε τὴν κόρην μεθ᾽ ὧν εἶπον,
ἡγήσομαι δὲ ἐγὼ καὶ σοὶ τοῦ πλοῦ κἀκείνῃ τῆς ὁδοῦ."

28   Πάνυ οὖν τεθορυβημένος ὁ Βρύαξις,[60] οὕτω γὰρ
ἐκαλεῖτο ὁ στρατηγός, ἀναπηδᾷ καὶ τῶν νεῶν καλέσας
τοὺς ἡγεμόνας ἐκέλευσε τὴν ταχίστην ἐν τοῖς αἰχμα-
λώτοις ἀναζητεῖσθαι Χλόην. 2. οἱ δὲ ταχέως καὶ
ἀνεῦρον καὶ εἰς ὀφθαλμοὺς ἐκόμισαν· ἐκαθέζετο γὰρ
τῆς πίτυος ἐστεφανωμένη. σύμβολον δὴ καὶ τοῦτο τῆς
ἐν τοῖς ὀνείροις ὄψεως ποιούμενος ἐπ᾽ αὐτῆς τῆς ναυ-
αρχίδος εἰς τὴν γῆν αὐτὴν κομίζει. 3. κἀκείνη ἄρτι
ἀποβεβήκει καὶ σύριγγος ἦχος ἀκούεται πάλιν ἐκ τῆς
πέτρας, οὐκέτι πολεμικὸς καὶ φοβερὸς ἀλλὰ ποιμε-
νικὸς καὶ οἷος εἰς νομὴν ἡγεῖται ποιμνίων, καὶ τά τε
πρόβατα κατὰ τῆς ἀποβάθρας ἐξέτρεχεν ἐξολισθαί-
νοντα[61] τοῖς κέρασι τῶν χηλῶν καὶ αἱ αἶγες πολὺ
θρασύτερον οἷα καὶ κρημνοβατεῖν εἰθισμέναι.

---

59 Jungermann: Χλόης V F   60 Βρύαξ F
61 οὐκ ἐξ. V

til around midday the commander fell into an inspired trance, where Pan himself appeared and spoke:

"You most impious and ungodly of mankind, by what 27 madness of heart have you dared such acts? You filled the countryside I love with war; you rustled herds of cattle, goats, and sheep under my care; 2. you dragged from a shrine a girl of whom Love intends to make a story; and you showed no respect for the Nymphs who looked on nor for me, Pan. If you set sail with such spoils you shall never see Methymna again, nor shall you escape this syrinx that rattled you. 3. No, I shall sink you and make you food for fish unless you return Chloe to the Nymphs at once, and the herds to Chloe, both the goats and the sheep. Get up now and put the girl ashore with the cargo I specified, and I will be your guide on your voyage and hers on her journey."

Very shaken, Bryaxis[29] (for that was the commander's 28 name) leapt up, summoned the ships' captains, and ordered them to look for Chloe among the captives on the double. 2. They were quick to find her and bring her before him, for she sat wearing a crown of pine. Regarding this as confirmation of his dream vision, he brought her ashore in his own flagship. 3. Just as she disembarked, the sound of a syrinx was again heard from the cliff, this time not warlike and terrifying but pastoral and like the sound that leads flocks to pasture. The sheep ran down the gangplank skittering on their horny hooves, while the goats went much more confidently, being used to walking on precipices.

---

[29] The name sounds non-Greek and suggests exuberant or wanton behavior (βρυάζειν).

29 Καὶ ταῦτα μὲν περιίσταται κύκλῳ τὴν Χλόην ὥσπερ χορὸς σκιρτῶντα καὶ βληχώμενα καὶ ὅμοια χαίρουσιν, αἱ δὲ τῶν ἄλλων αἰπόλων αἶγες καὶ τὰ πρόβατα καὶ τὰ βουκόλια κατὰ χώραν ἔμενεν ἐν κοίλῃ νηὶ καθάπερ αὐτὰ τοῦ μέλους μὴ κηλοῦντος.[62] 2. θαύματι δὲ πάντων ἐχομένων καὶ τὸν Πᾶνα εὐφη- μούντων ὤφθη τούτων ἐν τοῖς στοιχείοις ἀμφοτέροις θαυμασιώτερα· 3. τῶν μὲν Μηθυμναίων πρὶν ἀνα- σπάσαι τὰς ἀγκύρας ἔπλεον αἱ νῆες καὶ τῆς ναυ- αρχίδος ἡγεῖτο δελφὶς πηδῶν ἐξ ἁλός· τῶν δὲ αἰγῶν καὶ τῶν προβάτων ἡγεῖτο σύριγγος ἦχος ἥδιστος καὶ τὸν συρίττοντα ἔβλεπεν οὐδείς, ὥστε τὰ ποίμνια καὶ αἱ αἶγες προῄεσαν ἅμα καὶ ἐνέμοντο τερπόμεναι τῷ μέλει.

30 Δευτέρας που νομῆς καιρὸς ἦν καὶ ὁ Δάφνις ἀπὸ σκοπῆς τινος μετεώρου θεασάμενος τὰς ἀγέλας καὶ τὴν Χλόην μέγα βοήσας "ὦ Νύμφαι καὶ Πάν" κατ- έδραμεν εἰς τὸ πεδίον καὶ περιπλακεὶς τῇ Χλόῃ λειπο- θυμήσας κατέπεσε. 2. μόλις δὲ ἔμβιος ὑπὸ τῆς Χλόης φιλούσης καὶ ταῖς περιβολαῖς θαλπούσης γενόμενος ἐπὶ τὴν συνήθη φηγὸν ἔρχεται καὶ ὑπὸ τῷ στελέχει καθίσας ἐπυνθάνετο πῶς ἀπέδρα τοσούτους πολε- μίους. 3. ἡ δὲ αὐτῷ κατέλεξε πάντα· τὸν τῶν αἰγῶν κιττόν, τὸν τῶν προβάτων ὠρυγμόν, τὴν ἐπανθήσα- σαν τῇ κεφαλῇ πίτυν, τὸ ἐν τῇ γῇ πῦρ, τὸν ἐν τῇ θαλάσσῃ κτύπον, τὰ συρίσματα ἀμφότερα, τὸ πολε- μικὸν καὶ τὸ εἰρηνικόν, τὴν νύκτα τὴν φοβεράν, ὅπως αὐτῇ ὁδὸν ἀγνοούσῃ καθηγήσατο τῆς ὁδοῦ μουσική. 4. γνωρίσας οὖν ὁ Δάφνις τὰ τῶν Νυμφῶν ὀνείρατα καὶ τὰ τοῦ Πανὸς ἔργα διηγεῖται καὶ αὐτὸς ὅσα εἶδεν, ὅσα ἤκουσεν, ὅτι μέλλων ἀποθνήσκειν διὰ τὰς Νύμ- φας ἔζησε. 5. καὶ τὴν μὲν ἀποπέμπει κομίσουσαν τοὺς

These animals formed a circle around Chloe like a cho-   29
rus, frisking and bleating and looking joyful, while the
goats belonging to the other herdsmen, along with their
sheep and cattle, stayed where they were in the ship's
hold, inasmuch as the tune worked no magic on them. 2.
With everyone spellbound and praising Pan's name came
even more spellbinding sights in both elements. 3. The
Methymnaeans' ships started to sail before they had raised
the anchors, and the flagship was guided by a dolphin leaping from the water, while a very sweet sound of a syrinx
guided the goats and the sheep, though no one could see
the player. And so the sheep and the goats moved forward
in unison and grazed happily to the tune.

It was around the time of the second pasturing when   30
Daphnis, from a high lookout, spotted the herds and
Chloe. With a loud shout of "Nymphs and Pan!" he ran
down to the plain, hugged Chloe, and collapsed in a dead
faint. 2. Eventually revived by Chloe's kisses and warming
embraces, he went to their usual oak tree, sat beneath its
trunk, and asked how she had managed to escape such a
large enemy force. 3. She told him the whole story: the
goats' ivy, the sheep's howling, the pine sprouting on her
head, the fire on the earth and the noise at sea, the two
kinds of piping, martial and peaceful, the night of ter-
ror, how when she did not know a way home music had
shown her the way. 4. Recognizing the dream visions of the
Nymphs and the work of Pan, Daphnis told his own story
of what he had seen, what he had heard, that when on the
brink of death the Nymphs had given him life. 5. He sent
her off to fetch Dryas and Lamo and their families and

---

⁶² καλοῦντος F

ἀμφὶ τὸν Δρύαντα καὶ Λάμωνα καὶ ὅσα πρέπει θυσίᾳ, αὐτὸς δὲ ἐν τούτῳ τῶν αἰγῶν τὴν ἀρίστην συλλαβὼν καὶ κιττῷ στεφανώσας ὥσπερ ὤφθησαν τοῖς πολεμίοις καὶ γάλα τῶν κεράτων κατασπείσας ἔθυσέ τε ταῖς Νύμφαις καὶ κρεμάσας ἀπέδειρε καὶ τὸ δέρμα ἀνέθηκεν.

31   Ἤδη δὲ παρόντων τῶν ἀμφὶ τὴν Χλόην πῦρ ἀνακαύσας καὶ τὰ μὲν ἑψήσας τῶν κρεῶν, τὰ δὲ ὀπτήσας, ἀπήρξατό τε ταῖς Νύμφαις καὶ κρατῆρα ἐπέσπεισε μεστὸν γλεύκους καὶ ἐκ φυλλάδος στιβάδας ὑποστορέσας ἐντεῦθεν ἐν τροφῇ ‹τε› ἦν καὶ πότῳ καὶ παιδιᾷ καὶ ἅμα τὰς ἀγέλας ἐπεσκόπει μὴ λύκος ἐμπεσὼν ἔργα ποιήσῃ πολεμίων. 2. ᾖσάν τινας καὶ ᾠδὰς εἰς τὰς Νύμφας, παλαιῶν ποιμένων ποιήματα. νυκτὸς δὲ ἐπελθούσης αὐτοῦ κοιμηθέντες ἐν τῷ ἀγρῷ, τῆς ἐπιούσης τοῦ Πανὸς ἐμνημόνευον καὶ τῶν τράγων τὸν ἀγελάρχην στεφανώσαντες πίτυος προσήγαγον τῇ πίτυϊ καὶ ἐπισπείσαντες οἴνου καὶ εὐφημοῦντες τὸν θεὸν ἔθυσαν, ἐκρέμασαν, ἀπέδειραν, 3. καὶ τὰ μὲν κρέα ὀπτήσαντες καὶ ἑψήσαντες πλησίον ἔθηκαν ἐν τῷ λειμῶνι ἐν τοῖς φύλλοις, τὸ δὲ δέρμα κέρασιν αὐτοῖς ἐνέπηξαν τῇ πίτυϊ πρὸς τῷ ἀγάλματι, ποιμενικὸν ἀνάθημα ποιμενικῷ θεῷ. ἀπήρξαντο καὶ τῶν κρεῶν, ἀπέσπεισαν καὶ κρατῆρος μείζονος· ᾖσεν ἡ Χλόη, Δάφνις ἐσύρισεν.

32   Ἐπὶ τούτοις κατακλιθέντες ἤσθιον, καὶ αὐτοῖς ἐφίσταται Φιλητᾶς ὁ βουκόλος κατὰ τύχην στεφανίσκους τινὰς τῷ Πανὶ κομίζων καὶ βότρυς ἔτι ἐν φύλλοις καὶ κλήμασι, καὶ αὐτῷ τῶν παίδων ὁ νεώτατος εἵπετο Τίτυρος, πυρρὸν παιδίον καὶ γλαυκόν,

---

30 A programmatic pastoral name (cf. the opening of Virgil's

everything needed for a sacrifice, and in the meantime he rounded up the finest of his she-goats, garlanded her with ivy, just as they had appeared to the enemy, poured a libation of milk over her horns, and sacrificed her to the Nymphs. When he had hung and skinned her, he dedicated the skin.

Once Chloe and company were on hand, he lit a fire, 31 boiled some of the meat and roasted the rest, offered the firstlings to the Nymphs and as a libation poured out a bowl of new wine. He spread out leaves for couches and then was occupied with food, drink, and fun. He kept an eye on the herds in case a wolf should attack them and do an enemy's work. 2. They also sang some hymns for the Nymphs, compositions by shepherds of old. At nightfall they slept there in the field, and next day they turned their thoughts to Pan. Garlanding the chief goat of the flock with pine, they took him to the pine tree, poured a libation of wine over him, and praising the god's name they sacrificed him, then hung him up and skinned him. 3. After roasting and boiling the meat, they set it out nearby upon the leaves in the meadow, but they pegged the skin, horns and all, to the pine tree facing the statue, a pastoral offering to a pastoral god. Again they offered the firstlings and poured a libation from a larger bowl. Chloe did the singing while Daphnis played the syrinx.

At this point they lay down and were eating when 32 Philetas the cowherd came by chance onto the scene as he was bringing some small garlands for Pan and clusters of grapes still on their leafy stems. The youngest of his children, Tityrus,[30] was with him, a child ruddy and blue-eyed,

first *Eclogue*) used by Theocritus (and no doubt by Philitas); it is a Doric form of the word *satyros*.

λευκὸν δὲ καὶ ἀγέρωχον· καὶ ἤλλετο κοῦφα βαδίζων
ὥσπερ ἔριφος. 2. ἀναπηδήσαντες οὖν συνεστεφάνουν
τὸν Πᾶνα καὶ τὰ κλήματα τῆς κόμης τῆς πίτυος ἐξῆρ-
των καὶ κατακλίναντες πλησίον αὐτῶν συμπότην ἐποι-
οῦντο· 3. καὶ οἷα δὴ γέροντες ὑποβεβρεγμένοι πρὸς
ἀλλήλους πολλὰ ἔλεγον· ὡς ἔνεμον ἡνίκα ἦσαν νέοι,
ὡς πολλὰς λῃστῶν καταδρομὰς διέφυγον· ἐσεμνύνετό
τις ὡς λύκον ἀποκτείνας, ἄλλος ὡς μόνου τοῦ Πανὸς
δεύτερα συρίσας· τοῦτο τοῦ Φιλητᾶ τὸ σεμνολόγημα
ἦν.

33   Ὁ οὖν Δάφνις καὶ ἡ Χλόη πάσας δεήσεις προσ-
έφερον μεταδοῦναι καὶ αὐτοῖς τῆς τέχνης συρίσαι τε
ἐν ἑορτῇ θεοῦ σύριγγι χαίροντος. ἐπαγγέλλεται Φιλητᾶς καίτοι τὸ γῆρας ὡς ἄπνουν μεμψάμενος καὶ ἔλαβε
σύριγγα τὴν τοῦ Δάφνιδος· 2. ἡ δὲ ἦν μικρὰ πρὸς
μεγάλην τέχνην οἷα ἐν στόματι παιδὸς ἐμπνεομένη.
πέμπει οὖν Τίτυρον ἐπὶ τὴν ἑαυτοῦ σύριγγα, τῆς
ἐπαύλεως ἀπεχούσης σταδίους δέκα. 3. ὁ μὲν οὖν
ῥίψας τὸ ἐγκόμβωμα γυμνὸς ὥρμησε τρέχειν ὥσπερ
νεβρός, ὁ δὲ Λάμων αὐτοῖς ἐπηγγείλατο τὸν περὶ τῆς
σύριγγος ἀφηγήσασθαι μῦθον, ὃν αὐτῷ Σικελὸς αἰπόλος ᾖσεν ἐπὶ μισθῷ τράγῳ καὶ σύριγγι·

34   ῾Η σῦριγξ αὕτη τὸ πρῶτον[63] οὐκ ἦν ὄργανον ἀλλὰ
παρθένος καλὴ καὶ τὴν φωνὴν μουσική. αἶγας ἔνεμεν,
Νύμφαις συνέπαιζεν, ᾖδεν οἷον νῦν. Πὰν ταύτης νεμούσης, παιζούσης, ᾀδούσης προσελθὼν ἔπειθεν ἐς ὅ
τι ἔχρῃζε καὶ ἐπηγγέλλετο τὰς αἶγας πάσας θήσειν
διδυματόκους. 2. ἡ δὲ ἐγέλα τὸν ἔρωτα αὐτοῦ οὐδὲ
ἐραστὴν ἔφη δέξεσθαι[64] μήτε τράγον μήτε ἄνθρωπον

---

[63] West: ὄργανον V F
[64] Villoison: δέξασθαι V F

fair-skinned and lively; he capered lightly as he walked, like a kid. 2. So they jumped up and helped him to garland Pan, then hung the vine stems from the pine boughs and made Philetas recline next to them and join the party. 3. As old men do when tipsy, they started telling one another lots of stories: how they used to graze flocks when they were young, how they had dodged many a pirate raid; one boasted that he had killed a wolf, another that he was second only to Pan at playing the syrinx—this one was Philetas' boast.

So Daphnis and Chloe started pestering him with requests to share his art with them too, and to play the syrinx at a party for a god who loved the syrinx. Philetas consented, though he complained that old age makes for short breath, and took up Daphnis' syrinx. 2. But it was too small for his great artistry, being fit to be played on a boy's lips. So he sent Tityrus for his own syrinx, his farm being ten stades distant.[31] 3. He threw off his apron and without his clothes dashed away like a fawn. Meanwhile Lamo agreed to tell them the story of the syrinx, which a Sicilian goatherd had sung for him for the price of a goat and a syrinx.[32]

"This syrinx was originally not an instrument but a fair maiden with a musical voice. She grazed goats, played with the Nymphs, and sang as she still does. As she was grazing, playing, and singing, Pan approached her and tried to talk her into what he wanted by promising to make all her she-goats have twins. 2. But she scoffed at his love and refused to accept a lover who was not a full-fledged goat or man.

33

34

---

[31] About 1.8 km.

[32] For the story cf. Ovid. *Met.* 1.689–712 (probably from an Alexandrian source, perhaps Philitas), Achilles Tatius 8.6.7–11.

ὁλόκληρον. ὁρμᾷ διώκειν ὁ Πὰν ἐς βίαν. ἡ Σῦριγξ
ἔφευγε καὶ τὸν Πᾶνα καὶ τὴν βίαν· φεύγουσα κάμ-
νουσα ἐς δόνακας κρύπτεται, εἰς ἕλος ἀφανίζεται. 3.
Πὰν τοὺς δόνακας ὀργῇ τεμὼν τὴν κόρην οὐχ εὑρὼν τὸ
πάθος μαθὼν τὸ ὄργανον νοεῖ [καὶ][65] τοὺς καλάμους
κηρῷ συνδήσας ἀνίσους, καθότι καὶ ὁ ἔρως ἄνισος
αὐτοῖς· καὶ ἡ τότε παρθένος καλὴ νῦν ἐστι σῦριγξ
μουσική.»

35   Ἄρτι πέπαυτο τοῦ μυθολογήματος ὁ Λάμων καὶ
ἐπῄνει Φιλητᾶς αὐτὸν ὡς εἰπόντα μῦθον ᾠδῆς γλυκύτερον, καὶ ὁ Τίτυρος ἐφίσταται τὴν σύριγγα τῷ
πατρὶ κομίζων, μέγα ὄργανον καὶ αὐλῶν[66] μεγάλων,
καὶ ἵνα κεκήρωτο χαλκῷ πεποίκιλτο. 2. εἴκασεν ἄν τις
εἶναι ταύτην ἐκείνην ἣν ὁ Πὰν πρώτην ἐπήξατο. δι-
εγερθεὶς οὖν ὁ Φιλητᾶς καὶ καθίσας εἰς καθέδραν
ὄρθιος πρῶτον μὲν ἀπεπειράθη τῶν καλάμων εἰ εὔ-
πνοοι· 3. ἔπειτα μαθὼν ὡς ἀκώλυτον διατρέχει τὸ
πνεῦμα ἐνέπνει τὸ ἐντεῦθεν πολὺ καὶ νεανικόν. αὐλῶν
τις ἂν ᾠήθη συναυλούντων ἀκούειν, τοσοῦτον ἤχει τὸ
σύριγμα. κατ᾽ ὀλίγον δὲ τῆς βίας ἀφαιρῶν εἰς τὸ
τερπνότερον μετέβαλλε τὸ μέλος 4. καὶ πᾶσαν τέχνην
ἐπιδεικνύμενος εὐνομίας μουσικῆς ἐσύριττεν οἷον βοῶν ἀγέλῃ πρέπον, οἷον αἰπολίῳ πρόσφορον, οἷον
ποίμναις φίλον. τερπνὸν ἦν τὸ ποιμνίων, μέγα τὸ
βοῶν, ὀξὺ τὸ αἰγῶν. ὅλως πάσας σύριγγας μία σῦριγξ ἐμιμήσατο.

36   Οἱ μὲν οὖν ἄλλοι σιωπῇ κατέκειντο τερπόμενοι,
Δρύας δὲ ἀναστὰς καὶ κελεύσας συρίζειν Διονυσιακὸν
μέλος ἐπιλήνιον αὐτοῖς ὄρχησιν ὠρχήσατο καὶ ἐῴκει
ποτὲ μὲν τρυγῶντι, ποτὲ δὲ φέροντι ἀρρίχους, εἶτα

[65] Del. Villoison: καὶ τοὺς καλάμους ⟨ἐμπνεῖ⟩ Reeve

Pan started to chase her with force in mind. Syrinx started running from Pan and his force. When she tired from running, she hid in some reeds and vanished into a marsh. 3. Pan angrily cut away the reeds, could not find the girl, realized what had happened to her, and thought of the instrument after he had bound reeds together with wax, of unequal lengths just as their love had been unequal. And what was once a fair maiden is now a musical syrinx."

Lamo had just finished his storytelling, and Philetas 35 was complimenting him on telling a story sweeter than any song, when Tityrus returned with his father's syrinx, a big instrument with big pipes and decorated with bronze where it had been joined with wax. 2. One would have imagined it was the very one that Pan had originally crafted. So Philetas rose and sat upright on a chair, and first of all tried the reeds for good air flow. 3. When he was satisfied that his breath could pass through unobstructed, he began to blow loudly and lustily. One would have thought it was multiple pipes playing in unison, so substantial was the sound of his playing. Reducing the force by degrees, he modulated the tune into a sweeter mode, 4. and displaying every technique of pastoral musicianship he piped the sort of tune that befit a herd of cattle, that suited a flock of goats, that was right for sheep. The sheep's tune was sweet, the cattle's loud, the goat's shrill. Altogether, a single syrinx represented all syrinxes.

While the others reclined in silent enjoyment, Dryas 36 rose to request that he play a Dionysiac tune and danced them a dance of the vintage. First he suggested someone picking grapes, then carrying baskets, then treading the

---

66 (καὶ) καλάμων Villoison

πατοῦντι τοὺς βότρυς, εἶτα πληροῦντι τοὺς πίθους,
εἶτα πίνοντι τοῦ γλεύκους. 2. ταῦτα πάντα οὕτως
εὐσχημόνως ὠρχήσατο Δρύας καὶ ἐναργῶς ὥστε ἐδόκουν βλέπειν καὶ τὰς ἀμπέλους καὶ τὴν ληνὸν καὶ τοὺς
πίθους καὶ ἀληθῶς Δρύαντα πίνοντα.

37   Τρίτος δὴ γέρων οὗτος εὐδοκιμήσας ἐπ' ὀρχήσει
φιλεῖ Χλόην καὶ Δάφνιν, οἱ δὲ μάλα ταχέως ἀναστάντες ὠρχήσαντο τὸν μῦθον τοῦ Λάμωνος. ὁ Δάφνις
Πᾶνα ἐμιμεῖτο, τὴν Σύριγγα Χλόη· ὁ μὲν ἱκέτευε
πείθων, ἡ δὲ ἀμελοῦσα ἐμειδία· 2. ὁ μὲν ἐδίωκε καὶ ἐπ'
ἄκρων τῶν ὀνύχων ἔτρεχε τὰς χηλὰς μιμούμενος, ἡ δὲ
ἐνέφαινε τὴν κάμνουσαν ἐν τῇ φυγῇ. ἔπειτα Χλόη μὲν
εἰς τὴν ὕλην ὡς εἰς ἕλος κρύπτεται, 3. Δάφνις δὲ
λαβὼν τὴν Φιλητᾶ σύριγγα τὴν μεγάλην ἐσύρισε
γοερὸν ὡς ἐρῶν, ἐρωτικὸν ὡς πείθων, ἀνακλητικὸν ὡς
ἐπιζητῶν· ὥστε ὁ Φιλητᾶς θαυμάσας φιλεῖ τε ἀναπηδήσας καὶ τὴν σύριγγα χαρίζεται φιλήσας καὶ
εὔχεται καὶ Δάφνιν καταλιπεῖν αὐτὴν ὁμοίῳ διαδόχῳ.

38   Ὁ δὲ τὴν ἰδίαν ἀναθεὶς τῷ Πανί, τὴν μικράν, καὶ
φιλήσας ὡς ἐκ φυγῆς ἀληθινῆς εὑρεθεῖσαν τὴν Χλόην
ἀπήλαυνε τὴν ἀγέλην συρίζων νυκτὸς ἤδη γενομένης·
ἀπήλαυνε ⟨δὲ⟩ καὶ ἡ Χλόη τὴν ποίμνην τῷ μέλει τῆς
σύριγγος συνάγουσα, 2. καὶ αἵ τε αἶγες πλησίον τῶν
προβάτων ᾖεσαν ὅ τε Δάφνις ἐβάδιζεν ἐγγὺς τῆς
Χλόης, ὥστε ἐνέπλησαν ἕως νυκτὸς ἀλλήλους καὶ
συνέθεντο θᾶττον τὰς ἀγέλας τῆς ἐπιούσης κατελά-
σαι, καὶ οὕτως ἐποίησαν. 3. ἄρτι γοῦν ἀρχομένης
ἡμέρας ἦλθον εἰς τὴν νομὴν καὶ τὰς Νύμφας προτέρας
εἶτα τὸν Πᾶνα προσαγορεύσαντες τὸ ἐντεῦθεν ὑπὸ τῇ
δρυῒ καθεσθέντες ἐσύριττον, εἶτα ἀλλήλους ἐφίλουν,
περιέβαλλον, κατεκλίνοντο, καὶ οὐδὲν δράσαντες πλέον ἀνίσταντο. ἐμέλησεν αὐτοῖς καὶ τροφῆς καὶ ἔπιον
οἶνον μίξαντες γάλα.

clusters, then filling the jars, and finally drinking the new wine. 2. Dryas danced all this with such grace and vividness that they seemed to see the grapes, the wine press, the jars, and Dryas actually drinking.

So this old man by dancing was the third to win applause, and kissed Chloe and Daphnis, who quickly rose and danced Lamo's story. Daphnis took the part of Pan, Chloe of Syrinx; he implored her seductively, she smiled indifferently. 2. He gave chase and ran on tiptoe to suggest hooves, while she acted the girl tiring in her flight. Then Chloe hid in the woods as though in a marsh, 3. while Daphnis took Philetas' big syrinx and played a plaintive tune as of one in love, an amorous tune as of one wooing, and a recall tune as of one in pursuit. Philetas, amazed, leapt up and kissed Daphnis, then made him a present of the syrinx, and prayed that Daphnis would bequeath it to a successor just as good. 37

He dedicated his own syrinx, the small one, to Pan, kissed Chloe as if she were found after a real flight, and then drove his herd home, playing his syrinx, since night had fallen. And Chloe drove her flock home too, keeping them together with the tune of his syrinx. 2. The goats went along beside the sheep and Daphnis walked beside Chloe, and so they took their fill of one another until nighttime and made a plan to drive their herds down earlier than usual the next day, and this they did. 3. Day was just breaking when they came to the pasture. They greeted first the Nymphs and then Pan, then sat beneath the oak tree and played their syrinxes, and then started kissing, embracing, and lying down together, going no farther before they got up again. Food was also on their minds, and they drank wine mixed with milk. 38

39   Καὶ τούτοις ἅπασι θερμότεροι γενόμενοι καὶ θρα-
σύτεροι πρὸς ἀλλήλους ἤριζον ἔριν ἐρωτικὴν καὶ κατ᾽
ὀλίγον εἰς ὅρκων πίστιν προῆλθον. ὁ μὲν δὴ Δάφνις
τὸν Πᾶνα ὤμοσεν ἐλθὼν ἐπὶ τὴν πίτυν μὴ ζήσεσθαι
μόνος ἄνευ Χλόης μηδὲ μιᾶς χρόνον ἡμέρας, 2. ἡ δὲ
Χλόη τὰς Νύμφας εἰσελθοῦσα εἰς τὸ ἄντρον τὸν αὐτὸν
Δάφνιδι στέρξειν καὶ θάνατον καὶ βίον. τοσοῦτον δὲ
ἄρα τῇ Χλόῃ τὸ ἀφελὲς προσῆν ὡς κόρῃ ὥστε ἐξιοῦσα
τοῦ ἄντρου καὶ δεύτερον ἠξίου λαβεῖν ὅρκον παρ᾽
αὐτοῦ, "ὦ Δάφνι" λέγουσα "θεὸς ὁ Πὰν ἐρωτικός ἐστι
καὶ ἄπιστος· 3. ἠράσθη μὲν Πίτυος, ἠράσθη δὲ Σύριγγος, παύεται δὲ οὐδέποτε Δρυάσιν ἐνοχλῶν καὶ Ἐπι-
μηλίσι Νύμφαις πράγματα παρέχων. οὗτος μὲν οὖν
ἀμεληθεὶς ἐν τοῖς ὅρκοις ἀμελήσει σε κολάσαι κἂν ἐπὶ
πλείονας ἔλθῃς γυναῖκας τῶν ἐν τῇ σύριγγι καλάμων·
4. σὺ δέ μοι τὸ αἰπόλιον τοῦτο ὄμοσον καὶ τὴν αἶγα
ἐκείνην ἥ σε ἀνέθρεψε μὴ καταλιπεῖν Χλόην ἔστ᾽ ἂν
πιστή σοι μένῃ. ἄδικον δὲ εἰς σὲ καὶ τὰς Νύμφας
γενομένην καὶ φεῦγε καὶ μίσει καὶ ἀπόκτεινον ὥσπερ
λύκον." 5. ἥδετο ὁ Δάφνις ἀπιστούμενος καὶ στὰς εἰς
μέσον τὸ αἰπόλιον καὶ τῇ μὲν τῶν χειρῶν αἰγός, τῇ δὲ
τράγου λαβόμενος ὤμνυε Χλόην φιλήσειν φιλοῦσαν,
κἂν ἕτερον δὲ προκρίνῃ Δάφνιδος ἀντ᾽ ἐκείνης αὐτὸν
ἀποκτενεῖν. 6. ἡ δὲ ἔχαιρε καὶ ἐπίστευεν ὡς κόρη καὶ
νέμουσα καὶ νομίζουσα τὰς αἶγας καὶ τὰ πρόβατα
ποιμένων καὶ αἰπόλων ἰδίους θεούς.

Made hotter and bolder by all this, they began to compete with one another in a contest of love, and gradually went so far as to swear oaths of fidelity. Daphnis went to the pine tree and swore by Pan that he would not live alone without Chloe, not even for a single day, 2. while Chloe went into the cave and swore by the Nymphs that all she wanted was to live and die with Daphnis. But such was Chloe's girlish simplicity that she came out of the cave and demanded from him a second oath. "Daphnis," she said, "Pan is an amorous god and untrustworthy. 3. He fell in love with Pitys, he fell in love with Syrinx, and he never stops pestering the Dryads[33] and bothering the Nymphs who watch over the flocks. So if you neglect the oaths you swear by him, he will neglect to punish you, even if you go after more women than there are reeds in your syrinx. 4. Swear to me by this herd of goats, and by that she-goat who nursed you, never to desert Chloe as long as she stays faithful to you. But if she proves wrongful to you and the Nymphs, shun her, loathe her, and kill her like a wolf." 5. Daphnis enjoyed being distrusted. Standing in the middle of his flock and grasping a she-goat with one hand and a he-goat with the other, he swore to love Chloe as long as she loved him, and if ever she preferred another to Daphnis, he would kill himself rather than her. 6. She was delighted and trusted him, being a shepherd girl and regarding goats and sheep as the special gods of shepherds and goatherds.

[33] Cf. 1.4.1.

ΛΟΓΟΣ ΤΡΙΤΟΣ

1 Μιτυληναῖοι δὲ ὡς ᾔσθοντο τὸν ἐπίπλουν τῶν δέκα νεῶν καί τινες ἐμήνυσαν αὐτοῖς τὴν ἁρπαγὴν ἐλθόντες ἐκ τῶν ἀγρῶν οὐκ ἀνασχετὸν νομίσαντες ταῦτα ἐκ Μηθυμναίων παθεῖν ἔγνωσαν καὶ αὐτοὶ τὴν ταχίστην ἐπ᾽ αὐτοὺς ὅπλα κινεῖν, 2. καὶ καταλέξαντες ἀσπίδα τρισχιλίαν καὶ ἵππον πεντακοσίαν ἐξέπεμψαν κατὰ γῆν τὸν στρατηγὸν Ἵππασον, ὀκνοῦντες ἐν ὥρᾳ χειμῶνος τὴν θάλασσαν.

2 Ὁ δὲ ἐξορμηθεὶς ἀγροὺς μὲν οὐκ ἐλεηλάτει τῶν Μηθυμναίων οὐδὲ ἀγέλας καὶ κτήματα ἥρπαζε γεωργῶν καὶ ποιμένων, λῃστοῦ νομίζων ταῦτα ἔργα μᾶλλον ἢ στρατηγοῦ, ταχὺ δὲ ἐπὶ τὴν πόλιν αὐτὴν ‹ὥρμησεν›[67] ὡς ἐπεισπεσούμενος ἀφρουρήτοις ταῖς πύλαις, 2. καὶ αὐτῷ σταδίους ὅσον ἑκατὸν ἀπέχοντι κῆρυξ ἀπαντᾷ σπονδὰς κομίζων. 3. οἱ γὰρ Μηθυμναῖοι μαθόντες παρὰ τῶν ἑαλωκότων ὡς οὐδὲν ἴσασι Μιτυληναῖοι τῶν γεγενημένων ἀλλὰ γεωργοὶ καὶ ποιμένες ὑβρίζοντας τοὺς νεανίσκους ἔδρασαν ταῦτα μετεγίνωσκον μὲν ὀξύτερα τολμήσαντες εἰς γείτονα πόλιν ἢ σωφρονέστερα, σπουδὴν δὲ εἶχον ἀποδόντες πᾶσαν τὴν ἁρπαγὴν ἀδεῶς ἐπιμίγνυσθαι καὶ κατὰ γῆν καὶ

---

[67] Add. Huet

BOOK III

When the Mitylenaeans got word of the attack by the 1
ten ships, and some people came from the farms and informed them about the plundering, they considered such
treatment by the Methymnaeans intolerable and resolved
to take up arms against them immediately. 2. Enlisting
three thousand infantry and five hundred cavalry, they dispatched their commander Hippasus[34] by land, being wary
of the sea during the winter.

He did not plunder the Methymnaeans' farms as he 2
marched or seize herds and property from farmers and
shepherds, regarding that as the conduct of a brigand
rather than a commander, but rapidly moved on the city
itself, hoping to breach the gates while they were unguarded. 2. When he was some hundred stades[35] distant a
herald came to meet him with the offer of a truce. 3. For
the Methymnaeans had learned from the captives that the
Mitylenaeans knew nothing of what had happened but that
farmers and shepherds had treated the young men this
way because of their outrageous behavior. So they began to regret their rash action, more impetuous than pru-
dent, against a neighboring city and were anxious to return
all the plunder and resume secure relations by land and

34 The name suggests "knightly" Greek pedigree and com-
portment, by contrast with his Methymnaean counterpart,
Bryaxis.   35 About 18.5 km.

κατὰ θάλασσαν. 4. τὸν μὲν οὖν κήρυκα τοῖς Μιτυληναίοις ὁ Ἵππασος ἀποστέλλει καίτοιγε αὐτοκράτωρ
στρατηγὸς κεχειροτονημένος, αὐτὸς δὲ τῆς Μηθύμνης
ὅσον ἀπὸ δέκα σταδίων στρατόπεδον βαλόμενος τὰς
ἐκ τῆς πόλεως ἐντολὰς ἀνέμενε, 5. καὶ δύο διαγενομένων ἡμερῶν ἐλθὼν ἄγγελος τήν τε ἁρπαγὴν ἐκέλευσε κομίσασθαι καὶ ἀδικήσαντα μηδὲν ἀναχωρεῖν οἴ-
καδε· πολέμου γὰρ καὶ εἰρήνης ἐν αἱρέσει γενόμενοι
τὴν εἰρήνην εὕρισκον κερδαλεωτέραν.

3   Ὁ μὲν δὴ Μηθυμναίων καὶ Μιτυληναίων πόλεμος
ἀδόκητον λαβὼν ἀρχὴν καὶ τέλος οὕτω διελύθη· γίνεται δὲ χειμὼν Δάφνιδι καὶ Χλόῃ τοῦ πολέμου πικρό-
τερος. ἐξαίφνης γὰρ πεσοῦσα χιὼν πολλὴ πάσας μὲν
ἀπέκλεισε τὰς ὁδούς, πάντας δὲ κατέκλεισε τοὺς γεωρ-
γούς. 2. λάβροι μὲν οἱ χείμαρροι κατέρρεον, ἐπεπήγει
δὲ κρύσταλλος· τὰ δένδρα ἐῴκει κατακλωμένοις· ἡ γῆ
πᾶσα ἀφανὴς ἦν ὅτι μὴ περὶ πηγάς που καὶ ῥεύματα.
3. οὔτε οὖν ἀγέλην τις εἰς νομὴν ἦγεν οὔτε αὐτὸς
προῄει τῶν θυρῶν, ἀλλὰ πῦρ καύσαντες μέγα περὶ
ᾠδὰς ἀλεκτρυόνων οἱ μὲν λίνον ἔστρεφον, οἱ δὲ αἰγῶν
τρίχας ἔπεκον, οἱ δὲ πάγας ὀρνίθων ἐσοφίζοντο. 4.
τότε βοῶν ἐπὶ φάτναις φροντὶς ἦν ἄχυρον ἐσθιόντων,
αἰγῶν καὶ προβάτων ἐν τοῖς σηκοῖς φυλλάδας, ὑῶν ἐν
τοῖς συφεοῖς ἄκυλον καὶ βαλάνους.

4   Ἀναγκαίας οὖν οἰκουρίας ἐπεχούσης ἅπαντας, οἱ
μὲν ἄλλοι γεωργοὶ καὶ νομεῖς ἔχαιρον πόνων τε ἀπηλ-
λαγμένοι πρὸς ὀλίγον καὶ τροφὰς ἑωθινὰς ἐσθίοντες
καὶ καθεύδοντες μακρὸν ὕπνον, ὥστε αὐτοῖς τὸν χειμῶνα δοκεῖν καὶ θέρους καὶ μετοπώρου καὶ ἦρος αὐτοῦ
γλυκύτερον· 2. Χλόη δὲ καὶ Δάφνις ἐν μνήμῃ γινό-
μενοι τῶν καταλειφθέντων τερπνῶν, ὡς ἐφίλουν, ὡς
περιέβαλλον, ὡς ἅμα τὴν τροφὴν προσεφέροντο,

sea. 4. Although Hippasus had been elected commander with plenipotentiary authority, he sent the herald on to Mitylene while he made camp about ten stades[36] from Methymna and awaited orders from his city. 5. Two days later, a messenger arrived and instructed him to retrieve the plunder and return home without doing any damage. Given a choice between war and peace, they found peace more profitable.

Thus was resolved the war between Methymna and 3 Mitylene, ending as unexpectedly as it began. But for Daphnis and Chloe the winter was more bitter than the war, for a sudden heavy snowfall had closed all the roads and shut in all the farmers. 2. Torrents rushed boisterously down and the ice was frozen solid, the trees looked to be bent over, the ground was completely invisible except here and there around springs and brooks. 3. No one drove a flock to pasture or ventured outdoors himself, but instead built a big fire at cock-crow and spun flax or combed goat hair or designed clever bird traps. 4. At the same time there was thought for the cattle that ate bran at their mangers, for the goats and sheep that ate leaves in their pens, and for the pigs that ate acorns and mast in their sties.

With everyone thus forced to be housebound, the 4 farmers and herdsmen were glad of a short respite from their labors, to be eating meals in the morning and sleeping in late, so that to them winter seemed sweeter than summer and autumn and even spring. 2. But as Chloe and Daphnis looked back on the joys left behind—how they used to kiss, how they used to hug, how they used to take

36 About 1.8 km.

νύκτας τε ἀγρύπνους διῆγον καὶ λυπηρὰς ⟨ἡμέρας⟩[68]
καὶ τὴν ἠρινὴν ὥραν[69] ἀνέμενον ἐκ θανάτου παλιγ-
γενεσίαν. 3. ἐλύπει δὲ αὐτοὺς ἢ πήρα τις ἐλθοῦσα εἰς
χεῖρας ἐξ ἧς ἤσθιον ἢ γαυλὸς ὀφθεὶς ἐξ οὗ συν-
έπιⲥνον ἢ σύριγξ ἀμελῶς ἐρριμμένη, δῶρον ἐρωτικὸν
γεγενημένη. 4. ηὔχοντο δὴ ταῖς Νύμφαις καὶ τῷ Πανὶ
καὶ τούτων αὐτοὺς ἐκλύσασθαι τῶν κακῶν καὶ δεῖξαί
ποτε αὐτοῖς καὶ ταῖς ἀγέλαις ἥλιον, ἅμα τε εὐχόμενοι
τέχνην ἐζήτουν δι' ἧς ἀλλήλους θεάσονται. 5. ἡ μὲν δὴ
Χλόη δεινῶς ἄπορος ἦν καὶ ἀμήχανος· ἀεὶ γὰρ αὐτῇ
συνῆν ἡ δοκοῦσα μήτηρ ἔριά τε ξαίνειν διδάσκουσα
καὶ ἀτράκτους στρέφειν καὶ γάμου μνημονεύουσα· ὁ
δὲ Δάφνις οἷα σχολὴν ἄγων καὶ συνετώτερος κόρης
τοιόνδε σόφισμα εὗρεν ἐς θέαν τῆς Χλόης.

5   Πρὸ τῆς αὐλῆς τοῦ Δρύαντος ἐπ' αὐτῇ τῇ αὐλῇ
μυρρίναι μεγάλαι δύο καὶ κιττὸς ἐπεφύκει, αἱ μυρρίναι
πλησίον ἀλλήλων, ὁ κιττὸς ἀμφοτέρων μέσος, ὥστε
ἐφ' ἑκατέραν διαθεὶς τοὺς ἀκρεμόνας ὡς ἄμπελος
ἄντρου σχῆμα διὰ τῶν φύλλων ἐπαλλαττόντων ἐποίει,
καὶ ὁ κόρυμβος πολὺς καὶ μέγας ὅσος βότρυς κλημάτων ἐξεκρέματο. 2. ἦν οὖν πολὺ πλῆθος περὶ αὐτὸν
τῶν χειμερινῶν ὀρνίθων ἀπορίᾳ τῆς ἔξω τροφῆς·
πολὺς μὲν κόψιχος, πολλὴ δὲ κίχλη, καὶ φάτται καὶ
ψᾶρες καὶ ὅσον ἄλλο κιττοφάγον πτερόν. 3. τούτων
τῶν ὀρνίθων ἐπὶ προφάσει θήρας ἐξώρμησεν ὁ
Δάφνις, ἐμπλήσας μὲν τὴν πήραν ὀψημάτων μεμελι-
τωμένων, κομίζων δὲ ἐς πίστιν ἰξὸν καὶ βρόχους. 4. τὸ
μὲν οὖν μεταξὺ σταδίων ἦν οὐ πλέον δέκα, οὔπω δὲ ἡ
χιὼν λελυμένη πολὺν αὐτῷ κάματον παρέσχεν. ἔρωτι

[68] Add. Edmonds
[69] Valckenaer: εἰρήνης ὥραν V: ὥραν τῆς εἰρήνης F

their meals together—, they passed sleepless nights and tiresome ‹days› and looked forward to the spring season as a rebirth from death. 3. They felt pangs when a knapsack came to hand that they used to eat from, or they caught sight of a milk pail that they used to drink from, or a syrinx casually tossed away that had been a gift of love. 4. They prayed to the Nymphs and Pan to rescue them from these hardships too, and to show them and their flocks some sun, and while they prayed they also tried to think of a way to see one another. 5. Chloe was awfully helpless and stumped, for her reputed mother was always with her, teaching her how to card wool and turn the spindle, and mentioning marriage. But Daphnis, who had spare time and more sagacity than a girl, came up with the following ploy for seeing Chloe.

Right in front of Dryas' farmyard grew two large myr- 5 tles and an ivy bush, the myrtles close together and the ivy between them, so that it spread its tendrils over each of them like a vine and with its intertwining leaves formed a kind of cave, and many a cluster of berries, as big as grapes, hung from the stems. 2. So there was a crowd of winter birds around it, owing to the scarceness of food outside: many a blackbird, many a thrush, pigeons and starlings and every other winged ivy-eater. 3. Daphnis set out on the pretext of hunting these birds, filling his knapsack with honeyed tidbits and packing birdlime and snares to add credibility. 4. Although the trip was no longer than ten stades,[37] the still unmelted snow made considerable work

---

[37] About 1.8 km.

δὲ ἄρα πάντα βάσιμα, καὶ πῦρ καὶ ὕδωρ καὶ Σκυθικὴ χιών.[70]

6   Δρόμῳ οὖν πρὸς τὴν αὐλὴν ἔρχεται καὶ ἀποσεισάμενος τῶν σκελῶν τὴν χιόνα τούς τε βρόχους ἔστησε καὶ τὸν ἰξὸν ῥάβδοις μακραῖς ἐπήλειψε καὶ ἐκαθέζετο τὸ ἐντεῦθεν ὄρνιθας ⟨ἀναμένων⟩[71] καὶ τὴν Χλόην μεριμνῶν. 2. ἀλλ' ὄρνιθες μὲν καὶ ἦκον πολλοὶ καὶ ἐλήφθησαν ἱκανοί, ὥστε πράγματα μυρία ἔσχε συλλέγων αὐτοὺς καὶ ἀποκτιννὺς καὶ ἀποδύων τὰ πτερά· τῆς δὲ αὐλῆς προῆλθεν οὐδείς, οὐκ ἀνήρ, οὐ γύναιον, οὐ κατοικίδιος ὄρνις, ἀλλὰ πάντες τῷ πυρὶ παραμένοντες ἔνδον κατεκέκλειντο, ὥστε πάνυ ἠπορεῖτο ὁ Δάφνις ὡς οὐκ αἰσίοις ὄρνισιν ἐλθὼν καὶ ἐτόλμα πρόφασιν σκηψάμενος ὤσασθαι διὰ θυρῶν καὶ ἐζήτει πρὸς αὐτὸν ὅ τι λεχθῆναι πιθανώτατον. 3. "πῦρ ἐναυσόμενος ἦλθον." "μὴ γὰρ οὐκ ἦσαν ἀπὸ σταδίου γείτονες;" "ἄρτους αἰτησόμενος ἦκον." "ἀλλ' ἡ πήρα μεστὴ τροφῆς." "οἴνου δέομαι." "καὶ μὴν χθὲς καὶ πρῴην ἐτρύγησας." "λύκος με ἐδίωκε." "καὶ ποῦ τὰ ἴχνη τοῦ λύκου;" "θηράσων ἀφικόμην τοὺς ὄρνιθας." "τί οὖν θηράσας οὐκ ἄπει;" "Χλόην θεάσασθαι βούλομαι." 4. "πατρὶ δὲ τίς καὶ μητρὶ παρθένου τοῦτο ὁμολογεῖ;" πταίων δὴ πανταχοῦ, "ἀλλ' οὐδὲν τούτων ἁπάντων ἀνύποπτον. ἄμεινον ἄρα σιγᾶν· Χλόην δὲ ἦρος ὄψομαι, ἐπεὶ μὴ εἵμαρτο ὡς ἔοικε χειμῶνός με ταύτην ἰδεῖν." 5. τοιαῦτα δή τινα διανοηθεὶς καὶ σιωπῇ[72] τὰ θηραθέντα συλλαβὼν ὥρμητο ἀπιέναι, καὶ ὥσπερ αὐτὸν οἰκτείραντος τοῦ Ἔρωτος τάδε γίνεται.

7   Περὶ τράπεζαν εἶχον οἱ ἀμφὶ τὸν Δρύαντα· κρέα

[70] ἔρωτι . . . χιών habet O   [71] Add. Henderson
[72] ἀλλ' . . . διανοηθεὶς καὶ hic Hercher: post σιωπῇ V: om. F

for him. But love finds a way through everything, be it fire, water, or Scythian snow.

So he made tracks for the farmyard and, after shaking 6
the snow off his legs, set his snares, daubed long sticks with his birdlime, and sat down waiting for birds and thinking anxiously of Chloe. 2. Plenty of birds came, and enough were caught that he was endlessly busy collecting, killing, and plucking them, but no one emerged from the farm-house, not man, lass, or domestic fowl; instead, every-one was shut up indoors, staying close to the fire, so that Daphnis grew very baffled, wondering if he had come for birds of ill omen, and was working up the courage to find some pretext to barge through the door and asking himself what would sound most plausible. 3. "I came to get a light for the fire": "Why? Weren't there neighbors just a stade away?" "I'm here to ask for some bread": "But your knap-sack is full of food." "I need some wine": "You did have your vintage just the other day." "A wolf was after me": "Then where are the wolf's tracks?" "I'm here to catch the birds": "Well, now that you've caught them, why aren't you leaving?" "I want to see Chloe": 4. "Who admits such a thing to a girl's father and mother?" Tripped up on every side, he thought "not one of these is above suspicion, so better to keep quiet. I will see Chloe in the spring, since I'm apparently not meant to see her during the winter." 5. Reaching these conclusions, without a word he collected what he had caught and had just begun his return trip when, as if Love had taken pity on him, the following hap-pened.

Dryas and his family were at dinner: meat was being 7

διηρεῖτο, ἄρτοι παρετίθεντο, κρατὴρ ἐκιρνᾶτο. εἰς δὴ κύων τῶν προβατευτικῶν ἀμέλειαν φυλάξας, κρέας ἁρπάσας ἔφυγε διὰ θυρῶν. 2. ἀλγήσας ὁ Δρύας, καὶ γὰρ ἦν ἐκείνου μοῖρα, ξύλον ἀράμενος ἐδίωκε κατ' ἴχνος ὥσπερ κύων· διώκων δὲ κατὰ τὸν κιττὸν γενόμενος ὁρᾷ τὸν Δάφνιν ἀνατεθειμένον ἐπὶ τοὺς ὤμους τὴν ἄγραν καὶ ἀποσοβεῖν ἐγνωκότα. 3. κρέως μὲν καὶ κυνὸς αὐτίκα ἐπελάθετο, μέγα δὲ βοήσας "χαῖρε, ὦ παῖ" περιεπλέκετο καὶ κατεφίλει καὶ ἦγεν ἔσω <τῆς χειρὸς>[73] λαβόμενος. μικροῦ μὲν οὖν ἰδόντες ἀλλήλους εἰς τὴν γῆν κατερρύησαν, μεῖναι δὲ καρτερήσαντες ὀρθοὶ προσηγόρευσάν τε καὶ κατεφίλησαν, καὶ τοῦτο οἱονεὶ ἔρεισμα αὐτοῖς τοῦ μὴ πεσεῖν ἐγένετο.

8   Τυχὼν οὖν ὁ Δάφνις παρ' ἐλπίδας καὶ φιλήματος καὶ Χλόης τοῦ τε πυρὸς ἐκαθέσθη πλησίον καὶ ἐπὶ τὴν τράπεζαν ἀπὸ τῶν ὤμων τὰς φάττας ἀπεφορτίζετο καὶ τοὺς κοψίχους καὶ διηγεῖτο πῶς ἀσχάλλων πρὸς τὴν οἰκουρίαν ὥρμησε πρὸς ἄγραν καὶ ὅπως τὰ μὲν βρόχοις αὐτῶν, τὰ δὲ ἰξῷ λάβοι, τῶν μύρτων καὶ τοῦ κιττοῦ γλιχόμενα. 2. οἱ δὲ ἐπῄνουν τὸ ἐνεργὸν καὶ ἐκέλευον ἐσθίειν ὧν ὁ κύων κατέλιπεν. ἐκέλευον δὲ καὶ τῇ Χλόῃ πιεῖν ἐγχέαι, καὶ ἡ χαίρουσα τοῖς τε ἄλλοις ὤρεξε καὶ Δάφνιδι μετὰ τοὺς ἄλλους· ἐσκήπτετο γὰρ ὀργίζεσθαι διότι ἐλθὼν ἔμελλεν ἀποτρέχειν οὐκ ἰδών. ὅμως μέντοι πρὶν προσενεγκεῖν ἀπέπιεν, εἶθ' οὕτως ἔδωκεν. ὁ δὲ καίτοι διψῶν βραδέως ἔπινε, παρέχων αὑτῷ διὰ τῆς βραδύτητος μακροτέραν ἡδονήν.

9   Ἡ μὲν δὴ τράπεζα ταχέως ἐγένετο κενὴ ἄρτων καὶ κρεῶν, καθήμενοι δὲ περὶ τῆς Μυρτάλης καὶ τοῦ Λάμωνος ἐπυνθάνοντο καὶ εὐδαιμόνιζον αὐτοὺς τοιού-

[73] Add. Hercher

carved, bread passed, the wine bowl mixed. One of the sheepdogs, watching until no one was looking, snatched some meat and ran out the door. 2. Dryas, annoyed because it was his portion, grabbed a stick and followed its tracks like a dog. The chase had brought him to the ivy when he saw Daphnis with his catch on his shoulders and intent on scurrying away. 3. He forgot all about the meat and the dog, loudly cried "Hello there, boy!" and hugged him, gave him a kiss, took ⟨his hand⟩, and led him into the house. When they saw one other they nearly sank to the ground, but managing to stay upright they exchanged greetings and kisses, and this served as a support to keep them from collapsing.

So Daphnis got more than he hoped for: both a kiss   8 and Chloe. He settled by the fire, unloaded the pigeons and blackbirds from his shoulders onto the table, and told them how, sick of being housebound, he had gone out to hunt and caught some of them with snares and others with birdlime as they went after the myrtle berries and the ivy. 2. They applauded his energy and invited him to eat some of what the dog had left behind, and asked Chloe to pour them drinks. She gladly served the others first and Daphnis last, since she was pretending to be angry that he had come and meant to run off without seeing her. All the same, she took a sip before serving him, then gave it to him just so. And though he was thirsty he drank slowly, by slowness affording himself longer pleasure.

The table was soon empty of bread and meat, but they   9 remained sitting and asked after Myrtale and Lamo, and congratulated them on their good fortune in having such a

τοῦ γηροτρόφου εὐτυχήσαντας· 2. καὶ τοῖς ἐπαίνοις
μὲν ἥδετο Χλόης ἀκροωμένης, ὅτε δὲ κατεῖχον αὐτὸν
ὡς θύσοντες Διονύσῳ τῆς ἐπιούσης ἡμέρας μικροῦ
δεῖν ὑφ᾽ ἡδονῆς ἐκείνους ἀντὶ τοῦ Διονύσου προσ-
εκύνησεν. 3. αὐτίκα οὖν ἐκ τῆς πήρας προεκόμιζε
μελιτώματα πολλὰ καὶ τοὺς θηραθέντας δὴ τῶν ὀρνίθων, καὶ τούτους ἐς τράπεζαν νυκτερινὴν ηὐτρέπιζον.
4. δεύτερος κρατὴρ ἵστατο καὶ δεύτερον πῦρ ἀνεκάετο,
καὶ ταχὺ μάλα νυκτὸς γενομένης δευτέρας τραπέζης
ἐνεφοροῦντο, μεθ᾽ ἣν τὰ μὲν μυθολογήσαντες, τὰ δὲ
ᾄσαντες εἰς ὕπνον ἐχώρουν, Χλόη μετὰ τῆς μητρός,
Δρύας ἅμα Δάφνιδι. 5. Χλόη μὲν οὖν οὐδὲν χρηστὸν
ἦν ὅτι μὴ τῆς ἐπιούσης ἡμέρας ὀφθησόμενος ὁ
Δάφνις, Δάφνις δὲ κενὴν τέρψιν ἐτέρπετο· τερπνὸν
γὰρ ἐνόμιζε καὶ πατρὶ συγκοιμηθῆναι Χλόης, ὥστε
καὶ περιέβαλλεν αὐτὸν καὶ κατεφίλει πολλάκις, ταῦτα
πάντα ποιεῖν Χλόην ὀνειροπολούμενος.

10   Ὡς δὲ ἐγένετο ἡμέρα, κρύος μὲν ἦν ἐξαίσιον καὶ
αὔρα βόρειος ὑπέκαε πάντα, οἱ δὲ ἀναστάντες θύουσι
τῷ Διονύσῳ κριὸν ἐνιαύσιον καὶ πῦρ ἀνακαύσαντες
μέγα παρεσκευάζοντο τροφήν. 2. τῆς οὖν Νάπης
ἀρτοποιούσης καὶ τοῦ Δρύαντος τὸν κριὸν ἕψοντος
σχολῆς ὁ Δάφνις καὶ ἡ Χλόη λαβόμενοι προῆλθον
τῆς αὐλῆς ἵνα ὁ κιττὸς καὶ πάλιν βρόχους στήσαντες
καὶ ἰξὸν ἐπαλείψαντες ἐθήρων πλῆθος οὐκ ὀλίγον
ὀρνίθων. 3. ἦν δὲ αὐτοῖς καὶ φιλημάτων ἀπόλαυσις
συνεχὴς καὶ λόγων ὁμιλία τερπνή· "διὰ σὲ ἦλθον,
Χλόη." "οἶδα, Δάφνι." "διὰ σὲ ἀπολλύω τοὺς ἀθλίους
κοψίχους." "τίς οὖν σοι γένωμαι;" "μέμνησό μου."
"μνημονεύω νὴ τὰς Νύμφας, ἃς ὤμοσά ποτε εἰς ἐκεῖνο
τὸ ἄντρον ⟨εἰσελθοῦσα⟩[74] εἰς ὃ ἥξομεν εὐθύς, ⟨ἡνί-

[74] Add. Hercher

114

carer in old age. 2. He was delighted enough by these compliments in Chloe's hearing, but when they pressed him to
stay because they were going to make a sacrifice for Dionysus the next day, he was so delighted he nearly made obeisance to them instead of Dionysus. 3. So he promptly produced from his knapsack a great many honey cakes and the
birds he had caught, and they set about preparing these for
the evening meal. 4. Another wine bowl was set up and another fire lit, and after a very early nightfall they did justice
to the second table and then told stories and sang songs until they went to bed, Chloe with her mother, Dryas with
Daphnis. 5. For Chloe there was no gain except that tomorrow Daphnis would be there to see, while Daphnis was
pleased with an empty pleasure, for he considered it plea-
surable even to sleep beside Chloe's father, so that he
hugged and kissed him again and again, dreaming that he
was doing all this to Chloe.

When day came it was extraordinarily cold, and a north-   10
erly wind was parching everything. They got up and sacrificed a yearling ram to Dionysus, then built a big fire and
began to prepare a meal. 2. While Nape was baking bread
and Dryas was boiling the ram, Daphnis and Chloe used
the free time to go outside the farmyard to where the ivy
was, and once again placing snares and daubing birdlime,
they managed to catch no small number of birds. 3. And
they had the pleasure of continuous kissing and the enjoyment of conversation. "It was because of you that I came,
Chloe." "I know, Daphnis." "It's because of you that I'm
killing the poor blackbirds." "So what do you want me
to do?" "Remember me." "I do remember you, by the
Nymphs I once swore by when I entered that cave, where

κα>[75] ἂν ἡ χιὼν τακῇ." 4. "ἀλλὰ πολλή ἐστι, Χλόη, καὶ
δέδοικα μὴ ἐγὼ πρὸ ταύτης τακῶ"· "θάρρει, Δάφνι,
θερμός ἐστιν ὁ ἥλιος." "εἰ γὰρ οὕτως γένοιτο, Χλόη,
θερμὸς ὡς τὸ καῖον πῦρ τὴν καρδίαν τὴν ἐμήν." "παί-
ζεις ἀπατῶν με." "οὐ μὰ τὰς αἶγας, ἃς σύ με ἐκέλευες
ὀμνύειν."

11   Τοιαῦτα ἀντιφωνήσασα πρὸς τὸν Δάφνιν ἡ Χλόη
καθάπερ ἠχώ, καλούντων αὐτοὺς τῶν περὶ τὴν Νάπην
εἰσέδραμον πολὺ περιττοτέραν τῆς χθιζῆς θήραν
κομίζοντες, καὶ ἀπαρξάμενοι τῷ Διονύσῳ κρατῆρος
ἤσθιον κιττῷ τὰς κεφαλὰς ἐστεφανωμένοι. 2. καὶ ἐπεὶ
καιρὸς ἦν ἰακχάσαντες καὶ εὐάσαντες προέπεμπον τὸν
Δάφνιν, πλήσαντες αὐτοῦ τὴν πήραν κρεῶν καὶ ἄρτων.
ἔδωκαν δὲ καὶ τὰς φάττας καὶ τὰς κίχλας Λάμωνι καὶ
Μυρτάλῃ κομίζειν ὡς αὐτοὶ θηράσοντες ἄλλας ἔστ᾽ ἂν
ὁ χειμὼν μένῃ καὶ ὁ κιττὸς μὴ λείπῃ. 3. ὁ δὲ ἀπῄει
φιλήσας αὐτοὺς προτέρους Χλόης, ἵνα τὸ ἐκείνης
καθαρὸν μείνῃ φίλημα, καὶ ἄλλας δὲ πολλὰς ἦλθεν
ὁδοὺς ἐπ᾽ ἄλλαις τέχναις, ὥστε μὴ παντάπασιν αὐτοῖς
γενέσθαι τὸν χειμῶνα ἀνέραστον.

12   Ἤδη δὲ ἦρος ἀρχομένου καὶ τῆς μὲν χιόνος λυο-
μένης, τῆς δὲ γῆς γυμνουμένης καὶ τῆς πόας ὑπαν-
θούσης, οἵ τε ἄλλοι νομεῖς ἦγον τὰς ἀγέλας εἰς νομὴν
καὶ πρὸ τῶν ἄλλων Χλόη καὶ Δάφνις οἷα μείζονι
δουλεύοντες ποιμένι. 2. εὐθὺς οὖν δρόμος ἦν ἐπὶ τὰς
Νύμφας καὶ τὸ ἄντρον, ἐντεῦθεν ἐπὶ τὸν Πᾶνα καὶ τὴν
πίτυν, εἶτα ἐπὶ τὴν δρῦν ὑφ᾽ ἣν καθίζοντες καὶ τὰς
ἀγέλας ἔνεμον καὶ ἀλλήλους κατεφίλουν. ἀνεζήτησαν-
το καὶ ἄνθη στεφανῶσαι θέλοντες τοὺς θεούς· τὰ δὲ
ἄρτι ὁ ζέφυρος τρέφων καὶ ὁ ἥλιος θερμαίνων ἐξῆγεν·

75 Add. Reeve

we will go as soon as the snow melts." 4. "But there's a lot of it, Chloe, and I'm afraid I will melt before the snow does." "Take heart, Daphnis, the sun is hot." "If only it were as hot, Chloe, as the flame that burns this heart of mine." "You're beguiling me." "I'm not, so help me those goats that you told me to swear by."

Chloe responded this way to Daphnis like an echo,   11 then when Nape and the others called them they ran inside, bringing a much bigger catch than yesterday's. They poured from the bowl first to Dionysus, and ate their meal with their heads crowned with ivy. 2. When the time came, they cried "Iacchus" and "Evoe,"[38] filled Daphnis' knapsack with meat and bread, and saw him on his way. They also gave him the pigeons and thrushes to take to Lamon and Myrtale, saying that they would catch others themselves as long as the winter lasted and the ivy did not run out. 3. He took his leave, kissing them before Chloe, so that her kiss would remain pure. He made many other trips on various pretexts, and so their winter was not entirely without love.

Now spring was beginning, the snow was melting, the   12 earth was being uncovered, and the grass was beginning to grow. The herdsmen drove their flocks to pasture, Daphnis and Chloe before the others, since they were servants of a greater shepherd. 2. They ran straight to the Nymphs in the cave, then to Pan by the pine, then to the oak tree, where they sat grazing their flocks and exchanging kisses. Wishing to make garlands for the gods, they also looked for flowers, only just now coming up, nurtured by the west

---

38 Conventional ritual cries to Dionysus.

ὅμως δὲ εὑρέθη καὶ ἴα καὶ νάρκισσος καὶ ἀναγαλλὶς
καὶ ὅσα ἦρος πρωτοφορήματα. 3. ἠμέλχθη καὶ[76] ἀπὸ
αἰγῶν καὶ ὀΐων τινῶν γάλα νέον, καὶ τοῦτο στεφα-
νοῦντες τὰ ἀγάλματα κατέσπεισαν. 4. ἀπήρξαντο καὶ
σύριγγος καθάπερ τὰς ἀηδόνας ἐς τὴν μουσικὴν
ἐρεθίζοντες, αἱ δ᾽ ὑπεφθέγγοντο ἐν ταῖς λόχμαις καὶ
τὸν Ἴτυν κατ᾽ ὀλίγον ἠκρίβουν ὥσπερ ἀναμιμνησκό-
μεναι τῆς ᾠδῆς ἐκ μακρᾶς σιωπῆς.

13   Ἐβληχήσατό που καὶ ποίμνιον, ἐσκίρτησάν που
καὶ ἄρνες καὶ ταῖς μητράσιν ὑποκλάσαντες αὑτοὺς
τὴν θηλὴν ἔσπασαν· τὰς δὲ μήπω τετοκυίας οἱ κριοὶ
κατεδιώκοντες καὶ κάτω στήσαντες ἔβαινον ἄλλος
ἄλλην. 2. ἐγίνοντο καὶ τράγων διώγματα καὶ εἰς τὰς
αἶγας ἐρωτικώτερα πηδήματα· καὶ ἐμάχοντο περὶ τῶν
αἰγῶν καὶ ἕκαστος εἶχεν ἰδίας καὶ ἐφύλαττε μή τις
αὐτὰς μοιχεύσῃ λαθών. 3. κἂν γέροντας ὁρῶντας
ἐξώρμησεν εἰς ἀφροδίτην τὰ τοιαῦτα θεάματα· οἱ δὲ
νέοι καὶ σφριγῶντες καὶ πολὺν ἤδη χρόνον ἔρωτα
ζητοῦντες ἐξεκάοντο πρὸς τὰ ἀκούσματα καὶ ἐτήκοντο
πρὸς τὰ θεάματα καὶ ἐζήτουν καὶ αὐτοὶ περιττότερόν
τι φιλήματος καὶ περιβολῆς, μάλιστα δὲ ὁ Δάφνις. 4.
οἷα γοῦν ἐνηβήσας τῇ κατὰ τὸν χειμῶνα οἰκουρίᾳ καὶ
εὐσχολίᾳ[77] πρός τε τὰ φιλήματα ὤργα καὶ πρὸς τὰς
περιβολὰς ἐσκιτάλιζε καὶ ἦν ἐς πᾶν ἔργον περιερ-
γότερος καὶ θρασύτερος.

76 Jackson: ἡ μὲν Χλόη καὶ (Δάφνις add. V²) V F
77 Schäfer: ἀσχολίᾳ V: ἀσχαλίᾳ F

___

39 In the myth, Tereus, King of Thrace, wed the Athenian
princess Procne, but on a later visit to Athens raped her sister
Philomela, whose tongue he cut out to prevent her from telling

wind and warmed by the sun, but still they found violets, daffodils, pimpernels, and all the first bounty of spring-time. 3. They also took new milk from some of the goats and sheep and poured it in libation as they garlanded the statues. 4. They also offered the first fruits of the syrinx, as if encouraging the nightingales to sing, and the night-ingales did reply from the thickets, gradually perfecting their lament for Itys[39] as if remembering how to sing after a long silence.

Here and there sheep bleated, and lambs frisked and knelt beneath their mothers and sucked on the tit, while the rams chased after the ewes that had not yet lambed, each of them holding and mounting one. 2. There were he-goat pursuits too, and even more amorous mounting of the she-goats: they fought over the she-goats, for each had his own harem and kept guard against any clandestine adulterer. 3. Such sights would have spurred even old men to sexual desire as they watched, but as they were young, lusty, and long since questing after love, they were in-flamed by what they heard and melted away at what they saw, and they too tried to find for themselves something beyond kissing and hugging, especially Daphnis. 4. After a prime of youth spent in winter's idle domesticity, he grew taut at the kisses and horny at the embraces, and was bolder and more eager to try anything.

anyone. But she depicted the crime on an embroidery that she sent to Procne. The sisters avenged themselves by killing Itys, Procne's only child by Tereus, and serving him to his father for dinner. When Tereus chased the sisters with a sword, the gods changed him into a hoopoe, Procne into a nightingale, and Philomela into a swallow. The nightingale's song was regarded as a lament for Itys.

14 Ἤτει δὴ τὴν Χλόην χαρίσασθαί οἱ πᾶν ὅσον
βούλεται καὶ γυμνὴν γυμνῷ συγκατακλιθῆναι μακρό-
τερον ἢ πρόσθεν εἰώθεσαν· τοῦτο γὰρ δὴ λείπειν τοῖς
Φιλητᾶ παιδεύμασιν ἵνα γένηται τὸ μόνον ἔρωτα
παῦον φάρμακον. 2. τῆς δὲ πυνθανομένης τί πλέον
ἐστὶ φιλήματος καὶ περιβολῆς καὶ αὐτῆς κατακλίσεως
καὶ τί ἔγνωκε δρᾶσαι γυμνὸς γυμνῇ συγκατακλινείς,
"τοῦτο" εἶπεν "ὃ οἱ κριοὶ ποιοῦσι τὰς ὄις καὶ τράγοι
τὰς αἶγας. 3. ὁρᾷς ὡς μετὰ τοῦτο τὸ ἔργον οὔτε ἐκεῖναι
φεύγουσιν ἔτι αὐτοὺς οὔτε ἐκεῖνοι κάμνουσι διώκοντες
ἀλλ᾽ ὥσπερ κοινῆς λοιπὸν ἀπολαύσαντες ἡδονῆς συν-
νέμονται; γλυκύ τι ὡς ἔοικεν ἐστὶ τὸ ἔργον καὶ νικᾷ τὸ
ἔρωτος πικρόν." 4. "εἶτα οὐχ ὁρᾷς, ὦ Δάφνι, τὰς αἶγας
καὶ τοὺς τράγους καὶ τοὺς κριοὺς καὶ τὰς ὄις ὡς ὀρθοὶ
μὲν ἐκεῖνοι δρῶσιν, ὀρθαὶ δὲ ἐκεῖναι πάσχουσιν, οἱ μὲν
πηδήσαντες, αἱ δὲ κατανωτισάμεναι; σὺ δέ με ἀξιοῖς
συγκατακλινῆναι καὶ ταῦτα γυμνήν; καίτοιγε ἐκεῖναι
πόσον ἐνδεδυμένης[78] ἐμοῦ λασιώτεραι." 5. πείθεται
Δάφνις καὶ συγκατακλινεὶς αὐτῇ πολὺν χρόνον ἔκειτο
καὶ οὐδὲν ὧν ἕνεκα ὤργα ποιεῖν ἐπιστάμενος ἀνίστησιν αὐτὴν καὶ κατόπιν περιεφέρετο μιμούμενος τοὺς
τράγους. πολὺ δὲ μᾶλλον ἀπορηθείς, καθίσας ἔκλαεν
εἰ καὶ κριῶν ἀμαθέστερος εἰς τὰ ἔρωτος ἔργα.

15 Ἦν δέ τις αὐτῷ γείτων, γεωργὸς γῆς ἰδίας, Χρόμις[79] τὸ ὄνομα, παρηβῶν ἤδη τὸ σῶμα. τούτῳ γύναιον
ἦν ἐπακτὸν ἐξ ἄστεος, νέον καὶ ὡραῖον καὶ ἀγροικίας

---

78 ἐκδ- F
79 Edmonds cl. Theocr. 1.24: Χρόμης F: Χρῶμις V (ὄνομα
κύριον Suda χ 542).

He pressed Chloe to give him all that he wanted and to   14
lie together naked for longer than they used to before,
since this was the last untried step in Philetas' instructions,
so that the sole antidote for love could take effect. 2. She
asked what more there was than kissing, hugging, and actually lying down, and what he meant to do once they were
lying together naked. "What the rams are doing to the
ewes," he replied, "and the he-goats to the she-goats. 3. Do
you notice that after they do that, the females no longer
run away from the males and the males no longer wear
themselves out chasing the females, but instead they graze
together afterwards as if having shared a mutual pleasure?
Apparently this behavior has a sweetness that overcomes
the bitterness of love." 4. "Don't you also notice, Daphnis,
that the rams and the he-goats stand when they do this, and
the ewes and the she-goats stand when they have it done,
the males hopping onto the females and the females carrying them on their backs? And you ask me to lie down with
you, and naked to boot? Yet how much woollier these females are than I am, even with my clothes on!" 5. Daphnis
agreed. Reclining with her, he lay there a long time, and
not knowing how to do any of what he grew taut for, he
stood her up and clung to her from behind, imitating the
he-goats. But much more frustrated than before, he sat
down and started to weep, for being more inept than he-
goats in making love.

He had a neighbor who farmed his own land, named   15
Chromis[40] and physically past his prime. He had a lass, im-
ported from the city, young, pretty, and by country stan-

[40] The name appears in Theocritus 1.24 and Virgil, *Eclogue*
6.13.

ἁβρότερον· τούτῳ Λυκαίνιον ὄνομα ἦν. 2. αὕτη ὁρῶσα
τὸν Δάφνιν καθ᾽ ἑκάστην ἡμέραν παρελαύνοντα τὰς
αἶγας ἕωθεν εἰς νομήν, νύκτωρ ἐκ νομῆς, ἐπεθύμησεν
ἐραστὴν κτήσασθαι δώροις δελεάσασα. 3. καὶ δή ποτε
λοχήσασα μόνον καὶ σύριγγα δῶρον ἔδωκε καὶ μέλι
ἐν κηρίῳ καὶ πήραν ἐλάφου· εἰπεῖν δέ τι ὤκνει, τὸν
Χλόης ἔρωτα καταμαντευομένη· πάντα γὰρ ἑώρα
προσκείμενον αὐτὸν τῇ κόρῃ. 4. πρότερον μὲν οὖν ἐκ
νευμάτων καὶ γέλωτος συνεβάλετο τοῦτο, τότε δὲ ἐξ
ἑωθινοῦ σκηψαμένη πρὸς Χρόμιν ὡς παρὰ τίκτουσαν
ἄπεισι γείτονα κατόπιν τε αὐτοῖς παρηκολούθησε καὶ
εἴς τινα λόχμην ἐγκρύψασα ἑαυτὴν ὡς μὴ βλέποιτο
πάντα ἤκουσεν ὅσα εἶπον, πάντα εἶδεν ὅσα ἔπραξαν·
οὐκ ἔλαθεν αὐτὴν οὐδὲ κλαύσας ὁ Δάφνις. 5. συν-
αλγήσασα δὴ τοῖς ἀθλίοις καὶ καιρὸν ἥκειν νομίσασα
διττόν, τὸν μὲν εἰς τὴν ἐκείνων σωτηρίαν, τὸν δὲ εἰς
τὴν ἑαυτῆς ἐπιθυμίαν, ἐπιτεχνᾶταί τι τοιόνδε.

16   Τῆς ἐπιούσης, ὡς παρὰ τὴν γυναῖκα [λαβὴν][80] τὴν
τίκτουσαν ἀπιοῦσα, φανερῶς ἐπὶ τὴν δρῦν ἔνθα ἐκαθέζετο Δάφνις καὶ Χλόη παραγίνεται καὶ ἀκριβῶς
μιμησαμένη τὴν τεταραγμένην 2. "σῶσόν με" εἶπε
"Δάφνι, τὴν ἀθλίαν. ἐκ γάρ μοι τῶν χηνῶν τῶν εἴκοσιν
ἕνα τὸν κάλλιστον ἀετὸς ἥρπασε καὶ οἷα μέγα φορτίον ἀράμενος οὐκ ἠδυνήθη μετέωρος ἐπὶ τὴν συνήθη
τὴν ὑψηλὴν ἐκείνην κομίσαι πέτραν ἀλλ᾽ εἰς τήνδε τὴν
ὕλην τὴν ταπεινὴν ἔχων κατέπεσε. 3. σὺ τοίνυν πρὸς
τῶν Νυμφῶν καὶ τοῦ Πανὸς ἐκείνου ⟨συν⟩εισελθὼν εἰς

80 Del. Jungermann (λαβεῖν F): ταύτην Giangrande

41 "Little Wolf": similar names were borne by prostitutes (including comic ones, cf. Pollux 4.150 of the typical mask) and also

dards rather sophisticated. Her name was Lycaenium.[41]
2. Seeing Daphnis every day as he drove his goats down to
pasture in the morning and drove them back in the evening, she conceived a desire to acquire him as a lover by
enticing him with presents. 3. One day she waylaid him
when he was by himself and gave him a syrinx, honey in the
comb, and a deerskin knapsack, but divining his love for
Chloe, she hesitated to say anything; she observed that he
was completely devoted to the girl. 4. In fact she had already guessed as much by their nods and laughter. But
early that morning, pretending to Chromis that she was off
to visit a neighbor who was having a baby, she had tailed
them and, hiding in a copse so as not to be seen, overheard
everything they said and saw everything they did; not even
Daphnis' weeping did she miss. 5. She felt sorry for the
poor couple and thought she had a double opportunity: to
come to their rescue and serve her own desire as well. She
came up with the following scheme.

The next day, pretending to be off to visit the woman   16
who was having a baby, she showed up openly at the oak
tree where Daphnis and Chloe were sitting and gave an ac-
curate impression of a woman in distress: 2. "Come to my
rescue, Daphnis," she said, "I'm in a sorry state. An eagle
snatched one of my twenty geese, the best one, and it
was such a big load to carry that he couldn't get aloft and
bring it to his usual high rock over there, but crashed into
these woods down here still holding it. 3. So please, in
the name of the Nymphs and Pan there, come with me into

by respectable women, and they appear in pastoral and elegiac poetry; in Propertius 3.15 Lycinna's role is analogous to Lycaenium's,
as is Calypso's in the *Odyssey*.

τὴν ὕλην, μόνη γὰρ δέδοικα, σῶσόν μοι τὸν χῆνα μηδὲ
περιίδῃς ἀτελῆ μοι τὸν ἀριθμὸν γενόμενον. 4. τάχα δὲ
καὶ αὐτὸν τὸν ἀετὸν ἀποκτενεῖς καὶ οὐκέτι πολλοὺς
ὑμῶν ἄρνας καὶ ἐρίφους ἁρπάσει. τὴν δὲ ἀγέλην τέως
φρουρήσει Χλόη· πάντως αὐτὴν ἴσασιν αἱ αἶγες ἀεί
σοι συννέμουσαν."

17   Οὐδὲν οὖν τῶν μελλόντων ὑποπτεύσας ὁ Δάφνις
εὐθὺς ἀνίσταται[81] καὶ ἀράμενος τὴν καλαύροπα κατόπιν ἠκολούθει τῇ Λυκαινίῳ. ἡ δὲ ἡγεῖτο ὡς μακρο-
τάτω τῆς Χλόης, καὶ ἐπειδὴ κατὰ τὸ πυκνότατον
ἐγένοντο πηγῆς πλησίον καθίσαι κελεύσασα αὐτὸν
"ἐρᾷς" εἶπε "Δάφνι, Χλόης, καὶ τοῦτο ἔμαθον ἐγὼ
νύκτωρ παρὰ τῶν Νυμφῶν. 2. δι᾽ ὀνείρατος ἐμοὶ καὶ τὰ
χθιζά σου διηγήσαντο δάκρυα καὶ ἐκέλευσάν σε σῶσαι διδαξαμένην τὰ ἔρωτος ἔργα. τὰ δέ ἐστιν οὐ
φίλημα καὶ περιβολὴ καὶ οἷα δρῶσι κριοὶ καὶ τράγοι.
ἄλλα ταῦτα πηδήματα καὶ τῶν ἐκεῖ γλυκύτερα· πρόσ-
εστι γὰρ αὐτοῖς χρόνος μακροτέρας ἡδονῆς. 3. εἰ δή
σοι φίλον ἀπηλλάχθαι κακῶν καὶ ἐν πείρᾳ γενέσθαι
ζητουμένων τερπνῶν, ἴθι, παραδίδου μοι [τερπνὸν][82]
σαυτὸν μαθητήν, ἐγὼ δὲ χαριζομένη ταῖς Νύμφαις
ἐκείναις διδάξω."

18   Οὐκ ἐκαρτέρησεν ὁ Δάφνις ὑφ᾽ ἡδονῆς ἀλλ᾽ ἅτε
ἄγροικος καὶ αἰπόλος καὶ ἐρῶν καὶ νέος πρὸ τῶν
ποδῶν καταπεσὼν τὴν Λυκαίνιον ἱκέτευεν ὅτι τάχιστα
διδάξαι τὴν τέχνην δι᾽ ἧς ὃ βούλεται δράσει Χλόην, 2.
καὶ ὥσπερ τι μέγα καὶ θεόπεμπτον ἀληθῶς μέλλων
διδάσκεσθαι καὶ ἔριφον αὐτῇ σηκίτην δώσειν ἐπηγγείλατο καὶ τυροὺς ἁπαλοὺς πρωτορρύτου γάλακτος
καὶ τὴν αἶγα αὐτήν. 3. εὑροῦσα δὴ ἡ Λυκαίνιον

81 ἐγείρεται F   82 Del. Reeve

the woods—I'm afraid to go alone—and rescue my goose; don't just stand by while my roster is reduced. 4. Maybe you will kill the eagle too, and it will no longer be snatching lots of your lambs and kids. Chloe will look after your flock while you're gone. The goats must know her, since she is always grazing with you."

So having no suspicion of what was about to happen,   17 Daphnis got right up, picked up his crook, and followed behind Lycaenium. She led him as far away from Chloe as she could, and when they were in the thickest woods she told him to sit down by a spring and said, "Daphnis, you are in love with Chloe. I was told this by the Nymphs last night. 2. In a dream they described to me those tears of yours yesterday and bid me to come to the rescue by teaching you how to make love. It isn't merely kissing and hugging and what rams and he-goats do. It's a different kind of frolicking, sweeter than theirs, because the pleasure it brings lasts longer. 3. If you really want to be rid of your troubles and have a go at the delights that you're after, come on, give your [delightful] self to me as a pupil, and as a favor to these Nymphs I will teach you."

In his delight Daphnis could not resist, but coun-   18 try goatherd that he was, young and in love, he fell at Lycaenium's feet and begged her to teach him as soon as possible the skill that he wanted to use on Chloe. 2. As if about to learn something truly great and heaven-sent, he promised to give her a kid weaned in the fold, soft cheeses made from a she-goat's first milking, and the she-goat herself. 3. Discovering a pastoral generosity that she had not

αἰπολικὴν ἀφθονίαν οἵαν οὐ προσεδόκησεν ἤρχετο
παιδεύειν τὸν Δάφνιν τοῦτον τὸν τρόπον· ἐκέλευσεν
αὐτὸν καθίσαι πλησίον αὐτῆς ὡς ἔχει καὶ φιλήματα
φιλεῖν οἷα εἰώθει καὶ ὅσα καὶ φιλοῦντα ἅμα περιβάλ-
λειν καὶ κατακλίνεσθαι χαμαί. 4. ὡς δὲ ἐκαθέσθη καὶ
ἐφίλησε καὶ κατεκλίθη, μαθοῦσα ἐνεργεῖν δυνάμενον
καὶ σφριγῶντα ἀπὸ μὲν τῆς ἐπὶ πλευρὰν κατακλίσεως
ἀνίστησιν, αὐτὴν δὲ ὑποστορέσασα ἐντέχνως εἰς τὴν
τέως ζητουμένην ὁδὸν ἦγε, τὸ δὲ ἐντεῦθεν οὐδὲν περιειργάζετο ξένον· αὐτὴ γὰρ ἡ φύσις λοιπὸν ἐπαίδευσε
τὸ πρακτέον.

19   Τελεσθείσης δὲ τῆς ἐρωτικῆς παιδαγωγίας ὁ μὲν
Δάφνις ἔτι ποιμενικὴν γνώμην ἔχων ὥρμητο τρέχειν
ἐπὶ τὴν Χλόην καὶ ὅσα πεπαίδευτο δρᾶν αὐτίκα καθάπερ δεδοικὼς μὴ βραδύνας ἐπιλάθοιτο, ἡ δὲ Λυκαίνιον κατασχοῦσα αὐτὸν ἔλεξεν ὧδε· "ἔτι καὶ ταῦτά σε
δεῖ μαθεῖν, Δάφνι. 2. ἐγὼ γυνὴ τυγχάνουσα πέπονθα
νῦν οὐδέν· πάλαι γάρ με ταῦτα ἀνὴρ ἄλλος ἐπαίδευσε,
μισθὸν τὴν παρθενίαν λαβών, Χλόη δὲ συμπαλαί-
ουσά σοι ταύτην τὴν πάλην καὶ οἰμώξει καὶ κλαύσεται
κἂν αἵματι κείσεται πολλῷ [καθάπερ πεφονευμένη][83].
3. ἀλλὰ σὺ τὸ αἷμα μὴ φοβηθῇς ἀλλ' ἡνίκα ἂν πείσῃς
αὐτήν σοι παρασχεῖν ἄγαγε αὐτὴν εἰς τοῦτο τὸ χωρίον, ἵνα κἂν βοήσῃ μηδεὶς ἀκούσῃ κἂν δακρύσῃ
μηδεὶς ἴδῃ κἂν αἱμαχθῇ λούσηται τῇ πηγῇ· καὶ μέμνησο ὅτι σε ἄνδρα ἐγὼ πρὸ Χλόης πεποίηκα."

20   Ἡ μὲν οὖν Λυκαίνιον τοσαῦτα ὑποθεμένη κατ' ἄλλο
μέρος τῆς ὕλης ἀπῆλθεν ὡς ἔτι ζητοῦσα τὸν χῆνα, ὁ δὲ
Δάφνις εἰς λογισμὸν ἄγων τὰ εἰρημένα τῆς μὲν προτέρας ὁρμῆς ἀπήλλακτο, διοχλεῖν δὲ τῇ Χλόῃ περιτ-

---

[83] Del. Castiglioni, cf. 20.1

expected, Lycaenium began to educate Daphnis in the following way. She told him to sit beside her just as he was and to give her the same kind and number of kisses as usual, and as he kissed her, to put his arms around her and lie down on the ground. 4. So Daphnis sat down, kissed her, and lay down, and when she felt him distended and ready for action, she raised him from where he lay on his side, skillfully slipped under him, and guided him into the passage he had been looking for so long. From that point she had to make no extra effort: nature herself taught what was to be done.

When his lesson in love was over, Daphnis, still thinking 19 like a shepherd, was eager to run to Chloe and do everything he had learned right away, as if afraid that he would forget if he delayed. But Lycaenium held him back with these words: "There is something more you should know, Daphnis. 2. Because I'm a mature woman, this didn't hurt at all; long ago another man taught me this lesson and took my virginity as his reward. But when Chloe has this sort of wrestling match with you, she will scream and cry and lie bleeding heavily [as if murdered]. 3. But don't be afraid of the blood, though when you convince her to surrender herself to you, bring her to this spot so that if she yells no one will hear it, if she weeps no one will see it, and if she bleeds she can wash in the spring. And just remember that I made you a man before Chloe did."

Leaving him with this advice, Lycaenium went off to a 20 different part of the woods, saying that she was still looking for her goose, while Daphnis mulled over what she had said and abandoned his previous impulse. He was reluc-

τότερον ὤκνει φιλήματος καὶ περιβολῆς, μήτε βοῆσαι
θέλων αὐτὴν ὡς πρὸς πολέμιον μήτε δακρῦσαι ὡς
ἀλγοῦσαν μήτε αἱμαχθῆναι καθάπερ πεφονευμένην· 2.
ἀρτιμαθὴς γὰρ ὢν ἐδεδοίκει τὸ αἷμα καὶ ἐνόμιζεν ὅτι
ἄρα ἐκ μόνου τραύματος αἷμα γίνεται. γνοὺς δὲ τὰ
συνήθη τέρπεσθαι μετ᾽ αὐτῆς ἐξέβη τῆς ὕλης καὶ
ἐλθὼν ἵνα ἐκάθητο στεφανίσκον ἴων πλέκουσα τόν τε
χῆνα τοῦ ἀετοῦ τῶν ὀνύχων ἐψεύσατο ἐξαρπάσαι καὶ
περιφὺς ἐφίλησεν οἷον ἐν τῇ τέρψει Λυκαίνιον· τοῦτο
γὰρ ἐξῆν ὡς ἀκίνδυνον. 3. ἡ δὲ τὸν στέφανον ἐφήρ-
μοσεν αὐτοῦ τῇ κεφαλῇ καὶ τὴν κόμην ἐφίλησεν ὡς
τῶν ἴων κρείττονα καὶ τῆς πήρας προκομίσασα πα-
λάθης μοῖραν καὶ ἄρτους τινὰς ἔδωκε φαγεῖν καὶ
ἐσθίοντος ἀπὸ τοῦ στόματος ἥρπαζε καὶ οὕτως ἤσθιεν
ὥσπερ νεοττὸς ὄρνιθος.

21   Ἐσθιόντων δὲ αὐτῶν καὶ περιττότερα φιλούντων ὧν
ἤσθιον, ναῦς ἁλιέων ὤφθη παραπλέουσα. ἄνεμος μὲν
οὐκ ἦν, γαλήνη δὲ ἦν, καὶ ἐρέττειν ἐδόκει καὶ ἤρεττον
ἐρρωμένως· ἠπείγοντο γὰρ νεαλεῖς ἰχθῦς εἰς τὴν πόλιν
διασώσασθαι τῶν τινι πλουσίων. 2. οἷον οὖν εἰώθασι
ναῦται δρᾶν ἐς καμάτων ἀμέλειαν, τοῦτο κἀκεῖνοι
δρῶντες τὰς κώπας ἀνέφερον· εἷς μὲν αὐτοῖς κελευ-
στὴς ναυτικὰς ᾖδεν ᾠδάς, οἱ δὲ λοιποὶ καθάπερ χορὸς
ὁμοφώνως κατὰ καιρὸν τῆς ἐκείνου φωνῆς ἐβόων. 3.
ἡνίκα μὲν οὖν ἐν ἀναπεπταμένῃ τῇ θαλάσσῃ ταῦτα
ἔπραττον, ἠφανίζετο ἡ βοὴ χεομένης τῆς φωνῆς εἰς
πολὺν ἀέρα· ἐπεὶ δὲ ἄκρᾳ τινὶ ὑποδραμόντες εἰς κόλπον μηνοειδῆ καὶ κοῖλον εἰσήλασαν, μείζων μὲν ἠκούετο βοή, σαφῆ δὲ ἐξέπιπτεν εἰς τὴν γῆν τὰ τῶν
κελευστῶν[84] ᾄσματα. 4. κοῖλος γὰρ αὐλὼν[85] ὑπερκεί-

84 Cobet: κελευσμάτων V: λευκασμάτων F
85 Edmonds: τὸ πεδίον αὐλὼν V F

tant to pester Chloe for more than kissing and hugging: he
did not want her shouting at him as if he were an enemy, or
weeping as if in pain, or bleeding as if murdered. 2. This
was the first he had heard about the blood and he was
frightened, believing that surely blood comes only from a
wound. Having resolved to go on enjoying himself with her
in the usual ways, he left the woods and when he came to
where she sat plaiting a little garland of violets, he made up
a story about snatching the goose from the eagle's talons,
and then hugged her and kissed her the way he had kissed
Lycaenium at the height of his pleasure: that he could do
without risk. 3. She fitted the garland on his head and
kissed his hair, saying it was better than the violets, then
produced from her knapsack a piece of fruitcake and some
bread and gave it to him to eat. What he ate she snatched
from his mouth and ate it like a baby bird.

While they were eating, and doing more kissing than
eating, a fishing boat came into view as it sailed by. There
was no wind and the sea was calm, so they had decided to
row and were rowing hard, since they were in a hurry to
deliver some newly caught fish to a certain rich man in the
city while it was fresh. 2. As they pulled their oars they did
what sailors typically do to take their minds off their toil:
one, acting as boatswain, sang sea shanties while the others
piped up in unison, like a chorus, at the prompting of his
voice. 3. As long as they did this on the open sea, the noise
vanished as their voices were dispersed over an expanse of
air, but when they rounded a given cape and rowed into a
crescent-shaped and hill-rimmed bay, the noise was am-
plified and the boatswains' shanties carried clearly to the
land. 4. For situated above was a hill-rimmed glen that re-

21

μένος[86] καὶ τὸν ἦχον εἰς αὑτὸν ὡς ὄργανον δεχόμενος
πάντων τῶν λεγομένων μιμητὴν φωνὴν ἀπεδίδου, ἰδίᾳ
μὲν τῶν κωπῶν τὸν ἦχον, ἰδίᾳ δὲ τὴν φωνὴν τῶν
ναυτῶν, καὶ ἐγίνετο ἄκουσμα τερπνόν. φθανούσης γὰρ
τῆς ἀπὸ τῆς θαλάσσης φωνῆς ἡ ἐκ τῆς γῆς φωνὴ
τοσοῦτον ἐπαύετο βράδιον ὅσον ἤρξατο.

22   Ὁ μὲν οὖν Δάφνις εἰδὼς τὸ πραττόμενον μόνῃ τῇ
θαλάσσῃ προσεῖχε καὶ ἐτέρπετο τῇ νηὶ παρατρε-
χούσῃ τὸ πεδίον θᾶττον πτεροῦ καὶ ἐπειρᾶτό τινα
διασώσασθαι τῶν ᾀσμάτων, ὡς γένοιτο τῆς σύριγγος
μέλη· 2. ἡ δὲ Χλόη, τότε πρῶτον πειρωμένη τῆς
καλουμένης ἠχοῦς, ποτὲ μὲν εἰς τὴν θάλασσαν ἀπ-
έβλεπε τῶν ναυτῶν κελευόντων, ποτὲ δὲ εἰς τὴν ὕλην[87]
ὑπέστρεφε ζητοῦσα τοὺς ἀντιφωνοῦντας. 3. καὶ ἐπεὶ
παραπλευσάντων ἦν κἂν τῷ αὐλῶνι σιγή, ἐπυνθάνετο
τοῦ Δάφνιδος εἰ καὶ ὀπίσω τῆς ἄκρας ἐστὶ θάλασσα
καὶ ναῦς ἄλλη παραπλεῖ καὶ ἄλλοι ναῦται τὰ αὐτὰ
ᾖδον καὶ ἅμα πάντες σιωπῶσι. 4. γελάσας οὖν ὁ
Δάφνις ἡδὺ καὶ φιλήσας ἥδιον φίλημα καὶ τὸν τῶν
ἴων στέφανον ἐκείνῃ περιθεὶς ἤρξατο αὐτῇ μυθολογεῖν
τὸν μῦθον τῆς Ἠχοῦς, αἰτήσας εἰ διδάξειε μισθὸν
παρ᾽ αὐτῆς ἄλλα φιλήματα δέκα.

23   "Νυμφῶν, ὦ κόρη, πολὺ γένος, Μελίαι καὶ[88] Δρυ-
άδες καὶ Ἕλειοι, πᾶσαι καλαί, πᾶσαι μουσικαί. μιᾶς
τούτων θυγάτηρ Ἠχὼ γίνεται, θνητὴ μὲν ὡς ἐκ πατρὸς
θνητοῦ, καλὴ δὲ ὡς ἐκ μητρὸς καλῆς. 2. τρέφεται μὲν
ὑπὸ Νυμφῶν, παιδεύεται δὲ ὑπὸ Μουσῶν συρίζειν,
αὐλεῖν, ⟨ᾄδειν⟩[89] τὰ πρὸς λύραν, τὰ πρὸς κιθάραν,
πᾶσαν ᾠδήν· ὥστε καὶ παρθενίας εἰς ἄνθος ἀκμάσασα

---

86 ὑποκ- F   87 γῆν F   88 Μέλιαι καὶ Cobet:
μελικαὶ V: μέλι καὶ F   89 Suppl. Reeve

ceived the sound like a musical instrument and returned a voice that imitated everything that was said, the sound of the oars, the voices of the sailors, each distinct. It made for pleasant listening, the sound from the sea coming first, then the sound from the land ending as much later as it began.

Daphnis knew what was going on and fixed his atten- 22 tion on the sea, enjoying the boat as it scudded past the plain faster than a bird and trying to retain some of the songs so that they could be tunes for his syrinx. 2. But this was Chloe's first experience of what is called an echo, so she kept looking out to sea, where the sailors were calling the stroke, and then turning around toward the woods in search of the answering voices. 3. After they had sailed by and the glen was quiet, she asked Daphnis whether there was sea behind the cape too, with another ship sailing by and other sailors singing the same songs and all falling silent together. 4. Laughing sweetly and giving her an even sweeter kiss, Daphnis fitted the garland of violets on her and began to tell her the story of Echo, asking a fee of ten more kisses for teaching her.[42]

"Manifold is the race of Nymphs, my girl: there are 23 Meliae and Dryads and Heleii,[43] all beautiful, all musical. One of them had a daughter, Echo, mortal in having a mortal father but beautiful in having a beautiful mother. 2. She was brought up by Nymphs and taught by Muses to play the syrinx and the pipes, ‹to sing› tunes for the lyre, tunes for the cithara, every kind of song. So when she reached

---

[42] For the story cf. Ovid, *Met.* 3.356–401.

[43] Nymphs associated respectively with ash trees, oak trees, and marshes.

ταῖς Νύμφαις συνεχόρευε, ταῖς Μούσαις συνῇδεν. ἄρρενας δὲ ἔφευγε πάντας, καὶ ἀνθρώπους καὶ θεούς, φιλοῦσα τὴν παρθενίαν. 3. ὁ Πὰν ὀργίζεται τῇ κόρῃ, τῆς μουσικῆς φθονῶν, τοῦ κάλλους μὴ τυχών, καὶ μανίαν ἐμβάλλει τοῖς ποιμέσι καὶ τοῖς αἰπόλοις· οἱ δὲ ὥσπερ κύνες ἢ λύκοι διασπῶσιν αὐτὴν καὶ ῥίπτουσιν εἰς πᾶσαν τὴν γῆν ἔτι ᾄδοντα τὰ μέλη, 4. καὶ τὰ μέλη Γῆ χαριζομένη Νύμφαις ἔκρυψε πάντα καὶ ἐτήρησε τὴν μουσικὴν καὶ γνώμῃ Μουσῶν ἀφίησι φωνὴν καὶ μιμεῖται πάντα καθάπερ τότε ἡ κόρη, θεούς, ἀνθρώπους, ὄργανα, θηρία· μιμεῖται καὶ αὐτὸν συρίττοντα τὸν Πᾶνα, 5. ὁ δὲ ἀκούσας ἀναπηδᾷ καὶ διώκει κατὰ τῶν ὀρῶν οὐκ ἐρῶν τυχεῖν ἀλλ᾽ ἢ τοῦ μαθεῖν τίς ἐστιν ὁ λανθάνων μαθητής." ταῦτα μυθολογήσαντα τὸν Δάφνιν οὐ δέκα μόνον φιλήματα ἀλλὰ πάνυ πολλὰ κατεφίλησεν ἡ Χλόη· μικροῦ γὰρ καὶ τὰ αὐτὰ εἶπεν ἡ Ἠχὼ καθάπερ μαρτυροῦσα ὅτι μηδὲν ἐψεύσατο.

24   Θερμοτέρου δὲ καθ᾽ ἑκάστην ἡμέραν γινομένου τοῦ ἡλίου οἷα τοῦ μὲν ἦρος παυομένου, τοῦ δὲ θέρους ἀρχομένου, πάλιν αὐτοῖς ἐγίνοντο καιναὶ τέρψεις καὶ θέρειοι. 2. ὁ μὲν γὰρ ἐνήχετο ἐν τοῖς ποταμοῖς, ἡ δὲ ἐν ταῖς πηγαῖς ἐλούετο. ὁ μὲν ἐσύριζεν ἁμιλλώμενος πρὸς τὰς πίτυς, ἡ δὲ ᾖδε ταῖς ἀηδόσιν ἐρίζουσα. ἐθήρων ἀκρίδας λάλους, ἐλάμβανον τέττιγας ἠχοῦντας· ἄνθη συνέλεγον, δένδρα ἔσειον, ὀπώραν ἤσθιον. ἤδη ποτὲ καὶ γυμνοὶ συγκατεκλίθησαν καὶ ἓν δέρμα αἰγὸς ἐπεσύραντο, 3. καὶ ἐγένετο ἂν γυνὴ Χλόη ῥᾳδίως εἰ μὴ Δάφνιν ἐτάραξε τὸ αἷμα. ἀμέλει καὶ δεδοικὼς μὴ νικηθῇ τὸν λογισμόν ποτε πολλὰ γυμνοῦσθαι τὴν Χλόην οὐκ ἐπέτρεπεν, ὥστε ἐθαύμαζε μὲν ἡ Χλόη, τὴν δὲ αἰτίαν ᾐδεῖτο πυθέσθαι.

25   Ἐν τῷ θέρει τῷδε καὶ μνηστήρων πλῆθος ἦν περὶ τὴν Χλόην καὶ πολλοὶ πολλαχόθεν ἐφοίτων παρὰ τὸν

the flower of maidenhood she danced with the Nymphs, she sang with the Muses. She shunned all males, humans and gods alike, liking her maidenhood. 3. Pan grew angry with the girl, being jealous of her music and unsuccessful at winning her beauty. He afflicted the shepherds and goatherds with madness, and they tore her apart like dogs or wolves and scattered her limbs, still singing, over all the earth. 4. As a favor to Nymphs, Earth hid all her limbs and preserved their music, and by will of the Muses, she has a voice and imitates everything just as that girl once did: gods, humans, instruments, animals. She even imitates Pan himself as he plays the syrinx, 5. and when he hears her he jumps up and chases over the hills, yearning only to know who his invisible pupil is." When Daphnis finished this tale, Chloe gave not only ten but a great many kisses, for Echo had repeated virtually everything, as if to testify that he told no lies.

As the sun grew hotter by the day, spring winding down   24
and summer beginning, they again found new pleasures, summery ones. 2. He swam in the rivers, she bathed
in the springs. He played the syrinx in competition with
the pines, she sang in rivalry with the nightingales. They
hunted chattering locusts, caught noisy cicadas. They
picked flowers, shook trees, ate fruit. One day they even
lay down naked together and covered up with a single goatskin. 3. Chloe might easily have become a woman if the
thought of blood had not disturbed Daphnis. Indeed he
feared that some day his resolution might be overcome, so
he did not let Chloe take off her clothes very often. Chloe
wondered about this but was too modest to ask the reason
why.

This summer there was a throng of suitors around   25
Chloe. They came in great numbers from many places to

Δρύαντα πρὸς γάμον αἰτοῦντες αὐτήν, καὶ οἱ μέν τι
δῶρον ἔφερον, οἱ δὲ ἐπηγγέλλοντο μεγάλα εἰ ταύτης
τύχοιεν. 2. ἡ μὲν οὖν Νάπη ταῖς ἐλπίσιν ἐπαιρομένη
συνεβούλευεν ἐκδιδόναι τὴν Χλόην μηδὲ κατέχειν
οἴκοι πρὸς πλέον τηλικαύτην κόρην, ἢ τάχα μικρὸν
ὕστερον νέμουσα τὴν παρθενίαν ἀπολέσει καὶ ἄνδρα
ποιήσεταί τινα τῶν ποιμένων ἐπὶ μήλοις ἢ ῥόδοις,
ἀλλ᾽ ἐκείνην τε ποιῆσαι δέσποιναν οἰκίας καὶ αὐτοὺς
πολλὰ λαβόντας ἰδίῳ φυλάττειν αὐτὰ καὶ γνησίῳ
παιδίῳ (ἐγεγόνει δὲ αὐτοῖς ἄρρεν παιδίον οὐ πρὸ
πολλοῦ τινος)· 3. ὁ δὲ Δρύας ποτὲ μὲν ἐθέλγετο τοῖς
λεγομένοις, μείζονα γὰρ ἢ κατὰ ποιμαίνουσαν κόρην
δῶρα ὠνομάζετο παρ᾽ ἑκάστου, ποτὲ δέ, ⟨ἐννοήσας⟩[90]
ὡς κρείττων ἐστὶν ἡ παρθένος μνηστήρων γεωργῶν
καὶ ὡς εἴ ποτε τοὺς ἀληθινοὺς γονέας εὕροι μεγάλως
αὐτοὺς εὐδαίμονας θήσει, ἀνεβάλλετο τὴν ἀπόκρισιν
καὶ εἷλκε χρόνον ἐκ χρόνου καὶ ἐν τῷ τέως ἀπεκέρ-
δαινεν οὐκ ὀλίγα δῶρα. 4. ἡ μὲν δὴ μαθοῦσα λυπηρῶς
πάνυ διῆγε καὶ τὸν Δάφνιν ἐλάνθανεν ἐπὶ πολύ, λυπεῖν
οὐ θέλουσα· ὡς δὲ ἐλιπάρει καὶ ἐνέκειτο πυνθανόμενος
καὶ ἐλυπεῖτο μᾶλλον μὴ μανθάνων ἢ ἔμελλε μαθών,
πάντα αὐτῷ διηγεῖται, τοὺς μνηστευομένους ὡς πολλοὶ καὶ πλούσιοι, τοὺς λόγους οὓς ἡ Νάπη σπεύδουσα
τὸν γάμον ἔλεγεν, ὡς οὐκ ἀπείπατο Δρύας, ἀλλ᾽ εἰς τὸν
τρυγητὸν ἀναβέβληται.

26   Ἔκφρων ἐπὶ τούτοις ὁ Δάφνις γίνεται καὶ ἐδάκρυσε
καθήμενος, ἀποθανεῖσθαι μηκέτι νεμούσης Χλόης λέγων καὶ οὐκ αὐτὸς μόνος ἀλλὰ καὶ τὰ πρόβατα μετὰ
τοιοῦτον ποιμένα. εἶτα ἀνενεγκὼν ἐθάρρει καὶ πείσειν
ἐνενόει τὸν πατέρα καὶ ἕνα τῶν μνωμένων αὐτὸν

90 Add. Villoison

134

visit Dryas and ask for her hand in marriage. Some brought a present, some made big promises should they win her. 2. Nape was elated by the prospects; her advice was to marry Chloe off and not to keep a girl her age at home any longer, when pretty soon she would lose her maidenhood in the pasture and make a man of some shepherd in return for apples or roses. No, they should make her mistress of a household, get a windfall for themselves, and put it aside for their own natural child (a male child had been born to them not long before). 3. There were moments when Dryas was tempted by her rationale, since the gifts promised by each suitor exceeded the norm for a shepherd girl, but at other moments he thought that this maiden was too good for rustic suitors, and if she ever found her real parents she would make his family very well off. So he delayed his reply and played for time, and in the meantime he made no small profit in gifts. 4. When she heard about this she had a miserable time and managed to keep it from Daphnis for quite a while, not wanting to make him miserable. But he was insistent and pressed her for answers, and was more miserable not knowing than he would be if he knew, so she told him everything: that she had many rich suitors, the arguments Nape was using in her eagerness for the wedding, that Dryas had not said no but had put off his decision until the grape harvest.

At this Daphnis became distraught. He sat down and 26 burst into tears, saying that he would die if Chloe no longer grazed with him, and the sheep along with him, without such a shepherdess. Then he recovered and began to take heart, formed a plan to win over her father, started counting himself as one of the suitors, and was confident that he

ἠρίθμει καὶ πολὺ κρατήσειν ἤλπιζε τῶν ἄλλων. 2. ἓν
αὐτὸν ἐτάραττεν· οὐκ ἦν Λάμων πλούσιος[91]. τοῦτο
αὐτοῦ τὴν ἐλπίδα μόνον λεπτὴν εἰργάζετο. ὅμως δὲ
ἐδόκει μνᾶσθαι, καὶ τῇ Χλόῃ συνεδόκει. τῷ Λάμωνι
μὲν οὖν οὐδὲν ἐτόλμησεν εἰπεῖν, τῇ Μυρτάλῃ δὲ θαρ-
ρήσας καὶ τὸν ἔρωτα ἐμήνυσε καὶ περὶ τοῦ γάμου
λόγους προσήνεγκεν, ἡ δὲ τῷ Λάμωνι νύκτωρ ἐκοινώ-
σατο. 3. σκληρῶς δὲ ἐκείνου τὴν ἔντευξιν ἐνεγκόντος
καὶ λοιδορήσαντος εἰ παιδὶ θυγάτριον ποιμένων προ-
ξενεῖ μεγάλην ἐν τοῖς γνωρίσμασιν ἐπαγγελλομένῳ
τύχην, ὃς αὐτοὺς εὑρὼν τοὺς οἰκείους καὶ ἐλευθέρους
θήσει καὶ δεσπότας ἀγρῶν μειζόνων, ἡ Μυρτάλη διὰ
τὸν ἔρωτα φοβουμένη μὴ τελέως ἀπελπίσας ὁ Δάφνις
τὸν γάμον τολμήσῃ τι θανατῶδες ἄλλας αὐτῷ τῆς
ἀντιρρήσεως αἰτίας ἀπήγγειλε· 4. "πένητές ἐσμεν, ὦ
παῖ, καὶ δεόμεθα νύμφης φερούσης τι μᾶλλον· οἱ δὲ
πλούσιοι καὶ πλουσίων νυμφίων δεόμενοι. ἴθι δή,
πεῖσον Χλόην, ἡ δὲ τὸν πατέρα, μηδὲν αἰτεῖν μέγα καὶ
⟨δοῦναι⟩[92] γαμεῖν. πάντως δέ που κἀκείνη φιλεῖ σε καὶ
βούλεται συγκαθεύδειν πένητι καλῷ μᾶλλον ἢ πιθήκῳ
πλουσίῳ."

27   Μυρτάλη μὲν οὔποτε ἐλπίσασα Δρύαντα τούτοις
συντεθήσεσθαι μνηστῆρας ἔχοντα πλουσιωτέρους εὐπρεπῶς ᾤετο παρῃτῆσθαι τὸν γάμον, Δάφνις δὲ οὐκ
εἶχε μέμφεσθαι τὰ λελεγμένα. λειπόμενος δὲ πολὺ τῶν
αἰτουμένων τὸ σύνηθες ἐρασταῖς πενομένοις ἔπρατ-
τεν· ἐδάκρυε καὶ τὰς Νύμφας αὖθις ἐκάλει βοηθούς.
2. αἱ δὲ αὐτῷ καθεύδοντι νύκτωρ ἐν τοῖς αὐτοῖς ἐφίστανται σχήμασιν, ἐν οἷς καὶ πρότερον· ἔλεγε δὲ ἡ

___

91 πλούσιος V: πλούσιος ἀλλ᾽ οὐδὲ ἐλεύθερος εἰ καὶ
πλούσιος F   92 Add. Dalmeyda

would easily beat out the others. 2. One thing worried him: Lamo was not rich. This was the one factor that kept his hope slight. Even so, he thought that he should ask for her hand, and Chloe thought so too. He dared say nothing to Lamo but found the courage to reveal his love to Myrtale and to broach the subject of marriage, and that night she shared this with Lamo. 3. He adamantly rejected her advocacy and upbraided her for thinking to make a match between the daughter of shepherds and their son, who by his tokens was destined for great things and who, should he find his own family, would make the two of them free and masters of a larger spread. Because love was involved, Myrtale feared that if Daphnis' hope of marriage were completely disappointed he would do something lethal, so she gave him a different account of the rejection: 4. "We are poor people, my son, and look for a bride who will add some value, while they are rich and looking for rich bridegrooms. So come on, you convince Chloe, and get her to convince her father, to consent to the marriage without asking for a lot. I'm sure she loves you too and would rather sleep with a poor man who's handsome than a monkey who's rich."

Never expecting that Dryas would agree to this proposal as long as he had richer suitors, Myrtale thought that she had begged off the marriage in a plausible way, while Daphnis could find no fault with what she said. But falling far short of what he had asked, he did what penurious lovers usually do: he started to cry and appealed to the Nymphs once again for help. 2. As he slept that night they appeared to him in the same guise as before, and again it

27

πρεσβυτάτη πάλιν· "γάμου μὲν μέλει τῆς Χλόης ἄλλῳ
θεῷ, δῶρα δέ σοι δώσομεν ἡμεῖς ἃ θέλξει Δρύαντα. 3.
ἡ ναῦς ἡ τῶν Μηθυμναίων νεανίσκων, ἧς τὴν λύγον αἱ
σαί ποτε αἶγες κατέφαγον, ἡμέρᾳ μὲν ἐκείνῃ μακρὰν
τῆς γῆς ὑπηνέχθη πνεύματι, νυκτὸς δὲ πελαγίου ταρά-
ξαντος ἀνέμου τὴν θάλασσαν εἰς τὴν γῆν εἰς τὰς τῆς
ἄκρας πέτρας ἐξεβράσθη. 4. αὕτη μὲν οὖν διεφθάρη
καὶ <τὰ> πολλὰ τῶν ἐν αὐτῇ, βαλάντιον δὲ τρισχιλίων
δραχμῶν ὑπὸ τοῦ κύματος ἀπεπτύσθη καὶ κεῖται φυ-
κίοις κεκαλυμμένον πλησίον δελφῖνος νεκροῦ, δι' ὃν
οὐδεὶς οὐδὲ προσῆλθεν ὁδοιπόρος, τὸ δυσῶδες τῆς
σηπεδόνος παρατρέχων. 5. ἀλλὰ σὺ πρόσελθε καὶ
προσελθὼν ἀνελοῦ καὶ ἀνελόμενος δός. ἱκανόν σοι νῦν
δόξαι μὴ πένητι, χρόνῳ δὲ ὕστερον ἔσῃ καὶ πλούσιος."

28   Αἱ μὲν ταῦτα εἰποῦσαι τῇ νυκτὶ συναπῆλθον, γενομένης δὲ ἡμέρας ἀναπηδήσας ὁ Δάφνις περιχαρὴς
ἤλαυνε ῥοίζῳ πολλῷ τὰς αἶγας εἰς τὴν νομὴν καὶ τὴν
Χλόην φιλήσας καὶ τὰς Νύμφας προσκυνήσας κατῆλθεν ἐπὶ <τὴν> θάλασσαν ὡς περιρράνασθαι θέλων
καὶ ἐπὶ τῆς ψάμμου πλησίον τῆς κυματωγῆς ἐβάδιζε
ζητῶν τὰς τρισχιλίας. 2. ἔμελλε δὲ ἄρα οὐ πολὺν
κάματον ἕξειν· ὁ γὰρ δελφὶς οὐκ ἀγαθὸν ὀδωδὼς αὐτῷ
προσέπιπτεν ἐρριμμένος καὶ μυδῶν, οὗ τῇ σηπεδόνι
καθάπερ ἡγεμόνι χρώμενος ὁδοῦ προσῆλθέ τε εὐθὺς
καὶ τὰ φυκία ἀφελὼν εὑρίσκει τὸ βαλάντιον ἀργυρίου
μεστόν. 3. τοῦτο ἀνελόμενος καὶ εἰς τὴν πήραν ἐνθέμενος οὐ πρόσθεν ἀπῆλθε πρὶν τὰς Νύμφας εὐφη-
μῆσαι καὶ αὐτὴν τὴν θάλασσαν· καίπερ γὰρ αἰπόλος
ὤν, ἤδη καὶ τὴν θάλασσαν ἐνόμιζε τῆς γῆς γλυκυ-
τέραν ὡς εἰς τὸν γάμον αὐτῷ τὸν Χλόης συλλαμ-
βάνουσαν.

was the eldest who spoke: "Another god is in charge of Chloe's marriage, but we will give you presents that will entice Dryas. 3. The young Methymnaeans' boat, whose willow shoot your goats ate up, was blown far from land that day, but during the night an onshore wind churned the sea and the boat was cast ashore on the rocks of the cape. 4. The boat itself and most of its cargo were destroyed, but a purse containing three thousand drachmas was tossed up by the surf and is lying covered with seaweed beside a dead dolphin, so that no passerby has gone anywhere near it but gives it a wide berth because of the stench of the putrefaction. 5. But you approach it, and when you get there, retrieve it, and when you have retrieved it, make a present of it. It is enough for now that you not seem poor; in time you will actually be rich."

This said, they vanished with the night. At daybreak 28 Daphnis jumped up in high spirits and whistled loudly as he drove his goats to pasture. He gave Chloe a kiss and paid homage to the Nymphs, then went down to the sea as if wanting to have a splash and walked along the sand beside the breakers in search of the three thousand. 2. And apparently it would not take much effort, for the unpleasant odor of the beached and rotting dolphin assaulted him. Using its putrefaction to guide his way, he went straight to it, removed the seaweed, and found the purse full of money. 3. This he retrieved and put in his knapsack, and did not leave before praising the Nymphs' name and the sea itself, for though he was a goatherd he now thought the sea sweeter than the land, since it was the sea helping him marry Chloe.

29   Εἰλημμένος δὲ τῶν τρισχιλίων οὐκέτ᾽ ἔμελλεν ἀλλ᾽
ὡς πάντων ἀνθρώπων πλουσιώτατος, οὐ μόνον τῶν
ἐκεῖ γεωργῶν, αὐτίκα ἐλθὼν παρὰ τὴν Χλόην διηγεῖται τὸ ὄναρ, δείκνυσι τὸ βαλάντιον, κελεύει τὰς ἀγέλας φυλάττειν ἔστ᾽ ἂν ἐπανέλθῃ, καὶ συντείνας σοβεῖ
παρὰ τὸν Δρύαντα καὶ εὑρὼν πυρούς τινας ἁλωνο-
τριβοῦντα μετὰ τῆς Νάπης πάνυ θρασὺν ἐμβάλλει
λόγον περὶ γάμου· 2. "ἐμοὶ δὸς Χλόην γυναῖκα. ἐγὼ
καὶ θερίζειν[93] οἶδα καλῶς καὶ κλᾶν ἄμπελον καὶ φυτὰ
κατορύσσειν· οἶδα καὶ γῆν ἀροῦν καὶ λικμῆσαι πρὸς
ἄνεμον. ἀγέλην δὲ ὅπως νέμω μάρτυς Χλόη. πεντήκοντα αἶγας παραλαβὼν διπλασίονας πεποίηκα· ἔθρεψα καὶ τράγους μεγάλους καὶ καλούς, πρότερον δὲ
ἀλλοτρίοις τὰς αἶγας ὑπεβάλομεν. 3. ἀλλὰ καὶ νέος
εἰμὶ καὶ γείτων ὑμῖν ἄμεμπτος, καί με ἔθρεψεν αἲξ ὡς
Χλόην ὄις. τοσοῦτον δὲ τῶν ἄλλων κρατῶν οὐδὲ δώροις ἡττηθήσομαι· 4. ἐκεῖνοι δώσουσιν αἶγας καὶ
πρόβατα καὶ ζεῦγος ψωραλέων βοῶν καὶ σῖτον μηδὲ
ἀλεκτορίδας θρέψαι δυνάμενον, παρ᾽ ἐμοῦ δὲ αἵδε ὑμῖν
τρισχίλιαι. μόνον ἴστω τοῦτο μηδείς, μὴ Λάμων αὐτὸς
οὑμὸς πατήρ." ἅμα τε ἐδίδου καὶ περιβαλὼν κατεφίλει.

30   Οἱ δὲ παρ᾽ ἐλπίδα ἰδόντες τοσοῦτον ἀργύριον αὐτίκα τε δώσειν ἐπηγγέλλοντο τὴν Χλόην καὶ πείσειν
ὑπισχνοῦντο τὸν Λάμωνα. 2. ἡ μὲν δὴ Νάπη μετὰ τοῦ
Δάφνιδος αὐτοῦ μένουσα περιήλαυνε τὰς βοῦς καὶ
τοῖς τριβόλοις κατειργάζετο τὸν στάχυν· ὁ δὲ Δρύας
θησαυρίσας τὸ βαλάντιον ἔνθα ἀπέκειτο τὰ γνωρίσματα ταχὺς παρὰ τὸν Λάμωνα καὶ τὴν Μυρτάλην
ἐφέρετο μέλλων παρ᾽ αὐτῶν, τὸ καινότατον, μνᾶσθαι
νυμφίον· 3. εὑρὼν δὲ κἀκείνους κριθία μετροῦντας οὐ

93 Kairis: συρίζειν V F

With the three thousand in hand he waited no longer,   29
but feeling that he was the richest not only of the farmers
there but of all mankind, he went straight to Chloe, told
her about his dream, showed her the purse, told her to look
after the flocks until he got back, and bounded away to see
Dryas. He found him with Nape threshing some grain and
launched into a very bold proposal of marriage: 2. "Give
me Chloe as my wife. I know how to make a good harvest,
prune a vine, and plant trees. I know how to till the ground
and winnow in a wind, and Chloe can witness how I graze a
flock. I had fifty she-goats when I took over and doubled
their number. I have also raised nice big he-goats, where
before we used to mate our she-goats with other people's he-goats. 3. Furthermore, I am young and a faultless
neighbor to you, and a she-goat nursed me just as a ewe
nursed Chloe. In all this I outdo the others, and I will not
be beaten when it comes to gifts either: 4. they will offer
goats and sheep, a pair of mangy oxen, and grain that
couldn't even keep hens alive, while from me here's three
thousand for you. One thing: no one must know about this,
not even my own father Lamo." As he made the gift, he
hugged and kissed him.

At the unexpected sight of so much money they prom-   30
ised on the spot to give him Chloe and undertook to persuade Lamo. 2. Nape stayed there with Daphnis, driving
the oxen around and grinding the ears of corn under the
threshing boards, while Dryas stored the purse where the
tokens were kept and then hurried off to see Lamo and
Myrtale, intending something very novel: to ask for their
son's hand in marriage. 3. He found them measuring the

πρὸ πολλοῦ λελικμημένα ἀθύμως τε ἔχοντας ὅτι
μικροῦ δεῖν ὀλιγώτερα ἦν τῶν καταβληθέντων σπερ-
μάτων, ἐπ᾽ ἐκείνοις μὲν παρεμυθήσατο, κοινὴν ὁμο-
λογήσας αἰτίαν πανταχοῦ γεγονέναι, 4. τὸν δὲ Δάφνιν
ᾐτεῖτο Χλόη καὶ ἔλεγεν ὅτι πολλὰ ἄλλων διδόντων
οὐδὲν παρ᾽ αὐτῶν λήψεται, μᾶλλον δέ τι οἴκοθεν
αὐτοῖς ἐπιδώσει· συντεθράφθαι γὰρ ἀλλήλοις κἂν τῷ
νέμειν συνῆφθαι φιλίᾳ ῥᾳδίως λυθῆναι μὴ δυναμένῃ,
ἤδη δὲ καὶ ἡλικίαν ἔχειν ὡς συγκαθεύδειν μετ᾽ ἀλλήλων. 5. ὁ μὲν ταῦτα καὶ ἔτι πλείω ⟨τούτων⟩[94] ἔλεγεν,
οἷα τοῦ πεῖσαι λέγων ἆθλον ἔχων τὰς τρισχιλίας· ὁ δὲ
Λάμων μήτε πενίαν ἔτι προβάλλεσθαι δυνάμενος,
αὐτοὶ γὰρ οὐχ ὑπερηφάνουν, μήτε ἡλικίαν Δάφνιδος,
ἤδη γὰρ μειράκιον ἦν, τὸ μὲν ἀληθὲς οὐδ᾽ ὡς ἐξηγό-
ρευσεν, ὅτι κρείττων ἐστὶ τοιούτου γάμου, χρόνον δὲ
σιωπήσας ὀλίγον οὕτως ἀπεκρίνατο·

31   "Δίκαια ποιεῖτε τοὺς γείτονας προτιμῶντες τῶν
ξένων καὶ πενίας ἀγαθῆς πλοῦτον μὴ νομίζοντες
κρείττονα. ὁ Πὰν ὑμᾶς ἀντὶ τῶνδε καὶ αἱ Νύμφαι
φιλήσειαν. 2. ἐγὼ δὲ σπεύδω μὲν καὶ αὐτὸς τὸν γάμον
τοῦτον· καὶ γὰρ ἂν μαινοίμην εἰ μὴ γέρων τε[95] ὢν ἤδη
καὶ χειρὸς εἰς τὰ ἔργα δεόμενος περιττοτέρας ᾤμην[96]
καὶ τὸν ὑμέτερον οἶκον φίλον προσλαβεῖν ἀγαθόν τι
μέγα· 3. περισπούδαστος δὲ καὶ Χλόη, καλὴ καὶ
ὡραία κόρη καὶ πάντα ἀγαθή· δοῦλος δὲ ὢν οὐδενός
εἰμι τῶν ἐμῶν κύριος, ἀλλὰ δεῖ τὸν δεσπότην μαν-
θάνοντα ταῦτα συγχωρεῖν. φέρε οὖν ἀναβαλώμεθα
τὸν γάμον εἰς τὸ μετόπωρον· 4. ἀφίξεσθαι τότε λέγου-
σιν αὐτὸν οἱ παραγινόμενοι πρὸς ἡμᾶς ἐξ ἄστεος. τότε

---

[94] Add. Reeve   [95] Courier: εἰ μὴ γέροντες F: ἡμιγέ-
ρων τε V   [96] Courier: ὡς μὴ V F

barley that they too had just been winnowing and in low spirits because the barley was practically less than the seed that had been sown. He spoke comfortingly about this, saying that it was a common complaint everywhere. 4. Then he asked for Daphnis as a husband for Chloe, saying that while others were making large offers, he would accept nothing from them; instead, he would give Lamo and Myrtale some of his own property. After all, they had been brought up together and while grazing had been bonded by an affection that could not be easily broken; and now they were of an age to go to bed together. 5. He made these arguments and then some, as was natural for one whose prize for persuasion was three thousand. As an excuse Lamo could no longer plead poverty, since the other couple were not looking down on them, or Daphnis' age, since he was now a young man. Even so, he did not voice his true feeling, that Daphnis was too good for such a marriage, but after a brief silence he gave this answer:

"You are right to value neighbors over strangers and 31 not to think wealth better than honest poverty. For that may Pan and the Nymphs cherish you. 2. I'm eager for this marriage too: now that I'm an old man and need an extra hand for the work, I would be insane if I did not think it a great advantage to ally our households. 3. Besides, Chloe is much sought after too: she's a fine young girl and good at everything. But since I'm a slave without any authority over my affairs, my master has to be informed about this and give his consent. So look, let's postpone the wedding until the autumn: 4. the travelers from town say that he will be here at that time. Then they will be man and wife, but

ἔσονται ἀνὴρ καὶ γυνή· νῦν δὲ φιλείτωσαν ἀλλήλους
ὡς ἀδελφοί. ἴσθι μόνον, ὦ Δρύα, τοσοῦτον· σπεύδεις
περὶ μειράκιον κρεῖττον ἡμῶν." ὁ μὲν ταῦτα εἰπὼν
ἐφίλησέ τε αὐτὸν καὶ ὤρεξε πότον ἤδη μεσημβρίας
ἀκμαζούσης καὶ προύπεμψε μέχρι τινός, φιλοφρο-
νούμενος πάντα.

32   ὁ δὲ Δρύας οὐ παρέργως ἀκούσας τὸν ὕστερον
λόγον τοῦ Λάμωνος ἐφρόντιζε βαδίζων[97] καθ᾽ αὑτὸν
ὅστις ὁ Δάφνις. "ἐτράφη μὲν ὑπὸ αἰγὸς ὡς κηδομένων
θεῶν, ἔστι δὲ καλὸς καὶ οὐδὲν ἐοικὼς σιμῷ γέροντι καὶ
μαδώσῃ γυναικί. εὐπόρησε δὲ καὶ τρισχιλίων, ὅσον
οὐδὲ ἀχράδων εἰκὸς ἔχειν αἰπόλον. 2. ἆρα καὶ τοῦτον
ἐξέθηκέ τις ὡς Χλόην; ἆρα καὶ τοῦτον εὗρε Λάμων ὡς
ἐκείνην ἐγώ; ἆρα καὶ γνωρίσματα ὅμοια παρέκειτο
τοῖς εὑρεθεῖσιν ὑπ᾽ ἐμοῦ; ἂν ταῦτα ἀληθῆ φανῇ, καὶ
γένοιτο οὕτως[98], ὦ δέσποτα Πὰν καὶ Νύμφαι φίλαι,
τάχα οὗτος τοὺς ἰδίους εὑρὼν εὑρήσει τι καὶ τῶν
Χλόης ἀπορρήτων." 3. τοιαῦτα μὲν πρὸς αὑτὸν ἐφρόντιζε καὶ ὠνειροπόλει μέχρι τῆς ἅλω· ἐλθὼν δὲ ἐκεῖ καὶ
τὸν Δάφνιν μετέωρον πρὸς τὴν ἀκοὴν καταλαβὼν
ἀνέρρωσέ τε γαμβρὸν προσαγορεύσας καὶ τῷ μετο-
πώρῳ τοὺς γάμους θύσειν[99] ἐπαγγέλλεται δεξιάν τε
ἔδωκεν ὡς οὐδενὸς ἐσομένης ὅτι μὴ Δάφνιδος Χλόης.

33   Θᾶττον οὖν νοήματος, μηδὲν πιὼν μηδὲ φαγών,
παρὰ τὴν Χλόην κατέδραμε καὶ εὑρὼν αὐτὴν ἀμέλ-
γουσαν καὶ τυροποιοῦσαν τόν τε γάμον εὐηγγελίζετο
καὶ ὡς γυναῖκα λοιπὸν μὴ λανθάνων κατεφίλει καὶ
ἐκοινώνει τοῦ πόνου. 2. ἤμελγε μὲν εἰς γαυλοὺς τὸ

---

97 post βαδίζων usque ad 4.7.5 καὶ ἦν deest F
98 ἂν ταῦτα ἀληθῆ φανῇ, καὶ γένοιτο οὕτως Reeve: ἐὰν
ταῦτα οὕτως V   99 Elsner: θήσειν V

for now they must love one another like brother and sister. Here's one thing you should know, Dryas: the young man that you're promoting is a cut above the likes of us." With that, he kissed him and offered him a drink, for it was now high noon, and then walked him part of the way home, showing complete friendliness.

Dryas had not listened idly to Lamo's last remark, and 32 as he walked home he reflected about who Daphnis really was. "He was nursed by a she-goat, as if the gods cared about him. He's handsome and nothing like that pug-nosed old man and his balding wife. He got hold of three thousand, an amount a goatherd isn't likely to have even of wild pears. 2. Did someone expose him too, like Chloe? Did Lamo find him just as I found her? Were there tokens beside him like the ones I found? If this turns out to be true—and may it happen that way, master Pan and dear Nymphs—maybe when he discovers his own relations he will discover something about Chloe's mysterious circumstances too." 3. These were his reflections and daydreams all the way back to the threshing floor. When he got there, he bucked up Daphnis, who was anxiously awaiting the news, by addressing him as son-in-law, and promised that he would celebrate the wedding in autumn and, shaking his hand, that Chloe would belong to no one but Daphnis.

So quicker than a thought, and without stopping to eat 33 or drink, he ran back to Chloe and found her doing the milking and making cheese. He told her the good news and with no concealment kissed her as his bride-to-be, then pitched in with the work. 2. He milked the milk into the

γάλα, ἐνεπήγνυ δὲ ταρσοῖς τοὺς τυρούς, προσέβαλλε
ταῖς μητράσι τοὺς ἄρνας καὶ τοὺς ἐρίφους. καλῶς δὲ
ἐχόντων τούτων ἀπελούσαντο, ἐνέφαγον, ἔπιον, περι-
ήεσαν ζητοῦντες ὀπώραν ἀκμάζουσαν. 3. ἦν δὲ ἀφθονία πολλὴ διὰ τὸ τῆς ὥρας πάμφορον· πολλαὶ μὲν
ἀχράδες, πολλαὶ δὲ ὄχναι, πολλὰ δὲ μῆλα τὰ μὲν ἤδη
πεπτωκότα κάτω, τὰ δὲ ἔτι ἐπὶ τῶν φυτῶν, τὰ ἐπὶ τῆς
γῆς εὐωδέστερα, τὰ ἐπὶ τῶν κλάδων εὐανθέστερα· τὰ
μὲν οἷον οἶνος ἀπῶζε, τὰ δὲ οἷον χρυσὸς ἀπέλαμπε.
4. μία μηλέα τετρύγητο καὶ οὔτε καρπὸν εἶχεν οὔτε
φύλλον· γυμνοὶ πάντες ἦσαν οἱ κλάδοι· καὶ ἐν μῆλον
ἐπέττετο[100] ἐπ᾽ αὐτοῖς ἄκροις ἀκρότατον, μέγα καὶ
καλόν, καὶ τῶν πολλῶν τὴν εὐανθίαν ἐνίκα μόνον·
ἔδεισεν ὁ τρυγῶν ἀνελθεῖν καὶ ἠμέλησε καθελεῖν·
τάχα δὲ καὶ ἐφυλάττετο καλὸν μῆλον ἐρωτικῷ ποιμένι.

34   Τοῦτο τὸ μῆλον ὡς εἶδεν ὁ Δάφνις ὥρμα τρυγᾶν
ἀνελθὼν καὶ Χλόης κωλυούσης ἠμέλησεν. ἡ μὲν ἀμε-
ληθεῖσα ὀργισθεῖσα πρὸς τὰς ἀγέλας ἀπῆλθε, Δάφνις
δὲ ἀναδραμὼν ἐξίκετο τρυγῆσαι καὶ κομίσαι δῶρον
Χλόῃ καὶ λόγον τοιόνδε εἶπεν ὠργισμένῃ· "ὦ παρθένε,
τοῦτο τὸ μῆλον ἔφυσαν ὧραι καλαὶ καὶ φυτὸν καλὸν
ἔθρεψε πεπαίνοντος ἡλίου καὶ ἐτήρησε τύχη. 2. καὶ
οὐκ ἔμελλον αὐτὸ καταλιπεῖν ὀφθαλμοὺς ἔχων ἵνα
πέσῃ χαμαὶ καὶ ἢ ποίμνιον αὐτὸ πατήσῃ νεμόμενον ἢ
ἑρπετὸν φαρμάξῃ συρόμενον ἢ χρόνος δαπανήσῃ κείμενον, βλεπόμενον, ἐπαινούμενον. τοῦτο Ἀφροδίτη

---

100 Corais cl. Sapph. 105a (ἐρεύθεται): ἐπέττετο V: ἐπέκειτο
Villoison

44 This episode recalls a famous wedding song by Sappho (fr.
105a): for her bridegroom the bride has kept intact her virginity

pails, set the cheeses into baskets to harden, and put the lambs and kids under their mothers. When all this was in order, they had something to eat and drink, then walked about in search of ripe fruit. 3. There was a great abundance of it, since this was the most productive time of year: there were plenty of wild pears, plenty of cultivated pears, plenty of apples, some already fallen and some still on the trees. Those on the ground were more fragrant, those on the boughs more splendid; the former smelled like wine, the latter gleamed like gold. 4. One tree had been picked and wore neither fruit nor leaves; all of its boughs were bare. And one apple was ripening on its very topmost branches, a large fine one whose splendor by itself outshone many others put together. The picker had been afraid to climb up there and did not care to take it down. And maybe a fine apple was being reserved for a shepherd in love.[44]

When Daphnis spotted this apple he was eager to climb   34
up and pick it, and he ignored Chloe when she tried to stop him. Angry at being ignored, she went back to her flocks, while Daphnis climbed up and achieved his goal of picking the apple and bringing it to Chloe as a present. He spoke to her, angry as she was, this way: "Dear girl, fine seasons begot this apple, a fine tree nourished it under a ripening sun, and chance looked after it. 2. As long as I had eyes to see, I was not about to abandon it to fall to the ground, where a flock would trample it or a snake poison it or time waste it as it sat there being looked at and praised. This is what

"like a sweet apple ripening on the topmost bough, atop the very topmost, where the apple pickers have overlooked it, or no, not overlooked but were unable to reach it."

147

κάλλους ἔλαβεν ἆθλον· τοῦτο ἐγὼ σοὶ δίδωμι νικητή-
ριον. 3. ὁμοίους ἔχετε τοὺς[101] μάρτυρας· ἐκεῖνος ἦν
ποιμήν, αἰπόλος ἐγώ." ταῦτα εἰπὼν ἐντίθησι τοῖς κόλποις, ἡ δὲ ἐγγὺς γενόμενον κατεφίλησεν, ὥστε ὁ
Δάφνις οὐ μετέγνω τολμήσας ἀνελθεῖν εἰς τοσοῦτον
ὕψος. ἔλαβε γὰρ κρεῖττον καὶ χρυσοῦ μήλου φίλημα.

[101] ἔχετε τοὺς Cobet: ἔχομεν τοὺς σοὺς V

Aphrodite got as a beauty prize, and what I now give to you
as a victory prize. 3. You have the same sort of judges: that
one[45] was a shepherd, I am a goatherd." With these words
he put the apple into her bosom. As he came close, she
kissed him, so Daphnis did not regret daring to climb up so
high: he got a kiss that was better even than a golden apple.

45 Paris.

ΛΟΓΟΣ ΤΕΤΑΡΤΟΣ

1 Ἥκων δέ τις ἐκ τῆς Μιτυλήνης ὁμόδουλος τοῦ Λάμωνος ἤγγειλεν ὅτι ὀλίγον πρὸ τοῦ τρυγητοῦ ὁ δεσπότης ἀφίξεται μαθησόμενος μή τι τοὺς ἀγροὺς ὁ τῶν Μηθυμναίων ἐπίπλους ἐλυμήνατο. 2. ἤδη οὖν τοῦ θέρους ἀπιόντος καὶ τοῦ μετοπώρου προσιόντος παρεσκεύαζεν αὐτῷ τὴν καταγωγὴν ὁ Λάμων εἰς πᾶσαν θέας ἡδονήν· 3. πηγὰς ἐξεκάθαιρεν ὡς τὸ ὕδωρ καθαρὸν ἔχοιεν, τὴν κόπρον ἐξεφόρει τῆς αὐλῆς ὡς ἀπόζουσα μὴ διοχλοίη, τὸν παράδεισον ἐθεράπευεν ὡς ὀφθείη καλός.

2 Ἦν δὲ ὁ παράδεισος πάγκαλόν τι χρῆμα καὶ κατὰ τοὺς βασιλικούς. ἐκτέτατο μὲν εἰς σταδίου μῆκος, ἔκειτο δὲ ἐν χώρῳ μετεώρῳ, τὸ εὖρος ἔχων πλέθρων τεττάρων. 2. εἴκασεν ἄν τις αὐτὸν πεδίῳ μακρῷ. εἶχε δὲ πάντα δένδρα, μηλέας, μυρρίνας, ὄχνας καὶ ῥοιὰς καὶ συκᾶς καὶ ἐλαίας· ἑτέρωθι ἄμπελον ὑψηλήν, καὶ ἐπέκειτο ταῖς μηλέαις καὶ ταῖς ὄχναις περκάζουσα, καθάπερ αὐταῖς περὶ τοῦ καρποῦ προσερίζουσα. 3. τοσαῦτα ἥμερα. ἦσαν δὲ καὶ κυπάριττοι καὶ δάφναι καὶ πλάτανοι καὶ πίτυς. ταύταις πάσαις ἀντὶ τῆς ἀμπέλου κιττὸς ἐπέκειτο, καὶ ὁ κόρυμβος αὐτοῦ μέγας ὢν καὶ μελαινόμενος βότρυν ἐμιμεῖτο. 4. ἔνδον ἦν τὰ καρποφόρα φυτὰ καθάπερ φρουρούμενα· ἔξωθεν περιειστήκει τὰ ἄκαρπα καθάπερ θριγγὸς χειροποίητος,

46 The following description recollects oriental, especially

150

BOOK IV

One of Lamo's fellow slaves arrived from Mitylene with   1
the news that the master would be coming shortly before
the vintage to find out whether the Methymnaeans' raid
had done any damage to his lands. 2. Now that summer was
on its way out and autumn on its way in, Lamo began to
make his accommodations a pleasure to behold in every
way. 3. He cleaned out the springs so that their water
would be clean, carted the dung from the yard so that its
odor would not offend, and attended the park so that it
would look beautiful.

The park was a thing of consummate beauty even by   2
comparison with royal parks.[46] It was one stade long,[47] lay
on high ground, and was four plethra wide.[48] 2. One would
have compared it to a small plain. It had all sorts of trees:
apple, myrtle, pear, pomegranate, fig, and olive. On one
side was a towering vine that overspread the apple and
pear trees, its grapes darkening as if competing with them
in a contest of fruit. 3. These were the cultivated trees.
There were also cypresses, bays, planes, and pines. To
match the grape vine, ivy overspread all these, its large
darkening berries mimicking bunches of grapes. 4. The
fruit trees were on the inside as if under protection, and
on the outside the non-fruiting trees surrounded them

Persian, formal gardens, and recalls the garden of Alcinous in the
Odyssey.   [47] About 185 meters.   [48] About 120 meters.

καὶ ταῦτα μέντοι λεπτῆς αἱμασιᾶς περιέθει περίβολος.
5. τέτμητο καὶ διακέκριτο πάντα, καὶ στέλεχος στε-
λέχους ἀφειστήκει· ἐν μετεώρῳ δὲ οἱ κλάδοι συν-
έπιπτον ἀλλήλοις καὶ ἐπήλλαττον τὰς κόμας. ἐδόκει
μέντοι καὶ ἡ τούτων φύσις εἶναι τέχνης. 6. ἦσαν καὶ
ἀνθῶν πρασιαί, ὧν τὰ μὲν ἔφερεν ἡ γῆ, τὰ δὲ ἐποίει
τέχνη· ῥοδωνιαὶ καὶ ὑάκινθοι καὶ κρίνα χειρὸς ἔργα,
ἰωνιὰς καὶ ναρκίσσους καὶ ἀναγαλλίδας ἔφερεν ἡ γῆ.
σκιά τε ἦν θέρους καὶ ἦρος ἄνθη καὶ μετοπώρου
τρύγη[102] καὶ κατὰ πᾶσαν ὥραν ὀπώρα.

3   Ἐντεῦθεν εὔοπτον μὲν ἦν τὸ πεδίον καὶ ἦν ὁρᾶν
τοὺς νέμοντας, εὔοπτος δὲ ἡ θάλασσα καὶ ἑωρῶντο οἱ
παραπλέοντες· ὥστε καὶ ταῦτα μέρος ἐγίνετο τῆς ἐν τῷ
παραδείσῳ τρυφῆς. ἵνα τοῦ παραδείσου τὸ μεσαίτατον ἐπὶ μῆκος καὶ εὖρος ἦν, νεὼς Διονύσου καὶ
βωμὸς ἦν· περιεῖχε τὸν μὲν βωμὸν κιττός, τὸν νεὼν δὲ
κλήματα. 2. εἶχε δὲ καὶ ἔνδοθεν ὁ νεὼς Διονυσιακὰς
γραφάς· Σεμέλην τίκτουσαν, Ἀριάδνην καθεύδουσαν,
Λυκοῦργον δεδεμένον, Πενθέα διαιρούμενον· ἦσαν καὶ
Ἰνδοὶ νικώμενοι καὶ Τυρρηνοὶ μεταμορφούμενοι· πανταχοῦ Σάτυροι ⟨πατοῦντες⟩[103], πανταχοῦ Βάκχαι χο-

---

102 Jungermann: τρυφή V
103 Add. Schäfer

---

49 Semele, a Theban princess, was impregnated by Zeus and
then incinerated when she asked to see him undisguised; Zeus
rescued the fetal Dionysus and brought him to term sewn up in his
thigh.

50 Ariadne, daughter of King Minos of Crete, eloped with
Theseus after he had killed the Minotaur, was abandoned on
Naxos as she slept, and was carried off by Dionysus.

like an artificial fence, and around them in turn ran a deli-
cate stone wall. 5. All the trees were trimmed and spaced,
and each trunk stood apart from its neighbor, while over-
head the boughs met and entwined their foliage. Even
their natural growth looked like a work of art. 6. There
were flowerbeds too, some produced by the earth, others
by art: roses, hyacinths, and lilies were the work of human
hands, while the earth produced violets, daffodils, and
pimpernels. There was shade in summer, flowers in spring,
grapes for picking in autumn, and fruit in every season.

From this point there was a good view of the plain,   3
where those grazing their flocks could be seen, and a good
view of the sea, where those sailing along the coast were
in view, so that all this too was an aspect of the park's lux-
uriousness. At the very center of the park's length and
breadth was a shrine and altar of Dionysus; ivy covered the
altar, vine shoots the temple. 2. Inside, the temple had
paintings with Dionysiac themes: Semele in childbirth,[49]
Ariadne asleep,[50] Lycurgus in chains,[51] Pentheus being
torn asunder;[52] there were also Indians being conquered[53]
and Etruscans having their shapes changed;[54] everywhere
were satyrs ‹treading grapes›, everywhere maenads danc-

[51] King Lycurgus of Thrace opposed Dionysus and was bound
and torn apart by horses.   [52] King Pentheus of Thebes
opposed the advent of Dionysiac worship and was torn apart by
maenads, including his own mother.

[53] Dionysus, with Pan among his commanders, invaded India
after his successful campaigns in Greece.

[54] Etruscan pirates seized Dionysus as he sailed from Icaria to
Naxos, leaped overboard when his chains fell away and ivy
sprouted on the mast, and were transformed into dolphins.

ρεύουσαι. οὐδὲ ὁ Πὰν ἠμέλητο, ἐκαθέζετο δὲ καὶ αὐτὸς
συρίζων ἐπὶ πέτρας ὅμοιον ἐνδιδόντι κοινὸν μέλος καὶ
τοῖς πατοῦσι καὶ ταῖς χορευούσαις.

4　　Τοιοῦτον ὄντα τὸν παράδεισον ὁ Λάμων ἐθεράπευε,
τὰ ξηρὰ ἀποτέμνων, τὰ κλήματα ἀναλαμβάνων. τὸν
Διόνυσον ἐστεφάνωσε, τοῖς ἄνθεσιν ὕδωρ ἐπωχέτευ-
σεν ἐκ πηγῆς τινος ἦν[104] εὗρεν ἐς τὰ ἄνθη Δάφνις·
ἐσχόλαζε μὲν τοῖς ἄνθεσιν ὁ Λάμων, 2. παρεκελεύετο
δὲ καὶ τῷ Δάφνιδι[105] πιαίνειν τὰς αἶγας ὡς δυνατὸν
μάλιστα, πάντως που κἀκείνας λέγων ὄψεσθαι τὸν
δεσπότην ἀφικόμενον διὰ μακροῦ. 3. ὁ δὲ ἐθάρρει μὲν
ὡς ἐπαινεθησόμενος ἐπ᾿ αὐταῖς· διπλασίονάς τε γὰρ
ὧν ἔλαβεν ἐποίησε καὶ λύκος οὐδὲ μίαν ἥρπασε, καὶ
ἦσαν πιότεραι τῶν ὀΐων· βουλόμενος δὲ προθυμότερον
αὐτὸν γενέσθαι πρὸς τὸν γάμον πᾶσαν θεραπείαν καὶ
προθυμίαν προσέφερεν, ἄγων τε αὐτὰς πάνυ ἔωθεν καὶ
ἀπάγων τὸ δειλινόν. 4. δὶς ἡγεῖτο ἐπὶ ποτόν, ἀνεζήτει
τὰ εὐνομώτατα τῶν χωρίων· ἐμέλησεν αὐτῷ καὶ σκα-
φίδων καινῶν καὶ γαυλῶν πολλῶν καὶ ταρσῶν μειζόνων. τοσαύτη δὲ ἦν κηδεμονία ὥστε καὶ τὰ κέρατα
ἤλειφε καὶ τὰς τρίχας ἐθεράπευε· 5. Πανὸς ἄν τις ἱερὰν
ἀγέλην ἔδοξεν ὁρᾶν. ἐκοινώνει δὲ παντὸς εἰς αὐτὰς
καμάτου καὶ ἡ Χλόη καὶ τῆς ποίμνης παραμελοῦσα τὸ
πλέον ἐκείναις ἐσχόλαζεν, ὥστε ἐνόμιζεν ὁ Δάφνις δι᾿
ἐκείνην αὐτὰς φαίνεσθαι καλάς.

5　　Ἐν τούτοις οὖσιν αὐτοῖς δεύτερος ἄγγελος ἐλθὼν
ἐξ ἄστεος ἐκέλευσεν ἀποτρυγᾶν τὰς ἀμπέλους ὅτι
τάχιστα, καὶ αὐτὸς ἔφη παραμενεῖν ἔστ᾿ ἂν τοὺς
βότρυς ποιήσωσι γλεῦκος, εἶτα οὕτω κατελθὼν εἰς τὴν

---

[104] ἐκ πηγῆς τινος ἦν Brunck: πηγή τις ἦν V
[105] Christodoulou: ἐσχόλαζε μὲν ταῖς ἄνθεσιν ἡ πηγή,

ing. Nor was Pan neglected: he was there too, sitting on a
rock and playing the syrinx as if providing the music for
both the treaders and the dancers.

This was the park that Lamo started to put in order, cut- 4
ting away the dry wood, tying up the vine shoots. He put
a garland on Dionysus, and watered the flowers from a
spring that Daphnis had discovered for the flowers: Lamo
tended the flowers 2. and also urged Daphnis to fatten the
goats as much as he could, saying that the master would
surely inspect them, since he had not visited for so long.
3. Daphnis felt confident that he would be complimented
on that score: he had doubled the number that he had
taken over, no wolf had snatched even one, and they were
fatter than the sheep. But wanting the master to be enthu-
siastic for his marriage, he treated them with complete
care and attention, driving them out very early in the
morning and driving them back early in the evening. 4. He
led them to drink twice a day and looked for the best grazing spots. He took care to have new bowls, plenty of milk
pails, and larger cheese baskets, and he was so attentive
that he was even oiling their horns and combing their hair:
5. one would have thought it was Pan's sacred flock on view.
Chloe shared in all this work on them, neglecting her own
flock to tend to the goats, which made Daphnis think it was
her doing that they looked so fine.

While they were thus occupied a second messenger 5
came from town and told them to strip the vines as soon as
possible; he would remain on hand until they had turned
the clusters into new wine and only then return to the

Δάφνιδος δὲ ὅμως ἐκαλεῖτο πηγή. παρεκελεύετο δὲ καὶ τῷ
Δάφνιδι ὁ Λάμων V

155

πόλιν ἄξειν τὸν δεσπότην ⟨πεπαυμένης⟩[106] ἤδη τῆς
μετοπωρινῆς τρύγης. 2. τοῦτόν τε οὖν τὸν Εὔδρομον,
οὕτω γὰρ ἐκαλεῖτο, ὅτι ἦν αὐτῷ ἔργον τρέχειν, ἐδεξι-
οῦντο πᾶσαν δεξίωσιν καὶ ἅμα τὰς ἀμπέλους ἀπε-
τρύγων, τοὺς βότρυς ἐς τὰς ληνοὺς κομίζοντες, τὸ
γλεῦκος εἰς τοὺς πίθους φέροντες, τῶν βοτρύων τοὺς
ἡβῶντας ἐπὶ κλημάτων ἀφαιροῦντες, ὡς εἴη καὶ τοῖς
ἐκ τῆς πόλεως ἐλθοῦσιν ἐν εἰκόνι καὶ ἡδονῇ γενέσθαι
τρυγητοῦ.

6 Μέλλοντος δὲ ἤδη σοβεῖν ἐς ἄστυ τοῦ Εὐδρόμου,
καὶ ἄλλα μὲν οὐκ ὀλίγα αὐτῷ Δάφνις ἔδωκεν, ἔδωκε δὲ
καὶ ὅσα ἀπὸ αἰπολίου δῶρα, τυροὺς εὐπαγεῖς, ἔριφον
ὀψίγονον, δέρμα αἰγὸς λευκὸν καὶ λάσιον, ὡς ἔχοι
χειμῶνος ἐπιβάλλεσθαι τρέχων. 2. ὁ δὲ ἤδετο καὶ
ἐφίλει τὸν Δάφνιν καὶ ἀγαθόν τι ἐρεῖν περὶ αὐτοῦ πρὸς
τὸν δεσπότην ἐπηγγέλλετο. καὶ ὁ μὲν ἀπήει φίλα
φρονῶν, ὁ δὲ Δάφνις ἀγωνιῶν τῇ Χλόῃ συνένεμεν.
εἶχε δὲ κἀκείνη πολὺ δέος· μειράκιον γὰρ εἰωθὸς αἶγας
βλέπειν καὶ ὄρος καὶ γεωργοὺς καὶ Χλόην πρῶτον
ἔμελλεν ὄψεσθαι δεσπότην οὗ πρότερον μόνον ἤκουε
τὸ ὄνομα. 3. ὑπέρ τε οὖν τοῦ Δάφνιδος ἐφρόντιζεν
ὅπως ἐντεύξεται τῷ δεσπότῃ καὶ περὶ τοῦ γάμου τὴν
ψυχὴν ἐταράττετο μὴ μάτην ὀνειροπολοῦσιν αὐτόν.
συνεχῆ μὲν οὖν τὰ φιλήματα καὶ ὥσπερ συμπεφυ-
κότων αἱ περιβολαί, καὶ τὰ φιλήματα δειλὰ ἦν καὶ αἱ
περιβολαὶ σκυθρωπαὶ καθάπερ ἤδη παρόντα τὸν
δεσπότην φοβουμένων ἢ λανθανόντων. προσγίνεται
δέ τις αὐτοῖς καὶ τοιόσδε τάραχος.

7 Λάμπις τις ἦν ἀγέρωχος βουκόλος. οὗτος καὶ αὐτὸς

106 Add. Castiglioni

city to bring the master, when the autumn harvest ‹was over›. 2. So they very welcomingly welcomed this man Eudromus,[55] for that was his name, meaning that running was his job, and all the while kept on with the vine-stripping, taking the bunches to the presses, drawing off the new wine into the jars, and setting aside the prime bunches on the stem so that their visitors from the city too could experience the look and pleasure of a grape harvest.

When Eudromus was ready to hustle back to town, 6 Daphnis gave him a number of gifts, including the kind of gifts supplied by a herd of goats: firm cheeses, a kid born late in the year, a white woolly goatskin that he could throw on when running in winter. 2. He was delighted, kissed Daphnis, and promised to put in a good word for him with the master. He departed in a friendly mood, while Daphnis went on grazing with Chloe in an anxious frame of mind. She too was very apprehensive: he was a young man used to looking at goats, a mountain, country folk, and Chloe and was about to have his first sight of a master who until now had been merely a name. 3. So she worried for Daphnis' sake about the impression he would make on the master, and her heart was troubled by fear that their dream of marriage would never come true. So their kissing was continuous and their hugs were like fusion, but the kisses were timid and the hugs glum, as if the master were already there and they were afraid or shy of him. And then they were given yet another reason to feel troubled.

A certain Lampis[56] was a headstrong shepherd who was 7

---

[55] Not attested elsewhere, though the New Comic names Dromo and Dromio are similar.

[56] The name derives (ironically) from the verb "to shine."

ἐμνᾶτο τὴν Χλόην παρὰ τοῦ Δρύαντος καὶ δῶρα ἤδη
πολλὰ ἐδεδώκει σπεύδων τὸν γάμον. 2. αἰσθόμενος οὖν
ὡς εἰ συγχωρηθείη παρὰ τοῦ δεσπότου Δάφνις αὐτὴν
ἄξεται, τέχνην ἐζήτει δι᾽ ἧς τὸν δεσπότην αὐτοῖς
ποιήσειε πικρόν, καὶ εἰδὼς πάνυ αὐτὸν τῷ παραδείσῳ
τερπόμενον ἔγνω τοῦτον ὅσον οἷός τέ ἐστι διαφθεῖραι
καὶ ἀποκοσμῆσαι. 3. δένδρα μὲν οὖν τέμνων ἔμελλεν
ἁλώσεσθαι διὰ τὸν κτύπον, ἐπεῖχε δὲ τοῖς ἄνθεσιν
ὥστε διαφθεῖραι αὐτά. νύκτα δὴ φυλάξας καὶ ὑπερβὰς
τὴν αἱμασιὰν τὰ μὲν ἀνώρυξε, τὰ δὲ κατέκλασε, τὰ δὲ
κατεπάτησεν ὥσπερ σῦς. 4. καὶ ὁ μὲν λαθὼν ἀπελη-
λύθει, Λάμων δὲ τῆς ἐπιούσης παρελθὼν εἰς τὸν κῆπον
ἔμελλεν ὕδωρ αὐτοῖς ἐκ τῆς πηγῆς ἐπάξειν. 5. ἰδὼν δὲ
πᾶν τὸ χωρίον δεδῃωμένον καὶ ἔργον οἷον ἐχθρὸς οὐ
λῃστὴς ἐργάσαιτο, κατερρήξατο μὲν εὐθὺς τὸν χιτωνίσκον, βοῇ δὲ μεγάλῃ θεοὺς ἀνεκάλει, ὥστε καὶ ἡ
Μυρτάλη τὰ ἐν χερσὶ καταλιποῦσα ἐξέδραμε καὶ ὁ
Δάφνις ἐάσας τὰς αἶγας ἀνέδραμε, καὶ ἰδόντες ἐβόων
καὶ βοῶντες ἐδάκρυον.

8   Καὶ[107] ἦν μὲν καινὸν πένθος ἄνθων. ἀλλ᾽ οἱ μὲν
φοβούμενοι τὸν δεσπότην ἔκλαον, ἔκλαυσε δ᾽ ἄν τις
καὶ ξένος ἐπιστάς· ἀποκεκόσμητο γὰρ ὁ τόπος καὶ ἦν
λοιπὸν πᾶσα ἡ γῆ πηλώδης, τῶν δὲ εἴ τι διέφυγε τὴν
ὕβριν ὑπήνθει καὶ ἔλαμπε καὶ ἦν ἔτι καλὸν καὶ κείμενον. 2. ἐπέκειντο δὲ αὐτοῖς καὶ μέλιτται συνεχὲς καὶ
ἄπαυστον βομβοῦσαι καὶ θρηνούσαις ὅμοιον. ὁ μὲν
οὖν Λάμων ὑπ᾽ ἐκπλήξεως κἀκεῖνα ἔλεγε· 3. "φεῦ τῆς
ῥοδωνιᾶς, ὡς κατακέκλασται· φεῦ τῆς ἰωνιᾶς, ὡς πε-
πάτηται· φεῦ τῶν ὑακίνθων καὶ τῶν ναρκίσσων, οὓς
ἀνώρυξέ τις πονηρὸς ἄνθρωπος. ἀφίξεται τὸ ἦρ, τὰ δὲ

[107] Redit F

also asking Dryas for Chloe's hand and in his eagerness for the marriage had already given him lots of gifts. 2. So when he heard that Daphnis would marry her if he got his master's consent, he tried to think of a scheme to turn the master against them. Knowing that he took great pleasure in the park, he decided to ruin and deface it as much as he could. 3. If he tried to cut down trees, he would be caught because of the noise, so he targeted the flowers for destruction. He waited until nightfall, climbed over the wall, and dug some up, broke some off, and trampled the rest like a pig. 4. He got away unnoticed, but when Lamo arrived at the garden next morning to irrigate the flowers from the spring, 5. he saw the whole place devastated, more like the work of an enemy than a thief. He tore his tunic right off and with a great shout called on the gods. Myrtale dropped what she was doing and came running out, and Daphnis left his goats and came running up. They screamed when they saw it, and wept as they screamed.

This mourning for flowers was a novelty, but they were weeping in fear of the master, and even a stranger would have wept if he had been there: the place was thoroughly defaced and now all the ground was muddy, though any plant that had escaped the assault still kept some bloom, still shone, and still looked beautiful even on the ground. 2. The bees too still hung over them, buzzing continuously and without letup like mourners. In his shock Lamo even said, 3. "My poor rose bed, so broken down! My poor hyacinths and narcissi, that some troublemaker has uprooted! Spring will come, and they will not be flowering. It will be

8

οὐκ ἀνθήσει· ἔσται τὸ θέρος, τὰ δὲ οὐκ ἀκμάσει·
μετόπωρον ἄλλο, τὰ δὲ οὐδένα στεφανώσει. 4. οὐδὲ σύ,
δέσποτα Διόνυσε, τὰ ἄθλια ταῦτα ἠλέησας ἄνθη, οἷς
παρῴκεις καὶ ἔβλεπες, ἀφ᾽ ὧν ἐστεφάνωσά σε πολλάκις; πῶς δείξω νῦν τὸν παράδεισον τῷ δεσπότῃ; τίς
ἐκεῖνος θεασάμενος ἔσται; κρεμᾷ γέροντα ἄνθρωπον
ἐκ μιᾶς πίτυος ὡς Μαρσύαν, τάχα δὲ καὶ Δάφνιν, ὡς
τῶν αἰγῶν ταῦτα εἰργασμένων."

9   Δάκρυα ἦν ἐπὶ τούτοις θερμότερα, καὶ ἐθρήνουν οὐ
τὰ ἄνθη λοιπὸν ἀλλὰ τὰ αὑτῶν σώματα. ἐθρήνει καὶ
Χλόη Δάφνιν εἰ κρεμήσεται καὶ ηὔχετο μηκέτι ἐλθεῖν
τὸν δεσπότην αὐτῶν καὶ ἡμέρας διήντλει μοχθηρὰς ὡς
ἤδη Δάφνιν βλέπουσα μαστιγούμενον. 2. καὶ ἤδη
νυκτὸς ἀρχομένης ὁ Εὔδρομος αὐτοῖς ἀπήγγειλεν ὅτι
ὁ μὲν πρεσβύτερος δεσπότης μεθ᾽ ἡμέρας ἀφίξεται
τρεῖς, ὁ δὲ παῖς αὐτοῦ τῆς ἐπιούσης πρόεισι. 3. σκέψις
οὖν ἦν περὶ τῶν συμβεβηκότων, καὶ κοινωνὸν εἰς τὴν
γνώμην τὸν Εὔδρομον παρελάμβανον· ὁ δὲ εὔνους ὢν
τῷ Δάφνιδι παρῄνει τὸ συμβὰν ὁμολογῆσαι πρότερον
τῷ νέῳ δεσπότῃ καὶ αὐτὸς συμπράξειν ἐπηγγέλλετο
τιμώμενος ὡς ὁμογάλακτος. καὶ ἡμέρας γενομένης
οὕτως ἐποίησαν.

10   Ἧκε μὲν ὁ Ἄστυλος ἐφ᾽ ἵππου καὶ παράσιτος
αὐτοῦ, καὶ οὗτος ἐφ᾽ ἵππου, ὁ μὲν ἀρτιγένειος, ὁ δὲ
Γνάθων, τουτὶ γὰρ ἐκαλεῖτο, τὸν πώγωνα ξυρώμενος
πάλαι· ὁ δὲ Λάμων ἅμα τῇ Μυρτάλῃ καὶ τῷ Δάφνιδι
πρὸ τῶν ποδῶν αὐτοῦ καταπεσὼν ἱκέτευεν οἰκτεῖραι

---

57 A satyr who challenged Apollo to a musical contest and lost,
whereupon Apollo hung him from a tree and flayed him alive.
58 I.e. Eudromus' mother also nursed her mistress' baby.

summer, and they will not be in full bloom. There will be another autumn, but they will garland no one. 4. Did even you, Lord Dionysus, feel no pity for these sorrowful flowers? You were their neighbor and used to look at them, and many a time I used them to make garlands for you. How am I to show my park to the master now? How will he react when he sees it? He'll hang up an old fellow on one of the pines like Marsyas,[57] and maybe Daphnis too, if he thinks his goats did this."

After this their tears were more vehement, as now they were bewailing not the flowers but their own skins. Chloe bewailed Daphnis too, at the possibility that he might be hung up, and prayed that their master would not come after all. The days she endured were as miserable as if she could already see Daphnis being flogged. 2. One day as night was falling, Eudromus brought them news that the elder master would arrive in three days and that his son was coming ahead tomorrow. 3. So they reviewed what had happened and included Eudromus in their decision-making. Being fond of Daphnis, he advised them to admit everything to the young master beforehand and promised to help them personally, since he had influence as having been nursed at the same breast.[58] And next day they acted accordingly.

Astylus[59] arrived on horseback with his hanger-on, also on horseback. His first whiskers were just coming in, while Gnatho,[60] as the other one was called, had been shaving his beard for a while now. Lamo, along with Myrtale and Daphnis, fell at his feet and begged him to take pity on a

9

10

---

59 The name derives from *asty* "city."
60 "Jaws", a name typical of the comic "parasite."

γέροντα ἀτυχῆ καὶ πατρῴας ὀργῆς ἐξαρπάσαι τὸν
οὐδὲν ἀδικήσαντα, ἅμα τε αὐτῷ καταλέγει πάντα.
2. οἰκτείρει τὴν ἱκεσίαν ὁ Ἄστυλος καὶ ἐπὶ τὸν παράδεισον ἐλθὼν καὶ τὴν ἀπώλειαν τῶν ἀνθῶν ἰδὼν αὐτὸς
ἔφη παραιτήσεσθαι τὸν πατέρα καὶ κατηγορήσειν τῶν
ἵππων ὡς ἐκεῖ δεθέντες ἐξύβρισαν καὶ τὰ μὲν κατέκλασαν, τὰ δὲ κατεπάτησαν, τὰ δὲ ἀνώρυξαν λυθέντες. 3. ἐπὶ τούτοις ηὔχοντο μὲν αὐτῷ πάντα τὰ ἀγαθὰ
Λάμων καὶ Μυρτάλη, Δάφνις δὲ δῶρα προσεκόμισεν
ἐρίφους, τυρούς, ὄρνιθας καὶ τὰ ἔκγονα αὐτῶν, βότρυς
ἐπὶ κλημάτων, μῆλα ἐπὶ κλάδων. ἦν ἐν τοῖς δώροις καὶ
ἀνθοσμίας οἶνος· Λέσβιος ποθῆναι κάλλιστος οἶνος.

11   Ὁ μὲν δὴ Ἄστυλος ἐπῄνει ταῦτα καὶ περὶ θήραν
εἶχε λαγῶν, οἷα πλούσιος νεανίσκος καὶ τρυφῶν ἀεὶ
καὶ ἀφιγμένος εἰς τὸν ἀγρὸν εἰς ἀπόλαυσιν ξένης
ἡδονῆς· 2. ὁ δὲ Γνάθων, οἷα μαθὼν ἐσθίειν ἄνθρωπος
καὶ πίνειν εἰς μέθην καὶ λαγνεύειν μετὰ τὴν μέθην καὶ
οὐδὲν ἄλλο ὢν ἢ γνάθος καὶ γαστὴρ καὶ τὰ ὑπὸ
γαστέρα, οὐ παρέργως εἶδε τὸν Δάφνιν τὰ δῶρα
κομίσαντα, ἀλλὰ καὶ φύσει παιδεραστὴς ὢν καὶ κάλλος οἷον οὐδὲ ἐπὶ τῆς πόλεως εὑρὼν ἐπιθέσθαι διέγνω
τῷ Δάφνιδι καὶ πείσειν ᾤετο ῥᾳδίως ὡς αἰπόλον. 3.
γνοὺς δὲ ταῦτα θήρας μὲν οὐκ ἐκοινώνει τῷ Ἀστύλῳ,
κατιὼν δὲ ἵνα ἔνεμεν ὁ Δάφνις λόγῳ μὲν τῶν αἰγῶν, τὸ
δ' ἀληθὲς Δάφνιδος ἐγίνετο θεατής, μαλθάσσων δὲ
αὐτὸν τάς τε αἶγας ἐπῄνει καὶ συρίσαι τὸ αἰπολικὸν
ἠξίωσε καὶ ἔφη ταχέως ἐλεύθερον θήσειν τὸ πᾶν
δυνάμενος.

luckless old man and to rescue from his father's rage one who had done no wrong; at the same time he told him everything. 2. Astylus was moved to pity by this appeal. When he came to the park and saw the destruction of the flowers, he promised to intercede with his father and blame the horses, telling him that they had been tethered there and stampeded when they got loose, breaking down some of the flowers, trampling others, and uprooting the rest. 3. For this, Lamo and Myrtale wished him every blessing, and Daphnis brought him kids, cheeses, fowl and their chicks, grapes on the stem, and apples on the branch. Among the gifts was also wine with a floral bouquet: Lesbian wine makes the finest drinking.

Astylus expressed his appreciation for these gifts and 11 turned his attention to hunting hares, being a wealthy young man who spent all his time amusing himself and who was in the countryside to enjoy unfamiliar pleasure, 2. while Gnatho, being a fellow who knew only eating, drinking until he was drunk, and fornicating after he was drunk, and who was no more than a mouth, a belly, and the parts below the belly, had taken more than a casual look at Daphnis when he brought the gifts: having an ingrained taste for boys, and having found beauty of a kind unknown even in the city, he decided to move on Daphnis and thought that a goatherd would be easy to seduce. 3. This being the plan, he did not go hunting with Astylus but went down to where Daphnis was grazing his herd, to look at the goats, he said, but actually to look at Daphnis. To soften him up, he complimented the goats and asked him to play the goatherd's tune on the syrinx, and he said that he would soon make him a free man, since he had the power to make anything happen.

12   Ὡς δὲ εἶδε χειροήθη, νύκτωρ λοχήσας ἐκ τῆς
νομῆς ἐλαύνοντα τὰς αἶγας πρῶτον μὲν ἐφίλησε
προσδραμών, εἶτα ὄπισθεν παρασχεῖν ⟨ἐδεῖτο⟩[108] τοιοῦτον οἷον αἱ αἶγες τοῖς τράγοις. 2. τοῦ δὲ βραδέως
νοήσαντος καὶ λέγοντος ὡς αἶγας μὲν βαίνειν τράγους καλόν, τράγον δὲ οὐπώποτέ τις εἶδε βαίνοντα
τράγον οὐδὲ κριὸν ἀντὶ τῶν οἴων κριὸν οὐδὲ ἀλεκτρυόνας ἀντὶ τῶν ἀλεκτορίδων ἀλεκτρυόνας, οἷός τε ἦν ὁ
Γνάθων βιάζεσθαι τὰς χεῖρας προσφέρων, 3. ὁ δὲ
μεθύοντα ἄνθρωπον καὶ ἑστῶτα μόλις παρωσάμενος
ἔσφηλεν εἰς τὴν γῆν καὶ ὥσπερ σκύλαξ ἀποδραμὼν
κείμενον κατέλιπεν, ἀνδρὸς οὐ παιδὸς ἐς χειραγωγίαν
δεόμενον, καὶ οὐκέτι προσίετο ὅλως ἀλλὰ ἄλλοτε ἄλλῃ
τὰς αἶγας ἔνεμεν, ἐκεῖνον μὲν φεύγων, Χλόην δὲ
τηρῶν. 4. οὐδὲ ὁ Γνάθων ἔτι περιειργάζετο καταμαθὼν
ὡς οὐ μόνον καλὸς ἀλλὰ καὶ ἰσχυρός ἐστιν, ἐπετήρει
δὲ καιρὸν διαλεχθῆναι περὶ αὐτοῦ τῷ Ἀστύλῳ καὶ
ἤλπιζε δῶρον αὐτὸν ἕξειν παρὰ τοῦ νεανίσκου πολλὰ
καὶ μεγάλα χαρίζεσθαι θέλοντος.

13   Τότε μὲν οὖν οὐκ ἠδυνήθη· προσῄει γὰρ ὁ Διονυσοφάνης ἅμα τῇ Κλεαρίστῃ, καὶ ἦν θόρυβος πολὺς
κτηνῶν, οἰκετῶν, ἀνδρῶν, γυναικῶν· μετὰ δὲ τοῦτο
συνέταττε λόγον καὶ ἐρωτικὸν καὶ μακρόν. 2. ἦν δὲ ὁ
Διονυσοφάνης μεσαιπόλιος μὲν ἤδη, μέγας δὲ καὶ
καλὸς καὶ μειρακίοις ἁμιλλᾶσθαι δυνάμενος, ἀλλὰ καὶ
πλούσιος ἐν ὀλίγοις καὶ χρηστὸς ὡς οὐδεὶς ἕτερος. 3.
οὗτος ἐλθὼν τῇ πρώτῃ μὲν ἡμέρᾳ θεοῖς ἔθυσεν ὅσοι

---

[108] Add. Edmonds

[61] "Dionysus Manifest." The name is attested in various
Greek cities.

Sizing up Daphnis as being amenable, he waylaid him 12 that evening as he drove his goats back from the pasture. First he ran up and gave him a kiss and then asked him to present his backside the way she-goats do for he-goats. 2. After a while Daphnis caught on and replied that while it was fine for he-goats to mount she-goats, no one had ever seen a he-goat mounting a he-goat, or a ram mounting a ram instead of the ewes, or roosters mounting roosters instead of the hens. At this, Gnatho grabbed him and was ready to resort to rape, 3. but since he was drunk and barely able to stand, Daphnis pushed him off and tripped him onto the ground, then ran off like a puppy and left him lying there needing a man, not a boy, to lend a hand. After that, Daphnis allowed him to come nowhere near him, but grazed his goats in different places, avoiding him and looking after Chloe. 4. Nor did Gnatho interfere with him again, having discovered that he was not merely handsome but also strong. So he looked for an opportunity to speak with Astylus about him, hoping to get him as a gift from the young man, who was often willing to do him big favors.

He could not do it just then, for Dionysophanes[61] was 13 arriving with Cleariste,[62] and there was a great hubbub of animals, servants, men, and women, but later on he began to compose a long speech about love. 2. Dionysophanes' hair was now turning grey, but he was tall, handsome, and capable of competing with any young man. Few men were as rich, and none as good. 3. On the first day of his visit he

[62] "Best Renown." The name, appropriate for an upper-class character, appears twice in Theocritus (2.74, 5.88) but is also widely attested as an actual name.

προεστᾶσιν ἀγροικίας, Δήμητρι καὶ Διονύσῳ καὶ
Πανὶ καὶ Νύμφαις, καὶ κοινὸν πᾶσι τοῖς παροῦσιν
ἔστησε κρατῆρα· ταῖς δὲ ἄλλαις ἡμέραις ἐπεσκόπει τὰ
τοῦ Λάμωνος ἔργα, 4. καὶ ὁρῶν τὰ μὲν πεδία ἐν
αὔλακι, τὰς δὲ ἀμπέλους ἐν κλήματι, τὸν δὲ παράδεισον ἐν κάλλει, περὶ γὰρ τῶν ἀνθῶν Ἄστυλος τὴν
αἰτίαν ἀνελάμβανεν, ἥδετο περιττῶς καὶ τὸν Λάμωνα
ἐπῄνει καὶ ἐλεύθερον ἀφήσειν ἐπηγγέλλετο. 5. κατ-
ῆλθε μετὰ ταῦτα καὶ εἰς τὸ αἰπόλιον τάς τε αἶγας
ὀψόμενος καὶ τὸν νέμοντα.

14   Χλόη μὲν οὖν εἰς τὴν ὕλην ἔφυγεν ὄχλον τοσοῦτον
αἰδεσθεῖσα καὶ φοβηθεῖσα, ὁ δὲ Δάφνις εἱστήκει
δέρμα λάσιον αἰγὸς ἐζωσμένος, πήραν νεορραφῆ κατὰ
τῶν ὤμων ἐξηρτημένος, κρατῶν ταῖς χερσὶν ἀμφο-
τέραις τῇ μὲν ἀρτιπαγεῖς τυρούς, τῇ δὲ ἐρίφους ἔτι
γαλαθηνούς. 2. εἴ ποτε Ἀπόλλων Λαομέδοντι θητεύων
ἐβουκόλησε, τοιόσδε ἦν οἷος τότε ὤφθη Δάφνις. αὐτὸς
μὲν οὖν εἶπεν οὐδὲν ἀλλ' ἐρυθήματος πλησθεὶς ἔνευσε
κάτω προτείνας τὰ δῶρα, ὁ δὲ Λάμων "οὗτος" εἶπε
"σοί, δέσποτα, τῶν αἰγῶν αἰπόλος. 3. σὺ μὲν ἐμοὶ
πεντήκοντα νέμειν δέδωκας καὶ δύο τράγους, οὗτος δέ
σοι πεποίηκεν ἑκατὸν καὶ δέκα τράγους. ὁρᾷς ὡς
λιπαραὶ καὶ τὰς τρίχας λάσιαι καὶ τὰ κέρατα ἄθραυ-
στοι; πεποίηκε δὲ αὐτὰς καὶ μουσικάς· σύριγγος γοῦν
ἀκούουσαι ποιοῦσι πάντα."

15   Παροῦσα δὴ τοῖς λεγομένοις ἡ Κλεαρίστη πεῖραν
ἐπεθύμησε τοῦ λεχθέντος λαβεῖν καὶ κελεύει τὸν
Δάφνιν ταῖς αἰξὶν οἷον εἴωθε συρίσαι καὶ ἐπαγγέλλεται συρίσαντι χαρίσασθαι χιτῶνα καὶ χλαῖναν καὶ
ὑποδήματα. 2. ὁ δὲ καθίσας αὐτοὺς ὥσπερ θέατρον

sacrificed to the gods of the countryside, Demeter, Dionysus, Pan, and the Nymphs, and set up a wine bowl for everyone in attendance to share. The following days he spent
inspecting Lamo's work. 4. When he saw the plains fur-
rowed, the vines in shoot, the park in its beauty (for Astylus
was taking responsibility for the flowers), he was extraordinarily pleased, complimented Lamo, and promised to
make him a free man. 5. Then he went down to the goat
pasture to look at the goats and their goatherd.

Chloe fled into the woods, embarrassed and frightened   14
at such a large crowd, but Daphnis stood there with a
shaggy goatskin around his waist, a newly sewn backpack
hanging from his shoulders, and both hands full: one held
freshly set cheeses, the other unweaned kids. 2. If ever
Apollo did herd cattle for Laomedon, he must have looked
just as Daphnis looked that day.[63] Daphnis said nothing,
but blushed deeply and kept his head down as he proffered
his gifts. It was Lamo who spoke: "Here, master, is the
herdsman of your goats. 3. You gave me fifty to graze, plus
two he-goats, but he has turned them into one hundred for
you, plus ten he-goats. Do you see how sleek they are, with
thick coats and unbroken horns? He has made them musical too: when they hear the syrinx they do everything he
wants."

Cleariste was present for these remarks and was eager   15
to put her claim to the test. She asked Daphnis to play his
syrinx for the goats as usual, and promised to give him a tunic, a cloak, and a pair of shoes in appreciation of his playing. 2. He made them sit down as in a theater, then stood

---

[63] Apollo served King Laomedon of Troy for a year after an
attempt to revolt from Zeus.

στὰς ὑπὸ τῇ φηγῷ καὶ ἐκ τῆς πήρας τὴν σύριγγα
προκομίσας πρῶτα μὲν ὀλίγον ἐνέπνευσε, καὶ αἱ αἶγες
ἔστησαν τὰς κεφαλὰς ἀράμεναι· εἶτα ἐνέπνευσε τὸ
νόμιον, καὶ αἱ αἶγες ἐνέμοντο νεύσασαι κάτω· αὖθις
λιγυρὸν ἐνέδωκε, καὶ ἀθρόαι κατεκλίθησαν· 3. ἐσύρισέ
τι καὶ ὀξὺ μέλος, αἱ δὲ ὥσπερ λύκου προσιόντος εἰς
τὴν ὕλην κατέφυγον· μετ' ὀλίγον ἀνακλητικὸν ἐφθέγ-
ξατο, καὶ ἐξελθοῦσαι τῆς ὕλης πλησίον αὐτοῦ τῶν
ποδῶν συνέδραμον. 4. οὐδὲ ἀνθρώπους οἰκέτας εἶδεν
ἄν τις οὕτω πειθομένους προστάγματι δεσπότου. οἵ τε
οὖν ἄλλοι πάντες ἐθαύμαζον καὶ πρὸ πάντων ἡ Κλεαρίστη, καὶ τὰ δῶρα ἀποδώσειν ὤμοσε καλῷ τε ὄντι
αἰπόλῳ καὶ μουσικῷ· καὶ ἀνελθόντες εἰς τὴν ἔπαυλιν
ἀμφὶ ἄριστον εἶχον καὶ τῷ Δάφνιδι ἀφ' ὧν ἤσθιον
ἔπεμψαν. ὁ δὲ μετὰ τῆς Χλόης ἤσθιε καὶ ἥδετο γευόμενος ἀστικῆς ὀψαρτυσίας καὶ εὔελπις ἦν τεύξεσθαι
τοῦ γάμου πείσας τοὺς δεσπότας.

16   Ὁ δὲ Γνάθων προσεκκαυθεὶς τοῖς κατὰ τὸ αἰπόλιον
γεγενημένοις καὶ ἀβίωτον νομίζων τὸν βίον εἰ μὴ
τεύξεται Δάφνιδος, περιπατοῦντα τὸν Ἄστυλον ἐν τῷ
παραδείσῳ φυλάξας καὶ ἀναγαγὼν εἰς τὸν τοῦ Διονύσου νεὼν πόδας καὶ χεῖρας κατεφίλει. 2. τοῦ δὲ
πυνθανομένου τίνος ἕνεκα ταῦτα δρᾷ καὶ λέγειν κελεύ-
οντος καὶ ὑπουργήσειν ὀμνύντος, "οἴχεταί σοι Γνάθων" ἔφη "δέσποτα. ὁ μέχρι νῦν μόνης τραπέζης τῆς
σῆς ἐρῶν, ὁ πρότερον ὀμνὺς ὅτι μηδέν ἐστιν ὡραι-
ότερον οἴνου γέροντος, ὁ κρείττους τῶν ἐφήβων τῶν ἐν
Μιτυλήνῃ τοὺς σοὺς ὀψαρτυτὰς λέγων, μόνον λοιπὸν
καλὸν εἶναι Δάφνιν νομίζω. 3. καὶ τροφῆς μὲν τῆς
πολυτελοῦς οὐ γεύομαι, καίτοι τοσούτων παρασκευ-
αζομένων ἑκάστης ἡμέρας κρεῶν, ἰχθύων, μελιτω-
μάτων, ἡδέως δ' ἂν αἶξ γενόμενος πόαν ἐσθίοιμι καὶ

under the oak tree and took his syrinx from his knapsack. First he played softly, and the goats stood still and lifted their heads. Then he played the grazing tune, and the goats lowered their heads and began to graze. Next he struck a limpid tone, and all together they lay down. 3. He piped something shrill, and they fled into the woods as if a wolf was coming. A little later he sounded the recall, and they came out of the woods and assembled at his feet. 4. No one ever saw even human servants so obedient to a master's command. Everyone was amazed, especially Cleariste, who swore that she would come through with the gifts, since he was a fine goatherd and musician. They went back up to the farmhouse for lunch and sent Daphnis some of what they were eating. He shared it with Chloe and enjoyed a taste of urban cuisine; and he felt confident that he would persuade his masters and win the marriage.

But Gnatho was further inflamed by what had happened in the goat pasture and thought his life not worth living unless he won Daphnis. So waiting for Astylus to take a stroll in the park, he took him into the shrine of Dionysus and started kissing his feet and hands. 2. Astylus asked why he was doing this and told him to speak up, swearing that he would help him out. "Your Gnatho's done for, master," he said. "I'm the one one who until now loved only your table, who used to swear that nothing has a more youthful bloom than old wine, who said that your chefs are choicer than any boys in Mytilene, but now I think Daphnis is finer than anything. 3. I have no taste for expensive food, even though there's so much meat, fish, honey cakes prepared every day. I would gladly become a she-goat and eat grass and leaves so long as I could listen to

φύλλα τῆς Δάφνιδος ἀκούων σύριγγος καὶ ὑπ' ἐκείνου
νεμόμενος. σὺ δὲ σῶσον Γνάθωνα τὸν σὸν καὶ τὸν
ἀήττητον Ἔρωτα νίκησον. 4. εἰ δὲ μή, σὲ[109] ἐπόμνυμι
τὸν ἐμὸν θεόν, ξιφίδιον λαβὼν καὶ ἐμπλήσας τὴν
γαστέρα τροφῆς ἐμαυτὸν ἀποκτενῶ πρὸ τῶν Δάφνιδος
θυρῶν, σὺ δὲ οὐκέτι καλέσεις Γναθωνάριον ὥσπερ
εἰώθεις παίζων ἀεί."

17   Οὐκ ἀντέσχε κλάοντι καὶ αὖθις τοὺς πόδας κατα-
φιλοῦντι νεανίσκος μεγαλόφρων καὶ οὐκ ἄπειρος ἐρωτικῆς λύπης, ἀλλ' αἰτήσειν αὐτὸν παρὰ τοῦ πατρὸς
ἐπηγγείλατο καὶ κομίσειν εἰς τὴν πόλιν αὐτῷ μὲν
δοῦλον, ἐκείνῳ δὲ ἐρώμενον. 2. εἰς ἐνθυμίαν[110] δὲ καὶ
αὐτὸν ἐκεῖνον θέλων προαγαγεῖν ἐπυνθάνετο μειδιῶν
εἰ οὐκ αἰσχύνεται Λάμωνος υἱὸν φιλῶν ἀλλὰ καὶ
σπουδάζει συγκατακλιθῆναι νέμοντι αἶγας μειρακίῳ,
καὶ ἅμα ὑπεκρίνετο τὴν τραγικὴν δυσωδίαν μυσάτ-
τεσθαι. 3. ὁ δέ, οἷα πᾶσαν ἐρωτικὴν μυθολογίαν ἐν
τοῖς τῶν ἀσώτων συμποσίοις πεπαιδευμένος, οὐκ ἀπὸ
σκοποῦ καὶ ὑπὲρ αὑτοῦ καὶ ὑπὲρ τοῦ Δάφνιδος ἔλεγεν·
"οὐδεὶς ταῦτα, δέσποτα, ἐραστὴς πολυπραγμονεῖ, ἀλλ'
ἐν οἵῳ ποτὲ ἂν σώματι εὕρῃ τὸ κάλλος ἑάλωκε. 4. διὰ
τοῦτο καὶ φυτοῦ τις ἠράσθη καὶ ποταμοῦ καὶ θηρίου.
καίτοι τίς οὐκ ἂν ἐραστὴν ἠλέησεν ὃν ἔδει φοβεῖσθαι
τὸν ἐρώμενον; ἐγὼ δὲ σώματος μὲν ἐρῶ δούλου, κάλλους δὲ ἐλευθέρου. 5. ὁρᾷς ὡς ὑακίνθῳ μὲν τὴν κόμην
ὁμοίαν ἔχει, λάμπουσι δὲ ὑπὸ ταῖς ὀφρύσιν οἱ ὀφθαλμοὶ καθάπερ ἐν χρυσῇ σφενδόνῃ ψηφίς, καὶ τὸ μὲν
πρόσωπον ἐρυθήματος μεστόν, τὸ δὲ στόμα λευκῶν
ὀδόντων ὥσπερ ἐλέφαντος; 6. τίς ἐκεῖθεν οὐκ ἂν εὔξαι-
το λαβεῖν ἐραστὴς γλυκέα[111] φιλήματα; εἰ δὲ νέμοντος

109 Villoison: σοὶ V F

Daphnis' syrinx and have him take me to pasture. Please rescue your own Gnatho, and defeat invincible Love! 4. Otherwise, I swear by you, my own god, that I will take a dagger, cram my belly with food, and kill myself on Daphnis' doorstep, and no more will you be calling me Gnathipoo, as you always did when you were kidding."

Astylus, a big-hearted young man and not unac- 17 quainted with love's painfulness, could not resist him as again he wept and covered his feet with kisses, but promised that he would ask his father to give him Daphnis to take to the city as his own slave and Gnatho's beloved. 2. Wanting to steer him toward having his own second thoughts, he asked with a smile whether he felt no shame to be in love with a son of Lamo and indeed eager to bed down with a young man who herded goats; as he said this he burlesqued disgust at the reek of goats. 3. But Gnatho, a veteran of debauched drinking parties, was well schooled in the whole of erotic mythology and did not miss the mark in defending both himself and Daphnis: "No lover worries about any of that, master: in whatever body he finds beauty, he is smitten all the same. 4. That is why people fall in love even with a plant or a river or a beast, though who would feel no pity for a lover who needed to fear his beloved? Mine is a case of love for the body of a slave but the beauty of a free man. 5. Do you see how his hair is like hyacinth, how his eyes shine beneath his brows like a gem set in gold, how his face is flush with pinkness and his mouth with teeth whiter than ivory? 6. What lover wouldn't pray to get sweet kisses from that mouth? If I've fallen for a

---

110 Piccolos: εὐθυμίαν V: ἐπιθυμίαν F
111 Schäfer: λευκὰ codd.

ἠράσθην, θεοὺς ἐμιμησάμην. βουκόλος ἦν Ἀγχίσης,
καὶ ἔσχεν αὐτὸν Ἀφροδίτη· αἶγας ἔνεμε Βράγχος, καὶ
Ἀπόλλων αὐτὸν ἐφίλησε· ποιμὴν ἦν Γανυμήδης, καὶ
αὐτὸν ὁ τῶν ὅλων βασιλεὺς ἥρπασε. 7. μὴ καταφρο-
νῶμεν παιδὸς ᾧ καὶ αἶγας ὡς ἐρώσας πειθομένας
εἴδομεν, ἀλλ᾽ εἰ ἔτι μένειν ἐπὶ γῆς ἐπιτρέπουσι τοιοῦτον κάλλος, χάριν ἔχωμεν τοῖς Διὸς ἀετοῖς."

18   Ἡδὺ γελάσας ὁ Ἄστυλος ἐπὶ τούτῳ μάλιστα τῷ
λεχθέντι καὶ ὡς μεγάλους ὁ Ἔρως ποιεῖ σοφιστὰς
εἰπὼν ἐπετήρει καιρὸν ἐν ᾧ τῷ πατρὶ περὶ Δάφνιδος
διαλέξεται. ἀκούσας δὲ τὰ λεχθέντα κρύφα πάντα ὁ
Εὔδρομος καὶ τὰ μὲν τὸν Δάφνιν φιλῶν ὡς ἀγαθὸν
νεανίσκον, τὰ δὲ ἀχθόμενος εἰ Γνάθωνος ἐμπαροίνημα
γενήσεται τοιοῦτον κάλλος, αὐτίκα καταλέγει πάντα
κἀκείνῳ καὶ Λάμωνι. 2. ὁ μὲν οὖν Δάφνις ἐκπλαγεὶς
ἐγίνωσκεν ἅμα τῇ Χλόῃ τολμῆσαι φυγεῖν ἢ ἀποθανεῖν
κοινωνὸν κἀκείνην λαβών, ὁ δὲ Λάμων προκαλευάμε-
νος ἔξω τῆς αὐλῆς τὴν Μυρτάλην "οἰχόμεθα" εἶπεν "ὦ
γύναι· ἥκει καιρὸς ἐκκαλύπτειν τὰ κρυπτά. 3. ἔρρει
μοι[112] δὲ αἱ αἶγες καὶ τὰ λοιπὰ πάντα· ἀλλὰ μὰ τὸν
Πᾶνα καὶ τὰς Νύμφας οὐδ᾽ εἰ μέλλω βοῦς φασὶν ἐν
αὐλίῳ καταλείπεσθαι τὴν Δάφνιδος τύχην ἥτις ἐστὶν
οὐ σιωπήσομαι, ἀλλὰ καὶ ὅτι εὗρον ἐκκείμενον ἐρῶ καὶ
ὅπως ⟨εὗρον ὑπὸ αἰγὸς⟩[113] τρεφόμενον μηνύσω καὶ
ὅσα εὗρον συνεκκείμενα δείξω. μαθέτω Γνάθων ὁ

112 Hirschig: ἔρημοι codd.
113 Suppl. Arnott

64 Anchises and Aphrodite were the parents of Aeneas, *Iliad*
5.312–13.

herdsman, I've followed the gods' example. Anchises was a cowherd, and Aphrodite took up with him;[64] Branchus grazed goats, and Apollo held him dear;[65] Ganymede was a shepherd, and the king of the universe snatched him.[66] 7. Let us not look down on a boy whom, as we have seen, even she-goats obey as if they were in love with him; no, we should instead be grateful to Zeus' eagles for allowing such beauty to remain on earth."

Astylus laughed gaily, particularly at this last remark, and said that Love makes great rhetoricians. He started looking for an opportunity to speak with his father about Daphnis. But Eudromus had eavesdropped on this whole conversation. He liked Daphnis, considering him a fine young man, and disliked the prospect of such beauty used for Gnatho's drunken enjoyment, so he immediately told Daphnis and Lamo everything. 2. Daphnis was appalled, and decided to risk running away with Chloe or to take her with him in death, but Lamo called Myrtale out of the yard and said, "We are done for, wife. The time has come to reveal our secrets. 3. My goats are clean gone along with everything else, but by Pan and the Nymphs I will not keep silent about Daphnis' true circumstances, even if it means I'll be left like the proverbial ox in a stall.[67] No, I will say that I found him abandoned, I will reveal how I found him being nursed by a she-goat, and I will show everything that I found abandoned with him. That scum Gnatho needs to

18

[65] Branchus, to whom Apollo gave the gift of prophecy, was the eponymous ancestor of a family of influential Milesian seers.
[66] Zeus' eagle carried off Ganymede to be Zeus' beloved and cupbearer to the Olympian gods.
[67] Of something useless.

173

μιαρὸς οἷος ὢν οἴων ἐρᾷ. παρασκεύαζέ μοι μόνον
εὐτρεπῆ τὰ γνωρίσματα."

19 Οἱ μὲν ταῦτα συνθέμενοι ἀπῆλθον εἴσω πάλιν, ὁ δὲ
Ἄστυλος σχολὴν ἄγοντι τῷ πατρὶ προσρυεὶς αἰτεῖ
τὸν Δάφνιν εἰς τὴν πόλιν καταγαγεῖν ὡς καλόν τε ὄντα
καὶ ἀγροικίας κρείττονα καὶ ταχέως ὑπὸ Γνάθωνος καὶ
τὰ ἀστικὰ διδαχθῆναι δυνάμενον. 2. χαίρων ὁ πατὴρ
δίδωσι καὶ μεταπεμψάμενος τὸν Λάμωνα καὶ τὴν Μυρτάλην εὐηγγελίζετο μὲν αὐτοῖς ὅτι Ἄστυλον θεραπεύ-
σει λοιπὸν ἀντὶ αἰγῶν καὶ τράγων Δάφνις, ἐπηγγέλλετο δὲ δύο ἀντ᾽ ἐκείνου δώσειν αὐτοῖς αἰπόλους. 3.
ἐνταῦθα ὁ Λάμων πάντων ἤδη συνερρυηκότων καὶ ὅτι
καλὸν ὁμόδουλον ἕξουσιν ἡδομένων αἰτήσας λόγον
ἤρξατο λέγειν· "ἄκουσον, ὦ δέσποτα, παρ᾽ ἀνδρὸς
γέροντος ἀληθῆ λόγον· ἐπόμνυμι δὲ τὸν Πᾶνα καὶ τὰς
Νύμφας ὡς οὐδὲν ψεύσομαι. 4. οὐκ εἰμὶ Δάφνιδος
πατήρ, οὐδ᾽ εὐτύχησέ ποτε Μυρτάλη μήτηρ γενέσθαι·
ἄλλοι πατέρες ἐξέθηκαν τοῦτο τὸ παιδίον, ἴσως παίδων πρεσβυτέρων ἅλις ἔχοντες, ἐγὼ δὲ εὗρον ἐκκείμενον καὶ ὑπὸ αἰγὸς ἐμῆς τρεφόμενον, ἣν καὶ ἀποθα-
νοῦσαν ἔθαψα ἐν τῷ περικήπῳ, φιλῶν ὅτι ἐποίησε
μητρὸς ἔργα. 5. εὗρον αὐτῷ καὶ γνωρίσματα συνεκκείμενα, ὁμολογῶ, δέσποτα, καὶ φυλάττω· τύχης γάρ
ἐστι μείζονος ἢ καθ᾽ ἡμᾶς σύμβολα. Ἀστύλου μὲν οὖν
εἶναι δοῦλον αὐτὸν οὐχ ὑπερηφανῶ, καλὸν οἰκέτην
καλοῦ καὶ ἀγαθοῦ δεσπότου, παροίνημα δὲ Γνάθωνος
οὐ δύναμαι περιιδεῖν γενόμενον, ὃς ἐς Μιτυλήνην
αὐτὸν ἄγειν ἐπὶ γυναικῶν ἔργα σπουδάζει."

20 Ὁ μὲν Λάμων ταῦτα εἰπὼν ἐσιώπησε καὶ πολλὰ
ἀφῆκε δάκρυα, τοῦ δὲ Γνάθωνος θρασυνομένου καὶ
πληγὰς ἀπειλοῦντος ὁ Διονυσοφάνης τοῖς εἰρημένοις

learn what he is and what he lusts for. Just get the tokens ready for me."

They agreed on this and went back inside, while Astylus 19 sidled up to his father when he was unoccupied and asked permission to take Daphnis back to the city, on the grounds that he was handsome and too good for the country, and could soon be taught urban ways by Gnatho. 2. His father gladly gave his assent, summoned Lamo and Myrtale, and told them the good news that Daphnis would henceforth be serving Astylus instead of she-goats and he-goats, and promised to give them two goatherds in his place. 3. All the slaves were now crowding around, pleased at the prospect of having such a handsome fellow slave, when Lamo asked permission to speak. "My lord," he began, "hear a true story from an old man; I swear by Pan and the Nymphs that I will tell no lies. 4. I am not Daphnis' father, nor has Myrtale ever had the luck to be a mother. Other parents abandoned this child, perhaps because they had enough older children, and I found him exposed and being suckled by a she-goat of mine; when she died I buried her in the garden around the house, feeling affection because she had done a mother's job. 5. I also found recognition tokens exposed with him: I admit I did, master, and I have kept them safe, because they are signs of circumstances higher than ours. So while I do not consider him too good to be Astylus' slave, a handsome servant for a handsome and good master, I cannot stand by and watch him be used for the drunken enjoyment of Gnatho, who is eager to take him to Mitylene for service as a woman."

With this Lamo fell silent and wept copiously, while 20 Gnatho kept up a bold front and threatened to beat him. Dionysophanes was astonished by what he had heard and

ἐκπλαγεὶς τὸν μὲν Γνάθωνα σιωπᾶν ἐκέλευσε σφόδρα
τὴν ὀφρὺν εἰς αὐτὸν τοξοποιήσας, τὸν δὲ Λάμωνα
πάλιν ἀνέκρινε καὶ παρεκελεύετο τἀληθῆ λέγειν μηδὲ
ὅμοια πλάττειν μύθοις ἐπὶ τῷ κατέχειν τὸν[114] υἱόν. 2.
ὡς δὲ ἀτενὴς ἦν καὶ κατὰ πάντων ὤμνυε θεῶν καὶ
ἐδίδου βασανίζειν αὐτὸν εἰ ψεύδεται, ⟨συγ⟩καθημέ-
νης[115] τῆς Κλεαρίστης ἐδοκίμαζε[116] τὰ λελεγμένα. "τί
δ' ἂν ἐψεύδετο Λάμων μέλλων ἀνθ' ἑνὸς δύο λαμβάνειν
αἰπόλους; πῶς δ' ἂν καὶ ταῦτα ἔπλασεν ἄγροικος; οὐ
γὰρ εὐθὺς ἦν ἄπιστον ἐκ τοιούτου γέροντος καὶ
μητρὸς εὐτελοῦς υἱὸν καλὸν οὕτω γενέσθαι;"

21   Ἐδόκει μὴ μαντεύεσθαι ἐπὶ πλέον ἀλλ' ἤδη τὰ
γνωρίσματα σκοπεῖν εἰ λαμπρᾶς καὶ ἐνδοξοτέρας
τύχης. ἀπῄει μὲν Μυρτάλη κομίσουσα πάντα φυλατ-
τόμενα ἐν πήρᾳ παλαιᾷ, 2. κομισθέντα δὲ πρῶτος
Διονυσοφάνης ἐπέβλεπε, καὶ ἰδὼν χλαμύδιον ἁλουρ-
γές, πόρπην χρυσήλατον, ξιφίδιον ἐλεφαντόκωπον,
μέγα βοήσας "ὦ Ζεῦ δέσποτα" καλεῖ τὴν γυναῖκα
θεασομένην. 3. ἡ δὲ ἰδοῦσα μέγα καὶ αὐτὴ βοᾷ· "φίλαι
Μοῖραι· οὐ ταῦτα ἡμεῖς συνεξεθήκαμεν ἰδίῳ παιδί; οὐκ
εἰς τούτους τοὺς ἀγροὺς κομίσουσαν Σωφροσύνην[117]
ἀπεστείλαμεν; οὐκ ἄλλα μὲν οὖν ἀλλ' αὐτὰ ταῦτα.
φίλε ἄνερ, ἡμέτερόν ἐστι τὸ παιδίον· σὸς υἱός ἐστι
Δάφνις καὶ πατρῴας ἔνεμεν αἶγας."

22   Ἔτι λεγούσης αὐτῆς καὶ τοῦ Διονυσοφάνους τὰ
γνωρίσματα φιλοῦντος καὶ ὑπὸ περιττῆς ἡδονῆς
δακρύοντος ὁ Ἄστυλος συνεὶς ὡς ἀδελφός ἐστι ῥίψας

114 Brunck: ὡς V F
115 Suppl. Boden
116 Reeve olim: ἐβασάνιζε codd.
117 Σωφρόνην Courier

with a severe frown told Gnatho to be quiet. He began to question Lamo again, and warned him to tell the truth and fabricate no mythic tales in order to keep hold of his son. 2. But Lamo stuck to his story, swore by all the gods, and offered himself for torture to show if he was lying. So with Cleariste sitting at his side, Dionysophanes examined the testimony. "Why should Lamo lie when he stands to get two goatherds for one? How could a yokel make this up? In fact, was it not incredible from the very start that such a handsome son could have sprung from this sort of old man and shabby mother?"

It seemed best to stop guessing and examine the tokens 21 now, to see if they bespoke an illustrious and more distinguished station. Myrtale went off to bring all the items, which were kept in an old knapsack, 2. and when they arrived Dionysophanes was the first to start looking through them. When he saw a little purple mantle, a golden clasp, and a little sword with an ivory hilt, he loudly shouted "Lord Zeus!" and told his wife to come look. 3. When she saw them, she herself loudly shouted "Dear Fates! Aren't these the things we left with our own child? Isn't this the farm where we told Sophrosyne[68] to take him? They're none other than those very things. Dear husband, the child is ours. Daphnis is your son, and he was tending his father's goats!"

While she was still speaking and Dionysophanes was 22 still kissing the tokens and weeping with excessive joy, Astylus realized that he had a brother and, throwing off his

---

[68] "Modesty", the name of a nurse in Aristaenetus 1.6 and probably derived from New Comedy; Sophrone (Courier's emendation) is a nurse-name in Menander and Terence.

θοἰμάτιον ἔθει κατὰ τοῦ παραδείσου πρῶτος τὸν
Δάφνιν φιλῆσαι θέλων. 2. ἰδὼν δὲ αὐτὸν ὁ Δάφνις
θέοντα μετὰ πολλῶν καὶ βοῶντα "Δάφνι", νομίσας ὅτι
συλλαβεῖν αὐτὸν βουλόμενος τρέχει, ῥίψας τὴν πήραν
καὶ τὴν σύριγγα πρὸς τὴν θάλασσαν ἐφέρετο ῥίψων
ἑαυτὸν ἀπὸ τῆς μεγάλης πέτρας· 3. καὶ ἴσως ἄν, τὸ
καινότατον, εὑρεθεὶς ἀπωλώλει Δάφνις εἰ μὴ συνεὶς ὁ
Ἄστυλος ἐβόα πάλιν· "στῆθι, Δάφνι, μηδὲν φοβηθῇς·
ἀδελφός εἰμί σου καὶ γονεῖς οἱ μέχρι νῦν δεσπόται.
4. νῦν ἡμῖν Λάμων τὴν αἶγα εἶπε καὶ τὰ γνωρίσματα
ἔδειξεν. ὅρα δὲ ἐπιστραφεὶς πῶς ἴασι φαιδροὶ καὶ
γελῶντες. ἀλλ᾽ ἐμὲ πρῶτον φίλησον. ὄμνυμι δὲ τὰς
Νύμφας ὡς οὐ ψεύδομαι."

23   Μόλις μετὰ τὸν ὅρκον ἔστη καὶ τὸν Ἄστυλον
τρέχοντα περιέμεινε καὶ προσελθόντα κατεφίλησεν. ἐν
ᾧ δὲ ἐκεῖνον ἐφίλει, πλῆθος τὸ λοιπὸν ἐπιρρεῖ θερα-
πόντων, θεραπαινῶν, αὐτὸς ὁ πατήρ, ἡ μήτηρ μετ᾽
αὐτοῦ. οὗτοι πάντες περιέβαλλον, κατεφίλουν, χαίροντες, κλάοντες. 2. ὁ δὲ τὸν πατέρα καὶ τὴν μητέρα
πρὸ τῶν ἄλλων ἐφιλοφρονεῖτο καὶ ὡς πάλαι εἰδὼς
προσεστερνίζετο καὶ ἐξελθεῖν τῶν περιβόλων οὐκ ἤθε-
λεν· οὕτω φύσις ταχέως πιστεύεται. ἐξελάθετο καὶ
Χλόης πρὸς ὀλίγον καὶ ἐλθὼν εἰς τὴν ἔπαυλιν ἐσθῆτά
τε ἔλαβε πολυτελῆ καὶ παρὰ τὸν πατέρα τὸν ἴδιον
καθεσθεὶς ἤκουεν αὐτοῦ λέγοντος οὕτως·

24   "Ἔγημα, ὦ παῖδες, κομιδῇ νέος, καὶ χρόνου διελθόντος πατὴρ ὡς ᾤμην εὐτυχὴς ἐγεγόνειν· ἐγένετο γάρ
μοι πρῶτος υἱὸς καὶ δευτέρα θυγάτηρ καὶ τρίτος
Ἄστυλος. ᾤμην ἱκανὸν εἶναι τὸ γένος καὶ γενόμενον
ἐπὶ πᾶσι τοῦτο τὸ παιδίον ἐξέθηκα, οὐ γνωρίσματα

cloak, started to run from the park, wanting to be the first to give Daphnis a kiss. 2. When Daphnis saw him running with a great throng and crying "Daphnis!", he thought he was running because he wanted to carry him off. He tossed his knapsack and his syrinx away and headed for the sea to throw himself from the big rock. 3. And Daphnis, by a most strange turn, might have been lost because he was found, had Astylus not understood and cried out again: "Hold on, Daphnis, don't be afraid! I am your brother and your masters up till now are your parents! 4. Lamo has just now told us about the she-goat and showed us the tokens. Turn around and look how they come beaming and laughing. Come on, give me the first kiss! I swear by the Nymphs that I'm not lying."

At this oath Daphnis reluctantly held up and waited   23 for Astylus to run to him, and gave him a kiss when he came up. While he was kissing him, the rest of the throng streamed up, servants, maids, his father himself and his mother with him. Everyone hugged and kissed him, rejoicing and weeping. 2. But he embraced his father and mother before anyone else, and hugged them to his breast as if he had known them all along, and did not want to leave their embraces: so quickly does nature convince us! For a moment he even forgot about Chloe and returned to the house, where he donned expensive clothes and sat by his proper father to hear the story that he told.

"My sons, I married quite young, and after a while I   24 became a happy father, or so I thought. First I had a son, second a daughter, and third was Astylus. I thought my family was large enough, and when this child came along on top of all the others I abandoned him, leaving these things with him not as tokens of identity but as funeral of-

ταῦτα συνεκθεὶς ἀλλ᾽ ἐντάφια. 2. τὰ δὲ τῆς Τύχης ἄλλα βουλεύματα. ὁ μὲν γὰρ πρεσβύτερος παῖς καὶ ἡ θυγάτηρ ὁμοίᾳ νόσῳ μιᾶς ἡμέρας ἀπώλοντο· σὺ δέ μοι προνοίᾳ θεῶν ἐσώθης ἵνα πλείους ἔχωμεν χειραγωγούς. 3. μήτ᾽ οὖν σύ μοι μνησικακήσῃς ποτὲ τῆς ἐκθέσεως, ἑκὼν γὰρ οὐκ ἐβουλευσάμην, μήτε σὺ λυπηθῇς, Ἄστυλε, μέρος ληψόμενος ἀντὶ πάσης τῆς οὐσίας, κρεῖττον γὰρ τοῖς εὖ φρονοῦσιν ἀδελφοῦ κτῆμα οὐδέν, ἀλλὰ φιλεῖτε ἀλλήλους[118] καὶ χρημάτων ἕνεκα καὶ βασιλεῦσιν ἐρίζετε. 4. πολλὴν μὲν γὰρ ἐγὼ ὑμῖν καταλείψω γῆν, πολλοὺς δὲ οἰκέτας δεξιούς, χρυσόν, ἄργυρον, ὅσα ἄλλα εὐδαιμόνων κτήματα. μόνον ἐξαίρετον τοῦτο Δάφνιδι τὸ χωρίον δίδωμι καὶ Λάμωνα καὶ Μυρτάλην καὶ τὰς αἶγας, ἃς αὐτὸς ἔνεμεν."

25   Ἔτι αὐτοῦ λέγοντος Δάφνις ἀναπηδήσας "καλῶς με," εἶπε "πάτερ, ἀνέμνησας. ἄπειμι τὰς αἶγας ἄξων ἐπὶ ποτόν, αἵ που νῦν διψῶσαι περιμένουσι τὴν σύριγγα τὴν ἐμήν, ἐγὼ δὲ ἐνταυθοῖ καθέζομαι." 2. ἡδὺ πάντες ἐξεγέλασαν ὅτι δεσπότης γεγενημένος ἔτι ἦν[119] αἰπόλος, κἀκείνας μὲν θεραπεύσων ἐπέμφθη τις ἄλλος, οἱ δὲ θύσαντες Διὶ Σωτῆρι συμπόσιον συνεκρότουν. εἰς τοῦτο τὸ συμπόσιον μόνος οὐχ ἧκε Γνάθων ἀλλὰ φοβούμενος ἐν τῷ νεῷ τοῦ Διονύσου καὶ τὴν ἡμέραν ἔμεινε καὶ τὴν νύκτα ὥσπερ ἱκέτης. 3. ταχείας δὲ φήμης εἰς πάντας ἐλθούσης ὅτι Διονυσοφάνης εὗρεν υἱὸν καὶ ὅτι Δάφνις ὁ αἰπόλος δεσπότης τῶν ἀγρῶν εὑρέθη, ἅμα ἕω συνέτρεχον ἄλλος ἀλλαχόθεν, τῷ μὲν μειρακίῳ συνηδόμενοι, τῷ δὲ πατρὶ αὐτοῦ δῶρα κομίζοντες· ἐν οἷς καὶ ὁ Δρύας πρῶτος ὁ τρέφων τὴν Χλόην.

---

118 κρεῖττον . . . ἀλλήλους habet O   119 θέλει εἶναι F

ferings. 2. But Fate had other plans: my elder son and my daughter perished of the same illness in a single day, but you were saved by the gods' providence so that we would have more hands to support us. 3. Please, never bear a grudge against me for that abandonment, and Astylus, please bear no resentment that you will receive a portion of my wealth instead of the whole: for sensible people, no possession is greater than a brother. Come, love one another, and as far as money is concerned you will rival even kings. 4. For I shall bequeath you land, many competent servants, gold, silver, everything else that fortunate people possess. Only I award this place exclusively to Daphnis, along with Lamo and Myrtale and the she-goats that he himself used to graze."

While he was still speaking, Daphnis jumped up and said, "You were right to remind me, father: I'm off to take the goats to drink; they must be getting thirsty, waiting around for that syrinx of mine while I'm sitting here." 2. They all had a pleasant laugh to think that though he had become a master he was still a goatherd. Someone else was sent to look after the goats, while they all made sacrifice to Zeus the Savior and got busy preparing a party. Gnatho was the only one who did not attend this party: he was frightened and spent the whole day and night in the shrine of Dionysus like a suppliant. 3. Word spread rapidly to everyone that Dionysophanes had discovered his son and Daphnis the goatherd was discovered to be the master of these farms. At daybreak people came from all over to congratulate the young man and bring presents for his father. First among them was Dryas, Chloe's foster father.

25

26 Ὁ δὲ Διονυσοφάνης κατεῖχε πάντας κοινωνοὺς μετὰ τὴν εὐφροσύνην καὶ τῆς ἑορτῆς ἐσομένους. παρεσκεύαστο δὲ πολὺς μὲν οἶνος, πολλὰ δὲ ἄλευρα, ὄρνιθες ἕλειοι, χοῖροι γαλαθηνοί, μελιτώματα ποικίλα· καὶ ἱερεῖα δὲ πολλὰ τοῖς ἐπιχωρίοις θεοῖς ἐθύετο. 2. ἐνταῦθα ὁ Δάφνις συναθροίσας πάντα τὰ ποιμενικὰ κτήματα διένειμεν ἀναθήματα τοῖς θεοῖς· τῷ Διονύσῳ μὲν ἀνέθηκε τὴν πήραν καὶ τὸ δέρμα, τῷ Πανὶ τὴν σύριγγα καὶ τὸν πλάγιον αὐλόν, τὴν καλαύροπα ταῖς Νύμφαις καὶ τοὺς γαυλοὺς οὓς αὐτὸς ἐτεκτήνατο. 3. οὕτω δὲ ἄρα τὸ σύνηθες ξενιζούσης εὐδαιμονίας τερπνότερόν ἐστιν ὥστε ἐδάκρυεν ἐφ᾽ ἑκάστῳ τούτων ἀπαλλασσόμενος[120] καὶ οὔτε τοὺς γαυλοὺς ἀνέθηκε πρὶν ἀμέλξαι οὔτε τὸ δέρμα πρὶν ἐνδύσασθαι οὔτε τὴν σύριγγα πρὶν συρίσαι, 4. ἀλλὰ καὶ ἐφίλησεν αὐτὰ πάντα καὶ τὰς αἶγας προσεῖπε καὶ τοὺς τράγους ἐκάλεσεν ὀνομαστί. τῆς μὲν γὰρ πηγῆς καὶ ἔπιεν ὅτι πολλάκις καὶ μετὰ Χλόης· οὔπω δὲ ὡμολόγει τὸν ἔρωτα, καιρὸν παραφυλάττων.

27 Ἐν ᾧ δὲ Δάφνις ἐν θυσίαις ἦν, τάδε γίνεται περὶ τὴν Χλόην. ἐκάθητο κλάουσα, τὰ πρόβατα νέμουσα, λέγουσα οἷα εἰκὸς ἦν· "ἐξελάθετό μου Δάφνις· ὀνειροπολεῖ γάμους πλουσίους. 2. τί γὰρ αὐτὸν ὀμνύειν ἀντὶ τῶν Νυμφῶν τὰς αἶγας ἐκέλευον; κατέλιπε ταύτας ὡς καὶ Χλόην. οὐδὲ θύων ταῖς Νύμφαις καὶ τῷ Πανὶ ἐπεθύμησεν ἰδεῖν Χλόην. εὗρεν ἴσως παρὰ τῇ μητρὶ θεραπαίνας ἐμοῦ κρείττονας. χαιρέτω· ἐγὼ δὲ οὐ ζήσομαι."

28 Τοιαῦτα λέγουσαν, ταῦτα ἐννοοῦσαν ὁ Λάμπις ὁ βουκόλος μετὰ χειρὸς γεωργικῆς ἐπιστὰς ἥρπασεν

---

[120] οὕτω . . . ἀπαλλασσόμενος (-ττ-) habet O

Dionysophanes kept them all there to share his good 26
cheer and then his feast. Wine was provided in abundance,
as was wheat-meal bread, waterfowl, suckling pigs, as-
sorted honeycakes; and many victims were sacrificed to
the local divinities. 2. Now Daphnis collected all of his pastoral possessions and distributed them among the gods as
dedications. To Dionysus he dedicated his knapsack and
his goatskin, to Pan his syrinx and his transverse flute, to
the Nymphs his staff and the milk pails that he had made
himself. 3. What is familiar so truly gives more pleasure
than alien prosperity that Daphnis wept over each of these
possessions as he parted with it, and he did not dedicate
the pails until he had done the milking, nor the goatskin
before he had put it on, nor the syrinx before he had played
it, 4. but he actually kissed them all, said a word to the she-
goats, and called the he-goats by name. He also drank from
the spring, as many a time he had done with Chloe. But he
did not as yet reveal his love, waiting for the right moment.

While Daphnis was busy with sacrifices, this is what 27
was happening with Chloe. She sat weeping, grazing her
sheep, and saying what could be expected: "Daphnis has
forgotten me. He is dreaming of a wealthy marriage. 2.
Why did I make him swear by the she-goats instead of the
Nymphs? He has deserted them as he has deserted Chloe.
Not even when he was sacrificing to the Nymphs and Pan
did he feel any desire to see Chloe. Maybe he has found
maids in his mother's service who are better than me.
Good-bye to him! I won't go on living."

While she was speaking and thinking this way, Lampis 28
the cowherd came up with a gang of farmhands and

αὐτὴν ὡς οὔτε Δάφνιδος ἔτι γαμήσοντος καὶ Δρύαντος
ἐκεῖνον ἀγαπήσοντος. ἡ μὲν οὖν ἐκομίζετο βοῶσα
ἐλεεινόν, τῶν δέ τις ἰδόντων ἐμήνυσε τῇ Νάπῃ κἀκείνη
τῷ Δρύαντι καὶ ὁ Δρύας τῷ Δάφνιδι. 2. ὁ δὲ ἔξω τῶν
φρενῶν γενόμενος οὔτε εἰπεῖν πρὸς τὸν πατέρα ἐτόλμα
καὶ καρτερεῖν μὴ δυνάμενος εἰς τὸν περίκηπον εἰσελ-
θὼν ὠδύρετο, "ὦ πικρᾶς ἀνευρέσεως" λέγων 3. "πόσον
ἦν μοι κρεῖττον νέμειν; πόσον ἤμην μακαριώτερος
δοῦλος ὤν. τότε ἔβλεπον Χλόην, τότε ἤ‹κουον Χλόης
λαλούσης›,[121] νῦν δὲ τὴν μὲν Λάμπις ἁρπάσας οἴχεται, νυκτὸς δὲ γενομένης ‹συγ›κοιμήσεται.[122] ἐγὼ δὲ
πίνω καὶ τρυφῶ καὶ μάτην τὸν Πᾶνα καὶ τὰς αἶγας[123]
ὤμοσα."

29   Ταῦτα τοῦ Δάφνιδος λέγοντος ἤκουσεν ὁ Γνάθων
ἐν τῷ παραδείσῳ λανθάνων, καὶ καιρὸν ἥκειν διαλ-
λαγῶν πρὸς αὐτὸν νομίζων τινὰς τῶν τοῦ Ἀστύλου
νεανίσκων προσλαβὼν μεταδιώκει τὸν Δρύαντα 2. καὶ
ἡγεῖσθαι κελεύσας ἐπὶ τὴν τοῦ Λάμπιδος ἔπαυλιν
συνέτεινε δρόμῳ καὶ καταλαβὼν ἄρτι εἰσ‹αγ›άγοντα
τὴν Χλόην ἐκείνην τε ἀφαιρεῖται καὶ ἀνθρώπους γεωργοὺς συνηλόησε πληγαῖς. 3. ἐσπούδαζε δὲ καὶ τὸν
Λάμπιν δήσας ἄγειν ὡς αἰχμάλωτον ἐκ πολέμου τινὸς
εἰ μὴ φθάσας ἀπέδρα. κατορθώσας δὲ τηλικοῦτον
ἔργον νυκτὸς ἀρχομένης ἐπανέρχεται 4. καὶ τὸν μὲν
Διονυσοφάνην εὑρίσκει καθεύδοντα, τὸν δὲ Δάφνιν
ἀγρυπνοῦντα καὶ ἔτι ἐν τῷ περικήπῳ δακρύοντα.
προσάγει δὴ τὴν Χλόην αὐτῷ καὶ διδοὺς διηγεῖται
πάντα καὶ δεῖται μηδὲν ἔτι μνησικακοῦντα δοῦλον
ἔχειν οὐκ ἄχρηστον μηδὲ ἀφελέσθαι τραπέζης μεθ' ἣν
τεθνήξεται λιμῷ. 5. ὁ δὲ ἰδὼν Χλόην καὶ ἔχων ἐν ταῖς

---

[121] Suppl. Hercher   [122] Suppl. Valckenaer

snatched her, assuming that Daphnis would no longer be marrying her and that Dryas would be glad to have him. So she was carried off wailing piteously, but one of the by-standers who saw what happened told Nape, and she told Dryas, and Dryas told Daphnis. 2. He was beside himself, and though he dared not speak to his father, he could not bear it and went into the garden to lament: "What a bitter recognition! 3. How much better off I was as a herdsman! How much happier as a slave! Then I could look at Chloe, then ‹I could listen to her chatter,› but now Lampis has snatched her away, and tonight he will sleep with her. And here I am drinking and living in luxury, and my oaths by Pan and the she-goats meant nothing."

Gnatho, who was hiding in the park, overheard   29 Daphnis' speech and thought an opportunity had come for reconciliation with him. He rounded up some of Astylus' boys and set off after Dryas. 2. Telling him to lead the way, he made for Lampis' farmhouse at a run, caught him just as he was taking Chloe inside, took her away from him, and gave those farmhands a sound thrashing. 3. He wanted to tie Lampis up and march him off like some prisoner of war, but Lampis got away. This great exploit accomplished, Gnatho returned at nightfall. 4. He found Dionysophanes already in bed, but Daphnis was sleepless and still weeping in the park. He took Chloe to him, and as he presented her he told the whole story and asked Daphnis to bear no fur-ther grudge but rather to treat him as a slave not without his uses and not to sever him from a table without which he would starve to death. 5. At the sight of Chloe, and the feel

---

χερσὶ Χλόην τῷ μὲν ὡς εὐεργέτῃ διηλλάττετο, τῇ δὲ
ὑπὲρ τῆς ἀμελείας ἀπελογεῖτο.

30   Βουλευομένοις δὲ αὐτοῖς ἐδόκει τὸν γάμον κρύ-
πτειν, ἔχειν δὲ κρύφα τὴν Χλόην πρὸς μόνην ὁμολο-
γήσαντα τὸν ἔρωτα τὴν μητέρα· ἀλλ' οὐ συνεχώρει
Δρύας, ἠξίου δὲ τῷ πατρὶ λέγειν καὶ πείσειν αὐτὸς
ἐπηγγέλλετο. 2. καὶ γενομένης ἡμέρας ἔχων ἐν τῇ
πήρᾳ τὰ γνωρίσματα πρόσεισι τῷ Διονυσοφάνει καὶ
τῇ Κλεαρίστῃ καθημένοις ἐν τῷ παραδείσῳ, παρῆν δὲ
καὶ ὁ Ἄστυλος καὶ αὐτὸς ὁ Δάφνις, καὶ σιωπῆς
γενομένης ἤρξατο λέγειν· 3. "ὁμοία με ἀνάγκη Λάμωνι
τὰ μέχρι νῦν ἄρρητα ἐκέλευσε λέγειν. Χλόην ταύτην
οὔτε ἐγέννησα οὔτε ἀνέθρεψα, ἀλλὰ ἐγέννησαν μὲν
ἄλλοι, κειμένην δὲ ἐν ἄντρῳ Νυμφῶν ἀνέτρεφεν ὄϊς. 4.
εἶδον τοῦτο αὐτὸς καὶ ἰδὼν ἐθαύμασα καὶ θαυμάσας
ἔθρεψα. μαρτυρεῖ μὲν καὶ τὸ κάλλος, ἔοικε γὰρ οὐδὲν
ἡμῖν, μαρτυρεῖ δὲ καὶ τὰ γνωρίσματα, πλουσιώτερα
γὰρ ἢ κατὰ ποιμένα. ἴδετε ταῦτα καὶ τοὺς προσ-
ήκοντας τῇ κόρῃ ζητήσατε ἂν ἀξία ποτὲ Δάφνιδος
φανῇ."

31   Τοῦτο οὔτε Δρύας ἀσκόπως ἔρριψεν οὔτε Διονυσοφάνης ἀμελῶς ἤκουσεν, ἀλλ' ἰδὼν εἰς τὸν Δάφνιν
καὶ ὁρῶν αὐτὸν χλωριῶντα καὶ κρύφα δακρύοντα
ταχέως ἐφώρασε τὸν ἔρωτα καὶ ὡς ὑπὲρ παιδὸς ἰδίου
μᾶλλον ἢ κόρης ἀλλοτρίας δεδοικὼς διὰ πάσης ἀκρι-
βείας ἤλεγχε τοὺς λόγους τοῦ Δρύαντος. 2. ἐπεὶ δὲ καὶ
τὰ γνωρίσματα εἶδε κομισθέντα, ‹τὰ› ὑποδήματα
‹τὰ› κατάχρυσα, τὰς περισκελίδας, τὴν μίτραν,
προσκαλεσάμενος τὴν Χλόην παρεκελεύετο θαρρεῖν
ὡς ἄνδρα μὲν ἔχουσαν ἤδη, ταχέως δὲ εὑρήσουσαν
καὶ τὸν πατέρα καὶ τὴν μητέρα. 3. καὶ τὴν μὲν ἡ
Κλεαρίστη παραλαβοῦσα ἐκόσμει λοιπὸν ὡς υἱοῦ

of Chloe in his arms, Daphnis reconciled with Gnatho as with a benefactor, and apologized to Chloe for his neglect.

In discussing the situation, they decided that Daphnis 30 should hide his intended marriage and take Chloe in secret, confessing his love only to his mother. But Dryas did not agree: he asked to speak with Daphnis' father and promised that he himself would persuade him. 2. Next morning, he packed the tokens in his knapsack and visited Dionysophanes and Cleariste as they sat in the park; Astylus was present, as was Daphnis himself. When they were quiet he began his speech: 3. "Like Lamo, I am forced to tell what has until now gone untold. Chloe here is not my daughter and I did not nurse her. She has other parents, and a ewe fed her as she lay in a cave of the Nymphs. 4. I saw this with my own eyes and was amazed at the sight, and in my amazement I reared her. Her beauty bears witness, for she looks nothing like us, and these tokens bear witness too, for they are more valuable than befits a shepherd. Look at them and try to find the girl's relations, in case she turns out to be a suitable match for Daphnis."

Dryas did not drop this last comment without pur- 31 pose nor did Dionysophanes listen carelessly. Glancing at Daphnis and seeing him turning pale and hiding tears, he was quick to sense love. More anxious about his own son than someone else's daughter, he began to test Dryas' statements with the utmost exactitude. 2. When he saw the tokens that had been brought, the gilded sandals, the anklets, the headband, he called Chloe to him and told her to take heart, because she now had a husband and would soon find her father and mother. 3. Cleariste took charge of Chloe and began to dress her for her future role as

γυναῖκα, τὸν δὲ Δάφνιν ὁ Διονυσοφάνης ἀναστήσας
μόνον ἀνέκρινεν εἰ παρθένος ἐστί· τοῦ δὲ ὀμόσαντος
μηδὲν γεγονέναι φιλήματος καὶ ὅρκων πλέον, ἡσθεὶς
ἐπὶ τῷ συμποσίῳ[124] κατέκλινεν αὐτούς.

32   Ἦν οὖν μαθεῖν οἷόν ἐστι τὸ κάλλος ὅταν κόσμον
προσλάβηται. ἐνδυθεῖσα γὰρ ἡ Χλόη καὶ ἀναπλε-
ξαμένη τὴν κόμην καὶ ἀπολούσασα τὸ πρόσωπον
εὐμορφοτέρα τοσοῦτον ἐφάνη πᾶσιν ὥστε καὶ Δάφνις
αὐτὴν μόλις ἐγνώρισεν. 2. ὤμοσεν ἄν τις καὶ ἄνευ τῶν
γνωρισμάτων ὅτι τοιαύτης κόρης Δρύας οὐκ ἦν πατήρ. ὅμως μέντοι παρῆν καὶ αὐτὸς καὶ συνειστιᾶτο
μετὰ τῆς Νάπης, συμπότας ἔχων ἐπὶ κλίνης ἰδίας τὸν
Λάμωνα καὶ τὴν Μυρτάλην. 3. πάλιν οὖν ταῖς ἑξῆς
ἡμέραις ἐθύετο ἱερεῖα καὶ κρατῆρες ἵσταντο, καὶ ἀν-
ετίθει καὶ Χλόη τὰ ἑαυτῆς, τὴν σύριγγα, τὴν πήραν, τὸ
δέρμα, τοὺς γαυλούς· ἐκέρασε καὶ τὴν πηγὴν οἴνῳ τὴν
ἐν τῷ ἄντρῳ ὅτι καὶ ἐτράφη παρ᾽ αὐτῇ καὶ ἐλούσατο
πολλάκις ἐν αὐτῇ· 4. ἐστεφάνωσε καὶ τὸν τάφον τῆς
οἶος δείξαντος Δρύαντος καὶ ἐσύρισέ τι καὶ αὐτὴ τῇ
ποίμνῃ καὶ συρίσασα ταῖς θεαῖς ηὔξατο τοὺς ἐκθέντας
εὑρεῖν ἀξίους τῶν Δάφνιδος γάμων.

33   Ἐπεὶ δὲ ἅλις ἦν τῶν κατ᾽ ἀγρὸν ἑορτῶν, ἔδοξε
βαδίζειν εἰς τὴν πόλιν καὶ τούς τε τῆς Χλόης πατέρας
ἀναζητεῖν καὶ περὶ τὸν γάμον αὐτῶν μηκέτι βραδύνειν. 2. ἕωθεν οὖν ἐνσκευασάμενοι τῷ Δρύαντι μὲν
ἔδωκαν ἄλλας τρισχιλίας, τῷ Λάμωνι δὲ τὴν ἡμίσειαν
μοῖραν τῶν ἀγρῶν θερίζειν καὶ τρυγᾶν καὶ τὰς αἶγας
ἅμα τοῖς αἰπόλοις καὶ ζεύγη βοῶν τέτταρα καὶ ἐσθῆτας χειμερινάς, καὶ ‹ἐλεύθερόν τε αὐτὸν ἔθηκαν καὶ›[125]
ἐλευθέραν τὴν γυναῖκα, καὶ μετὰ τοῦτο ἤλαυνον ἐπὶ

---

124 Corais: συνωμοσίῳ V F   125 Add. Courier

daughter-in-law, while Dionysophanes took Daphnis aside
and privately asked whether Chloe was a virgin. When
Daphnis swore that nothing had happened beyond kisses
and vows, he was delighted and seated them both at the
party.

Then could be seen what beauty is like when enhanced 32
by adornment, for when Chloe had dressed, braided her
hair, and washed her face, she looked so much comelier
to everyone that even Daphnis hardly recognized her. 2.
Even without the tokens, anyone would have sworn that
Dryas was not the father of such a girl. Nevertheless, he
was there too, celebrating with Nape and sharing his own
couch with Lamo and Myrtale as drinking companions. 3.
Over the days that followed, more victims were sacrificed
and more wine bowls set up, and Chloe dedicated her possessions too, her syrinx, her knapsack, her goatskin, her
milk pails, and she also poured some wine into the spring
in the cave, because she had been nursed beside it and had
often bathed in it. 4. Dryas showed her the ewe's grave,
and she placed garlands on it, and as Daphnis had done,
she played a tune for her flock, and when the tune was finished she prayed to the goddesses that she would find the
ones who had abandoned her and that they would be worthy of her marriage to Daphnis.

When they had their fill of country festivities they de- 33
cided to go to the city to look for Chloe's parents and delay
the marriage no longer. 2. So they were packed up for the
trip early in the morning. They gave Dryas another three
thousand and Lamo a half share in the harvest and fruit-
picking on the farm, along with the goats and goatherds,
four pairs of oxen, and winter clothing; they also made him
a free man and his wife a free woman. Then they set off

Μιτυλήνην ἵπποις καὶ ζεύγεσι καὶ τρυφῇ πολλῇ. 3.
τότε μὲν οὖν ἔλαθον τοὺς πολίτας νυκτὸς κατελθόντες,
τῆς δὲ ἐπιούσης ὄχλος ἠθροίσθη περὶ τὰς θύρας
ἀνδρῶν γυναικῶν. οἱ μὲν τῷ Διονυσοφάνει συνήδοντο
παῖδα εὑρόντι καὶ μᾶλλον ὁρῶντες τὸ κάλλος τοῦ
Δάφνιδος, αἱ δὲ τῇ Κλεαρίστῃ συνέχαιρον ἅμα κομι-
ζούσῃ καὶ παῖδα καὶ νύμφην· 4. ἐξέπλησσε γὰρ κἀκείνας ἡ Χλόη κάλλος ἐκφέρουσα παρευδοκιμηθῆναι μὴ
δυνάμενον. ὅλη δὲ ἄρα ἐκίττα[126] ἡ πόλις ἐπὶ τῷ μειρακίῳ καὶ τῇ παρθένῳ, καὶ εὐδαιμόνιζον μὲν ἤδη τοῦ
γάμου, ηὔχοντο δὲ καὶ τὸ γένος ἄξιον τῆς μορφῆς
εὑρεθῆναι τῆς κόρης, καὶ γυναῖκες πολλαὶ τῶν μέγα
πλουσίων ἠράσαντο θεοῖς αὐταὶ πιστευθῆναι μητέρες
θυγατρὸς οὕτω καλῆς.

34 Ὄναρ δὲ Διονυσοφάνει μετὰ φροντίδα πολλὴν εἰς
βαθὺν ὕπνον κατενεχθέντι τοιόνδε γίνεται. ἐδόκει τὰς
Νύμφας δεῖσθαι τοῦ Ἔρωτος ἤδη ποτὲ αὐτοῖς κατα-
νεῦσαι τὸν γάμον, τὸν δὲ ἐκλύσαντα τὸ τοξάριον καὶ
ἀποθέμενον τὴν φαρέτραν κελεῦσαι τῷ Διονυσοφάνει
πάντας τοὺς ἀρίστους Μιτυληναίων θέμενον συμπότας, ἡνίκα ἂν τὸν ὕστατον πλήσῃ κρατῆρα, τότε
δεικνύειν ἑκάστῳ τὰ γνωρίσματα, τὸ δὲ ἐντεῦθεν ᾄδειν
τὸν ὑμέναιον. 2. ταῦτα ἰδὼν καὶ ἀκούσας ἕωθεν ἀνίσταται καὶ κελεύσας λαμπρὰν ἑστίασιν παρασκευ-
ασθῆναι τῶν ἀπὸ γῆς, τῶν ἀπὸ θαλάσσης καὶ εἴ τι ἐν
λίμναις, καὶ εἴ τι ἐν ποταμοῖς, πάντας τοὺς ἀρίστους
Μιτυληναίων ποιεῖται συμπότας. 3. ὡς δὲ ἤδη νὺξ ἦν
καὶ πέπληστο ‹ὁ› κρατὴρ ἐξ οὗ σπένδουσιν Ἑρμῇ,
εἰσκομίζει τις ἐπὶ σκεύους ἀργυροῦ θεράπων τὰ γνωρίσματα καὶ περιφέρων ἐνδέξια πᾶσιν ἐδείκνυε.

---

126 ἐκινεῖτο V

for Mitylene in great luxury, on horseback and in carriages. 3. Since it was dark when they arrived, they went unnoticed by the citizens until the following day, when a throng of men and women gathered outside their door. The men congratulated Dionysophanes on finding a son, especially when they saw how handsome Daphnis was, and the women rejoiced with Cleariste at bringing home both a son and his bride, 4. for Chloe's unsurpassable beauty stunned even them. The whole city was agog for the boy and the girl, and were already predicting a happy marriage and praying that the girl's family would be found to be worthy of her good looks. Many wives of the wealthiest husbands prayed to the gods that they themselves might be taken for mothers of such a lovely girl.

Dionysophanes, after much anxious thought, fell into a deep sleep and had the following dream. The Nymphs seemed to be asking Love now at last to consent to the marriage, and he unstrung his little bow, took off his quiver, and told Dionysophanes to invite all the leading citizens of Mitylene to a party, and when he filled the last wine bowl, to show the tokens to each of them and then sing the wedding hymn. 2. After seeing and hearing this, he got up in the morning and ordered a resplendent feast prepared with the produce of land and sea, and whatever is found in lakes and rivers, and invited as guests all the leading citizens of Mitylene. 3. When night came and the wine bowl was filled for the libation to Hermes,[69] a servant brought in the tokens on a silver tray and took them around from left to right for everyone to have a look.

[69] The last libation: Hermes presided over sleep, cf. Homer, *Odyssey* 7.136–38.

DAPHNIS AND CHLOE

35   Τῶν μὲν οὖν ἄλλων ἐγνώριζεν οὐδείς, Μεγακλῆς δέ
τις διὰ γῆρας ὕστατος κατακείμενος ὡς εἶδε γνωρίσας
πάνυ μέγα καὶ νεανικὸν ἐκβοᾷ· "τίνα ὁρῶ ταῦτα; τί
γέγονάς μοι, θυγάτριον; ἆρα καὶ σὺ ζῇς, ἢ ταῦτά τις
ἐβάστασε μόνα ποιμὴν ἐντυχών; 2. δέομαι, Διονυ-
σόφανες, εἰπέ μοι· πόθεν ἔχεις ἐμοῦ παιδίου γνωρίσματα; μὴ φθονήσῃς μετὰ Δάφνιν εὑρεῖν τι κἀμέ."
κελεύσαντος δὲ τοῦ Διονυσοφάνους πρότερον ἐκεῖνον
λέγειν τὴν ἔκθεσιν, ὁ Μεγακλῆς οὐδὲν ὑφελὼν τοῦ
τόνου τῆς φωνῆς ἔφη· 3. "ἦν ὀλίγος μοι βίος τὸν
πρότερον χρόνον· ὃν γὰρ εἶχον εἰς χορηγίας καὶ
τριηραρχίας ἐξεδαπάνησα. ὅτε ταῦτα ἦν γίνεταί μοι
θυγάτριον. τοῦτο τρέφειν ὀκνήσας ἐν πενίᾳ τούτοις
τοῖς γνωρίσμασι κοσμήσας ἐξέθηκα, εἰδὼς ὅτι πολλοὶ
καὶ οὕτω σπουδάζουσι πατέρες γενέσθαι. 4. καὶ τὸ μὲν
ἐξέκειτο ἐν ἄντρῳ Νυμφῶν πιστευθὲν ταῖς θεαῖς, ἐμοὶ
δὲ πλοῦτος ἐπέρρει καθ᾽ ἑκάστην ἡμέραν κληρονόμον
οὐκ ἔχοντι. 5. οὐκέτι γοῦν οὐδὲ θυγατρίου γενέσθαι
πατὴρ εὐτύχησα, ἀλλ᾽ ὥσπερ οἱ θεοὶ γέλωτά με ποι-
ούμενοι νύκτωρ ὀνείρους μοι ἐπιπέμπουσι δηλοῦντες
ὅτι με πατέρα ποιήσει ποίμνιον."

36   Ἀνεβόησεν ὁ Διονυσοφάνης μεῖζον τοῦ Μεγακλέ-
ους καὶ ἀναπηδήσας εἰσάγει Χλόην πάνυ καλῶς κε-
κοσμημένην καὶ λέγει· "τοῦτο τὸ παιδίον ἐξέθηκας.
ταύτην σοὶ τὴν παρθένον οἶς προνοίᾳ θεῶν ἀνέθρεψεν
ὡς αἶξ Δάφνιν ἐμοί. 2. λαβὲ τὰ γνωρίσματα καὶ τὴν
θυγατέρα, λαβὼν δὲ ἀπόδος Δάφνιδι νύμφην. ἀμφο-

---

70 "Great Fame", a conventional aristocratic name.

71 The seat of honor.

72 Among the civic expenses that the wealthy were required,

No one recognized them until a certain Megacles,[70]   35
who was seated last in order[71] because of his age, recognized them on sight and gave a cry as loud as a young man's:
"What's this I see? What has become of you, my little
daughter? Are you still alive too, or did some shepherd find
only these and pick them up? 2. Please tell me, Dionysophanes, how did you come by my child's tokens? After
discovering Daphnis, don't begrudge me my own discovery!" But Dionysophanes told him to speak first about the
abandonment, and without lowering his voice at all he replied, 3. "There was a time when I had little to live on: what
I had I had spent on fitting out choruses and warships.[72]
During that time a daughter came along. Reluctant to raise
her in poverty, I adorned her with these tokens and abandoned her, knowing that many men are eager to become
fathers even in that way. 4. So the child was left lying in a
cave of the Nymphs, entrusted to the goddesses, while for
me wealth started to pour in day after day, though I had no
heir. 5. For I never had the luck to become a father again,
even of a daughter, but as if having a laugh at my expense
the gods kept sending me dreams at night, that a sheep
would make me a father."

Dionysophanes cried out louder than Megacles and   36
leapt from his seat. He brought Chloe in, very beautifully
decked out, and said, "Here is the child that you abandoned. By the gods' providence a ewe nursed this maiden
for you, just as a goat nursed Daphnis for me. 2. Take your
tokens and your daughter, and when you have taken her,
return her to Daphnis as his bride. We abandoned them

but could also volunteer, to contribute; for Megacles' predicament cf. Xenophon, *Oeconomicus* 2.6.

τέρους ἐξεθήκαμεν, ἀμφοτέρους εὑρήκαμεν, ἀμφοτέρων ἐμέλησε Πανὶ καὶ Νύμφαις καὶ "Ερωτι." 3. ἐπῄνει
τὰ λεγόμενα ὁ Μεγακλῆς καὶ τὴν γυναῖκα 'Ρόδην
μετεπέμπετο καὶ τὴν Χλόην ἐν τοῖς κόλποις εἶχε, καὶ
ὕπνον αὐτοῦ μένοντες εἵλοντο. Δάφνις γὰρ οὐδενὶ
διώμνυτο προήσεσθαι τὴν Χλόην, οὐδὲ αὐτῷ τῷ
πατρί.

37   Ἡμέρας δὲ γενομένης συνθέμενοι πάλιν εἰς τὸν
ἀγρὸν ἤλαυνον· ἐδεήθησαν γὰρ τοῦτο Δάφνις καὶ
Χλόη μὴ φέροντες τὴν ἐν ἄστει διατριβήν, ἐδόκει δὲ
κἀκείνοις ποιμενικούς τινας αὐτοῖς ποιῆσαι τοὺς γάμους. 2. ἐλθόντες οὖν παρὰ τὸν Λάμωνα τόν τε Δρύαντα τῷ Μεγακλεῖ προσήγαγον καὶ τὴν Νάπην τῇ
'Ρόδῃ συνέστησαν καὶ τὰ πρὸς τὴν ἑορτὴν παρεσκευάζοντο λαμπρῶς. παρέδωκε μὲν οὖν ἐπὶ ταῖς Νύμφαις
τὴν Χλόην ὁ πατὴρ καὶ μετὰ ἄλλων πολλῶν ἐποίησεν
ἀναθήματα τὰ γνωρίσματα καὶ Δρύαντι τὰς λει-
πούσας εἰς τὰς μυρίας ἐπλήρωσεν.

38   Ὁ δὲ Διονυσοφάνης εὐημερίας οὔσης αὐτοῦ πρὸ
τοῦ ἄντρου στιβάδας ὑπεστόρεσεν ἐκ χλωρᾶς φυλλάδος καὶ πάντας τοὺς κωμήτας κατακλίνας εἱστία
πολυτελῶς. 2. παρῆσαν δὲ Λάμων καὶ Μυρτάλη, Δρύας καὶ Νάπη, οἱ Δόρκωνος προσήκοντες, ⟨Φιλητᾶς
καὶ⟩[127] οἱ Φιλητᾶ παῖδες, Χρόμις καὶ Λυκαίνιον· οὐκ
ἀπῆν οὐδὲ Λάμπις συγγνώμης ἀξιωθείς. 3. ἦν οὖν ὡς
ἐν τοιοῖσδε συμπόταις πάντα γεωργικὰ καὶ ἄγροικα. ὁ
μὲν ᾖδεν οἷα ᾄδουσι θερίζοντες, ὁ δὲ ἔσκωπτε τὰ ἐπὶ
ληνοῖς σκώμματα· Φιλητᾶς ἐσύρισε, Λάμπις ηὔλησε,
Δρύας καὶ Λάμων ὠρχήσαντο, Χλόη καὶ Δάφνις ἀλλήλους κατεφίλουν. 4. ἐνέμοντο δὲ καὶ αἱ αἶγες πλησίον ὥσπερ καὶ αὐταὶ κοινωνοῦσαι τῆς ἑορτῆς. τοῦτο

[127] Add. Boden

both, we have found them both, and both were cared for by Pan and the Nymphs and Love. 3. Megacles agreed to all this. He sent for his wife, Rhoda,[73] and clasped Chloe to his breast. They stayed and slept there, for Daphnis had vowed to surrender Chloe to no one, not even her own father.

The next day they all decided to drive back into the   37 countryside, at the request of Daphnis and Chloe, who were unable to bear life in town, and they too thought it right to put on a wedding in pastoral style. 2. When they got to Lamo's house, they presented Dryas to Megacles and Nape to Rhoda, and then began the splendid preparations for the feast. Chloe's father gave her away in the presence of the Nymphs and made numerous dedications, including her tokens, and he topped up Dryas' gift to make it an even ten thousand.

There in front of the cave Dionysophanes spread out   38 beds of green leaves, since the weather was fine, had all the villagers recline on them, and feasted them lavishly. 2. In attendance were Lamo and Myrtale, Dryas and Nape, Dorco's family, <Philetas and> Philetas' sons, Chromis and Lycaenium; not even Lampis stayed away, having been considered worth forgiving. 3. Appropriately for partygoers like these, everything was agricultural and rustic. Someone sang such songs as reapers sing, another cracked the jokes heard at wine presses; Philetas played the syrinx, Lampis played the pipes, Dryas and Lamo performed dances, Chloe and Daphnis kept exchanging kisses. 4. Even the goats were grazing nearby, as if they too were joining in the party; for the townspeople this was not very

---

[73] "Rose", a conventional name.

τοῖς μὲν ἀστικοῖς οὐ πάνυ τερπνὸν ἦν· ὁ δὲ Δάφνις καὶ
ἐκάλεσέ τινας αὐτῶν ὀνομαστὶ καὶ φυλλάδα χλωρὰν
ἔδωκε καὶ κρατήσας ἐκ τῶν κεράτων κατεφίλησε.

39   Καὶ οὐ τότε μόνον ἀλλ' ἔστε ἔζων τὸν πλεῖστον
χρόνον ⟨βίον⟩[128] ποιμενικὸν εἶχον, θεοὺς σέβοντες
Νύμφας καὶ Πᾶνα καὶ Ἔρωτα, ἀγέλας δὲ προβάτων
καὶ αἰγῶν πλείστας κτησάμενοι, ἡδίστην δὲ τροφὴν
νομίζοντες ὀπώραν καὶ γάλα. 2. ἀλλὰ καὶ ἄρρεν μὲν
παιδίον ὑπέθηκαν ⟨αἰγὶ⟩[129] καὶ θυγάτριον γενόμενον
δεύτερον ὄιος ἑλκύσαι θηλὴν ἐποίησαν καὶ ἐκάλεσαν
τὸν μὲν Φιλοποίμενα, τὴν δὲ Ἀγέλην. οὕτως αὐτοῖς καὶ
ταῦτα συνεγήρασεν. οὗτοι καὶ τὸ ἄντρον ἐκόσμησαν
καὶ εἰκόνας ἀνέθεσαν καὶ βωμὸν εἴσαντο Ποιμένος
Ἔρωτος, καὶ τῷ Πανὶ δὲ ἔδοσαν ἀντὶ τῆς πίτυος οἰκεῖν
νεών, Πανὸς Στρατιώτου ὀνομάσαντες.

40   Ἀλλὰ ταῦτα μὲν ὕστερον καὶ ὠνόμασαν καὶ ἔπρα-
ξαν· τότε δὲ νυκτὸς γενομένης πάντες αὐτοὺς παρέπεμ-
πον εἰς τὸν θάλαμον, οἱ μὲν συρίττοντες, οἱ δὲ αὐλοῦν-
τες, οἱ δὲ δᾷδας μεγάλας ἀνίσχοντες. 2. καὶ ἐπεὶ
πλησίον ἦσαν τῶν θυρῶν ᾖδον σκληρᾷ καὶ ἀπηνεῖ τῇ
φωνῇ, καθάπερ τριαίναις γῆν ἀναρρηγνύντες, οὐχ
ὑμέναιον ᾄδοντες. 3. Δάφνις δὲ καὶ Χλόη γυμνοὶ
συγκατακλιθέντες περιέβαλλον ἀλλήλους καὶ κατεφίλουν, ἀγρυπνήσαντες τῆς νυκτὸς ὅσον οὐδὲ γλαῦκες,
καὶ ἔδρασέ τι Δάφνις ὧν αὐτὸν ἐπαίδευσε Λυκαίνιον,
καὶ τότε Χλόη πρῶτον ἔμαθεν ὅτι τὰ ἐπὶ τῆς ὕλης
γενόμενα ἦν ποιμένων παίγνια.[130]

[128] Add. Reeve   [129] Add. Scaliger

[130] subscriptio: τέλος τῶν κατὰ Χλόην καὶ Δάφνιν Λόγγου
αἰπολικῶν V: τέλος Λόγου ποιμενικῶν τῶν περὶ Δάφνιν καὶ
Χλόην Λεσβιακῶν ἐρωτικῶν λόγοι τέσσαρες F

pleasant, but Daphnis called several of the goats by name, gave them some green leaves, and held them by their horns and gave them kisses.

Not only at that time but for as long as they lived, they led for the most part a pastoral life, worshipping Nymphs, Pan, and Love as their deities, owning a great many flocks of sheep and goats, and considering fruit and milk the sweetest food. 2. They also put a baby boy to a she-goat, and when their second came, a girl, they had her suckle at a sheep's nipple. They called the boy Philopoemen[74] and the girl Agele.[75] And in this fashion too the children grew old with them. They also adorned the cave, dedicated images, built an altar for Love the Shepherd,[76] and gave Pan a temple to dwell in instead of the pine, dubbing him Pan the Soldier.[77] 39

But it was later that they bestowed these names and performed these acts. Now, at nightfall, everyone conducted them to their bedroom, some playing the syrinx, some the pipes, some holding great torches aloft. 2. As they approached the doorway, they began to sing with voices rough and harsh, as if they were breaking up the ground with pitchforks instead of singing a wedding hymn. 3. Daphnis and Chloe lay together naked, hugged and kissed, spending that night more sleepless than any owl. Daphnis did some of what Lycaenium had taught him, and for the very first time Chloe learned that what had happened in the woods was nothing but shepherds' games. 40

---

[74] "Fond of Shepherds."   [75] "Flock."

[76] Cf. 2.5.4, 3.12.1.   [77] Commemorating his help against the Methymnaeans in Book II; and cf. Valerius Flaccus 3.48 *Pan nemorum bellique potens*.

XENOPHON OF EPHESUS

INTRODUCTION

The Story of Anthia and Habrocomes[1] attributed to Xenophon of Ephesus resembles the other four extant Greek
romantic novels in featuring invented (not mythical or historical) characters in a plot centered on a boy and a girl
who fall in love, remain true to one another despite obstacles, threats, temptations, and separations, and, by virtue
of their own goodness and the grace of friendly deities, live
happily ever after. In contrast to earlier Greek literature,
where erotic relationships are unequal in terms of age and
power, relationships and initiatives in the novels are more
equal and reciprocal, and marriage, the ultimate goal and
ideal, is based on romantic love and fidelity on the part of
both partners.

---

[1] The Suda and F, our only independent MS, entitle the novel
The Ephesian Story of Anthia and Abrocomes (for the most part F
also uses this spelling in the text), while Gregory Pardus (c. 1070–
1156) cites it as *The Story of Habrocomes and Anthia*. Because the
form *ta kata/peri* + girl's (or girl's + boy's) name(s) is common to
the titles of all five extant romantic novels but toponymic
descriptors (three different ones in the case of Longus) are not, I
assume that the former was the original and generic form. And because "Abrocomes" is meaningless in Greek, I adopt the aspirated
form of the name ("Graceful-Haired"), which is normal from classical through imperial times.

X.'s novel, like *The Story of Callirhoe* by Chariton of Aphrodisias, represents a "presophistic" mode of the genre, lacking the refinements of language, style, structure, narrative, rhetoric, literary allusion, and intertextuality that characterize the novels by Longus, Achilles Tatius, and Heliodorus. In terms of sophistication X. is indeed closer to *The Story of Apollonius of Tyre* than to *Callirhoe*, with some features more characteristic of oral storytelling and folktale than of literature. His language is simple, straightforward, and formulaic, an archaizing but unsystematic Attic that does not completely cover a *koine* base and pays less attention to such niceties as connection, subordination, rhythm, and avoidance of hiatus than in the other novelists. His narrative is rapid, paratactic, and schematic, with much repetition and parallelism but without large-scale shaping. Although he has literary interests (Herodotus, Xenophon, Thucydides, epic, drama, oratory, travel writing, geography, and mythography), there is no overt literary allusion or intertextual play, no mythological characters or situations, no artistic, philosophical, scientific, didactic, or sententious enhancements, and very little rhetorical ornamentation.

What X. gives us is not literature but action and adventure, in a form not unlike a screenplay for a television serial or action movie, or a graphic novel. The characters are functional, defined simply as good or bad of their type, motivated by basic and melodramatic emotions, and without moral or psychological depth. The focus is not so much on the overall plot as on the individual scenes and episodes, which are developed for their own interest and strung together with minimal, sometimes no, motivation, often simply a decision by a character, and with no great concern for smooth transitions and logical consistency. There is less direct speech (under a third of the whole) than in the other novels but, despite the work's relative brevity, far more episodes and subplots, some of them developed for their own interest, and an unusually large number of characters, no fewer than 44, 33 of whom are given names. The premium is on incidental vividness and variety, on suspense and surprise, so that from a literary point of view the novel looks uneven and ill-proportioned, some episodes and characters (especially in half of Book II, Book IV, and chapters 2–10 of Book V) being less well developed than others.

These features have led some to suppose that our text is the work of an epitomator, a supposition that suits the statement in the Suda, derived from a sixth-century source (see below), that the novel was in ten books, not the five which our text contains. While this cannot be disproved, we need not resort to an epitomator's intervention to account for our text's language, characterizations, plot, and narrative style: they are consistent throughout, and suitably effective and entertaining at the level of simple, probably orally derived, storytelling. Indeed it is hard to imagine that the action-crammed, cinematic story we have was originally conceived and composed at twice the length and in a more polished style.

Nonetheless X.'s novel is a good read: its overall structure, designed to accommodate both the basic plot (the couple's separation, quest, and ultimate reunion) and a wealth of secondary characters, incidents, and locales, is clear and economical, more in the manner of epic than the other novels. The protagonists begin their adventures in Ephesus and share the same cyclic and clockwise route through Ionia and the islands (notably Rhodes), Asia,

Egypt, Sicily, Italy, and then back again to Ephesus. From the point of their separation the perspective splits and broadens as more and more characters and subplots weave in and out of the action, until with accelerating pace and no little dexterity all the strands are gathered and sorted for a satisfyingly dramatic finale. Most of the characters, however memorable (e.g. the fierce females who beset Habrocomes), have only brief or functional roles, but the protagonists and the bandit Hippothous, who becomes connected to both of them, are given distinctive personalities: Anthia is active and resourceful, Habrocomes passive and morose (more a Jason than an Odysseus), and the sexually ambivalent Hippothous a complex mixture of good breeding and sociopathic violence, cruelty and compassion, selfishness and loyalty.

Unlike Chariton, X. sets his story not in the historical past but in an indefinite time that feels contemporary, though he avoids precise markers, never mentioning actual persons or events and identifying institutions and places only in vague terms. The names of his characters are ordinary or drawn from literature and mythology and seem to have no special significance or resonance. His geography too seems to be derived from books rather than personal experience: places are named but not described and are sometimes given defunct or variant identities (e.g. "Mazacus" for Mazaca, which had been renamed Caesarea under Tiberius; "Nucerium" for Nuceria); some of his itineraries are unlikely (e.g. the journey through Egypt in 4.1 and from Italy to Rhodes in 5.10); and his grasp of local information is often fuzzy (e.g. "local shepherds" instead of the well-known Boukoloi in 3.12.2; the titles ἄρχων and διοικῶν of the same official in 4.2).

The social strata in which most of X.'s story moves are

lower, the predicaments of the characters more extreme, and the worldview bleaker and more lurid than in Chariton, more akin to the realistic-picaresque novel or a modern western. And so fidelity and chastity, the only sure principles in a treacherous and bewildering world, are more central, as is the importance of the gods, without whose enmity (Eros) there would be no love and separation and without whose miraculous interventions (especially by Isis, Nile, and Helius) there would be no happy reunion.

Summary

Book 1. Young Habrocomes and fourteen-year-old Anthia, each from a leading family of Ephesus, possess nearly divine good looks, but Habrocomes is as arrogant as he is handsome. His contempt of Eros provokes the god, who afflicts Habrocomes and Anthia with mutual passion and, even after Habrocomes capitulates and begs the god's forgiveness, determines to punish them. Their concerned parents consult Apollo, who responds with an oracle foretelling for the children long wandering across the sea and much suffering before final redemption by Isis. The parents accordingly give them a wedding and send them on a honeymoon abroad, and the couple exchange vows of eternal fidelity. They sail to Samos and Rhodes, where they dedicate a golden panoply to Helius, but as they continue their voyage they are captured by Phoenician pirates led by Corymbus. On the way to his headquarters, commanded by Apsyrtus, Corymbus falls for Habrocomes and his friend Euxinus for Anthia. Habrocomes and Anthia stall for time.

Book 2. While Habrocomes and Anthia contemplate suicide as preferable to surrender, Apsyrtus claims them as his share of the booty and takes them as slaves to his estate in Tyre. Apsyrtus' daughter Manto falls for Habrocomes and with threats and inducements enlists the aid of Anthia, Anthia's loyal servant Rhoda, and her companion Leuco. She also writes a letter to Habrocomes. When he rejects her, she tells Apsyrtus that she was raped by Habrocomes, who is imprisoned and tortured. Anthia, Rhoda, and Leuco are awarded to Manto, now married to her original fiancé Moeris, and they all move to Syria, where Manto gives Anthia to a goatherd named Lampo, who however respects her chastity. Apsyrtus discovers Manto's letter, frees Habrocomes, and appoints him steward of his estate. When Moeris falls for Anthia, Manto orders Lampo to kill her, but instead he sells her to Cilician merchants. They are shipwrecked and Anthia is captured by the bandit Hippothous, who plans to sacrifice her to Ares, but she is rescued by Perilaus, a peace officer from Tarsus. Perilaus pressures Anthia to marry him, but she contrives a delay. Meanwhile, Habrocomes has gone off to search for Anthia, meets Hippothous, and decides to join with him in hopes of finding Anthia.

Book 3. As Hippothous recruits a new band, he tells Habrocomes the story of his first love, the boy Hyperanthes, and its sad dénouement that set him on his career as a bandit. Habrocomes responds with his own story of Anthia, and Hippothous promises to help him find her. Anthia decides to kill herself rather than marry Perilaus and asks a doctor for poison, but he gives her a soporific instead. She is given a lavish funeral but is rescued by tomb-robbers, who take her to Alexandria and sell her to slave dealers. Habrocomes hears about Anthia's stolen body, vows to die as soon as he finds it, and takes off for Alexandria. Psammis, an Indian merchant, purchases Anthia, who puts him off by claiming to be consecrated to Isis for one year. Habrocomes is shipwrecked, captured by bandits, and sold as a slave to Araxus, who treats him like a son but whose wife Cyno propositions him. Habrocomes agrees but reneges when Cyno kills Araxus. Cyno has the Prefect of Egypt arrest Habrocomes for the murder.

Book 4. Hippothous recruits a new band and rampages through Syria, Phoenicia, and Egypt. Habrocomes is ordered crucified but is rescued by the Nile and Helius, then ordered burned but rescued again by the Nile. The Prefect returns him to prison pending an investigation. Psammis, headed to India with Anthia, stops at Memphis, where Anthia asks Isis for help. Hippothous' band kill Psammis and capture Anthia, whom they do not recognize. The Prefect frees Habrocomes and crucifies Cyno. Habrocomes sets off for Italy. When Anthia kills Anchialus, one of Hippothous' men, as he tries to rape her, Hippothous has her thrown into a pit with hungry dogs, but the guard Amphinomus falls for Anthia and keeps the dogs at bay.

Book 5. Habrocomes arrives in Syracuse and joins the old fisherman Aegialeus, who has perpetuated a happy marriage by mummifying his deceased wife. Amphinomus takes Anthia to Coptus while Hippothous' gang operates to the north. Polyidus, a relative of the Prefect charged with putting down the bandits, crushes Hippothous' band at Pelusium. Hippothous escapes and heads for Sicily. Polyidus captures Amphinomus and Anthia and falls for her. When he pressures her in Memphis she takes refuge with Isis, then visits the temple of Apis, whose oracle predicts that she will soon regain Habrocomes. In Alexandria Polyidus' wife Rhenaea beats Anthia and turns her over to her slave Clytus with orders to take her to Italy and sell her to a pimp. Clytus reluctantly does so in Tarentum, but she preserves her virtue by feigning epilepsy. Habrocomes sails to Italy and takes work in a quarry. Hippothous marries a wealthy old woman who soon dies, leaving him her estate, and sails to Italy with a young boy named Cleisthenes in search of Habrocomes. Meanwhile, we learn that the couple's parents have died of grief, while Leuco and Rhoda have inherited their Syrian masters' large estate and stop at Rhodes en route back to Ephesus. Hippothous recognizes Anthia, buys her from the pimp, learns her true identity, and tells her of his affection for Habrocomes. Habrocomes decides to return to Ephesus, stops at Rhodes, and visits the temple of Helius, where he sees a dedication in honor of himself and Anthia made by Leuco and Rhoda, who meet him there and learn his identity. Hippothous and Anthia stop in Rhodes during the festival for Helius. Anthia dedicates a lock of hair, which leads to her recognition by everyone, Habrocomes being the last to hear the news. The couple reunite near the temple of Isis, and all sail back to Ephesus, where Habrocomes and Anthia honor Artemis and build tombs for their parents, while Hippothous builds a tomb on Lesbos for Hyperanthes, adopts Cleisthenes, and returns to Ephesus to live happily ever after with Habrocomes and Anthia.

Author and Date

A notice in the tenth-century Suda (ξ 50 Adler), drawn from an epitome of the *Dictionary of Notable People* by the sixth-century scholar Hesychius of Miletus, provides our only testimony for the author:

Ξενοφῶν Ἐφέσιος, ἱστορικός. Ἐφεσιακά· ἔστι δὲ ἐρωτικὰ βιβλία ιʹ περὶ Ἀβροκόμου καὶ Ἀνθίας· καὶ Περὶ τῆς πόλεως Ἐφεσίων, καὶ ἄλλα.

Xenophon of Ephesus, historiographer.[2] *Ephesian Story. It is a love story in ten books about Abrocomes and Anthia; also* The City of the Ephesians *and other works.*

Since the Suda also records novels by other Xenophons, a *Babylonian Story* by a X. of Antioch and a *Cyprian Story* by a X. of Cyprus, it could be that X. was a generic name adopted by early novelists (perhaps in homage to X. of Athens), and that our X. was Ephesian could be a mere inference from the home city of his protagonists and/or the novel's (alternate? cf. n. 1) title, since the text itself contains nothing that demonstrates native or even eyewitness familiarity with Ephesus. But the mention of other works by X., including one about Ephesus, may reflect real information. For the number of books, itacism of εʹ ("five"), which is the number given in the subscription to F, is a likelier explanation of the Suda's ιʹ ("ten") than the supposition that our text is an epitome.

X.'s vagueness about people, places, and events leaves us with no external evidence for dating the novel. If there are references to the Prefect of Egypt (but ἄρχων and

---

[2] This can also mean "story-teller" and designates both the setting of novels and local histories; cf. the Prologue of *Daphnis and Chloe* and Julian *Ep.* 8.

διοικῶν are used of the same person in 4.2) they give only a *terminus post quem* in the time of Augustus. Minas as currency (3.5) went out of use in the Hellenistic era, but X. may not have known or cared. Perilaus is called "the head officer of the peace in Cilicia" (2.13) and some have thought that he must be an *eirenarch*, an office whose earliest attestation is (currently) an Ephesian inscription from the reign of Trajan (98–117 CE), giving a *terminus post quem* in that era. But this is an unlikely inference: the *eirenarch* seems to have been only a municipal officer, whereas Perilaus apparently has charge of an entire region; there had long been other such "officers of the peace" in many places; and even if Perilaus was supposed to be an *eirenarch*, we do not know when or where this office originated: that our earliest attestation is Trajanic does not mean that the office was created only then, and we have no attestation from Cilicia.

Internal features, however, suggest a date earlier than the mid-first century CE. As already noted, X. and Chariton are both "pre-sophistic" writers, and in addition they have significant narrative elements in common. Chariton can be firmly dated between the second half of the first century BCE (mention of a Chinese bow and quiver in 6.4.2) and c. 150 CE (papyri), and his style, an educated *koine* without sophistic features, seems to place him earlier rather than later within this time frame; if Persius' mention (1.134) of *Callirhoe* as an example of trivial literature refers to Chariton's novel (the title occurs nowhere else), then it was already well known in Neronian Rome. If the narrative elements that both novels share is the result of borrowing, it is impossible to tell who borrowed from the other: is what we find in X. a clumsy borrowing from Chariton or something clumsy that Chariton found in X. and improved? Or did both draw independently from an existing stock of novelistic elements? In any event, it is clear that X. and Chariton treat their material, whatever its sources, differently, and if overall sophistication is a sign of progress in a genre, then X. should be dated earlier than Chariton.

Reception

No papyri have yet appeared, and although there are elements in the other ancient novels as well as Aristaenetus' letters (late 5th or early 6th century) and the *Acta Apocrypha* that may have been derived from X., they could also have come indirectly or from the common stock, so that the earliest sure reference is Gregory Pardus (see n. 1 above and the textual note on 1.1). The 33rd of the novellas of Masuccio Salernitano (born Tommaso Guardati) published in Naples in 1476 ("Mariotto and Giannozza") was likely drawn from Xenophon's story of Anthia and Perilaus (2.13, 3.8) and through subsequent treatments by Luigi da Porto, Matteo Bandello, and Arthur Brooke became the basis for Shakespeare's *Romeo and Juliet*. Politian cites X. in his *Miscellaneorum Centuria Prima* (1489). Parts of the story survive in oriental and modern Greek versions.

The Text

The 13th-century manuscript F (Florentinus Laurentianus Conv. Soppr. 627), which also contains Chariton, Longus, and part of Achilles Tatius, is the sole independent witness for X.'s novel. In F, X.'s spelling, forms, and syntax are not standardized, and this kind of variation may well reflect the author's own usage (see above). The first printed edition, with a Latin translation, was that of Antonio Cocchi (London, 1726); it was preceded by an Italian translation by Antonio Salvini (London, 1723). The chapter division traditionally follows the edition by A. von Locella (Vienna, 1796), the subchapter division that of R. Hercher (Teubner: Leipzig, 1858).

ΤΑ ΚΑΤΑ
ΑΝΘΙΑΝ ΚΑΙ ᾿ΑΒΡΟΚΟΜΗΝ

ΛΟΓΟΣ ΠΡΩΤΟΣ[1]

1   ᾿Ην ἐν ᾿Εφέσῳ ἀνὴρ τῶν τὰ πρῶτα ἐκεῖ δυναμένων,
Λυκομήδης ὄνομα. τούτῳ τῷ Λυκομήδει ἐκ γυναικὸς
ἐπιχωρίας Θεμιστοῦς γίνεται παῖς ᾿Αβροκόμης[2], μέγα
δή τι χρῆμα [ὡραιότητι σώματος ὑπερβαλλούσῃ][3]
κάλλους οὔτε ἐν ᾿Ιωνίᾳ οὔτε ἐν ἄλλῃ γῇ πρότερον
γενυμένου. 2. οὗτος ὁ ᾿Αβροκόμης ἀεὶ μὲν καὶ καθ᾿
ἡμέραν εἰς κάλλος ηὔξετο, συνήνθει δὲ αὐτῷ τοῖς τοῦ
σώματος καλοῖς καὶ τὰ τῆς ψυχῆς ἀγαθά· παιδείαν τε
γὰρ πᾶσαν ἐμελέτα καὶ μουσικὴν ποικίλην ἤσκει, καὶ
θήρα τε[4] αὐτῷ καὶ ἱππασία καὶ ὁπλομαχία συνήθη
γυμνάσματα. 3. ἦν δὲ περισπούδαστος ἅπασιν ᾿Εφε-
σίοις ἅμα καὶ τοῖς τὴν ἄλλην ᾿Ασίαν οἰκοῦσι, καὶ
μεγάλας εἶχον ἐν αὐτῷ τὰς ἐλπίδας ὅτι πολίτης ἔσοιτο
διαφέρων. προσεῖχον δὲ ὡς θεῷ τῷ μειρακίῳ, καί εἰσιν
ἤδη τινὲς οἳ καὶ προσεκύνησαν ἰδόντες καὶ προσ-

---

1 Ξενοφῶντος τῶν κατὰ ᾿Ανθίαν καὶ ᾿Αβροκόμην ᾿Εφεσι-
ακῶν λόγος πρῶτος: Suda ξ 50 ᾿Εφεσιακά· ἔστι δὲ ἐρωτικὰ
βιβλία ε´ (Salvini, cf. subscriptionem: ι´ codd.) περὶ ᾿Αβροκό-
μου καὶ ᾿Ανθίας: τὰ κατὰ ᾿Αβροκόμην καὶ ᾿Ανθίαν Greg. Pard.
Comm. in Hermog. Meth. Walz Rhet. Gr. 7.2 p. 1236
  2 Hemsterhuys: ᾿Αβρ- plerumque F

THE STORY OF
ANTHIA AND HABROCOMES

BOOK I

In Ephesus there was a man named Lycomedes,[1] one of 1
the most powerful people in the city. This Lycomedes and
his wife Themisto,[2] also a local, had a son Habrocomes,[3] a
paragon of handsomeness without precedent in Ionia or
anywhere else. 2. This Habrocomes grew handsomer by
the day, and his spiritual virtues blossomed along with his
physical excellences, for he pursued every field of study
and practiced a variety of arts, and hunting, riding, and
training with heavy weapons were exercises familiar to
him. 3. He was much sought after by all Ephesians and
by the inhabitants of the rest of Asia as well, and they had
high hopes that he would be a citizen of distinction. They
treated the young man like a god, and there were some
who at the sight of him even bowed down and offered

---

[1] An actual as well as mythical name, and attested for Ephesus
in the *Gospel of John* (II CE).

[2] An actual as well as mythical name.

[3] "Graceful-Haired"; for the name see Introduction.

---

[3] Tresling   [4] Higt: κιθαρὰ δὲ

ηὔξαντο. 4. ἐφρόνει δὲ τὸ μειράκιον ἐφ' ἑαυτῷ μεγάλα
καὶ ἠγάλλετο μὲν καὶ τοῖς τῆς ψυχῆς κατορθώμασι,
πολὺ δὲ μᾶλλον τῷ κάλλει τοῦ σώματος· πάντων δὲ
τῶν ἄλλων ὅσα δὴ ἐλέγετο καλὰ ὡς ἐλαττόνων κατεφρόνει καὶ οὐδὲν αὐτῷ, οὐ θέαμα, οὐκ ἄκουσμα ἄξιον
Ἀβροκόμου κατεφαίνετο· 5. καὶ εἴ τινα ἢ παῖδα καλὸν
ἀκοῦσαι ἢ παρθένον εὔμορφον, κατεγέλα τῶν λεγόντων ὡς οὐκ εἰδότων ὅτι εἷς καλὸς αὐτός. Ἔρωτά γε μὴν
οὐδὲ ἐνόμιζεν εἶναι θεόν, ἀλλὰ πάντη ἐξέβαλεν ὡς
οὐδὲν ἡγούμενος, λέγων ὡς οὐκ ἄν ποτε οὐ<δέ> τις
ἐρασθείη οὐδὲ ὑποταγείη τῷ θεῷ μὴ θέλων· 6. εἰ δέ που
ἱερὸν ἢ ἄγαλμα Ἔρωτος εἶδε, κατεγέλα ἀπέφαινέ τε
ἑαυτὸν Ἔρωτος παντὸς κρείττονα[5] καὶ κάλλει σώματος καὶ δυνάμει. καὶ εἶχεν οὕτως· ὅπου γὰρ Ἀβροκόμης ὀφθείη, οὔτε ἄγαλμα καλὸν κατεφαίνετο οὔτε
εἰκὼν ἐπῃνεῖτο.

2   Μηνιᾷ πρὸς ταῦτα ὁ Ἔρως, φιλόνεικος γὰρ ὁ θεὸς
καὶ ὑπερηφάνοις ἀπαραίτητος, ἐζήτει δὲ τέχνην κατὰ
τοῦ μειρακίου, καὶ γὰρ καὶ τῷ θεῷ δυσάλωτος ἐφαίνε-
το. ἐξοπλίσας οὖν ἑαυτὸν καὶ πᾶσαν δύναμιν ἐρωτικῶν
φαρμάκων περιβαλόμενος ἐστράτευεν ἐφ' Ἀβροκόμην. 2. ἤγετο δὲ τῆς Ἀρτέμιδος ἐπιχώριος ἑορτή· ἔδει
δὲ πομπεύειν[6] ἀπὸ τῆς πόλεως ἐπὶ τὸ ἱερόν, στάδιοι δέ
εἰσιν ἑπτά, πάσας τὰς ἐπιχωρίους παρθένους κε-
κοσμημένας πολυτελῶς καὶ τοὺς ἐφήβους, ὅσοι τὴν

---

5 Jackson: καλλίονα
6 ἔδει δὲ πομπεύειν post ἑπτά transp. Jackson

---

4 The theme of Eros despised was familiar in myth and folktale, cf. Euripides' Hippolytus and Theocritus' Daphnis.
5 The famous story of Acontius and Cydippe (Callimachus
Aetia 3, Ovid Her. 20 and 21) is similar.

prayers. 4. The young man held a high opinion of himself, glorying both in his spiritual accomplishments and even more so in his physical beauty. Everything generally reckoned fine he despised as inferior, and nothing seen or heard seemed to him worthy of Habrocomes. 5. Whenever he was told that a boy was handsome or a girl pretty, he would mock those who said so for not knowing that he alone was handsome. He did not even recognize Eros as a god but rejected him wholesale and paid no attention to him, holding that no one at all would ever fall in love or submit to this god unwillingly. 6. Whenever he saw a shrine or statue of Eros he would laugh and declare that he was superior to any Eros both in physical beauty and power. And that was the case: wherever Habrocomes appeared, no statue looked handsome and no picture was admired.

Eros grew furious at this,[4] being a competitive god and implacable against those who disdain him. He tried to find a stratagem to use against the young man, for even to the god he looked hard to catch. So he got himself fully armed and, equipping himself with a complete arsenal of love potions, set forth against Habrocomes.[5] 2. A local festival for Artemis[6] was underway, and from the city to her shrine, a distance of seven stades,[7] all the local girls had to march sumptuously adorned, as did all the ephebes[8] who were

2

---

[6] Patron goddess of the unmarried, whose shrines were typically situated in liminal places; she had an old and important cult at Ephesus, and her temple there was regarded as one of the "wonders" of the world.

[7] About 1.3 km.

[8] Originally "cadets" in military training; by Xenophon's time the *ephebeia* had become a largely symbolic association for young men from prominent families.

αὐτὴν ἡλικίαν εἶχον τῷ Ἀβροκόμῃ. ἦν δὲ αὐτὸς περὶ
τὰ ἑξκαίδεκα ἔτη καὶ τῶν ἐφήβων προσήπτετο καὶ ἐν
τῇ πομπῇ τὰ πρῶτα ἐφέρετο. 3. πολὺ δὲ πλῆθος ἐπὶ
τὴν θέαν, πολὺ μὲν ἐγχώριον, πολὺ δὲ ξενικόν, καὶ γὰρ
ἔθος ἦν ἐκείνῃ τῇ πανηγύρει καὶ νυμφίους ταῖς παρθένοις εὑρίσκεσθαι καὶ γυναῖκας τοῖς ἐφήβοις. 4.
παρῆσαν δὲ κατὰ στίχον οἱ πομπεύοντες, πρῶτα μὲν
τὰ ἱερὰ καὶ δᾷδες καὶ κανᾶ καὶ θυμιάματα, ἐπὶ τούτοις
ἵπποι καὶ κύνες καὶ σκεύη κυνηγετικά, ὧν τὰ μὲν
πολεμικά, τὰ δὲ πλεῖστα εἰρηνικά. ** ἑκάστη δὲ αὐτῶν
οὕτως ὡς πρὸς ἐραστὴν ἐκεκόσμητο. 5. ἦρχε δὲ τῆς
τῶν παρθένων τάξεως Ἀνθία, θυγάτηρ Μεγαμήδους
καὶ Εὐίππης, ἐγχωρίων. ἦν δὲ τὸ κάλλος τῆς Ἀνθίας
οἷον θαυμάσαι καὶ πολὺ τὰς ἄλλας ὑπερεβάλετο παρθένους. ἔτη μὲν ὡς τεσσαρεσκαίδεκα ἐγεγόνει, ἤνθει
δὲ αὐτῆς τὸ σῶμα ἐπ᾽ εὐμορφίᾳ, καὶ ὁ τοῦ σχήματος
κόσμος πολὺς εἰς ὥραν συνεβάλετο· 6. κόμη ξανθή, ἡ
πολλὴ καθειμένη, ὀλίγη πεπλεγμένη, πρὸς τὴν τῶν
ἀνέμων φορὰν κινουμένη· ὀφθαλμοὶ γοργοί, φαιδροὶ
μὲν ὡς καλῆς,[7] φοβεροὶ δὲ ὡς σώφρονος· ἐσθὴς χιτὼν
ἁλουργής, ζωστὸς εἰς γόνυ, μέχρι βραχιόνων καθει-
μένος, νεβρὶς περικειμένη, ὅπλα[8] γωρυτὸς ἀνημμένος,
τόξα < . . . >,[9] ἄκοντες φερόμενοι, κύνες ἑπόμενοι. 7.
πολλάκις αὐτὴν ἐπὶ τοῦ τεμένους ἰδόντες Ἐφέσιοι
προσεκύνησαν ὡς Ἄρτεμιν, καὶ τότ᾽ οὖν ὀφθείσης
ἀνεβόησε τὸ πλῆθος, καὶ ἦσαν ποικίλαι παρὰ τῶν
θεωμένων φωναί, τῶν μὲν ὑπ᾽ ἐκπλήξεως τὴν θεὸν
εἶναι λεγόντων, τῶν δὲ ἄλλην τινὰ ὑπὸ τῆς θεοῦ

---

7 O'Sullivan cl. Aristaenet. 1.10.7–8: κόρης
8 ὅπλα post τόξα transp. Peerlkamp
9 Lacunam participio desiderato suspicatur O'Sullivan

the same age as Habrocomes; he was about sixteen and already enrolled among the ephebes, and he headed the procession. 3. For the spectacle there was a large crowd both local and visiting, for it was customary at this assemblage to find husbands for the girls and wives for the ephebes. 4. The procession marched along in file, first the sacred objects, torches, baskets, and incense, followed by horses, dogs, and hunting equipment, some of it martial, most of it peaceful ‹ . . . › each of the girls was adorned as for a lover. 5. Heading the line of girls was Anthia,[9] daughter of Megamedes and Euippe,[10] locals. Anthia's beauty was marvelous and far surpassed the other girls. She was fourteen, her body was blooming with shapeliness, and the adornment of her dress enhanced her grace. 6. Her hair was blonde, mostly loose, only little of it braided, and moving as the breezes took it. Her eyes were vivacious, bright like a beauty's but forbidding like a chaste girl's; her clothing was a belted purple tunic, knee-length and falling loose over the arms, and over it a fawnskin with a quiver attached, arrows ‹ . . . ›, javelins in hand, dogs following behind. 7. Often when seeing her at the shrine, the Ephesians worshiped her as Artemis, so also at the sight of her on this occasion the crowd cheered; the opinions of the spectators were various, some in their astonishment declaring that she was the goddess herself, others that she

[9] "Blossomy." The usual form of the name is Antheia (which appears in a fragmentary novel, PSI 726), but Anthia, the form given in F and the Suda, is attested as an actual name in papyri.

[10] Aristocratic names; Megamedes is also the name of a character in the fragmentary novel *Chione*.

πε[ρι]ποιημένην, προσηύχοντο δὲ πάντες καὶ προσεκύνουν καὶ τοὺς γονεῖς αὐτῆς ἐμακάριζον, ἦν δὲ
διαβόητος τοῖς θεωμένοις ἅπασιν Ἀνθία ἡ καλή. 8. ὡς
δὲ παρῆλθε τὸ τῶν παρθένων πλῆθος οὐδεὶς ἄλλο τι ἢ
Ἀνθίαν ἔλεγεν, ὡς δὲ Ἁβροκόμης μετὰ τῶν ἐφήβων
ἐπέστη τοὐνθένδε, καίτοι καλοῦ ὄντος τοῦ κατὰ τὰς
παρθένους θεάματος, πάντες ἰδόντες Ἁβροκόμην ἐκείνων ἐπελάθοντο, ἔτρεψαν δὲ τὰς ὄψεις ἐπ᾽ αὐτὸν βοῶντες ὑπὸ τῆς θέας ἐκπεπληγμένοι, "καλὸς Ἁβροκόμης"
λέγοντες, "καὶ οἷος οὐδὲ εἷς καλοῦ μίμημα θεοῦ." 9.
ἤδη δέ τινες καὶ τοῦτο προσέθεσαν "οἷος ἂν γάμος
γένοιτο Ἁβροκόμου καὶ Ἀνθίας." καὶ ταῦτα ἦν πρῶτα
τῆς Ἔρωτος τέχνης μελετήματα. ταχὺ μὲν δὴ εἰς
ἑκατέρους ἡ περὶ ἀλλήλων ἦλθε δόξα, καὶ ἥ τε Ἀνθία
τὸν Ἁβροκόμην ἐπεθύμει ἰδεῖν καὶ ὁ τέως ἀνέραστος
Ἁβροκόμης ἤθελεν Ἀνθίαν ἰδεῖν.

3   Ὡς οὖν ἐτετέλεστο ἡ πομπή, ἦλθον δὲ εἰς τὸ ἱερὸν
θύσοντες ἅπαν τὸ πλῆθος καὶ ὁ τῆς πομπῆς κόσμος
ἐλέλυτο, ᾔεσαν δὲ ἐς ταὐτὸν ἄνδρες καὶ γυναῖκες,
ἔφηβοι καὶ παρθένοι, ἐνταῦθα ὁρῶσιν ἀλλήλους, καὶ
ἁλίσκεται Ἀνθία ὑπὸ τοῦ Ἁβροκόμου, ἡττᾶται δὲ ὑπὸ
Ἔρωτος Ἁβροκόμης καὶ ἐνεώρα τε συνεχέστερον τῇ
κόρῃ καὶ ἀπαλλαγῆναι τῆς ὄψεως ἐθέλων οὐκ ἐδύνατο,
κατεῖχε δὲ αὐτὸν ἐγκείμενος ὁ θεός. 2. διέκειτο δὲ καὶ
Ἀνθία πονήρως, ὅλοις μὲν καὶ ἀναπεπταμένοις τοῖς
ὀφθαλμοῖς τὸ Ἁβροκόμου κάλλος εἰσρέον δεχομένη,
ἤδη δὲ καὶ τῶν παρθένοις πρεπόντων καταφρονοῦσα·
καὶ γὰρ ἐλάλησεν ἄν τι, ἵνα Ἁβροκόμης ἀκούσῃ, καὶ
μέρη τοῦ σώματος ἐγύμνωσεν ἂν τὰ δυνατά, ἵνα
Ἁβροκόμης ἴδῃ. ὁ δὲ αὑτὸν ἐδεδώκει πρὸς τὴν θέαν
καὶ ἦν αἰχμάλωτος τοῦ θεοῦ. 3. καὶ τότε μὲν θύσαντες
ἀπηλλάττοντο λυπούμενοι καὶ τῷ τάχει τῆς ἀπαλ-

was someone else fashioned by the goddess, but all of them prayed, bowed down, and congratulated her parents, and the universal cry among all the spectators was "Anthia the beautiful!" 8. As the crowd of girls passed by, no one said anything but "Anthia," but as soon as Habrocomes followed with the ephebes, as lovely as the spectacle of the girls had been, at the sight of Habrocomes they all forgot about them and turned their gaze to him, stunned at the sight and shouting "Handsome Habrocomes! Peerless likeness of a handsome god!" 9. And now some added, "What a match Habrocomes and Anthia would make!" These were opening moves in Eros' stratagem. They were both quickly aware of each other's reputation; Anthia longed to see Habrocomes and Habrocomes, hitherto insensible to love, wanted to see Anthia.

And so when the procession was over, the whole crowd 3 repaired to the shrine for the sacrifice, the order of the procession was dissolved, and men and women, ephebes and girls, gathered in the same spot. There they saw each other. Anthia was captivated by Habrocomes, and Habrocomes was bested by Eros. He kept gazing at the girl and though he tried, he could not take his eyes off her: the god pressed his attack and held him fast. 2. Anthia too was in a bad way, as with eyes wide open she took in Habrocomes' handsomeness as it flowed into her, already putting maidenly decorum out of her mind: for what she said was for Habrocomes to hear, and she uncovered what parts of her body she could for Habrocomes to see. He gave himself over to the sight and fell captive to the god. 3. After the sacrifice they parted painfully, complaining about being

λαγῆς μεμφόμενοι ⟨καὶ⟩ ἀλλήλους βλέπειν ἐθέλοντες
ἐπιστρεφόμενοι καὶ ὑφιστάμενοι πολλὰς προφάσεις
διατριβῆς ηὕρισκον. 4. ὡς δὲ ἦλθον ἑκάτερος παρ᾽
ἑαυτὸν ἔγνωσαν τότε οἷ κακῶν ἐγεγόνεισαν, καὶ ἔννοια
ἑκάστῳ ὑπῄει τῆς ὄψεως θατέρου καὶ ὁ ἔρως ἐν αὐτοῖς
ἀνεκαίετο καὶ τὸ περιττὸν τῆς ἡμέρας αὐξήσαντες τὴν
ἐπιθυμίαν ἐπειδὴ εἰς ὕπνον ᾖσαν ἐν ἀθρόῳ γίνονται
τῷ δεινῷ καὶ ὁ ἔρως ἐν ἑκατέροις ἦν ἀκατάσχετος.

4   Λαβὼν δὴ τὴν κόμην ὁ Ἁβροκόμης καὶ σπαράξας
τὴν ἐσθῆτα "φεῦ μοι τῶν κακῶν" εἶπε, "τί πέπονθα
δυστυχής; ὁ μέχρι νῦν ἀνδρικὸς Ἁβροκόμης, ὁ κατα-
φρονῶν Ἔρωτος, ὁ τῷ θεῷ λοιδορούμενος ἑάλωκα καὶ
νενίκημαι καὶ παρθένῳ δουλεύειν ἀναγκάζομαι, καὶ
φαίνεταί τις ἤδη καλλίων ἐμοῦ καὶ θεὸν Ἔρωτα καλῶ.
2. ὦ πάντα ἄνανδρος ἐγὼ καὶ πονηρός. οὐ καρτερήσω
νῦν; οὐ μενῶ γεν⟨ν⟩ικός; οὐκ ἔσομαι κρείττων[10] Ἔρωτος; νῦν οὐδὲν ὄντα θεὸν νικῆσαί με δεῖ. 3. καλὴ
παρθένος· τί δέ; τοῖς σοῖς ὀφθαλμοῖς, Ἁβροκόμη,
εὔμορφος Ἀνθία, ἀλλ᾽ ἐὰν θέλῃς οὐχὶ σοί. δεδόχθω
ταῦτα· οὐκ ἂν Ἔρως ποτέ μου κρατήσαι." 4. ταῦτα
ἔλεγε καὶ ὁ θεὸς σφοδρότερος αὐτῷ ἐνέκειτο καὶ εἷλκεν
ἀντιπίπτοντα καὶ ὠδύνα μὴ θέλοντα. οὐκέτι δὴ καρτερῶν, ῥίψας ἑαυτὸν εἰς γῆν "νενίκηκας", εἶπεν,
"Ἔρως. μέγα σοι τρόπαιον ἐγήγερται κατὰ Ἁβροκόμου τοῦ σώφρονος· ἱκέτην ἔχεις. 5. ἀλλὰ σῶσον
τὸν[11] ἐπὶ σὲ καταπεφευγότα τὸν πάντων δεσπότην. μή
με περιίδῃς μηδὲ ἐπὶ πολὺ τιμωρήσῃ τὸν θρασύν.
ἄπειρος ὤν, Ἔρως, ἔτι τῶν σῶν ὑπερηφάνουν· ἀλλὰ
νῦν Ἀνθίαν ἡμῖν ἀπόδος· γενοῦ μὴ πικρὸς μόνον

10 Hemsterhuys: καλλίων
11 Jackson: ἔχεις ἄσωτον σὸν

parted so soon, <and> because they wanted to see each other they kept turning around and stopping, and found many an excuse for delay. 4. It was when each had come home that they realized what trouble had befallen them. For both of them the image of the other kept coming to mind, love flared up inside them, and having stoked their desire for the rest of the day, at bedtime they were in dire straits, and the love in each of them was uncontrollable.

Habrocomes pulled his hair and ripped his clothes. 4 "What troubles I have!" he exclaimed, "What bad luck! Until now Habrocomes was manly, contemptuous of Eros, a maligner of the god, and now I'm caught, vanquished, forced to be a girl's slave. As there now seems to be someone better looking than me, I acknowledge Eros as a god. 2. Wait: what an utterly worthless coward I am! Will I not resist this time? Will I not stand firm? Will I not remain stronger than Eros? It's time that I defeated this no-account god. 3. A girl is beautiful, but what of it? It's in your eyes, Habrocomes, that Anthia is attractive, not in your heart, if only you have the will. Let this be your decision: Eros shall never vanquish me!" 4. At these words the god attacked him more determinedly, dragging him along as he resisted and tormenting him as he balked. When he could hold out no longer, he threw himself to the ground and cried, "You win, Eros! Here stands your great trophy over Habrocomes the Chaste. He is your suppliant. 5. Now rescue one who takes refuge with you, the master of the universe! Don't abandon me or punish my rashness any further. It was through inexperience, Eros, that I scorned your powers. But now please give me Anthia! Don't be only

ἀντιλέγοντι, ἀλλ' εὐεργέτης ἡττωμένῳ θεός." ταῦτα
ἔλεγεν, ὁ δὲ Ἔρως ἔτι ὠργίζετο καὶ μεγάλην τῆς
ὑπεροψίας ἐνενοεῖτο τιμωρίαν [τὸ] πράξασθαι τὸν
Ἀβροκόμην. 6. διέκειτο δὲ καὶ ἡ Ἀνθία πονήρως καὶ
οὐκέτι φέρειν δυναμένη ἐπεγείρει ἑαυτὴν πειρωμένη
τοὺς παρόντας λανθάνειν. "τί" φησὶν "ὦ δυστυχὴς
πέπονθα; παρθένος παρ' ἡλικίαν ἐρῶ καὶ ὀδυνῶμαι
καινὰ καὶ κόρῃ μὴ πρέποντα. ἐφ' Ἀβροκόμῃ μαίνομαι
καλῷ μέν, ἀλλ' ὑπερηφάνῳ. 7. καὶ τίς ἔσται ὁ τῆς
ἐπιθυμίας ὅρος καὶ τί τὸ πέρας τοῦ κακοῦ; σοβαρὸς
οὗτος ἐρώμενος, παρθένος ἐγὼ φρουρουμένη· τίνα
βοηθὸν λήψομαι; τίνι ταῦτα κοινώσομαι; ποῦ δὲ
Ἀβροκόμην ὄψομαι;"

5   Ταῦτα ἑκάτερος αὐτῶν δι' ὅλης νυκτὸς ὠδύρετο,
εἶχον δὲ πρὸ ὀφθαλμῶν τὰς ὄψεις τὰς ἑαυτῶν, τὰς
εἰκόνας ἐπὶ τῆς ψυχῆς ἀλλήλων ἀναπλάττοντες. ὡς δὲ
ἡμέρα ἐγένετο ᾔει μὲν Ἀβροκόμης ἐπὶ τὰ συνήθη
γυμνάσματα, ᾔει δὲ ἡ παρθένος ἐπὶ τὴν ἐξ ἔθους
θρησκείαν τῆς θεοῦ. 2. ἦν δὲ αὐτοῖς καὶ τὰ σώματα ἐκ
τῆς παρελθούσης νυκτὸς πεπονηκότα καὶ τὸ βλέμμα
ἄθυμον καὶ οἱ χρῶτες ἠλλαγμένοι· καὶ τοῦτο ἐπὶ πολὺ
ἐγίνετο καὶ πλέον οὐδὲν αὐτοῖς ἦν. 3. ἐν τούτῳ ἐν τῷ
ἱερῷ τῆς θεοῦ διημερεύοντες ἐνεώρων ἀλλήλοις, εἰπεῖν
τὸ ἀληθὲς φόβῳ πρὸς ἑκατέρους αἰδούμενοι· τοσοῦτο
δὲ ἐστέναξεν ἄν ποτε Ἀβροκόμης καὶ ἐδάκρυσε καὶ
προσηύχετο[12] τῆς κόρης ἀκουούσης ἐλεεινῶς, 4. ἡ δὲ
Ἀνθία ἔπασχε μὲν τὰ αὐτά, πολὺ δὲ μείζονι τῇ συμφορᾷ κατείχετο· εἰ δέ ποτε ἄλλας παρθένους ἢ γυναῖκας ἴδοι βλεπούσας εἰς ἐκεῖνον, ἑώρων δὲ ἅπασαι
Ἀβροκόμην, δήλη ἦν λυπουμένη μὴ παρευδοκιμηθῇ
φοβουμένη. εὐχαὶ δὲ αὐτοῖς ἑκατέροις ἦσαν πρὸς τὴν
θεὸν κοινῇ, λανθάνουσαι μέν, ἀλλὰ ἐγίνοντο ὅμοιαι.

a harsh god toward the gainsayer but also a benefactor to the vanquished." This was his prayer, but Eros was still angry and determined to think of a great punishment to visit on Habrocomes for his scorn. 6. Anthia too was in a bad way: no longer able to bear it, she collected herself as she tried to hide her condition from those around her. "What is wrong with me?" she said, "I'm an underage maiden in love, and I hurt in ways strange and inappropriate for a girl. I'm crazy for Habrocomes, who is handsome but arrogant. 7. Where is the limit of my desire, and where is the end of my suffering? The one I love is haughty, and I am a maiden kept under surveillance. What helper can I find? To whom can I confide this? Where can I see Habrocomes?"

Each of them spent the whole night lamenting this way, and they held before their eyes the sight of the other as they refashioned their mental images of one another. Next day, Habrocomes went to his accustomed exercises and the girl went as usual to serve the cult of the goddess. 2. Their bodies were tired out after the previous night, their eyes listless, and their complexions altered, and this continued for quite a while with no change in their situation. 3. In the meantime, they spent their days watching each other in the goddess's temple, in their embarrassment fearful of telling each other the truth. Habrocomes went so far as moaning, weeping, and praying in pitiful fashion within earshot of the girl, 4. while Anthia felt the same way but was more deeply afflicted: whenever she spotted other girls or women looking at him—and they all eyed Habrocomes—she was visibly distressed, in fear of being outclassed. Each of them said prayers to the goddess that were private but

5

---

12 Hercher: προσείχετο

5. χρόνου δὲ προϊόντος οὐκέτι τὸ μειράκιον ἐκαρτέρει, ἤδη δὲ αὐτῷ καὶ τὸ σῶμα πᾶν ἠφάνιστο καὶ ἡ ψυχὴ καταπεπτώκει, ὥστε ἐν πολλῇ ἀθυμίᾳ τὸν Λυκομήδην καὶ τὴν Θεμιστὼ γεγονέναι οὐκ εἰδότας μὲν ὅ τι εἴη τὸ συμβαῖνον Ἁβροκόμῃ, δεδοικότας δὲ ἐκ τῶν ὁρωμένων. 6. ἐν ὁμοίῳ δὲ φόβῳ καὶ ὁ Μεγαμήδης καὶ ἡ Εὐίππη [καὶ] περὶ τῆς Ἀνθίας καθεισήκεισαν ὁρῶντες αὐτῆς τὸ μὲν κάλλος μαραινόμενον, τὴν δὲ αἰτίαν οὐ φαινομένην τῆς συμφορᾶς. εἰς τέλος εἰσάγουσι παρὰ τὴν Ἀνθίαν μάντεις καὶ ἱερέας ὡς εὑρήσοντας λύσιν τοῦ δεινοῦ. 7. οἱ δὲ ἐλθόντες ἔθυόν τε ἱερεῖα καὶ ποικίλα ἐπέσπενδον καὶ ἐπέλεγον φωνὰς βαρβαρικὰς ἐξιλάσκεσθαί τινας λέγοντες δαίμονας καὶ προσεποίουν ὡς εἴη τὸ δεινὸν ἐκ τῶν ὑποχθονίων θεῶν. 8. πολλὰ δὲ καὶ ὑπὲρ Ἁβροκόμου οἱ περὶ τὸν Λυκομήδην ἔθυόν τε καὶ ηὔχοντο, λύσις δὲ οὐδεμία τοῦ δεινοῦ οὐδὲ ἑτέρῳ αὐτῶν ἐγίνετο ἀλλὰ καὶ ἔτι μᾶλλον ὁ ἔρως ἀνεκαίετο. 9. ἔκειντο μὲν δὴ ἑκάτεροι νοσοῦντες, πάνυ ἐπισφαλῶς διακείμενοι, ὅσον οὐδέπω τεθνήξεσθαι προσδοκώμενοι, κατειπεῖν αὐτῶν τὴν συμφορὰν μὴ δυνάμενοι. τέλος ⟨δὲ⟩ πέμπουσιν οἱ πατέρες ἑκατέρων εἰς θεοῦ[13] μαντευσόμενοι τήν τε αἰτίαν τῆς νόσου καὶ τὴν ἀπαλλαγήν.

6   Ὀλίγον δὲ ἀπέχει τὸ ἱερὸν τοῦ ἐν Κολοφῶνι Ἀπόλλωνος διάπλουν ἀπὸ Ἐφέσου σταδίων ὀγδοήκοντα. ἐνταῦθα οἱ παρ᾽ ἑκατέρων ἀφικόμενοι δέονται τοῦ θεοῦ ἀληθῆ μαντεύσασθαι· ἐληλύθεσαν δὴ κατὰ ταὐτά, 2. χρᾷ δὲ ὁ θεὸς κοινὰ ἀμφοτέροις τὰ μαντεύματα ἐμμέτρως. τὰ ⟨δὲ⟩ ἔπη τάδε·

---

13 θεοῦ Cobet: θεοὺς (quod et in Plu. Mor. 245C corrigendum)

identical. 5. As time passed, the young man could go on no longer: already his physique had vanished entirely and his mind had collapsed. Lycomedes and Themisto were considerably depressed, not knowing what had happened to Habrocomes but frightened by what they saw. 6. Megamedes and Euippe had become equally frightened about Anthia as they saw her beauty fading away without an apparent reason for her affliction. Finally they brought in seers and priests to Anthia to find relief from her terrible state. 7. Upon arrival they sacrificed victims, made various libations, uttered exotic words to placate, so they said, certain divinities, and pretended that her terrible state came from the underworld gods. 8. Lycomedes' household also made plenty of sacrifices and prayers for Habrocomes, but there was no relief for either of them from their terrible state, but their love burned even stronger. 9. Both lay sick, in a condition so critical that they were expected to die at any moment, unable to acknowledge what was wrong. Finally their fathers sent a delegation to the god's shrine to have the cause and the cure of the sickness divined.

The temple of Apollo at Colophon is a short distance away, eighty stades from Ephesus by boat.[11] There the envoys for both parties came seeking a true response from the god. They had come with the same question, and the god gave the same response in verse to both. The lines were as follows:

[11] About 14 km. This shrine of Apollo in Claros had been a major oracular center since archaic times.

τίπτε ποθεῖτε μαθεῖν νούσου τέλος ἠδὲ καὶ
    ἀρχήν;
ἀμφοτέρους μία νοῦσος ἔχει, λύσις ἔνθεν
    ἀνυστή.[14]
δεινὰ δ' ὁρῶ τοῖσδεσσι πάθη καὶ ἀνήνυτα ἔργα·
ἀμφότεροι φεύξονται ὑπὲρ ἅλα λυσσοδίωκτοι,
δεσμὰ[15] δὲ μοχθήσουσι παρ' ἀνδράσι
    μιξοθαλάσσοις
καὶ τάφος ἀμφοτέροις θάλαμος καὶ πῦρ ἀΐδηλον.
ἀλλ' ἔτι που μετὰ πήματ' ἀρείονα πότμον
    ἔχουσι[16]
καὶ ποταμοῦ ἱεροῦ[17] παρὰ ῥεύμασιν Ἴσιδι σεμνῇ
σωτείρῃ μετόπισθε παριστᾶσ'[18] ὄλβια δῶρα.

7   Ταῦτα ὡς ἐκομίσθη τὰ μαντεύματα εἰς Ἔφεσον
εὐθὺς μὲν οἱ πατέρες αὐτῶν ἦσαν ἐν ἀμηχανίᾳ καὶ τὸ
δεινὸν ὅ τι ἦν πάνυ ἠπόρουν, συμβάλλειν δὲ τὰ τοῦ
θεοῦ λόγια οὐκ ἐδύναντο· οὔτε γὰρ τίς ἡ νόσος οὔτε τίς
ἡ φυγὴ οὔτε τίνα τὰ δεσμὰ οὔτε ὁ τάφος τίς οὔτε ὁ
ποταμὸς τίς οὔτε τίς ἡ ἐκ τῆς θεοῦ βοήθεια. 2. ἔδοξεν
οὖν αὐτοῖς πολλὰ βουλευομένοις παραμυθήσασθαι
τὸν χρησμὸν ὡς οἷόν τε καὶ συζεῦξαι γάμῳ τοὺς
παῖδας, ὡς τοῦτο καὶ τοῦ θεοῦ βουλ[ευ]ομένου δι' ὧν
ἐμαντεύσατο. ἐδόκει δὴ ταῦτα καὶ διέγνωσαν μετὰ τὸν
γάμον ἐκπέμψαι χρόνῳ τινὶ ἀποδημήσοντας αὐτούς.

---

14 Abresch: ἀνέστη   15 Ed. Cocchiana: δεινὰ
16 Hunc versum post δῶρα transp. Passow
17 Locella cl. 1.7.1: Νείλου
18 Passow: παραστῆς

---

12 Worship of the Egyptian goddess Isis became widespread

Why do you long to discover the end and the start of
 this illness?
Both are in thrall to one illness, and thence must the
 cure be accomplished.
Terrible their sufferings I can foresee and toils never-
 ending.
Both will take flight o'er the sea, pursued by a frenzy
 of madness;
Chains will they bear at the hands of men who
 consort with the ocean,
And one tomb and annihilating fire will be their
 nuptial bower.
Yet in time, when their sufferings are over, a happier
 fate is in store,
And alongside the streams of the sacred river to Isis
 the Holy,[12]
Isis the Savior, in time thereafter rich gifts shall they
 offer.

When this response was brought to Ephesus, their fa- 7
thers were immediately at a loss, had no idea what the danger was, and could not understand the god's utterance:
what was the illness? the flight? the chains? the tomb? the
river? the help from the goddess? 2. So after much deliber-
ation they decided to take as encouraging a view of the oracle as possible and join the children in marriage, since the
god too was expressing this wish in his response. This decided, they determined that after the wedding they should
send the couple on a trip out of town for a while. 3. Already

in the Hellenistic and Roman world, cf. Plutarch *Isis and Osiris*
and (for her role as savior) Book 11 of Apuleius' *Metamorphoses*.

3. μεστὴ μὲν ἤδη ἡ πόλις ἦν τῶν εὐωχουμένων, πάντα δ᾽ ἦν ἐστεφανωμένα καὶ διαβόητος ὁ μέλλων γάμος, ἐμακαρίζετο δὲ ὑπὸ πάντων ὁ μὲν οἵαν ἄξεται γυναῖκα [Ἀνθίαν], ἡ δὲ οἵῳ μειρακίῳ συγκατακλιθήσεται. 4. ὁ δὲ Ἁβροκόμης ὡς ἐπύθετο καὶ τὸν χρησμὸν καὶ τὸν γάμον ἐπὶ μὲν τῷ τὴν Ἀνθίαν ἕξειν μεγάλως ἔχαιρεν, ἐφόβει δὲ αὐτὸν οὐδὲν τὰ μεμαντευμένα ἀλλ᾽ ἐδόκει παντὸς εἶναι δεινοῦ τὰ παρόντα ἡδίονα. κατὰ ταὐτὰ δὲ καὶ ἡ Ἀνθία ἥδετο μὲν ὅτι Ἁβροκόμην ἕξει, τίς δὲ ἡ φυγὴ ἢ τίνες αἱ συμφοραὶ κατεφρόνει, πάντων τῶν ἐσομένων κακῶν Ἁβροκόμην ἔχουσα παραμυθίαν.

8 Ὡς οὖν ἐφέστηκεν ὁ τῶν γάμων καιρὸς ⟨καὶ⟩ παννυχίδες ἤγοντο καὶ ἱερεῖα πολλὰ ἐθύετο τῇ θεῷ, καὶ ἐπειδὴ ταῦτα ἐκτετέλεστο ἡκούσης τῆς νυκτός, βραδύνειν δὲ πάντα ἐδόκει Ἁβροκόμῃ καὶ Ἀνθίᾳ, ἦγον τὴν κόρην εἰς τὸν θάλαμον μετὰ λαμπάδων τὸν ὑμέναιον ᾄδοντες, ἐπευφημοῦντες, καὶ εἰσαγ⟨αγ⟩όντες κατέκλινον. 2. ἦν δὲ αὐτοῖς ὁ θάλαμος πεποιημένος· κλίνη χρυσῆ στρώμασιν ἔστρωτο πορφυροῖς καὶ ἐπὶ τῆς κλίνης Βαβυλωνία ἐπεποίκιλτο σκηνή· παίζοντες Ἔρωτες, οἱ μὲν Ἀφροδίτην θεραπεύοντες, ἦν δὲ καὶ Ἀφροδίτης εἰκών, οἱ δὲ ἱππεύοντες ἀναβάται στρουθοῖς, οἱ δὲ στεφάνους πλέκοντες, οἱ δὲ ἄνθη φέροντες. 3. ταῦτα ἐν τῷ ἑτέρῳ μέρει τῆς σκηνῆς. ἐν δὲ τῷ ἑτέρῳ Ἄρης ἦν οὐχ ὡπλισμένος ἀλλ᾽ ὡς πρὸς ἐρωμένην τὴν Ἀφροδίτην κεκοσμημένος, ἐστεφανωμένος, χλανίδα[19] ἔχων· Ἔρως αὐτὸν ὡδήγει λαμπάδα ἔχων ἡμμένην. ὑπ᾽ αὐτῇ τῇ σκηνῇ κατέκλιναν τὴν Ἀνθίαν ἀγαγόντες πρὸς τὸν Ἁβροκόμην, ἐπέκλεισάν τε τὰς θύρας.

9 Τοῖς δὲ ἑκατέροις πάθος συνέβη ταὐτὸν καὶ οὔτε

19 Hemsterhuys: χλαμύδα

the city was full of revelers, everything was festooned with garlands, and the impending wedding was much bally-hooed. Everyone saw a blessed future for him in marrying such a wife and for her in sharing her bed with such a young man. 4. When Habrocomes found out about the prophecy and the wedding, he was overjoyed at the prospect of marrying Anthia and the prophecies did not scare him at all: his present situation seemed nicer than any danger. Anthia took the same delight at the prospect of marrying Habrocomes: she paid no attention to what the flight or the disasters might be, since she had Habrocomes as a consolation for all future ills.

And so the time for their wedding arrived. There were   8
nightlong revels and many sacrifices to the goddess, and when these were performed and evening had come, though to Habrocomes and Anthia everything seemed to take too long, they escorted the girl to the bridal chamber with torches, singing the bridal hymn and shouting blessings, took her inside, and put her on the bed. 2. The chamber had been prepared for them: a golden bed had been spread with purple sheets, and above the bed a Babylonian canopy had been finely embroidered: there were Cupids at play, some attending Aphrodite, who was also represented, some riding mounted on sparrows, some plaiting garlands, some bearing flowers. 3. These were on one part of the canopy; on the other was Ares, not armed but garlanded and wearing a fine cloak, dressed for his lover Aphrodite; Eros, holding a lighted torch, was leading him on his way. Under the canopy itself they brought Anthia to Habrocomes, put her on the bed, and closed the doors.

The same passion overtook them both: they could no   9

προσειπεῖν ἔτι ἀλλήλους ἠδύναντο οὔτε ἀντιβλέψαι
τοῖς ὀφθαλμοῖς, ἔκειντο δὲ ὑφ᾽ ἡδονῆς παρειμένοι,
αἰδούμενοι, φοβούμενοι, πνευστιῶντες [ἡδόμενοι],
ἐπάλλετο δὲ αὐτοῖς τὰ σώματα καὶ ἐκραδαίνοντο αὐτοῖς αἱ ψυχαί. 2. ὀψὲ δὲ ὁ Ἁβροκόμης ἀνενεγκὼν
περιέλαβε τὴν Ἀνθίαν, ἡ δὲ ἐδάκρυε τῆς ψυχῆς αὐτῆς
σύμβολα προπεμπούσης τῆς ἐπιθυμίας τὰ δάκρυα.
καὶ ὁ Ἁβροκόμης "ὦ τῆς ἐμοὶ" φησὶ "ποθεινοτάτης
νυκτός, ἣν μόλις ἀπείληφα πολλὰς πρότερον νύκτας
δυστυχήσας. 3. ὦ φωτὸς ἡδίων ἐμοὶ κόρη καὶ τῶν
πώποτε λαλουμένων εὐτυχεστέρα, τὸν ἐραστὴν ἔχεις
ἄνδρα μεθ᾽ οὗ ζῆν καὶ ἀποθανεῖν ὑπάρξαι γυναικὶ
σώφρονι." εἰπὼν κατεφίλει τε καὶ ὑπεδέχετο τὰ δάκρυα
καὶ αὐτῷ ἐδόκει παντὸς μὲν εἶναι νέκταρος ποτιμώτερα
τὰ δάκρυα, παντὸς δὲ τοῦ πρὸς ὀδύνην φαρμάκου
δυνατώτερα. 4. ἡ δὲ ὀλίγα αὐτὸν προσφθεγξαμένη
"ναί" φησὶν "Ἁβροκόμη, δοκῶ σοι καλὴ καὶ μετὰ τὴν
σὴν εὐμορφίαν ἀρέσκω σοι; ἄνανδρε καὶ δειλέ, πόσον
ἐβράδυνας ἐρῶν χρόνον; πόσον ἠμέλησας; ἀπὸ τῶν
ἐμαυτῆς κακῶν ἃ πέπονθας οἶδα. 5. ἀλλ᾽ ἰδού, δάκρυα
μὲν ὑποδέχου τἀμὰ καὶ ἡ καλή σου κόμη πινέτω πόμα
τὸ ἐρωτικὸν καὶ συμφύντες ἀλλήλοις ἀναμιγῶμεν,
καταβρέχωμεν δὲ καὶ τοὺς στεφάνους τοῖς παρ᾽ ἀλλήλων δάκρυσιν ἵν᾽ ἡμῖν καὶ οὗτοι συνερῶσιν." 6. εἰποῦσα ἅπαν μὲν αὐτοῦ τὸ πρόσωπον ἠσπάζετο ἅπασαν δὲ
τὴν κόμην τοῖς αὑτῆς ὀφθαλμοῖς προσετίθει καὶ τοὺς
στεφάνους ἀνελάμβανε καὶ τὰ χείλη τοῖς χείλεσι
φιλοῦσα συνηρμόκει, καὶ ὅσα ἐνενόουν διὰ τῶν χει-
λέων ἐκ ψυχῆς εἰς τὴν θατέρου ψυχὴν [διὰ τοῦ φιλή-
ματος] παρεπέμπετο. 7. φιλοῦσα δὲ αὐτοῦ τοὺς ὀφθαλμοὺς "ὦ" φησὶ "πολλάκις με λυπήσαντες ὑμεῖς, ὦ τὸ
πρῶτον ἐνθέντες τῇ ἐμῇ κέντρον ψυχῇ, οἵ ποτε σοβα-

longer speak or meet each others' eyes but lay relaxed in pleasure, shy, fearful, breathing hard; their bodies were trembling and their hearts quivering. 2. At last Habrocomes recovered and embraced Anthia, and she started to cry as her heart itself poured forth the tears that were signs of her desire. Habrocomes sighed, "Ah night that I have most longed for and that was so hard to attain, after many previous nights in pain! Girl sweeter to me than the light of day, and luckier than any girl they talk about in stories, you have your lover as a husband: may it be yours to live and die with him as a chaste wife." With these words he kissed her and caught her tears, and he thought her tears sweeter to drink than any nectar and more potent against pain than any drug. 4. She spoke few words to him: "Truly, Habrocomes, do I look beautiful to you? Do I please you even after your own good looks? Unmanly coward, how long did you delay your love? How long did you neglect it? I know from my own ills what you suffered. 5. Here, catch my tears and let your beautiful hair drink a draught of love, let's cling together and become one, let's drench our garlands with each other's tears so that they too can share in our love." 6. With these words she pressed his whole face close, put all of his hair against her own eyes, took the garlands in her hands, and locked her lips on his in a kiss, and all their thoughts passed through their lips from one's heart to the other's. 7. As she kissed his eyes she said, "You're the ones that often caused me pain, you that first

ροὶ μέν, νῦν δὲ ἐρωτικοί, καλῶς μοι διηκονήσατε καὶ
τὸν ἔρωτα τὸν ἐμὸν καλῶς εἰς τὴν Ἀβροκόμου ψυχὴν
ὡδηγήσατε. 8. τοιγαροῦν ὑμᾶς πολλὰ φιλῶ καὶ ὑμῖν
ἐφαρμόζω τοὺς ὀφθαλμοὺς τοὺς ἐμοὺς τοὺς Ἀβροκόμου διακόνους, ὑμεῖς δὲ ἀεὶ βλέποιτε ταῦτα καὶ μήτε
Ἀβροκόμῃ ἄλλην δείξητε καλὴν μήτε ἐμοὶ δόξῃ τις
ἄλλος εὔμορφος. ἔχετε ψυχὰς ἃς αὐτοὶ ἐξεκαύσατε·
ταύτας ὁμοίως τηρήσατε." 9. ταῦτα εἶπε καὶ περιφύντες ἀνεπαύοντο καὶ τὰ πρῶτα τῶν Ἀφροδίτης
[ἐρώτων] ἀπήλαυον, ἐφιλονείκουν δὲ δι' ὅλης νυκτὸς
πρὸς ἀλλήλους, φιλοτιμούμενοι τίς φανεῖται μᾶλλον
ἐρῶν.

10   Ἐπειδὴ δὲ ἡμέρα ἐγένετο ἀνίσταντο πολὺ μὲν ἡδί-
ονες, πολὺ δὲ εὐθυμότεροι, ἀπολαύσαντες ἀλλήλων ὧν
ἐπεθύμησαν χρόνον πολύν.[20] 2. ἑορτὴ δὲ ἦν ἅπας ὁ
βίος αὐτοῖς καὶ μεστὰ εὐωχίας πάντα καὶ ἤδη καὶ τῶν
μεμαντευμένων λήθη, ἀλλ' οὐχὶ τὸ εἱμαρμένον ἐπελέ-
ληστο [ἀλλ'] οὐδὲ ὅτῳ ἐδόκει ταῦτα θεῷ ἡμέλει. 3.
χρόνου δὲ διελθόντος ὀλίγου ἔγνωσαν οἱ πατέρες
ἐκπέμπειν αὐτοὺς τῆς πόλεως κατὰ τὰ βεβουλευμένα,
ἤμελλόν τε γὰρ ἄλλην ὄψεσθαι γῆν καὶ ἄλλας πόλεις
καὶ τὸν τοῦ θεοῦ χρησμόν, ὡς οἷόν τε ἦν, παραμυθή-
σεσθαι ἀπαλλαγέντες χρόνῳ τινὶ Ἐφέσου. 4. παρεσκευάζετο δὴ πάντα αὐτοῖς πρὸς τὴν ἔξοδον, ναῦς τε
μεγάλη καὶ ναῦται πρὸς ἀγωγὴν ἕτοιμοι, καὶ τὰ ἐπιτήδεια ἐνεβάλλοντο, πολλὴ μὲν ἐσθὴς καὶ ποικίλη,
πολὺς δὲ ἄργυρος καὶ χρυσός, ἥ τε τῶν σιτίων ὑπερ-
βάλλουσα ἀφθονία. 5. θυσίαι δὲ πρὸ τῆς ἀγωγῆς τῇ
Ἀρτέμιδι καὶ εὐχαὶ τοῦ δήμου παντὸς καὶ δάκρυα
πάντων ὡς μελλόντων ἀπαλλάττεσθαι παίδων κοινῶν.
ἦν δὲ ὁ πλοῦς αὐτοῖς ἐπ' Αἴγυπτον παρεσκευασμένος.
6. ὡς δ' ἦλθεν ἡ τῆς ἀναγωγῆς ἡμέρα πολλοὶ μὲν

planted a goad in my heart! Once haughty but amorous now, you have served me well, and well have you guided my love into Habrocomes' heart. 8. For that I give you lots of kisses and join to you my own eyes, the servants of Habrocomes. May you always see just what you see now and not show Habrocomes any other beautiful girl, and may no other man appear good-looking to me. Own the hearts that you yourselves set afire, and look after them both alike." 9. With these words they relaxed in close embrace and for the first time enjoyed the gifts of Aphrodite, and all night long they competed with each other, ambitious to be revealed as the one more in love.

The next day, they arose much happier and in much   10
better spirits, now that they had enjoyed what they had for a long time desired from one another. 2. Their whole life was a festival, everything was full of enjoyment, and even the oracle was already forgotten. But fate had not forgotten, nor did the god neglect what he had decided. 3. A short while later, the fathers resolved to send them away from the city according to plan; they would see another country and other cities and soften the god's oracle, as far as they could, by being away from Ephesus for a time. 4. So everything was made ready for their departure: there was a large ship with a crew ready to sail, provisions were put on board, lots of clothing of various kinds, lots of silver and gold, and an excessive abundance of food. 5. Before their departure there were sacrifices for Artemis, prayers from the entire citizenry, and tears from everyone as if they were about to be separated from their own children. The voyage prepared for them was to Egypt. 6. When the

---

οἰκέται, πολλαὶ δὲ θεράπαιναι ⟨ἐνεβιβάζοντο⟩[21] μελλούσης δὲ τῆς νεὼς ἐπανάγεσθαι[22] πᾶν μὲν τὸ Ἐφεσίων ⟨πλῆθος⟩ παρῆν παραπεμπόντων, πολλοὶ δὲ καὶ τῶν ⟨ξένων⟩[23] μετὰ λαμπάδων καὶ θυσιῶν. 7. ἐν τούτῳ μὲν οὖν ὁ Λυκομήδης καὶ ἡ Θεμιστὼ πάντων ἅμα ἐν ὑπομνήσει γενόμενοι, τοῦ χρησμοῦ, τοῦ παιδός, τῆς ἀποδημίας, ἔκειντο εἰς γῆν ἀθυμοῦντες, ὁ δὲ Μεγαμήδης καὶ ἡ Εὐίππη ἐπεπόνθεσαν μὲν τὰ αὐτά, εὐθυμότεροι δὲ ἦσαν τὰ τέλη σκοποῦντες τῶν μεμαντευμένων. 8. ἤδη μὲν οὖν ἐθορύβουν οἱ ναῦται καὶ ἐλύετο τὰ πρυμνήσια καὶ ὁ κυβερνήτης τὴν αὑτοῦ χώραν κατελάμβανε καὶ ἡ ναῦς ἀπεκινεῖτο. 9. βοὴ δὲ τῶν ἀπὸ τῆς γῆς πολλὴ καὶ τῶν ἐν τῇ νηὶ συμμιγής, τῶν μὲν "ὦ παῖδες" λεγόντων "φίλτατοι, ἆρα ἔτι ὑμᾶς οἱ φύντες ὀψόμεθα;" τῶν δὲ "ὦ πατέρες, ἆρα ὑμᾶς ἀποληψόμεθα;" δάκρυα δὴ καὶ οἰμωγὴ καὶ ἕκαστος ὀνομαστὶ τὸν οἰκεῖον ἐκάλει μέγα εἰς ὑπόμνησιν ἀλλήλοις ἐγκαταλείποντες τὸ ὄνομα. 10. ὁ δὲ Μεγαμήδης φιάλην λαβὼν καὶ ἐπισπένδων ηὔχετο ὡς ἐξάκουστον εἶναι τοῖς ἐν τῇ νηὶ "ὦ παῖδες" λέγων "μάλιστα μὲν εὐτυχοῖτε καὶ φύγοιτε τὰ σκληρὰ τῶν μαντευμάτων, καὶ ὑμᾶς ἀνασωθέντας ὑποδέξαιντο Ἐφέσιοι, καὶ τὴν φιλτάτην ἀπολάβοιτε πατρίδα· εἰ δὲ ἄλλο ⟨τι⟩ συμβαίη, τοῦτο μὲν ἴστε οὐδὲ ἡμᾶς ἔτι ζησομένους, προίεμεν δὲ ὑμᾶς ὁδὸν δυστυχῆ μὲν ἀλλ' ἀναγκαίαν."

11 ἔτι λέγοντα ἐξιόντα ἐπέσχε τὰ δάκρυα, καὶ οἱ μὲν ἀπῄεσαν εἰς τὴν πόλιν, τοῦ πλήθους αὐτοὺς θαρρεῖν παρακαλοῦντος, ὁ δὲ Ἁβροκόμης καὶ ἡ Ἀνθία ἀλλήλοις περιφύντες ἔκειντο πολλὰ ἅμα ⟨ἐν⟩νοοῦντες, τοὺς πατέρας οἰκτείροντες, τῆς πατρίδος ἐπιθυμοῦντες, τὸν

---

[21] Zagoiannes   [22] O'Sullivan: ἐπανάξασθαι

day came for their departure, many servants and maids
‹were put aboard›, and as the ship made ready to sail, the
whole Ephesian populace was on hand to send them off,
including many ‹foreigners› with torches and sacrifices.
7. Meanwhile Lycomedes and Themisto, remembering
everything at once, the oracle, their child, the trip, lay
prostrate in despair, while Megamedes and Euippe had
the same experience but were in better spirits, since they
focused on the oracle's final outcome. 8. Then the crew was
bustling, the mooring cables were released, the pilot took
his position, and the ship was under way. 9. The cry from
those on shore was loud and was joined by those aboard the
ship: "Dear children, are we your parents going to see you
again?" and "Fathers, are we going to have you back?"
There were tears and lamentation, with each loudly calling
to a loved one by name, leaving one another their names
to remember. 10. Megamedes picked up a bottle, poured
a libation, and prayed audibly to those aboard the ship:
"Children, may you have the very best of luck and escape
the harsh terms of the oracle, may the Ephesians welcome
you back safely, and may you regain your beloved homeland! If anything else should happen, know that we will not
continue to live either; we are sending you away on a journey that is unfortunate but necessary."

Tears began to flow and prevented him from saying any　11
more. They returned to the city as the crowd tried to console them, while Habrocomes and Anthia lay in a close embrace with much on their minds—pity for their fathers,
homesickness for their country, worry about the oracle,

---

23 Cobet, cf. 1.1–2

χρησμὸν δεδοικότες, τὴν ἀποδημίαν ὑποπτεύοντες, παρεμυθεῖτο δ' αὐτοὺς εἰς ἅπαντα ὁ μετ' ἀλλήλων πλοῦς. 2. κἀκείνην μὲν τὴν ἡμέραν οὐρίῳ χρησάμενοι πνεύματι διανύσαντες τὸν πλοῦν εἰς Σάμον κατήντησαν τὴν τῆς Ἥρας ἱερὰν νῆσον κἀνταῦθα θύσαντες καὶ δειπνοποιησάμενοι πολλὰ εὐξάμενοι τῇ θεῷ τῆς νυκτὸς ἐπιγινομένης ἐπανήγοντο. 3. καὶ ἦν ὁ πλοῦς αὐτοῖς οὔριος, λόγοι δὲ ἐν αὐτοῖς πολλοὶ πρὸς ἀλλήλους· "ἆρα ἡμῖν ὑπάρξει συγκαταβιῶναι μετ' ἀλλήλων;" καὶ δή ποτε ὁ Ἁβροκόμης μέγα ἀναστενάξας ἐν ὑπομνήσει τῶν ἑαυτοῦ γενόμενος "Ἀνθία" ἔφησε "τῆς ψυχῆς μοι ποθεινοτέρα, μάλιστα μὲν εὐτυχεῖν εἴη καὶ σῴζεσθαι μετ' ἀλλήλων, 4. ἂν δ' ἄρα τι ᾖ πεπρωμένον παθεῖν καί πως ἀλλήλων ἀπαλλαγῶμεν ὀμόσωμεν ἑαυτοῖς, φιλτάτη, ὡς σὺ μὲν ἐμοὶ μενεῖς ἁγνὴ καὶ ἄλλον ἄνδρα οὐχ ὑπομενεῖς, ἐγὼ δὲ ὅτι οὐκ ⟨ἂν⟩ ἄλλῃ γυναικὶ συνοικήσαιμι." 5. ἀκούουσα δὲ Ἀνθία μέγα ἀνωλόλυξε καὶ "τί ταῦτα" ἔφησεν "Ἁβροκόμη; πεπίστευκας ὅτι ἐὰν ἀπαλλαγῶ σου περὶ ἀνδρὸς ἔτι καὶ γάμου σκέψομαι,[24] ἥτις οὐδὲ ζήσομαι τὴν ἀρχὴν ἄνευ σοῦ; ὡς ὀμνύω τέ σοι τὴν πάτριον ἡμῖν θεόν, τὴν μεγάλην Ἐφεσίων Ἄρτεμιν, καὶ ταύτην ἣν διανύομεν θάλατταν καὶ τὸν ἐπ' ἀλλήλοις ἡμᾶς καλῶς ἐκμήναντα θεὸν ὡς ἐγὼ καὶ βραχύ τι ἀποσπασθεῖσά σου οὔτε ζήσομαι οὔτε τὸν ἥλιον ὄψομαι." 6. ταῦτα ἔλεγεν ἡ Ἀνθία, ἐπώμνυε δὲ καὶ ὁ Ἁβροκόμης καὶ ὁ καιρὸς αὐτῶν ἐποίει τοὺς ὅρκους φοβερωτέρους. ἐν τούτῳ δὲ ἡ ναῦς Κῶ μὲν παραμείβει καὶ Κνίδον, κατεφαίνετο δὲ ἡ Ῥοδίων νῆσος μεγάλη καὶ καλὴ καὶ αὐτοὺς ἐνταῦθα ἔδει καταχθῆναι πάντως· δεῖν γὰρ ἔφασκον οἱ ναῦται

---

[24] καὶ γάμου σκέψομαι Arntzen: κατ' ἐμοῦ σκέψῃ

doubts about the voyage—though they felt reassured on all counts because they were making the voyage together. 2. Having a favoring wind that day, they completed the first stage of their journey and put in to Samos, the sacred island of Hera, where they made sacrifice and had a meal, and after many prayers to the goddess they set forth again the next evening. 3. Again the sailing was favorable, and they had many conversations: "Will we be allowed to spend our lives together?" Then Habrocomes groaned deeply as he recalled his own situation and said, "Anthia, dearer to me than my own life, my fondest hope is that together we will be happy and safe, 4. but if fate has some misfortune in store and we are somehow separated, let's take an oath, dearest, that you will stay chaste for me and submit to no other man, and that I will live with no other woman." 5. When she heard this, Anthia shrieked and said, "What are you saying, Habrocomes? How can you believe that if I am separated from you I would ever think about marrying a man, when I won't even stay alive without you? So I swear to you by our ancestral goddess, the great Artemis of the Ephesians, and by this sea that we are crossing, and by the god who has happily made us mad for each other that should I be separated from you even for the briefest moment, I will not continue to live or look upon the sun." 6. This was Anthia's oath, and Habrocomes made an oath too, and the circumstances made their oaths the more formidable. Meanwhile the ship passed by Cos and Cnidus, and the large island of Rhodes was coming into view; there they had to disembark completely, for the crew said that

καὶ ὑδρεύσασθαι καὶ αὐτοὺς ἀναπαύσασθαι μέλλον-
τας εἰς μακρὸν ἐμπεσεῖσθαι πλοῦν.

12　　Κατήγετο δὲ ἡ ναῦς εἰς Ῥόδον καὶ ἐξέβαινον οἱ
ναῦται, ἐξῄει δὲ καὶ ὁ Ἁβροκόμης ἔχων μετὰ χεῖρα
τὴν Ἀνθίαν· συνῄεσαν δὲ πάντες οἱ Ῥόδιοι τὸ κάλλος
τῶν παίδων καταπεπληγότες καὶ οὐκ ἔστιν ὅστις τῶν
ἰδόντων παρῆλθε σιωπῶν,²⁵ ἀλλ᾿ οἱ μὲν ἔλεγον ἐπιδημίαν ἐκ τῶν θεῶν, οἱ δὲ προσεκύνουν καὶ προσ-
επιτνοῦντο.²⁶ ταχὺ δὲ δι᾿ ὅλης τῆς πόλεως διεπεφοι-
τήκει τὸ ὄνομα Ἁβροκόμου καὶ Ἀνθίας, 2. ἐπεύχονται
δὲ αὐτοῖς δημοσίᾳ καὶ θυσίας τε θύουσι πολλὰς καὶ
ἑορτὴν ἄγουσι τὴν ἐπιδημίαν αὐτῶν. οἱ δὲ τήν τε πόλιν
ἅπασαν ἐξιστόρησαν καὶ ἀνέθεσαν εἰς τὸ τοῦ Ἡλίου
ἱερὸν πανοπλίαν χρυσῆν καὶ ἐπέγραψαν εἰς ὑπόμνημα
ἐπίγραμμα τῶν ἀναθέντων·

οἱ ξεῖνοι²⁷ τάδε σοι χρυσήλατα τεύχε᾿ ἔθηκαν,
Ἀνθία Ἁβροκόμης θ᾿, ἱερῆς Ἐφέσοιο πολῖται.

3. ταῦτα ἀναθέντες ὀλίγας ἡμέρας ἐν τῇ νήσῳ μείναν-
τες ἐπειγόντων τῶν ναυτῶν ἀνήγοντο ἐπισιτισάμενοι,
παρέπεμπε δὲ αὐτοὺς ἅπαν τὸ Ῥοδίων πλῆθος. καὶ
τὰ μὲν πρῶτα ἐφέροντο οὐρίῳ πνεύματι καὶ ἦν αὐτοῖς
ὁ πλοῦς ἀσμένο<ι>ς, κἀκείνην τε τὴν ἡμέραν καὶ
τὴν ἐπιοῦσαν νύκτα ἐφέροντο ἀναμετροῦντες τὴν Αἰ-
γυπτίαν καλουμένην θάλατταν· τῇ δὲ δευτέρᾳ ἐπέπαυ-
το μὲν ὁ ἄνεμος, γαλήνη δὲ <ἦν> καὶ ὁ πλοῦς βραδὺς
καὶ ναυτῶν ῥᾳθυμία καὶ πότος καὶ μέθη καὶ ἀρχὴ τῶν
μεμαντευμένων. 4. τῷ δὲ Ἁβροκόμῃ ἐν τούτῳ²⁸ ἐφί-

²⁵ Salvini: λυπῶν
²⁶ Elsner: προσεποιοῦντο　　　²⁷ ξεινοὶ κλεινοὶ
²⁸ ἐν τούτῳ post πότος transp. Hercher

they had to replenish their water and rest before embarking on a long sailing.

The ship put in to Rhodes and the crew disembarked; 12 Habrocomes left the ship too, holding Anthia by the hand. All the Rhodians gathered round, amazed at the youngsters' beauty, and not one of those who saw them passed by in silence: some called them a divine visitation, others worshiped and bowed before them. The names of Habrocomes and Anthia quickly made their way throughout the city. 2. They were accorded public prayers, and the Rhodians offered many a sacrifice and celebrated their visit like a festival. They toured the whole city and in the temple of Helius[13] dedicated a golden panoply and had an inscription from its donors inscribed on a plaque:

> The visitors dedicated to you these weapons of
>   beaten gold,
> Anthia and Habrocomes, citizens of sacred Ephesus.

3. When they had made this dedication and spent a few days on the island, at the crew's urging they took on supplies and set sail, and the entire Rhodian populace saw them off. At first they were carried along by a favoring wind and they found their journey pleasant, and that day and the following night they were carried along as they took the measure of the so-called Egyptian Sea. But by the next day the wind had dropped, there was a calm, their progress was slow, and among the crew there was relaxation, drinking, drunkenness, and a start of what had been prophesied. 4. At this point Habrocomes had a vision of a

[13] The sun-god Helius had major cult centers in Corinth and Rhodes, whose famous Colossus honored him.

σταται γυνὴ ὀφθῆναι φοβερά, τὸ μέγεθος ὑπὲρ ἄνθρωπον, ἐσθῆτα ἔχουσα φοινικῆν, ἐπιστᾶσα δὲ τὴν
ναῦν ἐδόκει καίειν καὶ τοὺς μὲν ἄλλους ἀπόλλυσθαι,
αὐτὸν δὲ μετὰ τῆς Ἀνθίας διανήχεσθαι. ταῦτα ὡς
εὐθὺς εἶδεν ἐταράχθη καὶ προσεδόκα τι δεινὸν ἐκ τοῦ
ὀνείρατος, καὶ τὸ δεινὸν ἐγίνετο.

13   Ἔτυχον μὲν ἐν Ῥόδῳ πειραταὶ παρορμοῦντες αὐτοῖς, Φοίνικες τὸ γένος, ἐν τριήρει μεγάλῃ, παρώρμουν
δὲ ὡς φορτίον ἔχοντες καὶ πολλοὶ καὶ γεννικοί. οὗτοι
καταμεμαθήκεσαν ⟨ἐν⟩ τῇ νηὶ ὅτι χρυσὸς καὶ ἄργυρος
καὶ ἀνδράποδα ⟨καὶ⟩ πολλὰ καὶ τίμια. 2. διέγνωσαν
οὖν ἐπιθέμενοι τοὺς μὲν ἀντιμαχομένους ἀποκτιννύειν,
τοὺς δὲ ἄλλους ἄγειν εἰς Φοινίκην πραθησομένους καὶ
τὰ χρήματα, κατεφρόνουν δὲ ὡς οὐκ ἀξιομάχων αὐτῶν. 3. τῶν δὲ πειρατῶν ὁ ἔξαρχος Κόρυμβος ἐκαλεῖτο, νεανίας ὀφθῆναι μέγας, φοβερὸς τὸ βλέμμα·
κόμη ἦν αὐτῷ αὐχμηρὰ καθειμένη. 4. ὡς δὲ ταῦτα οἱ
πειραταὶ ἐβουλεύσαντο τὰ μὲν πρῶτα παρέπλεον ἡσυ-
χῇ τοῖς περὶ ⟨τὸν⟩ Ἀβροκόμην, τελευταῖον δέ, ἦν μὲν
περὶ μέσον ἡμέρας, ἔκειντο δὲ πάντες οἱ ἐν τῇ νηὶ ὑπὸ
μέθης καὶ ῥαθυμίας, οἱ μὲν καθεύδοντες, οἱ δὲ ἀλύον-
τες, ἐφίστανται δὴ αὐτοῖς οἱ περὶ τὸν Κόρυμβον
ἐλαυνομένῃ τῇ νηὶ [τριήρης ἦν] σὺν ὀξύτητι πολλῇ.
5. ὡς δὲ πλησίον ἐγένοντο ἀνεπήδησαν ἐπὶ τὴν ναῦν
ὡπλισμένοι τὰ ξίφη γυμνὰ ἔχοντες, κἀνταῦθα οἱ μὲν
ἐρρίπτουν ἑαυτοὺς ὑπ' ἐκπλήξεως εἰς τὴν θάλασσαν
καὶ ἀπώλλυντο, οἱ δὲ ἀμύνεσθαι θέλοντες ἀπεσφάζον-
το. 6. ὁ δὲ Ἀβροκόμης καὶ ἡ Ἀνθία προστρέχουσι τῷ
Κορύμβῳ τῷ πειρατῇ καὶ λαβόμενοι τῶν γονάτων
αὐτοῦ "τὰ μὲν χρήματα" ἔφασαν "ὦ δέσποτα, καὶ
ἡμᾶς οἰκέτας ἔχε, φεῖσαι δὲ τῆς ψυχῆς καὶ μηκέτι
φόνευε τοὺς ἑκόντας ὑποχειρίους σοι γενομένους. μὴ

woman standing over him, fearsome to behold, superhumanly large, and wearing scarlet clothing, and as she stood over him she appeared to set the ship afire; everyone perished while he swam to safety with Anthia. He was instantly shaken up by this vision and expected something terrible to come of this dream, and this terrible something did come to pass.

It so happened that in Rhodes some pirates of Phoenician origin[14] were moored alongside them in a great trireme; they moored there as if carrying cargo and were a large and lusty lot. They discovered that there was gold, silver, slaves, and many valuable goods aboard the adjoining ship. 2. So they decided to attack, killing any who fought back and taking the rest to Phoenicia to sell along with the goods, but they thought little of them as opponents. 3. The leader of the pirates was called Corymbus,[15] a large young man with a fearsome glance, whose hair hung loose and unkempt. 4. When the pirates had settled on this plan, they first sailed quietly alongside Habrocomes' crew, but when it was midday and everyone on board lay about either sleeping or befuddled in the aftermath of carefree drinking, Corymbus' men finally attacked with their ship going full speed ahead. 5. As they drew near, they boarded the ship fully armed and with swords drawn; some on the ship threw themselves overboard in panic and drowned, while others, ready to defend themselves, were slaughtered. 6. Habrocomes and Anthia ran up to the pirate Corymbus, grasped him by his knees, and said, "Take the cargo, master, and take us as slaves, but spare our lives and stop killing those who willingly sur-

13

14 A typical venue for pirates, cf. *Daphnis and Chloe* I 28.
15 "Cluster" or perhaps "Top," attested as an actual name.

πρὸς αὐτῆς θαλάσσης, μὴ πρὸς δεξιᾶς τῆς σῆς,
ἀγαγὼν δὲ ἡμᾶς ὅποι θέλεις, ἀπόδου τοὺς σοὺς οἰκέτας, μόνον οἴκτειρον ἡμᾶς ὑφ᾽ ἑνὶ ποιήσας δεσπότῃ."

14 Ἀκούσας ὁ Κόρυμβος εὐθὺς μὲν ἐκέλευσε παύσασθαι[29] φονεύοντας, μεταθέμενος δὲ τὰ τιμιώτερα
τῶν φορτίων καὶ τὸν Ἁβροκόμην καὶ τὴν Ἀνθίαν
ἄλλους τε τινὰς τῶν οἰκετῶν ὀλίγους ἐνέπρησε τὴν
ναῦν, καὶ οἱ λοιποὶ πάντες κατεφλέχθησαν· τὸ γὰρ
πάντας ἄγειν οὔτε ἐδύνατο οὔτε ἀσφαλὲς ἑώρα. 2. ἦν
δὲ τὸ θέαμα ἐλεεινόν, τῶν μὲν ἐν τῇ τριήρει ἀνα-
γομένων, τῶν δὲ ἐν τῇ νηὶ φλεγομένων τὰς χεῖρας
ἐκτεινόντων καὶ ὀλοφυρομένων. 3. καὶ οἱ μὲν ἔλεγον
"ποῖ ποτε ἀχθήσεσθε, δεσπόται; τίς ὑμᾶς ὑποδέξεται
γῆ, καὶ τίνα πόλιν οἰκήσετε;" οἱ δὲ "ὦ μακάριοι,
μέλλοντες ἀποθνήσκειν εὐτυχῶς πρὸ τοῦ πειραθῆναι
δεσμῶν, πρὸ τοῦ δουλείαν λῃστρικὴν ἰδεῖν." ταῦτα
λέγοντες οἱ μὲν ἀνήγοντο, οἱ δὲ κατεφλέγοντο. 4. ἐν
τούτῳ δὲ ὁ τροφεὺς τοῦ Ἁβροκόμου πρεσβύτης ἤδη
σεμνὸς ἰδεῖν καὶ διὰ τὸ γῆρας ἐλεεινὸς οὐκ ἐνεγκὼν
ἀναγόμενον τὸν Ἁβροκόμην ῥίψας ἑαυτὸν εἰς τὴν
θάλασσαν ἐνήχετο ὡς καταληψόμενος τὴν τριήρη "τί
με καταλείπεις,[30] τέκνον" λέγων, "τὸν γέροντα, τὸν
παιδαγωγόν; 5. ποῖ δὲ ἀπερχόμενος, Ἁβροκόμη; αὐτὸς
ἀπόκτεινόν με τὸν δυστυχῆ καὶ θάψον· τί γάρ ἐστί μοι
ζῆν ἄνευ σοῦ;" ταῦτα ἔλεγε καὶ τέλος ἀπελπίσας ἔτι
Ἁβροκόμην ὄψεσθαι παραδοὺς ἑαυτὸν τοῖς κύμασιν
ἀπέθανε. 6. τοῦτο δὲ καὶ Ἁβροκόμῃ πάντων ἦν ἐλε-
εινότατον, καὶ γὰρ τὰς χεῖρας ἐξέτεινε τῷ πρεσβύτῃ
καὶ τοὺς πειρατὰς ἀναλαμβάνειν παρεκάλει, οἱ δὲ
οὐδένα λόγον ποιησάμενοι, διανύσαντες ἡμέραις τρι-

[29] Hirschig: φείσασθαι

render to you; by the sea itself, by your own right hand, please don't, but take us wherever you like, sell us as your own slaves, only take pity on us and give us to a single master."

At this Corymbus immediately ordered his men to stop the slaughter, transferred the most valuable cargo, including Habrocomes and Anthia and a few of the servants, and set the ship afire; everyone else was burned alive, since he could not transport them all and considered it unsafe. 2. It was a sad spectacle, some being brought aboard the trireme while the others, stretching out their hands and wailing, were burned alive on the ship. 3. The former were asking, "Where in the world are you being taken, masters? What land will receive you, in what city will you live?" The others were saying, "Blessed are those who will be lucky enough to die before they endure chains, before they know enslavement to brigands!" With this, the former were carried off while the latter were burned alive. 4. Meanwhile, Habrocomes' tutor, already an elderly man venerable in appearance and pitiful in his old age, was unable to bear Habrocomes' abduction, threw himself overboard, and swam after the trireme crying, "Why, my child, are you abandoning your old pedagogue? 5. Where are you headed, Habrocomes? Kill this unfortunate with your own hands and bury me, for what is life to me without you?" With these words he finally lost hope of seeing Habrocomes again, surrendered himself to the waves, and died. 6. For Habrocomes too this was sadder than anything else, and so he kept stretching out his hands to the elderly man and imploring the pirates to pull him aboard, but they paid

14

---

30 O'Sullivan, cf. Chariton. 3.5.4: ποῖ με καταλείψεις

σὶ τὸν πλοῦν κατήχθησαν εἰς πόλιν τῆς Φοινίκης
Τύρον ἔνθα ἦν τοῖς πειραταῖς τὰ οἰκεῖα. 7. ἦγον δὲ
αὐτοὺς εἰς αὐτὴν μὲν τὴν πόλιν οὐχί, εἰς πλησίον δέ τι
χωρίον ἀνδρὸς ἄρχοντος ⟨τοῦ⟩[31] ληστηρίου, Ἀψύρτου
τοὔνομα, οὗ καὶ ὁ Κόρυμβος ἦν ὑπηρέτης ἐπὶ μισθῷ
καὶ μέρει τῶν λαμβανομένων. ἐν δὲ τῷ τοῦ πλοὸς
διαστήματι ἐκ πολλῆς τῆς καθ᾿ ἡμέραν ὄψεως ἐρᾷ ὁ
Κόρυμβος τοῦ Ἀβροκόμου καὶ σφοδρὸν ἔρωτα, καὶ
αὐτὸν ἡ πρὸς τὸ μειράκιον συνήθεια ἐπὶ πλέον ἐξέκαιε.

15   Καὶ ἐν μὲν τῷ πλῷ οὔτε πεῖσαι δυνατὸν ἐδόκει
εἶναι, ἑώρα γὰρ ὡς διάκειται μὲν ὑπὸ ἀθυμίας πονήρως, ἑώρα δὲ καὶ τῆς Ἀνθίας ἐρῶντα, ἀλλὰ καὶ τὸ
βιάζεσθαι χαλεπὸν εἶναι αὐτῷ κατεφαίνετο, ἐδεδοίκει[32] γὰρ μή τι ἑαυτὸν ἐργάσηται δεινόν. 2. ἐπεὶ δὲ
κατήχθησαν εἰς Τύρον οὐκέτι καρτερῶν τὰ μὲν πρῶτα
ἐθεράπευε τὸν Ἀβροκόμην καὶ θαρρεῖν παρεκάλει καὶ
πᾶσαν ἐπιμέλειαν προσέφερεν, 3. ὁ δὲ ἐλεοῦντα τὸν
Κόρυμβον ἐνόμιζεν αὐτοῦ ποιεῖσθαι τὴν ἐπιμέλειαν.
τὸ δεύτερον δὲ ἀνακοινοῦται ὁ Κόρυμβος τὸν ἔρωτα
τῶν συλληστῶν τινι, Εὐξείνῳ τὸ ὄνομα, καὶ δεῖται
βοηθὸν γενέσθαι καὶ συμβουλεῦσαι τίνι τρόπῳ δυνήσεται πεῖσαι τὸ μειράκιον. 4. ὁ δὲ Εὔξεινος ἄσμενος
ἀκούει τὰ περὶ τοῦ Κορύμβου, καὶ γὰρ αὐτὸς ἐπ᾿
Ἀνθίᾳ διέκειτο πονήρως καὶ ἦρα τῆς κόρης σφοδρὸν[33]
ἔρωτα, λέγει δὲ πρὸς τὸν Κόρυμβον καὶ τὰ αὐτοῦ καὶ
συνεβούλευσε μὴ ἐπὶ πλέον ἔτι ἀνιᾶσθαι ἀλλὰ ἔργου

[31] O'Sullivan cl. 2.2.1
[32] Hemsterhuys: ἐδόκει
[33] Hemsterhuys, cf. 1.16.4, 5.4.5: φοβερὸν

no attention, completing their voyage in three days and putting in at Tyre, where the pirates had their base. 7. They brought them not into the city itself but to a nearby spot that was home to the leader of the gang, whose name was Apsyrtus,[16] to whom even Corymbus was subordinate, for a wage and a share of the booty. During the course of the voyage Corymbus fell passionately in love with Habrocomes from seeing him so often every day, and being at close quarters with the boy inflamed him all the more.

During the voyage he thought it impossible to seduce   15 him, since he saw how wretchedly off he was from despair and also saw that he was in love with Anthia; and then again it seemed to him difficult to resort to force, since he was afraid that Habrocomes might do himself some injury. 2. But after they had put in at Tyre he could no longer control himself. He began by taking care of Habrocomes, encouraging him to take heart and offering him every attention, 3. but he thought it was out of pity that Corymbus was showing him attention. Next, Corymbus confided his love to one of his fellow pirates, Euxinus[17] by name, and asked him to be his helper and advise him about how he could seduce the young man. 4. Euxinus was pleased to hear about Corymbus' situation because he himself was in a wretched state over Anthia and bore a fearsome passion for the girl, so he told Corymbus about his own situation and advised him to stop torturing himself and seize the ini-

---

16 Attested as an actual name but most famously borne by Medea's stepbrother, whom she murdered as she fled by sea with Jason and whose dismembered parts she threw overboard to distract their pursuers.   17 "Hospitable," an attested name more common in the form Euxenus, and an epithet of the Black Sea.

ἔχεσθαι· 5. "καὶ γὰρ" ἔφη "σφόδρα ἀγεννὲς κινδυνεύ-
οντας καὶ παραβαλλομένους μὴ ἀπολαύειν μετὰ ἀδεί-
ας ὧν ἐκτησάμεθα πόνων. δυνησόμεθα δὲ αὐτοὺς"
ἔλεγεν "ἐξαιρέτους παρὰ Ἀψύρτου λαβεῖν δωρεάν." 16.
ταῦτα εἰπὼν ῥᾳδίως ἔπειθεν αὐτὸν ἐρῶντα καὶ δὴ
συντίθενται κατὰ ταὐτὰ τοὺς ὑπὲρ ἀλλήλων ποιήσα-
σθαι λόγους καὶ πείθειν οὗτος μὲν Ἁβροκόμην, Κόρυμβος δὲ Ἀνθίαν.

16   ⟨Οἱ δὲ⟩ ἐν τούτῳ τῷ χρόνῳ ἔκειντο ἄθυμοι, πολλὰ
προσδοκῶντες, ἀλλήλοις διαλεγόμενοι, συνεχὲς ὀμνύ-
οντες τηρήσειν τὰ συγκείμενα. 2. ἔρχονται δὴ πρὸς
αὐτοὺς ὁ Κόρυμβος καὶ ὁ Εὔξεινος καὶ φράσαντες ἰδίᾳ
τι θέλειν εἰπεῖν, ἀπάγουσι καθ᾽ αὑτοὺς ὁ μὲν τὴν
Ἀνθίαν, ὁ δὲ τὸν Ἁβροκόμην. τοῖς δὲ αἵ τε ψυχαὶ
ἐκραδαίνοντο καὶ οὐδὲν ὑγιὲς ὑπενόουν. 3. λέγει οὖν ὁ
Εὔξεινος πρὸς τὸν Ἁβροκόμην ὑπὲρ Κορύμβου· "μειράκιον, εἰκὸς μὲν ἐπὶ τῇ συμφορᾷ φέρειν χαλεπῶς
οἰκέτην μὲν ἐξ ἐλευθέρου γενόμενον, πένητα δὲ ἀντ᾽
εὐδαίμονος, δεῖ δέ σε τῇ τύχῃ[34] πάντα λογίσασθαι καὶ
στέργειν τὸν κατέχοντα δαίμονα καὶ τοὺς γενομένους
δεσπότας ἀγαπᾶν. 4. ἴσθι γὰρ ὡς ἔνεστί σοι καὶ
εὐδαιμοσύνην καὶ ἐλευθερίαν ἀπολαβεῖν εἰ θελήσεις
πείθεσθαι τῷ δεσπότῃ Κορύμβῳ· ἐρᾷ γάρ σου σφοδρὸν ἔρωτα καὶ πάντων ἕτοιμός ἐστι δεσπότην ποιεῖν
τῶν ἑαυτοῦ. πείσῃ δὲ χαλεπὸν μὲν οὐδέν, εὐνούστερον
δὲ σεαυτῷ τὸν δεσπότην ἐργάσῃ. 5. ἐννόησον δὲ ἐν οἷς
ὑπάρχεις· βοηθὸς μὲν οὐδείς, γῆ δὲ αὕτη ξένη καὶ
δεσπόται λῃσταὶ καὶ οὐδεμία τιμωρίας ἀποφυγὴ
ὑπερηφανήσαντι Κόρυμβον. τί δέ σοι γυναικὸς δεῖ
νῦν καὶ πραγμάτων, τί δὲ ἐρωμένης τηλικῷδε ὄντι;

[34] Hemsterhuys: ψυχῇ

246

tiative. 5. "Look," he said, "it would be very abject of us to run risks and put ourselves in harm's way without confidently enjoying what we have won by our efforts. We will be able to get them," he said, "as our share from Apsyrtus, as a gift." 6. With this he easily convinced him, lovelorn as he was, and so they agreed to put in the same good word for each other, Euxinus to win over Habrocomes and Corymbus, Anthia.

Meanwhile ⟨the couple⟩ lay disheartened, beset by worries, as they talked with one another and constantly vowed to uphold their agreement. 2. Corymbus and Euxinus approached them and, explaining that they wanted a private word, Corymbus took Anthia aside while Euxinus took Habrocomes. Their hearts were pounding and they suspected nothing wholesome. 3. Euxinus duly spoke to Habrocomes on behalf of Corymbus: "Young man, it is only natural to take this disaster hard, now that you are a slave and no longer a master, a pauper and no longer rich, but you should chalk it all up to fortune, be content with your dominant fate, and show affection for your new masters. 4. Let me tell you that you can recover your happiness and freedom if you're willing to obey your master, Corymbus, because he's passionately in love with you and ready to make you master of all he possesses. Nothing bad will happen to you, and you will make your master better disposed toward you. 5. Reflect on your circumstances: there's no one to help you, this is a barbarian land, your masters are bandits, and there's no escape from retribution should you treat Corymbus with disdain. Why do you need a wife and responsibilities now? Why should someone your age need to love a woman? Toss all that

16

247

πάντα ἀπόρριψον· πρὸς μόνον δεῖ σε τὸν δεσπότην
βλέπειν, τούτῳ κελεύσαντι ὑπακούειν." 6. ἀκούσας ὁ
Ἀβροκόμης εὐθὺς μὲν ἀχανὴς ἦν καὶ οὐδέ τι ἀποκρί-
νεσθαι ηὕρισκεν, ἐδάκρυσε δὲ καὶ ἀνέστενε πρὸς αὐτὸν ἀφορῶν εἰς οἷα ἄρα ἐλήλυθε. καὶ δὴ λέγει πρὸς τὸν
Εὔξεινον "ἐπίτρεψον, δέσποτα, βουλεύσασθαι βραχὺ
καὶ πρὸς πάντα ἀποκρινοῦμαί σοι τὰ ῥηθέντα." 7. καὶ
ὁ μὲν Εὔξεινος ἀνεχώρει, ὁ δὲ Κόρυμβος τῇ Ἀνθίᾳ
διείλεκτο τὸν ἔρωτα τὸν Εὐξείνου καὶ τὴν παροῦσαν
ἀνάγκην καὶ ὅτι δεῖ πάντως αὐτὴν πείθεσθαι τοῖς
δεσπόταις· ὑπέσχετο δὲ πολλά, καὶ γάμον νόμιμον καὶ
χρήματα πεισθείσῃ καὶ περιουσίαν. ἡ δὲ αὐτῷ τὰ
ὅμοια ἀπεκρίνατο αἰτησαμένη βραχὺν βουλεύσασθαι
χρόνον. καὶ ὁ μὲν Εὔξεινος καὶ ὁ Κόρυμβος μετ'
ἀλλήλων ἦσαν περιμένοντες ὅ τι ἀκούσονται, ἤλπιζον
δὲ αὐτοὺς ῥᾳδίως πείσειν.

away! You should look only to your master, and to him show obedience when he has given an order." 6. At this Habrocomes was struck speechless and could find nothing at all to say in response, but burst into tears and groaned as he contemplated what he had truly come to. And so he said to Euxinus, "Please, master, give me a little time to think it over, and I will respond to everything you said." 7. Euxinus went away as Corymbus finished telling Anthia about Euxinus' love, her present constraint, and how she should obey her masters completely. He made a lot of promises if she obeyed: lawful marriage, money, prosperity. But she gave him the same answer as Habrocomes, asking for a little time to think it over. So Euxinus and Corymbus both started waiting to hear something, but they expected to win them over easily.

ΛΟΓΟΣ ΔΕΥΤΕΡΟΣ

1   Ὁ δὲ Ἁβροκόμης καὶ ἡ Ἀνθία ἧκον εἰς τὸ δωμάτιον
ἔνθα συνήθως διῃτῶντο καὶ πρὸς ἀλλήλους εἰπόντες
ἅπερ ἠκηκόεσαν, καταβαλόντες ἑαυτοὺς ἔκλαιον, ὠδύ-
ροντο, 2. "ὦ πάτερ" ἔλεγον, "ὦ μῆτερ, ὦ πατρὶς
φιλτάτη καὶ οἰκεῖοι καὶ συγγενεῖς." τελευταῖον δὲ
ἀνενεγκὼν ὁ Ἁβροκόμης "ὦ κακοδαίμονες" ἔφησεν
"ἡμεῖς, τί ἄρα πεισόμεθα ἐν γῇ βαρβάρῳ, [πειρατῶν]
ὕβρει παραδοθέντες πειρατῶν; ἄρχεται τὰ μεμαν-
τευμένα· τιμωρίαν ἤδη με ὁ θεὸς τῆς ὑπερηφανίας
εἰσπράττει· ἐρᾷ Κόρυμβος ἐμοῦ, σοῦ δὲ Εὔξεινος. 3. ὦ
τῆς ἀκαίρου πρὸς ἑκατέρους εὐμορφίας· εἰς τοῦτο ἄρα
μέχρι νῦν σώφρων ἐτηρήθην ἵνα ἐμαυτὸν ὑποθῶ
λῃστῇ ἐρῶντι τὴν αἰσχρὰν ἐπιθυμίαν; καὶ τίς ἐμοὶ
βίος περιλείπεται πόρνη μὲν ἀντὶ ἀνδρὸς γενομένῳ,
ἀποστερηθέντι δὲ Ἀνθίας τῆς ἐμῆς; 4. ἀλλ' οὐ μὰ τὴν
μέχρις ἄρτι σωφροσύνην ἐκ παιδὸς μοι σύντροφον
οὐκ ἂν ἐμαυτὸν ὑποθείην Κορύμβῳ, τεθνήξομαι δὲ
πρότερον καὶ φανοῦμαι <καὶ>[35] νεκρὸς σώφρων." 5.
ταῦτα ἔλεγε καὶ ἐπεδάκρυεν, ἡ δὲ Ἀνθία "φεῦ τῶν
κακῶν" εἶπε, "ταχέως γε τῶν ὅρκων ἀνα<μ>νησθῆναι
ἀνα>γκαζόμεθα,[36] ταχέως τῆς δουλείας πειρώμεθα·
ἐρᾷ τις ἐμοῦ καὶ πείσειν ἐλπίζει[37] εἰς εὐνὴν ἐλεύσεσθαι
τὴν ἐμὴν μετὰ Ἁβροκόμην καὶ συγκατακλιθήσεσθαι
καὶ ἀπολαύσειν <τῆς> ἐπιθυμίας. 6. ἀλλὰ μὴ οὕτως

---

[35] Zagoiannes cl. 3.10.2

BOOK II

Habrocomes and Anthia returned to the cubicle where 1
they were usually quartered, and when they told each
other what they had been told, they threw themselves to
the floor and began to weep and wail. 2. "Ah father," they
cried, "ah mother, dearest homeland, household, and family!" Habrocomes finally pulled himself together and said,
"We are so unfortunate! What will happen to us, now in a
barbarian land and turned over to wanton pirates? The
prophecies begin to come true. Now the god is working his
vengeance on me for my arrogance: Corymbus is in love
with me, and Euxinus with you. 3. How untimely is our
beauty for both of us! Is it for this that until now I have kept
myself chaste, only to submit to the sordid lust of an amorous pirate? And what sort of life lies ahead for me, once I
become a whore instead of a man and lose my own Anthia?
4. No, I swear by the chastity that has been my companion
since childhood that I will not submit to Corymbus! I will
die first and be revealed chaste even as a corpse!" 5. With
this he burst into tears, and Anthia said, "We're in such
trouble! How soon we are forced to remember our oaths,
how soon tested by slavery! Someone loves me and expects
to seduce me and join me in my own bed after Habrocomes, to sleep with me and indulge his desire. 6. But may

36 Hemsterhuys
37 Hercher: ἤλπιζεν

251

ἐγὼ φιλόζωος γενοίμην μηδ᾽ ὑπομείναιμι ὑβρισθεῖσα
ἰδεῖν τὸν ἥλιον. δεδόχθω ταῦτα· ἀποθνήσκωμεν,
Ἀβροκόμα. ἕξομεν ἀλλήλους μετὰ θάνατον ὑπ᾽
οὐδενὸς ἐνοχλούμενοι."

2   Καὶ τοῖς μὲν ταῦτα ἐδέδοκτο, ἐν δὲ τούτοις Ἄψυρτος ὁ προεστὼς τοῦ λῃστηρίου πυθόμενος ὅτι τε
ἥκουσιν οἱ περὶ τὸν Κόρυμβον καὶ ὅτι πολλὰ εἶεν καὶ
θαυμάσια κομίζοντες χρήματα ἧκεν εἰς τὸ χωρίον καὶ
εἶδέ τε τοὺς περὶ ⟨τὸν⟩ Ἀβροκόμην καὶ κατεπλάγη τὴν
εὐμορφίαν καὶ εὐθὺς μέγα κέρδος νομίζων ᾐτήσατο
ἐκείνους. 2. τὰ μὲν ἄλλα χρήματα καὶ κτήματα καὶ
παρθένους ὅσαι συνελήφθησαν διένειμε τοῖς περὶ τὸν
Κόρυμβον [πειραταῖς], ὁ δὲ Εὔξεινος καὶ ὁ Κόρυμβος
ἄκοντες μὲν συνεχώρουν τοὺς περὶ τὸν Ἀβροκόμην τῷ
Ἀψύρτῳ, συνεχώρουν δὲ οὖν ἀνάγκῃ. 3. καὶ οἱ μὲν
ἀπηλλάσσοντο, ὁ δὲ Ἄψυρτος παραλαβὼν τὸν Ἀβροκόμην καὶ τὴν Ἀνθίαν καὶ οἰκέτας δύο, Λεύκωνα καὶ
Ῥόδην, ἤγαγεν εἰς τὴν Τύρον. 4. περίβλεπτος δὲ ἦν
αὐτῶν ἡ πομπὴ καὶ πάντες ἐτεθαυμάκεσαν τὸ κάλλος
καὶ ἄνθρωποι βάρβαροι μήπω πρότερον τοσαύτην
ἰδόντες εὐμορφίαν θεοὺς ἐνόμιζον εἶναι τοὺς βλεπομένους ἐμακάριζον δὲ τὸν Ἄψυρτον οἵους οἰκέτας εἴη
κεκτημένος. 5. ἀγαγὼν δὲ αὐτοὺς εἰς τὴν οἰκίαν παρα-
δίδωσιν οἰκέτῃ πιστῷ δι᾽ ἐπιμελείας κελεύσας ἔχειν ὡς
μεγάλα κερδανῶν εἰ ἀπόδοιτο τῆς ἀξίας αὐτῶν τιμῆς.

3   Καὶ οἱ μὲν περὶ τὸν Ἀβροκόμην ἐν τούτοις ἦσαν.
ἡμερῶν δὲ διαγενομένων ὀλίγων ὁ μὲν Ἄψυρτος ἐπ᾽
ἄλλην ἐμπορίαν εἰς Συρίαν ἀπῆλθε, θυγάτηρ δὲ αὐτοῦ,
Μαντὼ ὄνομα, ἠράσθη τοῦ Ἀβροκόμου. ἦν δὲ καλὴ
καὶ ὡραία γάμων ἤδη, πολὺ δὲ τοῦ Ἀνθίας[38] κάλλους
ὑπελείπετο. 2. αὕτη ἡ Μαντὼ ἐκ τῆς συνήθους μετὰ

38 Hercher: Ἀβροκόμου

I never be so fond of life, may I never survive to look upon the sun if I am violated. Let this be our decision: that we die, Habrocomes. After death we will have each other and be molested by no one."

And that was their decision. Meanwhile Apsyrtus, the leader of the gang, heard that Corymbus' men had returned with a lot of marvelous booty and went to their place. When he saw Habrocomes' group he was astounded by their good looks, and right away recognizing a large profit he claimed them for himself. 2. The rest of the money, goods, and girls that had been captured he distributed to Corymbus' men. Euxinus and Corymbus surrendered Habrocomes' group to Apsyrtus unwillingly, but under compulsion nevertheless surrendered them. 3. They took their leave, while Apsyrtus seized Habrocomes and Anthia along with two slaves, Leuco and Rhoda,[18] and took them into Tyre. 4. The procession drew everyone's gaze, and all were struck by their beauty; barbarian people who had never before seen such good looks thought that they were looking at gods and congratulated Apsyrtus on possessing such slaves. 5. He brought them into his house and handed them over to a trusty slave, with instructions to take good care of them, since he expected a large profit if he could sell them for what they were worth.

And so this was the predicament of Habrocomes' group. A few days later Apsyrtus left for Syria on another venture, while his daughter, named Manto,[19] fell in love with Habrocomes. She was beautiful and already of marriageable age but far behind Anthia in beauty. 2. This

[18] "White" and "Rose," conventional names.

[19] An attested name, and in mythology the daughter and helpmate of the Theban seer, Tiresias.

τοῦ Ἀβροκόμου διαίτης ἁλίσκεται καὶ ἀκατασχέτως
εἶχε καὶ ἠπόρει ὅ τι ποιῆσαι· οὔτε γὰρ πρὸς τὸν
Ἀβροκόμην εἰπεῖν ἐτόλμα γυναῖκα εἰδυῖα ἔχοντα καὶ
πείσειν οὐδέποτε ἐλπίζουσα οὔτε ἄλλῳ τινὶ τῶν ἑαυτῆς
δέει τοῦ πατρὸς 3. δι᾽ ἃ δὴ καὶ μᾶλλον ἀνεκαίετο καὶ
διέκειτο πονήρως. καὶ οὐκέτι καρτεροῦσα ἔγνω πρὸς
τὴν Ῥόδην, τὴν σύντροφον τῆς Ἀνθίας οὖσαν ἡλικι-
ῶτιν καὶ κόρην, κατειπεῖν τὸν ἔρωτα· ταύτην γὰρ
μόνην ἤλπιζε συνεργήσειν αὐτῇ πρὸς τὴν ἐπιθυμίαν.
4. καὶ δὴ σχολῆς λαβομένη ἄγει τὴν κόρην πρὸς τὰ
πατρῷα ἐπὶ τῆς οἰκίας ἱερὰ καὶ δεῖται μὴ κατειπεῖν
αὐτῆς καὶ ὅρκους λαμβάνει καὶ λέγει τὸν ἔρωτα τὸν
Ἀβροκόμου καὶ ἱκετεύει συλλαβέσθαι καὶ πολλὰ
ὑπέσχετο συλλαβομένῃ. 5. ἔφη δ᾽ "ἴσθι μὲν οἰκέτις
οὖσα ἐμή, ἴσθι δὲ ὀργῆς πειρασομένη βαρβάρου καὶ
ἠδικημένης." ταῦτα εἰποῦσα ἀπέπεμπε τὴν Ῥόδην, ἡ
δὲ ἐν ἀμηχάνῳ κακῷ ἐγεγόνει· τό τε γὰρ εἰπεῖν Ἀβροκόμῃ παρῃτεῖτο φιλοῦσα τὴν Ἀνθίαν, πάνυ δὲ ἐδεδοίκει τῆς βαρβάρου τὴν ὀργήν. 6. ἔδοξεν οὖν αὐτῇ
καλῶς ἔχειν Λεύκωνι πρῶτον ἀνακοινῶσαι τὰ ὑπὸ τῆς
Μαντοῦς εἰρημένα· ἦν δὲ καὶ τῇ Ῥόδῃ κοινωνήματα
ἐξαιρέτως γενόμενα πρὸς Λεύκωνα καὶ συνῆσαν ἀλλήλοις ἔτι ἐν Τύρῳ.[39] 7. τότε δὴ λαβομένη μόνου "ὦ
Λεύκων" ἔφη, "ἀπολώλαμεν τελέως· νῦν οὐκέτι τοὺς
συντρόφους ἕξομεν· ἡ τοῦ δεσπότου θυγάτηρ Ἀψύρτου ἐρᾷ μὲν Ἀβροκόμου σφοδρὸν ἔρωτα, ἀπειλεῖ δὲ εἰ
μὴ τύχῃ δεινὰ ἡμᾶς ἐργάσασθαι. 8. σκόπει τοίνυν τί
δεῖ ποιεῖν· τὸ γὰρ ἀντειπεῖν τῇ βαρβάρῳ σφαλερόν,
τὸ δὲ ἀποζεῦξαι Ἀβροκόμην Ἀνθίας ἀδύνατον." ἀκούσας ὁ Λεύκων δακρύων ἐπλήσθη μεγάλας ἐκ τούτων

[39] O'Sullivan: Ἐφέσῳ

Manto was captivated through daily contact with Habrocomes, was uncontrollably smitten, and did not know what
to do about it. She dared not tell Habrocomes, knowing
that he had a wife and never expecting to seduce him, nor
tell anyone else in her circle, for fear of her father. 3. All
this made her burn even hotter, and she was in a bad way.
When she could contain herself no longer, she decided to
confess her love to Rhoda, Anthia's companion and a girl
her own age, expecting that she alone would help her
achieve what she desired. 4. So taking advantage of some
free time, she took her to the household's ancestral shrine,
asked her not to betray a secret, made her swear to it, con-
fessed her love for Habrocomes, begged her to assist, and
promised a great deal for her assistance. 5. "Be aware," she
said, "that you are my slave, and be aware that you will taste
the wrath of a barbarian if she is wronged." With this she
dismissed Rhoda, who found herself in an impossible di-
lemma: being devoted to Anthia, she could not bring herself to tell Habrocomes, but she was terrified of the barbarian girl's wrath. 6. So she decided that it would be well to
share Manto's revelation with Leuco first: Rhoda had a
special relationship with Leuco, and they were still inti-
mate with each other in Tyre. 7. So she found him alone
and said, "Leuco, it's all over for us: we are about to lose
our companions. Our master Apsyrtus' daughter is passionately in love with Habrocomes and threatens terrible
treatment for us unless she gets her way. 8. So consider
what we should do: opposing the barbarian girl is dangerous, but parting Habrocomes from Anthia is impossible."
9. Leuco listened and was overwhelmed with tears, as he

συμφορὰς προσδοκῶν· ὀψὲ δὲ ἀνενεγκὼν "σιώπα"
ἔφη, "Ῥόδη, ἐγὼ γὰρ ἕκαστα διοικήσω."

4   Ταῦτα εἰπὼν ἔρχεται πρὸς Ἀβροκόμην, τῷ δὲ ἄρα
οὐδὲν ἔργον ἦν ἢ φιλεῖν Ἀνθίαν καὶ ὑπ' ἐκείνης
φιλεῖσθαι καὶ λαλεῖν ἐκείνῃ καὶ ἀκούειν λαλούσης.
ἐλθὼν δὲ παρ' αὐτοὺς "τί" ⟨φησι⟩ "ποιοῦμεν, σύντροφοι; τί δὲ βουλευόμεθα, οἰκέται; 2. δοκεῖς τινι τῶν
δεσποτῶν, Ἀβροκόμη, καλός· ἡ θυγάτηρ ἡ Ἀψύρτου
πονήρως ἐπὶ σοὶ διάκειται, καὶ ἀντειπεῖν ἐρώσῃ βαρβάρῳ παρθένῳ χαλεπόν. σὺ οὖν ὅπως σοι δοκεῖ βουλευσάμενος σῶσον ἡμᾶς ἅπαντας καὶ μὴ περιίδῃς
ὀργῇ δεσποτῶν ὑποπεσόντας." 3. ἀκούσας ὁ Ἀβροκόμης εὐθὺς μὲν ὀργῆς ἐνεπλήσθη, ἀναβλέψας δὲ
ἀτενὲς εἰς τὸν Λεύκωνα "ὦ πονηρὲ" ἔφη "καὶ Φοινίκων
τῶν ἐνταῦθα βαρβαρώτερε, ἐτόλμησας εἰπεῖν πρὸς
Ἀβροκόμην τοιαῦτα ῥήματα καὶ παρούσης Ἀνθίας
ἄλλην παρθένον μοι διηγῇ; 4. δοῦλος μέν εἰμι, ἀλλὰ
συνθήκας οἶδα τηρεῖν. ἔχουσιν ἐξουσίαν μου τοῦ
σώματος, τὴν ψυχὴν δὲ ἐλευθέραν ἔχω. ἀπειλείτω νῦν
εἰ θέλει Μαντὼ ξίφη καὶ βρόχους καὶ πῦρ καὶ πάντα
ὅσα δύναται σῶμα ἐνεγκεῖν οἰκέτου· οὐ γὰρ ἄν ποτε
πεισθείην ἑκὼν Ἀνθίαν ἀδικῆσαι." 5. ὁ μὲν ταῦτα
ἔλεγεν, ἡ δὲ Ἀνθία ὑπὸ ⟨τῆς⟩ συμφορᾶς ἔκειτο ἀχανὴς οὐδὲ προσφθέγξασθαί τι δυναμένη, ὀψὲ δὲ καὶ
μόλις αὐτὴν ἐγείρασα "ἔχω μὲν" φησίν, "Ἀβροκόμη,
τὴν εὔνοιαν τὴν σὴν καὶ στέργεσθαι διαφερόντως ὑπὸ
σοῦ πεπίστευκα, ἀλλὰ δέομαι σοῦ, τῆς ψυχῆς [καὶ]
τῆς ἐμῆς δέσποτα, μὴ προδῷς ἑαυτὸν μηδὲ εἰς ὀργὴν
ἐμβάλῃς βαρβαρικήν, συγκατάθου δὲ τῇ τῆς δεσποί-
νης ἐπιθυμίᾳ· 6. κἀγὼ ὑμῖν ἄπειμι ἐκποδών, ἐμαυτὴν
ἀποκτείνασα. τοσοῦτον σοῦ δεήσομαι· θάψον αὐτὸς
καὶ φίλησον πεσοῦσαν καὶ μέμνησο Ἀνθίας." ταῦτα

expected this would lead to great calamities. But at last he pulled himself together and said, "Hush, Rhoda: I'll take care of everything."

With this he went to Habrocomes, who had no concern 4 beyond his love for Anthia and hers for him, talking to her and listening to her talk, and when he was with them he asked, "What are we going to do, my friends? What is our plan, my fellow slaves? 2. Habrocomes, one of our masters finds you handsome; Apsyrtus' daughter is in a bad way over you, and opposing an amorous barbarian girl is difficult. So it's up to you to think of a plan and rescue us all, and not stand by while we fall victim to the wrath of masters." 3. When Habrocomes heard this he was immediately consumed by anger. He looked straight at Leuco and said, "You scum, more barbaric than these Phoenicians! How dare you speak this way to Habrocomes, and tell me about another girl in Anthia's presence? 4. I am a slave, but I know how to keep promises. They have power over my body, but I keep a free soul. Let Manto threaten me this very moment if she likes, with swords, nooses, fire, and anything that a slave's body can bear, because I will never willingly agree to do Anthia wrong!" 5. That was his reply, but Anthia sat dumbfounded by her despair and unable to say a word. At last she roused herself and said, "I have your affection, Habrocomes, and I am convinced that I am uniquely cherished by you. But please, master of my heart, do not betray yourself, do not succumb to barbarian wrath, but acquiesce in your mistress' desire. 6. As for me, I will get out of your way by killing myself. Only this will I ask of you: bury me with your own hands, give me a kiss as I lie there, and remember Anthia." All this cast Habro-

πάντα εἰς μείζονα συμφορὰν τὸν Ἀβροκόμην ἦγε καὶ
ἠπόρει ὅστις γένηται.

5   Καὶ οἱ μὲν ἐν τούτοις ἦσαν, ἡ δὲ Μαντὼ χρονι-
ζούσης τῆς Ῥόδης οὐκέτι καρτεροῦσα γράφει γραμ-
μάτιον πρὸς τὸν Ἀβροκόμην, ἦν δὲ τὰ ἐγγεγραμμένα
τοιάδε· "Ἀβροκόμη τῶι καλῶι δέσποινα ἡ σὴ χαίρειν.
Μαντὼ ἐρᾶ σου μηκέτι φέρειν δυναμένη, ἀπρεπὲς μὲν
ἴσως παρθένῳ, ἀναγκαῖον δὲ φιλούσῃ. δέομαι μή με
παρίδῃς μηδὲ ὑβρίσῃς τὴν τὰ σὰ ᾑρημένην· 2. ἐὰν
γὰρ πεισθῇς πατέρα τὸν ἐμὸν Ἄψυρτον ἐγὼ πείσω σοί
με συνοικίσαι καὶ τὴν νῦν σοι γυναῖκα ἀποσκευα-
σόμεθα, πλουτήσεις δὲ καὶ μακάριος ἔσῃ· ἐὰν δὲ
ἀντείπῃς ἐννόει μὲν οἷα πείσῃ τῆς ὑβρισμένης ἑαυτὴν
ἐκδικούσης, οἷα δὲ οἱ μετὰ σοῦ [κοινωνοὶ] τῆς σῆς
ὑπερηφανίας σύμβουλοι γενόμενοι." 3. τοῦτο τὸ γράμ-
μα λαβοῦσα καὶ κατασημηναμένη δίδωσι θεραπαίνῃ
τινὶ ἑαυτῆς βαρβάρῳ, εἰποῦσα Ἀβροκόμῃ κομίζειν, ὁ
δὲ ἔλαβε καὶ ἀνέγνω καὶ πᾶσι μὲν ἤχθετο τοῖς ἐγ-
γεγραμμένοις, μάλιστα δὲ αὐτὸν ἐλύπει τὰ περὶ τῆς
Ἀνθίας. 4. κἀκείνην μὲν τὴν πινακίδα κατέχει, ἄλλην
δὲ ἐγγράφει καὶ δίδωσι τῇ θεραπαίνῃ· ἦν δὲ τὰ γε-
γραμμένα <τοιάδε>· "δέσποινα, ὅ τι βούλει ποίει καὶ
χρῶ σώματι ὡς οἰκέτου, καὶ εἴτε ἀποκτείνειν θέλεις
ἕτοιμος, εἴτε βασανίζειν ὅπως ἐθέλεις βασάνιζε, εἰς
εὐνὴν δὲ τὴν σὴν οὐκ ἂν ἔλθοιμι οὔτε ἂν τοιαῦτα
πεισθείην κελευούσῃ." 5. λαβοῦσα ταῦτα τὰ γράμματα ἡ Μαντὼ ἐν ὀργῇ ἀκατασχέτῳ γίνεται καὶ ἀνα-
μίξασα πάντα, φθόνον [καὶ], ζηλοτυπίαν, λύπην, φόβον, ἐνενόει ὅπως τιμωρήσαιτο τὸν ὑπερηφανοῦντα. 6.
καὶ δὴ καὶ ἐν τούτῳ ἔρχεται μὲν ἀπὸ Συρίας Ἄψυρτος

_____

20 The recipient normally erased the writing on the wax-

comes into greater despair, and he had no idea what he should do.

In the meantime, as Rhoda delayed, Manto could no 5 longer hold out and wrote a letter to Habrocomes containg the following message: "To the handsome Habrocomes from your mistress, greetings. Manto is in love with you and no longer able to stand it: unseemly perhaps for a girl, but compulsory for a girl in love. I beg you not to disdain or mistreat the girl who has taken your side, 2. for if you say yes, I will convince my father Apsyrtus to betroth me to you, we will get rid of your present wife, and you will be rich and prosperous; but if you say no, think what will happen to you when the mistreated girl takes her revenge, and what will happen to those who abetted your own arrogance." 3. She took this letter, sealed it, and gave it to one of her barbarian servants, telling her to deliver it to Habrocomes. He received it, read it, and was distressed by everything it contained; the part about Anthia pained him the most. 4. He kept the tablet, wrote on another one,[20] and gave it to the servant; what he wrote was as follows: "Mistress, do what you will and use my body as that of a slave; if you wish to kill me, I am ready, and if you wish to apply your choice of torture, then use torture. But I could not come to your bed and I would not consent to such a thing if you ordered it." 5. When she received this reply Manto flew into an uncontrollable rage, and in a confusion of emotions of every kind—envy, jealousy, pain, fear—she set about considering how she would take revenge on the one who was scorning her. 6. At this juncture Apsyrtus re-

coated tablet (*pinax*) and used the same tablet for the reply; here the preservation of the original letter is important for the plot.

ἄγων τινὰ τῇ θυγατρὶ νύμφιον ἐκεῖθεν, Μοῖριν ὄνομα.
ὡς δὲ ἀφίκετο εὐθὺς ἡ Μαντὼ τὴν κατὰ Ἀβροκόμου
τέχνην συνετάττετο καὶ σπαράξασα τὰς κόμας καὶ
περιρρηξαμένη τὴν ἐσθῆτα ὑπαντήσασα τῷ πατρὶ καὶ
προσπεσοῦσα πρὸς τὰ γόνατα "οἴκτειρον" ἔφη, "πάτερ, θυγατέρα τὴν σὴν ὑβρισμένην ὑπὸ οἰκέτου· 7. ὁ
γὰρ σώφρων Ἀβροκόμης ἐπείρασε μὲν παρθενίαν τὴν
ἐμὴν ἀφανίσαι, ἐπεβούλευσε δὲ καὶ σοὶ λέγων ἐρᾶν
μου. σὺ οὖν ὑπὲρ τηλικούτων τετολμημένων εἴσπρα-
ξαι παρ' αὐτοῦ τιμωρίαν τὴν ἀξίαν ἢ εἰ δίδως ἔκδοτον
θυγατέρα τὴν σὴν τοῖς οἰκέταις ἐμαυτὴν φθάσασα
ἀποκτενῶ."

6   Ἀκούσας ὁ Ἄψυρτος καὶ δόξας ἀληθῆ λέγειν αὐτὴν
ἠρεύνησε μὲν τὸ πραχθὲν οὐκέτι, μεταπεμψάμενος δὲ
τὸν Ἀβροκόμην "ὦ τολμηρὰ καὶ μιαρά" εἶπεν "κεφα-
λή, ἐτόλμησας εἰς δεσπότας τοὺς σοὺς ὑβρίσαι καὶ
διαφθεῖραι παρθένον ἠθέλησας οἰκέτης ὤν; ἀλλ' οὔτι
χαιρήσεις· ἐγὼ γάρ σε τιμωρήσομαι καὶ τοῖς ἄλλοις
οἰκέταις τὴν σὴν αἰκίαν ποιήσομαι παράδειγμα." 2.
εἰπὼν οὐκέτι ἀνασχόμενος οὐδὲ λόγου ἀκοῦσαι ἐκέ-
λευε περιρρῆξαι τὴν ἐσθῆτα αὐτοῦ τοῖς οἰκέταις καὶ
φέρειν πῦρ καὶ μάστιγας καὶ παίειν τὸ μειράκιον. 3. ἦν
δὲ τὸ θέαμα ἐλεεινόν· αἵ τε γὰρ πληγαὶ τὸ σῶμα πᾶν
ἠφάνιζον βασάνων ἄηθες ὂν οἰκετικῶν τό τε αἷμα
κατέρρει [πᾶν] καὶ τὸ κάλλος ἐμαραίνετο. 4. προσῆγεν
αὐτῷ καὶ δεσμὰ φοβερὰ καὶ πῦρ καὶ μάλιστα ἐχρῆτο
ταῖς βασάνοις κατ' αὐτοῦ τῷ νυμφίῳ τῆς θυγατρὸς
ἐνδεικνύμενος ὅτι σώφρονα παρθένον ἄξεται. 5. ἐν
τούτῳ ἡ Ἀνθία προσπίπτει τοῖς γόνασι τοῦ Ἀψύρτου
καὶ ἐδεῖτο ὑπὲρ Ἀβροκόμου, ὁ δὲ "ἀλλὰ καὶ μᾶλλον"
ἔφη "διὰ σὲ κολασθήσεται ὅτι καὶ σὲ ἠδίκησε γυναῖκα

turned from Syria with a bridegroom from that country for his daughter; his name was Moeris.[21] But as soon as he arrived, Manto launched her plot against Habrocomes. She mussed her hair and tore her clothes, ran to meet her father, fell at his knees and said, "Father, have pity on your daughter, outraged by a slave! 7. Your chaste Habrocomes tried to deflower me, and he also offended against you by declaring his love for me. So you must exact appropriate vengeance on him for audacity of such magnitude; otherwise, if you mean to deliver your own daughter into the hands of the slaves, I will kill myself first."

When Apsyrtus heard this he thought she was telling the truth. He made no further investigation into what had happened but sent for Habrocomes and said, "You brazen piece of filth! Did you dare behave insolently to your masters and were you ready, slave that you are, to defile a maiden? Well, you will not get away with it, because I am going to punish you and make your agony an example to the other slaves." 2. With that, he had no patience for listening to a word of explanation and ordered his slaves to rip off the young man's clothes, fetch fire and whips, and start beating him. 3. It was a piteous spectacle: the blows disfigured his whole body, unused to servile torments, his blood spilled out, and his beauty died away. 4. Apsyrtus also applied fearsome bonds and fire, and visited the worst tortures on him, demonstrating to his daughter's bridegroom that he would be marrying a chaste maiden. 5. Meanwhile Anthia fell at Apsyrtus' knees and pleaded for Habrocomes, but his answer was, "No, on your account he will be punished even more, because he wronged you too,

6

---

[21] "Destiny"; a conventional name.

ἔχων ἄλλης ἐρῶν." καὶ τότε ἐκέλευσε δήσαντας αὐτὸν
ἐγκαθεῖρξαί τινι οἰκήματι σκοτεινῷ.

7   Καὶ ὁ μὲν ἐδέδετο καὶ ἦν ἐν εἱρκτῇ, δεινὴ δὲ αὐτὸν
ἀθυμία καταλαμβάνει καὶ μάλιστα ἐπεὶ Ἀνθίαν οὐχ
ἑώρα, ἐζήτει δὲ θανάτου τρόπους πολλοὺς ἀλλ' εὕ-
ρισκεν οὐδένα πολλῶν τῶν φρουρούντων ὄντων. ὁ δὲ
Ἄψυρτος ἐποίει τῆς θυγατρὸς τοὺς γάμους καὶ ἑώρ-
ταζον πολλαῖς ἡμέραις. 2. Ἀνθίᾳ δὲ πάντα πένθος ἦν
καὶ εἴ ποτε δυνηθείη πεῖσαι τοὺς ἐπὶ τοῦ δεσμωτηρίου
εἰσῄει πρὸς Ἀβροκόμην λανθάνουσα καὶ κατωδύρετο
τὴν συμφοράν. 3. ὡς δὲ ἤδη παρεσκευάζοντο εἰς
Συρίαν ἀπιέναι προέπεμψεν ὁ Ἄψυρτος τὴν θυγατέρα
μετὰ δώρων πολλῶν ἐσθῆτάς τε [τὰς] Βαβυλωνίους
καὶ χρυσὸν ἄφθονον καὶ ἄργυρον ἐδίδου, ἐδωρήσατο
δὲ τῇ θυγατρὶ Μαντοῖ τὴν Ἀνθίαν καὶ τὴν Ῥόδην καὶ
τὸν Λεύκωνα. 4. ὡς οὖν ταῦτα ἔγνω ἡ Ἀνθία καὶ ὅτι εἰς
Συρίαν ἀναχθήσεται μετὰ Μαντοῦς δυνηθεῖσα εἰσ-
ελθεῖν εἰς τὸ δεσμωτήριον περιπλεξαμένη τῷ Ἀβροκόμῃ "δέσποτα" εἶπεν, "εἰς Συρίαν ἄγομαι δῶρον
δοθεῖσα τῇ Μαντοῖ καὶ εἰς χεῖρας τῆς ζηλοτυπούσης
παραδίδομαι, 5. σὺ δὲ ἐν τῷ δεσμωτηρίῳ μείνας
οἰκτρῶς ἀποθνήσκεις οὐκ ἔχων οὐδὲ ὅστις σου τὸ
σῶμα κοσμήσει. ἀλλ' ὀμνύω σοι τὸν ἀμφοτέρων δαίμονα ὡς ἐγὼ μενῶ σὴ καὶ ζῶσα κἂν ἀποθανεῖν δέῃ."
ταῦτα λέγουσα ἐφίλει τε αὐτὸν καὶ περιέβαλλε καὶ τὰ
δεσμὰ ἠσπάζετο καὶ τῶν ποδῶν προυκυλίετο.

8   Τέλος δὲ ἡ μὲν ἐξῄει τοῦ δεσμωτηρίου, ὁ δὲ ὡς
εἶχεν ἑαυτὸν ἐπὶ γῆς ῥίψας ἔστενεν, ἔκλαιεν "ὦ πάτερ"
λέγων "φίλτατε, ὦ μῆτερ Θεμιστοῖ, ποῦ μὲν ἡ ἐν
Ἐφέσῳ δοκοῦσά ποτε εὐδαιμονία; ποῦ δὲ οἱ λαμπροὶ
καὶ οἱ περίβλεπτοι Ἀνθία καὶ Ἀβροκόμης οἱ καλοί; ἡ
μὲν οἴχεται πόρρω ποι τῆς γῆς αἰχμάλωτος, ἐγὼ δὲ

a married man in love with another woman." Then he ordered them to tie him up and confine him in a dark cell.

And so he was bound and confined, and a terrible de- 7
pression overtook him, especially because he could not see
Anthia. He began to look for numerous ways to kill himself but could find none because his guards were numerous. Apsyrtus went ahead with his daughter's wedding and
the celebration lasted many days. 2. Anthia's unhappiness
was total, and whenever she could persuade the prison
guards she would secretly visit Habrocomes and bewail
their predicament. 3. Preparations were already underway
for the trip to Syria, and Apsyrtus sent his daughter off with
plenty of gifts, gave her Babylonian clothing and a gener-
ous amount of gold and silver, and to his daughter Manto
made a present of Anthia, Rhoda, and Leuco. 4. When
Anthia heard about this and realized that she was to be
sent to Syria with Manto, she managed to get into the
prison, embraced Habrocomes, and said, "Master, I am
being taken to Syria as Manto's present, delivered into the
hands of my jealous rival, 5. while you languish in prison
and await a miserable death, with no one even to deck out
your corpse. But I swear by our mutual guardian spirit that
I will be yours as long as I live and even if I must die." With
this she kissed him, embraced him, clung to his chains, and
rolled at his feet.

Finally she left the prison, and he threw himself to 8
the ground just as he was and began to weep and wail.
"Dearest father," he cried, " and mother Themisto! Where
is the happiness that we once thought was ours in
Ephesus? Where are Anthia and Habrocomes, the radiant,
the center of attention, the beautiful? She is gone to some
faraway land as a captive, while I am bereft of my only con-

καὶ τὸ μόνον ἀφήρημαι παραμύθιον καὶ τεθνήξομαι
δυστυχὴς ἐν δεσμωτηρίῳ μόνος." 2. ταῦτα λέγοντα
αὐτὸν ὕπνος καταλαμβάνει καὶ αὐτῷ ὄναρ ἐφίσταται.
ἔδοξεν ἰδεῖν αὐτοῦ τὸν πατέρα Λυκομήδη ἐν ἐσθῆτι
μελαίνη πλανώμενον κατὰ πᾶσαν γῆν καὶ θάλατταν,
ἐπιστάντα δὲ τῷ δεσμωτηρίῳ λῦσαί τε αὐτὸν καὶ
ἀφιέναι ἐκ τοῦ οἰκήματος· ⟨αὐ⟩τὸν δὲ ἵππον γενόμενον
ἐπὶ πολλὴν φέρεσθαι γῆν διώκοντα ἵππον ἄλλην θή-
λειαν καὶ τέλος εὑρεῖν τὴν ἵππον καὶ ἄνθρωπον γενέσθαι. ταῦτα ὡς ἔδοξεν ἰδεῖν ἀνέθορέ τε καὶ μικρὰ
εὔελπις ἦν.

9   Ὁ μὲν οὖν ἐν τῷ δεσμωτηρίῳ κατε⟨κέ⟩κλειστο, ἡ δὲ
Ἀνθία εἰς Συρίαν ἤγετο καὶ ὁ Λεύκων καὶ ἡ Ῥόδη. ὡς
δὲ ἧκον οἱ περὶ τὴν Μαντὼ εἰς Ἀντιόχειαν, ἐκεῖθεν γὰρ
ἦν Μοῖρις, ἐμνησικάκει μὲν καὶ τὴν Ῥόδην, ἐμίσει δὲ
καὶ τὴν Ἀνθίαν. 2. καὶ δὴ τὴν μὲν Ῥόδην εὐθὺς μετὰ
τοῦ Λεύκωνος κελεύει ἐμβιβάσαντάς τινας πλοίῳ πορ-
ρωτάτω τῆς Συρίας ἀποδόσθαι γῆς, τὴν δὲ Ἀνθίαν
οἰκέτῃ συνουσιάζειν ἐνενόει καὶ ταῦτα τῶν ἀτιμοτάτων
αἰπόλῳ τινὶ ἀγροίκῳ ἡγουμένη διὰ τούτου τιμωρήσα-
σθαι αὐτήν. 3. μεταπέμπεται δὲ τὸν αἰπόλον, Λάμπωνα τοὔνομα, καὶ παραδίδωσι τὴν Ἀνθίαν καὶ κελεύει
γυναῖκα ἔχειν καὶ ἐὰν ἀπειθῇ προσέταττε βιάζεσθαι.
4. καὶ ἡ μὲν ἤγετο ἐπ' ἀγρὸν συνεσομένη τῷ αἰπόλῳ,
γενομένη δὲ ἐν τῷ χωρίῳ ἔνθα ὁ Λάμπων ἔνεμε τὰς
αἶγας προσπίπτει τοῖς γόνασιν αὐτοῦ καὶ ἱκετεύει
κατοικτεῖραι καὶ ⟨ἁγνὴν⟩ τηρῆσαι. διηγεῖται δὲ ἥτις
ἦν, τὴν προτέραν εὐγένειαν, τὸν ἄνδρα, τὴν αἰχμα-
λωσίαν. ἀκούσας δὲ ὁ Λάμπων οἰκτείρει τὴν κόρην καὶ
ὄμνυσιν ἦ μὴν φυλάξειν ἀμόλυντον καὶ θαρρεῖν παρεκελεύετο.

solation and will die in prison, unfortunate and alone."
2. As he was speaking, sleep overtook him and he was
visited by a dream. He dreamt that he saw his father
Lycomedes dressed in black clothing, wandering over every land and sea, stopping at the prison, freeing him, and
releasing him from his cell, and that he himself became a
horse and traveled to many a land in pursuit of a second
horse, a mare, and finally found that mare and became a
man again. After this dream he sprang up and was slightly
more hopeful.

So he remained locked up in prison, while Anthia,   9
Leuco, and Rhoda were taken to Syria. When Manto's
group arrived in Antioch, where Moeris was from, she still
bore a grudge against Rhoda as well as hatred for Anthia.
2. She immediately ordered Rhoda to be put on a boat
along with Leuco and sold as far away as possible from Syrian territory, and her idea for Anthia was that she would go
with a slave, one of the lowest order to boot, a rustic goatherd, thinking that this way she would get her revenge on
her. 3. She sent for the goatherd, named Lampo,[22] handed
over Anthia, told him to make her his wife, and ordered
him to take her by force if she refused. 4. So she was taken
to the country to be with the goatherd, but when she got to
the place where Lampo grazed his goats, she fell at his
knees and begged him to take pity on her and to preserve
her chastity, and she told him who she was, her erstwhile
high estate, her husband, her captivity. Lampo listened
and felt pity for the girl, swore that he would surely keep
her undefiled, and encouraged her to take heart.[23]

[22] "Shining"; a conventional name.   [23] Paradigmatic is
Euripides' *Electra*, where Clytemestra punishes her daughter by
marrying her to a farmer who nevertheless respects her chastity.

10 Καὶ ἡ μὲν παρὰ τῷ αἰπόλῳ ἦν ἐν τῷ χωρίῳ πάντα χρόνον Ἀβροκόμην θρηνοῦσα, ὁ δὲ Ἄψυρτος ἐρευνώμενος τὸ οἰκημάτιον ἔνθα ὁ Ἀβροκόμης πρὸ τῆς κολάσεως διῆγεν ἐπιτυγχάνει τῷ γραμματιδίῳ τῷ Μαντοῦς πρὸς Ἀβροκόμην καὶ γνωρίζει τὰ γράμματα καὶ ὅτι ἀδίκως Ἀβροκόμην τιμωρεῖται ἔμαθεν. εὐθὺς οὖν λῦσαί τε αὐτὸν προσέταξε καὶ ἀγαγεῖν εἰς ὄψεις. 2. πονηρὰ δὲ καὶ ἐλεεινὰ πεπονθὼς προσπίπτει τοῖς γόνασι τοῖς Ἀψύρτου, ὁ δὲ αὐτὸν ἀνίστησι καὶ "θάρσει" ἔφη, "ὦ μειράκιον· ἀδίκως σου κατέγνων πεισθεὶς θυγατρὸς λόγοις, ἀλλὰ νῦν μέν σε ἐλεύθερον ἀντὶ δούλου ποιήσω, δίδωμι δέ σοι τῆς οἰκίας ἄρχειν τῆς ἐμῆς καὶ γυναῖκα ἄξομαι τῶν πολιτῶν τινος θυγατέρα, σὺ δὲ μὴ μνησικακήσῃς τῶν γεγενημένων, οὐ γὰρ ἑκὼν σε ἠδίκησα." 3. ταῦτα ἔλεγεν ὁ Ἄψυρτος, ὁ δὲ Ἀβροκόμης "ἀλλὰ χάρις" ἔφη "σοι, δέσποτα, ὅτι καὶ τὸ ἀληθὲς ἔμαθες καὶ τῆς σωφροσύνης ἀμείβῃ με." ἔχαιρον δὴ πάντες οἱ κατὰ τὴν οἰκίαν ὑπὲρ Ἀβροκόμου καὶ χάριν ᾔδεσαν ὑπὲρ αὐτοῦ τῷ δεσπότῃ. αὐτὸς δὲ ἐν μεγάλῃ συμφορᾷ κατὰ Ἀνθίαν ἦν, ἐνενόει δὲ πρὸς ἑαυτὸν πολλάκις "τί δὲ ἐλευθερίας ἐμοί; τί δὲ πλούτων καὶ ἐπιμελείας τῶν Ἀψύρτου χρημάτων; οὐ τοιοῦτον εἶναί με δεῖ· ἐκείνην καὶ ζῶσαν καὶ τεθνεῶσαν εὕροιμι." 4. ὁ μὲν οὖν ἐν τούτοις ἦν διοικῶν μὲν τὰ Ἀψύρτου, ἐννοῶν δὲ ὁπότε καὶ ποῦ τὴν Ἀνθίαν εὑρήσει. ὁ δὲ Λεύκων καὶ ἡ Ῥόδη ἤχθησαν εἰς Λυκίαν εἰς πόλιν Ξάνθον, ἀνώτερον δὲ θαλάσσης ἡ πόλις, κἀνταῦθα ἐπράθησαν πρεσβύτῃ τινί, ὃς αὐτοὺς εἶχε μετὰ πάσης ἐπιμελείας παῖδας αὐτοῦ νομίζων· καὶ γὰρ

So she was in the country with the shepherd, all the $\quad$ 10
while weeping for Habrocomes, while Apsyrtus, searching the small room where Habrocomes had lived before
his punishment, happened upon Manto's note to Habrocomes, recognized the writing, and realized that he was
punishing Habrocomes unfairly. So he gave immediate orders to release him and bring him into his presence. 2. A
victim of cruel and piteous treatment, he fell at Apsyrtus'
knees, but he made him rise and said, "Take heart, young
man: I believed a daughter's allegations and wrongly condemned you. But now I will make you a free man instead of
a slave, I will put you in charge of my own household, and I
will marry you to a daughter of one of our citizens; for your
part, bear me no grudge over what happened, because I
did not mean to wrong you." 3. To Apsyrtus' offer Habrocomes replied, "You have my gratitude, master, for learning the truth and rewarding me for my self-control." Indeed everyone in the household felt glad for Habrocomes
and expressed their gratitude to the master. But he himself remained in deep distress about Anthia, and she was
always on his mind: "What do I care about freedom? About
riches and stewardship of Apsyrtus' possessions? That
is not what I should be doing; I wish I could find Anthia
alive or dead!" 4. So this was his situation as he managed
Apsyrtus' affairs while pondering when and where he
would find Anthia. But Leuco and Rhoda had been taken
to the town of Xanthus in Lycia,[24] an inland town, where
they were sold to an old man who paid them every attention and thought of them as his own children, for he was

[24] Xanthus (modern Kinik in southwestern Turkey) was a
principal town of Lycia.

267

ἄτεκνος ἦν, διῆγον δὲ ἐν ἀφθόνοις μὲν πᾶσιν, ἐλύπουν
δὲ αὐτοὺς Ἀνθία καὶ Ἁβροκόμης οὐχ ὁρώμενοι.

11   Ἡ δὲ Ἀνθία ἦν μέν τινα χρόνον παρὰ τῷ αἰπόλῳ,
συνεχὲς δὲ ὁ Μοῖρις ὁ ἀνὴρ τῆς Μαντοῦς εἰς τὸ χωρίον
ἐρχόμενος ἐρᾷ τῆς Ἀνθίας σφοδρὸν ἔρωτα. καὶ τὰ μὲν
πρῶτα ἐπειρᾶτο λανθάνειν, τελευταῖον δὲ λέγει τῷ
αἰπόλῳ τὸν ἔρωτα καὶ πολλὰ ὑπισχνεῖτο συγκρύ-
ψαντι. 2. ὁ δὲ τῷ μὲν Μοίριδι συντίθεται, δεδοικὼς δὲ
τὴν Μαντὼ ἔρχεται πρὸς αὐτὴν καὶ λέγει τὸν ἔρωτα
τὸν Μοίριδος. ἡ δὲ ἐν ὀργῇ γενομένη "πασῶν" ἔφη
"δυστυχεστάτη γυναικῶν ἐγώ· τὴν ζήλην περιάξομαι
δι' ἣν τὰ μὲν πρῶτα ἐν Φοινίκῃ ἀφῃρέθην ἐρωμένου,
νυνὶ δὲ κινδυνεύω τοῦ ἀνδρός. ἀλλ' οὐ χαίρουσά γε
Ἀνθία φανεῖται καλὴ καὶ Μοίριδι· ἐγὼ γὰρ αὐτὴν καὶ
ὑπὲρ τῶν ἐν Τύρῳ πράξομαι δίκας." 3. τότε μὲν οὖν τὴν
ἡσυχίαν ἤγαγεν, ἀποδημήσαντος δὲ τοῦ Μοίριδος
μεταπέμπεται τὸν αἰπόλον καὶ κελεύει λαβόντα τὴν
Ἀνθίαν εἰς τὸ δασύτατον ἀγαγόντα τῆς ὕλης ἀποκτεῖναι καὶ τούτου μισθὸν αὐτῷ δώσειν ὑπέσχετο. 4. ὁ δὲ
οἰκτείρει μὲν τὴν κόρην, δεδοικὼς δὲ τὴν Μαντὼ ἔρχεται παρὰ τὴν Ἀνθίαν καὶ λέγει τὰ κατ' αὐτῆς δε-
δογμένα. ἡ δὲ ἀνεκώκυσέ τε καὶ ἀνωδύρετο "φεῦ"
λέγουσα, "τοῦτο τὸ κάλλος ἐπίβουλον ἀμφοτέροις
πανταχοῦ· διὰ τὴν ἄκαιρον εὐμορφίαν Ἁβροκόμης μὲν
ἐν Τύρῳ τέθηκεν, ἐγὼ δὲ ἐνταῦθα. 5. ἀλλὰ δέομαι
σοῦ, Λάμπων αἰπόλε, ὡς μέχρι νῦν εὐσέβησας, ἂν
ἀποκτείνῃς, κἂν ὀλίγον θάψον με τῇ παρακειμένῃ γῇ
καὶ ὀφθαλμοῖς τοῖς ἐμοῖς χεῖρας ἐπίβαλε τὰς σὰς καὶ
θάπτων συνεχὲς Ἁβροκόμην κάλει· αὕτη γένοιτ' ἂν
εὐδαίμων ἐμοὶ μετὰ Ἁβροκόμου ταφή." 6. ἔλεγε ταῦτα,
ὁ δὲ αἰπόλος εἰς οἶκτον ἔρχεται ἐννοῶν ὡς ἀνόσιον
ἔργον ἐργάσεται κόρην οὐδὲν ἀδικοῦσαν ἀποκτείνας

childless. They lived with an abundance of everything, but no longer seeing Anthia and Habrocomes pained them.

Anthia lived for some time with the goatherd, but 11 Manto's husband Moeris frequently visited the place and fell passionately in love with Anthia. At first he tried not to show it, but in the end he told the goatherd of his love and promised him a lot for his connivance. 2. The goatherd came to terms with him, but for fear of Manto he visited her and told her about Moeris' love. She became enraged and cried, "Of all wives I am the unluckiest! Must I take my rival with me everywhere? Because of her I first had a lover stolen away in Phoenicia, and now I risk losing my husband. But Anthia will be sorry for looking good to Moeris too, because I'm going to punish her for it, and also for what happened in Tyre!" 3. For the moment then she kept quiet, but when Moeris was out of town she summoned the goatherd and told him to seize Anthia, take her into the thickest woods, and kill her, and for this she promised to pay him. 4. He felt sorry for the girl, but for fear of Manto he went to Anthia and told her what had been decided in her case. She shrieked and began to wail, saying "Oh, how this beauty of ours conspires everywhere against us both! Because of our troublesome good looks Habrocomes is done for in Tyre, and I here. 5. But I ask you, goatherd Lampo, since you have thus far behaved respectfully, if you kill me, give me at least a shallow grave in the ground nearby, put your hands on my eyes, and invoke Habrocomes repeatedly as you bury me: for me this would make a happy funeral, in the presence of Habrocomes." 6. At this, the goatherd was moved to pity, aware that he was about to do an unholy deed by killing a girl who had done

οὕτω καλήν. 7. λαβὼν δὴ τὴν κόρην ὁ αἰπόλος φονεῦ-
σαι μὲν οὐκ ἠνέσχετο, φράζει δὲ πρὸς αὐτὴν τάδε·
"Ἀνθία, οἶδας ὅτι ἡ δέσποινα Μαντὼ ἐκέλευσέ μοι
λαβεῖν καὶ φονεῦσαί σε. ἐγὼ δὲ καὶ θεοὺς δεδιὼς καὶ
τὸ κάλλος οἰκτείρας βούλομαί σε μᾶλλον πωλῆσαι
πόρρω που τῆς γῆς ταύτης, μὴ μαθοῦσα ἡ Μαντὼ ὅτι
οὐ τέθνηκας ἐμὲ [μᾶλλον] κακῶς διαθήσει." 8. ἡ δὲ
μετὰ δακρύων λαβομένη τῶν ποδῶν αὐτοῦ ἔφη "θεοὶ
καὶ Ἄρτεμι πατρῴα, τὸν αἰπόλον ὑπὲρ τούτων τῶν
ἀγαθῶν ἀμείψασθε" καὶ παρεκάλει πραθῆναι. 9. ὁ δὲ
αἰπόλος λαβόμενος τῆς Ἀνθίας ᾤχετο ἐπὶ τὸν λιμένα,
εὑρὼν δὲ ἐκεῖ ἐμπόρους ἄνδρας Κίλικας ἀπέδοτο τὴν
κόρην καὶ λαβὼν τὴν ὑπὲρ αὐτῆς τιμὴν ἧκεν εἰς τὸν
ἀγρόν. 10. οἱ δὲ ἔμποροι λαβόντες τὴν Ἀνθίαν εἰς τὸ
πλοῖον ἦγον καὶ νυκτὸς ἐπελθούσης ἤεσαν τὴν ἐπὶ
Κιλικίας· ἐναντίῳ δὲ πνεύματι κατεχόμενοι καὶ τῆς
νεὼς διαρραγείσης μόλις ἐν σανίσι τινὲς σωθέντες ἐπ᾽
αἰγιαλοῦ τινος ἦλθον· εἶχον δὲ καὶ τὴν Ἀνθίαν. 11. ἦν
δὲ ἐν τῷ τόπῳ ἐκείνῳ ὕλη δασεῖα. τὴν οὖν νύκτα
ἐκείνην πλανώμενοι ἐν ⟨τ⟩αύτῃ[40] τῇ ὕλῃ ὑπὸ τῶν περὶ
τὸν Ἱππόθοον τὸν λῃστὴν συνελήφθησαν.

12   Ἐν δὲ τούτοις ἧκεν ἀπὸ τῆς Συρίας οἰκέτης [ὑπὸ]
τῆς Μαντοῦς γράμματα κομίζων τῷ πατρὶ Ἀψύρτῳ
τοιάδε· "ἔδωκάς με ἀνδρὶ ἐν ξένῃ· Ἀνθίαν δέ, ἣν μετὰ
τῶν ἄλλων οἰκετῶν ἐδωρήσω μοι, πολλὰ διαπραξα-
μένην κακὰ εἰς ἀγρὸν ⟨ . . . ⟩[41] οἰκεῖν ἐκελεύσαμεν.
ταύτην συνεχῶς ἐν τῷ χωρίῳ θεώμενος ὁ καλὸς Μοῖρις
ἐρᾷ, μηκέτι δὲ φέρειν δυναμένη μετεπεμψάμην τὸν

40 O'Sullivan
41 Lac. susp. O'Sullivan, supplere possis e.g. ἐξάγεσθαι καὶ
παρὰ αἰπόλῳ τινὶ

no wrong and was so beautiful. 7. Indeed when he seized the girl, the goatherd could not abide a murder, but said this to her: "Anthia, you know that my mistress Manto ordered me to seize and murder you. But I fear heaven and feel pity at your beauty, so I would rather sell you somewhere far from this country, in case Manto finds out that you are not dead and becomes ill disposed toward me." 8. She clung to his feet in tears, and said, "Please, you gods, and Artemis of my fatherland, reward the goatherd for these good deeds," and begged to be sold. 9. The goatherd took hold of Anthia and set off toward the shore, where he found some Cilician[25] merchants and sold the girl, and taking what he was paid for her he returned to the farm. 10. The merchants took Anthia and put her aboard their vessel, and at nightfall they set sail for Cilicia. But they were caught by an adverse wind and the ship broke up; some of the crew survived and on timbers only barely made it to a beach, taking Anthia too. 11. In that area there was a thick forest, so that night as they wandered in this forest they were captured by the bandit Hippothous' gang.[26]

In the meantime a slave arrived from Syria bearing a 12
letter from Manto to her father Apsyrtus, which read, "You gave me to a husband in a foreign land, but Anthia, whom you gave me as a present along with the other slaves, I ordered ‹to be taken› to the countryside ‹and› to live ‹with a goatherd› after she had committed numerous misdeeds. My handsome Moeris was constantly there gazing at her and is in love with her, and unable to bear this any longer I

---

[25] Cilicia (on the southeast coast of Turkey) was famous for its pirates, who were subdued by Pompey in 67 BCE.

[26] "Swift-Horse"; an epic and actual name.

αἰπόλον καὶ τὴν κόρην πραθῆναι πάλιν ἐκέλευσα ἐν
πόλει τινὶ τῆς Συρίας." 2. ταῦτα μαθὼν ὁ Ἁβροκόμης
οὐκέτι μένειν ἐκαρτέρει· λαθὼν οὖν τὸν Ἄψυρτον καὶ
πάντας τοὺς κατὰ τὸν οἶκον [εἰς] ἐπὶ ζήτησιν τῆς
Ἀνθίας ἔρχεται. ἐλθὼν οὖν < . . . >[42] ἐν τῷ ἀγρῷ ἔνθα
μετὰ τοῦ αἰπόλου ἡ Ἀνθία διέτριβεν. †ἄγει δὴ παρὰ
τὸν αἰγιαλὸν†[43] τὸν Λάμπωνα τὸν αἰπόλον ᾧ πρὸς
γάμον ἐδεδώκει τὴν Ἀνθίαν ἡ Μαντώ, ἐδεῖτο δὲ τοῦ
Λάμπωνος εἰπεῖν αὐτῷ εἴ τι οἶδε περὶ κόρης ἐκ Τύρου.
3. ὁ δὲ αἰπόλος καὶ τὸ ὄνομα εἶπεν ὅτι [καὶ] Ἀνθία καὶ
τὸν γάμον καὶ τὴν εὐσέβειαν τὴν περὶ αὐτὴν καὶ τὸν
Μοίριδος ἔρωτα καὶ τὸ πρόσταγμα τὸ κατ' αὐτῆς καὶ
τὴν εἰς Κιλικίαν ὁδόν, ἔλεγέ τε ὡς ἀεί τινος Ἁβροκόμου μέμνηται ἡ κόρη. ὁ δὲ αὐτὸν ὅστις ἦν οὐ λέγει,
ἕωθεν δὲ ἀναστὰς ἤλαυνε τὴν ἐπὶ Κιλικίαν ἐλπίζων
Ἀνθίαν εὑρήσειν ἐκεῖ.

13   Οἱ δὲ περὶ τὸν Ἱππόθοον τὸν λῃστὴν ἐκείνης μὲν
τῆς νυκτὸς ἔμειναν εὐωχούμενοι, τῇ δ' ἑξῆς περὶ τὴν
θυσίαν ἐγίνοντο. παρεσκευάζετο δὲ πάντα καὶ ἀγάλματα τοῦ Ἄρεος καὶ ξύλα καὶ στεφανώματα· 2. ἔδει δὲ
τὴν θυσίαν γενέσθαι τρόπῳ τῷ συνήθει. τὸ μέλλον
ἱερεῖον θύεσθαι εἴτε ἄνθρωπος εἴτε βόσκημα εἴη κρε-
μάσαντες ἐκ δένδρου καὶ διαστάντες ἠκόντιζον, καὶ
ὁπόσοι μὲν ἐπέτυχον τούτων ὁ θεὸς ἐδόκει δέχεσθαι
τὴν θυσίαν, ὁπόσοι δὲ ἀπέτυχον αὖθις ἐξιλάσκοντο.
ἔδει δὲ τὴν Ἀνθίαν οὕτως ἱερουργηθῆναι. 3. ὡς δὲ
πάντα ἕτοιμα ἦν καὶ κρεμᾶν τὴν κόρην ἤθελον ψόφος
τῆς ὕλης ἠκούετο καὶ ἀνθρώπων κτύπος. ἦν δὲ ὁ τῆς
εἰρήνης τῆς ἐν Κιλικίᾳ προεστώς, Περίλαος τοὔνομα,

[42] Lac. Jackson
[43] Obel. Hägg, cf. 5.1.2

sent for the goatherd and ordered the girl sold again in a city in Syria." 2. When Habrocomes found out about this, he could no longer bear to stay, so he slipped away from Apsyrtus and everyone else in the household and set off in search of Anthia. When he came ⟨ . . . ⟩ at the farm where Anthia had been living with the goatherd. †Down along the shore he brought† Lampo the goatherd, to whom Manto had given Anthia for marriage, and asked Lampo to tell him if he knew anything about a girl from Tyre. 3. The goatherd replied that her name was Anthia and told him about the marriage, his respectful behavior toward her, Moeris' infatuation, the order to kill her, and the journey to Cilicia. He added that the girl was constantly mentioning someone named Habrocomes. He did not reveal his identity but got up at dawn and rode to Cilicia, hoping to find Anthia there.

The bandit Hippothous' gang spent that night partying, and the next day they got busy with their sacrifice.[27] When everything was prepared—images of Ares, firewood, and garlands—2. the sacrifice was to be carried out in their usual manner: they hung the victim that was going to be sacrificed, whether human or animal, from a tree, stood at a distance, and tried to hit it with javelins, and the god was considered to accept the sacrifice of all who scored a hit, while those who missed tried to appease him a second time. It was Anthia who was to serve as this kind of sacrificial victim. 3. When all was ready and they were about to hang her up, they heard rustling in the woods and a din of men. It was the head officer of the peace in Cilicia, whose

13

[27] For this story compare *Asinus* 23 and Apuleius, *Met.* IV 22.

ἀνὴρ τῶν τὰ πρῶτα ἐν Κιλικίᾳ δυναμένων. 4. οὗτος ὁ
Περίλαος ἐπέστη τοῖς λῃσταῖς μετὰ πλήθους πολλοῦ
καὶ πάντας τε ἀπέκτεινεν, ὀλίγους δὲ καὶ ζῶντας
ἔλαβε. μόνος δὲ ὁ Ἱππόθοος ἠδυνήθη διαφυγεῖν
ἀράμενος τὰ ὅπλα. 5. ἔλαβε δὲ τὴν Ἀνθίαν Περίλαος
καὶ πυθόμενος τὴν μέλλουσαν συμφορὰν ἠλέησεν·
εἶχε δὲ ἄρα μεγάλης ἀρχὴν συμφορᾶς ὁ ἔλεος Ἀνθίας·
ἄγει δὲ αὐτὴν καὶ τοὺς συλληφθέντας τῶν λῃστῶν εἰς
Ταρσὸν τῆς Κιλικίας. 6. ἡ δὲ συνήθης αὐτῷ τῆς κόρης
ὄψις εἰς ἔρωτα ἤγαγε καὶ κατὰ μικρὸν ἑαλώκει Περίλαος Ἀνθίας. ὡς δὲ ἦκον εἰς Ταρσὸν τοὺς μὲν λῃστὰς
εἰς τὴν εἰρκτὴν παρέδωκε, τὴν δὲ Ἀνθίαν ἐθεράπευεν.
ἦν δὲ οὔτε γυνὴ τῷ Περιλάῳ οὔτε παῖδες καὶ περιβολὴ
χρημάτων οὐκ ὀλίγη. 7. ἔλεγεν οὖν πρὸς τὴν Ἀνθίαν
ὡς πάντα ἂν αὐτῇ γένοιτο Περιλάῳ, γυνὴ καὶ δεσπότις
καὶ παῖδες. 8. ἡ δὲ τὰ μὲν πρῶτα ἀντεῖχεν, οὐκ ἔχουσα
δὲ ὅ τι ποιήσει βιαζομένῳ καὶ πολλὰ ἐγκειμένῳ,
δείσασα μή κατι τολμήσῃ βιαιότερον συγκατατίθεται μὲν τὸν γάμον, ἱκετεύει δὲ αὐτὸν ἀναμεῖναι
χρόνον ὀλίγον ὅσον ἡμερῶν τριάκοντα καὶ ἄχραντον
τηρῆσαι· καὶ σκήπτεται ⟨μέν τι⟩, ὁ δὲ Περίλαος πείθεται καὶ ἐπόμνυται τηρήσειν αὐτὴν γάμων ἁγνὴν εἰς
ὅσον ἂν ὁ χρόνος διέλθῃ.

14   Καὶ ἡ μὲν ἐν Ταρσῷ ἦν μετὰ Περιλάου τὸν χρόνον
ἀναμένουσα τοῦ γάμου, ὁ δὲ Ἁβροκόμης ᾔει τὴν ἐπὶ
Κιλικίας ὁδόν, καὶ οὐ πρὸ πολλοῦ τοῦ ἄντρου τοῦ
λῃστρικοῦ, ἀπεπλάνητο γὰρ καὶ αὐτὸς τῆς ἐπ᾽ εὐθὺ
ὁδοῦ, συντυγχάνει τῷ Ἱπποθόῳ ὡπλισμένῳ. 2. ὁ δὲ
αὐτὸν ἰδὼν προ⟨σ⟩τρέχει τε καὶ φιλοφρονεῖται καὶ

---

28 A mythological and actual name.
29 The capital of Cilicia, Tarsus (on the coast of the Marsin dis-

name was Perilaus,[28] one of the most powerful men in
Cilicia. 4. This Perilaus attacked the bandits with a large
force and killed them all, except for a few that he captured
alive. Only Hippothous managed to collect his weapons
and make a clean getaway. 5. Perilaus took Anthia and pitied her when he heard about the misfortune that had been
in store for her, but this pity for Anthia spelled the beginning of further great misfortune. He took her along with
the captured bandits to Tarsus in Cilicia.[29] 6. The frequent
sight of the girl led Perilaus to passion, and by degrees he
fell captive to Anthia. When they arrived in Tarsus, he had
the bandits imprisoned and began to devote himself to
Anthia. Perilaus had no wife or children, and no small am-
plitude of possessions. 7. He declared to Anthia that she
would be everything to Perilaus, his wife, his mistress, and
his children. 8. At first she resisted, but she felt helpless to
act as he pressured her and kept insisting, afraid that he
might resort to something more violent, so she agreed to
the marriage but begged him to wait a little while, as much
as thirty days, and to leave her chastity intact. She offered
some sort of excuse, and Perilaus acquiesced, promising
that he would keep her pure of marital contact during the
specified interval.

So she found herself in Tarsus with Perilaus, awaiting   14
the deadline for her marriage, while Habrocomes was en
route to Cilicia. And not far from the bandits' cave, for
he himself had wandered off the high road, he encountered Hippothous, fully armed. 2. At the sight of him Hippothous ran over, offered a friendly greeting, and asked to

trict of southeastern Turkey) was an important agricultural and
commercial center.

δεῖται κοινωνὸν γενέσθαι τῆς ὁδοῦ· "ὁρῶ γάρ σε," <ἔφη> "ὦ μειράκιον, ὅστις ποτὲ εἶ, καὶ ὀφθῆναι καλὸν καὶ ἄλλως ἀνδρικὸν καὶ ἡ πλάνη φαίνεται πάντως ἀδικουμένου. 3. ἴωμεν οὖν Κιλικίαν μὲν ἀφέντες ἐπὶ Καππαδοκίαν καὶ τὸν Πόντον· ἐκεῖ[44] γὰρ λέγονται οἰκεῖν ἄνδρες εὐδαίμονες." 4. ὁ δὲ Ἀβροκόμης τὴν μὲν Ἀνθίας ζήτησιν οὐ λέγει, συγκατατίθεται δὲ ἀναγκά- ζοντι τῷ Ἱπποθόῳ καὶ ὅρκους ποιοῦσι συνεργήσειν τε καὶ συλλήψεσθαι· ἤλπιζε δὲ καὶ ὁ Ἀβροκόμης ἐν τῇ πολλῇ πλάνῃ τὴν Ἀνθίαν εὑρήσειν. 5. ἐκείνην μὲν οὖν τὴν ἡμέραν ἐπανελθόντες εἰς τὸ ἄντρον εἴ τι αὐτοῖς ἔτι περιττὸν ἦν αὐτοὺς καὶ τοὺς ἵππους ἀνελάμβανον, ἦν γὰρ <καὶ> τῷ Ἱπποθόῳ ἵππος ἐν τῇ ὕλῃ κρυπτόμενος.

[44] Ante Πόντον transp. Hercher

share the journey with him. "I can see, young man," he said, "whoever you are, that you are handsome to look at and manly to boot, and yours is clearly the trek of one who has been wronged. 3. Let's get out of Cilicia and head for Cappadocia and Pontus: they say that wealthy men live there." 4. Habrocomes said nothing of his search for Anthia, but under compulsion agreed to Hippothous' proposal, and they swore to be partners and help each other out. Habrocomes also hoped that in the course of their long trek he would find Anthia. 5. And so they returned to the cave for the rest of the day and used whatever they had left to refresh themselves and their horses, for Hippothous too had a horse hidden in the woods.

ΛΟΓΟΣ ΤΡΙΤΟΣ

1 Τῇ δὲ ἐξῆς παρῄεσαν μὲν Κιλικίαν, ἐποιοῦντο δὲ τὴν ὁδὸν ἐπὶ Μάζακον, πόλιν τῆς Καππαδοκίας μεγάλην καὶ καλήν· 2. ἐκεῖθεν γὰρ Ἱππόθοος ἐνενόει συλλεξάμενος νεανίσκους ἀκμάζοντας συστήσασθαι πάλιν τὸ λῃστήριον. ἰοῦσι δὲ αὐτοῖς διὰ κωμῶν μεγά- λων πάντων ἦν ἀφθονία τῶν ἐπιτηδείων· καὶ γὰρ ὁ Ἱππόθοος ἐμπείρως εἶχε τῆς Καππαδοκῶν φωνῆς καὶ αὐτῷ πάντες ὡς οἰκείῳ προσεφέροντο. 3. διανύσαντες δὲ τὴν ὁδὸν ἡμέραις δέκα εἰς Μάζακον ἔρχονται κἀνταῦθα πλησίον τῶν πυλῶν εἰσῳκίσαντο καὶ ἔγνω- σαν ἑαυτοὺς ἡμερῶν τινων ἐκ τοῦ καμάτου θερα- πεῦσαι. 4. καὶ δὴ εὐωχουμένων αὐτῶν ἐστέναξεν ὁ Ἱππόθοος καὶ ἐπεδάκρυ[σ]εν, ὁ δὲ Ἀβροκόμης ἤρετο αὐτὸν τίς ἡ αἰτία τῶν δακρύων. καὶ ὃς "μεγάλα" ἔφη "τἀμὰ διηγήματα καὶ πολλὴν ἔχοντα τραγῳδίαν." 5. ἐδέετο Ἀβροκόμης εἰπεῖν ὑπισχνούμενος καὶ τὰ καθ' αὑτὸν διηγήσασθαι. ὁ δὲ ἀναλαβὼν ἄνωθεν, μόνοι δὲ ἐτύγχανον ὄντες, ἐξηγεῖται τὰ καθ' αὑτόν.

2 "Ἐγὼ" ἔφη "εἰμὶ τὸ γένος πόλεως Περίνθου (πλη- σίον δὲ τῆς Θρᾴκης ἡ πόλις) τῶν τὰ πρῶτα ἐκεῖ δυναμένων. ἀκούεις δὲ καὶ τὴν Πέρινθον ὡς ἔνδοξος καὶ τοὺς ἄνδρας ὡς εὐδαίμονες ἐνταῦθα. 2. ἐκεῖ νέος ὢν ἠράσθην μειρακίου καλοῦ, ἦν δὲ τὸ μειράκιον τῶν

---

30 Properly Mazaca, which had been renamed Caesaraea in

They left Cilicia on the following day and headed for   1
Mazacus, a fine large town in Cappadocia,[30] 2. where Hippothous intended to recruit hardy young men and recon-
stitute his gang. As they traveled through large villages
they found abundant supplies of all kinds, since Hippothous was proficient in the Cappadocians' language and
they all dealt with him as one of their own. 3. They reached
Mazacus in ten days; there they settled in near the city
gates and decided to spend a few days recovering from
their fatigue. 4. In the course of their partying Hippothous
gave a groan and began to cry, and Habrocomes asked him
the reason for his tears. "My tale is long," he replied, "and
full of tragedy." 5. Habrocomes urged him to speak and
promised to tell his own tale. They happened to be alone,
and Hippothous told his story, starting from the beginning.

"My family," he said, "is among the most powerful in   2
Perinthus, a city near Thrace.[31] And you know the reputation of Perinthus as a renowned city whose men are prosperous. 2. There when I was young I fell in love with a
handsome youth, a youth who was a fellow countryman;

the time of Tiberius (modern Kayseri) and was a trade center and
seat of the Cappadocian kings until 14 CE.
    [31] Modern Eski Eregli on the Thracian Propontis, originally
a Samian colony; renamed Heraclea soon after the death of
Aurelian in 275 CE.

ἐπιχωρίων· ὄνομα Ὑπεράνθης ἦν αὐτῷ. ἠράσθην δὲ τὰ
πρῶτα ἐν γυμνασίοις διαπαλαίοντα ἰδὼν καὶ οὐκ ἐκαρ-
τέρησα. 3. ἑορτῆς ἀγομένης ἐπιχωρίου καὶ παννυχίδος
ἐπ᾽ αὐτῆς πρόσειμι τῷ Ὑπεράνθῃ καὶ ἱκετεύω κατ-
οικτείραι, ἀκοῦσαν δὲ τὸ μειράκιον πάντα ὑπισχνεῖται
κατελεήσάν με. 4. καὶ τὰ πρῶτά γε τοῦ ἔρωτος ὁδοι-
πορεῖ[45] φιλήματα καὶ ψαύσματα καὶ πολλὰ παρ᾽ ἐμοῦ
δάκρυα, τέλος δὲ ἠδυνήθημεν καιροῦ λαβόμενοι γενέσθαι μετ᾽ ἀλλήλων μόνοι καὶ τὸ τῆς ἡλικίας ἀλλήλοις
ἀνύποπτον ἦν. καὶ χρόνῳ συνῆμεν πολλῷ στέργοντες
ἀλλήλους διαφερόντως ἕως δαίμων τις ἡμῖν ἐνεμέ-
σησε. 5. καὶ ἔρχεταί τις ἀπὸ Βυζαντίου, πλησίον δὲ
τὸ Βυζάντιον τῇ Περίνθῳ, ἀνὴρ τῶν τὰ πρῶτα ἐκεῖ
δυναμένων, ὃς ἐπὶ πλούτῳ καὶ περιουσίᾳ μέγα φρονῶν
Ἀριστόμαχος ἐκαλεῖτο. 6. οὗτος ἐπιβὰς εὐθὺς τῇ Περίνθῳ ὡς ὑπό τινος ἀπεσταλμένος κατ᾽ ἐμοῦ θεοῦ ὁρᾷ
τὸν Ὑπεράνθην σὺν ἐμοὶ καὶ εὐθέως ἁλίσκεται, τοῦ
μειρακίου θαυμάσας τὸ κάλλος πάντα ὁντινοῦν ἐπά-
γεσθαι δυνάμενον. 7. ἐρασθεὶς δὲ οὐκέτι μετρίως κατεῖχε τὸν ἔρωτα, ἀλλὰ τὰ μὲν πρῶτα τῷ μειρακίῳ
προσέπεμπεν, ὡς δὲ ἀνήνυτον[46] ἦν αὐτῷ, ὁ γὰρ Ὑπεράνθης διὰ τὴν πρὸς ἐμὲ εὔνοιαν οὐδένα προσίετο,
πείθει τὸν πατέρα αὐτοῦ, πονηρὸν ἄνδρα καὶ ἐλάττονα
χρημάτων. 8. ὁ δὲ αὐτῷ δίδωσι τὸν Ὑπεράνθην προφάσει διδασκαλίας· ἔλεγε γὰρ εἶναι λόγων τεχνίτης.

45 ὁδοποιεῖ Schaefer   46 Jacobs: ἀδύνατον

32 "Exceedingly Blooming"; the name appears in Herodotus
(VII 224) as a son of Darius whose brother was named Habrocomes.

33 The transmitted text requires that we understand

his name was Hyperanthes.[32] I first fell in love with him
when I saw his tenacious wrestling in the gymnasium, and I
lost control of myself. 3. When a local festival with a nightlong celebration was held, I took that occasion to approach
Hyperanthes and begged for his pity. The youth listened,
promised everything, and took pity on me. 4. The first
stage of love's journey were kisses and caresses and many
tears from me, and in the end we took an opportunity to be
alone with each other, and the fact of our respective ages
went unsuspected.[33] We were together a long time, feeling
extraordinary affection for each other, until some divinity
took offense at our good fortune. 5. Someone came to town
from Byzantium, Byzantium being close to Perinthus, one
of the most powerful people there, a man priding himself
on his wealth and advantages, whose name was Aristomachus.[34] 6. As soon as this man set foot in Perinthus, as if
dispatched against me by some god, he saw Hyperanthes
with me and was captivated at once, marvelling at the
youth's good looks, which could attract anyone at all. 7.
Once in love he could no longer restrain his love, but
started by sending messages to the youth, and when that
was getting nowhere, since on account of his feelings for
me Hyperanthes let no one approach, he won over the
youth's father, a bad man with a weakness for money. 8.
The father gave him Hypranthes on the pretext of instruc-

$\dot{\alpha}\nu\dot{\upsilon}\pi o\pi\tau o\varsigma$ to mean "unsuspected" (as e.g. in Chariton VI 3.3 and
Heliodorus VI 7.8), for the narrative makes it clear that
Hyperanthes was younger than his suitors, as was conventional in
homoerotic relationships, though Hippothous himself is only just
old enough to make independent decisions.

[34] "Best in the Fight"; a conventional name.

παραλαβὼν δὲ αὐτὸν τὰ μὲν πρῶτα κατάκλειστον
εἶχε, μετὰ τοῦτο δὲ ἀπῆρεν ἐς Βυζάντιον. 9. εἱπόμην
κἀγὼ πάντων καταφρονήσας τῶν ἐμαυτοῦ καὶ ὅσα
ἐδυνάμην συνῆμεν τῷ μειρακίῳ. ἐδυνάμην δὲ ὀλίγα
καί μοι φίλημα σπάνιον ἐγίνετο καὶ λαλιὰ δυσχερής·
ἐφρουρούμην δὲ ὑπὸ πολλῶν. 10. τελευταῖον ⟨δὲ⟩
οὐκέτι καρτερῶν ἐμαυτὸν παροξύνας ἐπάνειμι εἰς
Πέρινθον καὶ πάντα ὅσα ἦν μοι κτήματα ἀποδόμενος
συλλέξας ἄργυρ⟨ι⟩ον εἰς Βυζάντιον ἔρχομαι. καὶ λαβὼν ξιφίδιον, συνδοκοῦν τοῦτο καὶ τῷ Ὑπεράνθῃ,
εἴσειμι νύκτωρ εἰς τὴν οἰκίαν τοῦ Ἀριστομάχου καὶ
εὑρίσκω συγκατακείμενον τῷ παιδὶ καὶ ὀργῆς πλησθεὶς παίω τὸν Ἀριστόμαχον καιρίαν. 11. ἡσυχίας δὲ
οὔσης καὶ πάντων ἀναπαυομένων ἔξειμι ὡς εἶχον
λαθὼν ἐπαγόμενος καὶ τὸν Ὑπεράνθην καὶ δι᾽ ὅλης
νυκτὸς ὁδεύσας εἰς Πέρινθον εὐθὺς νεὼς ἐπιβὰς
οὐδενὸς εἰδότος ἔπλεον εἰς Ἀσίαν. 12. καὶ μέχρι μέν
τινος διήνυστο εὐτυχῶς ὁ πλοῦς, τελευταῖον δὲ κατὰ
Λέσβον ἡμῖν γενομένοις ἐμπίπτει πνεῦμα σφοδρὸν
καὶ ἀνατρέπει τὴν ναῦν. κἀγὼ μὲν τῷ Ὑπεράνθῃ
συνενηχόμην ὑπ[ι]ὼν[47] αὐτῷ καὶ κουφοτέραν τὴν νή-
ξιν ἐποιούμην, νυκτὸς δὲ γενομένης οὐκέτι ἐνεγκὸν τὸ
μειράκιον παρείθη τῷ κολύμβῳ καὶ ἀποθνήσκει. 13.
ἐγὼ δὲ τοσοῦτον ἠδυνήθην τὸ σῶμα διασῶσαι ἐπὶ τὴν
γῆν καὶ θάψαι· καὶ πολλὰ δακρύσας καὶ στενάξας
ἀφελὼν λείψανα καὶ δυνηθεὶς εὐπορῆσαί που ἑνὸς
ἐπιτηδείου λίθου στήλην ἐπέστησα τῷ τάφῳ καὶ ἐπ-
έγραψα εἰς μνήμην τοῦ δυστυχοῦς μειρακίου ἐπίγραμμα παρ᾽ αὐτὸν ἐκεῖνον τὸν καιρὸν πλασάμενος·

[47] O'Sullivan

tion, since he claimed to be an expert in rhetoric. When he first received him he kept him locked up, and then he took him away to Byzantium. 9. I followed, disregarding all my own affairs, and spent as much time with the youth as I could, but that was seldom; kissing was infrequent and conversation difficult, since I was under heavy surveillance. 10. Finally unable to control myself any longer, I steeled myself, returned to Perinthus, sold all the possessions I had, got money together and went to Byzantium. I took a sword (Hyperanthes had also thought this best), entered Aristomachus' house at night, found him in bed with the boy, and filled with rage, I struck Aristomachus a fatal blow. 11. It was quiet and everyone was alseep. I left unnoticed and without difficulty, taking Hyperanthes with me. I travelled all night to Perinthus, immediately boarded a ship without being seen by anyone, and set sail for Asia. 12. For a while the voyage went favorably, but in the end a heavy wind struck us off Lesbos and sank our ship. I did manage to swim alongside Hyperanthes and make his swimming easier by supporting him, but when night fell the youth could no longer hold on, his swimming slackened, and he died. 13. I had only enough strength to salvage his body, bring it ashore, and bury it. With much weeping and lamentation I took away relics, and able to come up with only a single stone that somehow lay at hand, I placed it on his grave and inscribed it with this epitaph, composed on the spot, as a memorial to the unfortunate youth:

Ἱππόθοος κλεινῷ τεῦξεν τόδε σῆμ'[48] Ὑπεράνθη
οὐ φατὸν ἐκ θανάτοιο παθὼν[49] ἱεροῖο πολίτου,
ἐς βάθος Αἰγαίης[50] ἄνθος κλυτὸν ὁππότε[51]
    δαίμων
ἥρπασεν ἐν πελάγει μεγάλου πνεύσαντος ἀήτου.

14. τοὐντεῦθεν δὲ εἰς μὲν Πέρινθον ἐλθεῖν οὐ διέγνων,
ἐτράπην δὲ δι' Ἀσίας ἐπὶ Φρυγίαν τὴν μεγάλην καὶ
Παμφυλίαν, κἀνταῦθα ἀπορίᾳ βίου καὶ ἀθυμίᾳ τῆς
συμφορᾶς ἐπέδωκα ἐμαυτὸν λῃστηρίῳ. καὶ τὰ μὲν
πρῶτα ὑπηρέτης λῃστηρίου γενόμενος, τὸ τελευταῖον
δὲ περὶ Κιλικίαν αὐτὸς συνεστησάμην λῃστήριον
εὐδοκιμῆσαν ἐπὶ πολὺ ἕως ἐλήφθησαν οἱ σὺν ἐμοὶ οὐ
πρὸ πολλοῦ τοῦ σε ἰδεῖν. 15. αὕτη μὲν ἡ τῶν ἐμῶν
διηγημάτων τύχη· σὺ δέ, ὦ φίλτατε, εἰπέ μοι τὰ
ἑαυτοῦ· δῆλος γὰρ εἶ μεγάλῃ τινὶ ἀνάγκῃ τῇ κατὰ τὴν
πλάνην χρώμενος."

3   Λέγει δὲ ὁ Ἀβροκόμης ὅτι Ἐφέσιος καὶ ὅτι ἠράσθη
κόρης καὶ ὅτι ἔγημεν αὐτὴν καὶ τὰ μαντεύματα καὶ τὴν
ἀποδημίαν καὶ τοὺς πειρατὰς καὶ τὸν Ἄψυρτον καὶ τὴν
Μαντὼ καὶ τὰ δεσμὰ καὶ τὴν φυγὴν καὶ τὸν αἰπόλον
καὶ τὴν μέχρι Κιλικίας ὁδόν. 2. ἔτι λέγοντος αὐτοῦ
συνανεθρήνησεν ὁ Ἱππόθοος λέγων "ὦ πατέρες ἐμοί,
ὦ πατρίς, ἣν οὔποτε ὄψομαι, ὦ πάντων μοι Ὑπεράνθη
φίλτατε· σὺ μὲν οὖν, Ἀβροκόμα, καὶ ὄψει τὴν ἐρωμένην καὶ ἀπολήψῃ χρόνῳ ποτέ, ἐγὼ δὲ Ὑπεράνθην
ἰδεῖν οὐκέτι δυνήσομαι." 3. λέγων ἐδείκνυέ τε τὴν
κόμην καὶ ἐπεδάκρυεν αὐτῇ. ὡς δὲ ἱκανῶς ἐθρήνησαν

---

48 τόδε σῆμ' Salvini: τῶδ'   49 Jacobs: οὐ τάφον ἐκ
θανάτου ἀγαθὸν   50 Hemsterhuys: ἐκ γαίης
51 Jacobs: ὅν ποτε

284

Hippothous built this tomb for famous
    Hyperanthes,
In unspeakable suffering at the death of a holy
    countryman,
When once to the Aegean depths some god the
    illustrious blossom
Snatched, as a great gale o'erswept the face of the
    water.

14. I decided not to go back to Perinthus but travelled through Asia to Great Phrygia and Pamphylia, and there, in want of a livelihood and in distress at my misfortune, I took up banditry. At first I was an underling in a gang but in the end I put together a gang of my own in Cilicia. It had a substantial reputation until my men were captured not long before I spotted you. 15. This is the bad luck in my own tale, and now you, my friend, must tell me yours. It is obvious that you are under some great compulsion that accounts for your wandering."

Habrocomes explained that he was Ephesian and that   3 he had fallen in love with a girl and married her, and told of the prophecies, the voyage, the pirates, Apsyrtus and Manto, his imprisonment and flight, the goatherd and the journey to Cilicia. 2. While he was still speaking, Hippothous joined him in mourning, saying "Parents! Native land that I will never set eyes on again! Hyperanthes, dearest of all to me! You at least will set eyes on your beloved again, Habrocomes, and one day recover her, but I can never see Hyperanthes again." 3. As he spoke he showed the lock of hair and wept upon it. When they both had had

ἀμφότεροι ἀποβλέψας εἰς τὸν Ἀβροκόμην ὁ Ἱππόθοος
"ἄλλο" ἔφη "σοι [ὀλίγου]⁵² διήγημα παρῆλθον οὐκ
εἰπών· 4. πρὸ ὀλίγου τοῦ τὸ λῃστήριον ἁλῶναι ἐπέστη
τῷ ἄντρῳ κόρη καλὴ πλανωμένη τὴν ἡλικίαν ἔχουσα
τὴν αὐτὴν σοὶ καὶ πατρίδα ἔλεγε τὴν σήν· πλέον γὰρ
οὐδὲν ἔμαθον· ταύτην ἔδοξε τῷ Ἄρει θῦσαι. καὶ δὴ
πάντα ἦν παρεσκευασμένα καὶ ἐπέστησαν οἱ διώκοντες. κἀγὼ μὲν ἐξέφυγον, ἡ δὲ οὐκ οἶδα ὅ τι ἐγένετο.
5. ἦν δὲ καλὴ πάνυ, Ἀβροκόμη, καὶ ἐσταλμένη λιτῶς·
κόμη ξανθή, χαρίεντες ὀφθαλμοί." ἔτι λέγοντος αὐτοῦ
ἀνεβόησεν Ἀβροκόμης "τὴν ἐμὴν Ἀνθίαν ἑώρακας,
Ἱππόθοε. ποῦ δὲ ἄρα καὶ πέφευγε; τίς δὲ αὐτὴν ἔχει
γῆ; ἐπὶ Κιλικίαν τραπώμεθα, ἐκείνην ζητήσωμεν· οὐκ
ἔστι πόρρω τοῦ λῃστηρίου. 6. ναὶ πρὸς αὐτοῦ σε
ψυχῆς Ὑπεράνθους, μή με ἑκὼν ἀδικήσῃς, ἀλλ' ἴωμεν
ὅπου δυνησόμεθα Ἀνθίαν εὑρεῖν." ὑπισχνεῖται ὁ Ἱππόθοος πάντα ποιήσειν. ἔλεγε δὴ ἀνθρώπους δεῖν
ὀλίγους συλλέξασθαι πρὸς ἀσφάλειαν τῆς ὁδοῦ. 7.
καὶ οἱ μὲν ἐν τούτοις ἦσαν ἐννοοῦντες ὅπως ὀπίσω τὴν
εἰς Κιλικίαν ἐλεύσονται, τῇ δὲ Ἀνθίᾳ αἱ τριάκοντα
παρεληλύθεσαν ἡμέραι καὶ παρεσκευάζετο τῷ Περιλάῳ τὰ περὶ τὸν γάμον καὶ ἱερεῖα κατήγετο ἐκ τῶν
χωρίων πολλὴ δὲ ἡ τῶν ἄλλων ἀφθονία. συμπαρῆσαν
δὲ αὐτῷ οἵ τε οἰκεῖοι καὶ συγγενεῖς, πολλοὶ δὲ καὶ τῶν
πολιτῶν συνεώρταζον τὸν Ἀνθίας γάμον.

4   Ἐν δὲ τῷ χρόνῳ ὃν ἡ Ἀνθία ληφθεῖσα ἐκ τοῦ
λῃστηρίου ⟨διῆγεν παρὰ τῷ Περιλάῳ⟩⁵³ ἦλθεν εἰς τὴν
Ταρσὸν πρεσβύτης Ἐφέσιος ἰατρὸς τὴν τέχνην, Εὔδοξος τοὔνομα· ἧκε δὲ ναυαγίῳ περιπεσὼν εἰς Αἴγυπτον πλέων. 2. οὗτος ὁ Εὔδοξος περιῄει μὲν καὶ τοὺς

---

⁵² Dalmeyda   ⁵³ Bürger

their fill of mourning, Hippothous looked at Habrocomes and said, "I left something out of the tale I told you. 4. Shortly before my gang was captured, a beautiful girl came upon our cave in her wanderings; she was the same age as you and said that she was from your country. I found out nothing else. We decided to sacrifice her to Ares, and in fact everything was ready when the posse came upon us. I got away, but I don't know what became of her. 5. She was very beautiful, Habrocomes, and wearing inexpensive clothing; blonde hair, sexy eyes." While he was still speaking, Habrocomes cried out, "It was my Anthia you saw, Hippothous! But where has she fled? What land holds her? Let's go back to Cilicia, let's look for her! She cannot be far from the hideout. 6. By the soul of your own Hyperanthes, please don't deliberately wrong me, but let's go where we can find Anthia!" Hippothous promised to do all he could, and in fact said that they should recruit a few men for safety on the trip. 7. That was their situation as they made plans to return to Cilicia. Meanwhile, Anthia's thirty days had passed and preparations for Perilaus' wedding were underway: sacrificial victims were being brought in from the countryside and there was a great abundance of everything else. His friends and family were gathered, and many of the citizens were celebrating Anthia's marriage as well.

While Anthia, snatched from the hideout, ‹was so- 4
journing with Perilaus› there came to Tarsus an elderly Ephesian, a doctor by trade, named Eudoxus.[35] He arrived after being shipwrecked on a voyage to Egypt. 2. This Eudoxus made the rounds of the most respectable men in

[35] "Of Good Repute"; a conventional name.

ἄλλους ἄνδρας ὅσοι Ταρσέων εὐδοκιμώτατοι, οὓς μὲν
ἐσθῆτας, οὓς δὲ ἀργύριον αἰτῶν διηγούμενος ἑκάστῳ
τὴν συμφοράν, προσῆλθε δὲ καὶ τῷ Περιλάῳ καὶ εἶπεν
ὅτι Ἐφέσιος καὶ ἰατρὸς τὴν τέχνην. 3. ὁ δὲ αὐτὸν
λαβὼν ἄγει πρὸς τὴν Ἀνθίαν ἡσθήσεσθαι νομίζων
ἀνδρὶ ὀφθέντι Ἐφεσίῳ. ἡ δὲ ἐφιλοφρονεῖτό τε τὸν
Εὔδοξον καὶ ἀνεπυνθάνετο εἴ τι περὶ τῶν αὑτῆς λέγειν
ἔχοι· ὁ δὲ ὅτι οὐδὲν ἐπίσταιτο μακρᾶς αὐτῷ τῆς
ἀποδημίας τῆς ἀπὸ Ἐφέσου γεγενημένης· ἀλλ' οὐδὲν
ἧττον ἔχαιρεν αὐτῷ ἡ Ἀνθία ἀναμιμνησκομένη τῶν
οἴκοι. 4. καὶ δὴ συνήθης τε ἐγεγόνει τοῖς κατὰ τὴν
οἰκίαν καὶ εἰσῄει παρ' ἕκαστα πρὸς τὴν Ἀνθίαν,
πάντων ἀπολαύων τῶν ἐπιτηδείων, ἀεὶ δεόμενος αὐτῆς
εἰς Ἔφεσον παραπεμφθῆναι· ἐκεῖ[54] γὰρ καὶ παῖδες
ἦσαν αὐτῷ καὶ γυνή.

5   Ὡς οὖν πάντα τὰ περὶ τὸν γάμον ἐκτετέλεστο τῷ
Περιλάῳ, ἐφειστήκει δὲ ἡ ἡμέρα δεῖπνον μὲν αὐτοῖς
πολυτελὲς ἡτοίμαστο καὶ ἡ Ἀνθία ἐκεκόσμητο κόσμῳ
νυμφικῷ, ἐπαύετο δὲ οὔτε νύκτωρ οὔτε μεθ' ἡμέραν
δακρύουσα, ἀλλ' ἀεὶ πρὸ ὀφθαλμῶν εἶχεν Ἁβροκόμην. 2. ἐνενοεῖτο δὲ ἅμα πολλά, τὸν ἔρωτα, τοὺς
ὅρκους, τὴν πατρίδα, τοὺς πατέρας, τὴν ἀνάγκην, τὸν
γάμον. καὶ δὴ καθ' αὑτὴν γενομένη καιροῦ λαβομένη
σπαράξασα τὰς κόμας "ὦ πάντα ἄδικος ἐγὼ" φησὶ
"καὶ πονηρά, ὡς οὐχὶ τοῖς ἴσοις Ἁβροκόμην ἀμεί-
βομαι. 3. ὁ μέν γε ἵνα ἐμὸς ἀνὴρ μείνῃ καὶ δεσμὰ
ὑπομένει καὶ βασάνους καὶ ἴσως που καὶ τέθνηκεν,
ἐγὼ δὲ καὶ ἐκείνων ἀμνημονῶ καὶ γαμοῦμαι δυστυχὴς
καὶ τὸν ὑμέναιον ᾄσει τις ἐπ' ἐμοὶ καὶ ἐπ' εὐνὴν
ἀφίξομαι τὴν Περιλάου. 4. ἀλλ', ὦ φιλτάτη μοι πασῶν
Ἁβροκόμου ψυχή, μηδέν τι ὑπὲρ ἐμοῦ λυπηθῇς· οὐ
γὰρ ⟨ἄν⟩ ποτε ἑκοῦσα ἀδικήσαιμί σε· ἐλεύσομαι καὶ

Tarsus, begging clothing from some, money from others, recounting to each one his misfortune. He paid a visit to Perilaus too, and told him that he was an Ephesian and a doctor by trade. 3. Perilaus took him to meet Anthia, thinking that she would be glad to see someone from Ephesus. She kindly received Eudoxus and tried to find out if he had anything to tell her about her own family, but he replied that he knew nothing, having been away from Ephesus for so long. Nevertheless Anthia enjoyed his company, since he reminded her of her home town. 4. And so he became a friend of the family and saw Anthia each time he visited, enjoying every amenity and always asking her to send him back to Ephesus, for his wife and children were there.

When Perilaus had completed all preparations for the 5 wedding and the day had come, a lavish dinner was ready for them and Anthia was adorned in bridal array. But her tears did not stop night or day, and she kept Habrocomes ever before her eyes. 2. Much was on her mind all at once: her love, her oaths, her homeland, her parents, her predicament, her marriage. And so when she was by herself she took the opportunity to tear her hair and cry, "How utterly unfair I am, how vile, not to treat Habrocomes as he treats me! 3. He is the one who suffers imprisonment and torture, and for all I know is even dead, so that he can remain my husband, while I forget all that and unhappily marry. Yes, someone will sing my bridal hymn, and I will end up in Perilaus' bed. 4. Habrocomes, soul dearest of all to me, suffer no pain on my account: I would never willingly

---

54 O'Sullivan: καὶ

μέχρι θανάτου μείνασα νύμφη σή." 5. ταῦτα εἶπε καὶ
ἀφικομένου παρ' αὐτὴν τοῦ Εὐδόξου τοῦ Ἐφεσίου
ἰατροῦ ἀπαγαγοῦσα αὐτὸν ἐπ' οἴκημά τι ἠρεμαῖον
προσπίπτει τοῖς γόνασιν αὐτοῦ καὶ ἱκετεύει μηδενὶ
κατειπεῖν τῶν ῥηθησομένων μηδὲν καὶ ὁρκίζει τὴν
πάτριον θεὸν Ἄρτεμιν συμπρᾶξαι πάντα ὅσα ἂν αὐτοῦ δεηθῇ. 6. ἀνίστησιν αὐτὴν ὁ Εὔδοξος πολλὰ
θρηνοῦσαν καὶ θαρρεῖν παρεκάλει καὶ ἐπώμνυε πάντα
ποιήσειν ὑπισχνούμενος. λέγει δὴ αὐτῷ τὸν Ἁβροκόμου ἔρωτα καὶ τοὺς ὅρκους τοὺς πρὸς ἐκεῖνον καὶ
τὰς περὶ τῆς σωφροσύνης συνθήκας. 7. καὶ "εἰ μὲν ἦν
ζῶσαν" ἔφη "με ἀπολαβεῖν ζῶντα Ἁβροκόμην ἢ λαθεῖν ἀποδράσασαν ἐντεῦθεν περὶ τούτων ἂν ἐβου-
λευόμην, ἐπειδὴ δὲ ὁ μὲν τέθνηκε, φυγεῖν δὲ ἀδύνατον
καὶ τὸν μέλλοντα ἀμήχανον ὑπομεῖναι γάμον, οὔτε
γὰρ τὰς συνθήκας παραβήσομαι τὰς πρὸς Ἁβροκόμην οὔτε τὸν ὅρκον ὑπερόψομαι, σὺ τοίνυν βοηθὸς
ἡμῖν γενοῦ φάρμακον εὑρών ποθεν ὃ κακῶν με ἀπαλ-
λάξει τὴν κακοδαίμονα. 8. ἔσται δὲ ἀντὶ τούτων σοι
πολλὰ μὲν καὶ παρὰ τῶν θεῶν, οἷς ἐπεύξομαι καὶ πρὸ
τοῦ θανάτου πολλάκις ὑπὲρ σοῦ, αὐτὴ δέ σοι καὶ
ἀργύριον δώσω καὶ τὴν παραπομπὴν ἐπισκευάσω.
δυνήσῃ δὲ πρὸ τοῦ πυθέσθαι τινὰ ἐπιβὰς νεὼς τὴν ἐπ'
Ἐφέσου πλεῖν. ἐκεῖ δὲ γενόμενος ἀναζητήσας τοὺς
γονεῖς Μεγαμήδη τε καὶ Εὐίππην ἄγγελλε αὐτοῖς τὴν
ἐμὴν τελευτὴν καὶ πάντα τὰ κατὰ τὴν ἀποδημίαν ⟨καὶ⟩
ὅτι Ἁβροκόμης ἀπόλωλε λέγε." 9. εἰποῦσα τῶν ποδῶν
αὐτοῦ προυκυλίετο καὶ ἐδεῖτο μηδὲν ἀντειπεῖν αὐτῇ
δοῦναί τε τὸ φάρμακον. καὶ προκομίσασα εἴκοσι μνᾶς
ἀργυρίου περιδέραιά τε αὑτῆς, ἦν δὲ αὐτῇ πάντα
ἄφθονα, πάντων γὰρ ἐξουσίαν εἶχε τῶν Περιλάου,
δίδωσι τῷ Εὐδόξῳ. ὁ δὲ βουλευσάμενος πολλὰ καὶ τὴν

wrong you. I will be there, your steadfast bride until I die." 5. She had just finished speaking when Eudoxus, the Ephesian physician, arrived at her door. She took him away to a quiet room, fell at his knees, and begged him to say nothing to anyone of what she was about to tell him, making him swear by their ancestral goddess Artemis to assist her in everything she might ask of him. 6. Eudoxus made her get up as she bewailed her many sorrows, urged her to take heart, and promised on oath to do it all. Then she told him about her love of Habrocomes, her oaths to him, and her vows of chastity. 7. "If I could live to recover Habrocomes alive," she said, "or get away from here unnoticed, that would be my plan. But since he is dead, flight is impossible, and to endure my impending marriage is out of the question, for I will never transgress my pact with Habrocomes or disregard my oath, please come to my aid by finding some drug that will free me, so unhappy, from my torments. 8. For this you will have substantial rewards from the gods: before my death I will pray to them repeatedly on your behalf. And I myself will give you money and arrange for your transport home. You will be able to board a ship before anyone finds out and sail to Ephesus. When you get there, seek out my parents Megamedes and Euhippe and tell them how my life ended, everything that happened when I was away, and that Habrocomes is no more." 9. With these words she rolled at his feet and begged him not to refuse but to give her the poison. She produced twenty minas[36] in cash and her necklaces, for she had plenty of everything, having charge of all that Perilaus owned, and she gave this to Eudoxus.

[36] An anachronism, since the mina (worth 100 drachmas) went out of use in the Hellenistic era.

κόρην οἰκτείρας τῆς συμφορᾶς καὶ τῆς εἰς Ἔφεσον
ἐπιθυμῶν ὁδοῦ καὶ τοῦ ἀργυρίου καὶ τῶν δώρων ἡτ-
τώμενος ὑπισχνεῖται δώσειν τὸ φάρμακον καὶ ἀπῄει
κομιῶν. 10. ἡ δὲ ἐν τούτῳ πολλὰ καταθρηνεῖ τήν τε
ἡλικίαν κατοδυρομένη τὴν ἑαυτῆς καὶ ὅτι μέλλοι πρὸ
ὥρας ἀποθανεῖσθαι λυπουμένη, πολλὰ δὲ Ἀβροκόμην
ὡς παρόντα ἀνεκάλει. 11. ἐν τούτῳ ὀλίγον διαλιπὼν ὁ
Εὔδοξος ἔρχεται κομίζων θανάσιμον ⟨μὲν⟩ οὐχὶ φάρμακον, ὑπνωτικὸν δέ, ὡς μή τι παθεῖν τὴν κόρην καὶ
αὐτὸν ἐφοδίων τυχόντα ἀνασωθῆναι. λαβοῦσα δὲ ἡ
Ἀνθία καὶ πολλὴν γνοῦσα χάριν αὐτὸν ἀποπέμπει.
καὶ ὁ μὲν εὐθὺς ἐπιβὰς νεὼς ἐπανήχθη, ἡ δὲ καιρὸν
ἐπιτήδειον ἐζήτει πρὸς τὴν πόσιν τοῦ φαρμάκου.

6   Καὶ ἤδη μὲν νὺξ ἦν, παρεσκευάζετο δὲ ὁ θάλαμος
καὶ ἧκον οἱ ἐπὶ τούτῳ τεταγμένοι τὴν Ἀνθίαν ἐξαί-
ροντες. ἡ δὲ ἄκουσα μὲν καὶ δεδακρυμένη ἐξῄει ἐν τῇ
χειρὶ κρύπτουσα τὸ φάρμακον. καὶ ὡς πλησίον τοῦ
θαλάμου γίνεται οἱ οἰκ⟨εῖ⟩οι ἀνευφήμησαν τὸν ὑμέναιον, 2. ἡ δὲ ἀνωδύρετο καὶ ἐδάκρυεν "οὕτως ἐγὼ"
λέγουσα "πρότερον ἠγόμην Ἀβροκόμῃ νυμφίῳ καὶ
παρέπεμπεν ἡμᾶς πῦρ ἐρωτικὸν καὶ ὑμέναιος ἤγετο
ἐπὶ γάμοις εὐδαίμοσι. 3. νυνὶ δὲ τί ποιήσεις, Ἀνθία;
ἀδικήσεις Ἀβροκόμην τὸν ἄνδρα, τὸν ἐρώμενον, τὸν
διὰ σὲ τεθνηκότα; οὐχ οὕτως ἄνανδρος ἐγὼ οὐδὲ ἐν
τοῖς κακοῖς δειλή. δεδόχθω ταῦτα, πίνωμεν τὸ φάρ-
μακον· Ἀβροκόμην ⟨μόνον⟩[55] εἶναί μοι δεῖ ἄνδρα·
ἐκεῖνον καὶ τεθνηκότα βούλομαι." 4. ταῦτα ἔλεγε καὶ
ἤγετο εἰς τὸν θάλαμον. καὶ δὴ μόνη μὲν ἐγεγόνει, ἔτι
δὲ Περίλαος μετὰ τῶν φίλων εὐωχεῖτο. σκηψαμένη δὲ
τῇ ἀγωνίᾳ ὑπὸ δίψους κατειλῆφθαι ἐκέλευσεν αὐτῇ
τινι τῶν οἰκετῶν ὕδωρ ἐνεγκεῖν, ὡς δὴ πιομένη. καὶ δὴ
κομισθέντος ἐκπώματος λαβοῦσα οὐδενὸς ἔνδον αὐτῇ

He pondered the matter carefully, felt sorry for the girl's plight, wanted the trip back to Ephesus, was vanquished by the money and gifts, promised to give her the poison, and went off to get it. 10. In the interval she lamented copiously, bewailing her own youth and grieving that she was about to die before her time, and she called out to Habrocomes as if he were there. 11. Meanwhile Eudoxus was not gone for long and arrived with a drug that would cause not death but sleep, so that no harm would come to the girl and he would get his travel money and return safely. Anthia accepted the drug with deep gratitude and sent him on his way. He boarded a ship at once and sailed away, while she looked for a suitable opportunity to drink the poison.

Now it was night; the bridal chamber was made ready 6 and those assigned to the task had arrived to collect Anthia. She set forth unwillingly and in tears, hiding the poison in her hand. As she drew near the chamber, the family sang the bridal hymn. 2. But she grieved and wept: "This is the way," she said, "that I was once taken to my bridegroom Habrocomes. A fire of love escorted us and a bridal hymn celebrated a happy marriage. 3. But what will you do this time, Anthia? Will you wrong your husband Habrocomes, the one you love, the one who died for you? I am no such coward or so worthless in adversity. My decision stands: let us drink the poison. Habrocomes must be my ⟨only⟩ husband, and I want him even if he is dead." 4. With these words she was led into the bridal chamber. Now she was by herself, while Perilaus was still at the feast with his friends. Pretending that her anxiety had made her thirsty, she told one of the servants to bring her water to drink. And when a

---

55 Castiglioni cl. 4.5.3

παρόντος ἐμβάλλει τὸ φάρμακον καὶ δακρύσασα 5. "ὦ
φιλτάτου" φησὶν "Ἁβροκόμου ψυχή, ἰδού σοι τὰς
ὑποσχέσεις ἀποδίδωμι καὶ ὁδὸν ἔρχομαι τὴν παρὰ σὲ
δυστυχῆ μὲν ἀλλ᾽ ἀναγκαίαν. καὶ δέχου με ἄσμενος
καί μοι πάρεχε τὴν ἐκεῖ μετὰ σοῦ δίαιταν εὐδαίμονα."
εἰποῦσα ἔπιε τὸ φάρμακον καὶ εὐθὺς ὕπνος τε αὐτὴν
κατεῖχε καὶ ἔπιπτεν εἰς γῆν καὶ ἐποίει τὸ φάρμακον
ὅσα ἐδύνατο.

7   Ὡς δὲ εἰσῆλθεν ὁ Περίλαος εὐθὺς ἰδὼν τὴν Ἀνθίαν
κειμένην ἐξεπλάγη καὶ ἀνεβόησε θόρυβός τε πολὺς
τῶν κατὰ τὴν οἰκίαν ἦν καὶ πάθη συμμιγῆ, οἰμωγή,
φόβος, ἔκπληξις. οἱ μὲν ᾤκτειρον τὴν δοκοῦσαν τεθνηκέναι, οἱ δὲ συνήχθοντο Περιλάῳ, πάντες δὲ ἐθρήνουν
τὸ γεγονός. 2. ὁ δὲ Περίλαος τὴν ἐσθῆτα περιρρη-
ξάμενος ἐπιπεσὼν τῷ σώματι "ὦ φιλτάτη μοι κόρη"
φησίν, "ὦ πρὸ τῶν γάμων καταλιποῦσα τὸν ἐρῶντα
ὀλίγαις ἡμέραις νύμφη Περιλάου γενομένη, εἰς οἷόν
σε θάλαμον τὸν τάφον ἄξομεν. 3. εὐδαίμων ἄρα ὅστις
ποτὲ Ἁβροκόμης ἦν· μακάριος ἐκεῖνος ὡς ἀληθῶς,
τηλικαῦτα παρ᾽ ἐρωμένης λαβὼν δῶρα." ὁ μὲν τοιαῦτα
ἐθρήνει, περιβεβλήκει δὲ ἅπασαν καὶ ἠσπάζετο χεῖ-
ράς τε καὶ πόδας "νύμφη" λέγων "ἀθλία, γύναι δυστυ-
χεστέρα." 4. ἐκόσμει δὲ αὐτὴν πολυτελῆ[56] ἐσθῆτα
ἐνδύων, πολὺν δὲ περι‹τι›θεὶς χρυσόν. καὶ οὐκέτι
φέρων τὴν θέαν ἡμέρας γενομένης ἐνθέμενος κλίνῃ
τὴν Ἀνθίαν, ἡ δὲ ἔκειτο ἀναισθητοῦσα, ἦγεν εἰς τοὺς
πλησίον τῆς πόλεως τάφους κἀνταῦθα κατέθετο ἔν
τινι οἰκήματι πολλὰ μὲν ἐπισφάξας ἱερεῖα, πολλὴν δὲ
ἐσθῆτα καὶ κόσμον ἄλλον ἐπικαύσας.

8   Ὁ μὲν ἐκτελέσας τὰ νομιζόμενα ὑπὸ τῶν οἰκείων εἰς
τὴν πόλιν ἤγετο, καταλειφθεῖσα δὲ ἐν τῷ τάφῳ ἡ
Ἀνθία ἑαυτῆς γενομένη καὶ συνεῖσα ὅτι μὴ τὸ φάρ-

cup was brought, she took it when no one was in the chamber with her and put in the drug, weeping as she said, 5. "Soul of dearest Habrocomes, look: I am keeping my promises and coming to you, a journey sad but necessary. Welcome me with gladness, and make my life there with you a happy one." With these words she drank, at once fell into a deep sleep, and sank to the floor as the drug exerted its force.

As Perilaus came in and at once saw Anthia prostrate, he was stunned and cried out, and throughout the household there was considerable hubbub and confused emotions: grief, fear, astonishment. Some felt sorry for the girl who seemed to be dead, others shared Perilaus' grief, all lamented what had happened. 2. Perilaus tore his clothing and fell upon the body. "My dearest girl," he cried, "you have abandoned your lover before your marriage, after being Perilaus' intended bride for only a few days. To a fine bridal chamber will I be carrying you—the tomb! 3. Lucky Habrocomes, whoever he was, a man truly fortunate to receive such gifts from a beloved girl." Such were his lamentations as he embraced her all over and clung to her hands and feet, saying "Poor bride, unfortunate woman!" 4. He decked her out in fine clothing and adorned her with lots of gold. No longer able to bear the sight, he put Anthia on a bier the next day, for she still lay unconscious, and took her to the tombs near the town, where he laid her in a vault after sacrificing many victims and burning much clothing and other apparel.

After he had performed the customary ceremonies he was taken back to town by his household, but Anthia, left behind in the tomb, came to, realized that the drug had not

7

8

---

56 Schmidt: πολλὴν

μακον θανάσιμον ἦν, στενάξασα καὶ δακρύσασα "ὦ ψευσάμενόν με τὸ φάρμακόν" φησιν, "ὦ κωλῦσαν ὁδεῦσαι πρὸς τὸν Ἀβροκόμην ὁδὸν εὐτυχῆ· ἐσφάλην ἄρα παντάλαινα[57] καὶ τῆς ἐπιθυμίας τοῦ θανάτου. 2. ἀλλὰ ἔνεστί γε ἐν τῷ τάφῳ μείνασαν τὸ ἔργον ἐργάσασθαι τοῦ φαρμάκου λιμῷ· οὐ γὰρ ⟨ἂν⟩ ἐντεῦθέν μέ τις ἀνέλοιτο οὐδ᾽ ἂν ἐπίδοιμι τὸν ἥλιον οὐδ᾽ [ἂν] εἰς φῶς ἐλεύσομαι." ταῦτα εἰποῦσα ἐκαρτέρει τὸν θάνατον προσδεχομένη γενναίως. 3. ἐν δὲ τούτῳ νυκτὸς ἐπιγενομένης λῃσταί τινες μαθόντες ὅτι κόρη τέθαπται πλουσίως καὶ πολὺς μὲν αὐτῇ κόσμος συγκατάκειται γυναικεῖος, πολὺς δὲ ἄργυρος καὶ χρυσὸς ἦλθον ἐπὶ τὸν τάφον καὶ ἀναρρήξαντες τοῦ τάφου τὰς θύρας εἰσελθόντες τόν τε κόσμον ἀνῃροῦντο καὶ τὴν Ἀνθίαν ζῶσαν ὁρῶσι. μέγα δὲ καὶ τοῦτο κέρδος ἡγούμενοι ἀνίστων τε αὐτὴν καὶ ἄγειν ἐβούλοντο. 4. ἡ δὲ τῶν ποδῶν αὐτῶν προκυλιομένη πολλὰ ἐδεῖτο "ἄνδρες, οἵτινές ποτέ ἐστε" λέγουσα "τὸν μὲν κόσμον τοῦτον ἅπαντα ὅστις ἐστὶ καὶ ἅπαντα τὰ συνταφέντα λαβόντες κομίζετε, φείσασθε δὲ τοῦ σώματος. 5. δυοῖν ἀνάκειμαι θεοῖς, Ἔρωτι καὶ Θανάτῳ· τούτοις ἐάσατε σχολάσαι με. ναὶ πρὸς τῶν θεῶν αὐτῶν τῶν πατρῴων ὑμῶν, μή με ἡμέρᾳ δείξητε τὴν ἄξια νυκτὸς καὶ σκότους δυστυχοῦσαν." ταῦτα ἔλεγεν· οὐκ ἔπειθε δὲ τοὺς λῃστάς, ἀλλ᾽ ἐξαγαγόντες αὐτὴν τοῦ τάφου κατήγαγον ἐπὶ θάλατταν καὶ ἐνθέμενοι σκάφει τὴν εἰς Ἀλεξάνδρειαν ἀνήγοντο, ἐν δὲ τῷ πλοίῳ ἐθεράπευον αὐτὴν καὶ θαρρεῖν παρεκάλουν. 6. ἡ δὲ ἐν οἵοις κακοῖς ἐγεγόνει πάλιν ἐννοήσασα θρηνοῦσα καὶ ὀδυρομένη "πάλιν" ἔφησε "λῃσταὶ καὶ θάλασσα, πάλιν αἰχμά-

[57] Jacobs: πάντα καινὰ

been fatal, and with groans and tears said, "Ah, the drug has deceived me, has kept me from journeying a happy journey to Habrocomes. In my complete misery I have been foiled even in my desire for death! 2. But by staying in the tomb I can still fulfill the drug's purpose by starvation. No one would carry me off from here, I could not look upon the sun, and I will not move toward the light." With these words she steeled herself as she valorously awaited death. 3. Meanwhile some pirates heard that a girl had been given a lavish burial and that a lot of female finery as well as much silver and gold was interred with her. After nightfall they went to the tomb, broke open the door, entered the tomb, carried off the finery, and saw that Anthia was alive. Thinking this too a great windfall, they raised her up and wanted to take her away. 4. But she rolled at their feet and repeatedly entreated them. "Gentlemen, whoever you are," she said, "take away this finery, all there is of it, and everything buried with me, but spare my body. 5. I am an offering to two gods, Love and Death: let me devote myself to them. In the name of your own native gods, do not expose me to the light of day, when my misfortunes call for night and darkness." This was her plea, but she did not convince the pirates: they led her from the tomb, took her down to the shore, put her aboard a skiff, and set off with her toward Alexandria.[37] On the boat they looked after her and encouraged her to take heart. 6. But she was back again to dwelling on the enormity of her troubles, and with wails and lamentation said, "Once again pirates and

[37] The capital city of Egypt, founded in 332/1 BCE.

λωτος ἐγώ, ἀλλὰ νῦν δυστυχέστερον ὅτι μὴ μετὰ
Ἀβροκόμου. 7. τίς με ἄρα ὑποδέξεται γῆ; τίνας δὲ
ἀνθρώπους ὄψομαι; μὴ Μοῖριν ἔτι, μὴ Μαντώ, μὴ
Περίλαον, μὴ Κιλικίαν· ἔλθοιμι δὲ ἔνθα δὴ κἂν τάφον
Ἀβροκόμου μόνον ὄψομαι." ταῦτα ἑκάστοτε ἐδάκρυε
καὶ αὐτὴ μὲν οὐ ποτόν, οὐ τροφὴν προσίετο, ἠνάγκα-
ζον δὲ οἱ λησταί.

9   Καὶ οἱ μὲν ἀνύσαντες ἡμέραις οὐκ ὀλίγαις τὸν
πλοῦν κατῆραν εἰς Ἀλεξάνδρειαν κἀνταῦθα ἐξεβί-
βασαν τὴν Ἀνθίαν καὶ διέγνωσαν [ἐκ τοῦ πλοῦ]⁵⁸
παραδοῦναί τισιν ἐμπόροις· ὁ δὲ Περίλαος μαθὼν τὴν
τοῦ τάφου διορυγὴν καὶ τοῦ σώματος ἀπώλειαν ἐν
πολλῇ καὶ ἀκατασχέτῳ λύπῃ ἦν. 2. ὁ δὲ Ἀβροκόμης
ἐζήτει καὶ ἐπολυπραγμόνει εἴ τις ἐπίσταιτο κόρην
ποθὲν ξένην αἰχμάλωτον μετὰ λῃστῶν ἀχθεῖσαν, ὡς
δὲ οὐδὲν εὗρεν ἀποκαμὼν ἦλθεν οὗ κατήγοντο. δεῖπνον
δὲ αὐτοῖς οἱ περὶ τὸν Ἱππόθοον παρεσκεύασαν, 3. καὶ
οἱ μὲν ἄλλοι ἐδειπνοποιοῦντο, ὁ δὲ Ἀβροκόμης πάνυ
ἄθυμος ἦν καὶ αὐτὸν ἐπὶ τῆς εὐνῆς ῥίψας ἔκλαιε καὶ
ἔκειτο οὐδὲν προσιέμενος. 4. προιοῦσι δὲ τοῦ πότου⁵⁹
[ὁ κύριος]⁶⁰ τοῖς περὶ τὸν Ἱππόθοον παροῦσα καί τις
πρεσβῦτις ἄρχεται διηγήματος, ᾗ ὄνομα Χρυσίον.
"ἀκούσατε" ἔφη, "ὦ ξένοι, πάθους οὐ πρὸ πολλοῦ
γενομένου ἐν τῇ πόλει. 5. Περίλαός τις, ἀνὴρ τῶν τὰ
πρῶτα δυναμένων, ἄρχειν μὲν ἐχειροτονήθη τῆς εἰρήνης τῆς ἐν Κιλικίᾳ, ἐξελθὼν δὲ ἐπὶ λῃστῶν ζήτησιν
ἤγαγέ τινας συλλαβὼν λῃστὰς καὶ μετ' αὐτῶν κόρην
καλὴν καὶ ταύτην ἔπειθεν αὐτῷ γαμηθῆναι. 6. καὶ
πάντα μὲν τὰ πρὸς τὸν γάμον ἐκτετέλεστο, ἡ δὲ εἰς τὸν

⁵⁸ Locella   ⁵⁹ Hemsterhuys: προσ- et τόπου
⁶⁰ Salvini: εὐκαίρως Jacobs: καιρίως Peerlkamp

sea! Once again I am a captive, but this time more miserably, being without Habrocomes. 7. So what country will
have me? And what people will I see there? Not Moeris
again, not Manto, not Perilaus, not Cilicia. Let me go
where I might at least see Habrocomes' tomb." At these
thoughts she wept at every turn, and though she herself
would take no food, no drink, the pirates forced her.

They finished their rather lengthy voyage and made   9
port at Alexandria. There they put Anthia ashore and decided to hand her over to some slave dealers. Meanwhile
Perilaus, having learned of the break-in at the tomb and
the loss of the body, was in deep and uncontrollable pain,
2. while Habrocomes pursued his search and was busy asking if anyone knew anything about a foreign girl brought in
with pirates as a captive. Finding nothing, he returned ex-
hausted to their lodging. Hippothous' men made themselves a meal, 3. but while the others were having their
meal, Habrocomes was very dispirited, threw himself on
his bed, began to cry, and lay there without taking anything
to eat. 4. As Hippothous' gang progressed to the drinking,
an old lady by the name of Chrysium,[38] who was with them,
began a story. "Listen, strangers," she said, "to a sad story
that happened not long ago in the city. 5. A certain Perilaus,[39] one of its most powerful men, was elected officer of
the peace in Cilicia. He went out to look for pirates and
brought in some pirates that he had captured, and with
them was a beautiful girl whom he persuaded to marry
him. 6. When everything was ready for the wedding, she

38 "Goldie," a common name.
39 See 2.13.

θάλαμον εἰσελθοῦσα, εἴτε μανεῖσα εἴτε ἄλλου τινὸς
ἐρῶσα, πιοῦσα φάρμακόν ποθεν ἀποθνήσκει· οὗτος
γὰρ ὁ τοῦ θανάτου τρόπος αὐτῆς ἐλέγετο." ἀκούσας ὁ
Ἱππόθοος "αὕτη" ἔφησεν "ἐστὶν ἡ κόρη, ἣν Ἁβροκόμης ζητεῖ." 7. ὁ δὲ Ἁβροκόμης ἤκουε μὲν τοῦ
διηγήματος, παρεῖτο δὲ ὑπὸ ἀθυμίας· ὀψὲ δὲ καὶ
<μόλις>[61] ἀναθορὼν ἐκ τῆς τοῦ Ἱπποθόου φωνῆς
"ἀλλὰ νῦν μὲν σαφῶς τέθνηκεν Ἀνθία καὶ τάφος ἴσως
αὐτῆς ἐστιν ἐνθάδε καὶ τὸ σῶμα σῴζεται." 8. λέγων
ἐδεῖτο τῆς πρεσβύτιδος τῆς Χρυσίου ἄγειν ἐπὶ τὸν
τάφον αὐτῆς καὶ δεῖξαι τὸ σῶμα· ἡ δὲ ἀναστενάξασα
"τοῦτο γὰρ" ἔφη "τῇ κόρῃ <τῇ>[62] ταλαιπώρῳ τὸ δυστυ-
χέστατον· ὁ μὲν γὰρ Περίλαος καὶ ἔθαψεν αὐτὴν
πολυτελῶς καὶ ἐκόσμησε, πυθόμενοι δὲ τὰ συνταφέντα λησταὶ ἀνορύξαντες τὸν τάφον τόν τε κόσμον
ἀνείλοντο καὶ τὸ σῶμα ἀφανὲς ἐποίησαν, ἐφ' οἷς
πολλὴ καὶ μεγάλη ζήτησις ὑπὸ Περιλάου γίνεται."

10   Ἀκούσας ὁ Ἁβροκόμης περιέρρηξε τὸν χιτῶνα καὶ
μεγάλως ἀνωδύρετο καλῶς μὲν καὶ σωφρόνως ἀπο-
θανοῦσαν Ἀνθίαν, δυστυχῶς δὲ μετὰ τὸν θάνατον
ἀπολομένην. 2. "τίς ἄρα λῃστὴς οὕτως ἐρωτικὸς ἵνα
καὶ νεκρᾶς ἐπιθυμήσῃ σου, ἵνα καὶ τὸ σῶμα ἀφέληται;
ἀπεστερήθην σου ὁ δυστυχὴς καὶ τῆς μόνης ἐμοὶ
παραμυθίας. 3. ἀποθανεῖν μὲν οὖν ἔγνωσται πάντως,
ἀλλὰ τὰ πρῶτα καρτερήσω μέχρι που τὸ σῶμα εὕρω
τὸ σὸν καὶ περιβαλὼν ἐμαυτὸν ἐκείνῳ συγκαταθάψω."
ταῦτα ἔλεγεν ὀδυρόμενος, θαρρεῖν δὲ αὐτὸν παρεκάλουν οἱ περὶ τὸν Ἱππόθοον. 4. καὶ τότε μὲν ἀνεπαύ-
σαντο δι' ὅλης νυκτός, ἔννοια δὲ πάντων Ἁβροκόμην
εἰσήρχετο, Ἀνθίας, τοῦ θανάτου, τοῦ τάφου, τῆς ἀπωλείας. καὶ δὴ καὶ οὐκέτι καρτερῶν λαθὼν πάντας,
ἔκειντο δὲ ὑπὸ μέθης οἱ περὶ τὸν Ἱππόθοον, ἔξεισιν ὡς

entered the bridal chamber and, whether she was insane or in love with someone else, she drank poison from somewhere and died: people said this was the manner of her death." When Hippothous heard this he said, "That is the girl Habrocomes is looking for." 7. Habrocomes listened to the story but in despondency ignored it, until at length and with difficulty he leapt up when Hippothous spoke: "Now Anthia is clearly dead, but perhaps her tomb is here and her body is preserved." 8. With these words he asked the old lady Chrysium to lead him to her tomb and show him the body, but she cried out and said, "This is what was most unfortunate for the poor girl: Perilaus buried and adorned her lavishly, but pirates found out what was buried with her, dug up the tomb, snatched the finery, and made off with the body. Accordingly a search by Perilaus is underway far and wide."

When Habrocomes heard this he tore up his tunic and loudly mourned Anthia, dead in fine and chaste fashion but unfortunately lost after death: 2. "What pirate is so enamored as to desire you even dead, as to take even your body away? It is my misfortune to be deprived of the one part of you that would have been a consolation to me. 3. So I am wholly resolved to die, but first I will persevere until I find and embrace your body, then bury myself with it." With these words he mourned, while Hippothous' gang tried to console him. 4. At that point they turned in for the rest of the night, but Habrocomes kept thinking about everything: Anthia, her death, her tomb, her disappearance. Finally unable to bear it any longer, while Hippothous' gang lay prostrate from drinking he pretended to

10

---

61 Peerlkamp   62 Jacobs

δή τινος χρήζων καὶ καταλιπὼν πάντας ἐπὶ τὴν θάλατταν ἔρχεται καὶ ἐπιτυγχάνει νεὼς εἰς Ἀλεξάνδρειαν ἀναγομένης καὶ ἐπιβὰς ἀνάγεται ἐλπίζων τοὺς
λῃστὰς τοὺς συλήσαντας πάντα ἐν Αἰγύπτῳ κατα-
λήψεσθαι. ὡδήγει δὲ αὐτὸν εἰς ταῦτα ἐλπὶς δυστυχής.
5. καὶ ὁ μὲν ἔπλει τὴν ἐπ᾽ Ἀλεξάνδρειαν, ἡμέρας δὲ
γενομένης οἱ περὶ τὸν Ἱππόθοον ἠνιῶντο μὲν ἐπὶ τῷ
ἀπαλλαχθῆναι τοῦ Ἀβροκόμου, ἀναλαβόντες δὲ αὑτοὺς ἡμερῶν ὀλίγων ἔγνωσαν τὴν ἐπὶ Συρίας καὶ
Φοινίκης λῃστεύοντες ἰέναι.

11   Οἱ δὲ λῃσταὶ τὴν Ἀνθίαν εἰς Ἀλεξάνδρειαν παρ-
έδωκαν ἐμπόροις πολὺ λαβόντες ἀργύριον. οἱ δὲ ἔτρε-
φόν τε αὐτὴν πολυτελῶς καὶ τὸ σῶμα ἐθεράπευον,
ζητοῦντες ἀεὶ τὸν ὠνησόμενον κατ᾽ ἀξίαν. 2. ἔρχεται
δή τις εἰς Ἀλεξάνδρειαν ἐκ τῆς Ἰνδικῆς τῶν ἐκεῖ
βασιλέων κατὰ θέαν τῆς πόλεως καὶ κατὰ χρείαν
ἐμπορίας, Ψάμμις τὸ ὄνομα. 3. οὗτος ὁ Ψάμμις ὁρᾷ
τὴν Ἀνθίαν παρὰ τοῖς ἐμπόροις καὶ ἰδὼν ἁλίσκεται
καὶ ἀργύριον δίδωσι τοῖς ἐμπόροις πολὺ καὶ λαμβάνει
θεράπαιναν αὐτήν. 4. ὠνησάμενος δὲ ἄνθρωπος βάρ-
βαρος [καὶ][63] εὐθὺς ἐπιχειρεῖ βιάζεσθαι καὶ χρῆσθαι
πρὸς συνουσίαν· οὐ θέλουσα δὲ τὰ μὲν πρῶτα ἀντέ-
λεγε, τελευταῖον δὲ σκήπτεται πρὸς τὸν Ψάμμιν, δει-
σιδαίμονες δὲ φύσει βάρβαροι, ὅτι αὐτὴν ὁ πατὴρ
γεννωμένην ἀναθείη τῇ Ἴσιδι μέχρις ὥρας γάμων καὶ
ἔλεγεν ἔτι τὸν χρόνον ἐνιαυτοῦ τεθεῖσθαι[64]. 5. "ἢν οὖν"
φησιν "ἐξυβρίσῃς εἰς τὴν ἱερὰν τῆς θεοῦ μηνίσει μὲν
ἐκείνη, χαλεπὴ δὲ ἡ τιμωρία." πείθεται Ψάμμις καὶ τὴν
θεὸν προσκύνει καὶ Ἀνθίας ἀπέχεται.

[63] Hercher
[64] Lumb: -τῷ τίθεσθαι

need something, slipped away, and leaving everyone behind went to the shore, happened on a ship departing
for Alexandria, went aboard, and sailed off hoping to catch
in Egypt the pirates who had plundered everything. An
unfortunate hope it was that led him on this path. 5. In
the morning, while Habrocomes was sailing to Alexandria,
Hippothous' gang were annoyed at his departure, but after
a few days they recovered and decided to travel to Syria
and Phoenicia for banditry.

Meanwhile the pirates put in at Alexandria and made a   11
lot of money by selling Anthia to merchants, who kept her
at great expense and took care of her appearance, since
they were on the lookout for a buyer at the right price.
2. And indeed someone did come to Alexandria from India
to see the city and do some shopping, one of the kings
there by the name of Psammis.[40] 3. This Psammis saw
Anthia in the merchants' district and at the sight of her was
captivated, paid the merchants a lot of money, and took her
as a maidservant. 4. As soon as he bought her, the barbaric
fellow tried to force himself upon her and use her for sex.
She was unwilling and at first refused, but in the end made
Psammis the excuse—barbarians are naturally supersti-
tious—that her father had dedicated her at birth to Isis until she was of marriageable age, and she told him that there
was still a year before that time came. 5. "So if you violate
the goddess' protégé," she said, "she will be angry and your
punishment harsh." Psammis believed her, made obeisance to the goddess, and left Anthia alone.

[40] An Egyptian royal name (compare Psammetichus) in
Herodotus II 159–60.

12   Ἡ δὲ ἔτι παρὰ Ψάμμιδι ἦν φρουρουμένη, ἱερὰ τῆς
Ἴσιδος νομιζομένη. ἡ δὲ ναῦς ἡ τὸν Ἁβροκόμην
ἔχουσα τοῦ μὲν κατ᾽ Ἀλεξάνδρειαν πλοῦ διαμαρτάνει,
ἐκπίπτει δὲ ἐπὶ τὰς ἐκβολὰς τοῦ Νείλου τήν τε
παράλιον[65] καλουμένην καὶ Φοινίκης ὅση παραθα-
λάσσιος. 2. ἐκπεσοῦσι δὲ αὐτοῖς ἐπιδραμόντες τῶν
ἐκεῖ ποιμένων τά τε φορτία διαρπάζουσι καὶ τοὺς
ἄνδρας δεσμεύουσι καὶ ἄγουσιν ὁδὸν ἔρημον πολλὴν
εἰς Πηλούσιον τῆς Αἰγύπτου πόλιν καὶ ἐνταῦθα πι-
πράσκουσιν ἄλλον ἄλλῳ. ὠνεῖται δὴ τὸν Ἁβροκόμην
πρεσβύτης στρατιώτης, ἦν δὲ πεπαυμένος, Ἄραξος
τοὔνομα. 3. οὗτος ὁ Ἄραξος εἶχε γυναῖκα ὀφθῆναι
μιαράν, ἀκουσθῆναι πολὺ χείρω, ἅπασαν ἀκρασίαν
ὑπερβεβλημένην, Κυνὼ τὸ ὄνομα. αὕτη ἡ Κυνὼ ἐρᾷ
τοῦ Ἁβροκόμου εὐθὺς ἀχθέντος εἰς τὴν οἰκίαν καὶ
οὐκέτι κατεῖχε, δεινὴ καὶ ἐρασθῆναι καὶ ἀπολαύειν
ἐθέλειν τῆς ἐπιθυμίας. 4. ὁ μὲν δὴ Ἄραξος ἠγάπα τὸν
Ἁβροκόμην καὶ παῖδα ἐποιεῖτο, ἡ δὲ Κυνὼ προσφέρει
λόγον περὶ συνουσίας καὶ δεῖται πείθεσθαι καὶ ἄνδρα
ἔχειν ὑπισχνεῖτο [καὶ Ἄραξον ἀποκτενεῖν].[66] δεινὸν
ἐδόκει τοῦτο Ἁβροκόμῃ καὶ πολλὰ ἅμα ἐσκόπει, τὴν
Ἀνθίαν, τοὺς ὅρκους, τὴν πολλάκις αὐτὸν σωφροσύνην ἀδικήσασαν ἤδη, τέλος δὲ[67] ἐγκειμένης τῆς
Κυνοῦς συγκατατίθεται. 5. καὶ νυκτὸς γενομένης ἡ μὲν

---

65 Bürger cl. τὰ παράλια ap. Ach. Tat. 3.5.5, 19.2· παραίιων
66 Konstan AN 5 (2007) 38–40
67 τέλος δὲ Abresch: δὲ τέλος

---

41 These denizens of the Nile delta, more commonly known as
boukoloi ("herdsmen"), initiated a general Egyptian revolt against
the Romans in 172–73 CE and nearly succeeded in capturing Alex-

She remained under watch in Psammis' household, 12
held to be a protégé of Isis, while the ship carrying Habrocomes missed the route to Alexandria and went aground
at the mouth of the Nile on the so-called seaboard and
coastal area of Phoenicia. 2. Local shepherds[41] attacked
them when they were cast ashore, plundered their cargo,
bound the men and took them on a long desert road
to the Egyptian city of Pelusium,[42] and sold them there
to various buyers. An old retired soldier by the name of
Araxus[43] bought Habrocomes. 3. This Araxus had a wife
foul to behold, much worse to listen to, insatiable beyond
all bounds, named Cyno.[44] This Cyno developed a lust for
Habrocomes as soon as he was brought into the house and
soon could no longer restrain herself, being dreadfully
lustful and eager to indulge her passion. 4. While Araxus
liked Habrocomes and treated him like a son, Cyno propo-
sitioned him for sex, pressed him to give in, and promised
to take him as a husband [and kill Araxus].[45] Habrocomes
thought this dreadful and considered many factors together: Anthia, his oaths, the chastity that had already
done him so much harm. In the end, under pressure from
Cyno, he agreed to her proposition. 5. After nightfall she

andria before they were subdued as a result of internal factional-
ism (Dio Cassius 71.4); they figure prominently in the novels of
Achilles Tatius (III 9 ff.) and Heliodorus (III 5 ff.).   42 An
important trading center at the easternmost limit of the Nile
delta; modern Tell Farama, about 30 km southeast of Port Said.

43 A toponym not elsewhere attested as a personal name.

44 The name ("Bitch," suggesting shamelessness) is the name
of Cyrus' foster-mother in Herodotus 1.110–22.

45 Evidently an interpolation, in view of Habrocomes' reac-
tion below, when he is told of the murder.

ὡς ἄνδρα ἔξουσα τὸν Ἁβροκόμην τὸν Ἄραξον ἀποκτιννύει καὶ λέγει τὸ πραχθὲν τῷ Ἁβροκόμῃ, ὁ δὲ οὐκ
ἐνεγκὼν τὴν τῆς γυναικὸς ἀσέλγειαν ἀπηλλάγη τῆς
οἰκίας καταλιπὼν αὐτήν, οὐκ ἄν ποτε μιαιφόνῳ συγ-
κατακλιθήθεσθαι φήσας. 6. ἡ δὲ ἐν αὐτῇ γενομένη
ἅμα τῇ ἡμέρᾳ προσελθοῦσα ἔνθα τὸ πλῆθος τῶν
Πηλουσιωτῶν ἦν, ἀνωδύρετο τὸν ἄνδρα καὶ ἔλεγεν ὅτι
αὐτὸν ὁ νεώνητος δοῦλος ἀποκτείνειε καὶ πολλὰ ὅσα
ἐπεθρήνει καὶ ἐδόκει λέγειν τῷ πλήθει πιστά. οἱ δὲ
εὐθὺς συνέλαβον τὸν Ἁβροκόμην καὶ δήσαντες ἀν-
έπεμπον τῷ τῆς Αἰγύπτου τότε ἄρχοντι. καὶ ὁ μὲν
δίκην δώσων εἰς Ἀλεξάνδρειαν ἤγετο ὑπὲρ ὧν ἐδόκει
τὸν δεσπότην Ἄραξον ἀποκτεῖναι.

slew Araxus, intending to have Habrocomes for a husband, and told Habrocomes of her deed. But he could not bear the woman's depravity, left the house, and abandoned her, saying that he would never go to bed with a murderess. 6. When she recovered herself, she went at daybreak to the Pelusian assembly, started to bewail her husband and accuse the newly purchased slave of killing him, added to her lamentations much else of this sort, and seemed to the assembly to be speaking credibly. They arrested Habrocomes at once, bound him, and turned him over to the current prefect of Egypt. Found guilty on the charge of having murdered his master Araxus, he was taken to Alexandria for punishment.

ΛΟΓΟΣ ΤΕΤΑΡΤΟΣ

1   Οἱ δὲ περὶ τὸν Ἱππόθοον ἀπὸ Ταρσοῦ κινήσαντες
ᾔεσαν τὴν ἐπὶ⁶⁸ Συρίαν πᾶν εἴ τι ἐμποδὼν λάβοιεν
ὑποχείριον ποιούμενοι· ἐνέπρησαν δὲ καὶ κώμας καὶ
ἄνδρας ἀπέσφαξαν πολλούς. καὶ οὕτως ἐπελθόντες⁶⁹
εἰς Λαοδίκειαν τῆς Συρίας ἔρχονται κἀνταῦθα ἐπεδή-
μουν οὐκέτι ὡς λῃσταὶ ἀλλ᾽ ὡς κατὰ θέαν τῆς πόλεως
ἥκοντες. 2. ἐνταῦθα ὁ Ἱππόθοος ἐπολυπραγμόνει
⟨εἴ⟩⁷⁰ ποθεν Ἀβροκόμην εὑρεῖν δυνήσεται. ὡς δ᾽ οὐδὲν
ἤνυε ⟨ἀνα⟩λαβόντες⁷¹ αὑτοὺς ⟨διὰ⟩⁷² τῆς Φοινίκης
ἐτράποντο κἀκεῖθεν ἐπ᾽ Αἴγυπτον· ἐδόκει γὰρ αὐτοῖς
καταδραμεῖν Αἴγυπτον· 3. καὶ συλλεξάμενοι μέγα
λῃστήριον ἔρχονται τὴν ἐπὶ Πηλούσιον καὶ τῷ πο-
ταμῷ τῷ Νείλῳ πλεύσαντες εἰς Ἑρμούπολιν τῆς
Αἰγύπτου καὶ Σχεδίαν ἐμβαλόντες εἰς διώρυγα τοῦ
ποταμοῦ τὴν ὑπὸ Μενελάου γενομένην Ἀλεξάνδρειαν
μὲν παρῆλθον, ἦλθον δὲ ἐπὶ Μέμφιν τὴν ἱερὰν τῆς
Ἴσιδος κἀκεῖθεν ἐπὶ Μένδην· 4. παρέλαβον δὲ καὶ τῶν

---

68 Hemsterhuys: ἐπὶ τὴν   69 Dalmeyda: ἀπ-
70 Hemsterhuys   71 Hemsterhuys   72 O'Sullivan

---

46 A prosperous harbor city (Strabo 16.2.9), among those
named after Laodice by decree of her husband, Antiochus III, in
193 BCE; modern Latakia.   47 X. assembled the following,
rather unlikely, itinerary from literary sources.
48 Probably meaning Hermupolis Parva (modern Daman-
hur), about 70 km southeast of Alexandria.
49 An important commercial transport center (cf. Strabo

BOOK IV

Meanwhile Hippothous' gang moved out from Tarsus 1
and headed for Syria, subduing all opposition that they encountered. They set fire to villages and slaughtered many
men, and in this fashion they made their way to Laodicea
in Syria,[46] where they settled in no longer as bandits but as
if to see the sights of the city. 2. There Hippothous kept
poking around in hopes of somehow being able to find
Habrocomes. When he came up with nothing, they collected themselves and travelled through Phoenicia and
from there to Egypt, for they planned to ravage Egypt.[47] 3.
They collected a large bandit gang and went to Pelusium,
and after sailing on the Nile to the Egyptian Hermupolis[48]
and Schedia,[49] and putting in to the river canal built by
Menelaus[50] they passed by Alexandria but came to Memphis,[51] sacred city of Isis, and thence to Mendes.[52] 4. They

17.1.16) about 30 km southeast of Alexandria, near the modern
village of Kom-el Giza.

[50] An artificial channel connecting Alexandria with the
Canopic Nile; this Menelaus is probably the brother of Ptolemy I,
cf. Diodorus 20.21, 47–53 and Plutarch, *Demetrius* 15–17.

[51] A capital city about 20 km south of Cairo on the west bank
of the Nile, second only to Alexandria in importance; modern Mit
Rahina and Saqqara.

[52] Located where the Mendesian tributary of the Nile enters
the lake of Tanis; modern Tell El-Ruba. Mendes was important in
early times but by the early first century CE had been eclipsed by
neighboring Thmuis (Tema El-Amdid).

ἐπιχωρίων κοινωνοὺς τοῦ ληστηρίου καὶ ἐξηγητὰς τῆς
ὁδοῦ. διελθόντες μὲν δὴ Ταύ[τ]α[73] ἐπὶ Λεοντὼ ἔρχονται
πόλιν καὶ ἄλλας παρελθόντες κώμας οὐκ ὀλίγας, ὧν
τὰς πολλὰς ἀφανεῖς, εἰς Κοπτὸν ἔρχονται τῆς Αἰθιοπίας πλησίον. 5. ἐνταῦθα ἔγνωσαν ληστεύειν· πολὺ
γὰρ πλῆθος ἐμπόρων τὸ διοδεῦον ἦν τῶν τε ἐπ᾽ Αἰθιοπίαν καὶ τῶν ἐπὶ Ἰνδικὴν φοιτώντων· ἦν δὲ αὐτοῖς καὶ
τὸ ληστήριον ἀνθρώπων πεντακοσίων. καταλαβόντες
δὲ τῆς Αἰθιοπίας τὰ ἄκρα καὶ ἄντ<ρ>α[74] καταστη-
σάμενοι διέγνωσαν τοὺς παριόντας ληστεύειν.

2   Ὁ δὲ Ἁβροκόμης ὡς ἧκε παρὰ τὸν ἄρχοντα τῆς
Αἰγύπτου, ἐπεστάλκεσάν τε οἱ Πηλουσιῶται τὰ γενόμενα αὐτῷ καὶ τὸν τοῦ Ἀράξου φόνον καὶ ὅτι οἰκέτης
ὢν τοιαῦτα ἐτόλμησε. μαθὼν οὖν ἕκαστα οὐκέτι οὐδὲ
πυθόμενος τὰ γενόμενα κελεύει τὸν Ἁβροκόμην ἀγα-
γόντας προσαρτῆσαι σταυρῷ. 2. ὁ δὲ ἀπὸ μὲν τῶν
κακῶν ἀχανὴς ἦν, παρεμυθεῖτο δὲ αὐτὸν τῆς τελευτῆς
ὅτι ἐδόκει καὶ Ἀνθίαν τεθνηκέναι. ἄγουσι δὲ αὐτὸν οἷς
τοῦτο προσετέτακτο παρὰ τὰς ὄχθας τοῦ Νείλου· ἦν δὲ
κρημνὸς ἀπότομος εἰς <τὸ>[75] ῥεῦμα τοῦ ποταμοῦ βλέ-
πων· 3. καὶ ἀναστήσαντες τὸν σταυρὸν προσαρτῶσι
σπάρτοις τὰς χεῖρας σφίγξαντες καὶ τοὺς πόδας·
τοῦτο γὰρ τῆς ἀνασταυρώσεως ἔθος τοῖς ἐκεῖ· καταλιπόντες δὲ ᾤχοντο ὡς ἐν ἀσφαλεῖ τοῦ προσηρτη-

[73] Hemsterhuys   [74] Hemsterhuys
[75] Herwerden

---

[53] Hemsterhuys' plausible emendation; the town (modern
Tanta) was 130 km southeast of Alexandria.
[54] Probably meaning the city on the Pelusiac Nile 18 km.
north of Heliopolis; modern Tell el-Yahudiya.

recruited natives as partners in the bandit gang and guides for the journey. They passed through Taua[53] and came to Leontopolis,[54] and passing through not a few other cities, most of them obscure, they came to Coptus,[55] near Ethiopia. 5. There they decided to do their banditry, for there was a large crowd of merchants passing through on their way to Ethiopia and India,[56] and they now had a bandit gang of five hundred men. When they had taken the heights of Ethiopia and set up their caves, they determined to rob the wayfarers.

Meanwhile Habrocomes appeared before the prefect 2 of Egypt, and the Pelusians had written him a report of what had happened, both the murder of Araxus and that it was a slave who had dared such deeds. Hearing the particulars and making no further inquiry into what had happened, he ordered Habrocomes to be taken away and crucified.[57] 2. He was dumbfounded by his misfortunes, but the idea that Anthia too was dead consoled him about his own end. His assigned escort took him to the banks of the Nile, where there was a sheer cliff overlooking the stream of the river. 3. They raised the cross and bound him to it, tying his hands and feet tight with ropes, for this is the local custom in crucifixion. They left him hanging there and

[55] On the right bank of the Nile about 27 km north of Luxor; modern Qift. It was largely destroyed by Diocletian's forces after a revolt in 297 CE.

[56] As Strabo notes (17.1.45), a desert road developed by Ptolemy Philadelphus connected Coptus to the Red Sea, making it a center for trade from India, Arabia, and Ethiopia.

[57] There is a similar episode in Chariton IV 2.6.

μένου μένοντος. 4. ὁ δὲ ἀποβλέψας εἰς τὸν ἥλιον καὶ τὸ
ῥεῦμα ἰδὼν τοῦ Νείλου "ὦ θεῶν" φησὶ "φιλανθρωπότατε, ὃς Αἴγυπτον ἔχεις, δι᾽ ὃν καὶ γῆ καὶ θάλασσα
πᾶσιν ἀνθρώποις πέφηνεν, εἰ μέν τι Ἁβροκόμης ἀδι-
κεῖ καὶ ἀπολοίμην οἰκτρῶς καὶ μείζονα τιμωρίαν εἴ τις
ἐστὶ ταύτης ὑπόσχοιμι, 5. εἰ δὲ ὑπὸ γυναικὸς προ-
δέδομαι πονηρᾶς μήτε τὸ Νείλου ῥεῦμα μιανθείη ποτὲ
ἀδίκως ἀπολομένου σώματι[76] μήτε σὺ τοιοῦτον ἴδοις
θέαμα, ἄνθρωπον οὐδὲν ἀδικήσαντα ἀπολλύμενον ἐπὶ
τῆς σῆς ἐνταῦθα ‹γῆς." 6. ταῦτα›[77] ηὔξατο καὶ αὐτὸν ὁ
θεὸς οἰκτείρει καὶ πνεῦμα ἐξαίφνης ἀνέμου γίνεται καὶ
ἐμπίπτει τῷ σταυρῷ καὶ ἀποβάλλει μὲν τοῦ κρημνοῦ
τὸ γεῶδες εἰς ὃ ἦν ὁ σταυρὸς ἠρεισμένος, ἐμπίπτει δὲ ὁ
Ἁβροκόμης τῷ ῥεύματι καὶ ἐφέρετο οὔτε τοῦ ὕδατος
αὐτὸν ἀδικοῦντος οὔτε τῶν δεσμῶν ἐμποδιζόντων οὔτε
τῶν θηρίων [παρα]βλαπτόντων[78], ἀλλὰ παραπέμποντος τοῦ ῥεύματος· 7. φερόμενος δὲ εἰς τὰς ἐμβολὰς
ἔρχεται τὰς εἰς τὴν θάλασσαν τοῦ Νείλου κἀνταῦθα οἱ
παραφυλάσσοντες λαμβάνουσιν αὐτὸν καὶ ὡς δρα-
πέτην τῆς τιμωρίας ἄγουσι παρὰ τὸν διοικοῦντα τὴν
Αἴγυπτον. 8. ὁ δὲ ἔτι μᾶλλον ὀργισθεὶς καὶ πονηρὸν
εἶναι νομίσας τελέως κελεύει πυρὰν ποιήσαντας ἐπι-
θέντας καταφλέξαι τὸν Ἁβροκόμην. καὶ ἦν μὲν ἅπαντα παρεσκευασμένα καὶ ἡ πυρὰ παρὰ τὰς ἐκβολὰς τοῦ
Νείλου καὶ ἐπετίθετο μὲν ὁ Ἁβροκόμης καὶ τὸ πῦρ
ὑπετέθειτο[79], ἄρτι δὲ τῆς φλογὸς μελλούσης ἅπτεσθαι
τοῦ σώματος ηὔχετο πάλιν ὀλίγα ὅσα ἐδύνατο σῶσαι
αὐτὸν ἐκ τῶν καθεστώτων κακῶν. 9. κἀνταῦθα κυμα-
τοῦται μὲν ὁ Νεῖλος, ἐπιπίπτει δὲ τῇ πυρᾷ τὸ ῥεῦμα
καὶ κατασβέννυσι τὴν φλόγα. θαῦμα δὲ τὸ γενόμενον

---

[76] Peerlkamp cl. Ach. Tat. 8.3.2: σώματος

went away, thinking that he was secured. 4. But he gazed at the sun and looked at the Nile stream, and said, "Kindliest of gods, who hold sway over Egypt, through whom both earth and sky are revealed to all mankind, if Habrocomes has done any wrong, let me perish miserably and receive a worse punishment than this, if any there be, 5. but if I have been betrayed by an evil woman, may the Nile stream never be polluted by the body of one unjustly destroyed, and may you never see such a sight, a person who has done no wrong being destroyed on this your very own land." 6. This was his prayer and the god took pity on him: a sudden gust of wind arose, struck the cross, and blew away the soil on the cliff where the cross had been planted. Habrocomes pitched into the stream and was borne away; neither did the water harm him nor his fetters impede him nor the river beasts injure him, but the stream was his escort. 7. He was carried to the mouth of the Nile where it flows into the sea, and there the garrison arrested him and took him before the governor of Egypt as a fugitive from justice. 8. He was even angrier than before, and taking him for an utter criminal ordered them to build a pyre, put Habrocomes on it, and burn him up. Everything was made ready, the pyre by the mouth of the Nile, and Habrocomes was put on it while the fire was laid below, but just as the flame was about to reach his body he said more prayers, what little he could manage, to save him from his present misfortunes. 9. And now the Nile crested and its stream fell on the pyre and extinguished the flame.[58] To those present this event

---

[58] Compare the story of Croesus' salvation in Herodotus 1.87.

---

[77] Jackson   [78] O'Sullivan   [79] Abresch: ἐπε-

τοῖς παροῦσιν ἦν καὶ λαβόντες ἄγουσι τὸν Ἁβροκόμην πρὸς τὸν ἄρχοντα τῆς Αἰγύπτου καὶ λέγουσι τὰ
συμβάντα καὶ τὴν τοῦ Νείλου βοήθειαν διηγοῦνται.
10. ἐθαύμασεν ἀκούσας τὰ γενόμενα καὶ ἐκέλευσεν
αὐτὸν τηρεῖσθαι μὲν ἐν τῇ εἱρκτῇ, ἐπιμέλειαν δὲ ἔχειν
πᾶσαν, "ἕως" ἔφη "μάθωμεν ὅστις ὁ ἄνθρωπός ἐστιν
καὶ ὅ τι οὕτως αὐτοῦ μέλει θεοῖς."

3 Καὶ ὁ μὲν ἦν ἐν τῇ εἱρκτῇ, ὁ δὲ Ψάμμις ὁ τὴν
Ἀνθίαν ὠνησάμενος διέγνω μὲν ἀπιέναι τὴν ἐπ' οἴκου
καὶ πάντα πρὸς τὴν ὁδοιπορίαν παρεσκευάζετο, ἔδει δὲ
αὐτὸν ὁδεύσαντα τὴν ἄνω Αἴγυπτον ἐπὶ Αἰθιοπίαν
ἐλθεῖν ἔνθα ἦν τὸ Ἱπποθόου λῃστήριον. 2. ἦν δὲ πάντα
εὐτρεπῆ· κάμηλοί τε πολλαὶ καὶ ὄνοι καὶ ἵπποι σκευ-
αγωγοί· ἦν δὲ πολὺ μὲν πλῆθος χρυσοῦ,[80] πολὺ δὲ
ἀργύρου, πολλὴ δὲ ἐσθής· ἦγε δὲ καὶ τὴν Ἀνθίαν. 3. ἡ
δὲ ὡς Ἀλεξάνδρειαν παρελθοῦτα ἐγένετο ἐν Μέμφει,
ηὔχετο τῇ Ἴσιδι στᾶσα πρὸ τοῦ ἱεροῦ· "ὦ μεγίστη
θεῶν, μέχρι μὲν νῦν ἁγνὴ μένω λογιζομένη σὴ καὶ
γάμον ἄχραντον Ἁβροκόμῃ τηρῶ, τοὐντεῦθεν δὲ ἐπὶ
Ἰνδοὺς ἔρχομαι, μακρὰν μὲν τῆς Ἐφεσίων γῆς,
μακρὰν δὲ τῶν Ἁβροκόμου λειψάνων. 4. ἢ σῶσον οὖν
ἐντεῦθεν τὴν δυστυχῆ καὶ ζῶντι ἀπόδος Ἁβροκόμῃ ἢ
εἰ πάντως εἵμαρται χωρὶς ἀλλήλων ἀποθανεῖν ἔργα-
σαι τοῦτο· μεῖναί με σωφρονοῦσαν τῷ νεκρῷ." 5.
ταῦτα ηὔχετο καὶ προῄεσαν τῆς ὁδοῦ καὶ ἤδη μὲν
διεληλύθεισαν Κοπτόν, ἐνέβαινον[το][81] δὲ τοῖς Αἰθιό-
πων ὅροις καὶ αὐτοῖς Ἱππόθοος ἐπιπίπτει καὶ αὐτὸν
μὲν τὸν Ψάμμιν ἀποκτιννύει καὶ πολλοὺς τῶν σὺν
αὐτῷ καὶ τὰ χρήματα λαμβάνει καὶ τὴν Ἀνθίαν
αἰχμάλωτον. 6. συλλεξάμενος δὲ τὰ ληφθέντα χρή-

 [80] Locella: -ίου [81] Hirschig

was a marvel, and they took Habrocomes and brought him before the prefect of Egypt, told him what had come to pass, and described the Nile's assistance. 10. He marveled at hearing of these events and ordered him to be guarded in the prison but to have every consideration "until" he said "we find out who this person is and why the gods care about him so much."

And so he remained in prison, while Psammis, the pur- 3 chaser of Anthia, decided to travel homeward and began preparing everything for the journey. He had to travel through upper Egypt on his way to Ethiopia, where Hippothous' bandit gang was. 2. Everything was ready, many camels, asses, and packhorses, along with large quantities of gold and of silver, and lots of clothing. He took Anthia too. 3. When she had left Alexandria and arrived in Memphis, she stood before the temple[59] and prayed to Isis. "Greatest of goddesses, until now I have remained pure, being considered sacred to you, and I have kept my marriage to Habrocomes undefiled. But I am leaving here for India, far from the land of Ephesus and far from Habrocomes' remains. 4. So either rescue an unfortunate woman from this place and return her to a living Habrocomes or, if it is absolutely fated that we die apart, contrive this: that I remain chaste for his corpse." This was her prayer, and they set out on their journey. They had passed through Coptus and were crossing the boundaries of Ethiopia when Hippothous attacked them. He killed Psammis and many of his retinue, and captured the goods along with Anthia as a prisoner. 6. He collected the captured booty

59 Cf. Herodotus 2.176.

ματα ἦγεν εἰς ἄντρον τὸ ἀποδεδειγμένον αὐτοῖς εἰς
ἀπόθεσιν τῶν χρημάτων. ἐνταῦθα ἤει καὶ ἡ Ἀνθία, οὐκ
ἐγνώριζε δὲ Ἱππόθοον οὐδὲ Ἱππόθοος τὴν Ἀνθίαν.
ὁπότε δὲ αὐτῆς πύθοιτο ἥτις τε εἴη καὶ πόθεν τὸ μὲν
ἀληθὲς οὐκ ἔλεγεν, ἔφασκε δὲ Αἰγυπτία εἶναι ἐπιχώριος[82] καὶ τὸ ὄνομα Μεμφῖτις.

4   Καὶ ἡ μὲν ἦν παρὰ τῷ Ἱπποθόῳ ἐν τῷ ἄντρῳ τῷ
ληστρικῷ, ἐν τούτῳ δὲ μεταπέμπεται τὸν Ἁβροκόμην
ὁ ἄρχων τῆς Αἰγύπτου καὶ πυνθάνεται τὰ κατ᾿ αὐτὸν
καὶ μανθάνει τὸ διήγημα καὶ οἰκτείρει τὴν τύχην καὶ
δίδωσι χρήματα καὶ εἰς Ἔφεσον ἄξειν ὑπισχνεῖτο.
2. ὁ δὲ ἅπασαν μὲν ᾔδει χάριν αὐτῷ τῆς σωτηρίας,
ἐδεῖτο δὲ ἐπιτρέψαι ζητῆσαι τὴν Ἀνθίαν. καὶ ὁ μὲν
πολλὰ δῶρα λαβὼν ἐπιβὰς σκάφους ἀνήγετο τὴν ἐπὶ
Ἰταλίας, ⟨ὡς⟩ ἐκεῖ πευσόμενός τι [μαθεῖν][83] περὶ Ἀνθίας. ὁ δὲ ἄρχων τῆς Αἰγύπτου μαθὼν τὰ κατὰ τὸν
Ἄραξον μεταπεμψάμενος ἀνεσταύρωσε τὴν Κυνώ.

5   Τῆς δὲ Ἀνθίας οὔσης ἐν τῷ ἄντρῳ ἐρᾷ τῶν φρουρούντων αὐτὴν ληστῶν εἷς, Ἀγχίαλος τοὔνομα. οὗτος
ὁ Ἀγχίαλος ἦν μὲν τῶν ἀπὸ Συρίας Ἱπποθόῳ συν-
εληλυθότων, Λαοδικεὺς τὸ γένος, ἐτιμᾶτο δὲ παρὰ τῷ
Ἱπποθόῳ νεανικός τε ⟨ὢν⟩[84] καὶ μεγάλα ἐν τῷ ληστη-
ρίῳ δυνάμενος. 2. ἐρασθεὶς δὲ αὐτῆς τὰ μὲν πρῶτα
λόγους προσέφερεν ὡς πείσων καὶ ἔφασκε λόγῳ λήψεσθαι καὶ παρὰ Ἱπποθόου δῶρον αἰτήσειν. 3. ἡ δὲ
πάντα ἠρνεῖτο καὶ οὐδὲν αὐτὴν ἐδυσώπει, οὐκ ἄντρον,
οὐ δεσμά, οὐ ληστὴς ἀπειλῶν, ἐφύλασσε δὲ ἑαυτὴν ἔτι
Ἁβροκόμῃ καὶ δοκοῦντι τεθνηκέναι καὶ πολλάκις ἀνε-
βόα εἴποτε λαθεῖν ἠδύνατο· "Ἁβροκόμου μόνον γυνὴ

82 Cobet: -ίαν et -ιον   83 Suppl. et del. Hirschig
84 Hercher

and took it to a cave designated for the stashing of their booty. Anthia went there too, but she did not recognize Hippothous nor Hippothous Anthia. Whenever he asked her who she was and where from, she did not tell the truth but claimed to be a native Egyptian by the name of Memphitis.

So Anthia stayed with Hippothous in the bandits' cave,   4 but meanwhile the prefect of Egypt summoned Habrocomes, questioned him about himself, learned his story, pitied his lot, gave him money, and promised to send him to Ephesus. 2. He gave him every expression of thanks for his salvation but asked leave to keep searching for Anthia. And so he received many gifts, boarded a boat, and set sail for Italy, thinking to hear news of Anthia there. Meanwhile the prefect of Egypt discovered the truth about Araxus, summoned Cyno, and had her crucified.

While Anthia was in the cave, one of the bandits watch-   5 ing her, named Anchialus,[60] began to lust for her. This Anchialus, a native of Laodicea, was among those who had accompanied Hippothous from Syria, and he was prized by Hippothous, being lusty and of high standing in the bandit gang. 2. In his lust for her, he began by making propositions to seduce her, expecting to talk her into his clutches and ask for her as a gift from Hippothous. 3. But she refused everything, and nothing intimidated her, not the cave, not the fetters, not the bandit's threats, but she was still saving herself for Habrocomes, even if he seemed to be dead, and many a time when no one could hear her she would cry out, "Let me only remain Habrocomes' wife,

60 "Seaward"; a town on the Black sea and a proper name in Homer.

317

μείναι<μι>[85] κἂν ἀποθανεῖν δέῃ κἂν ὧν πέπονθα χείρω
παθεῖν." 4. ταῦτα εἰς μείζω συμφορὰν ἦγε τὸν Ἀγχίαλον καὶ ἡ καθ᾽ ἡμέραν τῆς Ἀνθίας ὄψις ἐξέκαεν αὐτὸν
εἰς τὸν ἔρωτα. οὐκέτι δὲ φέρειν δυνάμενος ἐπεχείρει
βιάζεσθαι τὴν Ἀνθίαν, 5. καὶ νύκτωρ ποτέ, οὐ παρόντος Ἱπποθόου ἀλλὰ μετὰ τῶν ἄλλων ὄντος ἐν λη-
στηρίῳ, ἐπανίστατο καὶ ὑβρίζειν ἐπειρᾶτο. ἡ δὲ ἐν
ἀμηχάνῳ κακῷ γενομένη σπασαμένη τὸ παρακείμενον
ξίφος παίει τὸν Ἀγχίαλον καὶ ἡ πληγὴ γίνεται καιρία·
ὁ μὲν γὰρ περιληψόμενος καὶ φιλήσων ὅλος ἐνενεύκει
πρὸς αὐτήν, ἡ δὲ ὑπενεγκοῦσα τὸ ξίφος κατὰ τῶν
στέρνων ἔπληξε. 6. καὶ Ἀγχίαλος μὲν δίκην ἱκανὴν
ἐδεδώκει τῆς πονηρᾶς ἐπιθυμίας, ἡ δὲ Ἀνθία εἰς φόβον
μὲν τῶν δεδραμένων ἔρχεται καὶ πολλὰ ἐβουλεύετο
ποτὲ μὲν ἑαυτὴν ἀποκτεῖναι, ἀλλ᾽ ἔτι ὑπὲρ Ἁβροκόμου
τι ἤλπιζε, ποτὲ δὲ φυγεῖν ἐκ τοῦ ἄντρου, ἀλλὰ τοῦτο
ἀμήχανον ἦν· οὔτε γὰρ ἡ ὁδὸς αὐτῇ εὔπορος ἦν οὔτε ὁ
ἐξηγησόμενος τὴν πορείαν. ἔγνω οὖν μένειν ἐν τῷ
ἄντρῳ καὶ φέρειν ὅ τι ἂν τῷ δαίμονι δοκῇ.

6   Κἀκείνην μὲν τὴν νύκτα ἔμεινεν οὔτε ὕπνου τυχοῦ-
σα καὶ πολλὰ ἐννοοῦσα, ἐπεὶ δὲ ἡμέρα ἐγένετο ἧκον οἱ
περὶ τὸν Ἱπποθοον καὶ ὁρῶσι τὸν Ἀγχίαλον ἀνη-
ρημένον καὶ τὴν Ἀνθίαν παρὰ τῷ σώματι καὶ εἰ-
κάζουσι τὸ γενόμενον καὶ ἀνακρίναντες αὐτὴν μαν-
θάνουσι πάντα. 2. ἔδοξεν οὖν αὐτοῖς ἐν ὀργῇ τὸ
γενόμενον ἔχουσι[86] τὸν τεθνηκότα ἐκδικῆσαι φίλον·
καὶ ἐβουλεύοντο κατὰ Ἀνθίας ποικίλα, ὁ μέν τις
ἀποκτεῖναι κελεύων καὶ συνθάψαι τῷ Ἀγχιάλου σώματι, ἄλλος δὲ ἀνασταυρῶσαι· 3. ὁ δὲ Ἱπποθοος
ἠνιᾶτο μὲν ἐπὶ τῷ Ἀγχιάλῳ, ἐβουλεύετο δὲ κατὰ
Ἀνθίας μείζονα κόλασιν. καὶ δὴ κελεύει τάφρον ὀρύ-
ξαντας μεγάλην καὶ βαθεῖαν ἐμβάλλειν τὴν Ἀνθίαν

even if it means my death, even if it means worse sufferings than I have already suffered." 4. This increased Anchialus' torment, and the daily sight of Anthia stoked his lust. When he could no longer bear it he tried to force Anthia, 5. and one night, when Hippothous was away with the others on a raid, he got up and attempted to rape her. In her helpless predicament she drew a sword lying nearby and stabbed Anchialus, and the stroke was fatal: trying to embrace and kiss her, he had got completely on top of her, and she brought up the sword from underneath and stabbed him in the chest. 6. And so Anchialus paid a fitting penalty for his evil passion, but Anthia grew fearful about her deed and did much pondering whether to kill herself, though she still had some hope for Habrocomes, or whether to flee the cave, though that was impractical: the road was not open to her, nor was there anyone to show her the way. So she decided to wait in the cave and face whatever her fate decreed.

All that night she waited, able to get no sleep and deep in thought. At daybreak Hippothous' gang arrived, saw Anchialus done in and Anthia beside his body, guessed what had happened, and got the whole story from her under questioning. 2. In their anger at what had happened they decided to avenge their dead friend and discussed various scenarios for Anthia: someone recommended that they kill her and bury her with Anchialus' body, another that they crucify her. 3. But Hippothous was distressed about Anchialus and determined a worse punishment for Anthia. He told them to dig a pit wide and deep and throw

6

85 Passow
86 Dalmeyda: ἔχειν

καὶ κύνας μετ᾽ αὐτῆς δύο, ἵνα ἐν τούτῳ μεγάλην δίκην
ὑπόσχῃ τῶν τετολμημένων. 4. καὶ οἱ μὲν ἐποίουν τὸ
προσταχθέν, ἤγετο δὲ ἡ Ἀνθία ἐπὶ τὴν τάφρον καὶ οἱ
κύνες· ἦσαν δὲ Αἰγύπτιοι καὶ τὰ ἄλλα μεγάλοι καὶ
ὀφθῆναι φοβεροί. ὡς δὲ ἐνεβλήθησαν ξύλα ἐπιτι-
θέντες μεγάλα ἐπέχωσαν τὴν τάφρον, ἦν δὲ τοῦ Νείλου ὀλίγον ἀπέχουσα, καὶ κατέστησαν φρουρὸν ἕνα
τῶν λῃστῶν Ἀμφίνομον. 5. οὗτος ὁ Ἀμφίνομος ἤδη
μὲν καὶ πρότερον ἑαλώκει τῆς Ἀνθίας, τότε δ᾽ οὖν
ἠλέει μᾶλλον αὐτὴν καὶ τῆς συμφορᾶς ᾤκτειρεν, ἐπε-
νόει δὲ ὅπως ἐπὶ πλεῖον αὐτὴ ζήσεται ὅπως τε οἱ κύνες
αὐτῇ μηδὲν ἐνοχλήσωσι καὶ ἑκάστοτε ἀφαιρῶν τῶν
ἐπικειμένων τῇ τάφρῳ ξύλων ἄρτους ἐνέβαλε καὶ ὕδωρ
παρεῖχε καὶ ἐκ τούτου τὴν Ἀνθίαν θαρρεῖν παρεκάλει.
6. καὶ οἱ κύνες τρεφόμενοι οὐδέν [ἔ]τι[87] δεινὸν αὐτὴν
εἰργάζοντο, ἀλλὰ ἤδη τιθασοὶ ἐγίνοντο καὶ ἥμεροι· ἡ
δὲ Ἀνθία ἀποβλέψασα εἰς ἑαυτὴν καὶ τὴν παροῦσαν
τύχην ἐννοήσασα "οἴμοι" φησί "τῶν κακῶν, οἵαν ὑπομένω τιμωρίαν· τάφρος [καὶ][88] δεσμωτήριον καὶ κύνες
⟨συγ⟩καθειργμένοι[89] πολὺ τῶν λῃστῶν ἡμερώτεροι·
τὰ αὐτά, Ἀβροκόμη, σοι πάσχω· 7. ἧς γάρ ποτε ἐν
ὁμοίᾳ τύχῃ καὶ σύ· καὶ σὲ ἐν Τύρῳ κατέλιπον ἐν
δεσμωτηρίῳ. ἀλλ᾽ εἰ μὲν ζῇς ἔτι, δεινὸν οὐδέν· ἴσως
γάρ ποτε ἀλλήλους ἕξομεν· εἰ δὲ ἤδη τέθνηκας, μάτην
ἐγὼ φιλοτιμοῦμαι ζῆν, μάτην δὲ οὗτος, ὅστις ποτέ
ἐστιν, ἐλεεῖ με τὴν δυστυχῆ." ταῦτα ἔλεγε καὶ ἐπεθρήνει συνεχῶς. καὶ ἡ μὲν ἐν τῇ τάφρῳ κατεκέκλειστο
μετὰ τῶν κυνῶν, ὁ δ᾽ Ἀμφίνομος ἑκάστοτε κἀκείνην
παρεμυθεῖτο καὶ τοὺς κύνας ἡμέρους ἐποίει τρέφων.

[87] Palairet   [88] O'Sullivan
[89] Hemsterhuys

in Anthia along with a couple of dogs: there she would pay
a heavy penalty for her audacious behavior. 4. They did as
they were told, and Anthia was taken to the pit and the
dogs along with her; they were Egyptian and altogether
huge and frightful to behold. After they threw them in,
they put big planks over the pit and piled dirt on top, for
the Nile was not far distant, and stationed Amphinomus,[61]
one of the bandits, as guard. 5. This Amphinomus was already captivated by Anthia, so he now felt all the more
sorry for her and pitied her situation. He figured out how
to keep her alive and the dogs from molesting her: at regular intervals he removed the planks covering the pit, tossed
in some bread, supplied some water, and this way encouraged Anthia to persevere, 6. and since the dogs were being
fed, they did nothing terrible to her but now became tame
and gentle. But as Anthia took stock of herself and considered her present situation, she cried "What misfortunes
are mine! What vengeance I endure! A pit for a prison,
shut in with dogs much gentler than the bandits! Habrocomes, my sufferings are the same as yours, 7. for you were
once in the same plight, where I left you behind imprisoned in Tyre. If you still live, it is not terrible at all, for perhaps we will hold one another someday, but if you are already dead, my own fight for life is pointless, and pointless
is this man's pity for my situation, whoever he is." In this
fashion did she cry out and mourn, shut in the pit with the
dogs, while Amphinomus at regular intervals consoled her
and gentled the dogs with his feedings.

[61] An epic and actual name.

ΛΟΓΟΣ ΠΕΜΠΤΟΣ

1   Ὁ δὲ Ἁβροκόμης διανύσας τὸν ⟨ἀπ'⟩[90] Αἰγύπτου
πλοῦν εἰς αὐτὴν μὲν Ἰταλίαν οὐκ ἔρχεται· τὸ γὰρ
πνεῦμα τὴν ναῦν ἀπῶσαν τοῦ μὲν κατ' εὐθὺ ἀπέσφηλε
πλοῦ, ἤγαγε δὲ εἰς Σικελίαν καὶ κατήχθησαν εἰς πόλιν
Συρακούσας μεγάλην καὶ καλήν. 2. ἐνταῦθα ὁ Ἁβροκόμης γενόμενος ἔγνω περιιέναι τὴν νῆσον καὶ ἀναζητεῖν ἔτι περὶ Ἀνθίας εἴ τι πύθοιτο. καὶ δὴ ἐνοικίζεται
μὲν πλησίον τῆς θαλάσσης παρὰ ἀνδρὶ Αἰγιαλεῖ
πρεσβύτῃ ἁλιεῖ τὴν τέχνην. 2. οὗτος ὁ Αἰγιαλεὺς
πένης μὲν ἦν καὶ ξένος καὶ ἀγαπητῶς αὐτὸν διέτρεφεν
ἐκ τῆς τέχνης, ὑπεδέξατο δὲ τὸν Ἁβροκόμην ἄσμενος
καὶ παῖδα ἐνόμιζεν αὐτοῦ καὶ ἠγάπα διαφερόντως. 3.
καὶ ἤδη ποτὲ ἐκ πολλῆς τῆς πρὸς ἀλλήλους συνηθείας
ὁ μὲν Ἁβροκόμης αὐτῷ διηγήσατο τὰ καθ' αὑτὸν καὶ
τὴν Ἀνθίαν εἰρήκει καὶ τὸν ἔρωτα καὶ τὴν πλάνην, ὁ δὲ
Αἰγιαλεὺς ἄρχεται τῶν αὑτοῦ διηγημάτων. 4. "ἐγὼ"
ἔφη, "τέκνον Ἁβροκόμη, οὔτε Σικελιώτης οὐδὲ ἐπιχώριος ἀλλὰ Σπαρτιάτης Λακεδαιμόνιος τῶν τὰ πρῶτα ἐκεῖ δυναμένων καὶ περιουσίαν ἔχων πολλήν. 5.
νέος δὲ ὢν ἠράσθην ἐν τοῖς ἐφήβοις καταλελεγμένος
κόρης πολίτιδος Θελξινόης τοὔνομα, ἀντερᾷ δέ μου

90 Hemsterhuys

62 "Coast Dweller," used especially of inhabitants of the

BOOK V

Habrocomes completed his voyage from Egypt but did 1
not reach Italy itself because the wind drove at his ship,
blew it off course, and took it to Sicily, where they disembarked at the large and beautiful city of Syracuse. 2. Once
there, Habrocomes decided to explore the island and continue his search for any news about Anthia. So he settled
himself near the coast with an old man, Aegialeus,[62] a
fisherman by trade. 2. This Aegialeus was a poor foreigner
who only just supported himself by his trade, but he was
happy to take Habrocomes in, treated him like his own son,
and showed him special affection. 3. When they reached
the point of great familiarity with each other, Habrocomes
told him his story: he spoke about Anthia, his love for her,
and his wanderings, and then Aegialeus started in on his
own story. 4. "Habrocomes my boy, I am not a Sicilian
Greek and not even a native,[63] but a Spartiate of Laconia,
from one of the most powerful families there and very
well-to-do. 5. When I was a young man just enrolled in the
ephebes,[64] I fell in love with a Spartan girl by the name of
Thelxinoe,[65] and Thelxinoe fell in love with me. We met

coastal Peloponnese (cf. Herodotus 5.68), where it is attested as a
personal name.

[63] I.e. a Sicel, cf. Thucydides 7.32.   [64] Cf. I 2.2.

[65] "Heart-Charming"; a cult-title of Hera at Athens, otherwise
a literary name used also by Aristaenetus and Nonnus.

ANTHIA AND HABROCOMES

καὶ ἡ Θελξινόη. καὶ τῇ πόλει παννυχίδος ἀγομένης
συνήλθομεν ἀλλήλοις, ἀμφοτέρους ὁδηγοῦντος θεοῦ,
καὶ ἀπηλαύσαμεν ὧν ἕνεκα συνήλθομεν. 6. καὶ χρόνῳ
τινὶ ἀλλήλοις συνῆμεν λανθάνοντες καὶ ὠμόσαμεν
ἀλλήλοις πολλάκις ἕξειν καὶ μέχρι θανάτου. ἐνεμέ-
σησε δέ τις ἄρα θεῶν. κἀγὼ μὲν ἔτι ἐν τοῖς ἐφήβοις
ἤμην, τὴν δὲ Θελξινόην ἐδίδοσαν πρὸς γάμον οἱ
πατέρες ἐπιχωρίῳ τινὶ νεανίσκῳ Ἀνδροκλεῖ τοὔνομα·
ἤδη δὲ αὐτῆς καὶ ἤρα ὁ Ἀνδροκλῆς. 7. τὰ μὲν οὖν
πρῶτα ἡ κόρη πολλὰς προφάσεις ἐποιεῖτο ἀναβαλ-
λομένη τὸν γάμον, τελευταῖον δὲ δυνηθεῖσα ἐν ταὐτῷ
μοι γενέσθαι συντίθεται νύκτωρ ἐξελθεῖν Λακεδαί-
μονος μετ' ἐμοῦ. καὶ δὴ ἐστείλαμεν ἑαυτοὺς νεανικῶς,
ἀπέκειρα δὲ καὶ τὴν κόμην τῆς Θελξινόης 8. ἐν αὐτῇ τῇ
τῶν γάμων νυκτί. ἐξελθόντες οὖν τῆς πόλεως ᾔειμεν
ἐπ' Ἄργος καὶ Κόρινθον κἀκεῖθεν ἀναγόμενοι ἐπλεύ-
σαμεν εἰς Σικελίαν. Λακεδαιμόνιοι δὲ πυθόμενοι τὴν
φυγὴν ἡμῶν θάνατον κατεψηφίσαντο. ἡμεῖς δὲ ἐνταῦθα διήγομεν ἀπορίᾳ μὲν τῶν ἐπιτηδείων, ἡδόμενοι
δὲ καὶ πάντων ἀπολαύειν δοκοῦντες ὅτι ἦμεν μετ'
ἀλλήλων. 9. καὶ τέθνηκεν ἐνταῦθα οὐ πρὸ πολλοῦ
Θελξινόη καὶ τὸ σῶμα οὐ τέθαπται, ἀλλὰ ἔχω γὰρ μετ'
ἐμαυτοῦ καὶ ἀεὶ φιλῶ καὶ σύνειμι." 10. καὶ ἅμα λέγων
εἰσάγει τὸν Ἀβροκόμην εἰς τὸ ἐνδότερον δωμάτιον καὶ
δεικνύει τὴν Θελξινόην γυναῖκα πρεσβῦτιν μὲν ἤδη,
καλὴν <δὲ>91 φαινομένην ἔτι Αἰγιαλεῖ κόρην· τὸ δὲ
σῶμα αὐτῆς ἐτέθαπτο ταφῇ Αἰγυπτίᾳ· ἦν γὰρ καὶ
τούτων ἔμπειρος ὁ γέρων. 11. "ταύτῃ οὖν" ἔφη, "ὦ
τέκνον Ἀβροκόμη, ἀεί τε ὡς ζώσῃ λαλῶ καὶ συγ-
κατάκειμαι καὶ συνευωχοῦμαι κἂν ἔλθω ποτὲ ἐκ τῆς
ἁλιείας κεκμηκὼς αὕτη με παραμυθεῖται βλεπομένη·

each other during a nightlong festival sponsored by the city, a god was guiding both of us, and we consummated what we desired when we met. 6. For a while we were together secretly, and again and again we pledged to remain together even unto death. But apparently some god was envious. I was still in the ephebes, and her parents betrothed Thelxinoe to a young Spartan named Androcles,[66] who was also now in love with her. 7. At first the girl made many excuses to postpone the wedding, until finally she managed to meet me and leave with me at night from Laconia. So we both dressed up as young men, and I also cut Thelxinoe's hair, 8. on the very night of the wedding. And so we left town for Argos and Corinth, and from there took a ship to Sicily. When the Spartans discovered our flight they condemned us to death. We had to struggle to make a living here, but we were happy and thought we enjoyed every advantage, since we had each other. 9. Thelxinoe died here not long ago and her body is not buried: I keep her with me and am always kissing her and being with her." 10. As he was speaking he took Habrocomes into the innermost bedroom and showed him Thelxinoe, now an old woman but in Aegialeus' eyes still a young girl. Her body was embalmed by the Egyptian method, for the old man was also experienced in this. 11. "And so, Habrocomes my boy," he said, "this way I can always talk to her as if she were alive, and lay with her and dine with her, and whenever I come home tired from fishing, the sight of her

66 A very common name, and one attested for the Peloponnese.

---

91 Hemsterhuys

οὐ γὰρ οἷα νῦν ὁρᾶται σοὶ τοιαύτη φαίνεται ἐμοί· ἀλλὰ
ἐννοῶ, τέκνον, οἷα μὲν ἦν ἐν Λακεδαίμονι, οἷα δὲ ἐν τῇ
φυγῇ· τὰς παννυχίδας ἐννοῶ, τὰς συνθήκας ἐννοῶ."
12. ἔτι λέγοντος τοῦ Αἰγιαλέως ἀνωδύρετο ὁ Ἁβροκόμης "σὲ δὲ" λέγων, "ὦ πασῶν δυστυχεστάτη κόρη,
πότε ἀνευρήσω κἂν νεκράν; Αἰγιαλεῖ μὲν γὰρ τοῦ βίου
μεγάλη παραμυθία τὸ σῶμα τὸ Θελξινόης καὶ νῦν
ἀληθῶς μεμάθηκα ὅτι ἔρως ἀληθινὸς ὅρον ἡλικίας οὐκ
ἔχει, 13. ἐγὼ δὲ πλανῶμαι μὲν κατὰ πᾶσαν γῆν καὶ
θάλασσαν, οὐ δεδύνημαι δὲ οὐδὲ ἀκοῦσαι περὶ σοῦ. ὦ
μαντεύματα δυστυχῆ. ὦ τὰ πάντων ἡμῖν Ἄπολλον
χρήσας χαλεπώτατα, οἴκτειρον ἤδη καὶ τὰ τέλη τῶν
μεμαντευμένων ἀπόδιδου."

2   Καὶ ὁ μὲν Ἁβροκόμης ταυτὶ κατοδυρόμενος παρα-
μυθουμένου αὐτὸν Αἰγιαλέως διῆγεν ἐν Συρακούσαις
ἤδη καὶ τῆς τέχνης Αἰγιαλεῖ κοινωνῶν, οἱ δὲ περὶ τὸν
Ἱππόθοον μέγα μὲν ἤδη τὸ λῃστήριον κατεστήσαντο,
ἔγνωσαν δὲ ἀπαίρειν Αἰθιοπίας καὶ μείζοσιν ἤδη
πράγμασιν ἐπιτίθεσθαι. 2. οὐ γὰρ ἐδόκει τῷ Ἱπποθόῳ
αὔταρκες εἶναι λῃστεύειν κατ᾽ ἄνδρα εἰ μὴ καὶ κώμαις
καὶ πόλεσιν ἐπιβάλοι. καὶ ὁ μὲν παραλαβὼν τοὺς σὺν
αὐτῷ καὶ ἐπιφορτισάμενος πάντα, ἦν δὲ αὐτῷ καὶ
ὑποζύγια πολλὰ καὶ κάμηλοι οὐκ ὀλίγαι, Αἰθιοπίαν
μὲν κατέλιπεν, ᾔει δὲ ἐπ᾽ Αἴγυπτόν τε καὶ Ἀλεξάνδρειαν καὶ ἐνενόει Φοινίκην καὶ Συρίαν <καταδρα-
μεῖν>[92] πάλιν· τὴν δὲ Ἀνθίαν προσεδόκα τεθνηκέναι·
3. ὁ δὲ Ἀμφίνομος ὁ φρουρῶν ἐν τῇ τάφρῳ αὐτὴν
ἐρωτικῶς διακείμενος οὐχ ὑπομένων ἀποσπασθῆναι

[92] O'Sullivan

326

comforts me, for the way you see her now is not the way I see her. My boy, I think of her as she was in Laconia, as she was when we eloped; I think of our festival, I think of our covenant."[67] 12. While Aegialeus was still speaking Habrocomes broke down. "And what about you," he cried, "most unfortunate girl of all? When will I find you again, even as a corpse? Thelxinoe's body is a great solace in the life of Aegialeus, and now I truly know that true love has no age limit. 13. But though I wander over every land and sea, I am unable even to get word of you. What unlucky prophecies! Apollo, who gave us the harshest of all oracles, take pity on us at last and bring your prophecies to their conclusion!"

And so Habrocomes lamented in this fashion, with   2
Aegialeus trying to console him, while he lived on in Syracuse and now took part in Aegialeus' trade. Meanwhile Hippothous' gang had now organized a large bandit force and planned to set out from Ethiopia and undertake bigger operations, 2. for Hippothous thought it unsatisfactory to be robbing individuals unless he also attacked villages and cities. So he rounded up his followers and packed everything for the trip; he had many pack animals and not a few camels. So he left Ethiopia behind and headed for Egypt and Alexandria, with thoughts of again ⟨ravaging⟩ Phoenicia and Syria. Anthia he presumed dead. 3. But Amphinomus was guarding her in the pit, amorously disposed, and loathe to be torn away from the girl because of

---

67 Cf. the models made for Admetus of his wife Alcestis and for Laodamea of her husband Protesilaus; their stories had been dramatized by Euripides. An actual instance was Nero's embalming of his wife, Poppaea, in 65 CE (Tacitus *Annals* 16.6).

τῆς κόρης διὰ τὴν πρὸς αὐτὴν φιλοστοργίαν καὶ τὴν
ἐπικειμένην συμφορὰν Ἱπποθόῳ μὲν οὐχ εἵπετο, λαν-
θάνει δὲ ἐν πολλοῖς τοῖς ἄλλοις καὶ ἀποκρύπτεται
ἐν ἄντρῳ τινὶ σὺν τοῖς ἐπιτηδείοις οἷς συνελέξατο.
4. νυκτὸς δὲ γενομένης οἱ περὶ τὸν Ἱππόθοον ἐπὶ
κώμην ἐληλύθεσαν τῆς Αἰγύπτου, Ἀρείαν[93] καλουμένην, πορθῆσαι θέλοντες, ὁ δὲ Ἀμφίνομος ἀνορύσσει
τὴν τάφρον καὶ ἐξάγει τὴν Ἀνθίαν καὶ θαρρεῖν παρεκάλει. 5. τῆς δὲ ἔτι φοβουμένης καὶ ὑποπτευούσης
τὸν ἥλιον ἐπόμνυσι <καὶ>[94] τοὺς ἐν Αἰγύπτῳ θεοὺς ἦ
μὴν[95] τηρήσειν γάμων ἁγνὴν μέχρι<ς>[96] ἂν καὶ αὐτή
ποτε πεισθεῖσα θελήσῃ συγκαταθέσθαι. πείθεται τοῖς
ὅρκοις Ἀμφινόμου Ἀνθία καὶ ἔπεται αὐτῷ· οὐκ ἀπελεί-
ποντο δὲ οἱ κύνες ἀλλ' ἔστεργον συνήθεις γενόμενοι.
6. ἔρχονται δὴ εἰς Κοπτὸν κἀνταῦθα ἔγνωσαν ἡμέρας
διαγαγεῖν μέχρις ἂν προέλθωσιν οἱ περὶ τὸν Ἱππόθοον τῆς ὁδοῦ. ἐπεμελοῦντο δὲ τῶν κυνῶν ὡς ἔχοιεν τὰ
ἐπιτήδεια. 7. οἱ δὲ περὶ τὸν Ἱππόθοον προσβαλόντες
τῇ κώμῃ τῇ Ἀρείᾳ πολλοὺς μὲν τῶν ἐνοικούντων
ἀπέκτειναν καὶ τὰ οἰκήματα ἐνέπρησαν καὶ κατῇεσαν
οὐ τὴν αὐτὴν ὁδὸν ἀλλὰ διὰ τοῦ Νείλου· πάντα γὰρ τὰ
ἐκ τῶν μεταξὺ κωμῶν σκάφη συλλεξάμενοι ἐπιβάντες
ἔπλεον ἐπὶ Σχεδίαν καὶ <Ἑρμούπολιν>[97] κἀντεῦθεν
ἐκβάντες παρὰ τὰς ὄχθας τοῦ Νείλου διώδευον τὴν
ἄλλην Αἴγυπτον.

3   Ἐν τούτῳ δὲ ὁ ἄρχων τῆς Αἰγύπτου ἐπέπυστο μὲν
τὰ περὶ τὴν Ἀρείαν καὶ τὸ Ἱπποθόου ληστήριον καὶ
ὅτι ἀπ' Αἰθιοπίας ἔρχονται, παρασκευάσας δὲ στρα-

---

93 Hemsterhuys, ut infra: ἄρειον   94 Locella
95 ἦ μὴν Abresch, cf. 2.9.4: σεμνὴν   96 Brunck
97 Hemsterhuys, cf. 4.1.3: spatium 6–7 litt. reliquit F

his tender affection for her and her dangerous situation, so he did not follow Hippothous but lost himself among the rest of the large gang and hid out in a cave with the provisions he had amassed. 4. After nightfall Hippothous' gang arrived in an Egyptian village called Areia,[68] which they wanted to plunder, while Amphinomus was excavating the pit, removing Anthia, and urging her to take heart. 5. But since she was still fearful and mistrustful, he swore by the sun and the gods of Egypt that he would surely keep her pure of intimacies until she herself was ready to consent willingly. Anthia trusted Amphinomus' oaths and followed him, nor were the dogs left behind but were happy to become their companions. 6. And so they went to Coptus and decided to spend a few days there until Hippothous' gang had gone farther ahead on the road, and they took care that the dogs had what they needed. 7. Meanwhile Hippothous' gang struck the village of Areia and killed many of the inhabitants, burned their houses, and moved out not by the same route but on the Nile, for they collected all the boats from the intervening villages, got aboard them, and sailed for Schedia and ‹Hermupolis›, and disembarking there they continued their journey through the rest of Egypt by the banks of the Nile.

In the meantime the prefect of Egypt had been informed of the events around Areia and of Hippothous' bandit gang, and that they were on the move from Ethio-

3

---

68   Otherwise unknown; perhaps X. has misplaced the Parthian region of Ar(e)ia, whose capital was another city named Alexandria.

τιώτας πολλοὺς καὶ ἄρχοντα τούτοις ἐπιστήσας τῶν
συγγενῶν τῶν αὑτοῦ Πολύιδον, νεανίσκον ὀφθῆναι
χαρίεντα, δρᾶσαι γεννικόν, ἔπεμψεν ἐπὶ τοὺς λῃστάς.
2. οὗτος ὁ Πολύιδος παραλαβὼν τὸ στράτευμα ἀπήν-
τα κατὰ Πηλούσιον τοῖς περὶ τὸν Ἱππόθοον καὶ εὐθὺς
παρὰ τὰς ὄχθας μάχη τε αὐτῶν γίνεται καὶ πίπτουσιν
ἑκατέρων πολλοί, νυκτὸς δὲ ἐπιγενομένης τρέπονται
μὲν οἱ λῃσταὶ καὶ πάντες ὑπὸ τῶν στρατιωτῶν φονεύ-
ονται, εἰσὶ δὲ οἳ καὶ ζῶντες ἐλήφθησαν. 3. Ἱππόθοος
μόνος ἀπορρίψας τὰ ὅπλα ἔφυγε τῆς νυκτὸς καὶ ἦλθεν
εἰς Ἀλεξάνδρειαν κἀκεῖθεν δυνηθεὶς λαθεῖν ἐπιβὰς
ἀναγομένῳ πλοίῳ ἐπανήχθη. ἦν δὲ αὐτῷ ἡ πᾶσα ἐπὶ
Σικελίαν ὁρμή· ἐκεῖ γὰρ ἐδόκει μάλιστα διαλήσεσθαί
τε καὶ διατραφήσεσθαι· ἤκουε δὲ τὴν νῆσον εἶναι
μεγάλην τε καὶ εὐδαίμονα.

4   Ὁ δὲ Πολύιδος οὐχ ἱκανὸν εἶναι ἐνόμισε κρατῆσαι
τῶν συμβαλόντων λῃστῶν ἀλλ᾽ ἔγνω δεῖν ἀνερευ-
νῆσαί τε καὶ ἐκκαθᾶραι τὴν Αἴγυπτον εἴ που ἢ τὸν
Ἱππόθοον ἢ τῶν σὺν αὐτῷ τινα ἀνεύροι. 2. παραλαβὼν
οὖν μέρος τι τοῦ στρατιωτικοῦ καὶ τοὺς εἰλημμένους
τῶν λῃστῶν ἵν᾽ εἴ τις φαίνοιτο οἱ μηνύσειεν⟩[98] ἀνέ-
πλει τὸν Νεῖλον καὶ τὰς πόλεις διηρεύνα καὶ ἐνενόει
μέχρις Αἰθιοπίας ἐλθεῖν. 3. ἔρχονται δὴ καὶ εἰς
Κοπτὸν ἔνθα ἦν Ἀνθία μετὰ Ἀμφινόμου. καὶ αὐτὴ μὲν
ἔτυχεν ἐπὶ τῆς οἰκίας, τὸν δὲ Ἀμφίνομον γνωρίζουσιν
οἱ τῶν λῃστῶν εἰλημμένοι καὶ λέγουσι τῷ Πολύιδῳ,
καὶ Ἀμφίνομος λαμβάνεται καὶ ἀνακρινόμενος τὰ
περὶ τὴν Ἀνθίαν διηγεῖται. 4. ὁ δὲ ἀκούσας κελεύει καὶ
αὐτὴν ἄγεσθαι καὶ ἐλθούσης ἀνεπυνθάνετο ἥτις εἴη
καὶ πόθεν. ἡ δὲ τῶν μὲν ἀληθῶν οὐδὲν λέγει, ὅτι δὲ

[98] Hemsterhuys

pia, so he readied a large number of soldiers, appointed as their leader one of his own kinsmen, Polyidus,[69] a young man fair to behold and lusty in action, and dispatched them against the bandits. 2. This Polyidus took his army and met Hippothous' forces at Pelusium, where at once battle was joined along the riverbanks and there were many casualties on both sides. At nightfall the bandits were routed and all were killed by the soldiers, though some were taken alive. 3. Only Hippothous threw away his weapons, fled during the night, and went to Alexandria, where he was able to stay out of sight, board a ship that was just departing, and sail away. His whole effort was focused on reaching Sicily: there he expected most easily to escape detection and make his living, for he had heard that the island was large and prosperous.

Polyidus did not consider it enough to defeat the bandits in an engagement but decided that he should also launch a thorough investigation and purge of Egypt, in hope of locating either Hippothous or any of his followers. 2. So he took a detachment of his army and the captured bandits, so that they would let him know in case any turned up, and set sail up the Nile, searched through the cities, and planned to go as far as Ethiopia. 3. And so they arrived in Coptus where Anthia was staying with Amphinomus. She happened to be in the house, but the captured bandits recognized Amphinomus and told Polyidus. Amphinomus was captured and under interrogation told them about Anthia. At this news he gave orders for Anthia to be produced, and when she arrived he questioned her closely about who she was and where from. In reply she spoke not

4

<hr />

[69] "Seeing Much," a mythical and actual name.

Αἰγυπτία εἴη καὶ ὑπὸ τῶν λῃστῶν εἴληπτο. 5. ἐν τούτῳ
ἐρᾷ καὶ ὁ Πολύιδος Ἀνθίας ἔρωτα σφοδρόν, ἦν δὲ
αὐτῷ ἐν Ἀλεξανδρείᾳ γυνή[99], ἐρασθεὶς δὲ τὰ μὲν
πρῶτα ἐπειρᾶτο πείθειν μεγάλα ὑπισχνούμενος, τελευταῖον δὲ κατῄεσαν εἰς Ἀλεξάνδρειαν, ὡς δὲ ἐγένοντο
ἐν Μέμφει ἐπεχείρησεν ὁ Πολύιδος βιάζεσθαι τὴν
Ἀνθίαν. 6. ἡ δὲ ἐκφυγεῖν δυνηθεῖσα ἐπὶ τὸ τῆς Ἴσιδος
ἱερὸν ἔρχεται <καὶ>[100] ἱκέτις γενομένη "σύ με" εἶπεν,
"ὦ δέσποινα Αἰγύπτου, πάλιν σῶσον ᾗ ἐβοήθησας
πολλάκις· φεισάσθω μου καὶ Πολύιδος τῆς διὰ σὲ
σώφρονος Ἁβροκόμῃ τηρουμένης." 7. ὁ δὲ Πολύιδος
ἅμα μὲν τὴν θεὸν ἐδεδοίκει, ἅμα δὲ ἤρα τῆς Ἀνθίας καὶ
τῆς τύχης αὐτὴν ἠλέει. πρόσεισι δὲ τῷ ἱερῷ μόνος καὶ
ὄμνυσι μήποτε βιάσασθαι τὴν Ἀνθίαν μήτε ὑβρίσαι
τι εἰς αὐτὴν ἀλλὰ τηρῆσαι ἁγνὴν ἐς ὅσον αὐτὴ θελή-
σει· αὔταρκες γὰρ αὐτῷ φιλοῦντι ἐδόκει εἶναι κἂν
βλέπειν μόνον καὶ λαλεῖν αὐτῇ. 8. ἐπείσθη τοῖς ὅρκοις
ἡ Ἀνθία καὶ κατῆλθεν ἐκ τοῦ ἱεροῦ. καὶ ἐπειδὴ ἔγνωσαν ἡμέραις τρισὶν αὐτοὺς ἀναλαβεῖν ἐν Μέμφει
ἔρχεται ἡ Ἀνθία εἰς τὸ τοῦ Ἄπιδος ἱερόν. διασημ-
μότατον δὲ τοῦτο ἐν Αἰγύπτῳ καὶ ὁ θεὸς τοῖς βουλο-
μένοις μαντεύει· 9. ἐπειδὰν γάρ τις προσελθὼν εὔξηται
καὶ δεηθῇ τοῦ θεοῦ αὐτὸς μὲν ἔξεισιν, οἱ δὲ πρὸ τοῦ
νεὼ παῖδες Αἰγύπτιοι ἃ μὲν καταλογάδην, ἃ δὲ ἐν
μέτρῳ προλέγουσι τῶν ἐσομένων ἕκαστα. 10. ἐλθοῦσα
δὴ καὶ ἡ Ἀνθία προσπίπτει τῷ Ἄπιδι. "ὦ θεῶν" ἔφη
"φιλανθρωπότατε, ὁ πάντας οἰκτείρων ξένους, ἐλέησον
κἀμὲ τὴν κακοδαίμονα καί μοι μαντείαν ἀληθῆ περὶ

---

[99] Ed. Cocchiana: συγγενής   [100] Locella

[70] Apis was a sacred bull well-known in the Greco-Roman

a word of truth but claimed to be an Egyptian captured by the bandits. 5. At this point Polyidus too began to feel a strong lust for Anthia, though he had a wife in Alexandria. In his lust he first tried to seduce her with great promises, but in the end they continued the journey down to Alexandria, and when they reached Memphis Polyidus tried to force Anthia. 6. She managed to escape, went to the temple of Isis, and became a suppliant. "Mistress of Egypt," she said, "who time and again have assisted me, please be my savior once more. Let Polyidus too spare me, as with your help I keep myself chaste for Habrocomes." 7. Polyidus at once respected the goddess, lusted for Anthia, and pitied her misfortune. He went to the temple alone and swore never to force Anthia or do her any violence but rather to keep her pure as long as she herself wished, for in his affection he considered it enough simply to look at her and talk with her. 8. Anthia, convinced by these avowals, came out of the temple, and when they decided to rest in Memphis for three days, Anthia went to the temple of Apis.[70] This temple was the most eminent in Egypt, and the god gave prophecies to those wanting them: 9. anyone who comes, prays, and makes an enquiry to the god, he emerges and the Egyptian boys in front of the temple foretell what the future holds in each case, sometimes in prose and sometimes in verse. 10. And so Anthia came and fell before Apis. "Most humane of gods," she said, "who show mercy to all strangers, take pity on me as well, an unlucky woman, and pronounce me a true prophecy about Habro-

world, where he had been naturalized in the Ptolemaic era as Serapis. For his oracular properties cf. Strabo 17.1.31–2, Aelian *NA* 11.10.

Ἀβροκόμου πρόειπε. 11. εἰ μὲν γὰρ αὐτὸν ἔτι ὄψομαι
καὶ ἄνδρα λήψομαι καὶ μενῶ καὶ ζήσομαι· εἰ δὲ ἐκεῖνος
τέθνηκεν ἀπαλλαγῆναι κἀμὲ καλῶς ἔχει τοῦ πονηροῦ
τούτου βίου." εἰποῦσα καὶ καταδακρύσασα ἐξῄει τοῦ
ἱεροῦ. κἂν τούτῳ οἱ παῖδες πρὸ τοῦ τεμένους παίζοντες
ἅμα ἐξεβόησαν·

Ἀνθία Ἀβροκόμην ταχὺ λήψεται ἄνδρα τὸν
αὐτῆς.

ἀκούσασα εὐθυμοτέρα ἐγένετο καὶ προσεύχεται τοῖς
θεοῖς. καὶ ἅμα μὲν ἀπῄεσαν εἰς Ἀλεξάνδρειαν.

5   Ἐπέπυστο δὲ ἡ Πολυίδου γυνὴ ὅτι ἄγει κόρην
ἐρωμένην καὶ φοβηθεῖσα μή πως αὐτὴ ἡ ξένη παρευ-
δοκιμήσῃ Πολυίδῳ μὲν οὐδὲν λέγει, ἐβουλεύετο δὲ
καθ' αὑτὴν ὅπως τιμωρήσηται τὴν δοκοῦσαν ἐπιβου-
λεύειν τοῖς γάμοις. 2. καὶ δὴ ὁ μὲν Πολύιδος ἀπήγ-
γελλέ τε τῷ ἄρχοντι τῆς Αἰγύπτου τὰ γενόμενα καὶ τὰ
λοιπὰ ἐπὶ τοῦ στρατοπέδου διῴκει τὰ τῆς ἀρχῆς,
ἀπόντος δὲ αὐτοῦ Ῥηναία, τοῦτο γὰρ ἐκαλεῖτο ἡ τοῦ
Πολυίδου γυνή, μεταπέμπεται τὴν Ἀνθίαν, ἣν δὲ ἐπὶ
τῆς οἰκίας, καὶ περιρρήγνυσι τὴν ἐσθῆτα καὶ αἰκίζεται
τὸ σῶμα 3. "ὦ πονηρὰ" λέγουσα "καὶ τῶν γάμων τῶν
ἐμῶν ἐπίβουλε, ματαίως ἔδοξας Πολυίδῳ καλή, οὐ γάρ
σε ὀνήσει τὸ κάλλος τοῦτο. ἴσως μὲν γὰρ πείθειν
λῃστὰς ἐδύνασο καὶ συγκαθεύδειν νεανίσκοις μεθύ-
ουσι πολλοῖς· τὴν[101] δὲ Ῥηναίας εὐνὴν οὔποτε ὑβρί-
σεις χαίρουσα." 4. ταῦτα εἰποῦσα ἀπέκειρε τὴν κόμην
αὐτῆς καὶ δεσμὰ περιτίθησι καὶ παραδοῦσα οἰκέτῃ

---

101 Palairet: τῆς

---

71 A ritual detail, cf. Aelian l.c.

comes. For if I am to see him again and recover him as my husband, I will remain among the living, but if he is dead, then it is well that I too take leave of this miserable life." With this tearful prayer she left the temple, whereupon the boys in front frolicked[71] as they cried out

> Anthia soon will recover Habrocomes, her very own
> husband.

Her spirits rose when she heard this, and she said a prayer to the gods. And with that they left for Alexandria.

Polyidus' wife found out that he was bringing home a 5 girlfriend and feared that this foreign girl might somehow surpass her in favor. So she said nothing to Polyidus but devised her own plot to take revenge on the girl who seemed to have designs on her marriage. 2. Polyidus was busy making his expeditionary report to the prefect of Egypt and in his camp carrying out other duties as commander, and in his absence Rhenaea,[72] for this was what Polyidus' wife was called, sent for Anthia, who was in the house, tore off her clothes, and abused her body. 3. "Wicked girl," she said, "with designs on my marriage, you attracted Polyidus in vain, because this beauty of yours will get you nothing. Maybe you could seduce bandits and sleep with a lot of drunken boys, but you will never get away with violating Rhenaea's bed!" 4. With this she cut off her hair, put her in chains, handed her over to a trusty servant, Clytus[73]

---

[72] An uninhabited island (var. Rheneia) just west of, and serving as an unpurified annex for, Delos (cf. Herodotus 6.97, Thucydides 3.104, Strabo 10.5.5), not otherwise attested as a personal name.   [73] "Renowned", attested (though in the form Κλύτος) as a personal name.

τινὶ πιστῷ, Κλυτῷ τοὔνομα, κελεύει ἐμβιβάσαντα εἰς
ναῦν ἀπαγαγόντα εἰς Ἰταλίαν ἀποδόσθαι πορνο-
βοσκῷ τὴν Ἀνθίαν. "οὕτω γὰρ" ἔφη "δυνήσῃ ἡ καλὴ
τῆς ἀκρασίας κόρον λαβεῖν." 5. ἤγετο δὲ ἡ Ἀνθία ὑπὸ
τοῦ Κλυτοῦ κλαίουσα καὶ ὀδυρομένη "ὦ κάλλος ἐπίβουλον" λέγουσα, "ὦ δυστυχὴς εὐμορφία, τί μοι
παραμένετε ἐνοχλοῦντα; τί δὲ αἴτια πολλῶν κακῶν μοι
γίνεσθε; οὐκ ἤρκουν οἱ τάφοι, οἱ φόνοι, τὰ δεσμά, τὰ
λῃστήρια, ἀλλ᾽ ἤδη καὶ ἐπὶ οἰκήματος στήσομαι καὶ
τὴν μέχρι νῦν Ἁβροκόμῃ τηρουμένην σωφροσύνην
πορνοβοσκὸς ἀναγκάσει με λύειν; 6. ἀλλ᾽, ὦ δέσποτα," προσπεσοῦσα ἔλεγε τοῖς γόνασι τοῦ Κλυτοῦ, "μή
με ἐπ᾽ ἐκείνην τὴν τιμωρίαν [ἅμα]¹⁰² προαγάγῃς ἀλλὰ
ἀπόκτεινόν με αὐτός· οὐκ οἴσω πορνοβοσκὸν δεσπό-
την· σωφρονεῖν, πίστευσον, εἰθίσμεθα." ταῦτα ἐδεῖτο,
ἠλέει δὲ αὐτὴν ὁ Κλυτός. 7. καὶ ἡ μὲν ἀπήγετο εἰς
Ἰταλίαν, ἡ δὲ Ῥηναία ἐλθόντι τῷ Πολυίδῳ λέγει ὅτι
ἀπέδρα ἡ Ἀνθία κἀκεῖνος ἐκ τῶν ἤδη πεπραγμένων
ἐπίστευσεν αὐτῇ. ἡ δὲ Ἀνθία κατήχθη μὲν εἰς Τάραντα, πόλιν τῆς Ἰταλίας, ἐνταῦθα δὲ ὁ Κλυτὸς δεδοικὼς
τὰς τῆς Ῥηναίας ἐντολὰς ἀποδίδοται αὐτὴν πορνο-
βοσκῷ. 8. ὁ δὲ ἰδὼν κάλλος οἷον οὔπω πρότερον
ἐτεθέατο μέγα κέρδος ἕξειν τὴν παῖδα ἐνόμιζε καὶ
ἡμέραις μέν τισιν αὐτὴν ἀνελάμβανεν ἐκ τοῦ πλοῦ
κεκμηκυῖαν καὶ ἐκ τῶν ὑπὸ τῆς Ῥηναίας βασάνων, ὁ
δὲ Κλυτὸς ἧκεν εἰς Ἀλεξάνδρειαν καὶ τὰ πραχθέντα
ἐμήνυσε τῇ Ῥηναίᾳ.

6   Ὁ δὲ Ἱππόθοος διανύσας τὸν πλοῦν κατήχθη μὲν
εἰς Σικελίαν, οὐκ εἰς Συρακούσας δὲ ἀλλ᾽ εἰς Ταυ-
ρομένιον καὶ ἐζήτει καιρὸν δι᾽ οὗ τὰ ἐπιτήδεια ἕξει. τῷ

¹⁰² Hercher

by name, and told him to put Anthia aboard a ship, take
her to Italy, and sell her to a pimp. "That way, my beauty"
she said, "you will be able to satisfy your insatiable lust."
5. Anthia was led away by Clytus in tearful lamentation.
"Treacherous beauty!" she cried, "Good looks that bring
only bad luck! Why do you stay and bother me? Why are
you the cause of so much trouble for me? Were the burials,
the murders, the chains, the banditry not enough? Must I
now be on display in front of a whorehouse, and will a pimp
force me to give up the faithfulness that until now I have
kept for Habrocomes? 6. No, master," she said, falling at
Clytus' knees, "please don't present me for that kind of
punishment but kill me yourself! I will not endure a pimp
for a master: believe me, I have always been virtuous!"
This was her plea, and Clytus felt pity for her. 7. While she
was being borne away to Italy, Rhenaea told Polyidus on
his return that Anthia had run off, and judging by the previous incidents he believed her. Anthia was taken to Tarentum, a city in Italy, where Clytus, anxious about Rhenaea's
orders, sold her to a pimp. 8. When he set eyes on such
beauty as he had never before beheld, he reckoned the
girl would make him a big profit, so for a few days he let her
recover from the exhaustion of the voyage and Rhenaea's
torments. Clytus returned to Alexandria and informed
Rhenaea what had been done.

Hippothous completed his voyage and put in to Sicily,   6
not at Syracuse but at Tauromenium,[74] and started seeking
an opportunity to provide for his needs. As for Habro-

---

[74] Modern Taormina, in eastern Sicily, a flourishing city during the early and middle empire.

δὲ Ἀβροκόμη ἐν Συρακούσαις, ὡς χρόνος πολὺς ἐγένετο, ἀθυμία ἐμπίπτει καὶ ἀπορία δεινὴ ὅτι μηδὲ Ἀνθίαν εὑρίσκοι μηδὲ εἰς τὴν πατρίδα ἀνασῴζοιτο. 2. διέγνω οὖν ἀποπλεύσας ἐκ Σικελίας εἰς Ἰταλίαν ἀνελθεῖν κἀκεῖθεν, εἰ μηδὲν εὑρίσκοι τῶν ζητουμένων, εἰς Ἔφεσον πλεῦσαι πλοῦν δυστυχῆ. ἤδη δὲ καὶ οἱ γονεῖς αὐτῶν καὶ οἱ Ἐφέσιοι πάντες ἐν πολλῷ πένθει ἦσαν οὔτε ἀγγέλου παρ᾽ αὐτῶν ἀφιγμένου οὔτε γραμμάτων, ἀπέπεμπον δὲ πανταχοῦ τοὺς ἀναζητήσοντας. 3. ὑπὸ ἀθυμίας δὲ καὶ γήρως οὐ δυνηθέντες ἀντισχεῖν οἱ γονεῖς ἑκατέρων ἑαυτοὺς ἐξήγαγον τοῦ βίου. καὶ ὁ μὲν Ἀβροκόμης ᾔει τὴν ἐπὶ Ἰταλίας ὁδόν, ὁ δὲ Λεύκων καὶ ἡ Ῥόδη, οἱ σύντροφοι τοῦ Ἀβροκόμου καὶ τῆς Ἀνθίας, τεθνηκότος αὐτοῖς ἐν Ξάνθῳ τοῦ δεσπότου καὶ τὸν κλῆρον, ἦν δὲ πολύς, ἐκείνοις καταλιπόντος διέγνωσαν εἰς Ἔφεσον πλεῖν, ὡς ἤδη μὲν αὐτοῖς τῶν δεσποτῶν σεσωσμένων, ἱκανῶς δὲ τῆς κατὰ τὴν ἀποδημίαν συμφορᾶς πεπειραμένοι[103]. 4. ἐνθέμενοι δὴ πάντα τὰ αὐτῶν νηὶ ἀνήγοντο εἰς Ἔφεσον καὶ ἡμέραις τε οὐ πολλαῖς διανύσαντες τὸν πλοῦν ἧκον εἰς Ῥόδον κἀκεῖ μαθόντες ὅτι οὐδέπω μὲν Ἀβροκόμης καὶ Ἀνθία σῴζοιντο, τεθνήκασι δὲ αὐτῶν οἱ πατέρες, διέγνωσαν εἰς Ἔφεσον μὴ κατελθεῖν, χρόνῳ δέ τινι ἐκεῖ γενέσθαι μέχρις οὗ τι περὶ τῶν δεσποτῶν πύθωνται.

7   Ὁ δὲ πορνοβοσκὸς ὁ τὴν Ἀνθίαν ὠνησάμενος χρόνου διελθόντος ἠνάγκασεν αὐτὴν οἰκήματος προεστάναι. καὶ δὴ κοσμήσας καλῇ μὲν ἐσθῆτι, πολλῷ δὲ χρυσῷ ἦγεν ὡς προστησομένην τέγους. ἡ δὲ μεγάλα ἀνακωκύσασα 2. "φεῦ μοι τῶν κακῶν" εἶπεν, "οὐχ ἱκαναὶ γὰρ αἱ πρότερον συμφοραί, τὰ δεσμά, τὰ λῃστήρια, ἀλλ᾽ ἔτι καὶ πορνεύειν ἀναγκάζομαι. ὦ κάλλος δικαίως ὑβρισμένον· τί γὰρ ἡμῖν ἀκαίρως

comes in Syracuse, after a long time had passed he was afflicted by terrible discouragement and despair, because he could neither find Anthia nor regain his homeland. 2. So he decided to sail from Sicily and go up to Italy and from there, should he succeed in none of his quests, to make an emptyhanded voyage back to Ephesus. By now their parents and all the Ephesians were very sorrowful, since from them no messenger had come and no letters, but still they dispatched people to search for them everywhere. 3. Through loss of spirit and old age, each one's parents were unable to hold out and released themselves from life. Habrocomes was on his way to Italy, while Leuco and Rhoda, the companions of Habrocomes and Anthia, decided to sail back to Ephesus after their master had died in Xanthus and left them his estate, a large one. They thought that their masters were safely home, and they had had enough of the complications of life abroad. 4. They put all their belongings on a ship and sailed for Ephesus, completing the voyage to Rhodes in only a few days. When they learned there that Habrocomes and Anthia had not yet come safely home and that their parents were dead, they decided not to return to Ephesus but to stay where they were for a while, pending some news of their masters.

In due course the pimp who had bought Anthia made 7 her display herself in front of the whorehouse. He dressed her up in a beautiful costume and lots of gold and took her to her spot outside a stall. But she raised a loud wail: "What troubles are mine!" she cried, "Are my previous predicaments not enough, the chains, the banditry? Must I now be a whore as well? Beauty of mine, you are justly violated, for

---

103 πεπειραμένων Bürger

παραμένεις; ἀλλὰ τί ταῦτα θρηνῶ καὶ οὐχ εὑρίσκω
τινὰ μηχανὴν δι᾽ ἧς φυλάξω τὴν μέχρι νῦν σωφροσύνην τετηρημένην;" 3. ταῦτα λέγουσα ἤγετο ἐπὶ τὸ
οἴκημα τοῦ πορνοβοσκοῦ τὰ μὲν δεομένου θαρρεῖν, τὰ
δὲ ἀπειλοῦντος. ὡς δὲ ἦλθε καὶ προέστη πλῆθος ἐπέρρει τῶν τεθαυμακότων τὸ κάλλος, οἱ δὲ πολλοὶ ἦσαν
ἕτοιμοι ἀργύριον κατατίθεσθαι τῆς ἐπιθυμίας. 4. ἡ δὲ
ἐν ἀμηχάνῳ γενομένη κακῷ εὑρίσκει τέχνην ἀπο-
φυγῆς· πίπτει μὲν γὰρ εἰς γῆν καὶ παρεῖται τὸ σῶμα
καὶ ἐμιμεῖτο τοὺς νοσοῦντας τὴν ἐκ θεῶν καλουμένην
νόσον, ἦν δὲ τῶν παρόντων ἔλεος ἅμα καὶ φόβος καὶ
τοῦ μὲν ἐπιθυμεῖν συνουσίας ἀπείχοντο, ἐθεράπευον
δὲ τὴν Ἀνθίαν· 5. ὁ δὲ πορνοβοσκὸς συνεὶς οἷ κακῶν
ἐγεγόνει καὶ νομίσας ἀληθῶς νοσεῖν τὴν κόρην
ἦγεν[104] εἰς τὴν οἰκίαν καὶ κατέκλινέ τε καὶ ἐθεράπευε
καὶ ὡς ἔδοξεν αὐτῆς γεγονέναι ἀνεπυνθάνετο τὴν
αἰτίαν τῆς νόσου. 6. ἡ δὲ Ἀνθία "καὶ πρότερον" ἔφη,
"δέσποτα, εἰπεῖν πρὸς σὲ ἐβουλόμην τὴν συμφορὰν
τὴν ἐμὴν καὶ διηγήσασθαι τὰ συμβάντα, ἀλλὰ ἀπ-
έκρυπτον αἰδουμένη. νυνὶ δὲ οὐδὲν χαλεπὸν εἰπεῖν
πρὸς σὲ πάντα ἤδη μεμαθηκότα τὰ κατ᾽ ἐμέ. 7. παῖς
ἔτι οὖσα ἐν ἑορτῇ καὶ παννυχίδι ἀποπλανηθεῖσα τῶν
ἐμαυτῆς ἧκον πρός τινα τάφον ἀνδρὸς νεωστὶ τεθνηκότος κἀνταῦθα ἐφάνη μοί τις ἀναθορὼν ἐκ τοῦ τάφου
καὶ κατέχειν ἐπειρᾶτο, ἐγὼ δ᾽ ἀπέφ<ε>υγον[105] καὶ
ἐβόων. 8. ὁ δὲ ἄνθρωπος ἦν μὲν ὀφθῆναι φοβερός,
φωνὴν δὲ πολὺ εἶχε χαλεπωτέραν. καὶ τέλος ἡμέρα
μὲν ἤδη ἐγίνετο, ἀφεὶς δέ με ἔπληξέ τε κατὰ τοῦ
στήθους καὶ νόσον ταύτην ἔλεγεν ἐμβεβληκέναι. 9.
ἐκεῖθεν ἀρξαμένη ἄλλοτε ἄλλως ὑπὸ τῆς συμφορᾶς

[104] Hemsterhuys: ἧκεν   [105] Hercher

why do you stay with me to my disadvantage? But why am I making these laments instead of finding some way to safeguard the virtue I have preserved until now?" 3. As she spoke she was taken to the whorehouse, the pimp alternately asking her to cheer up and making threats. When she got there and took her position out front, a crowd of men streamed over, marvelling at her beauty and many of them ready to lay out money for what they wanted. 4. But in her impossible predicament she found a means of escape: she fell to the ground, let her body go limp, and imitated the victims of the so-called sacred disease. Those present felt pity and fear, let go their desire for sex and tried to take care of Anthia. 5. The pimp, realizing what a mess he was in and thinking that the girl was truly sick, took her to his house, lay her down, and tried to treat her, and when she seemed to be herself again he questioned her about the nature of her sickness. 6. Anthia replied, "Master, I have been meaning to tell you about this condition of mine and to explain the circumstances, but I concealed it out of shame. But as it stands, there is no difficulty in telling you, since by now you know everything there is to know about me. 7. When I was still a girl, I wandered away from my friends during a nightlong festival and came upon the grave of a man recently deceased, and there someone appeared to leap up from the grave and started grabbing me. I tried to run away and screamed. 8. This being was frightening to behold and had a voice that was much worse. When daylight finally came, he let me go but hit me on the chest and said that he had cast this disease into me. From that time onward I have suffered from this condition

ANTHIA AND HABROCOMES

κατέχομαι. ἀλλὰ δέομαί σου, δέσποτα, μηδέν μοι
χαλεπήνῃς· οὐ γὰρ ἐγὼ τούτων αἰτία. δυνήσῃ γάρ με
ἀποδόσθαι καὶ μηδὲν ἀπολέσαι τῆς δοθείσης τιμῆς."
ἀκούσας ὁ πορνοβοσκὸς ἠνιᾶτο μέν, συνεγίνωσκε δὲ
αὐτῇ, ὡς οὐχ ἑκούσῃ ταῦτα πασχούσῃ.

8   Καὶ ἡ μὲν ἐθεραπεύετο ὡς νοσοῦσα παρὰ τῷ πορνο-
βοσκῷ, ὁ δὲ Ἁβροκόμης ἀπὸ τῆς Σικελίας ἐπαναχθεὶς
καταίρει μὲν εἰς Νουκέριον[106] τῆς Ἰταλίας, ἀπορίᾳ δὲ
τῶν ἐπιτηδείων ἀμηχανῶν ὅ τι ποιήσει τὰ μὲν πρῶτα
περιῄει τὴν Ἀνθίαν ζητῶν· 2. αὕτη γὰρ ἦν αὐτῷ τοῦ
βίου παντὸς καὶ τῆς πλάνης ἡ ὑπόθεσις· ὡς δὲ οὐδὲν
ηὕρισκεν, ἦν γὰρ ἐν Τάραντι ἡ κόρη παρὰ τῷ πορνο-
βοσκῷ, αὐτὸν ἀπεμίσθωσε τοῖς τοὺς λίθους ἐργα-
ζομένοις. 3. καὶ ἦν αὐτῷ τὸ ἔργον ἐπίπονον· οὐ γὰρ
συνείθιστο τὸ σῶμα οὐδ᾽ ὀλίγον[107] ὑποβάλλειν ἔργοις
εὐτόνοις ἢ σκληροῖς· διέκειτο δὲ πονήρως καὶ πολλάκις κατοδυρόμενος τὴν αὑτοῦ τύχην "ἰδοὺ" φησιν
"Ἀνθία, ὁ σὸς Ἁβροκόμης ἐργάτης τέχνης πονηρᾶς
καὶ τὸ σῶμα ὑποτέθεικα δουλείᾳ. 4. καὶ εἰ μὲν εἶχόν
τινα ἐλπίδα εὑρήσειν σε καὶ τοῦ λοιποῦ συγκατα-
βιώσεσθαι, τοῦτο ⟨ἂν⟩[108] πάντων ἄμεινόν με παρεμυ-
θεῖτο· νυνὶ δὲ ἴσως κἀγὼ δυστυχὴς εἰς κενὰ καὶ
ἀνόνητα πονῶ καὶ σύ που τέθνηκας πόθῳ τῷ πρὸς
Ἁβροκόμην. πέπεισμαι γάρ, φιλτάτη, ὡς οὐκ ἄν ποτε
οὐδὲ[109] ἀποθανοῦσα ἐκλάθοιό μου." 5. καὶ ὁ μὲν ταῦτα
ὠδύρετο καὶ τοὺς πόνους ἔφερεν ἀλγεινῶς, τῇ δὲ
Ἀνθίᾳ ὄναρ ἐπέστη ἐν Τάραντι κοιμωμένῃ· ἐδόκει μὲν
αὐτὴν εἶναι μετὰ Ἁβροκόμου καλὴν οὖσαν μετ᾽ ἐκεί-

106 Salvini: μουκέριον (et 5.10.1 –ίω)
107 O'Sullivan: οὐδὲ αὑτὸν   108 O'Sullivan
109 Palairet: οὔτε: οὔτε ⟨ζῶσα οὔτε⟩ O'Sullivan cl. 2.7.5, 10.3

342

at various times and in various ways. But please, master, don't be angry with me, for none of this is my fault. You could surely sell me and lose none of the price you paid." The pimp was annoyed to hear this but agreed that her suffering was involuntary.

And so she was treated at the pimp's house as if she 8 were sick, while Habrocomes had returned from Sicily and put in at Nucerium[75] in Italy. Lacking means and at a loss what to do, he first went around searching for Anthia, since she was his whole reason for living and wandering, but when he found nothing, for the girl was at the pimp's house in Tarentum, he hired himself out to a company working in the quarries. 3. The work was hard on him: he was not in the least accustomed to subjecting his body to strenuous or punishing tasks but fared poorly and frequently bemoaned his own bad luck. "Here, Anthia," he said, "behold your Habrocomes, a laborer in a low job, who have submitted my body to servitude. 4. And if I had any hope of finding you and spending the rest of our lives together, that would console me better than anything. But as it is, I may be just a wretch doing vain and unprofitable labor, and you may have died somewhere of longing for Habrocomes: for I am sure, dearest one, that even in death you would never have forgotten me." 5. Thus he lamented and bore his painful labors, but Anthia had a dream as she slept in Tarentum. She dreamt that she was with Habrocomes, she was

[75] That is, Nuceria (Alfaterna) in Campania, modern Nocera Inferiore, which was an important town about 16 km east of the modern coastline at Torre Annunziata; cf. Polybius 3.91.4, Strabo 5.4.11.

νου καλοῦ καὶ τὸν πρῶτον εἶναι τοῦ ἔρωτος αὐτοῖς
χρόνον, 6. φανῆναι δέ τινα ἄλλην γυναῖκα καλὴν καὶ
ἀφέλκειν αὐτῆς τὸν Ἀβροκόμην· καὶ τέλος ἀναβοῶν-
τος καὶ καλοῦντος ὀνομαστὶ ἐξαναστῆναί τε καὶ παύσασθαι τὸ ὄναρ. 7. ταῦτα ὡς ἔδοξεν ἰδεῖν εὐθὺς μὲν
ἀνέθορέ τε καὶ ἀνεθρήνησε καὶ ἀληθῆ τὰ ὀφθέντα
ἐνόμιζεν "οἴμοι τῶν κακῶν" λέγουσα "ἐγὼ μὲν καὶ
πόνους ὑπομένω πάντας καὶ ποικίλων πειρῶμαι δυστυχὴς συμφορῶν καὶ τέχνας σωφροσύνης ὑπὲρ γυναῖκας εὑρίσκω, Ἀβροκόμη· σοὶ δὲ ἴσως ἄλλη που
δέδοκται καλή· ταῦτα γάρ μοι σημαίνει τὰ ὀνείρατα.
8. τί οὖν ἔτι ζῶ; τί δ᾽ ἐμαυτὴν λυπῶ; κάλλιον οὖν ἀπο-
λέσθαι καὶ ἀπαλλαγῆναι τοῦ πονήρου τούτου βίου,
ἀπαλλαγῆναι δὲ τῆς ἀπρεποῦς ταύτης καὶ ἐπισφαλοῦς
δουλείας. 9. Ἀβροκόμης μὲν γὰρ εἰ καὶ τοὺς ὅρκους
παραβέβηκε μηδὲν οἱ θεοὶ τιμωρήσαιντο τοῦτον· ἴσως
ἀνάγκη τι εἴργασται· ἐμοὶ δὲ ἀποθανεῖν καλῶς ἔχει
σωφρονούσῃ." ταῦτα ἔλεγε θρηνοῦσα καὶ μηχανὴν
ἐζήτει τελευτῆς.

9   Ὁ δὲ Ἱππόθοος ὁ Περίνθιος ἐν τῷ Ταυρομενίῳ τὰ
μὲν πρῶτα διῆγε πονήρως ἀπορίᾳ τῶν ἐπιτηδείων,
χρόνου δὲ προϊόντος ἠράσθη πρεσβῦτις αὐτοῦ καὶ
ἔγημέ τε ὑπ᾽ ἀνάγκης τῆς κατὰ τὴν ἀπορίαν τὴν
πρεσβῦτιν καὶ ὀλίγῳ συγγενόμενος χρόνῳ ἀποθανού-
σης αὐτῆς πλοῦτόν τε διαδέχεται πολὺν καὶ εὐδαι-
μονίαν· πολλὴ μὲν οἰκετῶν παραπομπή, πολλὴ δὲ
[τῶν][110] ἐσθήτων ὕπαρξις καὶ σκευῶν πολυτέλεια.
2. διέγνω δὲ πλεῦσαι μὲν εἰς Ἰταλίαν, ὠνήσασθαι δὲ
οἰκέτας ὡραίους καὶ θεραπαίνας καὶ ἄλλην σκευῶν
περιβολὴν ὅση γένοιτ᾽ ἂν ἀνδρὶ εὐδαίμονι. ἐμέμνητο
δὲ ἀεὶ τοῦ Ἀβροκόμου καὶ τοῦτον ἀνευρεῖν ηὔχετο περὶ

beautiful and so was he, and it was the time when they first fell in love; then some other woman appeared, a beauty, and drew Habrocomes away from her; and finally, as he shouted and called to her by name, she sat up and the dream stopped. 7. When she had this dream she leapt straight up, let out a wail, and thought what she had seen was real. "What troubles!" she said, "I put up with every kind of struggle, I am beset in my misfortune by manifold predicaments, and I find resources of virtue beyond a woman's means, Habrocomes, but in your eyes some other woman perhaps seems beautiful, for that is what my dream signifies to me. 8. Then why should I keep on living? Why should I cause myself pain? Better then to perish and be rid of this wretched life, and be rid of this unseemly and dangerous servitude. 9. But even if Habrocomes has broken his vows, may the gods not punish him: perhaps he acted under compulsion, but for me the right course is to die virtuous." These were her words as she wailed and sought a way to end her life.

Meanwhile Hippothous of Perinthus spent the first 9 part of his sojourn in Tauromenium in poor condition through lack of means, but as time passed an old woman fell in love with him, and under compulsion of his poverty he married the old woman. He had lived with her a short time when she died, and he inherited great wealth and prosperity: a large retinue of servants, a large amount of clothing, and an extravagant array of belongings. 2. He decided to sail to Italy and buy young servants and maids and the rest of the list of belongings that become a prosperous gentleman. But he was always thinking of Habrocomes

110 Hercher

πολλοῦ ποιούμενος κοινωνῆσαί τε αὐτῷ τοῦ βίου παντὸς καὶ τῶν κτημάτων. 3. καὶ ὁ μὲν ἐπαναχθεὶς κατῆ-
ρεν εἰς Ἰταλίαν, εἵπετο δὲ αὐτῷ μειράκιον τῶν ἐν
Σικελίᾳ[111] εὖ γεγονότων, Κλεισθένης τοὔνομα, καὶ
πάντων μετεῖχε τῶν Ἱπποθόου κτημάτων καλὸς ὤν. 4.
ὁ δὲ πορνοβοσκὸς ἤδη τῆς Ἀνθίας ὑγιαίνειν δοκούσης
ἐνενόει ὅπως αὐτὴν ἀποδώσεται καὶ δὴ προῆγεν αὐτὴν
εἰς τὴν ἀγορὰν καὶ τοῖς ὠνησομένοις ἐπεδείκνυεν. 5. ἐν
τούτῳ δὲ ὁ Ἱππόθοος περιῄει τὴν πόλιν τὴν Τάραντα
εἴ τι καλὸν ὠνήσασθαι ζητῶν καὶ ὁρᾷ τὴν Ἀνθίαν καὶ
γνωρίζει καὶ ἐπὶ τῷ συμβάντι καταπλήσσεται καὶ
πολλὰ πρὸς ἑαυτὸν ἐλογίζετο· "οὐχ αὕτη ἡ κόρη, ἣν
ἐγώ ποτε ἐν Αἰγύπτῳ τιμωρῶν τῷ Ἀγχιάλου φόνῳ εἰς
τάφρον κατώρυξα καὶ κύνας αὐτῇ συγκαθεῖρξα; τίς
οὖν ἡ μεταβολή; πῶς δὲ σῴζεται; τίς ἡ ἐκ τῆς τάφρου
φυγή; τίς ἡ παράλογος σωτηρία;" 6. εἰπὼν ταῦτα
προσῆλθεν ὡς ὠνήσασθαι θέλων καὶ παραστὰς αὐτῇ
"ὦ κόρη" ἔφησεν, "Αἴγυπτον οὐκ οἶδας οὐδὲ λῃσταῖς
ἐν Αἰγύπτῳ περιπέπτωκας οὐδὲ ἄλλο τι ἐν ἐκείνῃ τῇ γῇ
πέπονθας δεινόν· εἰπὲ θαρσοῦσα· γνωρίζω γάρ σε ἐξ
ἐκείνου τοῦ χωρίου[112]." 7. Αἴγυπτον ἀκούσασα καὶ
ἀναμνησθεῖσα Ἀγχιάλου καὶ τοῦ λῃστηρίου καὶ τῆς
τάφρου ἀνῴμωξέ τε καὶ ἀνωδύρατο, ἀποβλέψασα δὲ
εἰς τὸν Ἱππόθοον, ἐγνώρισε δὲ αὐτὸν οὐδαμῶς, "πε-
πόνθαμεν" φησὶν "ἐν Αἰγύπτῳ πολλά, ὦ ξένε, καὶ
δεινά, ὅστις ποτὲ ὢν τυγχάνεις, καὶ λῃσταῖς περι-
πέπτωκα. ἀλλὰ σὺ πῶς, εἰπέ, γνωρίζεις τὰ ἐμὰ διηγήματα; 8. πόθεν δὲ εἰδέναι λέγεις ἐμὲ τὴν δυστυχῆ;
διαβόητα μὲν γὰρ καὶ ἔνδοξα πέπονθαμεν, ἀλλὰ σὲ οὐ

111 Cobet: εἰς Σικελίαν: ἐκ Σικελίας Hercher
112 Peerlkamp: ἐν ἐκείνῳ τῷ χωρίῳ

and prayed that he would find him, putting great value on sharing with him his whole way of life and his possessions. 3. And so he took ship and reached Italy, accompanied by a lad from one of the good families of Sicily named Cleisthenes,[76] who was handsome and so shared in all Hippothous' possessions. 4. Meanwhile the pimp thought Anthia was healthy again and made plans to sell her. And so he led her to the market and displayed her to prospective buyers. 5. At this juncture Hippothous was going about the city of Tarentum looking for something fine to buy when he saw Anthia, recognized her, was astounded at the coincidence, and had a long conversation with himself. "Isn't this the girl that back in Egypt I buried in a pit and shut up with dogs to avenge Anchialus' murder? What then is this turn-about? How was she rescued? What was her way out of the pit? What was her salvation against all odds?" 6. With this he stepped up as if wishing to buy her, and standing close to her he said, "My girl, don't you know Egypt? Didn't you fall among bandits in Egypt? And didn't you have another terrible experience in that country? Feel free to tell me, because I recognize you from that place." 7. When she heard mention of Egypt and was reminded about Anchialus, the bandit gang, and the pit, she groaned and wailed. She looked closely at Hippothous but did not recognize him at all. "I did have many terrible experiences in Egypt, stranger," she said, "whoever you may be, and I did fall among bandits. But tell me, please, how do you know my story? 8. Where do you say you got to know a wretch like me? No doubt my experiences are widely told

---

[76] A conventional name.

γινώσκω τὸ σύνολον." 9. ἀκούσας ὁ Ἱππόθοος καὶ
μᾶλλον ἐξ ὧν ἔλεγεν ἀναγνωρίσας αὐτὴν τότε μὲν
ἡσυχίαν ἤγαγεν, ὠνησάμενος δὲ αὐτὴν παρὰ τοῦ
πορνοβοσκοῦ ἄγει πρὸς ἑαυτὸν καὶ θαρρεῖν παρεκελεύετο καὶ ὅστις ἦν λέγει καὶ τῶν ἐν Αἰγύπτῳ
γενομένων ἀναμιμνήσκει καὶ τὴν φυγὴν καὶ τὸν ἑαυτοῦ πλοῦτον διηγεῖται[113]. 10. ἡ δὲ ᾐτεῖτο συγγνώμην
ἔχειν καὶ αὐτῷ ἐπεξηγεῖτο[114] ὅτι Ἀγχίαλον ἀπέκτεινε
μὴ σωφρονοῦντα καὶ τὴν τάφρον καὶ τὸν Ἀμφίνομον
καὶ τὴν τῶν κυνῶν πραότητα καὶ τὴν σωτηρίαν διηγεῖται. 11. κατῴκτειρεν αὐτὴν ὁ Ἱππόθοος καὶ ἥτις μὲν
ἦν ἐπέπυστο οὐδέπω, ἐκ δὲ τῆς καθημερινῆς σὺν τῇ
κόρῃ διαίτης εἰς ἐπιθυμίαν Ἀνθίας καὶ Ἱππόθοος
ἔρχεται καὶ συνελθεῖν ἐβούλετο καὶ πολλὰ ὑπισχνεῖται αὐτῇ. 12. ἡ δὲ τὰ μὲν πρῶτα ἀντέλεγεν αὐτῷ
ἀναξία εἶναι λέγουσα εὐνῆς δεσποτικῆς, τέλεον δὲ ὡς
ἐνέκειτο Ἱππόθοος οὐκέτ' ἔχουσα ὅ τι ποιήσει κάλλιον
εἶναι νομίζουσα εἰπεῖν πάντα αὐτῷ τὰ ἀπόρρητα ἢ
παραβῆναι τὰς πρὸς Ἁβροκόμην συνθήκας λέγει τὸν
Ἁβροκόμην, τὴν Ἔφεσον, τὸν ἔρωτα, τοὺς ὅρκους, τὰς
συμφοράς, τὰ λῃστήρια, καὶ συνεχὲς Ἁβροκόμην
ἀνωδύρετο. 13. ὁ δὲ Ἱππόθοος ἀκούσας ὅτι τε Ἀνθία
εἴη καὶ ὅτι γυνὴ τοῦ πάντων αὐτῷ φιλτάτου ἀσπάζεταί
τε αὐτὴν καὶ εὐθυμεῖν παρεκάλει καὶ τὴν αὐτοῦ πρὸς
Ἁβροκόμην φιλίαν διηγεῖται. καὶ τὴν μὲν εἶχεν ἐπὶ
τῆς οἰκίας πᾶσαν προσάγων ἐπιμέλειαν, Ἁβροκόμην
αἰδούμενος, αὐτὸς δὲ πάντα ἀνηρεύνα εἴ που τὸν
Ἁβροκόμην ἀνεύροι.

10   Ὁ δὲ Ἁβροκόμης τὰ μὲν πρῶτα ἐπιπόνως ἐν τῷ
Νουκερίῳ[115] εἰργάζετο, τελευταῖον δὲ οὐκέτι φέρων

___
[113] καὶ τὴν φυγήν post διηγεῖται transp. O'Sullivan

348

and famous, but I don't recognize you at all." 9. Hearing
this and recognizing her all the more from what she said,
Hippothous was quiet at first, but after he had bought her
from the pimp, he took her home, encouraged her, told her
who he was, reminded her of what had happened in Egypt,
and told the story of his own flight and wealth. 10. She
asked his forgiveness and also explained that she had killed
Anchialus for behaving intemperately, and told the story
of the pit, Amphinomus, the taming of the dogs, and
her salvation. 11. Hippothous felt sorry for her but had yet
to learn her identity. In daily contact with the girl Hippothous too came to desire her, wanted to go to bed with
her, and made many promises. 12. At first she refused him,
claiming that she was unworthy of a master's bed, but in
the end, as Hippothous kept pressing, she did no know
how to proceed, and thinking that it was better to tell him
all her secrets than to break her pact with Habrocomes,
she told him about Habrocomes, Ephesus, their love, their
vows, their predicaments, the bandit gangs, all the while
grieving over Habrocomes. 13. When Hippothous heard
that she was Anthia and the wife of his dearest friend, he
hugged her, told her to be of good cheer, and explained
his own affection for Habrocomes. He kept her in his
house and showed her every consideration out of respect
for Habrocomes, while he launched a full investigation in
hope of finding Habrocomes.

Habrocomes at first toiled very hard in Nucerium, but   10
in the end he could no longer bear his labors and decided

---

114 O'Sullivan: ἀπ-
115 Cf. ad 5.8.1

τοὺς πόνους διέγνω νεὼς ἐπιβὰς εἰς Ἔφεσον ἀνάγε-
σθαι. 2. καὶ ὁ μὲν νύκτωρ κατελθὼν ἐπὶ θάλασσαν
ἐπιφθάνει πλοίῳ ἀναγομένῳ καὶ ἐπιβὰς ἔπλει τὴν ἐπὶ
Σικελίαν πάλιν ὡς ἐκεῖθεν ἐπὶ Κρήτην τε καὶ Κύπρον
καὶ Ῥόδον ἀφιξόμενος κἀκεῖθεν εἰς Ἔφεσον γενησό-
μενος. ἤλπιζε δὲ ἐν τῷ μακρῷ πλῷ καὶ περὶ Ἀνθίας τι
πυθέσθαι. 3. καὶ ὁ μὲν ὀλίγα ἔχων τὰ ἐπιτήδεια
ἀναγόμενος καὶ διανύσας τὸν πλοῦν τὰ μὲν πρῶτα ἐπὶ
τὴν Σικελίαν[116] ἔρχεται καὶ εὑρίσκει τὸν πρότερον
ξένον τὸν Αἰγιαλέα τεθνηκότα· ἐπενέγκας δὲ αὐτῷ
χοὰς καὶ πολλὰ καταδακρύσας ἀναχθεὶς πάλιν καὶ
Κρήτην παρελθὼν ἐν Κύπρῳ γενόμενος ἡμέρας δια-
τρίψας ὀλίγας καὶ εὐξάμενος τῇ πατρίῳ Κυπρίων θεῷ
ἀνήγετο καὶ ἧκεν εἰς Ῥόδον. ἐνταῦθα πλησίον τοῦ
λιμένος εἰσῳκίσατο. 4. καὶ ἤδη τε ἐγγὺς ἐγίνετο Ἐφέσου καὶ πάντων αὐτὸν ἔννοια τῶν δεινῶν εἰσήρχετο,
τῆς πατρίδος, τῶν πατέρων, τῆς Ἀνθίας, τῶν οἰκετῶν.
καὶ ἀναστενάξας "φεῦ" ἔφη "τῶν κακῶν· εἰς Ἔφεσον
ἵξομαι μόνος καὶ πατράσιν ὀφθήσομαι τοῖς ἐμαυτοῦ
χωρὶς Ἀνθίας καὶ πλεύσομαι πλοῦν ὁ δυστυχὴς κενὸν
καὶ διηγήσομαι διηγήματα ἴσως ἄπιστα κοινωνὸν ὧν
πέπονθα οὐκ ἔχων· 5. ἀλλὰ καρτέρησον, Ἁβροκόμη,
καὶ γενόμενος ἐν Ἐφέσῳ τοσοῦτον ἐπιβίωσον χρόνον·
τάφον ἔγειρον Ἀνθίᾳ καὶ θρήνησον αὐτὴν καὶ χοὰς
ἐπένεγκαι· καὶ σαυτὸν ἤδη παρ' αὐτὴν ἄγε." ταῦτα
ἔλεγε καὶ περιῄει τὴν πόλιν ἀλύων ἀθυμίᾳ[117] μὲν τῶν
κατὰ τὴν Ἀνθίαν, ἀπορίᾳ δὲ τῶν ἐπιτηδείων. 6. ὁ δὲ
Λεύκων ἐν τούτῳ καὶ ἡ Ῥόδη διατρίβοντες ἐν Ῥόδῳ
ἀναθήματα ἀνατεθείκεσαν ἐν τῷ τοῦ Ἡλίου ἱερῷ παρὰ
τὴν χρυσῆν πανοπλίαν ἣν Ἀνθία καὶ Ἁβροκόμης

---

[116] O'Sullivan: τῆς Σικελίας   [117] Hemsterhuys: ἀπορίᾳ

to take ship and make for Ephesus. 2. One night he went down to the sea and found a ship just putting out, got aboard, and headed back to Sicily, so as to get from there to Crete and Cyprus and Rhodes and thence to Ephesus. He also hoped that during this long voyage he would hear some news of Anthia. 3. He sailed with few provisions and completed the first stage of the voyage to Sicily, where he discovered that his former host Aegialeus was dead. He poured libations for him and shed many a tear, then resumed his voyage, passed Crete, and arrived in Cyprus; after spending a few days and praying to the Cyprians' ancestral goddess,[77] he resumed his voyage and arrived in Rhodes, where he settled himself near the harbor. 4. Now that he was near Ephesus, all of his terrible experiences came to mind, his country, his parents, Anthia and their servants. With a deep sigh he said, "What troubles! I will arrive in Ephesus alone, my own parents will see me without Anthia, I will be a wretch making a useless voyage, and having no partner in my experiences I will tell stories that perhaps no one will believe. 5. But persevere, Habrocomes, and when you get to Ephesus, live on long enough to raise a tomb for Anthia, mourn her, and pour libations; then it will be time to put yourself beside her." With that he went around the city distraught with dejection about Anthia's case and with lack of provisions. 6. Meanwhile Leuco and Rhoda, who were staying in Rhodes, had set up a dedication in the temple of Helius beside the golden panoply that Anthia and

[77] Cyprus is a most unlikely stop on a voyage from Sicily to Crete to Rhodes unless the (unelaborated) point was a detour in order to pay homage to Aphrodite.

ἀνατεθείκεσαν· ἀνέθεσαν στήλην γράμμασι χρυσοῖς
γεγραμμένην ὑπὲρ Ἀβροκόμου καὶ Ἀνθίας, ἀνεγέ-
γραπτο δὲ καὶ τῶν ἀναθέντων τὰ ὀνόματα, ὅ τε Λεύκων
καὶ ἡ Ῥόδη. 7. ταύτῃ τῇ στήλῃ ὁ Ἀβροκόμης ἐπιτυγ-
χάνει· ἐληλύθει δὲ προσεύξασθαι τῷ θεῷ. ἀναγνοὺς
οὖν καὶ γνωρίσας τοὺς ἀναθέντας καὶ τὴν τῶν οἰκετῶν
εὔνοιαν πλησίον δὲ καὶ τὴν πανοπλίαν ἰδὼν μέγα
ἀνωδύρετο παρακαθεσθεὶς τῇ στήλῃ. 8. "ὦ πάντα"
ἔλεγεν "ἐγὼ δυστυχής· ἐπὶ τὸ τέρμα ἥκω τοῦ βίου καὶ
εἰς ἀνάμνησιν τῶν ἐμαυτοῦ συμφορῶν· ἰδοὺ ταύτην
μὲν τὴν πανοπλίαν ἐγὼ μετὰ Ἀνθίας ἀνέθηκα καὶ μετ'
ἐκείνης ἀποπλεύσας Ῥόδου ἥκω νῦν ἐκείνην οὐκ ἄγων,
εἰ δὲ αὕτη ἡ στήλη τῶν συντρόφων τῶν ἡμετέρων ὑπὲρ
ἀμφοτέρων τὸ ἀνάθημα, τίς οὖν γένωμαι μόνος; ποῦ δὲ
τοὺς φιλτάτους ἀνεύρω;" 9. ταῦτα ἐθρήνει λέγων. καὶ
ἐν τούτῳ ἐφίστα<ν>ται[118] ὁ Λεύκων καὶ ἡ Ῥόδη συνήθως εὐχόμενοι τῷ θεῷ καὶ θεωροῦσι τὸν Ἀβροκόμην
τῇ στήλῃ παρακαθεζόμενον καὶ εἰς τὴν πανοπλίαν
ἀποβλέποντα καὶ γνωρίζουσι μὲν οὐχί, θαυμάζουσι δὲ
ὅστις ὢν ἀλλοτρίοις ἀναθήμασι παραμένοι. 10. καὶ δὴ
ὁ Λεύκων ἔφη "ὦ μειράκιον, τί βουλόμενος ἀναθήμασιν οὐδέν σοι προσήκουσι παρακαθεζόμενος ὀδύρῃ
καὶ θρηνεῖς; τί δέ σοι τούτων μέλει; τί δὲ τῶν ἐνταῦθα
ἀναγεγραμμένων κοινωνεῖ σοι;" ἀποκρίνεται πρὸς αὐτὸν Ἀβροκόμης "ἐμά," φησὶν "ἐμὰ τὰ ἀναθήματα
Λεύκωνος καὶ Ῥόδης, οὓς ἰδεῖν εὔχομαι μετὰ Ἀνθίαν
Ἀβροκόμης ὁ δυστυχής." 11. ἀκούσαντες οἱ περὶ τὸν
Λεύκωνα εὐθὺς μὲν ἀχανεῖς ἐγένοντο, ἀνενεγκόντες δὲ
κατὰ μικρὸν ἐγνώριζον ἐκ τοῦ σχήματος, ἐκ τῆς φωνῆς, ἐξ ὧν ἔλεγεν, ἐξ ὧν Ἀνθίας ἐμέμνητο, καὶ πίπτου-

[118] Hercher

Habrocomes had dedicated. They set up a monument inscribed with golden lettering in honor of Habrocomes and
Anthia, and also inscribed their own names, Leuco and Rhoda,
as the dedicators. 7. Habrocomes, who had come to offer
prayers to the god, happened on this monument. When he
read it and recognized the dedicators and the goodwill of
his servants, and when he saw the panoply nearby, he sat
down beside the monument and heaved a loud groan. 8.
"How unlucky I am in everything!" he said, "I have come to
the end of my life and to a reminder of my own misfortunes. Look, this is the very panoply that I dedicated with
Anthia; with her I sailed away from Rhodes, and now I
have come back without her. If this monument is the dedication of our companions in honor of both of us, what then
should I do now that I'm on my own? Where am I to find
those dearest to me?" 9. So he lamented, but at this point
Leuco and Rhoda showed up for their usual prayers to the
god and beheld Habrocomes sitting by the monument and
looking at the panoply. They did not recognize him and
wondered who would be lingering beside someone else's
dedications. 10. And so Leuco said, "My lad, what do you
mean by sitting there groaning and lamenting beside dedications of no concern to you? What is your interest in this?
What have you in common with those inscribed here?"
Habrocomes replied to him by saying, "They are for me, for
me, these dedications by Leuco and Rhoda, whom after
Anthia I, Habrocomes the unlucky one, am praying to see."
11. On hearing this Leuco's party were struck speechless
on the spot, but little by little they recovered and recognized him by his appearance, his voice, what he said, and
his evocation of Anthia. They fell at his feet and told their

σι πρὸ τῶν ποδῶν αὐτοῦ καὶ τὰ καθ᾿ αὑτοὺς διηγοῦν
ται, τὴν ὁδὸν τὴν εἰς Συρίαν ἀπὸ Τύρου, τὴν Μαντοῦς
ὀργήν, τὴν ἔκδοσιν, τὴν πρᾶσιν τὴν εἰς Λυκίαν, τὴν
τοῦ δεσπότου τελευτήν[119], τὴν περιουσίαν, τὴν εἰς
Ῥόδον ἄφιξιν. 12. καὶ δὴ παραλαβόντες ἄγουσιν εἰς
τὴν οἰκίαν ἔνθα αὐτοὶ κατήγοντο καὶ τὰ κτήματα
αὑτῶν παραδιδόασι καὶ ἐπεμελοῦντο καὶ ἐθεράπευ
ον[το][120] καὶ θαρρεῖν παρεκάλουν. τῷ δὲ ἦν οὐδὲν
Ἀνθίας τιμιώτερον ἀλλ᾿ ἐκείνην ἐθρήνει παρ᾿ ἕκαστα.

11   Καὶ ὁ μὲν ἐν Ῥόδῳ διῆγε μετὰ τῶν συντρόφων ὅ τι
πράξει βουλευόμενος· ὁ δὲ Ἱππόθοος διέγνω τὴν Ἀν
θίαν ἀγαγεῖν ἀπὸ Ἰταλίας εἰς Ἔφεσον ὡς ἀποδώσων
τε τοῖς γονεῦσι καὶ περὶ Ἀβροκόμου ἐκεῖ τι πευσόμε
νος· καὶ δὴ ἐμβαλὼν πάντα τὰ αὑτοῦ εἰς ναῦν μεγάλην
Ἐφεσίαν μετὰ τῆς Ἀνθίας ἀνήγετο καὶ διανύσας
μάλα ἀσμένως τὸν πλοῦν 2. οὐ πολλαῖς ἡμέραις εἰς
Ῥόδον καταίρει νυκτὸς ἔτι κἀνταῦθα κατάγεται παρά
τινι πρεσβύτιδι, Ἀλθαίᾳ τὸ ὄνομα, πλησίον δὲ τῆς
θαλάσσης καὶ τήν τε Ἀνθίαν ἀνάγει παρὰ τὴν ξένην
καὶ αὐτὸς ἐκείνης μὲν τῆς νυκτὸς ἀνεπαύσατο. τῇ δὲ
ἑξῆς ἤδη μὲν περὶ τὸν πλοῦν ἐγίνοντο, ἑορτὴ δέ τις
ἤγετο μεγαλοπρεπὴς δημοσίᾳ τῶν Ῥοδίων ἁπάντων[121]
τῷ Ἡλίῳ καὶ πομπῇ τε καὶ θυσία καὶ πολιτῶν ἑορτα
ζόντων πλῆθος. 3. ἐνταῦθα παρῆσαν ὁ Λεύκων καὶ ἡ
Ῥόδη οὐ τοσοῦτον τῆς ἑορτῆς μεθέξοντες ὅσον ἀναζη
τήσοντες εἴ τι περὶ Ἀνθίας πύθοιντο. καὶ δὴ ἧκεν ὁ
Ἱππόθοος εἰς τὸ ἱερὸν ἄγων τὴν Ἀνθίαν, ἡ δὲ ἀπι
δοῦσα εἰς τὰ ἀναθήματα καὶ ἐν ἀναμνήσει τῶν πρότε
ρον γενομένη 4. "ὦ τὰ πάντων" ἔφησεν "ἀνθρώπων

---

119 Abresch: τῶν δεσποτῶν   120 Zagoiannes
121 Reeve: ἀγόντων

own story: their journey from Tyre to Syria, the wrath of Manto, their being bound over to her, their sale to Lycia, their master's end, their prosperity, their arrival in Rhodes. 12. And so they gathered him up and took him to the house where they were staying, turned their possessions over to him, took care of him, treated him, and tried to bolster his spirit. But for him nothing had as much value as Anthia, and at every turn he mourned for her.

So he lived in Rhodes with his companions, considering 11 a plan of action, while Hippothous decided to take Anthia from Italy to Ephesus, where he could return her to her parents and hear something of Habrocomes. And so he put all his belongings onto a large Ephesian ship and set out with Anthia. After a very pleasant voyage of not many days, they put in at Rhodes during the night and lodged near the sea with an old woman named Althaea;[78] he sent Anthia upstairs with their hostess and himself rested that night. Next day they were on the point of sailing, but a magnificent public festival for Helius was being put on by all the Rhodians,[79] with a procession and sacrifice, and a throng of citizens celebrating. 3. Leuco and Rhoda were on hand, not so much as participants in the festival as investigators after some news of Anthia. And so Hippothous came to the temple with Anthia, and when she looked at the dedications and remembered times past, "Helius," she said, "who oversee all human affairs and overlook only me in my bad fortune! When I used to live in Rhodes I wor-

[78] "Healer": a family of medicinal plants and a mythological name, e.g. the mother of Meleager.

[79] The Halieia, the city's most important annual festival, celebrated with special pomp every fourth year.

ἐφορῶν Ἥλιε, μόνην ἐμὲ τὴν δυστυχῆ παρελθών,
πρότερον μὲν ἐν Ῥόδῳ γενομένη εὐτυχῶς τέ σε προσεκύνουν καὶ θυσίας ἔθυον μετὰ Ἀβροκόμου καὶ εὐδαίμων τότε ἐνομιζόμην, νυνὶ δὲ δούλη μὲν ἀντ᾽ ἐλευ-
θέρας, αἰχμάλωτος δὲ ἡ δυστυχὴς ἀντὶ τῆς μακαρίας,
καὶ εἰς Ἔφεσον ἔρχομαι μόνη καὶ φανοῦμαι τοῖς
οἰκείοις Ἀβροκόμην οὐκ ἔχουσα." 5. ταῦτα ἔλεγε καὶ
πολλὰ ἐπεδάκρυε καὶ δεῖται τοῦ Ἱπποθόου ἐπιτρέψαι
αὐτῇ τῆς κόμης ἀφελεῖν τῆς αὐτῆς καὶ ἀναθεῖναι τῷ
Ἡλίῳ καὶ εὔξασθαί τι περὶ Ἀβροκόμου. 6. συγχωρεῖ ὁ
Ἱππόθοος, καὶ ἀποτεμοῦσα τῶν πλοκάμων ὅσα ἐδύνατο καὶ ἐπιτηδείου καιροῦ λαβομένη πάντων ἀπηλ-
λαγμένων ἀνατίθησιν ἐπιγράψασα ΥΠΕΡ ΤΟΥ ΑΝΔΡΟΣ
ΑΒΡΟΚΟΜΟΥ ΑΝΘΙΑ ΤΗΝ ΚΟΜΗΝ ΤΩΙ ΘΕΩΙ ΑΝΕΘΗΚΕ.
ταῦτα ποιήσασα καὶ εὐξαμένη ἀπῄει μετὰ τοῦ Ἱπποθόου.

12   Ὁ δὲ Λεύκων καὶ ἡ Ῥόδη τέως ὄντες περὶ τὴν
πομπὴν ἐφίστανται τῷ ἱερῷ καὶ βλέπουσι τὰ ἀναθήματα καὶ γνωρίζουσι τῶν δεσποτῶν τὰ ὀνόματα καὶ
πρῶτον ἀσπάζονται τὴν κόμην καὶ πολλὰ κατωδύ-
ροντο οὕτως ὡς Ἀνθίαν βλέποντες, τελευταῖον δὲ
περιῄεσαν εἴ που κἀκείνην εὑρεῖν δυνήσονται, ἤδη δὲ
καὶ τὸ πλῆθος τῶν Ῥοδίων ἐγνώριζον τὰ ὀνόματα ἐκ
τῆς προτέρας ἐπιδημίας[122]. 2. κἀκείνην μὲν τὴν ἡμέραν οὐδὲν εὑρίσκοντες ἀπηλλάγησαν καὶ τῷ Ἀβροκόμῃ τὰ ἐν τῷ ἱερῷ ὄντα ἐμήνυσαν. ὁ δὲ ἔπαθε μὲν τὴν
ψυχὴν ἐπὶ τῷ παραδόξῳ τοῦ πράγματος, εὔελπις δὲ ἦν
ὡς Ἀνθίαν εὑρήσων. 3. τῇ δὲ ἑξῆς ἧκεν ἡ Ἀνθία πάλιν
εἰς τὸ ἱερὸν μετὰ τοῦ Ἱπποθόου οὐκ ὄντος αὐτοῖς
πλοός, προσκαθίσασα δὲ τοῖς ἀναθήμασιν ἐδάκρυέ τε
καὶ ἀνέστενεν· ἐν τούτῳ δὲ ἐπεισίασιν ὁ Λεύκων καὶ ἡ
Ῥόδη τὸν Ἀβροκόμην καταλιπόντες ἔνδον ἀθύμως ἐπὶ

shipped you to my good fortune, offered you sacrifices with Habrocomes, and was considered blessed. But now I am a slave instead of a free woman, an unfortunate captive instead of that happy girl, and I am going to Ephesus alone to appear before my family without Habrocomes." 5. With these words and many tears she asked Hippothous to let her set aside a lock of her own hair and dedicate it to Helius with a few words of prayer about Habrocomes. 6. Hippothous agreed. She cut off as many of her locks as she could and found a suitable opportunity, when everyone had left the premises, to make her dedication, on which she wrote:

ON BEHALF OF HER HUSBAND HABROCOMES
ANTHIA DEDICATED HER HAIR TO THE GOD

With this act and a prayer, she left with Hippothous.

Leuco and Rhoda, who until now had been at the procession, stopped at the temple, saw the dedications, and recognized their masters' names. First they kissed the hair and lamented and wept copiously, as if they were looking at Anthia, and finally started walking around to see if they could find her anywhere; the Rhodian populace already knew the names from their previous visit. 2. Finding nothing that day, they departed and told Habrocomes what was in the temple. He was impassioned at heart by this unexpected occurrence and hopeful of finding Anthia. 3. The next day Anthia returned to the temple with Hippothous, since they could not sail. She sat by the dedications, crying and groaning, when along came Leuco and Rhoda, who had left Habrocomes at home, dispirited about his

12

---

122 Abresch: ἀπο-

τοῖς αὑτοῦ[123] διακείμενον· ἐλθόντες δὲ ὁρῶσι τὴν Ἀνθίαν καὶ ἦν μὲν ἔτι ἄγνωστος αὐτοῖς, συμβάλλουσι δὲ
πάντα[124], ⟨τὰ⟩[125] δάκρυα, τὰ ἀναθήματα, τὰ ὀνόματα,
τὸ εἶδος. 4. οὕτως κατὰ βραχὺ ἐγνώριζον αὐτήν,
προσπεσόντες δὲ τοῖς γόνασιν ἔκειντο ἀχανεῖς. ἡ δὲ
ἐτεθαυμάκει τίνες τε ἦσαν καὶ τί βούλοιντο· οὐ γὰρ ἄν
ποτε Λεύκωνα καὶ Ῥόδην ⟨ἰδεῖν⟩[126] ἤλπισεν. 5. οἱ δὲ ἐν
ἑαυτοῖς γενόμενοι "ὦ δέσποινα" ἔφασαν "Ἀνθία, ἡμεῖς
οἰκέται σοί, Λεύκων καὶ Ῥόδη, οἱ τῆς ἀποδημίας
κοινωνήσαντες καὶ τοῦ λῃστηρίου. ἀλλὰ τίς ἐνταῦθα
ἄγει σε τύχη; θάρσει, δέσποινα, Ἀβροκόμης σῴζεται
καὶ ἔστιν ἐνταῦθα ἀεί σε θρηνῶν." 6. ἀκούσασα ἡ
Ἀνθία ἐξεπλάγη τοῦ λόγου, μόγις δὲ ἀνενεγκοῦσα καὶ
γνωρίσασα περιβάλλει τε αὐτοὺς καὶ ἀσπάζεται καὶ
σαφέστατα τὰ κατὰ Ἀβροκόμην μανθάνει.

13   Συνέρρει δὲ ἅπαν τὸ πλῆθος τῶν Ῥοδίων πυνθα-
νόμενον τὴν Ἀνθίας εὕρεσιν καὶ Ἀβροκόμου. παρῆν δὲ
ἐν τούτῳ καὶ ὁ Ἱππόθοος ἐγνωρίσθη τε τοῖς περὶ τὸν
Λεύκωνα καὶ αὐτὸς ἔμαθεν οἵ τινές εἰσι. καὶ τὰ μὲν
ἄλλα ἦν[127] αὐτοῖς ἐπιτηδείως, τὸ δὲ ⟨οὐ τοῦτο,⟩[128] ὅτι
μηδέπω Ἀβροκόμης ταῦτα ἐπίσταται. ἔτρεχον δὲ ὡς
εἶχον ἐπὶ τὴν οἰκίαν. 2. ὁ δὲ ὡς ἤκουσεν ὑπό τινος τῶν
Ῥοδίων τὴν τῆς Ἀνθίας εὕρεσιν διὰ μέσης τῆς πόλεως
βοῶν "Ἀνθία" ἐοικὼς μεμηνότι ἔθεε. καὶ δὴ συντυγχάνει τοῖς περὶ τὴν Ἀνθίαν πρὸς τῷ ἱερῷ τῆς
Ἴσιδος, πολὺ δὲ τῶν Ῥοδίων πλῆθος ἐφείπετο. 3. ὡς δὲ
εἶδον ἀλλήλους εὐθὺς ἀνεγνώρισαν· τοῦτο γὰρ αὐτοῖς
ἐβούλοντο αἱ ψυχαί· καὶ περιλαβόντες ἀλλήλους εἰς
γῆν κατηνέχθησαν, κατεῖχε δὲ αὐτοὺς πολλὰ ἅμα

123 Peerlkamp: αὑτοῖς   124 Henderson: πάντα· ἔρωτα
125 Abresch   126 Naber

own situation. When they arrived they saw Anthia and did not yet recognize her, but they took everything in, her tears, the dedications, the names, her appearance. 4. In this way they gradually recognized her, and falling at her knees lay speechless. She wondered who they were and what they wanted, for she never expected to see Leuco and Rhoda. 5. When they recovered themselves they said, "Mistress Anthia, we are your servants, Leuco and Rhoda, who shared your yoyage and the pirate den. But what chance brings you here? Be of good cheer, mistress, Habrocomes is safe, and he is here, constantly mourning for you." 6. Anthia was shocked to hear this news, but when with an effort she recovered herself and recognized them, she threw her arms around them, kissed them, and got a very detailed report about Habrocomes.

When the Rhodians heard of the discovery of Anthia and Habrocomes, the whole populace streamed together; Hippothous too was among them. He was introduced by Leuco and Rhoda and in turn learned who they were. Everything was going the way they wanted, except for ⟨one detail⟩: Habrocomes did not yet know the news. They ran to the house just as they were. 2. When he heard from one of the Rhodians about Anthia's discovery, he began running through the middle of the city screaming "Anthia!" like a madman. He ran into Anthia's party at the temple of Isis, followed by a large throng of Rhodians. 3. They recognized each other as soon as their eyes met, for this is what their hearts desired, and joining in an embrace they fell to the ground. Many emotions seized them at once: joy,

13

---

127 Henderson: ἦν τὰ μὲν ἄλλα ἐν
128 Henderson

πάθη, ἡδονή, λύπη, φόβος, ἡ τῶν πρότερον μνήμη, τὸ
τῶν μελλόντων δέος. ὁ δὲ δῆμος ὁ Ῥοδίων ἀνευφή-
μησέ τε καὶ ἀνωλόλυξε μεγάλην θεὸν ἀνακαλοῦντες
τὴν Ἶσιν, "πάλιν" λέγοντες "ὁρῶμεν Ἀβροκόμην καὶ
Ἀνθίαν τοὺς καλούς." 4. οἱ δὲ ἀναλαβόντες ἑαυτοὺς
διαναστάντες εἰς τὸ τῆς Ἴσιδος ἱερὸν εἰσῆλθον "σοὶ"
λέγοντες, "ὦ μεγίστη θεά, τὴν ὑπὲρ τῆς σωτηρίας
ἡμῶν χάριν οἴδαμεν· διὰ σέ, ὦ πάντων ἡμῖν τιμιω-
τάτη, ἑαυτοὺς ἀπειλήφαμεν", προεκυλίοντό τε τοῦ τεμένους καὶ τῷ βωμῷ προσέπιπτον. 5. καὶ τότε μὲν
αὐτοὺς ἄγουσι παρὰ τὸν Λεύκωνα εἰς τὴν οἰκίαν καὶ ὁ
Ἱππόθοος τὰ αὐτοῦ μετεσκευάζετο παρὰ τὸν Λεύκωνα,
καὶ ἦσαν ἕτοιμοι πρὸς τὸν εἰς Ἔφεσον πλοῦν, ὡς δὲ
ἔθυσαν ἐκείνης τῆς ἡμέρας καὶ εὐωχήθησαν, πολλὰ
καὶ ποικίλα παρὰ πάντων τὰ διηγήματα, ὅσα τε
ἔπαθεν ἕκαστος καὶ ὅσα ἔδρασε, παρεξέτεινόν τε ἐπὶ
πολὺ τὸ συμπόσιον ὡς αὐτοὺς ἀπολαβόντες χρόνῳ.
6. ἐπεὶ δὲ νὺξ ἤδη ἐγεγόνει ἀνεπαύοντο οἱ μὲν ἄλλοι
πάντες ὅπως ἔτυχον, Λεύκων μὲν καὶ Ῥόδη, Ἱππόθοος
δὲ καὶ τὸ μειράκιον τὸ ἐκ Σικελίας τὸ ἀκολουθῆσαν εἰς
Ἰταλίαν ἰόντι αὐτῷ ὁ Κλεισθένης ὁ καλός, ἡ δὲ Ἀνθία
ἀνεπαύετο μετὰ Ἀβροκόμου.

14   Ὡς δὲ οἱ μὲν ἄλλοι πάντες κατεκοιμήθησαν, ἡσυ-
χία δὲ ἦν ἀκριβής, περιλαβοῦσα ἡ Ἀνθία τὸν Ἀβροκόμην ἔκλαεν "ἄνερ" λέγουσα "καὶ δέσποτα, ἀπεί-
ληφά σε πολλὴν γῆν πλανηθεῖσα καὶ θάλασσαν
λῃστῶν ἀπειλὰς ἐκφυγοῦσα καὶ πειρατῶν ἐπιβουλὰς
καὶ πορνοβοσκῶν ὕβρεις καὶ δεσμὰ καὶ τάφρους καὶ
ξύλα καὶ φάρμακα καὶ τάφους. 2. ἀλλ' ἥκω σοι τοιαύτη, τῆς ἐμῆς ψυχῆς Ἀβροκόμη δέσποτα, οἵα τὸ
πρῶτον ἀπηλλάγην εἰς Συρίαν ἐκ Τύρου, ἔπεισε δέ με
ἁμαρτεῖν οὐδείς, οὐ Μοῖρις ἐν Συρίᾳ, οὐ Περίλαος ἐν

pain, fear, memory of the past, fear about the future. The Rhodian people applauded and cheered, loudly invoking Isis: "Once again," they cried, "we see Habrocomes and Anthia, the beautiful couple!" 4. They recovered themselves, stood up, and went into the temple of Isis saying, "To you, greatest goddess, we are grateful for our salvation. Thanks to you, goddess that we esteem most of all, we have reclaimed each other." They prostrated themselves before the temple and fell before the altar. 5. Then they made their way to Leuco's house and went inside, Hippothous moved his own belongings to Leuco's house, and they were ready for the voyage to Ephesus. As they sacrificed and feasted that day, there were many different stories from everyone, what each one had experienced and done, and they extended the party until late, since they had found each other in the fullness of time. 6. When night came on, all the others retired where they happened to be—Leuco and Rhoda, Hippothous and the lad who had attended him on his trip from Sicily to Italy, the handsome Cleisthenes—but Anthia retired with Habrocomes.

When everyone else had gone to sleep and there was 14 absolute quiet, Anthia put her arms around Habrocomes and started to cry. "Husband and master," she said, "I have found you again after wandering over many a land and sea, after escaping threats from bandits, plots by pirates, insults from pimps, chains, pits, fetters, poisons, and burials. 2. But I have come back to you, Habrocomes master of my heart, the same as I was when I first left for Syria from Tyre. No one has persuaded me to misbehave, not Moeris in

361

Κιλικίᾳ, οὐκ ἐν Αἰγύπτῳ Ψάμμις καὶ Πολύιδος, οὐκ
Ἀγχίαλος ἐν Αἰθιοπίᾳ, οὐκ ἐν Τάραντι ὁ δεσπότης,
ἀλλ' ἁγνὴ μένω σοι πᾶσαν σωφροσύνης μηχανὴν
πεποιημένη. 3. σὺ δὲ ἆρα, Ἀβροκόμη, σώφρων ἔμει-
νας ἤ μέ τις παρευδοκίμησεν ἄλλη καλή; ἢ μή τις
ἠνάγκασέ σε ἐπιλαθέσθαι τῶν ὅρκων τε κἀμοῦ;" 4.
ταῦτα ἔλεγε καὶ κατεφίλει συνεχῶς, ὁ δὲ Ἀβροκόμης
"ἀλλ' ὀμνύω σοι" φησὶ "τὴν μόγις ἡμῖν ἡμέραν ποθει-
νὴν εὑρημένην ὡς οὔτε παρθένος ἐμοί τις ἔδοξεν εἶναι
καλή, οὔτ' ἄλλη τις ὀφθεῖσα ἤρεσε γυνή, ἀλλὰ τοιοῦτον εἴληφας Ἀβροκόμην καθαρόν, οἷον ἐν Τύρῳ κατ-
έλιπες ἐν δεσμωτηρίῳ."

15   ταῦτα δι' ὅλης νυκτὸς ἀλλήλοις ἀπελογοῦντο καὶ
ῥᾳδίως ἔπειθον ἀλλήλους ἐπεὶ τοῦτο ἤθελον. ἐπειδὴ δὲ
ἡμέρα ἐγένετο ἐπιβάντες νεὼς πάντα ἐνθέμενοι τὰ
αὑτῶν ἐπανήγοντο παραπέμποντος αὐτοὺς παντὸς τοῦ
Ῥοδίων πλήθους. συναπῄει δὲ καὶ ὁ Ἱππόθοος τά τε
αὑτοῦ πάντα ἐπαγόμενος καὶ τὸν Κλεισθένη· καὶ ἡμέραις ὀλίγαις διανύσαντες τὸν πλοῦν κατῆραν εἰς Ἔφεσον. 2. προεπέπυστο δὲ τὴν σωτηρίαν αὐτῶν ἡ πόλις
ἅπασα. ὡς δὲ ἐξέβησαν εὐθὺς ὡς εἶχον ἐπὶ τὸ ἱερὸν
τῆς Ἀρτέμιδος ᾖεσαν καὶ πολλὰ ηὔχοντο καὶ θύσαντες ἄλλα ἐνέθεσαν ἀναθήματα καὶ δὴ καὶ τὴν γραφὴν
τῇ θεῷ ἀνέθεσαν πάντων[129] ὅσα τε ἔπαθον καὶ ὅσα
ἔδρασαν. 3. καὶ ταῦτα ποιήσαντες ἀνελθόντες εἰς τὴν
πόλιν τοῖς γονεῦσιν αὐτῶν τάφους κατεσκεύασαν
μεγάλους, ἔτυχον γὰρ ὑπὸ γήρως καὶ ἀθυμίας προ-
τεθνηκότες, καὶ αὐτοὶ τοῦ λοιποῦ διῆγον ἑορτὴν ἄγον-
τες[130] τὸν μετ' ἀλλήλων βίον. 4. καὶ ὁ Λεύκων καὶ ἡ
Ῥόδη κοινωνοὶ πάντων τοῖς συντρόφοις ἦσαν, διέγνω
δὲ καὶ ὁ Ἱππόθοος ἐν Ἐφέσῳ τὸν λοιπὸν καταβιῶναι

Syria, nor Perilaus in Cilicia, not Psammis or Polyidus in
Egypt, not Anchialus in Ethiopia, not my master in Tarentum. No, I am still chaste, since I used every strategem of
virtue. 3. But what about you, Habrocomes? Have you remained true, or did some other beauty surpass me? Has no
one made you forget your vows, and me?" 4. As she spoke
she kissed him nonstop. "No, I swear to you," Habrocomes
replied, "by this day of ours, so longed for and hard won,
that I found no girl attractive nor any other woman pleas-
ing to my eyes. No, you have recovered Habrocomes just
as pure as when you left him in prison at Tyre."

In this fashion they defended themselves all night long   15
and easily convinced each other, because that was what
they wanted. When day came they boarded a ship, taking with them all their belongings, and set sail, and the
whole populace of Rhodes saw them off. Hippothous too
went with them, with Cleisthenes and all his belongings.
In a few days they completed their voyage and put in at
Ephesus. 2. The whole city had already heard the news of
their salvation. As soon as they disembarked they went
just as they were to the temple of Artemis, offered many
prayers and made sacrifice, then set up dedications, among
them dedicating to the goddess the inscription commemorating all that they had experienced and done. 3. When
they had done this, they went up to the city and built great
tombs for their parents, who from old age and dejection
had predeceased them, and went on to spend lives together that they celebrated like a festival. 4. Leuco and
Rhoda were their companions' partners in everything, and
Hippothous too decided to spend the rest of his life in

---

¹²⁹ Hemsterhuys: πάντα   ¹³⁰ Hercher: ἕξοντες

χρόνον. καὶ ἤδη Ὑπεράνθῃ τάφον ἤγειρε μέγαν κατὰ Λέσβον γενόμενος, καὶ τὸν Κλεισθένη παῖδα ποιησάμενος ὁ Ἱππόθοος διῆγεν ἐν Ἐφέσῳ μεθ᾽ Ἁβροκόμου καὶ Ἀνθίας.[131]

[131] Subscriptio: Ξενοφῶντος τῶν κατὰ Ἀνθίαν καὶ Ἁβροκόμην Ἐφεσιακῶν ε (i.e. ε´) λόγων τέλος

Ephesus. On Lesbos he now built a great tomb for Hyperanthes, and when he had adopted Cleisthenes as his son,
Hippothous spent his life in Ephesus with Habrocomes
and Anthia.

INDEX TO
DAPHNIS AND CHLOE

INDEX TO
ANTHIA AND HABROCOMES

INDEX